W9-AHB-019

The Binder's Road

Books by Terry McGarry

Illumination
The Binder's Road

TERRY McGARRY

The Binder's Road

TOR®

A TOM DOHERTY ASSOCIATES BOOK

NEW YORK

THE BINDER'S ROAD

This book is printed on acid-free paper.

Edited by Teresa Nielsen Hayden

Map by Ellisa Mitchell

A Tor Book
Published by Tom Doherty Associates, LLC
175 Fifth Avenue
New York, NY 10010

www.tor.com

Library of Congress Cataloging-in-Publication Data

McGarry, Terry.
The binder's road / Terry McGarry.—1st ed.
p. cm.
ISBN 0-765-30428-7
1.Women—Fiction. I. Title.

PS3613.C45 B56 2003
813'.54—dc21

2002040949

First Edition: March 2003

Printed in the United States of America

0 9 8 7 6 5 4 3 2 1

FOR KEVIN

Heartbreak piled on heartbreak for the man who could not die. Through shadow, storm, and shine he passed, but never into death. A nonned lifetimes he pressed on, and twice that, and thrice. Every road ended in loss. He could not follow brave comrades into the easeful arms of darkness. He could not join in passage the hearts he pledged. No one remained who had walked the roads he'd walked. No one remained who understood what his eyes had seen.

And so the man who could not die, despairing in his grief, sailed alone into the land beyond the mists, that he might never again love what he must lose. . . .

—Teller's Tale

NORTH
The Sea of Wishes
The Isle of Senana
The Sea of Charms
The Meri Isles
Maur Alna
The Khine
The Boot
The Ankle
The Strong Leg
The Heel
Maur Lengra
The Leeward Sea
Big Toe
The Weak Leg
The Toes
Wiggle
Cramp
Stub
Curl
The Little Toes
The Low Sea

The High Sea
Crown
The Sea of Storms
(The Windward Sea)
Nape
The Head
The High Arm
The Neck
Wrist
The Sea of Sorrows
Shrug
The Heartlands
The Muscle
The Belt
The Low Arm
The Thin Wrist
The Fist
The Elbow
Maur Aulein
Maur Bolein
Maur Gowra
Maur Sleith
The Forgotten Sea
The Dreaming Sea
Eiden Myr

The Binder's Road

❧

"Follow me!" the boy cried, and stepped into the passageway his mind had carved in the mountain.

Shivery air tickled his face, like a fizz of bubbles around a swimmer. The stone glowed the silvery white of the moon. Magestone shone for mages. He was no mage. Only a runner. A frightened, angry warder had called him "that lightless boy" in a voice hard and cold as stone. But there were mages behind him. Enough to turn the tunnel into an underground river of light. Injured mages. Counting on him to save them.

Triads could craft magestone, but it could not be cut with metal tools. Yet he reached out a fingertip and touched the smooth wall of a corridor that had not been there scant breaths ago.

I did this, *he thought.* I did this, with my dreams.

The only thing his dreams had ever wrought before was razored darkness. His face and arms were scored by the shadows' teeth and talons. His sleeves were torn and blood-soaked. His mind had fought hard to keep the Ennead off him.

Now, at last, the chance to be free. But what if he failed? What if they were caught? What if the Nine did to him what they'd done to the mages behind him?

"Follow me!"

His cry went out a plea. He forced himself to move forward.

The argent luminance of magestone cast no shadow, and there was no telling depth or distance or where the passage turned. He would have to feel his way through the light. The chill of stone seeped through the thin soles of his softboots, but a glance at his feet showed them suspended in pale nothingness.

He swayed with vertigo, and came up against the wall he had shaped. He laid his hands flat against it. Hang on, *he thought. He crabbed along the stone, and his body found a memory of doing something very like, once, long ago—*

Hang on, but don't look back. *Looking back was like looking down. He could not keep his balance if he looked back.*

The stone gave off a scent—strange, and not pleasant. Something like the heart of a daisy, but not as clean. Like all stone, it drew warmth from the flesh. Like all stone in the Holding, it felt of magecraft, like the twinge in a dinged elbow. But it was waxy. There was something about laying hands on it that was like laying hands on a live thing. It made a whispery silver sound. He did not know how or why. There were veins of magestone throughout the Holding, but if they spoke he'd never heard them. Here in the silver depths of the mountain, there was only magestone, and here its whispers were as loud as surf.

"This way!" he cried. Sound changed in this tunnel. He firmed his voice: "Follow me!"

Follow me. *How many times had he said those words? He had summoned young mages to this Holding, delivered the Ennead's call to the brightest when they took the triskele. He had ridden out of this mountain fastness into what felt like freedom, and never was, and he had brought mages back with him, full knowing, never warning. Every Holdingward step had been an agony of submission—*

Were they coming? The whispers were too loud. He would not be able to hear the tread of their bare feet. He did not trust mages, now, to follow the boy who had only ever led them to their doom.

He turned, an effort of will. The chamber he had left was lost to sight. The passageway had curved without him sensing it. Would the mages follow him if they couldn't see him? He should have herded, not led. Suppose they lost themselves in the watery light and could not feel their way?

Where his scored flesh had slid along stone there was a smear of black. Blood was black in the magestone's glow. The line hung on the wall like a wordsmith's mark—hovering in the shadowless space, as if he could scribe in blood on frozen currents.

"I'm here!" he cried, urgent now. "It's this way! Follow my voice!"

My voice, not my blood. *There was not blood enough in him to guide them all the way to freedom—and if they were pursued, it would guide their killers just as clearly.*

My voice. *It must be a strong voice, a voice worth following. A voice worth staking your life on. He had never spoken much. He was shy, he knew that, but it was fear, too—fear of saying the wrong thing, divulging too much.*

If the Ennead caught him, or their men did, no sleep would protect him. Behind him, good folk would soon be fighting for their lives against Ennead killers. Perhaps he should have stayed. Dying on a longblade might be better than what lay ahead if he tried to run, and failed.

Ennead. *Just the brush of the word against his mind was enough to set his heart pounding.*

"Come on!" *he cried again. His voice held and did not crack, as it had been wont to do of late, from grief, from fatigue, from the passage between childhood and manhood.* It was *a voice worth following. He would get them out of here.*

He had taken three steps back to see what was keeping them when the magestone's glow began to fade.

He had come too far. He was not a mage. The walls would not glow for him. He had never shown a magelight, though an illuminator had believed there was a light inside him, obscured by the years of pain and fear. He knew his life had been hard, but he didn't think it was so hard that it would seal off his own magelight. . . .

No. *This magestone, this fulgent river—it wanted him to remember. If he gave in to it, it would dissolve him where he stood. He would drown in memory as darkness pressed in, and he would lose the only hope he'd ever have of making things right.*

Groping along the solidity of stone, he moved back around the turn, and a silver crescent took shape, magestone lit by the presence of mages. They were following. They would dispel the darkness. The walls would glow again, for them.

"*This way!*" *he called, and now he could hear them: the wincing drag of a useless foot along the stone, the grunts and guttural sounds of the tongueless speaking among themselves.*

The magestone responded. Whatever the Ennead had taken from them, they still had light enough for that.

Now there was light to see them by.

Most of them were naked, or close enough, shreds of warders' white and reckoners' black hanging off them, the peeled skin of their former Holding positions. Their flesh was a webwork of white lines, deep scars carved by the Ennead's knives. Every third was missing one hand, or both; the eyelids of many others sank into hollows. The ones with no visible injury must be the binders, their songs forever silenced.

The Ennead had prevented them using their light as thoroughly as if they'd cored and sealed them. An illuminator could not cast without a casting hand. A wordsmith could not scribe if she could not see. A binder with no tongue could not control a bindsong; a binder with no feet could not gather casting materials. Three dozen of Eiden Myr's elite reduced to limping, sight-

less, inarticulate husks. He had heard them cry out for death, and he had heard the silence of those who were beyond hoping even for that.

This was how the Ennead repaid its brightest lights.

And he had called them. He had appeared in their towns, in his magecrafted, nine-colored cloak, and conveyed the Ennead's summons, and they had come with him, to be vocates in the Holding, to ward and protect all Eiden Myr, to practice magecraft at its highest.

He had called them, all of them, by proxy, even the ones he hadn't fetched, because he had never run away. Time and again he had had the opportunity, and he had fetched and returned as he was told to do. He had never said the word "complicity" aloud. He had said few words in his nine years and six, except the words the Ennead sent him to say. But that word hung in the air between himself and the mages like a line of blood.

Don't you know me? *he thought.* Was the pain so bad that you forgot who brought you to this? *He could not speak. Their smell came to him slowly through the still air of the tunnel: captivity, filth and blood and terror sweat and festering wounds. He gagged on it.*

"Well?" came a woman's hoarse voice. She stood in the center of the group. "I can't see you, boy, but you're the only one of us with boots, and I don't hear them moving."

I'm sorry, *he tried to say.*

"You cast passage," said another woman, nearer the front. Irony darkened her voice. Her eyes were flat as she gestured up the tunnel with the stump of a wrist. An illuminator. Their injuries made the triadic roles obvious as they were never meant to be. "The spirits of our dead found their own way, but you're going to have to lead the rest of us."

I'm sorry, *he tried again, but when he drew breath he inhaled only the damp choking tang of shame.*

"I saw a warder cut her throat rather than walk out the open cage door," called someone from the back. "There's some still believe the only way out is death. But we'll follow you, boy—so long as you bloody get on with it."

I'm sorry, *he thought, and he could have managed the words out loud now, but what he said was "Yes. Come on. Come ahead. I'll help you."*

He moved to the side of the group, prompting with hands and voice as they shuffled forward, just wanting to be sure of them before he took point again.

Far behind them, he heard a voice cry out. Someone else, trying to catch up. How could it be so far away? They hadn't come that far down the passageway. He turned, but could see nothing. The voice called again: "Ilorna!" He recognized it now: the warder who had scorned him as lightless, no use to them in the trap they'd been in. The trap he'd freed them of. Now she was trying to escape, using the passages he had dreamed. "Ilorna, I'm coming!"

A honey-haired wordsmith near the front of the group went very straight, then turned in blind response, started to go back.

"No," said the illuminator next to her. "Let her catch up. She's got two good feet."

But the calls were getting fainter.

"She's gone down some other tunnel," Ilorna said.

There were no other tunnels.

"I've got to go to her! She's my cousin, I can't leave her!"

"You can. You must go on. We must go on."

They struggled briefly, the illuminator wrapping her arms around the wordsmith to hold her back. The boy let go his purchase on rocky reality to go past them, into the middle of the group, trying to see down the depthless silver length of the tunnel behind them. The warder's voice had grown very faint. Where in the bloody spirits could she have gone? There were no other tunnels

Someone nearby cried out, and he saw a hobbling man tumble sideways— into *the wall? Could he have dreamed awry, could the walls be softening? He ran to help the man sit up—his was the leg that dragged, he'd been using the wall to prop himself up as he hopped along—and found the corridor as firm and wide as ever. The man had fallen into an opening. Forcing one good foot in front of the other, the boy made his way in—a threft, two threfts, six, and again the wall fell away into silver space under his hand—*

The tunnel branched.

That was why the warder couldn't reach them.

He froze. The tunnels turned, and the tunnels branched. How would he find the way?

"I've got him, lad," said the blind woman who'd spoken first. A wordsmith, once. She had the man's arm over her shoulders. She would be a good right leg for him. The others were helping, too—being each other's limbs and senses, trading hands for eyes and eyes for hands. "Which way, now?"

The clang of iron blades, the first death cries drifted faintly along the passageway, carried on silver currents from the chamber they had left. It seemed a nonned leagues away, and a lifetime ago. But the battle was happening now. It would be for nothing if they just stood there until the dying was done.

The close huddle of folk who had been mages turned ravaged faces to the boy and waited for his answer.

"This way," he said, moving into the main passage and past them to the front. He struck off up the incline, the way he had been going. He had always known his way through the Holding—most of it, anyway, even in the dark where the torchman had neglected his duties. He must trust that he knew it still. He had dreamed this. He could negotiate the twists and turns. "This way!"

He did not know how he made the choices he did. Sometimes space yawned under his hand, and he changed course and entered it. Sometimes he passed the branchings and continued down a straightaway or around the curve of a turn. But it was always upward, and the angle of ascent grew steeper. It took a long time for the sounds of battle to fall away, even faint as they were, even with the turnings. But when they did—because of distance, or the battle's ending?—he realized with a jolt that he would never know the outcome. He would never know if his friends had lived or died. His path had well and truly branched away from theirs now.

He was alone.

It's all right, *he told himself. He'd been alone before, on the trail, in his campsites; he'd been alone in the beds that strangers gave him as a passing traveler, alone in the midst of tavern revelries. He'd been alone when—*

"Are you all right, boy?" said the illuminator.

"It's this cursed stone," said the wordsmith who'd first spoken to him, who'd helped up the fallen man. Their voices were raw from screaming, the ones who still had voices at all, but he could tell them apart now. "It does something to the mind. They burned out my eyes, but my life's passed before my mind's eye as we walked. Don't let it plague you, lad."

"What's done is done," someone else agreed.

"It's getting less," said another. "It's not all magestone now, there's blackstone marbled in."

"Then we'll be in the dark, soon," the blind wordsmith said. "I'll wager no torchman's ever passed this way."

"Trust the boy," said the illuminator. "He made these tunnels. He'll see us through."

"Do you know where we'll be coming out?" said another. "There's some of us would do best in Crown, I think, and I don't know about the others. We'll all need care, and healing."

He'd thought the Ennead had broken them. But there was spirit in them still, and they were with him, and their words carried a double meaning: forgiveness. He was not alone.

They deserved an honest answer. "I don't know," he said. "It's sowmid. Still cold out. We'd starve. Before we got across the Aralinns. I think. We're going through them."

"Away from the sea, I hope," said the wordsmith.

"Yes," he said, though he couldn't say why he was so certain. "Into the mountains. Through them."

"Back into the Holding," said the illuminator.

"I don't know," he said, as the marbled walls became more nightstone than magestone, the flecks of mica in the one not sparkling in the glow of the other. "Maybe," he said.

"Let the boy be," said the wordsmith. "Let him do what he has to do."

There were grunts from the binders, sounds that had the inflection if not the shape of words. He heard no objection in them, or accusation, or mistrust. Given time, he thought, he might come to understand them as they seemed to understand each other. Perhaps they would all make a home together somewhere, if the stewards won their battle, if the rumored Darkmage and his rebel horde succeeded in bringing the Ennead down. They could start a village of their own, band together to put the horror of this place behind them forever, work to make a new life. He'd never had a real home. What joy, to find friendship, to find unity in survival, among those who understood where he had been. . . .

He shook off the waking dream. They had been mages, and could be mages no more. They would fight bitterness the rest of their days. They might go mad, as mages denied the use of their light were said to. They would have families somewhere, most of them, and they would want to return and be comforted in loved ones' arms, but they would fight pity the rest of their days, too, and helplessness. What the Ennead had done to them, no mage could heal.

But they had chosen life. They had chosen to follow him to freedom. He could not be responsible for how they used it, or hope for lasting bonds. He was still alone, in the end. No family to run to. He must see them on their way and then go on his. Whether or not he had anywhere to go.

As they came into full darkness, he let go of the future as he had let go of the past. He concentrated on the next step, on the feel of plain stone under his hand, on the cold smell of a rocky corridor new-cut in the mountain and not warded against damp. His nose caught a whiff of burning pitch as the passage abruptly narrowed, but he startled when splintery wood came under his hand, then the metal banding it. His fingers found a handle and the iron tongue that would lift a latch on the other side.

"Stop," he said softly, before the mages blundered into him. "There's a door."

They stood for a few moments, silent except for labored breath. He could smell their fear, and taste his own.

"We could go back," someone said at last. "Try a different turning."

"No," the boy said. "No. There'll be doors at the end of the others, too. Or blank walls."

"These tunnels are your mind, aren't they?" said the rasping voice of the blind wordsmith. It was close beside him. He felt her breath on his neck. "You dreamed these passages. They're a reflection of you."

"I guess they are," he said.

"They must have used you ill, that you could not even dream your way to freedom."

Not as ill as they used you, Wordsmith. *He drew himself up. "I'm going through. You should wait. Let me look."*

He felt movement, and when she spoke he knew it for a shake of the head. "We're together in this. Unwise, perhaps—but what's left to us if they capture you?"

"A chance," he said; but he grasped cold iron, levered the latch up, and pushed the wood outward to open their way back into the ancient corridors of the Holding.

Flickering torchlight, a tarry odor, a waft of smoke diverted into the doorway. In the more populous areas there were lampwells, not torches. Perhaps they had lucked out. Once he had his bearings, he might get them to the stables. He thought most of them could sit horses, and he knew which were the quiet mounts. He stood aside to let the three dozen mages limp and carry and guide each other into the greasy air of the corridor. He formed and discarded plans in his head as they moved. They would not do well on stairs. He did not know who watched the stables now or whether they were safe haven. Best to find a little-used chamber to hide the mages until he could see how things stood. He would scrounge food and water for them somehow—they were all skin and bones. Or park them in a pantry; who'd bother to prepare food now, with battles raging throughout the Holding?

"I don't smell any lights," the wordsmith said, her face raised as if she were actually sniffing the air. Mages could sense each other's lights, some as a taste, some as a scent, some as a warm glow as from a candle's flame. No warders or reckoners nearby, then; that was good. But it didn't mean there weren't stewards. Too many stewards supported the Ennead they'd served for generations.

"Good," he said. "But stay here. For a moment." He crossed the corridor to try a door on the other side. He heard someone shut the door they'd come through. Something told him to turn, make them open it again, not cut off the retreat. Before he could form the words he heard exactly the sound he'd feared: the tread of many boots on stone. Approaching along a cross-corridor. Moving fast.

"Friend or foe?" the illuminator asked him, as if stewards could sense in each other something like the quality of light a mage could sense—as if as a runner boy he was even a steward at all.

"I don't know," he said, but then they rounded the corner and he saw the ripple of nine-colored Ennead cloaks, saw pale faces never graced by sunshine floating over the dark velvet livery the Ennead had lately adopted for their private stewards. A dozen of them, with longblades sheathed at their sides. As they caught sight of the ragged mages, the first rank of three drew their blades, and the middle man of them called a halt and stepped forward.

"By all the spirits . . ." one of the stewards murmured before he was shushed by the man next to him.

"What's this?" the leader said. His glance passed right over the boy, found no one worth addressing among the half-naked huddle of adults, then

returned to the boy with a flicker of acknowledgment of his torn, but whole, black tunic and leggings. "A runner, are you? Where's your cloak? What are these people?" He squinted again at the mages. His eyes widened as he caught the glint of triskeles at their necks: the pewter pendants mages wore until the bonefolk took their corpses and left all metal things behind.

The boy thought quickly, his heart pounding. He didn't know these stewards, and their Ennead livery meant that invoking his master's name would not help him. Brondarion te Khine had standing only among stewards who opposed the Ennead. "The deepest chambers have been breached," he said, and if his voice shook it only made his case more plausible. "The Nine sent me to get these mages out before the other stewards killed them."

"Why would they kill them?" said one of the two standing behind the head steward, frowning. The other stood agape, his face drained of color.

The boy didn't know.

"To deprive the Ennead of their lights," said the leader. He'd lowered his blade, but was running a thumb back and forth along the crossguard. "Mages pledged their lives to the Ennead's needs in defense of the Holding against the Darkmage. Rebels would kill loyal mages, not spirit them away." He looked at the boy and came to a decision. "We'll bring you to the presence chamber, it's not far." He spoke in headlong bursts. "The Ennead will be glad to see you and you'll need an escort. We've put down most of the uprising but there are still rebels running loose. We'll see you safe."

No! Not the Ennead! *He bit down on panic. What could he offer instead? Who could he trust these mages to? Who would be known to loyal stewards as loyal? He didn't think there were any head warders anymore, and he'd never known any warders to trust anyway. There had been reckoners he trusted, once. Now there was no telling who remained in the Holding. Or what side they were on. "I'm supposed to . . ." he started. No name came to him. "I'm supposed to bring them to . . ."*

"Out with it, boy!" the leader said. "If you've orders from the Ennead let me hear them or I'll do with you as I see fit."

"Saraen, you're frightening the lad," said the man to the leader's right. Craggy-faced, with stooped shoulders. He had taken a step away from his commander. A subtle shift, but the wary evaluation in his eyes said he was wavering. The boy looked at the other stewards, saw shock mixed with some grim set jaws. He could use this, but he didn't know how. One of the mages behind him was tugging on what was left of his sleeve, murmuring something in his ear. The sound was so low he could barely hear it, and the shapeless moan of a binder to boot. He stopped trying to evaluate the stewards, and listened. The sound resolved into a name. Pelkin? Pelkin had been head reckoner. Pelkin was dead, or pledged to the Darkmage. Wait, not Pelkin . . . Burken. Yes, he knew Burken, a reckoner, a kind man others deferred to,

retired from the field. But was he known as a loyalist? One name could bring the whole construct of his story crashing down.

"I don't care if he's frightened," Saraen was saying, "we're all bloody fr—"

"Burken," the boy said, and swallowed hard.

Saraen frowned. "I thought he was staying out of this. But yes, all right. You're thrice lucky we came upon you in that case. The reckoners' level is the least secure part of the Holding. You'll need us to get there."

The other stewards were shifting, murmuring among themselves. "What's been done to them?" one burst out, a world of doubt on his face, doubt in everything he'd believed about the Ennead he served.

"What had to be done," Saraen said curtly. "They gave themselves up for this. Come on, you lot, turn out, it's back the other—"

"By Eiden's bloody balls, we did not," the wordsmith said.

Dead silence followed.

The mages were straightening, standing taller, in bitter display of their own mutilation. The wordsmith let fall the stained gray strips she had been holding across her body, the remnants of white velvet that would have held such authority as could have made these stewards bow to her. "I was a warder in this Holding," she said, "and two moons ago the Ennead bade me come to aid the defense against the Darkmage. It was not a request. They had use of my light, and that use required such torments of my flesh as nearly broke my spirit. Mark me, I didn't pledge myself to that."

"They never told us they were using anyone so!" cried the young steward to Saraen's left. "Grieving spirits—"

Saraen had turned and struck him so fast that the boy didn't register the blow, only the stagger and the other stewards catching him. The young steward raised his head and said, through bloody lips, "I pledged my life to them, and may all the powers of goodness forgive me." He shook off his fellows, unbuckled his belt, and let his sheathed blade fall to the stone. His eyes were wild, dazed from shock and the blow. "May you forgive me, mages." He turned and took two unsteady steps away.

"Hold," the leader said, and the young steward hesitated, turned. The other one, the craggy one with caution on his face, had moved behind Saraen now, awaiting the turn of events. Good, the boy thought, that was good, the wordsmith's words were convincing him, and now he was between the leader and the others.

Saraen said to the mages, "These are terrible times. The Ennead must take terrible measures. I grieve for your pain, but if what they asked of you was more than you could give . . . if you regretted your pledge to serve once you understood what they required . . ."

The wordsmith's mouth twisted. "What I've told you isn't enough, eh, steward? They burned out my eyes, that I might never scribe again, never again wield a wordsmith's tools. Their dark craft fed on my despair, their castings were fueled by the blazing light of my agonies. That is how they used me, and nonneds more—we you see here are but the survivors, those unlucky or late-come enough to have not yet escaped into death." Ripping off the rag that wrapped her eyes, she cried, "We did not pledge ourselves to this!"

Some stewards cried out at sight of her ruined, festering eyes, some turned their heads, some cast beseeching looks at their leader, desperate for denial or explanation. The mages, pressed close for warmth and support, had instinctively been hiding or protecting their injuries, but now they spread out to fill the corridor, raising blunted limbs, letting filthy wrappings fall, opening their mouths. Some stewards at the back broke and fled, ignoring Saraen's orders to stop. Helpless, swearing, he commanded the rest to form ranks and stand firm, then turned, shaken.

"Is this true, boy?" he asked.

The boy blinked. "What difference does what I say make?"

Saraen gestured at his clothes. "You wear the black. You serve the reckoners, and the Ennead. You're one of us." He ran a hand through his hair, his eyes going wild for a moment, then spat at the wall. "I can't very well ask the Nine, now, can I? Tell me true, boy, or I swear you'll regret it."

The boy stood up straight and forced his shadow-haunted eyes to fix unwavering on the steward's face. "It's true," he said. "And worse besides. I've seen it. I've been party to it. We all have. Every steward in this Holding. The revolt is only the others trying to make good. Trying to stop it. As best they know how." He had not strung so many words together in a long time. It exhausted him. Too much responsibility. Too long without food, water, genuine sleep. The battles inside his mind and out, the long upward climb to bring these mages here. They had suffered far worse, but that didn't make his knees less weak. He was shamed to feel naked, trembling mages move close to support him.

"They should have told us," Saraen said. His low voice was steady. His blade sank.

"I don't think they thought they could trust you."

The man rubbed a fist against his brow, his eyes shut tight, then mastered himself and said, "They were right. They could only have shown us. And they couldn't." He turned to his men. "But now they have. Are you—"

"Traitor," came a soft growl, and then a sucking gasp.

The boy understood what had happened only when Saraen fell. It cleared the way for him to see the craggy man beyond him with the blooded blade. The other stewards stumbled back in confusion and horror.

"Did you think defeating the Darkmage would not require terrible sacrifices?" the man said to Saraen as he died.

It had been Saraen's loyalty he was wary of. The boy had thought he was swayed by the mages' condition and considering taking over. He'd been only half right. He'd never been any good at gauging expressions.

This floated bemusedly through his mind as the corridor erupted in violence. Half the stewards lurched to craggy-face's side as the others attacked with bared blades. The two factions were evenly matched. For one suspended moment, iron clanged into deafening stasis. Neither side yielded.

Then mages were pushing past the boy to fall upon the nearer side. The mages who'd been supporting him drew him back and away. Blood flew through the air as some of the stewards turned blades on the mages and the others beat back the armed assault.

There were nearly three dozen mages and only half a dozen opposing stewards. Craggy-face's nearest cohorts went down under a mass of battering limbs. The rest, outnumbered, died on the blades of the stewards who had been their comrades. It was done in a matter of breaths, the stone floor of the corridor paved with death.

"Is that all they needed?" the blind wordsmith breathed into the awful silence. "To see us?"

The illuminator who had become her second raised himself from the crush of bodies, gave others his elbows to help pull themselves up, and staggered to the wordsmith and the boy and the weaker mages who had drawn back. He sank painfully to his knees on the blood-slick stone. Tears ran through the smears of red on his face. "It would seem so," he said, over the sobs of men who had just killed their friends. "Perhaps . . ." He took a moment to catch his breath. "Perhaps that is what we must do now. Show ourselves to the rest of them. Perhaps it isn't too late."

"Then you dreamed our way true," the wordsmith said to the boy. "Your mind brought us where we needed to go."

The boy looked at the corpses on the floor, at the shattered stewards beyond them, some on their knees beseeching forgiveness from the spirits, some standing in shock with their blades dangling from nerveless hands. Eiden Myr had never had blades before this last year. Eiden Myr had never had battles, or shed its own folk's blood. This Ennead had brought the world to this. He would never make good on his part in it. He was just a frightened boy.

One steward had made his way through the carnage to approach the mages. "You'll need care," he said quietly. "You'll need a place of safety. Let us take you to our quarters. We'll do what we have to do to see you safe."

"Will you help us turn the other Ennead loyalists?" the illuminator asked.

"We can try," the steward said. "It's too late, I think. But we can try."

Another came up beside him, her face a mask of hatred. "We can get close to the Ennead. We can put an end on this directly."

"Come with us for now," said the first. "I don't know how you got this

far, in the state you're in, but if you can make it a bit farther we'll . . . help, a little. As we can."

Some mages had died on stewards' blades, but more than three nines still lived. They looked done in, but they rose up, they lifted each other, they allowed the remaining stewards to bear them away down the corridor, to help the uprising as they could, to do what they could against the Ennead. The boy hung back, and when the wordsmith, sensing his absence, called for him, he caught the illuminator's eye and shook his head. The illuminator leaned over to the wordsmith and spoke. She lifted a hand in salute, and then was gone around the turn, leaving the boy alone with the dead.

He sank down cross-legged, put his elbows on his knees and his face in his hands, and cried for a long time. Then he rose and went down the corridor closing the eyes of the dead. When he got to the end, he sat again. He was freezing. He could not bring himself to strip a corpse of its nine-colored cloak, no matter how badly he longed to wrap himself in wool-lined velvet. He knew he must get up and go on. But there was nowhere to go. He could still follow the mages and stewards—they'd be moving slowly, and leave a trail of blood—but he was neither mage nor steward, he did not belong with them, and he was too shamed and too afraid of how much he wanted to be one of them. He could go back down to the chambers where he'd left his master and his friend, but that battle would be long over, and he could not put himself in the Ennead's hands again just for the certainty of having viewed their bodies. He could return to the passageways he'd dreamed, and drown in memory. Or he could leave the Holding, leave the reek of blood and death and agony and find true freedom, his heart's desire, in the clean mountain air outside.

He could make his way to the Shoulder and the High Arm, work for food; but he knew no trade except for the fetching of mages, and the care of horses he could not even shoe or stitch tack for—he was useless outside the Holding. He could take a mount and ride back through the Aralinns, back to the village he'd guided an illuminator from the last time he'd been sent out. There'd been sanctuary in a tavern there, a spill of warm light through the doorway. He might walk through that doorway again. But he could not go without news to give her folk, and he did not know what had become of her. He could go to Crown and take ship for the Boot or the Toes, clear around Eiden Myr, as far from the Holding as you could go, and see if some craftsfolk or traders would take on a boy too old to prentice.

Or he could sit here in torchlight with the dead.

Sitting with his head bowed, in a stupor of fatigue, he startled at a rustling sound as a long shadow fell across him. It would be some dead steward rising, some haunt sweeping down on him. The corridor was filled with them—

They were tall, clothed in tatters, white as the bones they consumed, silent in the presence of the dead they had come for. But they were not haunts.

He was too shocked even to scramble back. They seemed to come right through the stone walls, appearing like wraiths, but they were as solid and real as he was. One looked at him as they bent to their work—dark eyes, unblinking, too large for its thin face, swimming in tears that never fell—then looked away with no acknowledgment. They did not seem to mind that he was there, though no one had ever seen the bonefolk work. They would not come as long as humans held vigil; you had to leave the dead for them or the dead would rot where they lay. But he sat and watched, and they made no objection; and neither did they drag the bodies off around the next turn of the corridor, as they easily could have. They bent down, and lifted the dead in their spindly arms, gently, like cherished children. Perhaps he had dreamed so deep that he had seemed dead, and they'd come for him but gone off again on finding him alive. Perhaps he was a haunt himself, perhaps he'd died in the melee and had no memory of it now—was his one of the bodies whose eyes he had slid closed, had he failed to recognize his own face? He could feel his fingers digging into his own arms hard enough to hurt, but who knew what haunts felt—perhaps they believed they still had bodies, perhaps they didn't really know they were dead until the bonefolk took them. The bonefolk might be taking him now, and in moments he would fly apart, to haunt this corridor, forever unpassaged. No mages had cast passage for the stewards and other mages who'd died here. This corridor would be crowded with haunts. But if he were a haunt, wouldn't he see the others?

"I'm alive," he whispered, pulling back from the brink. The boneman who'd glanced at him stood holding a mage's body, and at his words it uncurled its long fingers, fanned them out and back in what looked like a rippling wave but might mean anything—a bid for silence, agreement that yes, he was alive . . . the flexing of stiff fingers.

The corridor went deathly cold. He'd been shaking already, but that was nothing compared with the chill that swept through now, an icy airless wind. The torches went dim without dying out, their flames burning low and smoky. In the gloom, the bonefolk became pale, insectile shadows, and for another moment of madness he feared he'd dreamed them, too. They would turn black and toothed and taloned and rend him. He would not have the strength to resist. He might have fallen asleep where he sat. He might be freezing to death, that would explain the terrible cold, and this a last, spectacular hallucination. . . .

"I'm awake," he said softly.

Again the boneman fanned its fingers.

Telling him something. Telling him, Yes, you are alive, you are awake. *Telling him,* Yes, I see you. You may stay. You may live.

The bonefolk cradled the bodies. The bodies took on a greenish glow, so bright he had to squint and was no longer sure what he saw. The bonefolk threw their heads back, mouths open in pleasure or pain or supplication. The corridor filled with a chalky scent cut with a harbinger of storm. The floor became a luminous green where blood had pooled. The glow intensified, an eerie, impossible phosphorescence, like something seen in darkest swampland, or Galandra's light running up a ship's rigging, only tinged with the color of storm, of moonlight filtered through the earliest spring leaves. He saw the bones within the flesh, starkly outlined in their joints and sockets, beautiful and supple in connection, and then the bones, too, were subsumed into radiance, and what the bonefolk held in their arms were human forms made of light itself.

The lights that had been the dead blazed so bright it made him weep, and then were gone; his eyes, seared by the memory of that light, were unable to distinguish the precise moment of their passing. He blinked at the afterimage, shifting his focus, and the bonefolk's arms were empty, falling back to their sides. A handful of pewter triskeles hit the floor, some knives, small tools, and a clatter of stones from a steward's pocket; the bag that had held them, like the clothes, the boots, the belts and scabbards, had been consumed along with the bodies.

Slowly the bonefolk's mouths closed, their heads came down, their eyes opened. Again one looked at him, with no expression, no recognition. Then they too were gone, stepping back into the walls, merging back into the stone.

The corridor was empty, the floor cleansed of blood, the air cleansed of smoke and the reek of dying. It smelled like a mountainside after a thunderstorm—every particle of existence scrubbed clean. The cold was gone, though there was no warmth to take its place, and the torches flared up, reasserting their presence with ordinary smoke that drifted off on ordinary air.

"I'm alive," the boy said. He fanned his fingers as the boneman had. "I'm alive. I have to go on."

He pushed himself to his feet and struck off up the corridor, opposite the way the stewards had taken the mages. A junction chamber at the end offered two other doors, and a spiral stair leading only down. One door was locked. The other opened on darkness. The stair, absurdly, ended one level down, and there were no doorways there.

He went back to the door he had come through with the mages. It opened on solid stone.

He looked down the corridor in the direction the stewards had gone. Back into the Holding. Back to the Ennead.

He returned to the junction chamber, took an oil lamp from its niche, and entered the doorway full of darkness. The passage beyond sparkled with nightstone, and led upward. He followed it until his legs ached and never came to a door. He began counting breaths, and at a nonned he turned to go back—then turned again and continued. Nothing would have changed where he had been, but if he kept going up, he might get out.

Or, he had to acknowledge when his legs gave way and he could not draw breath to keep climbing, he might not.

He rested. His breath came easier. The air chilled his sweat-damp clothes. His legs seized; he flexed and massaged them. He rose again, and climbed—it was steeper now, had been for some time, and there were clefts scored across the stone floor as footholds—and rested again when he could no longer climb, then climbed again. His breathing and his scuffling boots made the only sound. The passageway had no curve to it, did not spiral up the Holding to the top. That he had not come out by now meant that it must have led him straight into the mountain. He tried to still his heart, but terror was taking hold of him. This was the price of cowardice. Unwilling to face the Ennead, he had brought himself to this.

This was the price of courage. Choosing, at last, not to go back to them, as he had done time and again despite every opportunity to flee, he had come to this.

He could no longer climb. His belly was clenched in on itself with hunger. His throat and mouth burned for water while his bones and muscles ached with cold. He had nearly dropped the clay lamp so many times that he knew the next time it would shatter. He could not see how much oil remained in it, but the thin slosh when he shook it wasn't promising.

He turned. He began the slip-sliding descent. His trembling legs could not be trusted on the decline. He sat down for another measured rest, and for the first time in many breaths looked up from the floor, to the end of the lamplight's oval.

Downward, the passage ended in a blank wall.

"No," he said, just a rasp from his dry throat.

He no longer knew if he slept or woke.

He set the oil lamp beside him. It made a dull clink as it met stone—a welcome sound, a different sound, a sound. There was not much sound in dreams, as he recalled. But it was a hollow sound. Little oil left. He couldn't blow out the flame to conserve; he had no way to light the wick again. He pulled off a boot and folded the sock under one end of the lamp, so it wouldn't skitter away down the slope, and so the oil wouldn't pool away from the wick.

He lay back on the rocky floor, groaning as his back and head were drenched with cold.

He willed himself to sleep.

He never remembered his dreams, so if he knew he was dreaming when he dreamed he did not know he had known it when he woke.

I'm thinking, he thought. I'm not sleeping.

If he slept, if he dreamed, he could change the world.

He could change the tunnels, anyway. The passage had changed by itself, or because he was dreaming it. Maybe it was the mountain that slept, and dreamed, not him.

Stop thinking.

Before, when he was angry or afraid, he'd always been able to escape into sleep. He'd lie down, think how badly he wanted to be away from wherever it was, and be gone.

He must have gotten braver during that brief time with the mages, and the bonefolk after, because he was still lying here thinking about sleeping instead of doing it. And he very badly wanted to be away from here.

Unless he was already dreaming. He did not know if you could dream that you had gone to sleep. A dream within a dream—what would that do, in dreams like his?

Stop thinking!

He opened his eyes. The lamp was still burning. It was hard to keep his eyes closed, from fear that when he opened them it would have gone out. Taking a deep breath, he turned his head, lifted himself a little, and prepared to blow the flame out.

His breath died. He could not bring himself to extinguish the light. He forced himself up, the hardest thing he had ever done, and with the last energy in his spent limbs climbed away from the lamp and its illusory golden warmth. In this, the passage aided him; it curved now, where it had been straight before, so that not so much climbing was required before the light was gone. If the lamp kept burning, he could go back to it. If not, it would have gone out anyway.

Now, in darkness, with only the memory of flame hanging before him wherever he looked, there was no distraction.

He lay flat again, closed his eyes, and watched the phantom flame fade. He focused on the frantic beating in his chest, the longer rise and fall of his breathing over it. Nothing but that: the pulse of his heart, the surf of his breath, the life inside him. Both slowed, after a while. After a longer while, he could not feel the cold anymore. That quickened breath and heart—he might die, if he let the cold make him sleep. But he could not get out of here from behind, where the passage had closed to him, and he could not get out from ahead, which was only stone for many days' walk, if the stone even chose to take him that far. He could only get out sidewise. Or die anyway.

He knew how long a night was. He had lain awake for most of many nights, fighting the sleep he sought now, when he'd begun to realize that his sleep brought deadly dreams. He lay quiet for at least that long. Sleep never came. He had never felt more awake before, his mind ranging over his deeds, his wants, his guilts. The cold didn't take him; it was not as cold as snow, not winter-cold, not cold enough.

His dreams had deserted him.

He found his body again. It took a long time. There was a hand . . . here was his mouth . . . here were his eyes, though they were useless now. His legs came back as a pair. Every part of him was in agony from the cold. It took him a ninebreath just to get his elbows under him, twice that to sit up. But everything worked. A lifetime later, he was on his feet. Fumbling with his breeches, nearly too late, he relieved himself in the general direction of the wall; it stung coming out, and the trickling sound maddened him with thirst. It would mark this place. If the passage circled back into itself, he would know.

He was at the mercy of the passage now.

He walked. One foot, push up the incline, another foot, push up the incline. In this way he crabbed over to the wall. He kept a steadying hand on the vertical stone. After a while he realized he was trying to pull himself along the stone, but there were no handholds, and his fingernails were wet with what must be blood, and the wasted effort weakened him. He let his hand trail along the nubbly rock as through water over the side of a drifting boat.

He walked. The thick darkness was like a giant dreamshadow enfolding him. He kept reminding himself that he could breathe. Foot down, push forward, breathe in. Foot down, push forward, breathe out. It was just ordinary darkness. If he was dreaming, the shadows were outside, wherever his body lay. If not, then there would be no shadows.

He walked. His legs gave out. He slept by accident, but no dreams came, or if they did they changed nothing. Still the sandy wall under his hand, the scored stone under his feet. He walked again, not so far this time. How long had it been? Another day? How long would it be until he died of thirst? Wondering that, he found himself lying on his face with no idea if he had fallen or lain down. He was scrabbling along the stone, thinking he heard running water ahead of him. But it was below him, just there below a thin veneer of nightstone, and he was digging down to it, except the stone would not yield.

He woke up. He felt surprisingly rested, though still numb with cold. A bad dream, then. A powerless dream. He got up. He walked. He trailed his hand along the stone. He recoiled when it slid through a shock of cold—but it was water, a seep of water. He fell to his knees and slurped greedily at the mountain's gift, sobbing his thanks to unheeding stone, laughing in giddy victory, as if he could take credit for the decision that had brought him here. The stone had herded him. But it had given him water. It had given him a few more days of life.

Refreshed and strengthened, he walked. He could hear the water now, soft trickling rivulets at odd intervals, the stone weeping for him. How long until he starved? Long enough that it didn't matter. The rest of my life, he thought, and giggled, and went on even when his belly cramped so hard he cried out. After a while he wasn't even hungry anymore. He filled himself with water at every opportunity, marked his passage with it as it went through his body. He pushed on until his muscles failed and he felt himself sinking into the stone.

He woke up. How could it be a certain waking, when only the blanket of darkness greeted him? He prodded at his eyelids to be sure they were open. He went on, step by frozen, agonized step. If he'd dreamed, and his dreams changed the passageway, he would not know it in the dark. Groping along one wall, he might miss an opening or a door in the other. But where would doors lead to now? He was deep in the mountain, far beyond the reach of the Holding. No one ever came this far. There were no passages that led this far. But there was water. He would not die yet, not if there was water. Had he dreamed the water? Was it not the mountain's gift, but his own?

He woke up. He must have cried; he was trying to lick tears from his chin, scoop damp into his mouth with his fingers, which tasted of copper and salt. He screamed to the bonefolk, the only ones he could imagine reaching him here, but the scream came out a croak, and maybe it was better that way, because if the bonefolk came he wasn't dreaming, he was dead.

He woke up, still lying flat on the stone, still mad with thirst, no rivulets of water nearby, all the threfts he had covered gone with the dreaming, all of it to do again. I can't, *he thought,* I can't, *and* Get up, you must, you have to.

He woke, and woke, and woke, but never slept, and no change from the pitch dark and the numb chill. There was water, then there wasn't; there was thirst, then there was water. Which was real? There was never food. If he dreamed water, he could have dreamed food, but there was never food. If the mountain had given him water, it could have given him mushroom heather—that only needed spores and damp to grow, and no light or warmth at all. It was a cruel mountain. It taunted him. This was a cruel dream.

His foot caught on something, sent it skittering off to shatter against the wall. He followed it, bent down, touched wet shards of clay, sniffed oil on bloody fingers: his lamp. It had gone out. He sat down, held the broken pieces in his hands, and laughed until he felt faint. When he stopped to gasp breath, he could hear it: the river flowing over the clay bottom that had been dredged for the stuff to mold and bake into a lamp that would hold oil. Delighted, he followed the sound. He pushed damp fern fronds aside. He smelled mint and mulch and wet bark. Glorious smells. Life smells. They drew him into the blue-gold air, the tumbling buzzing dance of slipshod freedom. He could take it! He would be brave this time. No more the dragging chain of threat to haul him back. Death was good for blanking out the things you could lose. Not many, really—and that was a sad thing. Mostly his master. The other fosterlings. No friends. Well, the horses. But Purslane died. The mountain broke him. He flailed free of his grave, good strong brave fellow, brave Purslane, the color of brown river clay, knew his fool boy loved him and took every advantage of it, didn't he? But he was broken. He couldn't go on. Sometimes you were too broken to go on.

That was a bad place, a behind place, a place back in the dark tunnel. Ahead was mint and emerald fern in a depth of greenness, and the blue-gold dancing invitation, and he would take its hand, he would, because there was nothing to fear now. But he feared he was wrong. Death was the easy thing; life was the terror. He could see it now, and oh, he didn't want to. He tried to burrow back into the dark, to wake again in drynumb coldweary hunger, but it was beyond him now, and anyway there was no choice, his attention wouldn't tear away.

Lights. A world of lights. A great plane of lights, shifting, growing, blazing, flickering, burning calm and true. They hurt his dark-craving senses. Some were trying to save the world. He could have told them. He could have. But they didn't ask. Just went right on, headstrong, casting impossibility. It was going to break! They were going to break it!

He reached out. To stop it. To touch it. The light. And cracked open like a shell. Bloomed like a flame after the first tinder caught. Swell of golden radiance, eclipsing the sparkling world of lights, joining it, spirits, joining

never noticed the shy boy in the shadows

breaking the world in the saving of it

He screamed a name as the world-shell shattered and a burning hooked blade stabbed up through him and twisted, trying to withdraw, trying to core him like an apple, a blinding searing agony that left not ache, nor cold, nor thirst, nor hunger, nor shadows, nor anything at all beyond a yawning tunnel of darkness.

But it was only a dream, thought Mellas, spread flat on nightstone inside a dreaming mountain, a cruel fang of fired river clay clutched biting in his palm, and woke, shrieking, into the abyss.

The Isle

Halowen n'Tedra stared for many shallow breaths at a stray panel in what was assumed to be a dry accounting of inventory.

The threaded bamboo strips weren't the most unusual recording medium she had seen. In her time as a scholar, which was as long as the codices had been kept on the Isle of Senana, she had come across a variety of materials, from triangular oak rods to the most delicate rice parchment. She had seen a few of these bamboo-strip assemblages—but they were useful mainly for researching numeric representations rarely found in the codices proper, and otherwise considered mundane ephemera of little scholarly value. None of them had been well preserved since their mage wardings failed, and this one was suffering in the unsuitable damp.

It had clearly not been opened to its full extent in lifetimes; laid out with the strips laddered one above the other, it covered the width of the worktable. Its bindings, of animal gut or sinew, had crumbled despite the care she'd taken in unfolding it, and she'd spent the morning removing the rotted strings and binding it afresh. The bamboo panels now ran freely along waxed hemp threaded through holes to either end, knotted under the top and bottom strips. The original had been neatly constructed; grooves in each strip compensated for the bulk of the threads, allowing the unfolded whole to lie flat. She'd replicated the binding as closely as possible, right down to the knots.

She was proud of her work—the old pride she had taken as a binder in crafting good casting materials—but at the same time reluctant for anyone to see her do it. It had taken much to overcome the head scholar's blind adherence to the triadic disciplines. Because of his strict prejudices, there were few binders on the scholars' isle, and the others kept mainly to the workshops, restoring and preserving the materials. She had stayed—but for many moons, even as she learned to read and scribe, she had feared she would never be permitted to do research. Her chief interest lay in the theory that bindsongs once had words of their own, separate from the rendering of wordsmiths' glyphs in sung form. Having earned her way at last to the privilege of exploring rather than maintaining the codices, she felt uncomfortable—and oddly ashamed—to do anything that backslid into her former role.

She had been close. So close. She had found verses unrelated to the wordsmiths' canon, and aerate marks that could translate as singing notation. She had sensed incipient discovery, as awesome as the rediscovery of a lost language. Song *was* language, or it could blend with language, with rules and forms and patterns as intricate and powerful as words'. She *knew* it.

But she would not have the luxury of proving it now.

She was the first scholar of the new age to examine the inner panels of this collection. She had only bothered because a similar bamboo codex was arguably a collection of songs, perhaps kept as an aid to memory by some binder or singer of old. She had hoped to find additional materials to support her belief.

And perhaps she had. But she had found much more than that.

The center panel did not match the others. Some binder's error of old, a simple mixup, the panels of two codices switched in the midst of rethreading such as she had done. The other strips bore the discrete blocky glyphs of Ghardic, the language of trade. The center panel was scribed in curling, exuberant, lyrical, ornamented Celyrian. She'd repaired the binding anyway; the switch might prove to be an historical clue, and she would inform the keeper of codices in case a panel of Ghardic turned up in a Celyrian codex.

Then she read the panel. It was a verse of such profound magnitude that reading it for the third time left her feeling faint, as though her own body had dissipated and she hovered in the midday air, weightless, suspended between exultation and terror.

It's quite a day for shocks, she thought, firmly prosaic, to ground herself. *We're all reeling. I'm no exception.* Jhoss n'Kall's departure had rocked the island to its foundations. That the enigmatic former beekeeper had been at odds with Graefel n'Traeyen, the head scholar, was well known. But no one expected him to break with Graefel outright. That he should leave Senana entirely was unthinkable. Yet this very dawn his solitary form had been seen descending the winding trail to the limestone beach, and boat tenders there said he had taken a coracle to the mainland, bound for his Heel home. It was a dangerous crossing in winter.

She would have to make that crossing herself.

The certainty of it stabbed her like a blade of ice, cruel and chill. She had not left the island in five and a half years. She had never left the island at all; she had come here, and stayed here.

She could seek out the seeker. She could show her this. She *should* show her this. Nerenyi n'Jheel had taken her side when she had begged admittance to the scribed mysteries. Nerenyi had been illuminator as well as seeker, and her battles with former wordsmith Graefel were legendary. Falowen trusted her wisdom and relied on her backbone. But Nerenyi did not abide secrets. The philosophy of seekers was disclosure. They talked compulsively, without discretion. It would be all over the mainland in a matter of ninedays, and this had to be handled with more care than that.

It would change everything. It could not be entrusted to the head scholar; he would hoard the knowledge, perhaps use it to gain leverage over those he felt threatened their scholars' way of life. She would go to Graefel, and he would take the bamboo codex from her and lock it up, telling no one, forbidding her to tell.

Graefel would hide it. Nerenyi would shout its contents from the hilltop.

Only Jhoss would know what best to do.

Send him a message, she thought. It would be madness to make the journey herself. Leave it to some runner who traveled for a living.

Yet runners could not be trusted to refrain from reading the messages they bore, and Jhoss could not be trusted to believe a message sent by a third-rung scholar. He would certainly not return to Senana at her behest.

She could leave it here, and go to him. Probably no one else would look at it in the meantime. But he'd be no more inclined to believe her story in person than in a message, and she would have wasted too much time in the journey.

He would have to see this for himself, and she would have to bring it. Bearing an artifact off the island, though it was not a bound parchment or vellum codex, was forbidden. When the appropriation was discovered, as it would be, quickly, she would be hunted down, relieved of her stolen goods, and prohibited from returning. Then she would have no proof to show Jhoss, and either Nerenyi would make its contents known or Graefel would bury it.

Somehow she would have to keep ahead of them until she'd caught up to Jhoss and shown him. Then the decision would be his.

He was qualified. He had served as advisor to Torrin Wordsmith himself, the liberator of the codices. Some on Senana, following Graefel's lead, held that Torrin was the dark betrayer, the man who drove the light from Eiden Myr and toppled the Ennead that protected it from disaster and storm. Falowen knew otherwise. She had spent long evenings listening to Jhoss recount the tales. She felt the great mage's death as if she had known him.

Could he have been aware of the information this bamboo flitch contained? He was deeply learned; he had read as many of the codices as it was possible for one man to read in the time he'd had, and made a start at translating several of the old languages. She had pored over the notes scribed in his flowing, slanted hand. But he had known the old Ennead might read them. He had been circumspect. He had kept secrets. Like Graefel, who had stored vast tracts of knowledge in his mind in the days when all triadic scribings dissipated in castings, he had done most of his work in his head. And he had not had access to everything they had here.

He could not have known. He would not have kept something like this from his closest folk. He would have told Jhoss.

She must tell Jhoss.

"Something interesting?" Bofric n'Roric leaned over from the table behind her to peer at what had thrust her into contemplation.

Somehow Falowen managed not to snap the codex shut. Bofric was a meddling old man and she didn't like him. She had no grounds for mistrust, beyond his tendency to stick his knobby nose in things that didn't concern him, but his insatiable thirst for languages came with a furtiveness that made her uneasy even when she had nothing to hide.

With a sigh, she obscured his view with a weary wave of her forearm. "Accounts," she said. "And in a numeric system that's been well researched. I fear I've wasted my time repairing it." She folded it with unrushed care, closing in the lines of verse.

"Pity," Bofric said, and returned to his own work. Had his sharp eyes lingered just a bit too long?

Falowen packed up her materials and went out the door that led to the collection she had drawn the bamboo codex from.

Then she slipped through an adjoining door, hid the codex under a heavy stack of sedgeweave on a storage shelf, and proceeded to her dormitory to dress for a brisk walk.

• • •

The brisk walk became a terrified descent to the limestone beach, burdened with the codex she had retrieved and the light snack that was all she could justify bringing with her beyond the wool outerwear and thick cloak she wore. She was certain she was followed, but glances behind her showed nothing. If there were no boats at the dock, all was lost. The evening check of the collections would show that she had not returned what she had left her mark for. The community of scholars had grown to several nonned, but that was not so many that a quick check wouldn't turn up that Falowen n'Tedra was missing, too. Someone would remember that she had gone for a walk down the hill. Someone would be sent to check the docks. In winter, there was nowhere to hide.

One coracle remained.

She did not take the time to call or search for its owner. She got in, unmoored it, laid oars in oarlocks, and rowed.

The seas were rough. Her arms burned after a dozen strokes. The coracle took on water. She feared the light craft would overturn and dump her into the whitecapped swells in her heavy woolens. She feared the willow laths would break apart in the chop. She feared she would freeze. She feared the current that bore her Headward of where she meant to land, then the winter waves that gouged the beach she thought to choose instead. This was madness. She was mad. She was a scholar, she wasn't fit. But she had been a binder once. She had been strong once. Somehow she gained a shell-strewn strand on the mainland, tethered the coracle to a spike driven deep in the sand, and made her way on foot up the dunes and onto a semblance of road before the light failed.

She rested, and when the moon rose she began the long journey across the Hand to where she might ship for the Strong Leg, in the heel of which was Jhoss n'Kall's home.

She was haunted by what she sensed as a shadow, but she could never trick it into revealing itself. No one could have followed her so far. If Nerenyi's folk had tracked her, they would confront her directly. *You'd make a conspiracy of the cracks in a stone*, she told herself, and continued on, day after dogged day.

Illness was everywhere, but she stayed nowhere long enough to court it. She missed her studies; she missed her colleagues. She thought often of turning back. Then she looked at the verses on the bamboo strip and continued on. Jhoss *must* see this for himself. Jhoss would know what to do, how to keep the knowledge from being misused. Jhoss would know how to deliver to Eiden Myr the salvation this slim strip prophesied.

One day, two-thirds of the way to her destination, she coughed up black phlegm, and knew that her race was lost.

Still she went on. She redoubled her pace. She begged rides, she told lies. As her health failed, she sought a runner. Better to entrust her burden now than die with it on her person, to be consumed along with her body in the bonefolk's arms, or have it stolen from her while she lay ill. But she could find no runner to the Heel before she fell.

She lay insensible for days. Her lungs came out of her in hacking pieces, black and rotten. Fever seared her, then subsided, then returned. Her extremities swelled. Unknown folk took care of her. They should shun her contagion, but they bathed her, warmed her, cooled her, fed her, administered herbs to ease her pain.

"The children," she babbled, "it's the children, I must tell Jhoss." No one answered. "The children are our salvation," she said, her wasted fists clenched in a linen shirtfront, shoving her face up close to a caretaker. "You must find me a runner!"

"Of course," the woman said, and disengaged. No runner came.

"It's the children!" she cried, and someone said, "Hush, now. You're dying. Don't make it harder on yourself. Give me the codex."

She couldn't understand the blunt words. She must have misheard. "Jhoss . . . must handle . . . with great care . . . this knowledge . . . proof . . . the children . . ."

"Leave it to me, scholar. I'll see it gets into the best possible hands, and no other." She felt the threaded bamboo stack slip from her. Had she been reading? Had she fallen asleep reading? It was too dark to read. Silly of her, to try to read in the dark.

"The children," she said for the last time, as the dark closed in.

I

Shadow

GIR DOEGRE

i!" Jiondor Stallholder's shout set sheets of tin trembling, rang walls and roofs like coarse bells, jingled in the trinkets down Vanity Short. "*Come back here, you!*"

Pelufer danced.

With a hop and a skip-turn she had cleared two sprawled waysiders and switched direction to eel through a clutch of gawpers at the opposite stall. Why did hungry people with nothing to work at spend all day ogling food they couldn't afford? Why did waysiders even come here, stuffing the longstreets with their skinny bodies and their need? All right, the maur had risen, the mountains had quaked—but flooded banks brought sea-things you could eat, and she'd rather be crushed than starve. Waysiders all had the same arch in their necks and slump in their shoulders. Their bodies were shaped into an appeal. They came here looking like somebody should take *care* of them.

She rounded a stall piled with bulbs and tubers, evaded the blur of a kick from the stallholder, chewed the candied sedgeroot she'd had off Jiondor. He was still thundering. She swallowed, and belched up a grin. *Too late*, she sang in silence, *too late*. The treat was in her belly now. She shot back across Hunger Long, a quick deft weave through the sluggish current of people. A keeper loomed between her and escape, the little alley between Jifadry's soups and Toudin's stews. His arm was bent into a crook, his mouth a slice of smile that meant *I've got you*. Her grin widened. She picked up speed. She hurtled toward him. His body set for impact. Then a skidding whirl in the dust, a dip, a twist, and she was away. He was braced too firm to turn in time.

She was through Scarves Short, out the other side, and to the middle of Tin Long before nine breaths had passed. A good dance: the pouches at her belt bulged with loaves, her pockets sagged with plums and nuts, her belly was full of treats. Hunger Long was still Harvest Long, for her—its old name, from before the floods and quakes and waysiders, from before the poisoned rivers. She was small, and she knew how to move in a crowd, keep tall folk between her and her target until the moment came to snake a hand out and pluck her choice from fryspit or hangline. She looked like every other ragged child in this Strong Leg tradertown, neither boy nor girl, hair neither blond nor brown, face and arms so dirty that her skin had no color of its own. The town keepers never bothered to learn the children one from another, wouldn't know her when they saw her again. Tomorrow she'd dance down Copper Long, then Bronze Long, and shortstreets thereafter, and in a sixday Hunger Long would have forgotten her, and she would dance there again.

If they left here, as they had to, *had* to, soon, no matter what Elora said, she would need quick and practiced steps. No one else would feed them. No one else would take what they couldn't charm or barter. No one else would see Caille safe and sheltered by night, fed and watered by day. Elora's shoulds-and-shouldn'ts would be the end of them if Pelufer's steps faltered.

Elora's rights-and-wrongs came straight from Father's mouth, and they'd been lies when he said them. Elora believed them; Elora believed in honesty, and fair trading, and Elora believed in Father. But belief and honesty didn't fill a rumbling belly. And anyway, Father was dead.

Tin Long was not as thronged as Hunger Long. Waysiders stayed clear till nightfall or were swept aside or trampled. Copper Long was buffed and rounded, pliable; Bronze Long was muscular, shining; Tin Long was sharp and brittle, all glints and angles, sheets of metal hammered so thin that they'd cut you just for thinking of them. It stretched from its Bronze Long point to its Copper Long end through sticky air hazed with dust: a muted sparkle of pots and spoons and plates glinting in the humid sunshine, a rattle of tin and tinsmiths' calls and here and there a tinkers' wagon creaking back from some long overland journey only to restock, turn around, go out again. Horse sweat and the drone of flies thickened vapors of mold and rot. The shacks and houses climbing the upleg hills in jumbled wedges would not block the sun until well after noon. Noxious mists rolled through the streets like tumbleweeds, never higher than a man's head, never climbing the hills. Heat off the tin roofs made a lazy shimmer in air almost too dense to breathe. All the water in the world hung suspended in that air, absorbing grit and dull-baked sunlight until you'd think it would just go solid and all movement would grind to a halt. No rain since harvestmid last; just this laden air, and dewmongers to harvest it, and drip pits with their tarps and stones, and whatever they could import across Maur Lengra, from the Weak Leg, where folk had marshes to drain, or from the Girdle, where the rain never stopped.

Pelufer slipped into the gutter behind the stalls, to pass close by the shortstreets that opened on the long every dozen threfts. Safe from roadway traffic, she would blend with the tinkers' children, though most her age slaved at bending brake or jennie. A band of young ones surrounded her in some ring-a-lo game. She lunged with a hard stamp of foot and a jut of jaw too overacted to be serious. The ring burst and the children flew giggling and tumbling away through billows of mist. Conversation drifted back on the settling vapor, the gossip and byplay of experienced customers and traders. "We're losing this town," she heard, and "We've lost it already, all the waysiders to feed," and "I've patched and rehammered all I can, it's new tin we need."

You hear that, Elora?

River waters had fed Gir Doegre even when they could no longer slake its thirst, and there were still the roads: maur-to-Knee, Boot-to-Girdle, Heel-to-Highlands. A good place for traders, an easy pitch. But you had to have something to trade, and if you made things out of other things, you had to bring something here from somewhere else, or send someone to fetch it.

That would be good work for us, Elora. If there was tin out there, and copper, and the miners and sifters weren't all dead of flood or plague or the dozen other disasters invented or garbled by too many tellings . . .

She might as well speak to the dead. Elora clung to this place like a haunt.

Far above, in the sickly haze that was the sky, thunder rumbled. Gawpers sighed in anticipation. From away, they were; Pelufer ignored the sky. It was helpless thunder. It rolled across them all the time, on its way Heartward. Never gave a drop of rain. Only lightning, now and then, to stitch the sky, or strike what houses had stood firm against rot and mites and borers.

At the next stall, the same conversation, repeated up and down both shorts and longs: This town is rotting, it's starved for metals, it's as good as dead, just look around you. "The Khinish will wake before you see the end of this place, it's always been here and always will," she heard, a trader's optimism, and then something else, something she must have heard wrong, except she heard it again, a low sound-shape of promise and menace:

The Khinish are waking.

Her heart leaped, part fear and part exhilaration. If it was true . . . if they came . . . there would be an end on the dancing then, the Khinish wouldn't abide that, but there would be work, too, real work for her, for them, no more mooning at tinkers' get with their useful chores or being turned away from harvests so poor that not even cottars were needed to bring them in. The Khinish were strong. The Khinish were capable. The Khinish could put the world to rights. If they woke. If they came.

But rumors were hardly ever true. And if this one was, it would give Elora enough to beat her at stay-or-go. And then she would never be free of *them*.

She kept moving. Pewter Short, Brass Short, Stone Short, each with stalls crowded right up to the end. The longstreet side of any stall was its weak side—accessible but not closely watched. Custom passed in front, and no one expected trouble from the backs of Tin Long traders watching their own wares. Most end stalls had baffles to shield them against quick-fingered children. And traders knew better than to let their wares spill over the front of the stall onto crates and shelves beyond the reach of their arms. But times were hard. They had to display all the stock they could. The smallest items, the least likely to be missed, the most eye-catching but least valuable, migrated out and down and away from the protection of the stall like waysiders seeking something better for themselves.

That was how two glittering stones made their way from Mireille's stall into Pelufer's pocket.

Too late, she sang in silence, *too late*, as Mireille's snub nose came up and her head turned as if pulled on a string. Quick as a cat she was out from behind her planks. Her little mouth was a round dark opening. In another breath, curses would fly out of it like bats. Her narrow-eyed gaze speared the hand that had dropped near Pelufer's pocket. So she hadn't seen the stones go in. She wouldn't call the keepers unless she was sure. Pelufer had tricked her too many times.

With lazy ease, Pelufer unlooped her water ladle from where it hung next to her left tunic pocket. She didn't have to look back at Mireille as she slid into the queue by the public barrels. She could feel the spite through the misty air. Mireille would be counting stones for the rest of the day, then recounting them to make sure the mistake wasn't her own. It was so hard not to burst out laughing that tears leaked from the corners of her eyes.

The woman who had been last in line, stiff with impatience or the effort of waiting, went soft in the spine and shoulders and expansively gestured Pelufer ahead of her. A generous hostess welcoming a guest into space that was not hers to offer. The motion jostled the man before them. He turned, puffing up in preparation to take affront. "The child's crying with thirst!" the woman said.

His stance relaxed into something lazy, hipshot, but still balanced, still ready for . . . what? *Best not rile this one*, Pelufer thought, beginning to regret her choice of ruse. "Bit inefficient, wouldn't you say?" he remarked. "Cry less, drink less."

Pelufer sniffled and rubbed a bare toe in the sticky dirt, eyes downcast. She needn't see the man's face to know that he'd dismissed her with wry amusement and returned to contemplating the wait. The way he moved spoke louder than any word or smile. People were shapes and subtle shifts of weight, angles of shoulder and cant of legs. Eyes and voices could hide a nonned things. The language of limbs could not.

"Are you hungry?" the woman said. "Does anyone look after you?" She was standing too close. Pelufer smelled travel sweat and the moldflowers keepers washed with after hauling the dead away. She shouldn't smell like a keeper. This wasn't right.

"Water's free," Pelufer said vaguely, glancing over her left shoulder. She could run, now; she could leave Mireille counting, forget the ruse. But Mireille was talking to a keeper. Mists shifted, and brief dilute sunlight rounded the pommel of his sheathed longblade to a muted shine. Mireille's hands danced a pattern over her planks, then fluttered at Pelufer. The keeper turned to look. Pelufer was staring to the left, as if watching a mange-ridden dog forage in the midden behind a shack, but she had them clear in her side vision.

A pattern, she thought. Poxy Mireille. She didn't need to count. She'd laid them out some way that she knew when the shape had changed. It was what Pelufer would have done. She'd never expect it of Mireille, always so quick to pounce on sacrilege.

"I'm sure you wouldn't say no to a treat," the not-right woman behind her said. Her hands fell on Pelufer's shoulders. A protective gesture. People were always trying to mother her. She hated it. But this was something more. There was something wrong with those hands. Her insides felt strange.

"I don't take handouts," Pelufer said, harsher than she should. This too-kind woman might keep the keeper off her. But there was something bubbling inside. The not-rightness was growing, radiating from the woman into her and forming into a thing inside her, connected with the light hands flat on her shoulders.

The keeper was heading over. Mireille's complaints goaded him like little missiles. Pelufer had to watch him without watching, had to gauge sternness or exasperation from the way he moved, to tell if he was on Mireille's side or not.

"Not a handout. Something in trade. Perhaps you'd tell me a little about this place, I've only just come and I'd be grateful for a local guide and you could earn yourself a treat, even a meal, perhaps your mother and father and sisters and brothers . . ."

Be quiet! Pelufer needed to sense the movements, the dance around her. She could tell the keeper she was with this woman. She might use this. But too much was happening too fast. The woman wasn't right. She offered work, a day's work, that was all Pelufer had ever wanted, that was all Father had ever wanted, a day's work to feed his family, but Pelufer knew a ruse when she heard one, she felt the lie running tense down the woman's fingers, *don't try to use someone who would use you, it twists on you—*

They were only four from the barrels now. The water keeper was bladed, too, but water keepers didn't handle the dead. "Three more," he said, the customary warning as the barrels ran low, "the rest of you try down the long," and the customary moans slid along the queue as obedient folk moved on to the next station, there were three for every long, they never all went empty at once.

Her own ruse had run out with the water.

It was the woman, or the keeper, or the dance now.

She couldn't use the woman against the keeper or the keeper against the woman. She wanted to. She wanted to be clever and do that. But adults had a nasty habit of siding with each other.

She felt as though she'd swallowed a cup of freezing bubbles.

"It's all right," said the dangerous man ahead of her, beginning to turn, "I'll be the last, you'll both share mine."

She wouldn't. Too much was wrong here. She couldn't sort it. Time to dance. She tensed to spring.

The woman sensed it. Her hands closed reflexively on Pelufer's shoulders. The thing inside her burst out like a rotten center:

"*Ardis.*"

No, no, not now—

"Traig." She could not stop it. "Areil." She bit her tongue, tasted rust. "Bendik."

The woman jerked stiff but did not release her. The man's body betrayed nothing, but his face drained of blood, sometimes you *could* tell things from faces— Names vomited out of her, a gush of names right here in the middle of Tin Long, this was disaster, she had to run—

Fingers arched into claws dug into nerves between the bones of her shoulders. Her arms went tingly-numb. Names poured from her mouth. Impressions not her own poured through her head. She cut them off, an old vicious reflex: She made an axe fall in her mind and cut off the limb of a tree of names. But still they battered at her. Never so many in one place since the bilechoke fever had run through Highhill. Except for the spirit wood. She couldn't control her mouth or her throat, couldn't strangle it. Glittering black tar oozed around the edges of her vision.

"It's some kind of fit," the dangerous man said. The stalls keeper stopped next to them. Traders and customers turned curious heads. The water keeper left the spent barrels and joined them with the same wary slow movements as his bladed brother. Fear cleared her mind but couldn't shut her mouth. The dangerous man, the flowery woman—Pelufer felt their connection through the closing of their bodies, they meant to keep her from the keepers, too late, too late, *they steal lone children like you to give the bonefolk*, nonsense spouted by angry stallholders but if it was nonsense why did the bladeless woman wash with flowers why was everything funneling in not right this was not right—

Back was stopped by the woman's body, sidewise by her hands, forward by the man, but down was clear. She was a child having a fit. People having fits fainted. That wasn't so hard. She'd been close enough a breath ago. She melted her legs. The pinching fingers could not support her dangling weight. She hit the ground like a full sack. The fingers came with her, closed on her shirt. She spun hard in the dirt—outward, away from the approaching stalls keeper. Old linen gave but did not tear. The woman would not let go. Her arms were numb. She had only her legs. Her teeth, if she had to.

The stalls keeper was bending down to her. She drove herself upward into the woman's clinging fingers. The woman swore and snatched them back. The man said, "We must get her out of the sun, it's a heat palsy, I'm a healer, let me take her," but the keepers weren't having it, maybe sometimes keepers *could* help you, and she was whirling, spinning into the dangerous man, and the keeper reaching for her blundered into him, and their grabbing arms muddled, and she was away, across the long, through the jagged teeth of tin stalls, up the reeking midden path behind rows of hovels and then between the hovels, still small enough to fit though soon she wouldn't be, old limewashed clay scraped her, she lost a loaf-stuffed pouch in the tight squeeze and she'd left another behind on the ground when she dropped and spun, that food had been for Elora and Caille, they'd have to leave here before she was too big to get through the boltholes, they'd have to leave here sooner than that if claw-fingered strangers were stealing children, how would she explain this, a fit right in Tin Long in front of everyone, Elora would kill her, she had to get back . . .

Up a steep short, down again, up again, over, hurdling dogs, ducking clotheslines, ducking the paddles clothesbeaters turned on her for the disruption, barking apology. She never danced where folk lived, she never ventured up this hill, too many had died here. She shut her ears, tried not to shut her eyes. It wouldn't help. She felt the whispering tickle of names in her throat. She concentrated on material shapes, objects to avoid, elude, slip between in a calculation of speed and angles. She ran out of breath halfway along the remaining stretch of Tin Long. She realized she was falling. She forced her steps wide. Just another few threfts.

A manger beckoned. She went down, rolled under. Stifled a sneeze. Ignored the curious snuffling of soft donkey muzzles until it stopped.

Her head was pounding. Her heart was pounding. She was patient. She let the pounding slow. She didn't think about what happened. In a few slowbreaths, then she would think. When her breaths were coming slow enough, she'd count nine of them and then she'd think.

Ardis. A baker who loved the sweet smell of fresh flour. A . . .

She conjured the axe in her mind, raised it high, cut the Ardis limb off hard.

Traig. He made beds. The sheets were soft in his hands, silky, not crisp like linen or downy like flannel. Who'd think to make sheets out of silk?

She cut the Traig limb off. Then the Areil limb—some kind of teacher, showing patterning to young people. Then Bendik, before he came clear. She swallowed a whimper. It was too much. One was too much. She couldn't count how many this had been.

I'm Pelufer, she thought very clearly at herself. *I'm getting up now. I'm going back to my sisters.*

She elbowed out from under the manger, got to shaky feet, peered around to get her bearings. She'd come mostway up the hill. Down behind her, the long was a tin-spiked river of mist.

What had those strangers been, how were they linked, what had they wanted, why was the world a twistedness around them, *where had all those names come from?* The treats in her belly had curdled, and she was, perversely, thirsty. On a renewed burst of fear, she broke into a trot, then made herself walk. Damp air came hard into her lungs; she swore on every outbreath. Better to swear than to say names. She cursed Mireille and keepers and dangerous, flowery strangers. She tried on a laugh. It didn't work. Another name burped out at the end of it, and a woman near her looked up stricken from a butter churn. She quickened her step and held a soiled kerchief over her mouth to muffle the sounds. She never came here, into the tangle of shortstreets at the upland end of town. She never came past the hovels at the front, all tin sheets and sod, never went beyond, to where the rot had not taken so many of the original structures, to the shantytown where people crammed in under any roofs they could find and camped under precarious tinsheet or tarp lean-tos, sleeping chocked against the decline. She never ventured back to where one-family cottages now hosted three, or six, beds bunked and the occupants sleeping—and dying—in shifts. She never came to Highhill. This was why.

She picked her way around the fetid knots of shelters, through alleys and byways, down toward the head of Copper Long. The lightning-slashed clouds moved Girdleward and the watery sun moved Khineward. Angling light changed the shape of the vapors that haunted Gir Doegre. All shapes had changed; that brief shock in Tin Long had twisted the fabric of her world, and now everything seemed a wrongness, off kilter, out of place. She sensed threats lurking in byways that had been avenues of escape.

Understanding none of it, drained and frayed and knowing her own dogged bravery for a ruse tried in vain on herself, she crossed Tin Long as furtive as a cat hearing wagons rumble. She dodged and twisted and turned with the twisting, turning shorts, deep inside the triangle of Tin and Copper and Bronze Longs, the center of Gir Doegre town. Hunger Long bisected the triangle, from point to base, another furtive crossing, wedge to wedge. On instinct she avoided the cold places where the names would come. She knew them all, knew every fingerspan of the traders' wedges. There was no thought now of filching untended wares. Just the drive to return to where she had begun at sunup, the debris-strewn lot inside the intersection of Copper Long and Bronze Long, where the rot had crumbled all the shacks and now the junkmongers displayed their pitiful offerings on ragged blankets or raveled silk or stained linen, or no more than a little space cleared on the ground.

Elora sat at the lot's edge, a slim, silk-haired beacon among the drab huddles of fallen wrights and traders, by a linen cloth smoothed neat on the scrap of ground they had fought hard to defend for the last two years. Their pitch.

Caille, absorbed in some complex arrangement of mounds and pebbles in the dirt nearby, felt Pelufer's approach and raised her head without turning, spoke a word to their older sister. There was anger in Elora's body as she twisted to see.

Normal, Pelufer thought. *Act normal. People are all around.*

"Here," she said before Elora could ask her where in the raving spirits she'd been, and deposited on a corner of their cloth the contents of one pouch—glazed buns, no longer square, with a cluster of berries crushed into them.

Elora screeched, plucking at the sticky mass. "You'll stain it, Pel—oh, look, you *idiot*—"

"I'll clean it, I always do." She kept her voice reasonable. Normal. Elora went dead stubborn when she was cranky. Say, *Pack up, we have to go, we have to go home and stay there for the rest of the day*, and Elora would set her jaw and sit tight until she'd had the whole story. It wasn't safe to tell it here.

"And all those cleanings will add up and it will fray and look dingy and be no good to us at all—it's our last linen, you know that, why do you *do* these things?"

"I don't."

"You do."

"Do not."

"Do too."

"All right I do. Don't you like what I brought? Caille likes it. Look, there's dourberries, and bannock, we hardly ever get that—"

"It's all squished together."

"So? It'll still taste good."

"It's disgusting."

"It all goes together in your stomach!" Real annoyance ground in her. Elora was such a *pest*, and this was important, they couldn't afford to be cranky right now.

"Berrybread," Caille pronounced, with a beatific smile. She separated one sticky bun from another, rotated it so that the berry-smeared side was toward her, opened her mouth wide, and shoved the whole thing into her pudgy face.

Elora should have softened, sharing a smile with Pelufer at their cute little sister. Caille was cute on purpose, to effect just such a softening. But neither had a smile to share. "Not a thing we can set out on the pitch," Elora said. "You haven't brought us a single new thing in a nineday."

"I'm feeding us, Elora, that's more than I can say for you. Did you shift *any* of this lot today?" The paltry selection of junk on the linen didn't look any smaller, only rearranged to make it seem that there were new wares. It was artfully done; Elora was good. But it was not enough.

"Custom isn't moving as it should. Something's wrong today."

You don't know the third of it.

"Come on, then," she said. "Let's close up. Let's eat at home. We never eat at home anymore, like a proper family." A calculated appeal: Elora, the oldest at nine-and-four, was always trying to make them the proper family they could never be again.

Elora squinted at her, then shook her head. "We'll eat here, while we work. We can't lose even part of a day, not when custom is thin."

Panic edging in, Pelufer cast about for inspiration, and found it in the wary, envious eyes of the downtrodden traders around them. Folk who'd be waysiders themselves soon enough. Most of them had no shack to go to, no remnant of shelter left. They slept on the blankets they laid their wares on during the day. Come winter, they would freeze. They were always hungry.

"Look," she said, tension giving the word a nasty bite. "Look at what else I brought." She tossed two more pouches on the cloth, shook out the contents of one, and began to empty her pockets. A blatant display. A keeper's tithe of bounty.

"Pelufer, stop it!" Elora scooped bruised peppers and squashed loaves back into pouches, glancing quickly around from under her lashes. It was too much, she said in the secret way, with her fingers, hands held low. The others would know she'd stolen it.

And they'd be wanting it for themselves, Pelufer fingered back, merciless. "So let's go home and eat."

Elora hissed in frustration. But she acquiesced. She pressed the filled pouches back into Pelufer's hands, then cleared Caille off the edge of the cloth so she could bundle it into a sack, which she then slung over her shoulder. They rose as one, from long habit. All their wares, a hodgepodge of nails and ribbons, tapers and tacks, buckles without belts and laces without shoes, jumbled into a sack that a slim young girl could sling with ease.

"I don't know what's got into you," Elora growled low, for Pelufer's ears only, "but you'll pay for it later, you mark me." They looked at no one as they walked. They did not have to negotiate the lot's patchwork of pitches when they closed up; they crossed the tail end of Copper Long and disappeared into what seemed a tangle of thickets and thorn bramble, up a track that only they remembered and no waysiders had yet found. At the end of that track, half a mile on, was a shed that had once stored a crafter's tools. A cozy place tucked away in the thick brush that separated town and forest, far enough above the Heel Road to work in isolated peace. The rot had not touched the shed, though mites and borers were eating it now. It had been their mother's workplace. They had bartered the tools away four years ago, and come home sobbing after, to a cottage whose contents went for the drink that killed their father two years past. A year ago, in winter, they had bartered the cottage itself for clothing and footgear and blankets; now they lived in the shed, a ninefoot-by-ninefoot space where they slept on mite-pocked boards, one of them always tucked up against the boltless, out-of-plumb door to keep it closed.

If Caille did not relent—and Pelufer knew she would not, she could best Elora to get her way but never Caille, not on something like this—the shed would fall to the mites and borers, and they would have only the pitch left then. The space of their world had decreased in a slow agony of subtraction, season by season, since Pelufer was five. Caille's age.

They would leave this town. They *would*. And then the world would open to them, instead of closing down, year by year, foot by foot, person by person, until only one of them was left, or none.

As they made their way along the faint trail, escorted by clouds of midges, careful not to let the only clothes they owned snag or tear on thorns, Pelufer was already in the shed in her mind. She would sit cross-legged against the door while Elora and Caille ate. The only light in the shed came in filtered shafts through the holes where their chinking had crumbled. They had not yet traded their battered old broom, but no amount of sweeping kept the molds at bay, and the close air was choking. But it was their place. They would be safe there while she told her sisters what had happened, while they figured out what to do. Elora would eat slowly, pretending to savor every bite, to be sure that Caille was full before she finished what was left. Caille, Pelufer knew, always stopped before she was full, pretending to an attack of pickiness after the edge of hunger was off, and Elora always believed her. She'd long ago ceased trying to get Pelufer to eat. Pelufer ate what she could cadge when she cadged it, and if she didn't cadge enough for all of them, she went hungry, and that was that.

She would not partake of the keepers' tithe. That was for waysiders. Refugees. Beggars. She saw to it that her sisters were fed well enough to disdain it, too.

"Tell me now," Elora said, moving sidewise through a place where brush had grown nearly across the track. "While we walk. We're far enough."

Pelufer smiled. She knew Elora had been dying to ask.

She told her—all but the fit.

"For spirits' sake!" Elora cried. "Is that it? That's why all your antics today? Gossip and a run-in with smelly strangers? When does a day pass that we're not up to our necks in both?"

Elora thought she was so bloody hardheaded and practical. "You better listen to me, Elora! You said yourself something's wrong today. I can feel it! Everything's wrong!"

"You had a scare, that's all. You don't want to admit it because you don't like to admit you get scared. You're making it into more than it is so you won't seem a fool. But we all get scared. Don't we, Caille."

Caille was having none of the argument. She returned Elora's gaze, blinked impassively, and said nothing.

Pelufer burst out, "I had a fit of names. In the middle of Tin Long. That flowery woman put her hands on me and names came out."

Elora stopped dead in the track, but didn't turn. "That's never happened before."

"No. It was her. She was wrong somehow. They came off her. And the way she smelled . . . she . . ." It came together in her mind, the horrible thought. "But it can't be," she breathed, refusing the idea. "The man said he was a healer. Maybe that was it. Maybe they were the names of the ones they couldn't save."

"So maybe they're not wrong. Maybe they're right, and good, and have never hurt anyone, and you were just upset because you've never been touched by someone who touched death."

Their eyes met, both minds spinning.

"They weren't wearing white," Pelufer said. "And that man's no healer—he's a fighter if I ever saw one, he wore a blade even though he didn't."

"And the keepers don't feel wrong like that, do they," Elora said, "and they haul the dead to the bonefolk, and they touch you sometimes when they're trying to catch you, and names don't come out. Nolfi doesn't feel like that, and his brother died in his arms. Everyone in this town has touched death. They don't feel wrong."

"Father never felt wrong like that," Pelufer added softly. She didn't look at Caille, but Elora understood. Mother had died in birthing Caille. Caille herself had come from death.

Names didn't come off people who had touched death. They could only have come off people who caused it. "We'll have to hide you till the keepers forget what they saw. And the gawpers." Elora's shoulders slumped. "Oh, Pel, how could you?"

"I didn't mean to. I never mean to. It just happens."

"Yes. I know that. I'm sorry. But if we have to go . . . spirits, Pel, *Mireille* saw you, she'll *never* forget something like that . . . I can't go, Pel . . . I can't leave Mamma and Padda. . . ."

"*They left us!*"

Elora stared. "I can't believe you said that."

"Well, they did."

"They did? Then why did we have to trade the cottage? Why did we have to give our home away for the price of a winter's warmth?"

Pelufer clamped her teeth. That wasn't what she'd meant. She knew they were still here. Mother had died in that cottage. Father had died in that cottage. That was why she couldn't stay here. She couldn't bear it, having them so close yet not really there. And that was why Elora couldn't leave.

She had lost her advantage. It was always like that, with Elora. She could force her, sometimes, but on even ground she could never outnegotiate her. Elora was their father's daughter, their father the trader, who'd tended a copper stall his life long, who'd pledged a woman who'd made copper sing in her hands. A fair man, but canny. You'd come in sure you had the stones to outplay Elora on any table, and she'd turn the game upside down.

She wanted Elora to decide. But she wanted Elora to decide the way she wanted her to.

The rest of the argument unrolled in her head like a carpet whose weave never changed. *Then let's find somewhere else to live*, she'd say. *We can't afford anywhere else to live*, Elora would say. *Then I'll go to the spirit wood*, Pelufer would say. *You will not*, Elora would say. *You will not steal from the dead*. But they were dead, they didn't care anymore about whatever had been in their pockets and around their necks, the things the bonefolk left behind. *It's stealing from the living if it's anything at all, and I do that all the time*, she'd say, and Elora would say, *This would be worse. This would be things with sentimental value. Things people would recognize. They'd know where you'd been. That ground is sacred*. She'd say, *Then I'll travel to another town and trade them there and come back, I'll hitch a ride with carters*, and Elora would say they must never split up, and she'd say *Then we'll go together*, and Elora would say *We'd lose the pitch, we have to be there every day or squatters will have it*. Around and around, for every solution an obstacle.

She felt suddenly, deeply, desperately tired. "I wish Mamma was here," she said. She knew she shouldn't say such things in front of Caille. It just came out. She was so tired.

"So do I, Pelufer. But she's not. And I'm the oldest."

"Only by two years, that's not so much."

"I'm the oldest, and I'll decide." Her face was grim, pained. It was as hard for Elora to walk through the dying brush as it was for Pelufer to walk through the places where people died. "We'll lay low for a few days. You're not to go out anywhere, for any reason. That man and woman were traveling through. They'll be on their way and then we just have to hope that nobody understood what they saw on Tin Long today and they'll forget about it."

"Mireille will tell."

"Mireille won't know what happened. She wasn't close enough to hear you say the names, right? And she wouldn't understand what that meant anyway."

"The woman understood. And the man. They went dead pale."

"And if—" Elora glanced at Caille, who was listening patiently, but continued, because there was never any point in trying to keep things from her; there was only one thing they had ever successfully kept from her, and it was the only thing worth worrying about. "If that woman did kill those people, and that's why the names came off her, then she won't be announcing it, will she? She won't be going to the keepers and saying, 'I must find that child, she knows the names of everyone I've killed.' "

"The keepers wouldn't know me anyway."

"Maybe not. But some trader would."

"Traders don't tell tales about their own to strangers."

"No? Not even hungry ones? Or threatened ones? Or the ones you steal from? And it's not the point anyway. The point is that the woman will probably leave here as fast as she can. You scared her. She's probably already gone."

"Or she's asking about us. Searching for us. Telling people she's worried about the little girl who had a fit in Tin Long today, and does anyone know where she lives?"

This frightened them both into silence. Then Pelufer whispered, looking down the track, "No one knows where we live now."

Elora followed her gaze, but neither of them moved to continue onward. "Can we be sure?"

Caille squeezed between them, pressed close, eyes wide. Sensing their fear? Or something else?

Pelufer twisted to look behind them. This path was the only way to the shed. The dangerous man and the flowery woman would have gone to their pitch first. That location would have been easy enough to get out of people if Elora was right. It would take them longer to find out about the shed. If someone knew to tell them.

"Come on," Pelufer said. "We can still get there ahead of them."

Elora stopped her. "And what? Hide? They'll knock that door down with a breath."

"Get our things," Pelufer replied, struggling past her.

Elora took her by the shoulders as if to shake sense into her. "What things, Pel? *We haven't got any things left.*"

Pelufer went still, searching Elora's face, amazed that Elora might not know that she knew about the faces under the floorboards, more amazed that she would be willing to leave them behind. She put a hand slowly into her left tunic pocket, felt down past seeds and nuts and the remains of a season's stolen food, brought out the two stones she'd nicked from Mireille's stall, displayed them on soiled fingertips. Even grotty with crumbs and lint, they sparked with green fire.

"Eyes," she told her sister. "I brought you eyes."

Elora's mouth worked, but nothing came out. Then she said, "You stole these."

"Well, yes," Pelufer said. Didn't Elora care that she knew about the workings? "But only from Mireille."

"And that's supposed to make it all right? Because no one likes that poor lonely woman, it's all right to steal from her? She hates us already, Pel, you're only making things harder for us. Have you done *anything* today that wouldn't make things harder for us?"

"She's not a woman. She has only four years on you."

"I'm nearly a woman."

"You're not."

"I am. Oh, this is stupid, Pel, we've got to run, we can't go home now. . . ."

"We can. We have time. We're going back for your things." She paused. "I'll go, if you're afraid."

Elora went first. She quickened the pace, took less care about skin and clothes. They kept Caille close between them, Pelufer's arms out to shield her face from sharp branches, and the old dead tough vines that could cut you just as deep. Pelufer tried not to shy at the dry rustle of startled birds, the quick start-stop-start of startled rodents. There was a rise at the end, to the shed on higher ground. They came sweaty and breathless into the fly-haunted clearing.

Pelufer knew the man and woman could not possibly have headed them off, but she gave a quick glance to either side as they emerged, checking the periphery of brown grass. She blundered hard into Elora, who had stopped cold, and Caille, between them, cried out in protest.

Then Pelufer and Caille looked, too, and none of them moved for many short breaths.

The shed had fallen.

The rot had not touched it because Elora had strengthened the old wood. That was something she could do, though she'd been exhausted for a day after. But the mites had tunneled deeply, gorged themselves. All they needed was warmth and moisture and wood, and there was plenty of that in the musty shed. The woodworms were slower, you could collect them and put them out, but that only enlarged the holes and the moths only laid more eggs, and there'd been nothing to trade for the camphor that would ward the place against them. They'd chinked the holes with earth and twigs and ivy and prayed to Eiden the shed would stand through winter.

It was only sowmid. Eiden had not obliged them.

"Oh, why now?" Elora breathed, shutting her eyes tight, clutching Caille to her side with one hand, the other reaching out toward the jumble of boards that had been their home.

"It was the mites or us," Pelufer said. She was trembling with rage, while her mind sang in silence, *Too late, too late.* She couldn't yell at Caille, but she could yell at Elora about her. "Why did she have to be so *bleeding stubborn?*"

"Don't be cruel," Elora snapped, whipping around. Caille eeled free, of Elora and the inevitable row, and started across the clearing.

"She didn't have to kill them!" Pelufer cried. "She could have just made them itchy or ill or something so they'd go chew on dead trees instead!"

"That's not something she would do."

Elora's words were calm. But she dropped slowly to her knees, staring at the end of her world.

Caille had come to within a threft of the collapsed shed. With an oath, Pelufer ran to pull her back.

"Leave her, Pel. She only wants to look."

Pelufer grimaced. She had seen the kind of looking Caille did. Late in the winter of the six fevers, when droplimb had afflicted all who'd partaken of the flour tithe, the keepers made holes for the fallen arms and feet and hands and legs and buried them, but the first hole wasn't deep enough and starving dogs dug it up during the night. They'd happened by the scene at dawn, before the keepers found it. Elora had been off protecting the pitch. Caille had watched the dogs gnaw the human limbs without emotion. Pelufer, unable to chase the dogs off, had doubled over retching, and come up to find Caille fascinated by the teeming white lives that had grown in the decaying flesh of a man's arm. She had dragged Caille away and said nothing of it to Elora. Now, at Pelufer's feet, with Pelufer poised to snatch her away should the pile of boards shift, Caille squatted down and looked intently at the insects scrambling around the ruined shed. *It was their home, too,* Pelufer thought, randomly, strangely, watching her unfathomable sister. They had only been doing what mites and grubs do.

"Broken," Caille said, and pointed.

Pelufer followed the angle of gesture and saw it right away. The round impressions of a hammer on one of the boards.

"We'll build it up again," Elora said, rising. "We have some nails. We'll get more somehow. And a hammer."

Pelufer snorted. A whole box of nails wouldn't be enough to put this right. "Maybe whoever knocked it down will let us borrow the hammer they used."

Elora came over and looked. When she closed her eyes, tears leaked out. "I won't run away," she said. "Gir Doegre is our home. Mother and Father's home." She whirled on Pelufer, her eyes flying open. "We'll ask the keepers for help."

Help. It always came down to help. Pelufer would *not* ask for help! Then you got beholden. Get beholden to too many people and your life wasn't your own anymore. "No."

"Why not? Because of your stupid pride? Someone did this to us! That's what keepers are for, to stop people doing things like this!"

"We can't trust anyone. Not traders, not keepers. Only us."

Elora gritted her teeth. "Then we'll stack the wood up and hide it and sleep on the pitch till it gets cold and then we'll trade it as firewood for lodgings and . . ." Her own attempts to find trader solutions failed, as they had failed so many before her. They had bargained away everything of value but their bodies, and those were no use to anyone either.

"We're waysiders," Pelufer said. "Don't you see? *We're waysiders in our own home now.*"

"We've already been that, Pel. We've been that since Padda died."

"Stop calling him that! You sound like a baby. He was a sodden old snock and a liar too, and 'Father' was too much respect for him!"

The flat sting of Elora's slap opened into a throbbing oval ache. Pelufer stood firm. Elora's body recoiled. Hitting Pelufer had made her instantly smaller, pulled into herself, but she would not let Pelufer see that on her face. Elora always thought that faces were the only thing about people that you could gauge.

Caille cried out, just after the crack of palm on cheek. It always took her the split of a breath to feel things. She drew breath to wail.

Elora pulled Caille's face against her stomach to muffle the sound and said, "You get my workings. Obviously you know where I keep them. You get them, and then we'll go and hide and figure out what's next."

Pelufer moved. This was something she could do. Mother would have told her to wear gloves, but she had no gloves. So she shifted the boards one by one, mindful of protruding nails, until she'd cleared a space over the back right corner of the shed. She didn't have to pull up the two loose floor planks; they'd bounced askew when the rest fell. Three small bundles wrapped in oiled cloth looked up at her from under wood dust. She replaced the oatbread in one of her pouches with them, drawing the string tight and double-knotting the end around her belt. The woven belt sagged.

Each of them had a blanket. She fished them out of the wreckage and tied them in a bundle at the end of a fallen branch from the edge of the clearing. She picked the stoutest branch she could find. She'd coveted the keepers' blades for as long as she could remember. But she'd settle, now, for a club. Her sisters needn't know of its double purpose.

The brush lengthened into shadow and then contracted as the sun sank. They returned the way they had come. Dusk would help them. Anyone searching would have to bring a lamp that would betray them. They would probably not see three girls squeezed between thornbushes where no bodies could fit. If Caille could stay quiet . . .

But it didn't come to that. They crossed the point of Copper and Bronze Longs and went over the maurbridge into Lowhill. The longs were quiet, stalls empty and battened. Dim lights burned along the row of public houses by the river. Nothing seemed amiss.

Smelling an inn's cookfire, Pelufer wondered how long it would be before whoever had knocked their shed down returned for the fuel. She knew it must have been Mireille, but she was too scared to summon more than cursory anger at her. She was always angry at Mireille. Mireille had tormented Elora as a child—some old feud between their mother and her mother that Pelufer never understood. That alone made Pelufer hate her. But then she had persuaded the alderfolk that Elora's workings were sacrilege. It was a whole group of them, but she was the worst, the loudest, with the most convincing words. Elora didn't think Pelufer knew about that. It had happened before Father died, when Elora was trying even harder to be Mother, when she tried to trade her workings to keep them going, when everything they had or earned went for Father's drink. Elora said to be forgiving, she said to pity Mireille. Pelufer pitied no one. Pelufer trusted no one. Pelufer relied on no one.

"Only to hide," Elora whispered to Caille. They stood in front of a locked byre. Animals rustled within. "Only to hide, not to frighten, not to steal their food."

Caille squinted at Pelufer to be sure Elora wasn't speaking only for herself. Then she accepted the rusty hairpin Elora held out. She slid it into the lock. She moved it up and down and sidewise, feeling around. Then she pulled it out, rolled it in her fingers, reinserted it, and turned the lock.

They went in. A dog rose up snarling, then snuffled at Caille and flopped back down as if it were their own dog, only startled out of sleep. The stock shifted, nervous, but Caille touched each one in turn and they calmed. "Donkey, ox, ox, donkey, donkey, donkey," she said to her sisters. Letting them know what they shared the space with.

They'd eaten most of Pelufer's crushed takings on the trail. They finished the rest now in silence, and the water in the gourd Elora carried. Faint misty light fell in bars through ventilation slats high in the back wall of the byre when the moon rose.

"They're beautiful eyes," Elora said suddenly.

A peace offering.

Embarrassed, Pelufer shrugged and said, "It smells like Father after a bad night in here. But you picked a good one, Elora."

"Donkey farts," Caille said with relish. Pelufer heard her lips pull back from her baby teeth in a grin. She felt Caille drag the dog out of sleep into a hug, heard its halfhearted protesting whine become a contented whuffle, felt both little sister and big, warm dog settle in for sleep between her and Elora.

"You were his favorite, Pel, you know you were," Elora said. "You know you're only angry at him for leaving us. He loved you so much."

Pelufer hated it when they talked about this. But Elora was trying. She would try, too. "No, it was you." She had to make herself say it, but it wasn't that hard, because it was true. "You were his girl." She paused. "You looked like Mamma."

"You don't know that."

"Do too."

"Do not. You don't remember her face."

"Do too!" But not the way Elora meant. She remembered a shape, a softness. Defensive, hopeless, she said, "It was kind."

"Ah," Elora said, softly, if Pelufer had proved her wrong. But in the last sweep of cloud-free moonlight they both saw Caille, cuddled in between them, thumb on her cheek and chubby fingers curled against her mouth, the whole assemblage buried in the dog's ruff. Caille had had only one glimpse of Mother, when all life and kindness had already gone from her, and had never felt the gentle touch of her living hand. If something happened to them, what would Caille remember?

"It won't," Elora said. "We won't let it."

"You don't know what I was thinking."

"Do too."

"All right you do." Pelufer picked in vain at splinters she hadn't felt enter palms and finger pads, slivers of what had been foursquare shelter, and thought, *It already did, and we let it.*

"You can't go into the wood," Elora said.

"I have to now."

"You don't."

"I do. We'll need things to barter in other towns. Awayfolk won't recognize any of it. It'll be safe to trade."

"You can't go into that place."

"Yes I can. I went through Highhill today. It wasn't so bad."

"But that was just the ones who died in Highhill."

The spirit wood was where they brought all the dead, from every part of Gir Doegre. A clearing, a gentle place that had been sacred once, a place where people of light had done their work. In other towns and other times, the tellers said, the dead were left where they'd died, for the bonefolk to collect. But here they delivered them, the last act the living could do in respect for the lost. In other times, passage would have been provided for the dying; there'd be nothing in the clearing for Pelufer to fear. But those times were gone. Pelufer could barely remember them. Elora could, but she rarely spoke of them; it was like talking about food you couldn't have or things you missed about living with Mamma and Padda, it was a torment and it wasn't fair to Caille.

That clearing in the woods was where all the dead went, and wherever the dead had been, Pelufer felt them, and named them.

"I came back from there before all right."

"You weren't all right."

"I'm older now. I'm strong."

"You're not."

"Am too."

Sigh. "All right you are. But I'm coming with you."

"You can't, Elora. You know you can't. You *really* know you can't. And if you came, we'd have to bring Caille."

"No," said Caille, but there was no telling what she meant, and she might have spoken from dreams, the word was so slurred.

The woods had been dying for a long time. The edges of them were sere and brown and drooping. The drought had done it, mostly, but Gir Doegre's river came from the Druilor Mountains, and Druilor runoff was poison to trees the same as it was to people. Dewmongers had worked for years to provide enough water to save them, and in the end had given up. Dowsers had searched in vain for underground springs. No one would use wood from the bonefolk's forest—at least, no one had yet, though next winter would tell—and so the dying trees stood uncut. None would harvest them, and none could save them.

Elora could not go into that place.

"I can barter my workings in other towns," Elora said. "I'd rather that, than have you go there."

"You have only three." Pelufer untied the heavy pouch from her belt and passed it to Elora in the dark. "And I've seen them. You can't trade these."

"I will if I have to."

"They might get just as angry in other towns as they did here. They might take these, too, and burn them."

She could feel Elora flinch.

"It's the only way. You know it and I know it." She whispered, "Is she really asleep?"

"No," Caille murmured from deep in dreams, and "No" again, but Pelufer slipped from her side without rousing her, and though the dog woke—she heard its breathing change—it took no interest in her movements. She started for the door. In her mind she was already in the woods, already approaching the place of her nightmares, already putting one foot in front of the other to force herself there, to root in humus and bracken and haunts. She jumped when a hand gripped hers hard in the dark. Elora, catching her as she passed.

"I'm glad you'll get to leave here," Elora said. "I know it's what you wanted. I'm glad you'll get what you wanted, Pel, really. Please come back so we can leave together."

"I know it's my fault," Pelufer said. She made herself grip the hand in return. "I didn't mean for this to come of it. I didn't work it out this way."

"I know you didn't."

"I only want to go home, Elora."

"I know. I know." A ragged breath. "But home's gone."

"I know. I'll be back. At Nolfi's barrow, if you have to leave here." She tried to pull her hand free, but couldn't.

"Please, Pel." Elora's grip became painful. Pelufer knew that she had her eyes squeezed shut just as tight, as she sent a prayer to whatever spirits still listened to frightened children. "Please, please come back."

Dindry Leng

Every muscle in Louarn's body clenched as a heart-piercing cry jerked the drowsing village awake. He snatched up stick and carrysack as he rose from his cross-legged vigil, and was half-way across the trampled brown triangle that had been the village green before its itinerant occupants had struggled from their bedding.

A lone peacekeeper trotted inside the moving sphere of a lantern's glare, her path converging on Louarn's. No candles flickered to life in the cottages around the green, though anxious eyes gleamed through cracked shutters as the keeper's light moved past. Louarn fell in silently behind, where the keeper would not see him and order him back. Ahead of them, down the single road that led into and out of the loop-end village, another keeper would be coming toward them through the darkness, bearing no lantern to betray his presence and ruin his night-sight in the moonless gloom.

The cry of discovery had become a sustained keening. It was difficult to locate under the howling and barking of dogs in response, the wailing of wakened infants. Not the blacksmith's, opposite the green's point; not the first few crafteries along the road beyond it. Louarn heard geese, but couldn't work out what that meant. The lantern turned down an alley between two dovecotes cooing and fluttering with the drowsy surprise of those within. Down the path was a cottage; the distressed honking came from beyond it. The down-mongers', then. Louarn followed.

The sour dryness of bird droppings was cut by the unmistakable reek of blood. An eerie creaking was accompanied by a slow, erratic drip, both just audible as the keening died to whimpers. Louarn slipped through the open cottage door behind the silhouettes of three peacekeepers. The whimpers came from somewhere near the floor below the leftmost one. The middle one raised her lantern high.

"Sweet, merciful spirits," she said.

Turning slowly in the gloom, suspended from a rafter by cords around their necks, were a man, a woman, and a younger woman. Wounds to their heads were evident only as deeper shadow, the stains that had run down their faces and into their nightclothes.

Louarn swallowed his gorge.

"Where are their *hands?*" breathed a peacekeeper.

They'd be in the closest midden heap. But Louarn could not tell them that without calling suspicion onto himself. Others were pushing in around him now, gasping at what they saw—enfolding him in anonymity. More gathered beyond the door.

"Cut them down cut them *down,*" sobbed the voice that had been keening, and two folk detached from the crowd to draw a young man up from his knees, restrain him when he lunged wildly for a peacekeeper's blade.

"Fetch a ladder," someone said, before they saw that there was one right there—the loft ladder that had been used to string the family up. Judging from the rafter's groan, it wouldn't support the dead weight of three bodies much longer as it was.

"We could only meet at night, her father didn't approve of me, I never knew why but I'd come after midnight when they were sleeping and we'd sit together . . . we'd . . ." The explanation fractured into another keening wail. The young man's friends tried to drag him from the cottage and the sight of his sweetheart's body. "No," he said, "no, for Eiden's sake let me say goodbye to her before they come, cut her down and let me . . ."

"We'll bring her to them," the tallest peacekeeper said as the others struggled to lower the bodies. "You can carry her to the boneyard, son, but only if you come away now and compose yourself."

Louarn moved aside as the peacekeeper herded the friends bearing the youth's sagging weight out of the cottage, clearing a way through the crowd beyond with low, firm words. He would interrogate that poor grieving boy. But there was nothing to be done for it.

The youth's story would ring true. He had not done this thing.

The other peacekeepers had the bodies down now. Someone had taken a lantern up to the loft. "Blood in this bed too," she said. "They were all three brained in their sleep."

It was better that way. Better quick, oblivious death under the end of a cudgel, than what Louarn had pictured.

"But the *hands*," said someone, staring at the blood-soaked dirt floor.

A horrified cry from out back told Louarn they had been found.

He was replacing a crumbling section of hearth in the bakers' cottage in Salmer Leng when he heard the rumors of the first. Clearing out the broken shards of brick, mixing the mortar, dampening the old brick before he mortared in the first of the new lest the dry bricks suck the moisture from the mortar while it cured and make it crack. He'd tapped the new bricks into place one by one, adding mortar at the top of each crack to even it out with the surrounding brick, then scraping off the excess. Always moistening as he went, because wet mortar was more easily worked than dry. The new section would have to be misted for the first few days, to help it cure evenly, then let dry for five days. It was always hard to believe that the new-mixed wet mortar, a dour unattractive gray, would cure to the neat whiteness of the brick. He wished he would be here to admire it. Creating a protection, a shelter, where there had been only loose-piled pieces was good. But it gratified him most deeply to repair, to make a neat, mended surface of tumbledown fragments. Fitting parts into a joined whole that would endure. Filling in the gaps so that you'd never know there had been a brokenness there.

The master bricklayer had come in from the heat, for a cool drink, to check Louarn's work, and no doubt to share some juicy news he had heard while making similar repairs to the bakers' ovens. They'd become friends, in their brief time together. Croy had hoped that Louarn would stay in Salmer Leng. Louarn had come to enjoy the older man's propensity for gossip. He relished a good tale the way others relished strong drink. Gossip inebriated him, made him charming and silly when ordinarily he was hard-baked as the materials he worked with.

But this time he had looked pained. He'd kept his voice low as he related the news of a death just outside Thandera Veẓh, a village two leagues Beltward. Details were thin. Some kind of accident with a scythe. Both hands lost, though that couldn't be true, it must have been one, the story garbled. Man bled to death, they said, though he'd seemed to have hit his head when he fell. Louarn shared Croy's discomfort. All folk worked with their hands. The loss of limbs was the worst that could happen short of death, and when the two were linked it was hard news indeed. But death itself was not uncommon news.

They'd been fortunate here in the winter just past—not so many agues and fevers as there had been.

"Ech, you're right," Croy had said, downing his drink and rising to dust himself off. "We're blessed indeed, and I'm glad for you to remind me of it."

It was days before news reached them of a singer disappearing on the way from a herd-band encampment near Amir Vezh, six leagues Beltward. Though the bonefolk had taken the body, her hands had been found in a midden heap, her stone and metal belongings in a pile just beside the road out of town. It couldn't be true, Croy had said. The tale must have warped in the telling. He'd winced down at his rough hands, examined the crazing of fine cracks in the mortar dust that caked them. No one would do such a thing. No one would mutilate the dead like that.

They still had not thought it killing until it happened again, this time in their own village. Louarn had told Croy that day that he would be leaving. He had waited long in the tavern where they'd agreed to share a farewell drink. Croy would relent and come to wish him well. They could have had the drink at home; Croy had hosted him during his time in Salmer Leng, paying him in hospitality what he could not pay in tallystones, then paying him in tallystones anyway, forcing them upon him, when they'd completed an unusually lucrative job. There had been little enough new building in recent years, little enough need for the bricklayer's skills, beyond repairs. Louarn had accepted the tallystones with a silent vow to convert them to an imported brandy the brickman craved but could not afford.

He knew I would go sometime, Louarn had thought. These leavetakings were always hard; some took it better than others. Perhaps Croy was snubbing him as punishment. Grief hit hard folk in hard ways. Louarn had traded all his tallystones, and all the kisses the publicans' daughter could extract from him before closing time, for a small cask of the finest Neck brandy. He had carried it back to the modest brick cottage Croy had built himself, with his strong, rough hands—and found a drenching of blood, and neighbors who'd come at the sounds of a struggle, and peacekeepers bearing those strong, rough hands in theirs, rescued from the midden. The man himself had lain in the middle of the floor where Louarn had slept. He'd suffered a blow to the head, but a neighbor insisted there was still breath in him when they'd found him. If there was, it had drained with the blood.

Louarn, the journeyman outsider, was questioned. The claims of the smitten publicans' daughter, the only one with him between the time the last customer left and midnight, were greeted with suspicion. But her father, once they roused him, confirmed where Louarn had been. They released him to go on his way. While they had questioned him outside, the bonefolk had come; it was not the custom in those parts to bear the dead to the bonefolk's places. Croy was gone.

Louarn believed he was looking for more than one killer. Croy was a big man and not lax or stupid. When a teller disappeared—all but her cast-off hands, and the objects the bonefolk left in a pile by her Foir Druile hearth—he knew the killers were heading Legward, confirmed when a healer went the same way in Gir Seille.

He also knew that he must be at once stealthy and forthright. Suspicious whispers that would have died out in his wake as he moved would follow him as he followed the killers. But he was always one town behind, or two. Alderfolk were dying now. The trail took him into the Leg, but he could not trace out a straight line in his mind—no roads in the Leg went straight, meandering along rivers or around hills—and nothing clearly linked the circumstances of the deaths. A stranger wherever he went, he was hampered in his inquiries, wary of accruing suspicion, equally wary of alerting the killers to his search should they double back. He approached runners, hungry for their knowledge, and was told that two of their number had been similarly dispatched in the Lowlands in late winter. Two days later, news reached him of the grisly death of one of the runners he'd approached.

He stopped asking questions. He merely listened, eavesdropping in every tavern, at every teller's hearth, on every village green.

He began to wonder whether he himself was somehow the link.

A third cry came, as nearly full of horror as the responses of those who'd found the bodies and their extremities.

"Eiden wept," said a villager beside Louarn, lifting his gaze to the loft from whence the cry had come. "Not another."

This echoed Louarn's own fear, but the blanched villager who came to the edge of the loft to display what she'd found bore in her arms no younger sibling's body, but a sheaf of vellum.

"Perhaps they were saving it against the day of the return," said a peacekeeper, rising.

For answer the woman in the loft turned the vellum in her hands to display the topmost leaf, holding the sheaf by the lantern she had set on the loft's edge. Details were unclear in the flame's yellow light, but that the vellum was inscribed, illuminated, was unmistakable.

The peacekeeper swore. "They'll have to be burned."

"Burn the cottage," said someone next to Louarn, and he turned to see a feverish, chilling hunger in the eyes of the man who'd spoken.

"And the bodies with it," said the woman next to him.

"We'll do no such thing," the peacekeeper snapped. "Out, the two of you. Now." When they hesitated in complying, she took a looming step in their direction, and they slid backward out of the reeking cottage, as Louarn slid himself further into the small clutch of folk remaining inside.

His mind was hard at work. He did not know the Strong Leg well. But he knew they frowned on the secular use of a dead craft's tools. He knew they clung to the prohibitions of a vanished way of life. Tradition was deep-rooted here and did not pull up easily. He hadn't thought much on it, as his own crafts did not tend in directions that would be forbidden here. But this was a piece of his puzzle, a terribly important piece, if he could find the shape of it and place it in the right gap. Geese. Doves. Illuminated vellum . . .

They were bearing the dead away now. He felt a frustrated urge to examine the bodies, and instead examined the urge itself. What did his fingers feel they would have found, if they could have searched? He glanced around the desecrated cottage, but sensed nothing that would help him, nothing sight or smell or touch could tell him. He let himself be borne outside in the wake of the dead, but he eased into the shadows by the path rather than follow to wherever their boneyard was.

He was not alone. Two peacekeepers had stayed. To supervise the burning of the materials found in the loft, he soon saw. There was far more than just the sheaf of vellum the woman had displayed. Parchment and sedgeweave, quills and boards—what they mounded in the little dirt yard and set aflame was years of hoarded work. The bonfire pained him less than did the grim satisfaction of the villagers who had stayed. This was craft, though it was not his own, and the burning of it was an ill deed.

But he could not stop it. And his mind was turning, turning. Vellum, sedgeweave, parchment, quills. Geese and doves. Downmongers. A farmer. A singer. A bricklayer. A teller. A healer. Alderfolk. Runners. Half-formed links weakened and broke as the next loop in the chain failed to fit.

"They just couldn't give up their craft," said a woman beside him, too softly for the others to hear. He chanced a look at her and saw tears glistening on round cheeks.

"Their craft?" he said, as softly. A cold certainty gripped his intestines. His body understood before his mind had laid the pieces in.

The woman startled. She hadn't meant for anyone to hear. Finding a stranger next to her, she seemed at once relieved and newly wary.

But there were itinerants everywhere. In the Heartlands, that made villages pull into themselves, give more importance to their own. In the Legs, it made all villages one village, all places one place.

"Their craft," she said at last. "They were only downmongers since the Lightbreaker's time. Spirits, this is a hard loss for us."

"I grieve with you," Louarn said, a standard reply, but he kept his gaze on her until she realized that he was waiting for her to finish, though she thought she had.

"Their craft from the time of the light," she said. "Magecraft. They were our village triad."

The last brick went in and mortared itself smooth.

Some wordsmiths became tellers when the light died. Binders became singers, healers. Reckoners became runners. Mages—the ones folk had looked to for help, guidance, advice, arbitration, because they were wise, because they were special, because they had power—became alderfolk and village leaders.

And some went back into their family trades.

Croy had been a mage. He never spoke of it; it was no part of the man Louarn had known. But there had been a profound, abiding grief in him, as at the loss of a home, or a loved one—or a limb. The loss of a light that gave the power to heal and ward . . . such a loss would grieve a man that deeply. Louarn had seen the triskele once, tossed in a jumble of chain on the mantel, nearly obscured by years of dust, and thought no more of it than he would have of an old tool neglected at the bottom of a box. Mages' work, a dead craft that he would never learn, meant nothing to him. But Croy had been a mage.

He had lagged one town or two behind the killers until now. It was mostly luck that had kept him from losing them entirely, with the slow rate news traveled and the half-blind way in which he had moved. What he had lacked was a means of heading them off. Something that would tell him why they killed the folk they killed, so he could find more of those folk before the killers did.

What sort of folk they killed would serve as well as why.

"Where are there the most who used to be mages?" Louarn said to the woman beside him.

"Where are what?" she said, returning her attention to him as if after a long time away.

He'd been thinking aloud as much as asking her. He could mumble some demurral now, say *never mind*. He asked, "Where was the light strongest in this region?"

She frowned and took a step away.

He cursed himself for an overeager fool.

"That's what those other two asked, too," she said.

His heart went into his throat.

That there were two or more he now had no doubt—the dead weight of an adult was no easy thing to string from a cottage rafter, and if one man had hauled them up, chances were the old wood would have given way. They had been lifted and hanged. "What other two?" he asked, trying to sound offhand.

"A man and a woman, they were here yesterday. They said they were healers but they weren't wearing white."

"No one wears white around here if they know what's good for them," said a man just beyond and behind her. Louarn hadn't noticed him in the leaping shadows cast by the bonfire. He was the one who'd suggested they burn the cottage.

"That's not true," said the woman from the loft, now that the conversation had become loud enough to overhear. "The menders do worthy work."

"They use the tools of magecraft," the man said. "They'll use them up, and there'll be nothing for when the light returns."

"Then they'll make more," said someone else.

"Don't be an idiot—you know what I mean. It's not the *things*, it's the *use* of them. That's what gave magecraft its power, that only mages scribed and sang and painted."

Everyone in the small group was being drawn into what was clearly an old debate in these parts, and threatened to flare up as bright as the bonfire they'd made to show its consequences.

"What did they look like?" Louarn pressed the woman, turning his body, trying to parlay his question into a side conversation while the rest argued the foundations of a craft that was dead and not coming back. "The two who were here?"

"One man, one woman, as I said. Girdlers, from the look of them. The tall kind, the Highland kind, hair like wheat."

"And what answer did they get to their question?" Louarn asked, his heart pounding.

"The Knee," the woman said, scornful that he did not know this simplest bit of history, mistrusting him now because she did not understand why the others were so important to him or who they were. He saw her gaze flicker toward the peacekeepers. "The light was always strongest in the Knee."

Louarn slipped into the shadows as she made the decision to point him out. He heard them call after him. He had to move slowly, by touch and hearing, until his eyes lost the lingering glare of flames. The fluttering of rock doves in their coops. The gravel of the path giving way to the packed-dirt road under his boots. He slung his carrysack on the stick over his shoulder, found the balance of long years of travel. Shouts went up behind him. He strode quickly up the road, past where the peacekeeper would have been stationed if not for the killings. The bulk of cottages on either side gave way to shacks, then a sense of space in the darkness, rolling black land under lowering night sky. Suddenly a white blur caught his eye—the road marker at the fork, a thigh-high slab of granite lower on one side than the other. You could give directions by such a marker. That made it as much symbol as any glyph painted on a leaf. But that irony would not sway the folk whose lanterns bobbed in the dark up the road behind him.

There were fields all around as far as he could sense, and his questing toe found only shallow ditches to either side of the road. He could not run in darkness so deep; he'd turn an ankle and be laid up for a nineday, or break a bone and die of blood poisoning.

He looked again at the marker. There was a deeper darkness, a depression behind the stone. In the stone's shadow, with his cloak over him, it might be enough to hide him.

He moved with care around the stone and down. His worn sole slipped on gravel, then caught on a root. He let himself go to his knees in the deep gloom behind the stone, which was now over his head.

His knees met something at once bony and yielding. He realized his error only just in time to fumble for the mouth and clamp a hand down over it. His palm pressed on beard stubble and drool. He whispered quick, desperate words of reassurance. The head nodded. He tested the acquiescence by removing his hand. The man under him remained silent, and even shifted to better accommodate the new addition to his sleephole.

The searchers came only as far as the end of their road. Their hearts were not in it; they didn't really believe he'd had anything to do with the killings, or they also had deduced that there must have been two—in which case good thing they didn't find him holed up here with whoever this was—or they were unwilling to venture any farther from their own ground.

When their voices had gone, when he sat up and wiped his hands on his worn trousers, he saw, far off across an Armward field, the green glow of bonefolk feeding, and knew what had chilled the searchers into returning to the comfort of their village.

The man he'd fallen on was chuckling low in his chest. "Not much of a town for waysiders like us, is it?" he said, a toothless slur.

"No, I suppose it's not," Louarn said, understanding that the man had been run out. Dindry Leng had seemed tolerant of its itinerants, but there were reasons they employed peacekeepers, and there were things they would not abide besides the undermining of a base of power that no longer existed. He got up and straightened his clothing. Before he lifted his carrysack again, he pulled out a half loaf of stale bread and bent to press it into the itinerant's hands. "For waking you," he said, and struck off along the downleg road.

The sound of the man's laughter followed him for a long way.

At dawn he came to a crossroads, uncertain whether he had passed any other crossroads in the dark, content to have stayed on the road and not broken his neck in a ditch. There he sat and rested, spasming awake at a brief vision of Croy in a halo of buttery light to find that workers had come into the fields around him. Still husbanding the ailing land, pulling weeds that thrived in conditions that were killing the crops they'd sown.

"I'm headed for the Knee," he called out. "What town should I aim for, to get there the fastest?"

"Gir Doegre," came the reply. "But that's no place for you. They have too many waysiders, it's not fair on them. Go up this road"—the man pointed—"but take the Bootward turning when it comes, there'll be someone there you can ask. It's Andry Leng you want, or Gir Mened."

"May you have a full belly by sundown," someone else bade him. "But don't go to Gir Doegre. You don't want to go there."

Yes, Louarn thought, even as he nodded and thanked them for their advice and said he'd take it, for the benefit of pursuers who would not come. *Yes, I'm afraid I do.*

He hefted his sack and headed up the Kneeward road.

Gir Doegre

Pelufer listened long at the edge before she stepped into the bonefolk's wood. Names would come off her, too many to muffle with the tattered kerchief she held bunched by her mouth. She had to be sure no one living was around to hear.

The hike here had taken her well past midnight, avoiding keepers' lanterns all the way up Copper Long, dodging into and out of dark shorts, then feeling her way along the Boot Road verge till she found the spirit-wood path. Didn't a lot of people die just before dawn?

Her heart was pounding too hard to count beats. Her breaths came almost as fast. She couldn't gauge time that way. So she sat amid the rustling whisper of dying trees until her heart slowed, and her breath slowed, and some inner sense told her it was safe.

The trees were alive the last time she'd been here. Old-growth stands of yews and pale-barked, silver-leafed bonewood. The forest had been a lush, dark greenness, redolent of resins and rich earth, alive with the trills and flutter of nightbirds. There had been no names before that. The last time she'd been here was when the names had first come. It was the night her mother died.

She could feel the border. If she leaned forward, bubbles roiled and expanded in her belly, in her veins. If she leaned back, the pressure eased. She'd come the long way round, avoiding the Knee Road and the wider logging track where keepers might be carting bodies. She'd crept up the path beaten by countless feet avoiding the straight route through. You were supposed to say benisons if you went through the spirit wood. You were supposed to honor the dead. If you were in a hurry, or if the forest scared you, you had to go around. If the forest would make you spout names like a poisoned fountain, you *really* had to go around.

Now it was time to go in.

She rose from her crouch and took a step.

Unease expanded inside her. She remembered this feeling. She had been six years old. That was five years ago. It felt as if no time had passed at all. The pressure inside, increasing, as if she were a small cask being filled by a stream. If she kept walking forward, the stream would become a river. Stay put or advance, either way she would overflow.

"I'm stronger now," she whispered, to hear regular words come out. "I'm older and stronger now."

There was no moon behind the haze above the trees. These were the spirit days. Her night-sight was good, but useless here in the pitch dark of a clouded, moonless midnight; she had to go slow, using her shape-sense to keep from blundering into trees.

She took another step, and the names began to come.

"Melledor," she said. "Amtreor. Ofrander. Jimni. Morlor."

Strong Leg names. Local names. She forced them down to a whisper, muffling them behind the cloth. Barely on the verge, and already so many that she had trouble snatching breaths between them. But she wasn't even nearly far enough yet. The spirit wood was a nonnedfoot band of trees around a glade. The glade was up ahead somewhere. Three ninesteps? Four?

"Aifrin, Nomulor, Bardor, Donfa," she said, gasping. "Jimurin, Ronderas, Feraille, Andorlin . . ." She had known some of these people, they had been shopkeepers and traders—one a friend of her mother's, she thought, one a trading acquaintance of her father's, but she couldn't hang on long enough to be sure, more kept coming, there were too many— "Anondry, Nemolle, Belu, Noluorin . . . Valenya, Erileka, Jerulon, Herik, Fesalyn . . ."

Their lives eddied in her mind like mists, rolling and merging. Cobblers and coppersmiths and fullers and tinkers and bakers, herders and wheelwrights and hillwomen and chandlers, publicans and ironsmiths and carters. Too many lives, too many to hold. So many waysiders crowding in, Weak Leg names, Girdle names, Boot names, so much unfamiliar. Snatches of attitudes and customs she could barely understand.

Run. She didn't think the word, there was no room for it in her bursting mind, but the impulse went through her limbs like a thread of lightning. Her legs and arms twitched, then jerked her around. She grit her teeth and turned back and made herself take another step. The third step.

The rush of names came on so strong that she went to her knees in the hard bracken. This was why she ran. She always ran before it got like this. She dragged in air and was still saying names on the inbreath. It was almost funny, she used to make Caille laugh by talking this way except it always ended up making her feel faint and burpy and she'd have to stop because her head was spinning and her chest hurt. Her head was spinning now. Her chest hurt.

She could go on. There was no one to hear. No one to learn the secret. She dropped forward and crawled. Leaves crumbled and twigs broke under her palms, bracken crackled. Names gasped out of her and sobbed in. She was getting breath. She was dizzy but she was getting enough breath to go on.

Lives tumbled over each other inside her, knowledge she didn't want, couldn't contain, until she couldn't have told which snatches of memory went with which names. The feel of a baby's hair. A dazzle of polished copper in sunshine. Burning heat, fevers, retching, agony. Jagged lances of heartbreak at leaving the world behind crossed spikes of ecstasy she couldn't comprehend. Triumph and despair. Highlit glimpses, like dapples of sunshine through the nodding canopy of a living forest. Here a perfect golden droplet of joy, there a setting stain of guilt. The dead were all shreds and flutters, little bits left over of the most intense moments in their lives, and ordinary moments that lingered for no good reason, the damp beaded coolness of a tankard of ale in the hand on a hot day, a puff of choking dust along a roadside, that time the kiln cracked and the sound it made, the way he gazed out over the maur with sunrise pink and gold in his hair, the reek of a bad oyster. "Beoni Luander Altreille Nilu," she said, the names running together into one name, "JedfaDiludelGrotelynEldomon," then coming so fast and hard and insistent that she couldn't get a whole name out or absorb a vision before the next came. The names were only impulses stacked one atop another but none of them able to come forth whole, "ChafBorAilDomGra," and she was choking on them, her mind a shifting wash of sensation that she could no longer isolate except for one overlapping memory of being like this once before of how this swept over her once before in this same wood when it was alive and embedded inside that an even older memory of a freak wave at maurside and her mother unable to hold on—

The names stopped.

She dragged in a long searing breath and coughed out mist. She raised her head into a deafening silence.

Her hands and knees were bleeding. Cold particles of water brushed her face, fog rolling through the woods. She blinked drops from her eyelashes. Her hair was plastered to her head. She breathed again, her throat burning, and coughed until she retched. Her lungs hurt. Her heart hurt. Her belly cramped, then eased.

She got on her feet, reaching to steady herself on the trunk of a yew. No rough bark came under her hand. There was nothing to hold on to but mist. Disoriented, she stumbled. Her heart took a dip. Where had the trees gone? There was nothing but tumbling gray going to white. The way the mist moved suggested open space. She had come full into the bonefolk's glade. Lost in the roil of names and lives, she had crossed the threfts between without knowing it.

Without turning, to stay oriented, she made herself take a step back the way she had come, to see if the whole thing started again. It didn't. No names. No lives. No memories, no other-selves. Just the slow drip of condensed fog. But another step back, and another, did not bring her to the edge of the trees.

All right. She was in the middle of the glade, that was all. She could cross it in any direction and find the periphery. It would be hard to find the path she'd come in by, but the logging track was wide and clear and it ran right past the glade. She'd never been in so thick a fog, but eventually it would lift, the mists were always fickle. And if it didn't, how much harder could it be to feel her way in mist than in dark? Why should fog make her feel lost when night didn't?

Night. It was no longer night. The mist was too pale for that. A bolt shot through her gut: Elora would miss her when she didn't return at dawn. How late was she? How far out of the night had she come while the names and selves were roiling inside her?

She couldn't waste more time wondering. There was work to do. She got back on her hands and knees, grunting in denial of small pains, and began to feel her way through the bark and leaf mold. There were small things growing here. Things that could root shallow in the fog-damped bracken, things that didn't need the deep watering of rain or poisoned streams but could live on mist, in the clean top-cover of what had fallen. Mosses and mushrooms. Little greennesses, tiny living viny stems and leaves.

And between them, down in among them, metal things.

The bonefolk consumed flesh and fibers. Here were all the things they left: stones and buckles, knives and chisels, the oddments folk carried in their pockets and stuffed in their belts, the kind of oddments Elora made a trade of. She had to take care with the blades—most were rusted, and a rusty cut would make you ill. She found entire collections of stones, scattered near each other when some player's pouch dissolved in a boneman's arms. Pairs of shoe buckles. A whole set of artisan's tools. Something metallic and strangely warm, a sinuous rounded weave that after several breaths she recognized as the pendant of a person of light.

She stuffed her belt and pouches, filled her pockets. It was an unthinkable bounty, far more than she'd imagined. Other pendants. A ring with a graven face. Rings with cut stones set in them and braided metals. Waysider things that keepers would have confiscated if they'd found them. She should have come to this glade long ago. Who'd have known one Gir Doegre chisel from another? She could have traded the carven things with Boot merchants or Girdle carters who didn't care about Strong Leg customs. It would have been worth the risk. Elora's shoulds-and-shouldn'ts had held her back too long. If the dead didn't like this, wouldn't they tell her? Of all people, wouldn't she be the one who'd know a thing like that?

There were no dead here. Only dry, drifted remnants of memory, like the dead leaves she was crawling around in. Leftover mists, that clung to her for a while and then burned off. She didn't even need the axe she used to conjure in her mind, to cut them off. She could brush them off, like stray hairs or lint.

The fog was thinning, rolling off townward. She planted one foot in the forest's detritus and pushed herself up with the other, rising victorious, laden with riches. She'd come battered but triumphant through her night of struggle. She'd faced the worst and bested it. She could see the trees now, see where they went sparse between the glade and the logging track. She sauntered toward the track, shaking the stiffness from her limbs, even whistling a little, low at first and then stronger. Whistling was forbidden, and added a delicious thrill to her victory. At the trees' edge, she kicked up drifted leaves in a gleeful flouting of sound, reckless and free. She whirled to scatter them with her foot so she could watch them flutter back to earth, harmless.

Her eye was drawn up by a differentness in the tree-shapes across from her.

There was a man standing in the yews and bonewood, a third of the way around the glade's edge.

He stood very still, but hipshot, relaxed, ready to move in any direction on a breath. His face was shaped like a hatchet, more severe for his long hair pulled tight and bound behind his head. She could not gauge intent from the cant of his body; he intended everything, and nothing.

He was the dangerous man who'd stood in front of her on the water queue. He'd claimed to be a healer, but he wasn't wearing mender's white, and now she saw a hint of grip and crossguard to one side of his head—a longblade strapped to his back.

She stood frozen in surprise for one breath too many. Fog billowed in and obscured him, and in the next moment he wasn't there. He'd moved silently in rustling, crackling underbrush that did not allow silence.

Pelufer bolted. The fog had come around her now, it flowed and ebbed in waves, but she had a beeline on the logging track. He'd gone from view as if fading back, not sidling off, so she'd have a jump on him, to head her off he'd have had to be moving already—

He was standing in the grooved ruts of the track. He lunged into an impact that drove the breath from her. He bore her back into the clearing, pushed her down onto her rear so that to run she'd have to scramble up. Bubbles were rising inside her. Her limbs were nerveless as she waited for air to come back into her. It felt as though it never would. The pressure was an agony with no breath in her to vent it. A sore spot bloomed on her breastbone, and her eyes rolled up, caught sight of what she'd crashed into—a sheathed knife at his belt. She wanted to reach for it, but she couldn't move for lack of breath.

Suddenly she was dragging in air, and on the outgasp came "Deilyn, Niseil, Astael, Sowryn." Sharpness, agony, rage . . . She swayed back, and the man crouched before her and took her by the shoulders and shook her, and "Vaen, Coenn, Daeriel" spewed out, and none of these were the glade's names, they were names she'd never heard before, alien names, and he was shaking her and saying, "What *are* you?," and she said "Perchis, Vebryn," and then "Yours, they're yours, they're yours," babbling, insensible with horror, the shrieking pain of all those violent deaths.

The glade went abruptly cold. Pelufer could feel it in her skin. The living heat had been leached right out. The man flowed upright, drawing his knife in a silken whisper, eyes scanning the clearing, the trees. Pelufer crimped away from him, pushing with the heels of her hands and feet. "Stay put," the man snapped.

It was a deep, dangerous command that compelled her to obey. But a queer warmth was growing inside her, offsetting the deathly chill. A profound sense of safety. It was the feeling her insides got when her father's arms enfolded her. She felt the cold now as a kind of embrace, and the dangerous man and his wicked blade seemed to recede, moving out and away into a periphery of danger that couldn't touch her, held warm and safe at its center.

An illusion, something told her. In moments he would grab her, he was just at arms' reach and he was faster than anyone had a right to be, she wasn't safe yet, but she *could* be—she was free to run, and what cupped her in its warming hands was the potential of escape, a pause in time, a breath of space in which options lay open to her in every direction, a sphere of possibility.

Go, you foolish child, she thought, a thought that couldn't be her own, and she flipped over and scrabbled up into a tripping run. The man barked at her to stop. It carried such hard authority that she faltered, and turned, and saw him engulfed in a bank of cold fog that condensed impossibly from the thinning mists, an unnatural thing, thick and blinding.

Keeping him from chasing her.

Father, she thought, the voice of her own heart, as she fled from the glade the way she had come, bore down until she found the trampled trail, slipslid around its dew-muddy curves, skirted its sink-holes on hard tufts of poisoned yellow grass. *Father!* she thought, a wail of separation now, as the otherworldly cold and mist passed away behind her. She burst out onto the Boot Road, barely dodging the hooves of mules, running back past a driver's curse and a brake's screech and rumbling cartwheels, back down the rutted road, toward town, safety, Elora.

Father, she thought, slowing to a winded trot, then a walk as the shakes came on, the energy of flight drained. Of all the names she had said during the night, none had been Nimorin n'Belu, none had been Prendra n'Anondry, though the bonefolk's glade had them both. Her pains flared up, her scraped hands and knees, her bruised chest, her rasped throat, and there was no one to soothe them, no warmth of comfort at her core anymore, and for one moment she wanted to turn, go back, find again that touch of her father in the forest of the dead.

Copper Long was abustle with midmorning activity. Pelufer came onto it through the Bootside shanties and moved quickly away from the Tin Long end, where the roads to Bootward and Kneeward crossed, where the dangerous man might come down the Knee Road from the logging track. The sun was finally burning through the haze, heating the mists and the middens, its heat rising back in dust-sticky waves. It was much later than she'd realized. Elora would be frantic. Caille would be cranky. But she slowed herself—softening, blending. She seeped like a wisp of fog into the fabric of Gir Doegre. She was a rasp, a mist, a haunt. She was the color of the earth. No one would notice her.

Nowadays Nolfi set up his barrow in the space between two cousins' stalls midway down Copper Long. Elora would be waiting there, as they'd agreed.

Her pulse was calming, the shakes easing. She was hungry and thirsty, and angry about a pouch she had lost when the man threw her to the ground in the glade. She wanted to tell Nolfi about the dangerous man, rally their friends to turn the tables on him. There were plenty of tricks they could play on him and never get caught. They could drive him away, and the woman with him. But Nolfi hadn't been inclined toward pranks since he took over his brother's barrow. Nolfi wouldn't like her taking things from the dead. Nolfi would be more afraid of the dangerous man than she was. Nolfi was becoming a grownup. And their friends weren't hers or even Elora's, just his. They had roamed in gangs when they were little, playing games, playing tricks, filching trinkets. But then Mother died, and the secret came on her and her sisters, and they couldn't have friends anymore, because someone might find out. Elora had been the smartest, Pelufer the fastest, Nolfi the bravest. But that was a long time ago. And Nolfi was almost a grownup now.

She saw him before she saw his barrow. He was partway out in the long, hawking his wares in a singsong voice that came just short of sacrilege. Soon she was close enough to see the sheen of sweat on his face and neck. It made her aware that she was shivering. Noon closed the air in like an oven, though it was only sowmid. Good. It would help her forget the scares she'd had, the sleep she hadn't. It would bake the deep cold from her bones.

She slipped between stalls and came around behind and hunkered down between the shafts of Nolfi's barrow. She could smell the heat-warmed copper. It smelled like Mother's craftery. Elora and Caille were nowhere to be seen; that was good, they were hiding well. The trader at the next stall saw her and gestured to Nolfi, spoiling the surprise. Pelufer popped up anyway, still quick enough to startle him when he turned to look for her. "Where's Elora?" she asked.

"Pel," he said. She frowned at the twist of his chin, the way his shoulders shrugged up, his hands turning outward. "Pel," he said, "I'm sorry . . ."

Sorry for what? People were sorry for death, sorry for disaster. Something had happened to her sisters—

A keeper stepped up next to Nolfi. She felt presences behind her.

"Don't grab her," Nolfi warned, "she'll go mad."

She dropped her upper body and drove back with her legs, pushing between the two behind her and underneath the sweep of their arms, but she came up hard against a third—*four keepers, they sent* four *for me*—and he hugged her arms tight against her sides while one of the others got an arm around her legs. *Then* she went mad. Nolfi's warning was nothing compared with the way she fought, bucking and twisting and biting, pounding her hard head back into one's chestbone as she got one leg free and kicked another, pulling them all off balance and crashing into Nolfi's cousin's stall, *serves him right for giving me up*—

"Stop it, stop it, you'll hurt yourself," Nolfi cried, elbowing in to get near her. She snarled and would have scratched him if she could have reached with the clawed hand pinned to her side. But the keepers were big and there were too many of them. They wrapped arms around her until they had her immobilized on her side off the ground. In response, she shrieked. It came out horrible, her throat rasped raw by the night before, but that made it even worse on the ears, and Nolfi stumbled back as the keepers winced and swore and turned their heads. "Bloody spirits, we'll have to gag her," she heard one say as she drew breath for a renewed assault—but it was clear they weren't going to drop her, she didn't have enough lung power to force it, and though a gag would stop them hearing any names that might come out, she couldn't let them do that until they'd told her what happened to her sisters.

She went limp and turned pleading eyes to Nolfi. "Elora," she said. "Caille."

"They're fine, they're all right, the keepers will take you to them, they're all right. *Spirits*, Pel!"

She wanted to hit him for making it sound as if she was the one making all this trouble. Relief won out, and then, in the same heartbeat, fury that he'd made her think the worst. " 'I'm sorry'!" she spat. "You'll be sorry, all right!" She followed that with a string of invective that would have made her father blush, and she'd learned the art from him. Nolfi looked hurt but not chastened.

"Let her down," he said, "don't carry her like an old carpet!"

Two of the keepers laughed outright, looking from spitting, twisting, swearing Pelufer back to Nolfi.

"It's not my fault," he said as they carried her off.

She called him every name she knew and then began inventing new ones. His voice, righteous and regretful, followed her down the long as the keepers bore her toward the pitches, and cut through the expletives that grew faint as her voice went hoarse.

"It wasn't me!" Nolfi called, as if across the gulf of years that separated them from the childhood friends they had been. "Elora sent them!"

"I was worried sick," Elora said, and her hand twitched as if it wanted to slap her, although it was only dabbing a wet cloth on facial scratches Pelufer hadn't felt until her sister started tending them. "I had to get help. It was the only good choice."

"You could have trusted me," Pelufer growled. Her throat was so sore that everything she said sounded jaded and threatening, a satisfying effect. "And now look where we are."

In a tavern on the river side of Bronze Long, the Mute Swan, named for the birds that congregated behind it before the crowfever had them all, and a good bit of Lowhill with them. The sound of the River Doegri lapped over the sills of the unshuttered back windows, and she could almost hear the grinding of the mill over on its maurbound tributary. Their house had been in Lowhill, across the river; if she looked out the window now, she could probably point to it. The singing whisper of river currents and the stony rumble of the mill had made her sleep, when she was very small. But she'd had her fill of memories—other people's, and her own. She knew perfectly well that she'd been saying goodbye to Gir Doegre in her heart ever since she set out last night, ever since Elora had agreed to leave. Goodbye, forest. Goodbye, roads. Goodbye, warm-copper smell. Goodbye, grinding millstones. Goodbye, whispering river. Next it would be "Goodbye, Mamma" and "Goodbye, Padda," and it made her sick, it made her want to spit, it made her want to hit something. *It's time to go it's time to go!*

But they couldn't go until the men and women seated around the tavern's tables said they could. All the alderfolk of the town assembled here, three senior and three junior, and not a few traders once the word got out that some big decision was in the works regarding trader children. All this attention brought to bear on them, all because Elora had to run to the keepers instead of trusting Pelufer and waiting as she was supposed to.

"I did trust you," Elora said. "I trusted you to be back by dawn. That's what we agreed. Dawn at the byre, and at Nolfi's barrow if Caille and I had to leave there."

It was true. But you had to be more adaptable than that. You had to keep your head when things didn't go as planned.

And if that man had decided to kill me, I'd have been glad to see keepers then, wouldn't I. That was Elora's kind of sense. She tried it on, and decided she didn't care for it. No keepers had been anywhere near there. He could have cut her throat and the bonefolk would have had her before anyone ever knew, and no one like her to tell the tale, no one like her to say "Pelufer" and explain how she had died.

She was the only one like her. Elora and Caille were the only ones like them. They could not afford this kind of scrutiny. *It's time to go!*

"But it's all right now," Elora said. "I negotiated with them. I made a deal. It'll get us out of Gir Doegre, the way you wanted."

"What kind of deal?" Pelufer said uneasily, straightening.

Elora glanced over her shoulder. "You'll see when she comes back, she had arrangements to make for us. It's brilliant, Pel, you'll be so proud of me. I know you're angry that I went to the keepers, and I was sorry too right afterward because it got them worried about all of us and they brought Caille and me to the alderfolk and it really was getting out of hand, but I met this woman, just wait, you'll see."

The terrible thought that went through Pelufer's mind could not be what Elora meant. "What does this woman look like, Elora?" She swallowed. "What does she smell like?"

Doubt flickered over Elora. "She was in town looking for prentices," she said with a frown. "She didn't know anything about us, she was just sitting in here with the alderfolk, and when they started to talk about putting us into care, I . . ." She shook her head and threw down the wet cloth. "You said it was a woman and a man, Pel, and you didn't tell me what they *looked* like, you never say what color people are or how tall they are or anything useful, and they were dangerous and scary and this woman isn't, and there was no man with her—"

"Because he was in the spirit wood." Pelufer didn't need her raspy voice now to sound dark. "Trying to catch *me*. I got away and now it turns out *you've* given us to *her*. You idiot, you idiot . . ."

"It's not her." Elora had made up her mind. "It's not. You'll see. You wanted work for us, honest work, and I've found us some, I've found us a way out. We'll prentice as healers, and if we don't like it we'll run away. It's simple. It's perfect. You'll see."

The low murmur of adult conversation had faded into the sound of the river, but one of the senior alderfolk turned to them now—Anifa, a sallow, graying woman whose family had traded on Tin Long for generations—and said, "Have you explained it to her, Elora?"

Elora gripped Pelufer's arm and sat up straight with a prim nod. At her feet, Caille sat cross-legged with the tavern cat upside down in the cradle of her legs, its eyes squinched shut and its head flung blissfully back against her as she stroked its throat. Someone's lean cowdog lay with its head on her knee.

Pelufer shrugged Elora off and stood up. "No, she hasn't."

"We've had an offer to prentice you," Anifa said. "It's a good offer. You'll learn a trade. You'll get to see the world."

"We have a trade," Pelufer said.

"Your sister has a precarious excuse for a trade. It is insufficient to support the three of you. You run wild, thieving and spirits know what else. We don't know where the youngest sleeps, whether she's cared for properly, whether she eats—"

"She eats well!" Pelufer said. "We all eat, and not your poxy keepers' tithe either! We take care of ourselves!"

Anifa pulled up, huffy at being interrupted, and Denuorin, the senior alderman next to her, leaned forward to say, "Where do you sleep, child? Do you have blankets? Enough for winter?"

We had a place till someone knocked it down! Pelufer swallowed the words at a glare from Elora, but still said, "We do better than waysiders. They sleep in the roads."

"With their mothers and fathers," Anifa said. "Waysider orphans are fostered. You're traders' children. Gir Doegre children. We let you fend for yourselves as long as we dared, but it can't continue. You're a danger to yourselves. You'll have to go into care, one way or another. With the help of your sister, we've worked out something that benefits all of us. The spirits were working this day. Ah, here she comes now."

Caille deposited the cat on the floor, smoothed its disarrayed fur, and stood up, pressing close to Pelufer, with the dog standing by her. "It's all right, none of this means anything," Pelufer whispered. "I'll undo whatever Elora's gotten us into." Elora heard that, and she stood up, too, resentful and frightened. She was afraid of what she had done, but still determined to prove it was good and clever. Her back was stiff as a board, her mouth a grim line, all the parts of her braced and straight.

Footsteps sounded on the porch.

It took a long time for Pelufer to turn. Her back was to the door. It could still be someone else, some well-meaning journeyer who *would* get them out of this bind and out of Gir Doegre and away from the man and the woman who were killers. Anifa was saying, "You'll prentice to this healer, and come back to us with skills and lore that will save lives," and she meant it, she meant well, her narrow shoulders squared, her thin chest puffed out, she thought she was doing something grand, saving three trader children and investing in Gir Doegre's future at the same time, a bargain that would benefit them all, a fine traders' solution.

The person in the doorway was the flowery woman.

She stepped in, greeted the alderfolk and the traders, nodded at Elora, all business.

Pelufer's fingers pressed against Elora's back to say that it was her.

Elora's fingers pressed into her arm to say that it wasn't.

She fingered that it was.

Elora fingered that if it was, Pelufer was wrong about her.

Her step was forthright. Her spine was straight. There was no crook to her posture, no subterfuge in her movement.

The cowdog gave a low whine, and Caille moaned and gave a wriggle as both sisters' hands fell on her and tightened. Both certain and both doubting. Maybe there was a good reason for the names, maybe not the reason they'd reasoned out, maybe they'd reasoned themselves into a hole and it was all wrong and the woman was all right. But what was the man doing in the spirit wood? Could it be there was no connection between them after all? They'd seemed strangers at first, on the water queue, and what she'd sensed during her fit of names could have been wrong. . . .

Pelufer shook herself and gritted her teeth. "No," she said, as loud and as firm as she could. "We won't go with her."

"But it's all arranged."

Traders were crowding into the tavern's greatroom now. Nolfi and his cousins and Elander and Ofalador from Copper Long, Jifadry and Toudin and Jiondor from Hunger Long, Seldra and Prenaille from Tin Long, some Bronze Longers she didn't know, and a handful from the shorts: Befendry, flowing in scarves; Nemrina sweating in her own woolens to show off her wares; and Mireille, smirking, as if she knew what was going on and had even had some hand in it.

"What's all arranged?" said Toudin the stewmonger.

"We're prenticing Nimorin and Prendra's lot," said the senior alderwoman Jeolle, still busty and pink-cheeked for all her fall of snow-white hair. "Making the best of a hard situation. Risalyn's offer is a good one. Two mounts and a fortnight's provisions for the children, and in five years we get back what not one waysider has provided us in all this time: a resident healer, to keep our folk from dying."

"Menders heal," a trader said with a frown. It was Jiondor, the sweetsmonger from Hunger Long. Only yesterday Pelufer had filched treats from him, laughed at him as she danced away.

"Menders use the things of light. Risalyn uses acceptable tools. It's a new way, developed by ordinary folk, to do no harm."

"She doesn't look a healer to me," Jiondor said. "She looks . . ." He glanced at Pelufer and shut his mouth, and Nolfi was cutting him off anyway, crying, "You can't just prentice them off!"

"The eldest agreed to it," Anifa said. "In fact, it was her idea. Jiondor, Risalyn spent the night with the sick in Pointhill, and her draughts and decoctions have worked wonders. I'm sorry, Nolfi, I know they're your friends, but I'll ask you to keep quiet, you're not of age and—"

"You're trading us," Pelufer said. "It has nothing to do with what Elora offered or didn't. It's you. You're bartering us, like sheets of tin."

Anifa nodded. "Yes, love. I'm afraid we are. It's for the best, for you and for Gir Doegre."

"Who decided this?" Jiondor persisted. "There was no traders' meeting."

"This is a matter for the alderfolk," said Jeolle. "It's not a trader concern."

"It certainly is, if you're trading our children now."

"They must be fostered," Anifa explained patiently. "They can't provide for themselves. The middle one runs wild—"

Jiondor halted her recitation: "Then foster them to me."

Pelufer gaped. Alderman Denuorin said, "They've done nothing but steal from you lot for the last five years!"

"I wouldn't call it stealing," Jiondor said. "Young Pel might, I suppose, but she's too proud to take the keepers' tithe and it's all tasteless gruel anyway, no offense, and it's meant for waysiders, not children of our own. They keep better fed by thinking they've snatched it off us, and keep their pride in the bargain. You've done them a wrong by forcing it out, but I might as well tell you, if it's the difference between keeping them here and letting strangers cart them off."

"The healer is better off than we are. She'll give the girls a better life. She has more to offer them than we do here."

"She can't feed them herself if she's bartering for their food," Jiondor said. "With me and mine they'll be fed and clothed and sheltered. What more do you want?"

"Elora n'Prendra to come back to us a healer."

"Then buy the healer. A fortnight's provisions and two mounts, for training three girls on the road? What would it cost to keep her here, to serve us and prentice them? We'll take up a collec—"

"I'm a journeyer," said the woman—Risalyn, a High Girdle name. "I cannot stay. It's not my way."

"You won't take our children," Jiondor said. His jaw was set and his bulk drawn up in a shape of stubborn defiance. Pelufer had never seen him like this. It made his thundering anger at her a joke. "If they must foster, they'll foster to their own."

"You'll feed them sweets off your stall?" Denuorin said.

"Don't insult me, Alderman. Nursed your brood on pewter, did you?"

"You have two of your own, Jiondor, and another coming. How do you think you'll support six?"

"I'll find a way. This is their home. She won't be carting Gir Doegre girls off to some hut in the Girdle!"

"They'll travel the length and breadth of Eiden Myr, learning a craft you won't have here so long as you shun white," Risalyn said.

"You can count that little one's years on one hand! You plan to haul her from Heel to Crown? She's a baby!"

"I come from a community of healers. We care for our children collectively. They'll be well looked after."

"Healers." Jiondor looked to spit, then thought better of it, and appealed to the alderfolk. "You can't trade our children to f—to strangers. It's madness."

"You can't feed them, Jiondor."

There was a pause.

"He can if I help him," said Toudin.

"And if I do," said Jifadry.

The soupmonger and the stewmonger. A dozen more spoke up, traders from up and down Hunger Long, the people Pelufer had filched from and taunted for almost as long as she could remember. Nemrina the weaver promised blankets, Meloni the seamer promised clothes. "Their mother was a coppersmith," said Tiloura from Copper Long, "either of the younger can prentice to me, it's in their blood and the rasping cough took my own girl." Jifadry said, "It needn't break the deal. Prentice off some youngling who *wants* to be a healer, there must be some old enough to make the choice."

Denuorin turned to Anifa. "Their father was a good stallholder in his day, and his eldest remembers. She'd do well by Jiondor. It would honor Nimorin's memory."

Anifa surveyed the other alderfolk, then said to Risalyn, "It seems we're all agreed. If there's some other way we could . . ."

"Not all." Mireille oozed out from the back of the trader group like a worm after a hard rain. "I say they should go. Not every trader they've stolen from has been happy about it. They had two stones off me only yesterday—I bet you'd find them if you searched them. Are you forgetting Elora's sacrilege?"

Floorboards creaked under feet shifting.

"Those things were burned," Elora said, her eyes on the floor.

"Who's to say you haven't made more?"

Nolfi said, "You've had it in for Elora since you were little."

"And you've defended her just as long, even when she turned her back on you," Mireille shot back. "They're no friends of yours. They didn't want to know you once their mother died. They think they're too good for the rest of us, too good to ask for help."

"That's enough," Anifa said.

"But they—"

"You're still a child yourself, Mireille, and however much I may have agreed with you in the past, you have no more say among traders than Nolfi does until you've come of age—"

"Tell me what Pelufer has in those pouches. Tell me what Elora has in that sack. Tell me that, and I'll be quiet." Mireille folded her arms across her chest and stood with her nose up and her nostrils flared. She had gone from worm to rat. Sniffing for their defeat as for the scent of scraps.

"Their private belongings," Anifa replied, "and if you're suggesting we search them, that's out of the question. They're here for our protection, not to be judged on a charge of theft."

"Maybe they should be," said one of the traders. He drew glares, but he said, "Some of my bronze could be in those sacks. Look how they sag. If those girls leave, I'd like to know something of mine isn't going with them."

"If it's stolen goods," Jiondor said, "we'll find out when I get them home, and we'll make restitution." He turned to Anifa and Jeolle and Denuorin. "Let me take them home now? My word as a trader, there'll be no sacrilege, no thieving."

Pelufer winced. *But we'll be gone*, she thought. *He'll be embarrassed, but his word will stand*. She said, "Elora made a mistake. We want to go live with Jiondor."

"I'm sorry." Elora put a hand at her throat as if to push the words up and out. "I should have talked it over with my sister first. You're very generous, Jiondor. Thank you."

For one breath of relief, it seemed that would be it. Jiondor and the alderfolk were discussing details. The flowery woman was conceding; whatever she'd wanted, she'd lost and she couldn't very well make a fuss. Nolfi was walking toward them, and so she didn't see Mireille coming, Mireille used him as cover until she was close enough to dart out a hand to yank one of the pouches from her belt.

Pelufer cat-hopped back with an oath. Mireille failed to pull the pouch free. But the fabric was old, and never meant for holding pointy objects. Mireille's finger snagged in a tear, and the battered pouch ripped open. Its contents spilled out.

Rusted awls with no handles. Braidmetal rings set with cut stones. A tarnished silver ring with a flat graven face. The three-armed pewter pendants of people of light.

Everyone in the room stared at the jangling mess. Mireille went pale, as if she'd expected to release a hoard of her own stones and instead had dug her claws into a nest of wasps.

"Those are things the bonefolk leave," she breathed.

Anifa rose from her seat and caned her way across the room, her entire body as stiff as the leg that no longer bent and the arm that braced the cane.

Her gaze rose from the spill to Pelufer's face. "You thieved from the spirit wood," she said. Pelufer set her jaw. What she'd done wasn't wrong. The dead didn't care. But Anifa didn't know that, and she couldn't tell her. "This changes everything."

"It's sacrilege," Mireille said.

"And a rude act that revealed it," Anifa snapped. "I'll have words for you, Mireille. You've overstepped yourself. No, don't even start—I don't care that we'd never have known if not for you. Get out. Go tend your stall, and mind your step."

Mireille slunk out of the tavern. Anifa caned her way back to her seat through a silent room. Pelufer made herself look at the traders who'd stuck up for her. A clump of disappointment, an edge of outrage. Nolfi was still standing near Elora, and it came to Pelufer, as he knuckled his brow and turned away, that he'd been sweet on Elora, and maybe she on him. When Elora stopped being his friend it was more because she didn't trust herself not to tell him their secret than that she was afraid he'd guess it. There had been sacrifice there and she'd been blind to it.

It was the last of her worries now. This was a serious offense. They didn't have to preach at her to tell her that. If you stole a cow, or a set of tools, or anything big, they kept you around long enough to return the goods or work off your debt, and then they booted you out of town. They sent you off.

Her heartbeat quickened. They would have to run. There was a back door to the tavern. Was anyone near it? Chancing a look would give her away. She made her face into stone, but her belly churned.

"Will you have them now, given this?" Anifa said to Risalyn.

"Of course I will. We'll return those things, ask the dead for forgiveness, and then we'll go, and spirits willing in a few years I'll return you a set of fine young women who will obey the rules and ply a useful trade with honor."

Pelufer's stone face flushed hot with blood. *Liar!* she thought. *Killer killer killer!*

She tensed to spring, with no idea what she would do but maddened, goaded into doing *something*. Elora grabbed her hard, strong though she was trembling with confusion and shame. Caille was crushed between them. The dog growled, its hackles up, looking around as if it didn't know who to attack, and the tavern cat was hissing, its tail blown up huge, its back arched. Caille's face was screwed up as if with the effort of holding back tears.

That was when Pelufer heard the sound in the walls.

The walls, and the floor—inside the walls, under the floor. Scratchings and scrabblings and squeakings.

"No," she whispered to Caille, "no, stop it, no," but it was too late, she and Elora had done the damage, their distress had flowed into Caille and through her into the floorboards of the tavern and every living thing felt it now, even the traders.

Motion erupted from each crack and cranny of the tavern. The walls crawled with mites and spiders, beetles and silverfish. Wasps poured in the window, disturbed from a nest under the eaves. Rats and mice skittered from cellar and pantry. People leaped from their seats, raised their arms and looked around with amazed wild eyes.

Caille could have done this on purpose. She hadn't; she was upset, beside herself, she'd lost control. But it was the perfect diversion. Pelufer herded her sisters around and prepared to drag or shove them out the back door. Two keepers stood in her way.

If only she'd been able to look.

"No more running," one of them said—she knew that face, but it wasn't smiling now, he'd been playing with her yesterday when he let her duck under his arms, their whole life here had been a game of grownups letting them think they were quick and clever when the whole time they'd been *taken care of*. Pelufer wanted to throw herself at him, pummel him, curse him for tricking her. But the game was over. She had to be smarter than that now.

She crouched down to Caille. "You've got to stop it," she said, softly, so no one would understand what she was saying to her terrifying, powerful sister.

People were stamping at insects, kicking at mice; someone had a broom raised. Caille screeched in horror. "No! No kill! *No kill!*" A baby's words. She hadn't talked like that when she was three let alone five. "*No kill!*" Her face was a boiled, swollen beet. Her body was bent nearly double, as if the blast of her shriek could stop all movement like a great wind.

Pelufer turned Caille firmly back to her and said, "The way to stop it is to calm yourself. *Now*. Or they'll squash all the mice."

Elora hunkered down with them. It was she and Pelufer who had to calm themselves. They took deep breaths, holding on to each other and Caille, watching each other. Caille fixed on them, breathed with them. Hysteria deflated into pouting, uncomprehending hurt. The scuttlings and squeakings faded. The creatures slipped back into their cracks and holes.

"Will they figure out it was her?" Elora said, voice low.

Pelufer shook her head: *I don't know*.

"Come on, girls," said one of the keepers. "Your running days are over. It's into the pantry with you until this is sorted."

What a stupid place to put three little girls with rats running mad. The cowdog thought so, too, or at least didn't like the keepers' actions, but it backed off at a soft, sad touch from Caille, then trotted reluctantly back to its master. Pelufer let herself be guided with her sisters into the windowless storage space. She took careful note of how the pantry door stood in a wall perpendicular to the back door. The back of the pantry would be the side wall of the tavern.

When the keeper had closed the door on them, shutting out the sound of voices in the main room, Pelufer said, "It would be better to wait till dark, but I think you should do it now, Elora."

Elora had huddled down and didn't look ready to do anything. "Too much has happened. I need to think."

"There isn't time. They're thinking, too. They'll figure out that Caille is special, it won't take much if that woman helps them, she already knows I'm special and she can lead them to it, you know she can. Or they'll just get over the rats and spiders and give us to her."

"If I do it," Elora said, "they'll know for sure."

"But we'll be gone."

"I don't want to go forever. I want to be able to come back."

"We still can, no matter what they know. When we're grownups, and they can't do whatever they want with us."

Elora wasn't convinced. She had less confidence than Pelufer in the power of growing up, even though she held age over Pelufer's head all the time and was always deferring to the grownups' rules.

"If I do it, they still might catch us."

Pelufer started to say something bold about how once they were out on the long no one could ever catch them, but she didn't know that for sure anymore, not if all the keepers had been humoring her. "Then they'll catch us, and at least they'll keep us then instead of giving us to that woman. I'd rather have our secrets come out than be dead."

It all came down to that, didn't it. That was the decision.

"If the secret gets out," Elora said, "everyone in the world will be trying to catch us, and we'll never be safe no matter how far we run."

That was what Father had told them. It was the admonition that had ruled their lives. *Never tell. Never let anyone see.*

Pelufer looked desperately around the pantry. It doubled as a tool room, and in two breaths she found what she needed: a shovel, to prop in the corner against the back wall. "Can you make it look like that did it?"

"We're not strong enough to do it with a shovel."

"They'll think we were scared. That makes people strong. They'll think they didn't hear the noise for their own arguing."

"I'm sorry," Caille said. They both turned in surprise, thinking she was talking to them, but the words were addressed to a mouse on her knee, nibbling grain she'd taken from a bag beside her. It was a wild mouse; she didn't pet it, just watched it eat and said, "I'm sorry, mouse. I didn't mean it. I was scared. I'm glad you didn't get killed."

Pelufer looked at Elora. Caille was talking to them after all.

"All right," Elora said, and gave Pelufer the sack made of their blankets and linen cloth. It had her workings in it, and their bits and pieces. Pelufer still had enough of her spirit-wood haul, in her pockets and her one remaining pouch, to get them started in another town, but they'd need the blankets after dark. The desire for sleep was an agony. She pushed it aside as Elora laid her hands on the cedar wall.

"It's not a natural thing," she warned. "I'll be tired afterward. I might be too tired to run."

"Stop putting it off," Pelufer replied. "Just do it."

Elora closed her eyes and applied herself, and Pelufer watched with a wicked glee as the laths of the wall went gray and brittle under Elora's hands. She poked a knot out with her finger and used the hole for a grip to lever the laths off the support beams. They came away easily, and she stacked them to the side.

"They don't like it," she said. "They fit where they were."

"No helping that," Pelufer told her. "Keep going."

The boards on the outside were trickier, and it took both of them to angle them inside. But they were lucky: beyond the hole Elora had made was the back of a refuse bin. No one had seen shingle fall mysteriously away from boards that then lifted themselves and slid from sight.

"Can you get through there?" Pelufer asked, gauging Elora's slim frame against the spaces in the framing.

"I'll have to," she said. She couldn't compromise support beams, and without knowing the framers' craft they couldn't be sure which those were.

Pelufer went through first, then took the sack from Elora and reached for Caille, who slid through like an otter, without help. Elora was through to the waist when she got stuck.

"Twist the other way," Pelufer whispered. "No, more sideways."

It was no good. She was going to have to remove a section of beam.

"Just long enough for you to get out, then you can put it back and fix it," Pelufer said.

"I can't, Pel, I'm so tired already . . ."

"You have to. You *really* have to."

"I can't."

Choking back a growl, Pelufer wrapped her arms around Elora for one last pull. Hips grinding against wood, her tunic tearing, Elora came abruptly free—and the two of them tumbled against the bin with a jarring thud.

They went still and listened for footsteps. They heard nothing but their own breathing. Then Caille tapped Pelufer on the shin.

She looked up into Nolfi's blinking face, then down at the prybar in his hand.

"Well, that's half the job done," he said. "Get into the barrow."

It wasn't his barrow. It was some old, weathered thing that smelled of vegetable rot. A woman Pelufer didn't know stood casually at the shafts. Around the barrow, as if lounging there trading gossip on a break, was a collection of bronzemongers. At the head of the alley were bronze stalls, and not one of the stallholders paying a bit of attention to what was going on behind them—but deftly turning the attention of customers away from it.

Elora got in first, curling herself like a potato peeling to fit, and Pelufer fit herself into the curl, hugging Caille in close and putting the blanket sack under her head. A big smelly piece of burlap was tossed over them, and their feet lifted as the woman took up the shafts and wheeled the barrow away onto Bronze Long.

"Wiggle your foot if you can hear me," Nolfi said in a conversational tone. When Pelufer wiggled, he said with a forced smile in his voice, "This is Jiondor's pledge, Beronwy. He's still inside arguing for you." Pelufer wiggled again, to make up for what she couldn't say out loud. "All the traders pulled together to keep you out of that woman's hands." Again Pelufer wiggled. "Stop wiggling. You can thank us later." Everything he said after that, and everything Beronwy said back, was ordinary trader talk until the barrow was plunked unceremoniously down on its back support legs and Nolfi said, "Stay put until dark and don't move even then. Stay put until I come to fetch you." Stray objects were piled on top of the burlap. Pelufer wiggled her foot in protest. "I'll be a ninefoot away shelling peas and paying no attention to this barrow," Nolfi said, "but if I hear this rubbish move I'll come over here and club you over your thick stupid head, Pel."

When his footsteps had receded, she tensed her muscles for the painstaking job of sliding out without disturbing whatever rattly junk he had piled on them. Elora pinched her extra hard, and Caille locked her hands in with her strong little forearms.

It was a long wait, unable even to whisper to her sisters—she tried it and earned another pinch—sweltering and soaking under the rough burlap throw meant to keep produce fresh in the sun, not hold in the body heat of three nervous girls. Pelufer resigned herself to using the time to take stock of what had happened, maybe figure a few things out. The next thing she knew Nolfi was shaking her awake and helping her lift Caille from the barrow, and Elora was already out and talking quietly with Beronwy and Jiondor off to the side.

She'd thought they were by Jiondor's house, but of course that was the first place anyone would look for the escaped girls he'd wanted to foster. The barrow was parked by cottars' crofts off the High Road, just the other side of the river from Pointhill. Only a couple of the crofts were still tended.

"You'll have to give Jiondor what you took from the spirit wood," Nolfi said. "Every bit of it, so he can return it."

Pelufer wasn't all awake yet, and her refusal came out whiny and peevish. "We need those things to get started somewhere else."

"Consider it a trade, then. Your spirit-wood goods for that donkey and the food they've packed for the trip. And me."

Pelufer snorted. "We don't need you."

"Jiondor thinks you do, so I'm going. I have only my cousins here anyway; otherwise I'm just like you."

She knew that he meant having no parents or other family, but it came out anyway: She said, "You're not."

He nodded. "I know that much," he said. "Now, you listen to me. You'll want to come back here someday. You're going to need people who can help you. Jiondor and Beronwy went to a lot of trouble for you today. I think that proves you can trust them. So I want you to tell them whatever it is before we go. You don't have to tell me. You can tell me later, or not tell me ever, I don't care as long as we're all safe. But you owe it to them."

"It's not that kind of secret," Pelufer said. "It's bigger than that. It's bigger than owing people things. Anyway, we promised my father."

"Your father's dead, Pel."

"Only mostly."

He regarded her in silence. Then he said, "Maybe he'll come with you." His voice was low, as if he might embarrass himself and wanted as few people as possible to hear. "Maybe he's always with you."

The spirit wood was a long way from their house in Lowhill. The feeling she had gotten there was more than just the jabs and punches of other people's lives and selves. He'd been *with* her, in some way she didn't understand. Not like right after he died, not like in the house he died in. But more *there* than any of the things she'd thought were haunts and now it seemed were only echoes.

"Maybe," she said at last, and felt a cold wind blow through her, an intimation of profound things she didn't understand.

Jiondor and Elora were bidding Beronwy good night—she was going back to spell whoever had been looking after their children. Elora joined Pelufer and Caille, and then Jiondor did, and the five of them sat together in the dark and the quiet for a while, and then Jiondor said, "I'm sending you to my cousin's place below Gir Nuorin. Country's a bit more rugged than what you're used to, right up against the mountains there, but the water's pure, not like this Druilor runoff that's killing us. And it's not so hot. If you're not happy there, you send us word, and we'll work out something else. Nolfi will see you as far as their place, make sure you're settled in."

Make sure we don't run away the first night, Pelufer translated. Well, they wouldn't. Not if this cousin was kind, and not too bossy, and there was work for them to do. Not the first night, anyway.

"In exchange for that, since we're all traders here, I want the truth."

Pelufer didn't check with Elora before she answered. Elora's head was down, she could see it from the point of her eye; she was tired, and she'd never been any good at lying. This was a job for Pelufer. "I can feel haunts," she said. "I can tell how people died. I go to where the dead were, and their names come out of me, and I . . . see things, or feel things, there's no word for it . . . I *know* things. About them."

Jiondor considered this, then shook his head and said, "You went to the spirit wood with a gift like that."

"It's not a gift. Every time names come out of me it might give me away. I can't stop it when it happens. If people knew I could do that, they'd be wanting me to talk to their dead, and find out things for them, and . . ."

"You might make a good trade of that. Why not tell?"

"Because I promised my father I wouldn't."

"What did he think might happen if someone found out?"

She shrugged, lowering her lashes. "I don't really know." "*They'll use you,*" he'd said. "*They'll control you, and use you, and your lives won't be your own anymore.*" Their lives *had* to remain their own.

"And all this time, you turned away from your friends, you kept to yourselves, all three of you, to keep this secret that you can talk to the dead?"

She nodded. "Except I don't think I can really talk to them. Hear them, maybe, but that's not it either. I don't know what it is. It's just a thing I can do. Other things I can't do." She frowned. This part, the true part, she was trying to explain right, to make up for all she was leaving out, so they'd believe her when she said *That's it. That's the whole secret*. But she wasn't doing it very well. She didn't know how to describe it. She didn't know how it worked.

"That woman wanted you," Jiondor said. "I watched her close today, and it was you she wanted, Pelufer, not your sisters. No offense to your father, but I've seen drunks look at drink with less interest than that woman looked at you. Like a fever in her eyes. I don't think she even knew why. Do you?"

"She wants to kill me," Pelufer said. "Because I know the names of the people she's killed. And her friend too." She explained about the fit of names on Tin Long, about the man in the spirit wood, and all the while the back of her mind was saying, *Good. This is good. It keeps them thinking and wondering about something besides Caille and Elora.*

Jiondor opened his mouth to respond, but a terrible thought came to her and she cut him off. "They might— You were the one who— Suppose they—"

"Ah." Jiondor gave a slow, cold smile and said, "No, I don't imagine they will. But Beronwy and me might welcome them trying."

"They're killers," Elora said. Her voice was dulled by the effort of what she had done in the tavern. "Someone should . . ."

"You let me worry about that," Jiondor said. "We'll keep our end of the bargain, young Pel. You've told us the truth. I'll keep it tucked in my own thick noggin. You get yourselves on that donkey. There's food for a threeday in the smaller bag, and hay for old Bristlecone in the canvas sacks."

Though his instructions were goodhearted and his manner kind, there was something in Jiondor now that made the chill go through Pelufer again, and she was relieved to be on the donkey and away up the High Road, with Highhill passing to the left and Pointhill to the right, and Nolfi talking softly to the donkey from where he walked up at its head, and Elora's arms around her from behind and Caille snugged close in front. It was still the spirit days, the between-days, the dark of the moon. The way was black between blacker hills, and it would be a long trip round the back of Highhill and over to the Knee Road on the narrow dirt path. Caille's head lolled against her chest, and Elora's bobbled loosely, giving a half-snore now and then in her ear.

She woke when the dim, scattered lights of Gir Doegre were

almost lost behind them, like guttering candles engulfed in mist.

Goodbye, Mamma, she said, deep in the privacy of her heart. *Goodbye, Padda.*

She listened with every sense she had, but felt no answer.

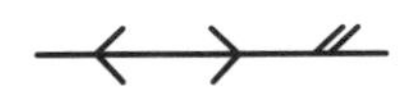

The boy crept out of his bedchamber as his mother was chalking a casting circle on the floor of the common room. The stone looked smooth, but the chalk bounced over tiny bumps and the line came out raggedy. He smiled. His lines came out raggedy, too. "You'll never be a wordsmith, my boy, with lines like that," his father would say. "Nor illuminator, either." "Why not?" his mother would reply, with a funny sidelong look at their own illuminator—their pledge, his other father, Ellerin. "It never stopped him." They were always teasing each other. It came from when they were vocates together. Vocates were mages called to serve the Holding because they were powerful. Bright lights. He'd never seen the light in them. That was fair. They'd never seen the light in him either. But he wasn't six yet. Almost. As good as. But not quite. When he was six, he might show a light. "You've a whole year of being six ahead of you," his mother would say. "It might not show right away." But it would. He knew it would. The moment he turned six, there it would be. He'd look down at his hand and see it glowing. He'd look up and see his mother glowing, and his father, and his second father. His mother would hug him and say, "I knew it!" His father would slap him on the back, a little too hard like he always did, and Ellerin would ruffle his hair, like he always did. It wouldn't be that different from not showing a light, except for how proud they'd be. And maybe then they'd let him go out into the Holding instead of keeping him here all the time. They kept him here because they loved him, they said. They said he could explore the Holding when he was older. He'd slipped out of their chambers once, and

nothing bad had happened, there was only a corridor with walls and lampwells the same as in their chambers, but he still felt the sting of the spanking. His mother had cried after she was done being angry. He was afraid she would cry if he showed a light, too. He knew she didn't want him to. He didn't understand why. When she saw it, she'd be happy. She would. When he was six.

"How many days until I'm six?" he asked. They'd settled down on the casting circle now, after all the big rush and excitement. They made a triangle, the way they sat. Circles and triangles were powerful. Their proxy rings had circles carved inside a triangle, and the faces of the rings were circles too. That meant that they were powerful enough to be proxies for the Ennead. Proxy meant "in place of." It meant you could do things the Ennead would do if there were more of them, and there had to be proxies because nine wasn't enough to do everything. Being proxy meant you could speak for the Ennead, except that there were two kinds of proxies, reckoners and warders, and his parents were warders, which meant they stayed here in the Holding to work for the Ennead. They had to stay in the Holding the way he had to stay in their chambers. That was fair. But he'd like to get a proxy ring, only be a reckoner instead. Reckoners went out into the world to speak for the Ennead. The silver rings shone in the lamplight. That shine was something he could see. When he was six, his whole body would shine like that. When he showed a light, it would be so bright that the Ennead would call him to be a vocate, and then he could get a ring and be a reckoner. And wear black. He'd never seen black clothes. They'd be mysterious and powerful. His parents always wore white, but reckoners got to wear black.

He had startled them. They hadn't heard him come out. "Go back to your chamber," his father said, as Mother set out the last of the quills and started mixing pigment in a saucer. Preparing the casting materials. That always took a little while. The binder had a lot to do in the beginning, getting everything ready. He didn't know if he wanted to be a binder, but if he drew squiggly lines then he wasn't going to be an illuminator or a wordsmith when he showed a light, when he was six.

"How many days till I'm six?" he said again, peeved. This was important! What was all the rush about anyway?

Father whipped around fast and said "Now!" in a tone so sharp it didn't sound like his voice at all.

It was like a stranger had spoken. He fell back a step, stung. There was a pained looked on Mother's face, but she didn't stop what she was doing. He looked to Ellerin for aid. Ellerin always stuck up for him. Ellerin always made a joke to take the edge off any scolding. But Ellerin's eyes were closed. He was meditating. They had to meditate before important castings. Ellerin called it "centering." He had to pull into himself so that the guiders would form to show him the way to illuminate the manuscript when his turn came. It was like he wasn't even listening.

The boy turned wide eyes back on his father, afraid of the angry face he'd see, and Father seemed to sink into himself.

"You were born in sowmid," he said. He looked very tired. "In a few breaths it will be Ve Galandra. That's the sowmid equinox. It'll be soon, son. Too soon. Spirits willing, the light will skip you. Being lightless keeps you safe. Now, what did I say to you before?"

"To stay in my bedchamber. But I like to watch you cast!"

"Not this time, son. Do as I say, please. We must cast this warding now. It's very important."

An emergency, they'd said. It was an emergency. They'd never had an emergency before. He had memorized a lot of instructions about what to do in different emergencies—if there was a fire, if someone came into the chambers he didn't know, if he was ever left alone for a very long time. But he didn't know which kind this was, and there was no stranger in the common room, or smell of smoke, or anything scary or different at all. It made no sense.

He opened his mouth to object, then closed it. His father was always fair. His father had answered his question. Now he should be a good boy and go inside.

Just one more question. One more question, one more answer, and he would go and be good. "Which day of sowmid, Father?"

Mother and Father looked at each other. There was a little pause. They never thought he noticed things like that, but he did. It meant he'd made them think of some important grownup thing they didn't want to tell him. Then Father said to Mother, as if it summed up all the sadness in the world, "We know the triplets' day, yet we don't know our own boy's."

"You don't know?" he burst out. Was that what they were keeping from him? Was that the terrible thing that always hung over them? Was that why he couldn't go outside their chambers? Because he didn't have a day of his own?

"Oh, my sweet," Mother said, swaying toward him as if to take him in her arms . . . but she couldn't get up, you weren't supposed to leave the casting circle once you sat down, and her hands were pressed together into her shins so hard he could see the white where the blood couldn't reach. It frightened him. He went to her. He couldn't help it.

"Pirra . . ." Father warned.

"I know, I know," she said, as her arms and her scent—wax and oak gall and linseed oil—closed around him. She buried her face in his hair and he could feel the damp of tears seeping through to his head. "But if we fail . . ."

"We should have brought the others in," Ellerin said. "If we fail, there won't be anyone to . . ." He trailed off in a way that the boy knew meant

he was talking with his face or hands, but he twisted around too late to see. Then his mother took him by the shoulders and stood him up straight, facing her.

"We can't fail," she said to Ellerin. "But he knows what to do, if we do. Right, sweetling? What did I tell you?"

"I'm Flin," he recited, the words to say if strangers came and he couldn't hide or run or there was a fire and he had to go out into the corridor. "My mother was called a vocate. She brought me here and told me to hide. Now I can't find her."

"What's her name?" his mother said.

"I don't know. She's Mother. I call her Mother."

"What does she look like?"

"She's tall and fair."

"And what else?"

"That's it. That's all I'm to say, ever. I'm Flin . . ."

"It's madness," Father said.

Mother glanced at him sharply. "It will keep him alive."

"His foster name would alert the others—"

"We can't trust the others now. We can't trust anyone."

"I'm not Flin?" Flin said softly, hopelessly confused and now frightened too. He had no name and no day. . . .

"Of course you're Flin, my sweet. You're you, you're Flin, you know the words to say, that's all that matters."

"There's no purpose to this confusion, Pirra, there's no light in him, no danger to him, I'm telling you—"

"We can't have this debate again," Ellerin cut in. "We must begin now, or Pirra's fears will come to pass."

"I'm Flin," Flin whispered.

His mother pushed him gently from the circle. He walked past his father, too scared to lower his eyes, and turned only once, when he got to the door of his bedchamber, to see them bent over their casting, Father's quill scritch-scritching on parchment, Ellerin so centered he seemed no longer to be there at all, the skin around Mother's eyes and mouth scrunched and stretched as if waiting for her wordsmith and illuminator to do their work was the hardest thing she had ever done. Then he went into his bedchamber as he'd been told. His head swam with names and days. He'd only wanted to know how long he'd have to wait before he showed a light. He didn't want to know that names and days were more important even than that, not if they wouldn't tell him why. He crawled into his bed, missing his mother's hand smoothing his hair, smoothing him into sleep, his father's firm weight on the bed until the weight of dreams took him. He loved bedtime. Now he slept and rose alone and stumbled to the doorway and found they were still casting. "We might be at it till midday or even midnight next," he remembered Ellerin saying, and Father saying, "I'll set out food for him, he'll be all right." The food was there on the side table, cream and honey and dry cooked wheat, and he knew they'd want him to eat it, so he mixed it and spooned it into his mouth and swallowed it, and by the time it was gone he was more awake, and had decided to make a list of questions for them to answer when they were finished. He would present them like a good proxy, in order. He would be very grownup about it, and they would answer because they'd see that during the night he'd grown up, he'd grown a night closer to being six.

Outside, they said, it got light during the day and dark during the night, as if the spirits lit a great candle overhead, in something called the sky, and at the end of the day it had burned down and things got dark until the spirits lit another. Well, that was how he thought of it. He so wished to see the sky. He wished it so badly, and he felt so alone, that he started to cry, and went to the doorway again, but he could hear the quick, soft, sure whisper of Ellerin's brushes over parchment and knew they were still casting, still, how long could it take, castings took forever but he'd slept and woken, they never took that long, and then he started to get angry, but he heard his mother's weary voice raised in bindsong, the voice as warm and delicious as hot porridge, and that meant the casting was ending, the binder always sang last and then the manuscript went away and the casting was complete. So he went to the doorway again, thinking it was pretty silly going back and forth and back and—

Mother's song tore into a shriek.

He ran through the doorway and skidded to a stop just inside the common room.

Ellerin's body spasmed backward as if something had hit him.

Father doubled over himself, his head turned enough to the side that Flin could see the flesh of his face. It was blackening and . . . twisting, like a lemon peel tossed on the fire.

Ellerin's eyes, rolling wildly, caught sight of the boy, and he flung an arm out to push him into his bedchamber, but missed. He fell over sideways, screaming, clutching his arms to himself and kicking his legs out like he was fighting something off.

Mother no longer looked like Mother. She looked like a shadow of Mother in a bowl of dark water. Blackening, melting, all her skin shriveling, starting to peel.

He was still sleeping. He had to wake up. He yelled, "Wake up!" It came out a squeak.

He ran to his mother. He touched her. It was horrible. He touched her harder, trying to make her be her.

Baby, her mouth said, but no sound came out. My baby boy.

Father could still talk.

"Run," he said.

Flin gripped his mother's arm. He could not let go. His hands were burning. He screamed.

Father's blow took him in the shoulder and sent him sprawling.

"Do as I tell you!" rasped the thing that wasn't Father anymore. "Go, son. Run!"

Flin fumbled at the forbidden door with his burned hands. Father had told him to run. Father was out there, somewhere, with Mother and Ellerin. He looked back into the chamber. They weren't there. They ran from the thing that made everyone black. Flin had to run or it would get him too. They were out here somewhere, at the end of this corridor, or the next one.

He ran down the corridor. He ran through an opening in the wall. There was no floor beyond it, only little black stone not-floors, one after another, down and down until there was a wall. He fetched up hard against the wall and cried for Mama. He raised his arms to be carried. The thing that made everyone black was inside him now. It was behind his eyes. He couldn't see. "Mama," he said, reaching for her, but where she should have been was only empty air, and he reached too far.

The blackthing tumbled and battered him for a long time before it took him.

The Head

It was always night in the holding, and there was no sleeping sound there. The air, no longer circulated by magecraft, was thick with haunts, with the dry revenants of agony. No one pinched out their candles, and oil had long since run short; where the corridor lamps were unlit, where there was no pitch for torches, few cared to walk. Folk gravitated to the common areas, crammed into the old vocates' beds so as not to be alone, pooled their wax and oil so as not to have to sleep in darkness. In darkness, despair coated the walls, sliding down the droplets of condensation that could no longer be warded away. In darkness, some said, you could still hear the screams deep in the stone.

Rubbish, Dabrena thought, rising from her pallet and stepping carefully around her daughter, who moved listless and frowning through troubled dreams. *We are haunted only by our failures.*

Yet how long since she had slept sound?

Seven years. Coming with child had been the end of her own childhood; what should have brought joy had brought only betrayal. The Ennead had surreptitiously removed the freedom when they cast her warder. They had wanted more mageborn children. Dabrena had celebrated her silver ring with the prettiest boy she knew, an oblivious coupling in the glow of magestone. Now the Ennead was dead. Their Holding glowed no longer. And for Dabrena, pretty boys held no more allure.

She would have preferred to bed down in the sleephall. It was what she'd been accustomed to, and the warmth and sound and smells of sleeping bodies had always comforted her. But her folk would not hear of it. "You must have your own chamber," they'd said. Not one with windows, of course—daylight was rationed to scribes—but a private chamber with its own bathing alcove. She didn't like it. Haunted or not, it felt both too cramped and too lonely. But she'd learned to acquiesce on small matters.

She moved from flickering candleshadow through the deeper shadow of the alcove's hangings, and into the blackness within, feeling her way to the washstand.

There she leaned over the the basin and cried, as long and as hard as she could. Her hands gripped the splintered edges of the washstand, her body curled over, her belly convulsed. Tears ran down to drench her chin like drool. They wet the basin in smeared droplets. Such a little liquid, for such a hard, hot flow of tears. She purged herself of tears as she would purge bad ale or a stew that had gone off. A cloth soaked in soiled water, she wrung herself hard. When she was through, she poured fresh water into her hand and bathed her face, cool liquid on swollen skin, waiting for her flesh to resume its pale semblance of calm.

That's done then.

Once a night was usually sufficient. Once a night, for six years. Tears enough to fill the parched riverbeds of the Heartlands. But she was warder no longer, and had no power to divert a single tear or raindrop to where it could do some good.

She returned to the outer chamber and sat cross-legged beside her daughter, whose first whimpers, when they came, would signal the first blush of dawn against the mountain's skin.

Seven years since she had arched in naive, victorious ecstasy under her closest friend. Six years since she'd betrayed him to the Ennead, to save the child they'd made.

"Do you dream of him?" Dabrena whispered, not quite touching the smooth head, reluctant to wake the child. "Do you remember your father, Kara?"

The inadequate light of their struggling candle darkened Kara's cap of honey hair to the color of her father's. When she woke—in tears, as she always did just before morning bells—the brown eyes she turned to Dabrena would be his eyes.

It was a sick and dirty thing for a child to cry each day before waking. Kara would never say why—whether it was bad dreams, or a bellyache, or missing the father she'd known a scant three moons.

Whatever the cause, it could be healed only if acknowledged, and that was the last thing Kara would do.

What have you done to our baby, Dabrena?

Mind wandering and ears alert for whimpers that never came, Dabrena realized that the child had awakened only when she sat up wide-eyed, pointed, and said, "He's here."

Dabrena's heart clutched in her chest. She had the child behind her and a wall at their backs before she knew she'd moved. All she could feel was her heartbeat squeezed to a rapid, painful thread, all she could see was the muted sparkle of mica around her, the twin oval stains of their sleeping pallets at her feet, the black of the bathing alcove.

The strangled throbbing in her chest opened into a pounding rush of anger.

This child. This child and her fantasies.

"There's no one there, Kara." She just barely maintained control of her voice.

"Well, no, not now," Kara said. She elbowed out from behind Dabrena and rubbed her eyes, her tone and stance peevish. "You moved too fast. You scared him."

As quickly as that, Dabrena's rage melted into sadness. Her own fault. An overreaction—the terror of her year under the Ennead had never quite left her. Her own fault. She knew perfectly well that Kara had concocted an imaginary friend. Her own fault, for raising a child so lonely she had need of one.

"Does he frighten very easily?" she asked. She tilted her head down at her daughter but was unable to stop her eyes scanning the shadows, which jumped wildly now as the candle guttered and created the suggestion of form where there was nothing.

Kara made a face. "You mean me. You think when I talk about him I'm talking about me. You think he's really just me. He's not. He's him. *I* don't frighten easy. I don't know about him. How would *I* know? But you frighten all the time."

These insights were so many, and so biting, that it took Dabrena a breath to catch up to them.

She said, "You know I always believe you, Kara—" But that was a lie. She had not believed. She had interpreted. "I thought it was a game we both knew we—" But she could not articulate something as fine as the shared comprehension of what was pretend and what was not. "I'm *not* always frightened!"

Justifying herself to a child. Justifying protective instincts she should be praised for! *I'm not a good mother, I'm a terrible mother, we all know I was never cut out for this, but above all else I have protected you!*

But that excused nothing. She'd thought herself a snarling mountain cat defending her young. Her daughter thought her a coward, an anxious woman who spooked at shadows.

"If you had seen what I . . ." But she could not put such horrors on her child. The girl was only six and a third years old, a magical age, an age of intelligence still shielded by the vestiges of babyhood.

Are you planning on finishing one of these sentences, Dabrena?

"If I saw what you saw, I still wouldn't frighten easy," Kara said. Responding to the words Dabrena had swallowed—bloody irritating child! But now Dabrena drew her gaze from the mocked shadows and said, quietly, brows raised, "You wouldn't?" And more frightening than any spectre in the shadows was to see smug pride flicker across the little face, see the girl puff up, about to assert, "No, I wouldn't!"—only to falter under the dark implication of her mother's tone.

"Easily," Dabrena corrected, gentling her voice, and knelt down to pull the child into her arms.

Now the tears came.

The little-girl body was so tiny in her embrace. Her father had been a wiry man, not tall, and Dabrena had been taunted for her size all her life—called doll, toy, trinket, for her small stature and honey hair and long-lashed hazel eyes. Now she was the big girl. She tried to soak up the racking sobs, take them into her, another thing to be purged after the long day ahead. *If I could spare you this*, she thought. *If I could have spared you this . . .*

This what? This life? Was that it, in the end? That she had never meant to have this child, and now was saddled with her, failing and failing to make her world a happy place?

What have you done to our baby, Dabrena?

She set Kara away from her and combed the damp bangs with her fingers. Kara's eyes slid closed under the caress, then opened with a kind of yearning. For what? What was it she cried for? Dabrena tried to lighten the mood. She tapped the button nose, three times for luck, then said, "You're a very brave girl."

"Why do you *spoil* things?" Kara cried, the morning bells ringing in her voice, and whirled away to dress herself in a wild flurry of silks and woolens.

Dabrena just knelt there, helpless. *Get me away from this* child! she thought. *Shielders and Khinish cannot be worse than this!*

"You say things to make them be true." On went a sock. "I *am* brave! But you don't know that. You think I'm a baby." On went a pair of breeches, with much hopping and stamping. Dabrena winced as she heard a seam tear. "You tell me and tell me how grownup I am because you want to make it be true—because you think it isn't!"

"I—I'm a wordsmith," she said, on reflex, forgetting that it was no longer true in the sense she meant. "That's . . . what I do . . ."

Kara glared as if to say, *That's what you do. Make words. As if they could change things. And they never do.*

It was too much. She was reading insight into the tantrum of a six-year-old. "Put your shoes on, then clean your face and teeth. We'll be late."

"I can't find them!"

"Your face and teeth?"

"My shoes!"

"How can you lose a pair of shoes in a chamber this size?"

"You moved them!"

"I haven't touched them."

"Then maybe *he* took them."

Your make-believe friend did not take your shoes. No, that would not help. Kara meant to rile her. They searched the room in silence, finding the shoes under a sack of unused outerwear moved last evening when Dabrena tidied. Her fault, again. Vindication only entrenched Kara's sulk. In silence they walked the long lamplit corridors to the cookroom, in silence they ladled out porridge and prepared a dull salad of crumbled cheese on mushroom heather, and in silence they ate. No one ever disturbed Dabrena with news or business until she and her daughter had broken their fast, just as no one would disturb her once they had retired to their chamber for the night. She wished someone *would* interrupt—save her from these blighted silences, hand her a task, give her something possible to do.

But they would not. The moment she dropped spoon into empty bowl, Selen or Corle would appear as if out of the stone of the walls with a nonned critical items requiring her attention. Let her call for one of them during the meal, to discuss some plan for the day, and they would be nowhere about. Let her try to bed the child down on a cot in a maphall so she could work into the night, and Ronim or Narilyn would hound her until she took Kara off to her own bed.

A bitter laugh came out of her: *My own folk, forcing me to spend time with my child. As if I didn't keep her by me every breath.*

"It's not funny," Kara mumbled through porridge.

"I wasn't laughing at you, sweet."

"Nothing's funny! I'm angry at you!"

"You're too young to be angry at me. You're not supposed to be angry at me for another six years, till you discover something called 'boys,' which spirits help me I'm going to have to—"

Kara flung her breakfast bowl to the floor. It hit with a dull, unsatisfying clatter. She stared at it for a moment, like a baby vaguely aware that her rattle was no longer in her hand. Then, with a despairing snarl, she scrambled down and began bashing it against the black stone. Dabrena was on her knees next to her just as the wood cracked jaggedly apart, gripping her hard by the wrists before she could cut herself, snatching the pieces from her hands. "Kara, Kara, Kara, what in all the world—"

"*Get away!*"

Peripherally aware of a concerned group gathering, Dabrena tried to enfold the tantrum in her arms. Kara resisted with the tensile strength of hysteria. Dabrena stopped pulling. *Try another tack.* That's what the child's father would have advised. "Look at me, Kara." In her voice was all the command of the harvestmaster she had once been, before ever she was warder or mender. She could tell Kara a dozen times to do a thing and she would not, but use that tone and the child snapped to obey. A tone could have nearly the power of a binder's song. But Kara covered her face with her porridge-smeared arms. "No," she sobbed. "I hate you."

Dabrena's awareness of the crowd melted away, and there was only the child in front of her. "Why, Kara?" she whispered, letting her hands drop—then lifting them again, only to pull back when Kara batted at her. "Why do you cry? Why are you so angry? Is it your father? Do you miss him? Is it friends you miss? Other children? You have so many friends here, everyone loves you, Narilyn loves you, Selen loves you, I love you. You're safe, Kara, I will let no harm come to you. *Why are you so angry with me?*"

The child, past speech, would only sob—forced, fierce sobs calculated to demand attention, to tell the world she was angry, she was hurt. But never why. Did she even know?

"Let me take her." Reiligh, rising behind Kara like a tree. Dabrena followed the legs up the trunk to the ruddy face of the herbmaster. He was a gentle soul, a male child of Neck hillwomen fostered into a craftery. Unlike so many here, he had been neither mage nor seeker; just a kind man with a body too big for him, better at growing things than making things, who saw a need when the magelight failed and found his way here to fill it. "We could take a walk. Go down to the cataract. That's her favorite place. A dip in the fizzy basin! You'd like that, Kara, wouldn't you?"

"No," Dabrena said—snappish, overly harsh, and it shut down the brief hope that focused Kara's eyes. That was too bad. But this was one line they could never cross. "You know better than that."

"Then come with us," Reiligh persisted, calm and inexorable.

"We'll all three of us go. Make an outing of it. How long since we've had an outing, eh?"

Golden Narilyn, off to the right, said, "Our visitors are gathering in the presence chamber. Dabrena must attend them."

"But Kara doesn't have to," Ronim said. Like Narilyn and Selen, he'd been a vocate with her, and would speak as few others dared; the bond among those called by the Ennead was strong, and stronger for what that Ennead had done to them. Dabrena caught the tap of a foot. Ronim thought the child should be packed off to Dabrena's family in the Fingers.

It was the same on all the faces, even Selen's and Corle's. Pity, embarrassment, irritation. She could not afford a display like this in front of the junior menders. So many of them had come here since the uprisings. The others hadn't seen what she had seen. They didn't understand what it was like, what she had done, why she must always keep the child near, keep the child safe.

Kara's sobs died to a sniffle. Poor Kara, tiny Kara, forgotten in the midst of a crowd centered on her. "We have to go now, sweet," Dabrena said. "This is an important day. People have come a long way to see us. We have to be strong and smart today. Tonight we can cry, all right? Tonight we can be angry. All right, Kara? All right, sweet?"

The child rose obediently, accepted the wet cloth Selen offered her to wipe her face and hands. But her shoulders were slumped. The clear angry light had gone from her eyes.

I think I'd prefer the tantrum, however inconveniently timed.

What have you done to our baby, Dabrena?

She denied the voice that haunted her, the guilt that ran like an old dark bindsong under all her thoughts. With Kara firmly in hand, she turned to fetch the food and drink she would be bringing for the holding's guests.

Selen stopped her.

The others exchanged glances. Then everyone left the dining hall but her most senior folk.

"We must talk, Dabrena," Selen said.

"Whatever it is, we'll sort it out later. The runners and Khinish and shieldmaster will be waiting—"

"Let them wait. There will never be a later. Later is always later. Now is now."

Selen gently disengaged Dabrena from her daughter. Reiligh took Kara's hand. Kara looked to Dabrena for permission. Dabrena said, "No," and reached for her. Selen took Dabrena's arm and said, "Yes,

Bre. This once, let's try it. She'll be right there at the other end of the hall. She'll never be out of your sight."

Dabrena, flummoxed, let herself be herded toward the far end of the hall. Midway there she said "*No*" and turned for Kara, now seated and babbling nonstop to Reiligh as if her tantrum had never happened, her mouth full of gooey breadroot. *Don't let her do that, she's overexcited, she'll choke on her food*—but Selen and Corle had a firm grip on her, and before she knew it she was seated at the other table, and Corle was behind her, pressing down on her shoulders with his chubby hands, not letting her rise.

"Dabrena," Selen said in a low voice, sitting beside her, leaning in close. "You can see her. She's with Reiligh. She adores him. He'd die for her. She's *right there*."

"You've done all you could to see that I spend time with her, and now—"

"Yes, all we could. And we've just seen what's come of it. We've seen it every morning for three moons now."

Dontra barred the door, to keep the conversation private; both door and bar were new since the uprisings. Then she sat down with Dabrena, Selen, Ronim, Narilyn, Loris, and Corle. Except for Jerize, Eltarion, and Cinn, who were in the field, these were all who remained of their vocate sleephall. Tolivar was dead; Terrell and Garran were assumed dead; Jonnula had died in the Fist; and Karanthe, Herne, and Annina, like so many reckoners, had become runners. There had been nine-and-eight of them when they were called. Seven of them left alive here, six in the field. Four dead or missing. Their losses had been minor compared with other halls'.

Well, they were all one hall now. But these were her closest advisors, her head folk. Only Reiligh had penetrated the inner circle Dabrena had formed with those who'd earned the ring with her, who'd stood by her in the last days, and the first.

"What is this?" Dabrena said warily.

Corle glanced at Selen, as though it should fall to her, but when she hesitated he said, "You've got to let Kara go."

"The child is a misery," Ronim said.

"The child is miserable," Selen snapped. "There's a difference."

"I'm not having this discussion again. Not today of all days." Dabrena tried to rise. Narilyn, beside her, pressed her down by the forearm. She shook the grip off, but could not shake off their combined gazes. It was hard to read them and watch Kara at the same time. Was that the strategy?

"You must, Dabrena. We can no longer endure this." Again Corle looked at Selen, a bulge-eyed goading to speak up, and Selen said, "To your family, that would be best, I think."

"I've already told you no."

"She's a hindrance," said Ronim.

"She's my daughter!"

"She's a possession you guard with a ferocity bordering on obsession," said Corle, head bowed. "And you are killing her."

"Not to mention the rest of us."

"Shut up, Ronim."

"I'm not unsympathetic—"

"Yes you are. And it's irrelevant."

"We shouldn't gang up on her," Dontra said.

"This has to be done," Selen replied.

"To send her away would be the worst kind of betrayal." Dabrena looked from one of them to another, then across at Kara, then to the next. "Think what it would do to her!"

"That's not what you're thinking, Dabrena. You're thinking what it will do to you."

Dabrena opened her mouth to object, and tasted lies, and swallowed hard. "You don't know," she said.

"I think we do, a little," Dontra said. She spoke softly. Dabrena's heart flew into her throat. If Dontra guessed—

"We know it was bad, whatever it was. It had to be. Everything then was bad. The Ennead did terrible things. That's all we need to know. What else could have made you the way you are?"

"It wasn't so bad when she was little. She could stay by you night and day, amuse herself alone in the midst of adults hard at work. Her mother's presence was enough for her then. Now she needs company. She needs children. She needs *freedom*."

"She's not interested in children's games."

"You've taught her not to be."

"It comes down to this, Dabrena. Send her home to your village in the Fingers, or we will all go permanently into the field."

This was madness. "You'd leave the holding? With so much half done? You'd leave your work, your friends?"

"I'm afraid we would."

"Then *I'll* go into the field, I'll take her with me and—"

"You'd keep her on as tight a rein outside as you do here. Tighter! If you won't let her run the corridors of the holding, how will you treat her when there's a whole world to get lost in? You'll tighten your stranglehold on that child until she gags. She doesn't want to go adventuring. She wants a home, a real home in the sunlight, where she can run free in blithe safety."

"She'd only love my village because it would be a holiday, full of gifts and treats. When the holiday wore off . . ."

"Why would it? They'd cherish her. They'd adore her."

"I cherish her. I adore her."

"Do you? Do you really? Dabrena, do you even love that child at all?"

Dabrena was too appalled to answer.

Loris said, "She's a precious stone, Dabrena, a beautiful glowing stone you were handed out of nowhere and never wanted but protected with your life because you knew she was precious, even though you couldn't see it yourself, even though the stone was never something you wanted and all it ever did was weigh you down."

Dabrena stared at the barred door.

"You can let her go, Bre," said Selen. "It's all right. She'll still love you. She does love you, though you cripple her. Her love for you will only grow stronger for her learning to love the world, too. Let her go. Let her go to a place where she'll be happy."

After Karanthe had left, Selen had been closest to her. She relied heavily on Selen's judgment, her equanimity. "They wouldn't look after her properly, they'd—"

"Oh, spirits, Dabrena, of course they would!" said Dontra.

"Children are dying out there. Fevers, injuries—"

"At least they lived a little!" Ronim cried. "That child is dying *here*, can't you see it? As surely as if you'd let her take a fever or fall off a cliff. Living in the dark, among people too driven, too *busy* to be with her, living among haunts in the shadows, denied the company of other children, pets . . . You will kill her if you keep her with you, no matter where you go."

"And we need you here," said Narilyn.

"You must think I'm a very bad mother," Dabrena said softly.

"You were a good mother," Selen said. "You were, Dabrena. The way you made her laugh, the patient way you taught her, the way you touch her when you aren't thinking about it, which is when she *feels* it because that burning intensity of your focus is diverted from her for long enough to let her feel. But she doesn't laugh anymore. She's secretive. She throws tantrums. When is she happy? *When she's away from you*. Look at her there with Reiligh, look how animated she is. You are smothering that child. She is a flame that has no air to breathe that she might burn bright. Let her go, for this little while. Just a few moons. If your village is ailing, send her to Glydh. She's a piece of Tolivar, still living in the world. Entrust her to his family. Let them touch her. Let them love her. Let them see him living on in her."

After a long silence, Dabrena said, "There's so much I should have done, Selen." Gone to Glydh, to see Tolivar's folk. *But I'd have had to tell them what became of him. I could not tell them how he died. When he went for a proxy, they knew they might never see him again. Better to leave it at that. Better to wonder, than to know what I would tell them.* Let the child run free and happy through the passageways. *But she might have fallen, gotten lost somewhere I couldn't reach her.* Brought her home. *But there's fever in the Hand, symptoms we've never heard of, an illness we might not be able to outsmart . . .*

Saved that infant from the Ennead.

But I couldn't.

Saved Tolivar.

"I'll let her have minders," she said abruptly. Negotiating, like a petitioner. It had come to this. "Reiligh can look after her in the mornings and Belwyn can have her with the other children in the afternoons."

"Listen to yourself. Every one of those words was a tooth being pulled. You can barely stand to sit across from her in the same hall."

You weren't there you don't know . . .

"Something terrible happened."

"We know that."

"But it happened six years ago."

"*It's a new world now.*"

Like proxies, all speaking with one voice, as they had been trained to do. She would not sway them with words. She would have to prove it to them.

"I cannot delay the meeting any longer." She rose. She called across the room: "Reiligh, could you look after Kara until sunset bells?" She heard Kara's gasp of hope. She saw Reiligh's surprised, pleased nod. "Would you like that, Kara? Just until suppertime?"

Kara clapped her hands in delight, a gesture Dabrena had never seen her make. Her beaming smile cut deep.

But she had done it. "You see?" she said, turning.

"Yes," Selen said quietly. "Do you?"

Head high, Dabrena fetched the tray she had prepared, then set it on a table by the door. She unbarred the door, opened it. The corridor beyond stretched long. She stepped out.

It was like ripping off a limb. All she could feel was that soft weight pulled from her arms, over and over again. Held before her, that tiny precious life in the balance. The echo of the strangled cry, the infant who was not her own, but could have been. All she could think was *I can't I can't I can't I can't.*

The child was part of her. The child belonged to her. They could not be separated. Not even for Kara's sake.

She fetched her daughter.

When Verlein n'Tekla l'Sayal had left this holding, at the end of the magewar, it had been a chaos of fleeing stewards, a slaughterground of mages. Its warders, newly deprived of their magelight, had been exhausted and demoralized. By rights the place should have been abandoned. It should stand now a deserted memorial to the failure of magecraft, its only denizens some refugees weathering the gales that battered its coastal village, perhaps some former mages and stewards clinging at peril of starvation to the only home they'd ever known.

It should not, by any means, be a thriving community. It should not have its own sources of food or suppliers of materials; it should have nothing to trade or barter.

She had assessed this holding as a casualty of the magewar. She should have known better. Never count the dead till you see the bodies. There had been life in it still. Not much, but a flicker. Enough. And Dabrena n'Arilda l'Desarde, against all odds, had fanned that ember, and made this mountain holding a force to be reckoned with once again.

Oh, they were struggling. You could see it through the cracks in the rotting wood of the privies, smell it in the cheap candle drippings. They were living on fungus and goat cheese, wearing castoffs, shivering in their stone chambers—but they were fed, they were clothed, and they were sheltered, which was more than many could claim. They went bladeless not because forged iron was beyond their means but because danger, here, was beyond their ken. Above all, they had purpose. They moved through their smoky passageways with vigor. They discussed their work over meals, at chance meetings, in their sleephalls, with laughter and eagerness.

This had been a terminus of torment and death. A petite cottar from the Fingers had made it a nexus of healing and life.

How the woman had done it was not entirely clear. She'd built somehow on the structure of proxies. Verlein had paid little attention to the ins and outs of magecraft. She had never fully understood its hierarchies. Why understand what you were set to behead? She had dedicated herself wholly to the Ennead's downfall. She had mustered an armed force to effect it. *An "army,"* she thought wryly. *Thanks to little squiggles on parchment leaves I could tear with my fingers, we have a word for it. They were my fighters. The Ennead called them rebels—a horde of rebels. And now we know: They were an "army."*

It was a word from an ancient world, speaking like a haunt through the medium of ink and leaf. There was more power in those squiggles than she'd allowed for; they were a window on a warring world she would never have heard of without them, and folk who could read them. There were volumes of such leaves, bound into codices. She'd found them cached here when she took the place.

Burn them—her lips had formed the words, but her throat had given them no voice. She'd taken a torch from the wall and prepared to cast it into the chamber piled high with codices. You burned off the leaves of autumn, the detritus of the dying year. Those codices represented an order that had taken her folk and returned nothing, ignored her and then killed those she loved. Every particle of her being had wanted to see them burn.

She didn't know what stopped her. Not Evrael; though he took credit for snatching the torch from her hand, she had already let the arm fall, the command die on her lips. Certainly not a promise made to a mage who had betrayed her. He'd asked her to salvage them at all cost. She had agreed. Then he had abandoned her. The promise was forfeit. Yet she kept it.

And here she was, in this holding again, six long years after sparing the codices, sparing the warders, six long years of vigil along Eiden Myr's shores. The presence chamber was empty now, serene in lamplight, hung with colored tapestries that would have been a sacrilege in another time. They had only tangible wardings against cold and damp here now. The blood had been scrubbed from the stone by hand.

She had come here to meet with the remains of the mages she had spared. She had come here to say, "Your folk are gelded. Send them home to provide for their families, or send them to us if they can learn the blade." She had thought to make this dead mountain a fortification against attack. But she had found it thriving.

What she had done was not so different from what Dabrena n'Arilda had done. She had encircled Eiden Myr with her fighters, so that no ninemile stretch of coast was left unguarded. When the magecrafted warding around Eiden Myr was broken, it left them vulnerable to the outer realms. On the rare clear days, they could see the strip of land on the horizon off the Fist. "That's where we came from," the scholars said, and tellers took up the tale, and spread it. "That's where mages lived once, long ago, before we fled to exile here. What we thought was the world was an island. We live in an island realm. There really was a land beyond the mists."

Verlein had taken charge. If there were real folk in the land beyond the haze, they would have real ships and real blades, and they would covet this fertile bit of country laid out on the waters. They would fear and hate its mages, whether or not they knew the light had gone.

Where there had been a magecrafted shield she put a human shield, bristling with iron. From the Holding she had headed into the Midlands, where folk had been primed to fight her, and turned them to her cause. They were ready to fight *something*; a threat from the outside was more palatable than the threat from her, and at any rate she had beaten them. She was the victor. The Ennead had been corrupt and she had routed it. Chastened but still battle-ready, young Midlanders had flocked to her. Cored and directionless, mages had flocked to her too, for the structure and stability her cadre offered. She had a clear goal and a chain of command. Lightless, useless, they welcomed the tasks she set them. They had spent their lives protecting Eiden Myr through their craft; with their craft denied them, they turned readily to her. Oh, some had gone back to the trades they were born to, becoming cobblers and weavers and sheepherds again, where their villages would have them; and some had fled to the Isle of Senana, where a pale shadow of magecraft's routine could be found. But many had come to her. And some, it seemed, had come here.

None of it was more important than what she was doing. If hordes of fighters, invaders, *armies*, came over the Forgotten Sea, or the Dreaming Sea, or the Sea of Sorrows, or slipped around and came at them from top or bottom or back, there would be no cobbling then, no scholars, no sheepherds. Eiden Myr would be conquered and enslaved. That was something else they had learned from those codices of theirs. In the outer realms, in the realms of old, that was how it was done: You invaded, you conquered, and you ruled.

She would not have it. Her folk would fight to the death, to the last one of them, before they would let outworlders set foot on Eiden's body.

She ran her finger along the rounded edge of the triangular table in the center of the chamber, surprised that they used this space at all, even more surprised at how little they had altered it. Welcoming guests into a slaughter chamber . . . was it to remind them what they had fought, or what they had been, or what they had lost? If there was message in this, Verlein could not translate it.

No matter. She would evaluate whatever they offered, negotiate for what aid they could provide, and get out—back to her windy hillsides, her outcroppings, her seawalls, her guardposts, where she belonged. Scanning the hazy waters for the first prick of sail or swell of hull on the horizon. She was not healer, or seeker, or scholar, or reckoner, or whatever these Holding folk had become. This was a dark, unhealthy place. She had conquered it once. She had better things to do than conquer it again.

"Verlein."

Eowi's soft voice carried only into the chamber, from his post just inside the doorway. She nodded: They were coming. She had made sure to be early, with Eowi and Girayal, her seconds—a day early for the meet, to wander the Holding and gauge the changes against the rumors she had heard, and so early to this chamber that their wretched bells had barely tailed off when she'd finished inspecting it for hiding places and weaponry. Forgoing breakfast always put her in a sour frame of mind, but Girayal had the foresight to save some supper, and since these folk ate the same swill three times a day, it made no difference. Nor did the swill, when you came down to it. Her fighters were doing no better, living on seaweed at their coastal posts, clothed and sheltered by the generosity of local villages. How long could Eiden Myr go on, when their protectors and healers were reduced to wearing castoffs and eating swill? She flicked a crumb of dry cheese off the polished table.

The blond man who strode in, with the air of a ship's master coming on deck, was midway through his seventh nineyear, lean and deeply tanned, ruggedly handsome under hair and beard so sun-bleached that there was no telling how much gray was in them. He was flanked by two swarthy Khinish sailors. They carried the scent of the sea on them, as if they'd only just arrived.

"Cutting it a bit close, aren't you, Evrael?"

"Verlein." He gave her a slight nod and the barest glance, as his sailors, a man and a woman, stationed themselves by the open door, one inside, one out. Both wore cudgels and longstaffs; the outline of dagger sheaths showed through the soft material of their high boots. He did not bother to introduce them to her, but Eowi and Girayal welcomed them. Her shield and the Khinish seafolk had become well acquainted over the years.

She seated herself with a view of the entry, seeing no reason to wait on the others, and after a moment he did the same. He sat as if unaccustomed to straight-backed chairs set on carpeted floors that didn't move. Verlein, herself used mainly to camp stools, rubbed her mouth to hide a grin. "The place has changed," she said, an opening to benign chatter. She and he had come to an understanding six years ago, standing at the portal to that chamber of codices. He was a known quantity.

"This place changed a generation ago," he said. "No, more than that." His mouth was set and grim. His restless eyes, the pale green of an angry sea, roved the walls as if threats might lurk behind the tapestries. After that first acknowledgment, his gaze had never returned to her. That, too, they had in common, the continual scanning wariness of those who held guard against attack.

"I hear you've stepped up production of ships," she said. "Good thing your quinces and apricots came in, or I don't know how you'd get the timber."

Watching his man at the door as if awaiting some particular signal, Evrael replied, "It was Streln who commissioned the shipbuilding; it's only mastwood that we don't grow on Khine; and we had other goods to trade besides fruit. White pines don't grow only in the Gerlocs. But we had fruit, and needed mastwood. They had mastwood and they had scurvy and the High Arm is easily accessible by sea. This holding made the match."

This time Verlein let the grin blossom. In one elegant deflection, he had told her that her information was flawed, that he still deferred to headman Strelniriol te Khine, that his adopted island was quite healthy, thank you, and that thus far they were allied to this holding. *Nicely done*, she thought. *Could that understanding we forged need stropping and oiling after all?*

Bootsteps sounded in the passageway. Evrael's man gave a shake of the head so slight that anyone else would have missed it, and through the door came not the Khinish headman, as Verlein had expected, but two men and a woman dressed in black tunics and hose. Verlein rose to her feet at the unlikely sight. When she'd heard the Khinish were coming, she'd assumed that this would be a gathering of leaders. Those who still wore reckoner's black were merely message runners. She could have been no more surprised if three children had walked into the chamber.

"Good morning," said the oldest of them—a Norther, judging from the blunt accent and pale complexion. He did not bear himself like someone who'd stumbled into the wrong place; he believed he was expected here. As tall and lean as Evrael, with eyes and hair the color of aged silver, he was old indeed, by the standards of the day. Few saw their ninth nineyear anymore, fewer still of them former mages, and none of those were scribing messages with their arthritic hands, let alone running them hither and yon. He gave a fluid bow, as did his unarmed aides, and beside her Evrael stiffened before returning it—with awkward grace, as if remembering a gesture long forgotten.

"Evrael n'Vonche," the old man said. "It has been many years."

"A lifetime," Evrael replied. There was a strange light in his sea-distant eyes. "And it was n'Daivor, as it turns out, though I am wholly Evrael te Khine."

The old man's brows arched. "Was it now?" he said softly.

"If my brother's message can be believed."

"Evonder your brother was a sound man, Evrael. I wish you could have known him."

Verlein had stood over the body of this Evonder—n'Vonche, n'Daivor, it made no difference to her—in this very chamber. He had been one of the Ennead, felled in the magewar as the Nine's final casting against the Lightbreaker failed. If Evrael was his brother, Evrael himself had been Ennead spawn. That he was of Head stock was evident in his coloring, his name, his diluted Khine drawl, and she'd always known he'd forsaken the light when he was young. She had not known that it was Ennead light. This old man was more than he seemed, and Evrael . . .

"Yes," he said without turning, sensing her evaluation. "I was born in this Holding and groomed for the Ennead. I told you the changes began more than a generation ago. I was here. I saw it. I denied it, and went to Khine." Something passed between him and the old man then, something deeper than Verlein could follow.

She felt old forces rising, arraying against her. There was a forest of history here. She must tread carefully. Breaking the magelight had not broken the bonds between these people, or the ambitions this mountain had fostered.

"You recall some of the old courtesies, but not all," the old man chastised gently—another statement more significant than it sounded. Verlein became aware that she was fingering the guard of her longblade. *They are divesting me of arms*, she thought, *as the weapons become words and the field of battle the past*. "I am Pelkin n'Rolf, of Drey, in the Neck," he said to her with exaggerated gallantry, "and I was once the Ennead's head reckoner. Now my folk make their way carrying messages. And information."

Ah, Verlein thought. *And thus your importance to this holding*. Were they spies for Dabrena, as well? Eiden's bloody balls, what had she walked into here?

"Verlein Blademaster," she said, "and I never did understand why you folk persist in wearing black."

Ignoring the gibe, he continued, "I present to you Jimor n'Loflin of the Strong Leg, and Chaldrinda n'Poskana of the Haunch. Jimor, Chaldrinda, I present to you Evrael te Khine, master of the Khinish fleet, and Verlein n'Tekla, first of Eiden's shield." He waited for the introduction of Evrael's seafolk and Verlein's seconds. When neither came, he returned his attention to her, as if there had been no breach of his outdated protocol. "What better way to identify ourselves as runners when we travel? Times are hard. One commission is hardly enough to cover the cost of bearing a message by hand. We depend upon customers waylaying us as we pass."

"You are a black reminder of the Ennead that brought a darkness on this world."

His eyes narrowed. *Good*, she thought. *Let's get a rise out of you, see what you're made of, old man.* But his expression remained courteous. "Black was considered a color of grieving, in another world. We grieve the light we have lost." He manufactured a genial smile, but his eyes cautioned her to accept what he offered next: "Would you have us wear pigeon feathers on our heads?" *Respond in kind*, those eyes said, *or I will take your goading personally*.

She was meant to come back with a joke—take him up on the opportunity to abandon her aggressive position. She understood the maneuver. She could work with it—say something like *Perhaps only the dovekeepers among you*, which in the code of this conversation would convey her understanding that he was more than a message boy while reminding him that she wore a longblade. But she was not yet prepared to acknowledge any authority on this man's part. Reckoners had failed her folk in desperate times.

Better feathers on your heads than silver rings on your fingers, she started to say, but pulled her thrust when she caught a nod from Evrael's man. The arrival, at last, of the Khinish headman. The nod was relayed to Evrael by his woman inside the chamber. The step he took to the side cleared his line of sight to the door, which the runners had blocked, and also distanced him from physical alliance with Verlein.

So much could be conveyed and confirmed by so little. Evrael straightened, but did not quite come to attention as his folk did. His sweeping gaze fixed on the doorway. As Streln entered, their eyes locked, and for a long moment it was apparent that for the two of them no one else existed.

The headman of Khine made up in breadth and muscle what he lacked in height. His complexion was darker than Verlein's, shading to bronze rather than olive and further deepened by the sun; his eyes, which might have been brown in natural light, looked so dark that their whites startled. He had the stance of a fighter, but not the easy grace of the fighters Verlein trained. Every movement spoke discipline and control. A Khinish blade curved to his flank as if molded there, and one gloved hand rested with care on its belt rather than its pommel. A cloak was folded, not flung, across the opposite forearm. Two men stood braced and square-shouldered precisely one pace behind him and to either side.

The scent that wafted to her was of horseflesh. The silent confrontation of headman and fleetmaster clearly followed some time apart. Streln had not sailed here on one of Evrael's ships. He might have made the crossing from Khine on one, but he had ridden from the Boot all the way to the Head. Four nonned leagues or more, by horseback.

No wonder there were whispers that the Khinish were waking.

"Headman," Evrael said at last, on a rising tone, and laid his fist on his heart.

"Fleetmaster," the headman replied, a flat statement, and laid his fist on his.

It was a customary Khinish greeting. Verlein had seen it a nonned times. But in the rarefied atmosphere of this chamber the gesture took on strange layers of significance. She scowled.

"You must have had an arduous journey, and no host as yet to give you welcome," said Pelkin n'Rolf. "Why don't we sit while names are exchanged—there's no telling how long our wait will be."

"Evrael and his fleetmates are known to me," said Streln, "and he has spoken my title. That is Eiden's self-proclaimed first shield and those are two of her seconds. You were a reckoner once, are now a bearer of tidings and possibly more, and those are your aides. These are my men. That is all any of us needs to know."

"As you say, Headman." With that neutral deferral, Pelkin gestured his folk into seats that gave their backs to the door, and engaged them in ordinary conversation. Verlein took her own seat again, with a glance to Eowi and Girayal to confirm that they should stay in place, and stretched out at an angle to the chairback, crossing her legs at the boot and her arms at her chest. Streln posted his men with the lift of a finger, then moved aside to await their hosts. After the briefest hesitation, Evrael went to him, and they exchanged even briefer words, too low for Verlein to make out. Then Evrael returned to the table and sat, one chair away from hers, still facing the door, still on the same side. His hands lay lightly on the stone surface, perhaps an unconscious display: he held no weapon, but his longstaff was propped in easy reach. His gaze still swept the chamber and lit on his guards at intervals, but slowly now; what absorbed him was visible only to his mind's eye.

Verlein produced a toothpick and worked at a nutshell lodged in her teeth.

Did you learn what you sought? he had asked. Streln had answered, *Yes. And she was right.*

Five words, whose message he had already read in Streln's reserve, in the refusal to take the chair beside his. Five words, rising like unmarked shoals in a seaway he had not wanted to enter. This mountain holding was a rocky point he had sailed ever to windward of. Now, in the next few breaths, he would find out whether it would be the wreck of him at last.

Evrael had never thought to return here—not even once, let alone this second time. He had left at two nineyears of age, the day after taking his triskele. Ordinary mages went journeying for a year after receiving the pewter symbols of their craft. He went to sea, which was the journeying of a lifetime. Mages were always needed on shipboard, particularly bindsmen with journey trusses. Somehow he never triaded, as if the spirits knew that magecraft was not his true calling. After a year he landed on Khine, forged friendships, became the bonded son of a prominent family. Streln, of an age with him, became his bonded brother, then far more. They had labored side by side in the vineyards and groves of that rich, sun-drenched island, where all families were landholders and all leaders were chosen by consensus. The rigor of the lifestyle had suited his Holding upbringing just as its warmth had neutralized it. On Khine, hard work and discipline were rewarded with honest, open acclamation. His speech slowed, his pallor darkened, his sandy hair bleached blond in the sun. He woke to life and love and honor. He never looked back.

Yet he could not resist the sea's call. Though it kept him from Streln at times, he made a place for himself as shipwright, later as shipmaster. It gave him standing apart from Streln's family, put them on equal footing: the seafolk chose their own leaders, answering only to the headman of all Khine. He himself became their fleetmaster, just as Streln, his rise unrelated to Evrael's, came one step away from headman—and just as rumors of dissension on the mainland began to reach them.

In among those rumors he received a message from the youngest member of the Ennead. In all his long lifetime away, no one else had contacted him—not parent, not the brother she claimed was born nine moons after his departure. Then this young woman sent to him, the master of the Khinish fleet, seeking to forge an alliance.

As binder, never mind seaman, he should not have been able to read it, but the last two Enneads had trained their successors in all three triadic disciplines, so he did not require a wordsmith to translate for him or scribe a reply. He'd thought she was her father at first, not knowing Rigael was dead, seeing his mark, the rune *riol*, at the foot of her messages, but in context her identity came clear. He rebuffed her, and failed to acknowledge several subsequent advances. Her pleas kept coming. When he could no longer deny the thickening rumors of darkcraft, he constructed replies that led her to believe he would bring his fleet to her aid.

He had no intention of doing so. She was party to this darkcraft, if not in practice then in complicity. He meant only to sabotage her schemes by promising help he would fail to provide—a small way in which he was willing to help those fighting that faraway Ennead. But then, thoroughly duped by his lies, she revealed the plan for a great casting to be worked by the leading triad of her Ennead. It was to happen on the balance day of the following sowmid equinox. The casting would satisfy an ancient vengeance against the outer realms, and sacrifice the leading triad, clearing the way for rulers to arise. She would have him, and the Khinish, by her side when that time came.

He had to go. He had to stop it.

Trusting in the love they bore each other, he told Streln everything—and that, he knew now, was the trunk from which all subsequent errors branched. "*I must return to the place of my birth and set things to rights,*" he'd said. "*I would take six ships.*"

"*And so you shall,*" Streln had said. "*We have slept too long here on our sunny island, I fear, while darkness has crept across the mainland. We have remembered our beginnings only in dreams. We must awaken from those dreams now, and assert our heritage.*"

Evrael was not born to Khine, not of Streln's blood. He was pressed for time, could not stop to ponder awakenings; he left immediately for the Holding, and even then, battered by the front of what he later learned was a Great Storm, cored of his magelight in what he later learned was a loss suffered realmwide, he arrived past noon on the balance day of Ve Galandra. Verlein's rebel horde had burrowed through the mountain and joined a stewards' uprising, while warders reduced to little more than stewards themselves had pulled together to divert the Storm. All was changed, irrevocably, the home of his youth soiled, castrated, freed. There was little left for him to do but stay Verlein's murderous fury, save the warders, the materials, the codices.

But he'd captured the last surviving member of that doomed Ennead: Lerissa n'Lessa l'Rigael, who called herself Lerissa n'Rigael in negation of her lightless, banished mother, who signed her messages with *riol*, her father's mark, the frost hawthorn. The youngest member of the Nine. The scheming girl who had sent him messages and expected his fleet to save her.

He had thought her a devious, naïve child, not worth bloodying a blade on, perhaps redeemable, and no longer his concern.

He had brought her home with him, and delivered her to Streln.

Now he sat in the new holding that had risen from those ashes, at the very table where his brother had died. He hadn't believed the girl's claims that he had a brother. But the resemblance had been inarguable. His parents had lain not two threfts away, poisoned. The remains of a triskele had strewn the table, and in death Evonder clutched the tools that had shattered it. When Evrael returned home, a message from his brother awaited him, having wended its slow way to Khine through the proxies who now made a trade of bearing such messages. *I am your brother Evonder*, it had said, *the son of Naeve and nominally Vonche. I will probably be dead when you read this, and there is a thing you must know. The shade of Daivor, the binder who trained you, the binder who trained me, the man who was triaded with our parents, was bound into his own triskele by those who murdered him, more than two nineyears after you left. I have touched that triskele and felt his spirit as though casting passage, and I tell you true, brother I have never known: He was my father, and believed, hoped, that he was yours as well. I have lived in your shadow all my life, golden Evrael, but gravely wronged you by failing to reach out. Understand that silence was necessary, given the circumstances here. I could never take the risk. It has grieved me always. Spirits willing, I will live to look on your face one day. Strive well, and die with honor.*

Like the girl's messages, it was scribed in Ghardic, a language in disuse, and signed with a rune—*deis*, Daivor's mark, the blackthorn, no doubt taken up when Evonder took Daivor's place on the Ennead, to differentiate him from Vonche, whose rune *vol* would otherwise have been his in that vowelless script. No common wordsmith could have read either message or rune. No one but a son of the Ennead. But only a son of Khine would have understood that last exhortation. It was how they bid each other farewell when they believed they would never meet again.

He'd grieved, in the austere Khinish way, and moved on. It was not his calling to set Eiden Myr to rights. He was a sailor, a shipwright, a farmholder. Khine was untouched by the mainland's troubles, unfazed by their aftermath. They had never relied entirely on their mages. They were robust folk not prone to illness or injury; their island was self-supporting. He carried surplus goods to struggling coastal villages. In hall, he spoke in support of accepting a certain number of refugees into quarantine when the Boot was racked by earthquake; when the land settled, his ships carried them back again. He'd aided the mainland as he could. He'd persuaded himself it was enough.

Streln, the consummate Khinishman, had felt quite the opposite. His inclination in times of crisis was to take command. Thanks to the codices Evrael had salvaged, they now possessed historical precedent for such leanings, relayed through the scribes on Senana: The Khinish descended from a martial seafaring race—a race of conquerors. When that race's mages fled into exile from the outer realms, they isolated themselves on Khine. In prosperous safety, they suspended their domineering ways. But in Streln it became clear that they hadn't lost them. They had oiled and stored their weapons for twice nine nonned years; it was the work of three moons to craft new handles for the existing blades and forge twice their number anew from the model they provided. Khinish society had retained its structure, through all those generations of peace, and their blood had never entirely lost its cold fire. They chose leaders they would follow into death. All they lacked was a cause.

Lerissa n'Rigael was judged and incarcerated. Streln was perversely moved by her courage, her dignity, her resistance to pain. Intrigued, he visited her in her captivity. She told him stories about Khine's forebears, their glorious ancient history. Evrael could not refute them; Evrael had read them, too, and the scholars would only confirm anything he challenged. She dropped offhand suggestions; when the results were pleasing, Streln began to actively seek her advice. He had her transferred to his estate. Slowly he lifted the prohibitions on her, allowed her to interact and find productive work. He would not see what was clear to Evrael: that he was the work she had set herself. She had years . . . and the burning ambition Evrael lacked. In Streln the desire to rule was instinctive but tempered. In Lerissa it was an edged stone. She sliced her way into Streln, made herself seem indispensable, drove a wedge between him and Evrael—and replaced Evrael in his bed, as she replaced Evrael's counsel in his ear.

She told Streln what he secretly longed to hear. *Eiden Myr needs your strong hand. The Khinish alone have the discipline to set that poor ailing land to rights. They are starving! They are dying! And all for lack of effective leadership. You cannot sit idly by on your pleasant island and allow it.*

Streln had not been wholly, or easily, convinced. Though nearly estranged from Evrael, he owed him debts of love and honor. He could not forget the years of wisdom and companionship his brother and lover had given him. And he could not ignore the attraction that charged the air whenever they caught sight of each other. But Lerissa's insidious influence had rooted deep. She played on parts of Streln hidden even to himself. She gave advice that Streln was predisposed toward. Streln *wanted* her to be right.

And Evrael persisted in advising against intervention. He did so publicly, at the midwinter hall. Many leading families spoke in support of him. Once Streln would have respected opposition as Evrael's right; Lerissa whispered in his ear that it was betrayal.

Evrael would have preferred to attack the problem directly, on grounds that a woman nearly executed for collusion in darkcraft could not be permitted to counsel a headman; but such a maneuver would have been too easily dismissed as a spurned lover's bitter fruit, and until Streln installed her in some official capacity, there was technically nothing to object to. He could not seek hall censure for a man's choice of bedmate. In the meantime, the woman labored selflessly on behalf of the refugees pouring in from the beleaguered mainland, redeeming herself, good deed after good deed, in the eyes of Khinish who valued hard, honorable work above all else. She behaved as an exemplary Khinishwoman for six years. Soon they would forget her corrupt past, which they had not witnessed and, so long as she continued to render impeccable service, could forgive as the misguided error of youth. It was only a matter of time until Streln bestowed land upon her and some philanthropic title. There would be grounds for attack then—but it would be too late. No doubt she knew that; perhaps she had already been offered land and name and had demurred, further entrenching Streln's belief that her ambition burned pure.

To kill her would bring suspicion immediately upon him. It could be contrived for her to die of some rampant mainland illness, but only if she ventured onto the mainland. He had seafolk keeping watch for ailing refugees, in hope that some one of her beggared charges might become his unwitting assassin; but such plots sickened him, and sometimes he believed she was herself an illness, twisting hearts as grotesquely as the sprain palsy twisted limbs.

In hall, where reputation and probity held sway, he knew his footing. Backed by coastal landholders, with members of Streln's own family taking his part, he had made it necessary for Streln to justify his desire to intervene. It is understandable, they said. We were bred to rule; the codices on Senana have proven it. But it would stretch our resources. It would cost us. And thus far it seems unnecessary. Eiden Myr is an honorable, resilient land. Let it effect its own recovery if it can.

And so Streln had watched, and waited, and capitalized on the opportunity when it came: word that the remnants of the Holding warders planned to meet on what most mainlanders called Spindle Day, four ninedays after Ve Galandra, with Verlein n'Tekla and a representative from the Isle of Senana. The shieldmaster would be petitioning for resources, perhaps some official alliance. The scholars, the menders, and the homegrown soldiers were the closest the mainland had come to consensus leadership. It is possible, Streln claimed in hall, that this is a sign of their development. I will go to that council. Perhaps I may advise them. At the least we must hear the words spoken there. I will journey on horseback, with a hand of my best men.

It was pointed out, and of course it was true, that this was madness. Go by sea, he was told. Or send a delegate—send the fleetmaster in your stead. You might not survive such an overland journey, through villages racked by disaster and plague.

What Streln wanted was firsthand proof that what Lerissa whispered was true—that the mainland would be lost without Khinish intervention. But he turned it back beautifully, ever the inspired orator; even as the waters roughened, Evrael felt a surge of pride and old love. If the mainland is as dangerous as you claim, Streln said, then we *must* intervene, to save it from itself. If not, I risk nothing but my winter grain by making the journey ahorse.

The hall acquiesced. And Evrael, still unsure whether his reasons were political or personal, said, "And I shall sail there, to bear you home again."

That pleased the hall, which wanted the two of them at peace. It disquieted Streln, though only Evrael noticed. It no doubt infuriated Lerissa, who pictured Evrael alone with his old lover on shipboard, where he might slice him free of her glamorous netting. Evrael himself grew short of breath at the prospect.

But it was not to be. Streln had traveled up the mountainous length of Eiden Myr, through Leg and Girdle and Belt, through Heartlands and Neck and Head, to see for himself whether matters were as grave as Lerissa claimed.

Whatever he had experienced or observed had caused him to conclude that they were. If this council did not dissuade him, he would make of the mainland a Khinish precinct.

Why do I care? Evrael asked himself. *The Khinish way is strict and honorable. Mainlanders might welcome the order and stability it would bring. Does it grieve me only that she will have won?*

And when did it become "they" and not "we"?

Dabrena n'Arilda had not yet arrived. There might still be time for him to warn her how much now rested on her performance here. She had no way of knowing what was at stake. Could the girl he remembered carry this off? Dabrena Wordsmith was little more than two nineyears of age when he met her, but she had rallied frightened, downtrodden warders to fight off the last Great Storm. It was an admirable feat. She might have grown strong enough to convince Streln that his intervention was unnecessary, or cunning enough to bluff him that it could be resisted. Evrael had seen firsthand how formidable young girls could grow up to be. If she had weathered well, there was a chance that Streln, no matter what he had seen, would board Evrael's ship, go home, and stay.

When she came rushing harried through the door, a diminutive creature looking no older than when he last saw her, wisps of honey hair escaping their band, her white hose stained, bearing refreshments like a clumsy steward and towing a sullen child, he felt an axe cut the moorings to all his hopes.

Dabrena deposited her tray of breadroot loaves and watered wine on the stone table and Kara on a stool off to the side, plunked herself into a seat without ceremony, and said, "I'm Dabrena n'Arilda, I welcome you, I'm sorry I'm late. I've brought Selen and Loris, who have expertise in recordkeeping. I know some of you have titles, but we don't, and none are needed here. Has my delay allowed you to introduce yourselves to those you didn't know? Good." The Khinish headman looked as if someone had rammed him down on a fencepost. "Won't you sit?"

"I will stand."

With a slight shrug, she gestured Loris into the last seat, between Verlein and Evrael. The three-sided table was designed to seat nine, and though they'd tried with various chairs they could not comfortably change that loaded number. This was the only available chamber large enough to accommodate a group; the dining halls, sleephalls, scriptoria, and maphalls were always in use. They'd lined up plenty of stools by the entry, for aides and companions, but when Senana had declined to attend she'd thought to seat only four at the table itself—Pelkin, Verlein, Streln, and her. She had not counted on armed guards, or on the fleetmaster asserting an equal authority with the Khinish headman, or on Pelkin making a show of equality among runners.

No matter. Empty stools gave Kara room to stretch out and nap if she liked. It would be easier for Selen and Loris to scribe on a table than on binding boards. If the headman had piles and the others saw absurd need to guard against attack, it only left more room for her people.

She did not meet Selen's eyes, and Loris applied himself to the preparation of a quill. On the way here, they had not spoken of the confrontation in the dining hall. She turned her mind from it.

That a sowmid meeting with Verlein had become perceived as a council of leaders peeved her. She'd hoped to reallocate some of the shield's growing number of fighters, who were wasted on their vain, lonely seaside vigil. She wasn't sorry the Khinish fleetmaster was here; if she could persuade him to assign some of his trading vessels double duty as coastal patrol, it would give her firmer footing with Verlein, who would be tricky to manage. She'd hoped the head scholar from Senana could be enticed to come as well. He'd been terse and uncooperative of late, all but accusing her of siphoning off his best folk—as if the dry swotters he considered their best were any use in the productive endeavors of this holding! She'd hoped to demonstrate their activities personally, to prove that they were not in competition for the brightest minds. But in main she'd seen an opportunity to sit him and Verlein down to discuss the ostensible outer-realms threat face-to-face. He'd declined her invitation, but word of its issuance had reached the Khinish headman, apparently leading him to believe that he was being overlooked in some consolidation of power, and he had messaged his intent to attend. It had not been a request. *Bullheaded man*, she had thought; she could not refuse him, but it opened her way to ask the runners to send representation as well. If she had to put up with the imposition of Khine, she'd bloody well get *something* out of it. Her former warders had been leery of too close association with former reckoners, and she gathered the feeling was mutual: each felt the other must have known more than they admitted about the Ennead's corruption, each blamed the other for not acting against it. The rift between warder and reckoner had begun under that Ennead, was one of its nasty byblows. With this meeting she might begin to bridge that rift. They had sore need of the runners' aid in their work.

A small gathering to foster cooperation. It was more like some teller's land-beyond. Three folk still wearing the black, and her folk no better in warder's white, though it was mender's white now. A man the very image of the old Ennead's Evonder, though aged and brined, sitting here at the old Ennead's table. The Lowlander who had ravaged this holding to no purpose, picking her teeth past lips drawn back in a snarl. A Khinishman out of some ancient history in which swarthy invaders came armored in boiled animal skin and metals. Half of them bristled with weapons and had sentries posted in her corridor. You'd need a blade to cut the tension—and there were plenty of those.

"Why are these runners here?" said Verlein.

All right, Dabrena thought. *That speech you prepared was goat fodder anyway. Let it go as it goes.* "For the same reason you are. Pelkin n'Rolf, like yourself, has not been here since the magewar. This is a new holding. I wanted to show it to you." The two with Pelkin she had not met until last night when they arrived. She'd been disappointed and relieved. Three of his closest comrades had been vocates with her. It would have been both joy and anguish to see them again. Doubtless he knew that, and so brought strangers. Pelkin himself she did not know as well as she should. If she could rectify that with all of them . . . "Evrael te Khine also has not been here since the magewar. Strelniriol te Khine has never been here."

"As you have never been to Khine, nor anywhere besides here since the magewar," said Streln. "You live in obscurity behind stone walls, just as your predecessors did."

"What predecessors?" she shot back. He was probing for a nerve. He'd struck one, but inadvertently, and she wouldn't let it force her off the point. "This holding was established six years ago when an old way of life died forever. We have no predecessors."

"Then you have no heritage."

"We make our own heritage."

"And your own rules?"

"There are no rules. There are goals. Learn. Heal. Soothe. Mend. Gather knowledge and give it out again. Do you object to that?"

In dulcet tones, he said, "Not yet."

"An atmosphere of antagonism will be counterproductive." Her gaze dismissed him and swept the rest. "This is neither conspiracy nor competition. Some of you I asked here, some of you asked yourselves. It makes no difference. You've all come a long way. Let's find out how we can help each other."

"How do you propose to meet these lofty goals of yours?" Verlein said, scowling at Selen and Loris, who were scribing accounts on sedgeweave.

Dabrena suppressed a sigh. *By keeping codices instead of burning them*, she thought. "I was hoping to lead you all in a tour of the premises, show you our scriptoria and maphalls—"

"You could show me a nonned folk like these scratching the itchy skin of dead sheep, and it would tell me no more than you could sitting right here."

Because you never learned to read, like most of the rest of Eiden bloody Myr, despite every opportunity. Dabrena had to bite down to check her temper. Verlein, like Streln, was testing her. These were bladed folk. Their patterns of thought had developed differently from hers. She must make allowance for that.

"We compile information," she said. "Our folk in the field learn how one region heals an illness, say, or solves a problem of irrigation; they bring that information back here, we compile it so that it can be quickly referenced, we make copies of the resulting codices, and we send them back out into the field, to provide answers for problems in other regions. We have nearly completed a set of maps of our land, to better understand its needs, such as quality of soil and distribution of water. We've kept records of weather patterns, settlement and movement of people; we are midway through a rough head count, and we are beginning to see patterns in the spread of illness, the incidence of births and deaths, the—"

"*That's* what you're doing?" Verlein burst out. "Binding sheaves of sheepskin to arm your folk, as a substitute for *magecraft*? You're as useless as those inkmongers on Senana!"

Dabrena smiled. She'd had this debate with her own folk in the early days, and won. "Quite the contrary," she said. "On the Isle of Senana they analyze the past. We analyze the present. I cannot speak for them, and their head scholar declined my invitation. But I assure you that what we do here we do actively. We accumulate knowledge. We believe that we can compensate for the loss of magecraft by cooperating in the application of knowledge."

"You haven't solved the problem of the weather," Verlein said.

"And your knowledge is nothing without a strong arm to see it put into practice," Streln said.

Dabrena was bemused. "People welcome the knowledge we bring."

"If they won't act on your knowledge, you must compel them."

"We don't *compel* anyone. We offer ideas they haven't thought of or couldn't see from their vantage point."

"You could lie."

"I don't see what that would gain us. We lie, our recommendations fail, we lose the respect we've earned. Folk trust those in white because we can be relied upon to help them. What we do works only because we do it accurately and honorably."

Streln gave a thoughtful nod. *That got through to him*, she thought. Then he said, "But sometimes folk cannot see what is best for them. Have you the authority to make them bend?"

"Your insistence on compulsion has no relevance. If a thing makes sense and has worked before, folk try it. If they don't, the consequences are their own to bear. We present the known alternatives. Eight times out of nine they choose the right one."

"You are a fool."

"And you are clearly very wise. Tell me what I've missed."

"You've missed everything. You've missed the world."

Evrael spoke up—quickly, as if to belay something: "What you describe is not unlike our halls on Khine. We decide by consensus, and the consensus of training and experience always chooses the wisest path. We are not unalike, in this way."

It seemed he would have gone on, but Verlein broke in, "You

claim to traffic in cures, yet you have no cure for this weather, nor any idea why it is the way it is."

"Not yet. But we will."

"You can't cause rain to fall in the Heartlands by diverting the flow of rivers. You can't stop the storms that batter the village outside your own front door."

"We cured bonebreak fever in the Toes. We introduced rice crops to hopelessly flooded Girdle bottomlands—"

"What you have done," Streln said, "has been an admirable allocation of resources over a large landmass. We ourselves recently benefited from one of your suggestions. You have taken solutions discovered in isolated areas and efficiently shared them with the rest of Eiden Myr. You are yourselves a valuable resource. But you fail to adequately control a land in chaos."

"We have not failed because our intent has never been to control, Streln. Your reiteration grows tedious. With help, and time, we will do more to soothe the troubled land. 'Chaos' is far too strong a word."

"What kind of help?" Verlein asked. "The only aid my folk can give you is some tips on building seawalls."

"Your folk could be dispersed inland to show your seawalls to Midlanders trying to build dikes."

Verlein grinned widely. "Aha! You would see my shield dismantled that we might coach farmers in crop watering."

"Not dismantled. A reduced watch. Your folk have expertise that could be valuably developed."

"And we are not valuable now?"

"You produce nothing. You're a burden on every coastal village."

"My folk are the warders now, Dabrena."

"And where is this great bladed storm you ward against? In six years, why has no one come?"

"Someone sank the ships we sent."

"Perhaps they just sank. Perhaps they got lost. Perhaps there are no outer realms anymore at all."

"You haven't been to the Fist since it happened. You know nothing, buried here in your black rock. You can see the land on the horizon!"

"Perhaps it's a trick of the light. Perhaps Galandra's warding wasn't broken but only breached, so that we might go out but nothing might come in—or back. There are a nonned possible answers, Verlein, and no way to study the question."

"Senana might have shed some light," Pelkin said. "Graefel n'Traeyen was ever stubborn and self-absorbed, but you have other scholars here, don't you? This bears more discussion. Summon one of them, and let us proceed more . . . knowledgeably."

Whether Verlein had bristled at the reference to Senana or to Pelkin's home-village association with its head, Dabrena could not tell, but she snarled, "You don't run your proxy circle any longer, old man, and this is no Ennead to report to. Don't pretend to power you no longer have."

The old man smiled. Verlein looked away from whatever she saw in his eyes, but she persisted, "Those ships were sunk by outworlders. They know of us now. They'll be coming. You mark me."

"Then why haven't they come?" Pelkin said. "We'd be a little difficult to miss."

"You're the spymaster. You tell me."

"The what?" Pelkin said, still smiling, head cocked, but his eyes as flat as silver plates.

"Have they come already? Have you spirited them off somewhere that we might not know of them, not interrogate them, find out what it is we can expect when the main forces come?"

Dabrena began, "Verlein, you've gone far b—"

"Then you explain it! You tell me! But until you can, do not consider for one moment that you may have even one blade of mine."

"I can't explain it, Verlein. We haven't the means. The scholars haven't, either, Pelkin, though I too would have liked to hear Graefel's thoughts."

"Then perhaps you should go to him," Pelkin said. "Perhaps you should find out if his island is what you have concluded it to be, from accounts delivered to you here in your holding."

Pelkin's quiet words were as much a challenge as Verlein's and Streln's blunt attacks. She could not untangle the dual threads of his statement. Was his point that she was too cloistered here? Or were the runners more closely allied with the isle than she had known? Pelkin was not, as she had expected him to be, on her side. She had expected them all to be on her side, once she had explained things to them.

Verlein would not give up her argument. "When they come, if some Ennead pretender like you has sent my people inland to carve ruts in the dirt with their longblades—"

Exasperated, Dabrena snapped, "I don't want to send your people anywhere!"

Her own words flowed down the long corridors of her mind and echoed back with the words she hadn't said. *I don't want to send your people anywhere. I want you to send them.*

She had mastered this holding by delegating. You go here, you go there, you both come back and report. It was all based on that, at heart. For all her weariness, for all the dead ends, for all the agonizing slowness of the work, she was proud of what she had built and how. *She* had rallied the warders to divert the last Great Storm, when the Ennead—who existed not to control Eiden Myr, not to head a hierarchy of mages, but simply *to guard the land against those Great Storms*—was busy trying to destroy the outer realms instead of saving their own. *She* had persuaded the best warders to stay, when, stunned by the loss of their magelight, they'd been poised to flee the Holding in droves. *She* had pulled them from their stupor, *she* had convinced them there was reason to go on. With her inconvenient child strapped to her back, she had harangued and pleaded and contrived work for them to do, and they had gradually found their way, creating something where there had been nothing. Something wonderful. Something to be proud of.

These folk argued as her warders had, in the beginning. But these folk were not warders. Even Pelkin, who had been a mage and a proxy, was a foreigner to her now. She did not have the words to sway them. They had become something new and incomprehensible while she was buried in her maps and reports. The Khinish she had known were strong, sensible folk with their heads on straight who could be relied upon in a pinch, not dark, antagonistic strangers from a culture alien to hers. The runners she had known had been reckoners at heart, mages accustomed to working in proxy—not adversaries.

These people shared her goals: to restore Eiden Myr to safe prosperity. She had expected them to share her methods as well, once she made them clear. Hers was so obviously the right way to proceed.

But she had not been in the world, as they had. She had been watching the world through the window of her menders' accounts. It had changed profoundly during her time here, and she had no direct experience of it.

We all think our way is the only way. Who is to say that I am right and they are wrong?

The debate had continued while she was lost in thought. Some aides had spoken up and been shushed. Now Streln was speaking to her. "You have made a craft of efficiently allocating resources," he said. "Now you seek to allocate us. Verlein will not permit it. She is leader of her folk and intends to remain so, guarding our coasts as she sees fit. Let her keep her vigil. The villagers who support her folk are happy enough to do it, to know they are guarded. You seem to be the only one perturbed by what you perceive as an imbalance in what they consume to what they provide. They provide an illusion of safety. Let them provide it."

"It is no illusion," Verlein growled low in her throat.

Streln ignored her. "What I have seen in my journey here is unacceptable." His face was dark. His arms were crossed. His legs were spread. Dabrena felt a queer flutter in her belly, perhaps a response to the way Evrael shifted in his obviously unaccustomed chair, the way Pelkin's silver brows drew down, the way inked quills paused over sedgeweave. They had lost control of this meeting. They had all arrived here with causes, and none of this was going the way any of them had planned. Not even Streln.

"Conflict," Streln said. "Riots. Brigandage. Killings." He paused to let them take this in, then said, "Chaos."

Dabrena shot a look at Selen, who received the initial reports of all their folk returned to the holding; she shrugged with a slight, amazed shake of her head. Loris, their birdmaster, opened his hands and stared back wide-eyed.

"We know nothing of such horrors," she said. "We have suffered drought, flood, plague, fire, earthquake, blight, every natural disaster that magecraft kept from us, but in every case folk have worked together to overcome them. Doggedly. Rationally. Peacefully. What you describe is . . . a nightmare born of your own fears."

"I have seen what I have seen," Streln said. "With waking eyes. You have failed your land. It is coming apart as we speak. You have not been in it, so you do not know."

Unless he was lying—*he must be lying we would have heard we would have known of this*—his eyewitness account superseded anything she or Selen or Loris might say. None of them had been in the field in years. Dontra went out periodically, sometimes as far as the Neck or Shrug, but that was not far enough. She must call in the menders sent most recently along the route Streln had traveled. "Where?" she said sharply. "When? Give me details."

"I am not one of your obedient talebearers."

"Tell me, Streln. You've left this far too late."

"So you do take responsibility."

"If there is a problem we can mend it. No one riots over nothing. Perhaps trade routes have been blocked by some local calamity, perhaps food has run short. You've made a claim. Support it with details or admit the claim was a false one designed to test this sense of responsibility you keep harping on."

"We saw a man killed for his clothes in the Boot two moons ago. We were set upon by brigands in the Strong Leg. A miners' water squabble in the Druilors left their camp deserted but for the bodies. In the Girdle we heard of men and women killed in their own huts.

At the foot of the Oriels, more brigands, out for our horses. In the Heartlands they were rioting for food."

Selen pushed a sedgeweave leaf across the table. Dabrena had thought she was noting the incidents, but the scribing said, *Porfinn was in the Boot. No one has come from the other areas more recently than Streln.* They had not heard from Porfinn in at least two moons. They had been more irritated with her than concerned, but sometimes messages got lost or menders declined to send word until they had completed their tasks. Was that the first of many signs she should have recognized?

She shoved the leaf away. "If things were as bad as you claim, our folk would have sent birds." She glanced at Loris. He shook his head. "I'm sorry, Streln, but I cannot respond to your claims as the crisis you believe them to be. You saw localized conflicts. No doubt they were resolved after you passed. We will send extra folk in case problems persist and we may be of aid, and I do thank you for telling us," *though it took you long enough, you bloody bullock,* "but for the purposes of this discussion I'm afraid I must conclude that you are overreacting. The mainland is not Khine. Perhaps you misunderstood. If not, then we can only do what we have always done. Overcome the fundamental problem that has brought folk into conflict, and the conflict dissolves."

"It is too late for that," Streln said. "Order must be restored."

Dabrena ground her teeth. "Order restores itself as difficulties are overcome. You insult our mainland folk, Streln. They are controlled by decency and common sense."

"Some towns employ bladed guards," Verlein said.

"Which is their decision," Dabrena began, but Streln cut her off with "Who came from you, no doubt, and bear weapons they do not know how to wield."

"You're just itching for a fight, aren't you, Headman," Verlein replied. She broke the toothpick she'd been toying with and tossed the pieces on the table. "What is it you actually want, besides to see us all at odds?"

He gazed at her with a mildness that could not disguise contempt. "I supported your futile vigil, Shieldmaster."

"Deriding me all the way. My gratitude is boundless."

"No. But it will be. Just so long as your blades remain pointed seaward."

Verlein rose to her feet. The guards at the doorway tensed, stepped away from each other, shifted weapons more easily to hand.

The headman smiled for the first time. "Would you raise your blade against a Khinishman?"

"Would you raise yours against a blademaster?"

"You are no blademaster, though perhaps you were trained by one," Streln said. "The tradition is dilute in you, more dilute still in those who emulate you. If your shield were twice nine nonned *blademasters* strong, I would fear you indeed."

Verlein slid a hooked dagger from one of the many sheaths at her belt. Dabrena cursed herself for not disarming them all at the door, but the breath she drew to object caught in her throat. Lamplight swirled into the dagger's strange metal and was swallowed in quicksilver vortices. Verlein held point and pommel in her fingertips, tilting the dagger to augment the effect, and said, "Do you know what this is?"

"A magecrafted blade," Streln said. "A very old one. A very little one."

The corner of Verlein's mouth pulled up and back. "This is a cheit, one of a kenai's three weapons, each of which must be passed to a worthy student before death. I received it from a kenai, who received it from the kenai who trained her. A flesh-and-blood kenai, who found me worthy." She sheathed the hypnotic weapon abruptly and said, "You've relearned your heritage through dusty tomes. I look at you and want to sneeze."

"It was always in us," Streln replied, unperturbed. "It survived in the blood, in our way of life. I have heard of the kenai blademasters. They worked alone. You have tried to create a legion of kenaila, an unnatural thing. Your kenai master, if such she truly was and not merely the descendant of thieves, has rejected you. You have turned a rare art into something rough and crass. Your 'blademasters' are cottars wielding sharpened sticks."

The insults bit so deep that even Dabrena felt a twinge. She had been a cottar once, in a way still was. Verlein grinned, a feral baring of teeth that made the blood run cold. Her eyes shone. Her face was flushed. "Try me, Streln."

"Sit down, the both of you," Dabrena said.

"And if we won't?" There was nothing bellicose in Streln's question. He seemed genuinely curious—but with an intensity suggesting that her answer would matter very much to him. "What will you do then?"

Dabrena was through with his tests. "Lock you in here and let you lop each other's limbs off," she said, "and solve the irritation of yourselves. We've gotten—"

"That might ruin your tidy chamber," Streln persisted, taking a step closer to the table, to her. "Drench your tapestries in blood. Nick your pretty table."

Dabrena raised her eyes and met his steadily. She had not asked him here. He was an irritant, a self-styled killer who had no place in the lightless world she was trying to shepherd. Until he'd imposed his physical presence on her holding, it had had productive dealings with Khine. Yes, she had thought to delegate those at this table. Yes, that was a misjudgment. She would reevaluate. She would investigate his unsettling claims. But she did not have to endure his instigations. "If you have something straightforward to say, Streln, say it."

Pelkin, Evrael, and Verlein all started to speak, but Dabrena belayed them with a gesture.

"You may call me Headman." Pleasure curled in Streln's voice.

"I will not accommodate you," she said, and waited.

"You see no use in this world for blades. You think to reason with those who wield them. You think to bleed the shieldmaster's hard-won ranks, send trained fighters inland to reinforce ditches. Perhaps you think to make use of the ships I've commissioned, brokering our mastwood trade with an eye toward a patrol of your mainland coasts. Perhaps you would rather waste Khinish seafolk on what you believe is a fool's vigil. But imagine, for a moment, that that child in the corner is Eiden Myr. And suppose, just for argument's sake, that one of my men . . . Eldrisil . . . were to take that child and hold a blade to her . . ."

It happened before Dabrena could translate whatever subtle sign of genuine command he sent his guard. Kara was squealing, suspended by the back of her tunic at the length of a muscled arm, punching and kicking the air. The other muscled, banded arm held a blade curved like a scythe.

". . . and, with one nod from me, were to—"

Dabrena's chair was in her hands and driving toward the brown bulk of the Khinish guard. He was pinned between its legs, against a tapestry, turned two-thirds to her, one elbow bashed against the wall, the arm dropping loose. Kara was scrambling to her feet, *uninjured, the fall didn't hurt her*, and blood was pouring from the guard's neck. The chair's legs had ripped his tunic and probably the flesh underneath. Why was his neck . . .

Dabrena's wild focus did not take in that a knife had pierced his throat until she saw him grab for it. His eyes, a mirror of the shock in her own, slid away, seeking guidance from his leader, but the life went from them before he found it.

She shoved herself back. The chair's legs grated against stone through the tapestry before it fell and the wood jarred apart against the floor. Some visceral part of her wanted it to be the guard's bones. She reached for Kara without looking, pulled her tight against her side. A palsied trembling took hold of her body. She wrapped every nerve, every muscle tight.

"Waste of a good blade," said Verlein. "That stone will have ruined the point." The hand that had launched the knife was only now dropping back to her side. Her words were brusque, but she looked shaken. Not because she had just killed a man without a moment's reflection. Not because Evrael held a dagger against the cavity below her ribs. She was staring at Kara, the way you'd stare at a child just snatched from beneath a wagon's wheels, still seeing the averted disaster.

A nonned things could have caused that blade to go wild and hit Kara instead.

Dabrena wrenched her gaze around to Streln. "What lesson did you hope to teach by this display?" Kara's heart was pounding against her hip, her little hands fisted in the skirt of her white velvet tunic. Dabrena tightened her grip, not letting her look at the dead man.

"What lesson have you taken from it?" Streln said. His voice was silk. It did not belong to a man that stony.

What could she say to such a man? He wasn't foreign because he was Khinish. He was foreign because when you put blades in people's hands they became something that no human language would reach. "That you are the kind of man who would waste a life to make an irrelevant point," she said at last.

"The shieldmaster took the life," Streln said.

Verlein could have killed Kara as easily as the Khinishman.

Streln went on, "I have demonstrated that under threat you would use force to defend what you cherish and you would be unable to control the shieldmaster. Perhaps my man would not have harmed the child. Perhaps I would not have given the order. It would have been irrational, absurd, yes? But perhaps I would have. Verlein did not wait to find out. Neither did you."

"Your demonstration is lost on me. Get out."

"And if I refuse?"

She would have snatched the blade from Verlein's scabbard and plunged it into his heart, *if I didn't have the child if there were hands I trusted to put her in while I did it—if it wouldn't betray everything I stand for.*

You wear mender's white, but you are no mender.

You do understand his point, it's a valid point despite the madness of its making, you just don't want to hear it.

This wasn't even the issue under discussion.

He's trolling for something else.

But what? She couldn't think. Had he sacrificed a man and threatened her flesh and blood to *throw her off kilter*?

"If you refuse, I will call for your removal. Some of the armed folk in this chamber will press to effect it and some will resist. You will then find out which are which. Perhaps that serves your purposes. It does not interest me. Our work here has nothing to do with you. Go back to your island and stay there."

Streln pressed his fist to his heart, looking her straight in the eyes, before he turned to leave. The gesture chilled her. In the ancient codices, martial forces were pictured giving fealty to their leaders with such gestures. Among the Khinish in her lifetime it had ever been an open hand. Now it was a fist.

The lonely, cadenced tap of one pair of boots echoed down the passageway. Everyone turned toward the sound; even the runner being sick in the far corner lifted his head to watch the door. Weapons came up, guards adjusted the lines of their bodies.

"Am I late?" said a voice from beyond the doorway.

When the weapons lowered a fraction, their bearers assessing him as no threat, a short man in scholar's gray stepped into the chamber. He looked around, brows rising as he took note of those assembled; then something made him turn, and he saw the man slumped among overturned stools under a blood-smeared tapestry.

"Ah," he said, very softly. "Yes, it appears I am."

Evrael stared at the scholar with no comprehension and no interest. What he was seeing was an afterimage of Streln's movements as he set up his own man to die. Eldrisil was a good man, young and earnest if sometimes coarse, from a family of moderate stature. He might have risen, given time. A hard worker. A loyal son. His death was a loss to Khine.

Streln had thrown him away.

He would have to justify this in hall. Evrael saw no way for him to do it except to claim a preemptive, hotheaded overreaction from the shieldmaster. Did Streln hope to leverage conflict with the shield? Put the mainland at odds with him, defying any need for alliance, spitting on their ideal of cooperation? Evrael had watched him work Dabrena as he would work an opponent in a dirt wedge. He changed lines on her fluidly, now supporting Verlein, now mocking her, now praising the holding, now challenging it. Dabrena had put up her blade. It was the correct response. Let him tire himself rather than chase after his whimsical shifts. What Streln had done shocked him to the core. This was not the man he knew.

What a fool he was, not to have realized how deeply Streln had steeped in Lerissa's poisons.

The appearance of the scholar was so ill timed it was humorous. Verlein felt hilarity bubble up. She quashed it. A reaction to shock. Streln had ordered his man to threaten a child. It was unthinkable. She had not expected Dabrena to react so quickly, so fiercely. That was too bad; she would have spared the man's life. But it was done now. She had Dabrena's measure. She had Khine's, as well, though not its fleet's. And here came the Isle of Senana, in the form of a bald Weak Legger as thick and tough as a stump, pale-eyed and ash-skinned, bearing no weapon but a penknife and a sack of quills and scrolls. This was not the head scholar, who was a pale, redheaded Highlander. Nor was it the keeper of codices, who was a woman and black as night. Just some lackey.

And he had the misfortune to walk in on this.

"What should we do with him?" Selen said under her breath. Dabrena thought she meant the scholar. *Find the dullest task you can and set him to it*, she thought, *and let that be our response to Graefel's insult*. Then Selen prompted, "They won't come for him if we just stand here," and she was glad she'd kept her mouth shut.

She turned to Evrael. "Is there a ceremony you observe? We have a chamber where the bonefolk . . ."

"Take him to your chamber," Streln said over his shoulder. "The fleetmaster would cast him into the sea."

Dabrena did nothing until Evrael nodded; then she looked at Verlein, who moved toward the dead man. Eldrisil. Eldrisil tul Khine, Eldrisil who was of Khine. Their connectives cast the dead in the past.

To the scholar, she said, "You are late, you are not Graefel n'Traeyen, and you can tell him his mockery missed its mark by as much as you missed the meeting. Stay and work, or go back to Senana, it's up to you." She took Kara's shoulders firmly in her hands and crouched before her. "I must bear the dead to the bonefolk's chamber," she said. "I am partly responsible for the loss of his life. Will you follow me quietly?"

"No," Kara said. "I want to help carry."

Sweet spirits, absolutely not. I don't even want you to get a good look at him. "Are you sure?" *You'll bear the scar of this the rest of your life. Streln made good on his threat to harm you, though your body is whole. I should have kept you closer. I should have placated him. I should have silenced him. I should have killed him.* But Streln had gone, and his remaining man with him.

"I want to help carry him," Kara said again.

"We'll all do it," Pelkin said, "we were all party to this act," and they did, bearing him down passageways and stone steps, Verlein at the head to take the most weight, Pelkin and Evrael at the sides, Dabrena and her tiny daughter at the feet. Kara never faltered, and when they left him in the cold, dark chamber, she was the one who gave him into the spirits' keeping. She looked to Evrael for aid in getting his full name right, as if she understood something of how the adults around her were connected, when Dabrena thought she'd been daydreaming or counting her beads in the corner. At the last moment she bent down to whisper something into the dead man's ear. Taking her hand as they left that chamber, Dabrena asked what she had said, but Kara wouldn't tell her.

The child and her secrets.

"There was more for us to discuss," Pelkin said outside in the corridor, with a neutral glance toward the scholar, who despite Dabrena's dismissal had followed at a respectful distance, with the other runners, Verlein's seconds, Selen and Loris, and the handful of holding folk who had joined them as they passed. "Perhaps in one of those scriptoria or maphalls you wished to show us?"

The noon bells had not yet rung. Dabrena felt a brief vertigo, that so much had passed in the space of less than a morning. She still had not recovered from seeing her child held aloft by a man with a blade. *They don't know, they can't know what happened, what I did. . . .* She realized that both the old man and the fleetmaster were standing closer than propriety dictated, as if to buttress her with their respective strength and years. Verlein stood at the closed door to the bonefolk's chamber, saying something in a low voice; her woman, though watching the passageway, mouthed the same words silently. Selen and Loris awaited her, as Narilyn and Reiligh and Corle and the others would await all three of them at noon, to hear the report. It would be disheartening to give them news of only petty strife and pointless death. Perhaps something could be salvaged. She must not let Streln win.

As if reading her thoughts, Evrael stepped even closer, shielding his words from his sailors' ears, and said, "He's made you hate him, and he's made you fear him. Do not permit him to wield that power. Step down from your position if you must. Somewhere deep inside you will always fear, now, the moment when he comes for your child and you are too late to stop him. It will hinder you in what is to come."

"I have always feared the moment when someone comes for my child and I am unable to save her," Dabrena murmured. "What difference if it's your headman? I fear shadows and nightmares, I fear the heat, I fear the chill. Streln has gained no ground he didn't already own."

"Nonetheless," he said, and stepped away.

So did Pelkin. She felt diminished. He held a reserved strength and wisdom too easily overlooked until you felt its absence.

Dabrena faced Verlein, whose chanting or recitation at the bonefolk's door had come to an end. "You must leave this holding, Shieldmaster," she said. "You took a life here. Stay the night if you must, but be gone by morning bells."

Verlein nodded. "You may call on my blades should you need them again," she said. "For defense, not ditches. But you take my meaning."

If I need you to kill someone else I've already incapacitated, I will send word immediately, Dabrena thought. But "I do" was all she said, and she bowed to Verlein, who had been a harvestmaster once, as she had, and Verlein, though not of the holding, returned the bow before she went.

Evrael followed suit, with his seafolk and no further acknowledgment.

Dabrena turned to find Pelkin dismissing his aides to find rest or food. He wanted his word with her in private. "There is a maphall you might find interesting," she replied at last.

"Maps!" said the scholar. "I'd love to see some maps."

Dabrena had forgotten him. Moving toward them through the ill-lit passageway, he looked like some smoky, stunted reversal of a boneman. "I gave you your instructions."

"Don't punish me because you're peeved at Graefel."

"It was Graefel I invited, not an aide, and he declined."

"He was wrong."

"Yes, he was. Now go on with you."

"I'd get lost, like any vocate. Rather follow you."

Her flare of exasperation guttered into weary puzzlement. Did he think he was a vocate, wearing the dove gray the vocates had worn under the old Ennead? Was he some crackpot who'd wandered in here looking for a hierarchy gone the better part of a nineyear? "Graefel didn't send you," she guessed.

A bright, happy smile lit up his whole face, like a child's. "His exact words were 'Bleeding spirits, go then, if it means so much to you, but leave me in peace.' Does that qualify?"

Loris came forward bearing a short sedgeweave scroll that looked the worse for wear and was crimped in the center, borne by a bird. "This came in under Senana's seal," he said, reading as he walked. "It says that should Adaon n'Arai l'Ivrel become an irritant, pack him off without hesitation, but . . . uh . . ." He lifted his eyes from the message and blinked. ". . . under no circumstances send him back."

Dabrena rubbed her face. "Give him a meal, Loris, and find him some copying to do. We'll discuss assignments later."

Loris frowned. "I should accompany you and the—"

"Selen can record. We are fewer now, there's no need for two scribes, and I know you have work to do."

It came out like a dismissal. That wasn't how things worked here. But he knew she was tired. He handed the scroll and his own sedge-weave leaf to Selen—all right, that was a bit petulant, the equivalent of saying "Fine then, *you* compile the report"—and moved to follow the small crowd that was dispersing down the passageway. There were fewer dead these days—now and then someone succumbed to old age, or some field injury they could not heal, or what used to be called magesickness, poisoning from improper handling of certain pigments—but holding folk remembered when the dead lined the corridors, and stopped whatever they were doing to show respect.

Dabrena made a gesture of encouragement to the scholar with her chin. "You follow him," she said, and added a nod, as if he had failed to understand that he was free to go.

"I'll follow you," he affirmed cheerfully.

She couldn't be bothered. Taking Kara by the hand, she led Pelkin to the nearest maphall, the scholar at their heels. Kara kept turning to look at him, and twice Dabrena's grip saved her from a fall. Once she giggled, and Dabrena looked back to see the quick-smoothed innocence of someone who had just made a face.

"My name is Kara," she said over her shoulder as they entered the hall. "Kara n'Dabrena l'Tolivar."

Dabrena herself nearly tripped. Kara resolutely refused to speak to strangers. It was one reason Dabrena was loath to take her home to the Fingers. All her relatives would be strangers.

Inside, the low hubbub of banter fell silent and the scene went as still as a picture in an illuminated codex. Someone froze with a chalk sketch in her outstretched hand; someone searching through a large volume let it fall open with a thump, ignoring whatever spread it revealed.

Carry a dead man through the corridors, and people moved to follow, somber but long past shock. Lead the Ennead's head reckoner into a hall of onetime warders, and the world ground to a halt.

"Good morning," Pelkin said, and bowed to them. The noon bells rang, as if the holding itself were bent on correcting him.

The hall emptied, although there was good light at noontime and they generally worked through till supper.

"What did you say to the dead man when you gave him to the spirits?" the scholar asked Kara.

Frowning, distracted, Dabrena said to Pelkin, "They were warders, take no notice of them. Here, let me show you . . ."

"His name was Eldrisil," Kara said to the scholar as Dabrena led her to the table by the far wall, under the high window, where sunlight never fell directly to bleach the enormous, sectioned representation of Eiden's body assembled there, leaf by leaf.

"You were a warder, too," Pelkin said, "and I abandoned you as surely as I did them." He smiled at the impressive cartographical assemblage, and for a moment Dabrena saw another face under his face, a familiar one from long ago, and felt a pang she didn't understand. It reminded her of a light so bright it would have bleached these leaves of ink as no sunshine could.

"Did you wish Eldrisil a smooth journey to the spirits?" the scholar said, and Dabrena turned, sensing a shift in his voice. He was on one knee in front of Kara, and Kara leaned forward, her free hand cupped over her mouth, to whisper an answer in his ear.

Leave my daughter alone! was making its way from Dabrena's mind to her mouth as the scholar said, "Ah. That's a fine journey wish, young Kara," and stood up to examine the map. What Dabrena found herself saying was "How did you get her to do that?"

"Why don't you ask Kara?" he said, looking sidelong at Dabrena, then back at the map.

The child's stubborn face gave a clear answer. Then she pressed between them so she could see the map, too.

"She has to have *some* secrets from you," the scholar said, peering closely at the long, smooth rivers veining the Low Arm.

"That's the River Koe," Kara said, pointing with a care not to touch the sedgeweave. "Up here it splits off into the River Loge, which runs down into Maur Aulein."

He has no idea what he's saying. Dabrena watched her daughter happily gloss the unlabeled map for this man she had met scant moments before. He might have just explained to Dabrena something she had agonized over for moons. Kara had to have *some* secrets . . . if she couldn't have secret chambers to play in, quiet places for private time alone or with special friends, she would make secret chambers in her mind, and Dabrena could never go there.

What have you done to our baby, Dabrena?

Shut up! Shut up! I have to keep going!

"As you can see," she said to Pelkin, "we've chalked in the bits we're still working on, as we transfer them from the smaller sectional maps you see in progress, or bound into codices, around the hall. This is the third revision. It's taken us five years to get this far. It'll take another five, I think, before the details are accurate enough to be useful, and we're still developing methods to work out the distances and elevations. The seekers among us have been a great help in that."

"It's progressing well," Pelkin said. "I'm impressed, though I expected no less. There were some very ancient maps in the codices sent to Senana. Did you . . . ?"

"They copied them for us," Dabrena confirmed. "Twice, in fact, which helped us differentiate copying errors from the original mapmakers' errors. They'd only mapped the coastline and indicated the mountain ranges and anchorages. Whoever they were, it seems they had no intent of landing and coming inland."

"It was a wasteland then. Attempts at reclamation had failed so often they'd given up. It would have been merely a stopping point for mariners. Perhaps an aid—or a hazard—to navigation."

"I wish we knew more," she said, in a near-whisper, not really meaning to say the words aloud.

"We're working on it," the scholar said, and winked. "Do you have any more detailed maps of the Southlands?"

Thank the spirits—a way to get rid of you for long enough to breathe. She pointed him to the correct volumes. Kara followed him, still reeling off place names. Dabrena reached to pull her back, but Selen touched her arm lightly, then interposed herself between the child and the new-come scholar. It was just enough to ease Dabrena back on her heels. But her leg jiggled nervously. She saw Pelkin notice it.

"You are never comfortable unless you are touching her."

She shrugged, an eye on Kara. "I've gotten better about it, over the years."

He did not comment. Instead he said, "You'd like the runners' help. Tell me how."

"Information," she replied immediately. "Weather patterns, terrain, a corrective eye on maps such as these. A report on any trends you've noticed in illness, p—"

"You wish us to be reckoners again."

Kara was reaching around Selen to help the scholar find the right page in a battered codex. *I can't allow this.* "Did you ever stop?"

"We reckon other things now," Pelkin said softly. "And the patterns you seek to track are warders' work—menders' work. Your work. Not ours."

You were trying to allocate his runners, too. She scrubbed a hand through her hair as if to root the voice out like a louse. "All right," she said. "What did you have in mind?"

He smiled. "You invited us here."

"For the wrong reasons, I fear." She felt very weary. *I've got to part them*, she thought, hearing Kara giggle at something the scholar said. He was patient with her even though he was clearly intent on whatever he'd found in the codex. *I don't know him from a stick in the road, but even if I did, she can't get attached.* Anger flared briefly, jealousy, then ebbed back into weariness. *She has Reiligh, she has Loris and Corle, she doesn't need this stunted shadow of a boneman.* Reiligh had tried to take Kara off her hands for the day. If she had let him, Streln would have had to make his hideous point some other way. *But she doesn't really have them at all. She has no one but me. Because I won't let her.*

"Perhaps," Pelkin said. "And in truth I would not have come, had I not something to tell you myself, without intermediaries."

This was important, whatever it was. She had to face Pelkin with her full attention. "Kara," she said, "come away now, come to me." She held out her hand. She tried not to see Kara's face shut down, her shoulders fall, her dragging, obedient steps. She just concentrated on the hand slipping into hers. Her chest lightened. Now she could think. "Go ahead."

Pelkin did not look at the scholar or Selen as he said, "To tell you, Dabrena. Only you."

With a wide-eyed shrug at Selen, Dabrena asked her to remove the scholar to the scriptorium across the corridor.

"The child should go as well," Pelkin said.

"She won't understand."

"Oh, I doubt that very much."

Kara looked up hopefully, thinking to be sent after the scholar. With a harsh sigh, Dabrena said, "There's sedgeweave in the corner, Kara, and ink and quills prepared. Why don't you draw one of your maps? Come show us when it's finished."

Kara, delighted, immediately ran off to comply. She was rarely permitted sedgeweave, and she had a passion for drawing invented maps, some desire to elaborate on her perception of the real ones. Eiden Myr was as imaginary to her as any realm in her mind.

Dabrena gave Pelkin her attention.

He said, "You have a betrayer in your holding."

Dabrena's throat closed on a breath, so that she made a strange inadvertent sound—like a snore interrupted when a sleeper was jostled.

"Senana must beware as well. Messages have gone between here and Khine, between Khine and Senana. I do not know what they said. But there is a pattern."

"Do you know the source?"

"Only on Khine. And I only suspect it. I have no proof."

"Your suspect, then."

"Lerissa Illuminator."

The Ennead mage name spun her mind through possibilities that veered and branched until she could no longer follow. She put a finger on the edge of the map table to balance herself. "The Nine died. They combined in the hein-na-fhin, and it killed them."

"Only the leading triad. The others killed each other, as best I can piece it together from what was seen before the bonefolk came. Poison, for the most part, but the throat of one was cut, and the hearts of two elders may have failed. The youngest was removed to Khine, where she was imprisoned. But she has not been idle in her captivity. I believe she maneuvers to regain the power she considers herself entitled to as a daughter of the Ennead."

"How?"

"I don't know. But she is aided in her efforts. All the Nine had dedicated servants. Whatever she promised or threatened, hers are loyal to her still, and roam at large to work her bidding. There is no doubt that some remained here. There is little doubt that at least one went to the scholars."

"You've deduced this from the paths of messages you haven't read?"

"I've constructed this from rumors and facts that combine into unavoidable probability."

Verlein had called the runners spies. Dabrena had thought the accusation born of resentment. Now it seemed there was truth in it.

"You are not inclined to believe the spy warning you of spies, eh?" Pelkin's gray eyes gleamed.

"Perhaps no one is better suited," Dabrena said. "But who . . ."

"It could be any of your folk, from a steward whose name you never knew to one of your closest colleagues. And there could be more than one."

Her mind ran through the names before she could stop it. Not Dontra. Not Ronim. Not Corle. Spirits . . . not Selen. Yet it could be any of them, any of the six folk here who'd earned the ring with her. Only Reiligh came from outside. Did that mean it was him? Or did that make him the only one she could trust?

"Why should I believe you?"

"You shouldn't. You should trust nothing. But if you begin to wonder, to question, to watch, then I will have done what I came here for."

"You had no interest in our meeting."

He shrugged, though it was obvious now; he'd only used it as an excuse to make contact without being seen to initiate it. "It could never have come to good."

"Has it done harm?"

"Oh, it showed us much. But I must return to my folk, to work on this among other things, in the knowledge that any of them could be compromised as well. Streln's behavior . . . No. It's too soon to say."

"And if it's me?" Dabrena said.

He smiled. "It could have been, once. You would have done anything those nine demanded of you, to save your child."

Dabrena paled. "But no longer?"

"I don't believe so. I know more about you than you may think possible. You've met your worst darkness and made amends as you could. It's worth the risk, at any rate. Someone had to know, and who else would I tell? One of your scribes? Evonder is gone. Brondarion is gone. The head warders were gone a young man's lifetime ago. This is not the holding I knew."

"It's not the world we knew."

"No. It will never be that again."

Evrael strode down a corridor that in his childhood had led to bakeries. They had quartered Verlein on an old stewards' level. She was slow in answering his knock but admitted him at last. He moved from the oily lamplight of the passage into the smoky flicker of a single candle's flame.

"Six years ago," he said without preamble, "we stood at the threshold to a chamber full of the past, you and I. I told you of the shield. I told you it was broken and the light destroyed in its breaking. You conceived the idea of a human shield to replace it."

Verlein stretched out on her bed. "Tell me something interesting, Evrael."

He could tell her that he had encouraged her idea of a shield in order to give her homegrown soldiers something to do besides ravage his family home. It would interest her to know that he had considered occupying the Holding with his Khinish seafolk until he was certain that Verlein would make no attempt to control Eiden Myr by force. He had diverted her horde just as Dabrena n'Arilda had diverted a Great Storm: by splitting it into parts that would go around Eiden

Myr rather than down the center of it. But there was no more need to tell her this now than there had been then.

"You asked for my fleet to be a shield at sea beyond your shore-bound shield," he went on. "I denied it to you as I would have denied it to Dabrena had Streln not circumvented her request. Now I will pledge those patrols to you, if in return you pledge your folk to fight the Khinish. They will invade the mainland shortly after Streln's return." Unless Pelkin could dissuade them. Through an aide Pelkin had conveyed a desire to sail with Evrael to Khine, to address the hall. Evrael would take him. But it would do no good. Two Northers trying to tell the Khinish their business. In the end they would follow Streln. "Streln retains enough private ships to ferry ground forces to the Boot, though if I can subvert them he'll have to build a bridge, which will delay him. Either way, they will have no fleet." *Unless you or one of your folk divulges this arrangement too soon, and he gains time to leverage my command from me in hall. A risk I must live with.* "Streln will send forces upland by ground, securing the inland trade routes as he goes. You can hem them in, if you adapt your coastal positions quickly and I transport reinforcements by ship. You can surround them, and stop them, with my fleet at your back, with my ships defending your shores."

"I can stop your unfaithful lover, you mean. Whoever that woman is he's in bed with now, that's what's really got your goat. I don't think I feel like sending my folk in to avenge your wounded heart."

"The woman he's in bed with now," Evrael said quietly, "is Lerissa n'Lessa l'Rigael, the last surviving member of the Nine."

Evrael had seen Verlein prepared to cast a torch on generations of codified learning because to her it epitomized the hierarchy headed by those nine. He had calculated precisely the reaction an Ennead name would engender. Across her face flashed surprise, outrage, and . . . something else, an emotion he couldn't identify.

"They have sunset bells here, don't they?" she said. "They have bells for every bloody movement of the bloody sun, you'd think they'd just go out and live under it like normal folk. Leave me until sunset bells. I'll give you my answer then."

It would be yes. He saw it in the duck of her chin, the hand on her blade. She merely needed time to justify it to herself, or summon her seconds and make a show of consulting them, though there was no question who was first in the hierarchy she had built.

He left her, as requested; and in the corridor he braced his hands on cold black stone and leaned into the wall, barely restraining the impulse to smash his head against it.

Whispering in his lover's ear, Lerissa had accused him of betrayal.

It had been unwarranted. Now he had made it true.

I am not punishing him for choosing her, he told himself, listening for any hint of defensiveness or deceit. *I no longer know him. He is poisoned past recognition. He sows conflict. He holds children to the blade. The man I knew is gone.*

He bit down on a wailing grief, straightened himself, and moved along the lamplit passageway to join his seafolk. They commanded their own ships in his fleet, and had agreed to accompany him in case a hall had to be convened. He had consulted them, and they had reached consensus. It remained, now, only to inform them of the shieldmaster's expected answer, and wait with them until the bells of sunset freed them to return to the sea.

A hooded figure stepped from an obscure corner of Verlein's chamber and moved with care toward a stool by the low sprucewood table.

"You must kill Lerissa n'Rigael. If she is the reason the Khinish have woken, it is she you contend with, and she you must eliminate. Put Streln back where he belongs, in Evrael's peaceful, well-meaning hands."

"In the hands of a long-lost scion of this holding," Verlein said. "You would love that, wouldn't you." She paced the confines of the chamber. She poured wine she did not bother to sample. It took that long for the figure to reach the stool, to brace an arm on the table and lower itself toward the seat. Stiff knees and elbow gave out, and the last half-foot of the descent came in a barely controlled rush. Dark robes billowed briefly and then settled. The hood fell back to reveal long gray hair braided in the intricate style of the Boot, and a woman's face, deeply grooved, that might have been carved from the blackstone around them.

In a way it had been. Lerissa n'Rigael was not the sole surviving member of the Nine.

"How can there be Ennead partisanship when there is no longer an Ennead?" the woman said, plumping her robes with strong-boned hands swathed in wasted flesh. "I had no love for Evrael when he was his parents' bright hope, and he fled in cowardice from forces I sought to channel. But it is a new world now. We work with what is."

"In the hope of restoring what was," Verlein said. She lifted the winecup, changed her mind, set it back down. "I don't know how far I trust your historical motives, Worilke."

"We have never trusted each other," Worilke n'Karad said. "Yet here we are." She took the cup of wine and drank it off. "Twice nine nonned years ago, Galandra na Caille le Serith established Eiden Myr as a haven for persecuted mages, warding it from the outer realms in a display of power unparalleled thereafter. Her warding was never meant to be broken. It was meant to have a lifespan, like any living thing. That span was cut short, and all was changed. I saw that, as I saw her vision with the clarity of a mage casting passage for the dying. What it showed me went far deeper than ephemeral allegiances formed in my mortal lifetime. You fear the realignment of old powers in the transformation of former reckoners, warders, Ennead. Pelkin and Evrael spoke of old times and raised your guard dog's hackles. Well, fear nothing of the sort from me. What I have told you remains true: I seek now only to realize Galandra's plans despite their violent disruption. Lerissa can only exacerbate that disruption, and thwart the natural capacity of Eiden's body to heal itself. She is an artificial creature with the outdated ambitions of an artificial world. Though Morlyrien seduced his soul, Evrael's heart is wholly Eiden's."

Verlein scowled with the effort of separating the teller's rhetoric and the mystic's blather from the political observations she had come to rely on. Her fighter's heart longed to be directed by a wise intelligence, but her harvestmaster's will took umbrage at being told what to do. She feared manipulation by one more clever and erudite than herself even as she yearned to give herself over to it. With Worilke, she faced a continual struggle between wariness and need.

"Cold-blooded killing is not my bailiwick," said Verlein. "That's your brand of scheming. I'm a harvestmaster, a fighter. I'll fight to put Eiden Myr back to rights. I'll fight through the Khinish until I reach this Lerissa of yours, but I'll have killed the lot of them by then."

"You could avoid fighting them at all if you eliminate her before they've moved up the Strong Leg."

"I don't want to avoid fighting them!"

"No, of course you don't. You have been looking for a fight these six years long, and never found it, and now Evrael has handed you a battle and you will gleefully engage, destroying the Strong Leg to no good purpose."

"You sound like the Lightbreaker," Verlein said with scorn.

Worilke's laugh racked her spent frame. "Torrin was a good boy," she said. "I underestimated him. I should have listened to him. You keep me for my counsel, Verlein, much as Streln must keep Lerissa. Don't let Ennead ghosts manipulate the two of you into a battle that will leave only Lerissa standing. Ally with Evrael, support his cause, it is a just one. But send someone for Lerissa. Try, at least. Try to avoid the bloodshed if you can. We have harmed the world too much already. This was not what Galandra wanted."

"You and bloody blighted Galandra."

Yet it was worth a try.

"Assassins were a thing of the old world, the outer realms," Worilke mused. It was the scholar in her surfacing. Her obsession with Galandra long preceded their moment of communion in the magewar. She'd been compiling a life story of the woman when the magewar interrupted her. She'd steeped as deeply in the ancient codices as anyone on Senana—probably deeper. "We have nothing like those now, nor time to train one."

Verlein touched the small dagger at her belt, remembering hot blue eyes in a pugnacious face, long afternoons in long grass, dizzying whirlwind attacks, a fierce spirit that never relented.

"Yes we do," she said. "Oh, yes we do."

Dabrena stared at the ninefoot-by-sixfoot image of Eiden as if waking from a long sleep to find it spread before her in all its wide, wild danger.

This holding had become her world. Despite all the maps, despite reports that linked her to every corner and byway of Eiden Myr, despite the picture in her mind of Eiden's body from Curl to Crown and Boot to Head, she had ceased to exist in the world. The mountain was her world.

"What does Lerissa want?" she asked Pelkin.

"Control," he answered simply. "And by wanting it, she will make others want it, by her leave or in her stead, and we will have only battles where once we had unquestioning, untroubled peace." He touched the edge of the map. "This new world is young yet. It can still be shaped. It can still be saved, or torn asunder."

"Don't put that on my shoulders, Reckoner."

"You became head warder, my dear. It has rested on your shoulders since that day. On mine as well, spirits help us." He sighed, then said, "My folk have found a site by Maur Gowra. We have been adapting it to serve as a kind of holding in its own right. A place to preserve the arts of magecraft against the light's return, whether it ever comes or not."

"We preserve those arts. Graefel preserves those arts. And the light is gone, Pelkin. Surely you feel it. That dead place inside."

"I feel it—or feel nothing, as the case may be. I, too, believe it gone forever. But even then . . . You use magecraft's tools for mundane, practical purposes. Graefel uses them to further theoretical pursuits. My folk have vowed to keep the art of their use alive, *as magecraft*, lest twice nine nonned years of craft be lost. Even should the light to actuate it never burn again."

"A noble pursuit," Dabrena said, though she considered it as vain as Verlein's shield.

"Only a bit of the old world, saved for the new, should it need it. We cannot see the future. We prepare as we can."

"I don't know the world, old or new." Her voice had fallen lower than the near-whispers they had spoken in.

"That was a failing of the last Ennead's as well. They believed they had risen above the world they were meant to shepherd."

"And you let them!"

He smiled. It was the old argument, the old enmity. Helpless to prevent the corruption at their head, the proxies fragmented into distrust and mutual blame rather than joining forces to contain it. "Yes," he said. "I let them. I worked against them as I could. I aided insurrection as I could. Evonder n'Daivor worked from within, Torrin n'Maeryn from without, and I aided them both as I continued to run my reckoners rather than openly defy the Ennead and be destroyed by them. They destroyed Alliol's triad, after which the warders had no head, until you. We won, in the end, though it cost us. But yes. I let them."

"You were with the Lightbreaker?"

He laughed. "I was. And that response is precisely why the fact is not more widely known."

"Then you were with . . ."

Kara came running over with a half-drawn map. It was a lovely construct, and Dabrena told her so, though her mind was not on it, and though it bore an odd resemblance to a section of the Strong Leg.

Pelkin praised it as well, and then replied to Dabrena's hanging question. "Yes. I was with the Lightbreaker's illuminator in the magewar. I was her grandfather."

"I was a vocate with her."

Pelkin nodded. "She spoke of you. Now you know part of how I know what I know about you. Pity. I work so hard to be mysterious."

Dabrena closed her eyes tight, and only realized she had also closed her fists when Kara made a pained sound and tried to extricate her sedgeweave, which was crumpling.

"I'm sorry, sweet," she said, releasing the leaf, but she turned her head away to hide the sting in her eyes.

"Did she know my father?" Kara asked in a small voice.

"You were right," Dabrena said to Pelkin, "she understands more than I credit her with, clever girl." But to Kara she replied, wryly,

"She knew your father rather better than I can explain until you're older." Then she saw how Kara had pulled into herself—as if expecting an outburst. *Is that why she never asks about him?*

It was too much to take in, but she could not escape. She could never escape the consequences of Tolivar's death, not while she remained a part of the black rock that had killed him. Pelkin said, "Do you know what became of him?"—as if he knew, somehow, and would tell her if she shook her head. But of course . . . Karanthe n'Farine, who had been a vocate with them, and who had heard the account of Tolivar's end from its only witness, was one of Pelkin's now. She would have told him, if his granddaughter hadn't. At least he'd heard it in person. Karanthe's message of condolence, scribed in a childish hand as soon as she learned how, had been brief and assumed that Dabrena knew, and had arrived while Dabrena still had hope that Tolivar lived. *How would I have known? The bonefolk took him!* Dabrena had messaged back, beside herself. *How would I have known, in this black rock of secrets?* Karanthe's reply had been long in coming. The reckoners had not yet fully turned to messengers in those early days. *I am sorry, I am sorry, I am so sorry*, it had said, and gone on to claim that his end was quick. It was a palpable lie, in a shaking hand. And Karanthe had never come. Dabrena would not forgive that.

"He died," she said.

She could not admit the rest in front of Kara. She could not say, *The Ennead killed him*. She could not say, *I betrayed him to them*.

"He was a sailor," Kara said. "From the Knee."

Pelkin said, "Then you must think of him whenever you hear the sea, and know that his spirit carries his love for you on the winds that touch your face."

It was a kind and lovely thing to say, and a fitting cap on a conversation Dabrena could no longer bear. But Kara said, "Oh, no. He's not on the winds or in the sea."

"He's not?" Pelkin shifted, no doubt concerned that he'd overstepped himself and contradicted whatever gentling tale her mother had told her.

Kara shook her head, very serious. With a wary glance at Dabrena, she tugged on Pelkin's sleeve with her free hand. He obliged her by bending down, his eyes on Dabrena. Kara whispered in his ear as she had in the scholar's. She was a good whisperer; Dabrena couldn't hear a word. But Pelkin's wince was too much.

"What is it?" she snapped. "Tell me."

"I . . ." he began, but Kara's vigorous shake of the head gave him pause. "I'm afraid it appears to be a secret."

"This is madness, Pelkin, tell me. She cries every morning. She has bad dreams. Well, so do we all, but she's a *child*, she's my child and I can't help her if she won't *tell me what's wrong*."

"I don't think this is what's wrong," Pelkin said with care.

"Don't tell," Kara warned. "It's a secret! Don't tell!"

Dabrena's anger went cold and hard. "These games have gone too far. For spirits' sake, she's concocted an imaginary . . ."

She fell silent.

No. That can't be it.

Pelkin said to Kara, "She's figuring it out herself."

"Don't . . ." Kara's warning was a plea now, not for Pelkin to keep the secret but for Dabrena not to guess it.

"She already knows, pet," Pelkin said. "And a word to the wise, for the next time: You have to make the person promise not to tell before you give the secret, eh?"

To a child, it made inescapable sense. Pelkin waited for Kara's nod before he turned to Dabrena.

"She said she sees him in your chamber. She says he's a haunt. She says he tells her things. Important things."

Dabrena's knees went weak. Well, they had always done that around Tolivar, hadn't they. But she had thought . . . she had been so sure that the voice in her head . . .

A childish fantasy, she tried to say, and couldn't. *It's rubbish, the worst kind of sentimental rubbish. I won't have it*. But if a haunt was all the father Kara had, how could she deny it?

"I have much to think on, Pelkin." She tried to ignore the relief on Kara's face when it appeared her mother would not burst a seam.

"Did you think before you diverted the last Great Storm?"

"Is a Great Storm coming?"

"Perhaps. A human one. What are storms formed of? The clash of great bodies of air, differing in temperature, pressure?"

"One of our seekers would happily regale you with theories."

"It is the same with people as with winds and currents. Listen to me, Dabrena. I do not know what Streln truly saw on his way here. I do not trust his account. Perhaps he saw what he wanted to see in order to justify what he wants to do. Perhaps he saw events that were contrived for his view. But his folk are a wind rising. And one more thing I can tell you, though I hope it remains our problem alone: Someone is killing runners. Whether it's onetime reckoners they target I do not know. But they are killing those of us in black."

"Eiden's bloody . . . Why did you say nothing in the meeting?"

"And support Streln's argument? He was a nocked arrow, he needed no more tension on his bow. That's not your concern. We'll warn your folk in white where we see them in our travels. You must look to your own walls and passageways now."

"Yet with an eye on the wide world."

"With a hand in it. Or more."

They heard an opening door and then footsteps in the corridor, and with a cry Kara snatched her sedgeweave to show Adaon. Dabrena and Pelkin followed; as Dabrena asked Selen to tell the mapmakers they could return to their work, Pelkin regarded Adaon with one of his evaluating smiles. "The head scholar's message implies that you've been a bit of trouble."

"My notoriety dogs me. You pledged in the scholar's village, Pelkin—was Graefel n'Traeyen as insufferable when he was a boy?"

"And as bright," Pelkin said.

Adaon gave a thoughtful nod, as if this oblique reply had enlightened him. Then he clasped his hands behind his back and made a graceful pivot that left his body at a formal incline toward Dabrena. "I will give you no trouble, mender."

"And will you be staying on?" Pelkin said casually.

"Not if the general meeting has dispersed," Adaon said, stepping into the maphall to return the codices he'd perused. "In fact, I'll be on my way in either event, with my thanks for your brief hospitality."

"Oh, stay, Adaon!" Kara cried. "Here, look what I made."

He looked long at the map she showed him. "Perhaps I'll see you in this place, one day."

With a wink to Kara and a bow to Pelkin and Dabrena, he was gone, and Pelkin said his farewells then, too, his business concluded. Dabrena was left standing in the corridor with Kara's map in one hand and Kara's hand in the other.

Though she was accustomed to conferring with dozens of people during the course of a day, advising, assigning, providing encouragement and ideas, it felt as though she'd conferred enough for a nineday in the course of this one morning and noon. Still she looked down at her daughter and said, "We have to talk."

At first, in the quiet of their chamber, it was she who did the talking, while Kara ate the midday meal she'd fetched for her on the way. She apologized. She explained. All in vain; Kara was unmoved, ground into stone by a trying day and half a lifetime of resentment. It could not be undone in an afternoon. But at last Dabrena said, "What things does your father tell you?" And Kara, the floodgates opened by even a pretense at belief, told her.

"He says you have to come. He says there's treasure. He's tried to tell you, but you won't listen. You turn a deaf ear. You don't want him to forgive you. What did you do that he has to forgive you for?"

Dabrena felt struck to the heart.

The child could not be that perceptive.

It could not be the shade of her old lover speaking through their daughter. Yet it could only be Tolivar.

"Where?" she said, not sure if she was more yearning or more terrified, rejecting both. "Where am I to go?"

"Here," Kara said, and smoothed out the crinkled sedgeweave map. "Where he was from."

"And did he say I should take you along?" She tried to be gentle, but bitterness roughened her voice. Selen claimed the child didn't want to go adventuring. If this was an elaborate bid for a journey . . .

Kara frowned. "I don't know. I could ask him. But I don't think he'll come tonight. He might not come anymore ever. He used to be with me all the time. But now . . ."

"Now not so much?" Dabrena prompted. "Now that you're older?"

"No," Kara said cautiously, then chanced a look up. "Because *he* is. Can I finish the map now? It was only partly done but I wanted to show it."

Dabrena mixed ink for her and trimmed a quill, and experienced a queer dislocation as she set up the inkpot for the child, handed her the pen, heard the point begin to score the lay of the sedge. As if she had played binder. As if she had forgone her own part, the scribing part, and given a casting into an illuminator's hands.

She shook it off. Tolivar was dead, the light was dead; Kara would never triad her wordsmith mother and bindsman father, never cast with them, never shine bright. Her child, her strange, ineffable child, had not cried for the first three moons of her life; and then the light went, and thereafter it seemed as though she'd never stopped crying. Dabrena had thought at first that breaking the Storm was what unmaged her and stressed her calm baby to tears. But it was the breaking of the light. They had been cored. Even the baby had felt it. There *had* been a light in there. She had done grieving it, and her own. She should be done grieving Tolivar, as well, and yet she felt she never would be.

There were betrayers in her holding. Folk plotting with the Ennead's ghost to gain control of Eiden Myr. She could wait, and watch; but she went back over the past days and ninedays and moons in her mind, and found nothing amiss. She trusted her folk with her life. She trusted her folk with Eiden Myr's life. If there was wrongdoing, it would not be seen by her.

"*You've missed everything. You've missed the world,*" Streln had said.

"*Resign your position, if you must,*" Evrael had said.

"*I'll come to you, Dabrena,*" Tolivar had said, his last words to her. "*I won't die inside a rock.*"

But then he had. And now he wanted her to come to him.

If she stayed here, everything would stay the same.

If she left, it would leave a hole. Someone would try to fill it. Mistakes would be made. Truths would come out.

But someone would have to watch.

Who could she trust to watch in her stead?

She didn't know the world anymore. She couldn't subject her daughter to risks she hadn't evaluated herself.

She couldn't put her daughter in strangers' hands.

She couldn't tear her away from everything she knew and the people who, for good or ill, had become her family.

If Tolivar had something to show her, she had to find out what it was. Even if it was madness to go.

To see the world she no longer knew, to learn how to mend it. To see what Tolivar wanted her to see. To save her daughter from her own smothering love. To create a hole, to flush a betrayer.

When Kara handed her the sedgeweave leaf—a remarkable representation of the Knee's highlands sloping down to the lowlands by Maur Lengra—Dabrena said, "If you were in terrible trouble, if you were afraid for your life, who would you call for?"

Wary of tricks, Kara said, "You."

"Besides me."

"Is there a blade? Is there a big man?"

Dabrena cursed herself for a fool—and then it sank in how Kara had brightened, and the relish she took in saying, "Will he cut me in two if I don't escape? Will he lop my head off?"

"Kara!"

Immediately the grisly pleasure was quenched. Kara ducked her head and began picking at her shoe.

Sweet spirits . . . once the scare wore off, she thought it was . . .

"All right," she said. "If you like. Or maybe you're clinging by your fingernails to something very high, and you need someone to catch you when you fall."

"A hole?" Kara said. "A deep hole? So deep you'd fall forever? There's a hole like that, it talks to you, I always wanted to—" She cut herself off with a groan and flopped back on her pallet.

Waiting for me to cry "Who told you that? Who told you of that place?" and march off to scold them raw.

She had been horrible to this child.

"Yes," she said. "The deepest hole in the world. And only one person will be in time to snatch you back from it. It would be me, of course, but suppose you could choose someone else to save you. Who would it be, Kara?"

"Reiligh," Kara said, bored and offhand, no longer interested in the game now that she was being saved.

"Reiligh," Dabrena murmured. "Yes. I think I will trust that wisdom over all the dead-end reasoning I could produce."

They visited Reiligh in his garden galleries, and Dabrena sat talking long with him while Kara played in mushroom heather.

Then she and her tired daughter ate a quiet supper, undisturbed by any of her folk, and returned to their chamber together. Kara fell asleep instantly. Dabrena lit a fresh candle and sat up the night watching it melt. She stroked her daughter's hair and remembered when baby Kara had turned toward her in her sleep rather than away, had sought warmth and comfort rather than the privacy of dreams. She watched and waited for the haunt, searching the jumping shadows for some suggestion of his wiry form, his soft brown eyes, his sailor's hands.

Tears streaming down her face, she said, "Tell me if I'm doing right, Tolivar."

You do what you must, came the answer from her mind. *As you always have.*

The shadows said nothing, and if the stone screamed, it was only in her heart.

She left the mountain at dawn, shocked by the vast inverted bowl of sky, drinking deep of that shock lest she see again the vision of her daughter's awed face when she told her that she'd be going into the field and Reiligh would have the care of her till she'd returned.

It was already too hot to hug herself close, to drive away the flesh's memory of Kara's little-girl body, stiff in her farewell embrace, straining to be released.

Gir Doegre

From the crest of a mint-scented rise Louarn had climbed for just this view, the town looked typical of the region. Strong Leg towns were wedged—into the fork of a road, the tines of a river, two rivers coming to confluence, a depression among hills. This one sloped up the surrounding hills rather more than smaller villages did, but otherwise was remarkable only for its three angled crossroads and for the misty pall that hung over it.

The wind was out of the Sea of Charms, not strong but constant. It seemed to blow crosswise to the movement of the clouds. Though it set brown leaves skittering across the hilltops, it touched the town only lightly. There was a chill within the sweltering heat, a kiln dryness beneath the humidity. Damp air and dry seemed unable to blend. Mists shifted, settled, shifted, as if finding no seat to their liking.

A town like this would never lie easy. It drew him. It challenged him to learn its byways, make its unfamiliar streets his own, to solve the puzzle of itself. He would stay here no longer than it took to earn or beg a meal and some transportation faster than his own legs. But he felt, if things were different, that he might have bided awhile here, given Gir Doegre time to reveal itself to him. It would be wanting to show him things. He would have liked to stay long enough to see them.

As he moved downhill, sidling from tussock to tussock past uninterested sheep, he could see crowds flowing up and down the long streets that defined the town's wedge shape. More than their share of waysiders, a man near Dindry Leng had said. What attracted them? Maur Lengra had flooded its banks, not once but three times in recent years, driving maurside dwellers inland. But in the Weak Leg they had flowed down to the seaside and out into the Haunch and deep into the Toes. They found cracks and fissures to sink into, villages that had need of their skills and space for them to settle in. Were there no cracks or fissures in these hills?

He regained the road and walked the rest of the way into town, passing fallow cottars' crofts at the point where his road crossed one that angled upland, then coming to a choice between three market streets. Down the center, a redolence of cooking—herbs and roast vegetables, fried plantains and simmering leeks, rich oils and spiced sauces, all mixed unpleasantly with the reek of whatever the cooks burned for fuel. To the left and right, a cacophony of metalworking and hawkers' cries. The center street was the more crowded, and slightly less of an assault on the ears, but the smells turned his empty stomach. He took the leftward, the downland side of which was a long row of inns and public houses. He would blend here, in his subdued, road-worn attire, and if he asked questions he might be able to hear the answers.

Between the public houses he saw steps, some of chipped stone, some of rickety wood, leading down to a river that one might bathe in but not drink from. Though he had come midway into the Strong Leg, he was not yet out of the Druilors' shadow. The Blooded Mountains, they were called, for the iron rust they bled, and they stretched far enough into the leg to poison the water table with their deadly minerals. Another town or two Kneeward he should find clean water. Here, it seemed, they drank dew and mist from barrels guarded by peacekeepers with longblades. He stood in line to drink with the rest, and was told that the keepers' tithe would be dispensed at noon, from a tavern called the Owls' Barn.

He went there. Families waited in weary patience, children making no fuss. "Inside's already full," someone told him. He stuck his head through into dimness long enough to make out an equally quiet crowd around the tables inside, and catch a whiff of old droppings that had never quite been scrubbed out of the planks. It reminded him of the Dindry Leng downmongers. No barn owls were evident, although the close rafters would have suited them well, and clearly they had once been made welcome, droppings or no. That reminded him of the Dancing Gull, in Esklin, on the Dreaming Sea. One gull there, long ago, had developed a stamping footwork that jiggled small sand creatures loose in the receding tide, and eventually whole flocks had learned the trick. He would have liked to see the sight. Old-timers there claimed it gave them no end of laughter. But disease had swept the local bird life like a tidal surge, and the gulls of Esklin danced no more.

His nose must have wrinkled as he pulled his head out and found a seat by the porch steps, for someone said, "The owls used to eat out of your hand in there, but if the publicans caught you feeding them, they'd bar you. Birds kept the vermin down better than cats, the last fever we had. Then the next one got the birds—owls and swans and swifts and all, and a good bit of Lowhill with them. A sad tale, that."

A sad tale repeated wherever Louarn roamed, with as many versions as there were villages. At least illness was a natural thing. He whiled away the slow breaths till noon weaving box puzzles for the children out of floor rushes he had them collect, and was pleased to lighten their spirits; but he was more pleased to hear no tales of unnatural deaths in their mist-haunted town.

The keepers' tithe was a vat of cooling porridge, some unidentifiable meal boiled in sheep's milk. He took it in the same battered cup with which he'd drunk their water, and though he tried to give half his portion to a family next to him, they refused it, saying that there was plenty for all and he should go for seconds or even thirds if he was road-weary. He waited to be certain this was true, then forced another helping down himself despite the taste. It seemed unwise to share food among so many, but when he asked "Do you not fear sickness?" the reply came from several at once: "Better tomorrow to fear than die today."

"Is the keepers' tithe why you stay here?" he asked the father who had declined his offering.

The man looked as though he'd never considered the reason. "No," he said at last, "there's tithes and alms in other towns. But there's no more work there than here. So we stay here."

He got no clearer answer from anyone else he spoke to that day, and the man was right—there was no work to be had. Wherever he went, another itinerant had got there first, and his goal—to earn a horse—would not be realized in this region, where the frothing sickness had hit hard. He sought everywhere to cadge a ride, but an afternoon haunting smithies and wheelwrights', cartwrights' and carters', yielded nothing bound Kneeward. "Perhaps in a threeday," a merchant told him. "Ships are due in Ulonwy and Glydh, some might be making their way up to meet them."

That was not soon enough. He needed to be under way today, or first thing in the morning. But he had come many leagues on his tired legs. He would not last much longer on foot.

He did not think the killers were on horseback. If they were, they tarried long in each town where they struck, taking care with their choice of victims, for he had not lagged far behind them even on foot. But if he did not head them off, he would be no better than a death-chaser. He didn't mean to track them. He meant to meet them directly, and stop them.

He considered theft. The consequences in these parts, as best he could tell, were not so severe as in the Lowlands, where they'd mark you for all to see. But of all the skills he had acquired, that was the first, and least. Only a horse or mule would be worth stealing, and those were far too closely watched.

He considered sharing his burden at last, in this region where life's essentials were so generously shared. He looked everywhere for folk dressed in black or white. Menders or runners would have the means to send word ahead, have their people waiting in the Knee, knowing who to warn and what to guard against. But there was no black or white among these Strong Leg folk, who clung hard to the old ways. There would be no aid for him from those quarters. Anyone else would think him a madman, or, more frightening, concoct some justification for the killers' deeds. And he would just as soon stand by his decision to say nothing. Anyone he spoke to could be one of the killers. Anyone he spoke to might know one of them, or sympathize with them. He deeply feared that there was more than just a pair of darkhearts. Some deep instinct had told him, when he realized the dead had been mages, that there was more to this than the bit he could see, from ground level, with his ordinary eyes.

The sun's hazed disk sank toward the Knee, mocking his inability to follow. He moved through the shifting vapors, gauging the progress he would have made if each step had been Kneeward rather than along the same streets on the same vain quest.

"What kind of work?"

"I can turn my hand to just about anything."

"A lad-of-all-crafts, so."

"Yes."

"No crafts want doing here, I'm afraid."

"Yes, I'd heard as much."

"Easiest way up the Knee Road is in a cart to the bonefolk."

"That would cut the journey rather short."

"It would, so. What's in the Knee for you?"

"Friends to meet. They won't wait if I'm delayed."

"That's a pity. But I can't help you."

It was the same wherever he turned. Then he chanced to turn off the long tinmongers' street onto a stonemongers' row, and three things happened almost at once, as was so often the way of it. A young woman at the first stall eyed him, suspicion rising into interest, and he lifted a foot to approach her; young women tended to offer him sweeter trades. At that moment the nearer end of the stall next to hers gave a creak that he knew all too well. On reflex he was already reaching out when the wooden lattice holding up that end gave way. He caught the board by the corners—an old door, judging from the heft, and the hinge seating under his fingers. A few jostled playing stones rolled off, but most held firm on their bed of felt, and even the tallest of the clay vessels in the center did not totter. He nudged pieces of rotten pinewood away with his boot that he might get closer and better support the weight until the proprietor, an elderly woman now quite flustered, could decide what to do. While he was standing thus, he heard a nearby tinker say, "My driver's ill, and I guaranteed delivery. If that load's not there by tomorrow noon, there goes my custom in the Knee." The elderly woman was thanking him profusely rather than solving the problem. "If you could find some crates," he said tightly. Her mouth moved, but his ear was fixed on the tinkers' conversation. "I'd run it up there for you," he heard, "but . . ."

". . . *sure* there are some about," the elderly stonemonger said, not looking very hard. "There are crates everywhere, I could break my neck on crates a dozen times a day yet when I find myself in need of some . . ."

He could no longer hear the other conversation. He considered dropping the board and letting the goods fall, or calling over his shoulder, or telling the proprietor to hush. But he felt the young woman at his shoulder before he saw her, before she could reach to help—him, he sensed, not her competitor—and he said, "Be a love, will you, and go tell those tinkers back there I'll be their driver if they still need one?"

Confused but willing, the girl bade the older woman watch *her* stall while she delivered Louarn's message. Unable to turn and observe the exchange, he cast about for some means of propping the board up until repairs could be made. Most stalls here were hammered concoctions of sheet metal. This hybrid of wood and tin must predate the rot that had claimed its fellows. "Can you bring that barrel over?" he said to the woman, gesturing with his chin at what had served as her seat. She eyed it dubiously—physical labor was either beyond or beneath her—but when he grunted as if the board's weight were becoming too much for him, she managed to roll the barrel on its end, maneuvering it into place that he might lay the board down on it.

"Oh, that will do nicely!" she said, and reeled off still more gratitude—her way, he realized, of fending off a request for compensation. He decided to pity hard circumstances rather than scorn tightfistedness, and turned.

"I'll be going with you," said the tinker, who had been standing directly behind him. Two arms in slings attested to why he hadn't moved in to help. "And sprained wrists don't stop me from cold-cocking a man who might think to make off with my goods."

Louarn gave his most brilliant smile. It wasn't hard; dark bluster suited the man's kind face so badly it was harder not to laugh. "Your goods, wagon, and team will be safe with me. All I want is passage to the Knee. But you'll need to drive them back again. Perhaps you'd prefer someone who can make the round trip."

They agreed to meet before closing in a public house called the Chimney Swift; if Louarn had found a surer ride or the man had found a there-and-back driver, they'd part ways with no hard feelings.

"Was it a healing stone you were looking for, then?" the young woman said, drawing him back toward her own stall. "Perhaps you'd want some playing stones now, to pass the time at the Swift?"

"I have my own set, thanks." Louarn was assessing the older woman's stall much as the young woman was assessing him. Seeing his attention wander, she said, "Then reward my message-running with your company. Help me close up at sunset, and I'll treat you to that ale."

He couldn't help but smile at her trader's patter, casting even the smallest exchanges in her favor while making them sound like favors to him. He accepted, and until sunset occupied himself in making small repairs to the older woman's stall with borrowed tools and tin scraps he charmed from tinkerwomen. What was still serviceable of the pinewood supports he fashioned into a three-legged stool to replace her barrel perch, weaving a barrel-hoop seat of cattail and bulrush, which resisted the river's poisons but were available in profusion since they were no longer safe to eat. The children he sent to collect them from the river he repaid with twistleaf puzzles. In all, a satisfying job of work, and the stonemonger was so well pleased, despite her protestations throughout, that she tried to press on him a trinket, an oddly shaped pale stone. "It's no good to me, no one wants it," she said, "but with a knack like yours who knows what use you'd find for it." In the end he demurred with reasonable grace—he'd been amply repaid by the enjoyment of the task itself, and the last thing he needed was useless trinkets weighing him down. Then it was time to help her younger competitor pack up her goods, and before he knew it he was sitting down with her as dusk closed in and the Chimney

Swift's publican lit rushlights in clay jars, filling his house with smoke to rival the restless mists outside.

"You must tell me all about yourself," the young stonemonger said as she got the ales in. The publicans' daughter gave her a sour look as she served them, reassessed her after sizing up Louarn, then left them to their drinks, though her eyes strayed often to Louarn from across the smoky room.

This made Louarn reassess the stonemonger as well. "And you," he replied politely, regretting his decision now and wondering how long he could nurse this ale to avoid owing her for another. She was younger than she looked. "For example"—he crooked a half-smile at her, not too much lest he promise something he would not now give—"what is your name?"

"Mireille n'Jenaille," she said, and took a breath.

When the tinker met him, though he came early, the girl was long gone in a huff, and Louarn said, "I'm afraid it turns out my business may keep me here another day." The tinker, relieved, said, "My sister will do the run for me after all. But if you still need a ride, she said, be on the Knee Road at midnight with a light. She'll watch for you, she said."

What Louarn needed was a way to make a man who didn't know him, a sweetsmonger named Jiondor n'Timlin, tell him where he'd put a little pickpocket who was in more danger than she could guess.

A little girl with a pouch that spilled out stolen mages' things. A tall woman named Risalyn, a Girdler from the look of her, the tawny Highlands kind, who collected those spilled things carefully when the girl had gone, and claimed she would return them to the spirit wood from whence the girl had ostensibly stolen them. A woman with a keen interest in the girl—a little girl with other pouches, still full and in her possession when she disappeared.

All this had come from Mireille, though he had a job extracting it from a tangle of bitter grievances. At first he'd barely listened. Then he'd had her repeat some recent details. Again he'd lost the main thread, as his mind seized on the contents of the pouch and the way the Girdler had collected it. His hands remembered, then, what they would have sought had he searched the bodies in Dindry Leng—what they would not have found. His mind's eye recalled the dusty mantel in Croy's home. There had been a triskele on that mantel. Croy *had* been a mage, as the downmongers had been mages. But what Louarn had not noted, when he returned to find the man dead, his inner eye remembered: a clear space on the mantel, a triskele shape in the dust. The pendant had been removed.

The killers took trophies.

The killers had passed through here, and a little girl, known for her thieving, had filched those trophies while feigning a fit on a water queue, and the killers wanted them back. Some the woman had retrieved, but sympathetic traders had spirited the girl away before they got the rest. There would be more than a dozen that he knew of, perhaps many he did not.

The killers would be seeking that girl.

Again he had surfaced, questioning Mireille about the girl's disappearance, the names of the traders who must have helped her, the barrow boy who had disappeared the same time she had. Mireille, as he intended, had taken his interest to be in her, in the clever way she believed she had influenced events to rid herself of rivals and her town of dangerous subversives. But when he had what he needed, his interest flagged, and he sank again into strategies—how to approach this sweetsmonger, earn his trust or compel his help—and he tried too late to charm Mireille into leading him to Jiondor's home. His smile would still have got him a bed for the night, but he misjudged her self-involvement past that point, and she scented manipulation.

To her dubious credit, she tried to work him in return. Her own questions grew hooks. He let them drag information from him—just enough for her to conclude that he was a secret trafficker in mages' goods, trading triskeles and reckoners' rings on a shadow market. She was appalled, good Strong Legger that she was, burner of crafts and carvings, suppressor of arts that harmed no one. He took some pleasure in appalling her, though she would run straight to the alderfolk she aspired to join, and he would have to complete his new task before he was run out of town. But better to have her spread that lie than spread something approaching the truth and flush the killers before he was ready.

At least they had drained their third tankards, and he suffered only a dousing in vitriol, not a dousing in ale, when she quit him.

When the tinker would not stay for a drink—a relief, since Louarn could not afford to offer one—the publicans decided to close up early. Swept from the Swift with stained rushes and pipe ash, Louarn stood for a time gazing down the lane between the fronts of taverns and the backs of stalls, letting his eyes adjust to darkness after the porch lamp went out, listening to itinerants snore. He drew his cloak close and considered where to go next. There would be no finding the sweetsmonger until morning. The alderfolk would have folk looking for him then, too, but Mireille would be busy at her trade, and with his battered hat angled low he would be difficult to identify based on her description alone. They might also watch Jiondor's stall, but he would surmount that when he got there. Surely their peacekeepers had better things to do than chase a young woman's whimsy.

Three lanterns flaring to life in front of a tavern down the row and heading up toward him through the mist told him the extent to which he had misjudged. He didn't wait to see if it was he they sought, but eased down the porch and around the corner of the public house. Through the decaying balustrade he watched three bladed peacekeepers go up the steps. A soft knock on the door was answered by the publican. No, there was no one left inside. They'd closed early for lack of custom. Yes, there'd been a man drinking with Mireille, but they chucked him out so they could get some sleep, and if these good folk wouldn't mind . . .

One of the peacekeepers requested entry to search the premises. One of the others began rousing the sleepers in the lane, shining lanternlight on bewildered faces; the third moved off a ways and dimmed her light, watching for anyone rising to slip away. A pale blur of Mireille's blunt features leaned into the searcher's light. She peered at a man and shook her head. He could just make out her hooded form following the light to the next sleeper.

Arms slid around him from behind. He barely kept from gasping. They drew him deeper into the shadows. They were sinuous arms—caressing, not capturing. "Who are we hiding from?" said a sweet voice, and the publicans' daughter nuzzled the back of his neck.

You can take me to Jiondor's home, he thought, and turned so that she felt his smile on her cheek, and pressed her lightly against the wall, stifling her giggle with his lips just in time. *It will be a game,* he thought, and when she whispered, "If it's Mireille, you're well shut of *that,*" he silenced her with another kiss and thought, *Or perhaps to spite a girl you don't like. Whatever will sway you, we'll do.* Then she did giggle, and it was his own oath he had to stifle. River sounds and the protests of disturbed itinerants damped the peacekeepers' hearing, but it was her keen-eared father who opened the side door and said, "Berilise? You've picked the wrong night to go lad-chasing."

The outward-opened door blocked the light from inside. Louarn set the girl away from him and faded farther into the dark. Too far and he'd be tumbling down the river slope. Too near and the light of an outswung lantern would catch him.

"No lad, Father," Berilise said, but another giggle betrayed her, and now a peacekeeper's boots were descending the side stair within. In moments a lantern would be thrust out. Louarn quested with his toe, and only managed to send a skitter of loose stones down into the river.

"No lad indeed," said a deeper voice. As the peacekeeper's lantern moved beyond the door, its light falling just short of where Louarn stood plastered to the siding, a plump man stepped into view from across the alley. His cheeks were flushed with drink, and his stance was chastened. "Only me. Afraid I startled the girl. Thought she might be someone else."

"Jiondor?" said the publican, herding his daughter inside. "Bit far from the Swan, aren't you? My daughter's a third your age, man." Louarn's breath caught, but whether it was at the name of the man he sought or the kiss the girl blew him on her way in, he couldn't have said. Neither father nor peacekeeper saw the kiss.

"I was in the Mute Swan," Jiondor said agreeably, and then told the peacekeeper, "I overheard the goings-on with Mireille and the alderfolk. Thought I'd lend an eye searching, since it had somewhat to do with me. I've no lantern, though."

"Well, it's for nothing," said the peacekeeper. "Unless they've got the fellow out front, that's an end on searching tonight. If he's not found by now, he's slipped off. Go on home, Jiondor. But keep an eye peeled tomorrow all the same."

"I will, so," Jiondor said, and bid the publican goodnight, let the peacekeeper go on ahead, let the side door close and the bolt slide home within. Then he was on Louarn before Louarn had taken two steps toward him, hustling him down uneven stone stairs and swinging him around against a tumble of weed-choked rock on the steep riverbank. A hand closed on Louarn's throat; thumb and middle finger pressed on points just below the jawbone's hinges. "Go for a blade," the man said, his low voice blending nearly into the river's song, "and I'll crush this."

Louarn raised his hands out to the sides. The pressure eased, but the hand remained.

"Where's the woman?" Jiondor said.

Louarn was too long in answering, unable to work out what the man meant. As the hand on this throat squeezed in warning, he said all he could think to say, afraid it was too much: "That's what I'd like to know."

"Lose her, did you?"

"I never had her."

They stood frozen that way for long breaths, with the river twining and untwining its invisible currents beside them.

Any itinerant out in that lane was more likely to be one of the killers than was this ordinary foodmonger, protecting little girls he had offered to foster. What were his motives? He must believe Louarn was some threat to them. Or was Louarn a competitor? Could there be some trade in children, for labor perhaps, or was that a dark thought unfair to decent folk doing their best in hard times? Trailing darkness so closely, he feared his own spirit had darkened, so that it was more difficult to recognize what was good and genuine. A market in child labor would be untenable—they'd consume as much as they earned. Assume the man wanted to shield them, then. But if his motives were protective, why not let the peacekeepers take the threat away?

He was hiding something. He had some connection to this that he did not want the alderfolk to discern.

"You're wondering why I saved you from the keepers," the man said.

"It would betray a trust. But you won't tell me whose."

He could feel through the man's hand that he had guessed rightly, but the man said, "Keepers won't take a life. But I will if I have to. Now you'll tell me why I shouldn't."

He thinks I am one of the killers. He knows that they have killed, but he thinks there may have been reason for it. Jiondor knew that there was more than one. A man and a woman, both Highlands Girdlers from the look of them, the woman in Dindry Leng had said. Louarn did not look a Highlands Girdler; he hadn't the height or the coloring. A plains Girdler, perhaps, though his hair was too dark even for that, but hair could be dyed. Had Jiondor gotten a good look at him, while he stood in lamplight on the Chimney Swift's porch?

"How long were you watching?" He tried to calculate how long Mireille had been gone, how much Jiondor would have had to overhear of her appeal to the alderfolk before he slipped off to his own ends. If he'd sought and seen a man of Louarn's description, the man Mireille described, and thought him one of the killers, there could be three killers. He'd been so sure he was following two. More than three and their stealth would be compromised . . . but three was a number of power, they might well be working as three, a dark inversion of an old-time triad . . .

"Answer me," Jiondor said.

Louarn had to wade upstream through leagues of thoughts before he retrieved the demand still hanging there.

"You won't kill me," he said quietly, making his decision, "because I have not yet become what I hunt." *Because taking a life is the worst abomination to the spirit, and I would not put that stain on your soul.* "You shouldn't kill me, because the children you protect are in grave danger."

Jiondor's fingers dug hard, then eased, as if the reaction was involuntary. "The only danger those girls were in was being prenticed to that so-called healer, and she won't find them now."

"She will," Louarn said, and told him how.

Jiondor swore. "That wee one always had a way with beasts. Thought the worst it would bring her was heartache, in these ill times." He released Louarn and straightened. Louarn could just make him out now in the dim glow of a nail-paring moon filtered through the sky's haze. Mist coiled around their feet, but clung to the river, refusing to rise. "What are you?" the man said.

"A journeyman crafter," Louarn said, "no more than that. But I am hunting a pair of killers. Possibly three, I thought a moment ago, but now I don't know what I think."

"I thought they were . . ." Jiondor swore again, eloquently, a talent of these Strong Leggers. "This gets us nowhere. Two men with secrets. I won't tell you mine, you won't tell me yours, and meanwhile those girls could be in it up to their necks. I'll have to go."

"Go?" Louarn said, prompting more than asking.

"Fetch them, rescue them, whatever it amounts to. I can't involve keepers. I won't involve my pledge, she's put up her blade for good. But you can come; you will anyway, whatever I do, I couldn't borrow or beg a ride and you'll trail me on foot."

"It's hard to get rides Kneeward," Louarn agreed, and watched.

Jiondor nodded. "Yes, they're Kneeward. That's not enough for you to find them. But if I bring you I can keep an eye on you. We leave now. No stops, no messages except mine to my pledge."

"I am hunting these people, Jiondor, not working with them."

"That's as may be. I've had enough lies and secrets to last me a good long while. Right now it's all a lie until I find otherwise. But I'll risk being wrong about some of it, on the chance of keeping those girls from harm."

"Then we must go now," Louarn said, and rose stiffly, rubbing the hard memory of rocks from his tailbone. "There'll be a ride for us on the Knee Road, if we're in time, and if those publicans will give you a light for the driver to see us by."

While they awaited the sound of wagon wheels on the side of the road by a slumbering shantytown, the sweetsmonger holding the borrowed candle lantern ready, Louarn mused on the tight weave this tradertown turned out to be—a box puzzle, a twistleaf puzzle, a braid of mists and currents.

The Fist

Razhe's cheekbone cracked against the table. No pain in the back of her head—a shove from behind, not a blow. She was on her feet in the time it took an eye to open, with an instant field awareness of the posture and position of every form in the room. No threat from front or sides. The stool her rising knocked backward scraped and tottered but did not hit flesh. Whoever had smashed her head down was not directly behind her. He was likely right-handed. There was no blade in her. He was either reaching his bare hand for a weapon or drawing his fist back.

She spun left, blade hand sweeping a knife from her belt. Her off elbow whipped through air. She jerked her blade arm back hard to halt the rotation even as the carry knife came fluidly into a thrusting grip.

No one there. No one diving through door or window. Just a side wall of chinked gray stone, hung with horse shoes, mule shoes, ill-matched halves of steer shoes.

Though she had pulled up, the low, smoky room continued to rotate. The floor tilted. She came full around and braced herself on the table. The flamewood's grain ran in queasy waves.

"All right there?" A man set a tankard of dark beer down on a cluster of rings in the old waxseed polish. Publican? Innkeeper? Taverner—place was too small for an inn, and in a public house she would have smelled stew.

"Your furniture's making me seasick."

"That'd be the stout," the man said cheerfully. "Chuck bucket's in the corner there."

She fingered her cheekbone and found it numb but not bloody. Low rafters, smoke-filled air, tables stained and scarred. The drink spill smelled rich and bitter, the pipe smoke piquant. The Fist, then. She was still in the Fist, where they drank stout and crumbled dry crampbark into their briar pipes. Hobblebush, they called it. She wasn't anywhere near numb enough if she could remember a thing like that.

A set of ninestones strewed the table. A winning configuration, possibly arranged by the impact of her face. Beside her was a modest pile of old clenched nails. Beside a larger pile, across from her, sat another tankard, empty. Who'd finish his drink but leave his stones?

The boot knife plunged point-first into the table beside the stones gave partial answer. She worked it out and slid it home. "Sorry about that," she said to the taverner.

"The cut'll wax in, like all the others," he said. "And nice work, by the way. I was in the cellar, but my boy saw it. Will the fellow come back for his stones, do you think?"

Kaẓhe gauged the time of day from the shuttered windows and oily lampglow and said, "Not tonight. Why don't you keep them safe for him?" She scooped the nails into their box but left the stones for the taverner, not trusting herself to cope with the drawbag

"*It's more than nails I'm rolling for,*" he'd said, with a tense, expectant glance as he rattled the stones in his cupped hands, and she'd snorted and told him to yank a younger pair of breeches.

She remembered now—the offer of a friendly game, the way he demanded the strongest stout. Called himself Arron, a Heartlands name but in a Highlands accent. She'd let him stand her the drinks, although the taverner gave her all she asked. For keeping the peace. She remembered now. The Blue Dunnock had thrown her out for starting more brawls than she stopped. She'd packed the blasted Fist in, set off for home. But now she was here.

She remembered. It was a partner Arron wanted, but the bladed kind. "*A rousing workout once a nineday, when the caravans come through,*" he'd said, "*and you'll never have to wipe up another tavern.*"

She hadn't heard of roadside attacks in the Fist, though merchants traveled in caravans for fear of just that, with hired blades to protect them. The folk they hired wouldn't know a point from a buttcap—she'd said as much when they tried to hire her—but this lout didn't know that, or didn't want to find out the hard way that he was wrong.

At least they fear me enough to want me, she'd thought. The merchants, and the lout.

She'd turned him down. He'd turned nasty. Said she was selling herself cheap, working protection for crossroads fleatraps.

"*Aren't you tired of being a washed-up legend? Kazhe n'Zhevra, bodyguard to the Lightbreaker. Can't make choices for yourself, without some darkmage pulling your strings?*"

"*His name was Torrin,*" she'd growled.

"*His name was traitor,*" Arron had said, his burred accent thickening, and that was when her knife went into the wood and he stumbled up and away. He'd mistaken her for someone else, she said, and if she saw him again she wouldn't be aiming for the table.

"*I only made one mistake,*" he'd said as he backed to the door. "*I didn't wait for you to get through the next barrel of stout.*"

Bleeding spirits, she hated Highlanders.

She retrieved her stool and gripped the seat to guide herself onto it. She picked up her tankard with two hands. It seemed like years since the last draught, as if in the moment of keeling face-first into the table she had journeyed to a far time and place. The shakes eased as the bitter, creamy liquid went down. A meal in a mug, that's what this stuff was. Forget your ales and shandies. You could live on this. Forget careering brigandage you could have prevented with a maiming blow. Forget the insults you shouldn't have let pass.

Forget the past. That was the point. Somewhere was the memory of drinking with shielders—the looks of disgust, even pity, as they went on their way. Today? The day before? It didn't matter. Lift the tankard, take a swallow, there went the memory. Somewhere below that, the memory of driving Benkana off; lift, swallow, drown that memory a little deeper. Worse hurts lay wrecked in the depths. The draughts of stout blended into draughts of ale and beer and wine, a stream running backward through the years and disappearing into a swallowhole, down and down into the darks of the earth.

Yet somehow the bottom of even the dullest tankards showed the same clear moment. Only when they were filled would the vision of Torrin Wordsmith's fall ripple and grow dark.

"I see you're still keeping your back to the wall."

The familiar voice made her blink, though she was too well greased to startle. She'd taken no interest in the woman who came through the door. Folk came, folk went; it was a tavern. Now she absorbed the watchful demeanor, the grip of a longblade peeping over the shoulder, the extra belt sheaths. She should have noticed this one. Shielder or brigand, someone that bladed deserved her attention. How many tankards had she downed since kissing the table?

She took in the long black hair, the olive skin, the green eyes, and knew: Not enough. Not nearly enough.

"Verlein."

"Hello, Kaȥhe. Long time."

"Not long enough."

"Longer than you know." Verlein n'Tekla swung a leg around the lout's stool and sat. "A lot's happened while you wallowed in the bottom of a cask."

Kaȥhe's lips drew back in a snarl that would have passed for a grin in other company. "Straight to the point. I taught you to dance better than that."

"I've made some modifications in your teachings."

"I saw," Kaȥhe said on a belch. "Your shielders waddle by now and then. You've done ill by those blades, lengthening them. *Tapering* them."

"To a finer point," Verlein said. "They thrust through the holes in mail."

"The hole's in the opponent's guard. If it's down to his mail he's dead already."

"I'm not here to argue bladecraft. We do things my way now."

Kaȥhe barked out a laugh and wiped spittle from her mouth with the back of her hand. "And may the spirits save you all."

"How long since you've eaten, Kaȥhe?"

Kaȥhe lifted her tankard. "This is the only food they serve here. And you won't buy me with this or any other meal, whatever it is you want." She drained it off, and the serving boy was right there to take it for a refill.

"You've trained him well," Verlein said after passing him a tallystone to fetch her a brandy.

"Better than I did you."

"I took what I could use and left the rest."

Kaȥhe made a sloppy gesture toward a particular sheath at Verlein's belt. "Yet you still wear that."

Verlein touched the yellowed grip of the cheit and said, "A relic. It reminds me there's a world out there. It's proof that I can fight it when it comes."

They didn't know what substance the grip was crafted from, any more than they knew what black material, inset with bone-white triangles, wrapped the grip of Kaȥhe's longblade. Some kind of animal horn, Kaȥhe thought, though how the makers had come by it she didn't know. Perhaps they didn't have bonefolk in the ancient world. She wondered if the bonefolk here would take it when Verlein fell, or leave it behind with the tang. That would answer the animal-ormineral question. If Verlein had become blademaster, she'd bequeath that cheit to a successor when she died. But Kazhe had chosen ill in choosing her.

The boy brought her freshened tankard. She washed the tightness from her throat with a long pull, then kept pulling, and handed it back to him empty. Her father's shade was long gone to the spirits. If they were kind, he'd never know the fate of the dagger that had been his, and his master's before him.

"Aren't you going to tell me the outer realms are a tellers' tale?" Verlein said.

Tellers. Holes. Didn't they have tellers in this hole? She felt the maudlins coming on. A wistful tale to bring a tear to the eye, now, that would suit her. To have her heart lifted and crushed by events that hadn't touched her, to exult and ache and grieve for things that never were. She wanted a teller, a fantasy, not some haunt of the past made flesh.

"You should have come at another time," she said. Her words were blurred, distant. "Earlier. Or another day."

Now was a time to be mawkish, to laugh and cry at wisps and vapors, to find the illusory camaraderie of vine and grain among shadowy strangers in a wayside place whose name she didn't even know. To feel, for a space of breaths, something that felt like sentiment. To paint an illumination of life over the hard numb plank of herself—and then go black, know nothing, and wake under a table or in a ditch with simple, burning needs that could be met. A piss. A drink of water. A mug of elderbark tea. A thirst that could be quenched, an ache that could be soothed. She'd plunge her head into a stream, then spend the time from waking till noon with her longblade driven hilt-down into the ground. Watching its shadow contract against it. Waiting to see whether midday came before she accepted the blade's justice. When midday won, she could unearth the blade, and sheath it, and walk through some alehouse door and feel the first cool blessed flow of relief in her gullet.

She would be happy then. She would be entertaining and entertained, she would welcome reminiscences of youth and fervent beliefs. That would have been the time for this. Not now.

"All the days are the same, for you," Verlein said, and in that faraway voice, on that faraway face hazed by smoke and long years, Kazhe thought there was a quiet pity.

"Why do you *plague* me?" she snarled, expanding from her seat. Her voice came out of that distant, muted place and swelled into a roar: "*Why do you plague me?*"

"I need you, Kazhe. Sit down."

No tales. No laughter. No sweet tears. She sank back onto the stool, dead weary. "Go away, Verlein. You're a ghost. Haunt someone else."

"I'm real, Blademaster, and I have need of you."

Kazhe drank, and when the mouthful struggled back up as bile, she drank again to wash it down. She waved a hand in resignation: *Say what you will.* She laughed, belatedly noting the honorific, and then sighed. *Blademaster.* Her father's name. She'd never been meant to take it up so soon. But when she killed the turncloaks who'd killed him, she'd done it with his blade.

"We fought the Ennead," Verlein was saying. "Together or apart, it was the same fight. But it's not over. There's one left of the Nine. There's one left of you to kill her."

Ennead. How long since she had heard that word? How much longer since she had cared? "*We both only ever tried to keep what we loved alive,*" someone had said to her once. "*For me it was a way of life. For you it was a man.*"

But Torrin fell, and Torrin died, while she was bashing herself against the magecrafted warding that kept her from his side, her throat screamed raw, her blade useless, and Torrin fell, and Torrin died, and all the long stream of ale had done nothing to soothe the burning screams.

"There's no one left to fight, Verlein," she said, so clearly that for a moment she thought someone spoke for her. "I lost the only fight that ever counted."

"No, there's one fight left," Verlein replied. "And you're losing that one."

Kazhe came back to herself at the table, saw the undulating grain in the flamewood, the gouge her boot knife had made, the layers of polish, the pewter tankard in her hand. She tilted it, peering close, but the gray metal gave back no reflection.

As dull as the metal, she said, "Tell me who you want me to kill."

"No. Not while you're like this." Verlein sipped her brandy—the first sip she'd taken—then rose from her seat. "I'm staying in the inn in Tilgard, down the road. Your blade was sworn to protect, Kazhe. The man you protected is gone. I'll give you all Eiden Myr to protect in his stead—if you come to me tomorrow at sunset, clean and with no drink in you."

Kazhe huffed in disbelief. "I won't join your fool shield."

"I wouldn't have you. You don't follow orders."

"*What*, then?"

"Meet my terms and I'll tell you."

"Fine," Kazhe said, throwing her hands up. Then, with a twist to her mouth that was meant to be wry but turned out crafty, she said, "You going to drink that?"

Verlein stared at the brandy cup and said, "I remember the night we met." *No*, Kazhe thought, *don't*, but Verlein didn't hear. "You were two nineyears old, all white-blond fluff of hair and blazing eyes. Full of rage and courage. Don't drown that wild, bright flame. I loved you, Kazhe. So did Torrin, in his way. But my heart is still beating. My heart can still be broken."

Then she was gone, on a swell of pain, leaving Kazhe alone in the midst of strangers, with a tankard of dark grief and failure at one hand, a cup of pungent Koeve brandy in the other.

"Till tomorrow," she said, lifted the cup in a toast to the closing door, and downed the brandy in three searing gulps.

She was wet. Not the river. From the stink, not a ditch.

"Wake up," someone crooned, not for the first time. Then, harder, "Wake up, runt. I have to see you take the lesson."

A fist in her shirt, pulling up, shoving back. The ooze and squish of an open midden under her back. She smelled a barn or stable. Another voice, lower. More than one of them. Life came back into her limbs on a surge of exhilarating fear, but she left them limp. She kept her eyes closed, and listened.

Only two. One was Arron. She knew the voice. He'd been alone. Or so she'd thought. The rest blurred. It didn't matter. He had a friend now.

"Pick her up."

"I'm not touching that. You pick her up."

An oath. Muffled thuds of boots on dirt. A bucket swung by its handle, slapping into a stream. Maybe nine feet away. She cracked open a crusty eye. One had turned to watch the other fill the bucket.

Novices.

She took the near one out with an elbow across the jaw as he turned at the sound of her sucking rise, then a knee to the crotch, all before her body's state caught up with her. She shoved him into the dungheap; she wobbled but didn't go down. Arron was visible in the light of stars and a hangnail moon. Running from the stream, awkward with the bucket. She stepped back into the shadow of the barn. The bucket was too heavy to swing around in time. He flung the water at where she'd been, a pale arc. She came at him from the side, less an attack than a headlong stumble. He was just off balance enough for the impact to knock him down. In the Fist they wrestled for sport. But he was a Highlander. Even impaired, she got his arms locked while he was still trying to flip over.

He swore at her, and she jerked hard, feeling ligaments strain—not all his. "Wasting your time," she managed through a swollen, grit-thick mouth. "Taverner has your stones. Taverner has twice your bloody stones."

He answered with a choking sound. The smell was unbearable. She grinned, feeling it soak into his clothes.

A yellow light came around the side of the stable barn. The taverner and his boy. The boy held the lantern. The taverner held her scabbarded longblade.

She pushed away from Arron and stumbled up. Not graceful, and she dropped the weapon when the overeager taverner tossed it to her, but once she had the grip in her hand the blade centered her. She stepped away as the louts got their feet. The friend had the worse of it, and was swearing at Arron, something about how this was supposed to be an easy one-off, just a scare. Kazhe frowned.

The taverner said, "They kicked through the bolt on the door. Good thing you were sleeping there, Blademaster. From the looks of it nothing was taken. But I told you you should have hung on to your weapon."

The bloody taverner had heard the crash and cowered in his room while the two men dragged her out and around the side of the stable. Kazhe wanted to close her eyes and hold her head, but her line of sight along the blade was the only reason she hadn't fallen. She supposed she should credit him for coming down to bring her the blade. She didn't remember entrusting it to him, but at least that kept it out of the dungheap. Any of her eight smaller blades would have done if it came to that. Some instinct must have told her that Arron might return while she was passed out and take her blade as a consolation prize.

"I'll only need the flat of this," she said. "Neither of you will do much robbing with broken arms, I'd say, and if you're careful, the gangrene shouldn't get you."

"Bloody spirits!" cried the friend. "We're not robbers!"

"You could have just asked for the stones back," Kazhe went on. "And if you take such insult from a knife stuck in a tabletop, you have no business drinking in taverns."

"We were sent," said the friend, ignoring Arron waving him to silence.

"*Sent?*" Her own raised voice sent a spike through her head, but didn't kill the ironsmith using her skull for an anvil. She bit down on a groan. A fractured, painful glare haloed the lantern, and all movement took on a throbbing translucence in the approach of dawn.

"Her shielders saw you drinking here, couple of days ago, and she sent us on ahead to see how far you could be pushed, then knock some sense into you," Arron said at last, bitterly. "She told us the day you lost a fight because of drink, you'd never look at an alehouse again. She said if we could shame you enough . . . But there'll be no deal now that I've told you."

"The deal broke when I didn't lose the fight." A little stable muck never hurt anyone, though it was going to be a cold job washing it off in the stream.

"They came here to mess you about?" the taverner said. "If not for you and them, I'd still have a bolt on my door?"

Kazhe nearly burst out laughing, but it would have hurt too much. Poor, naïve taverner. It was so nice when he was legendstruck. She'd be sleeping rough the rest of this night.

Unless she put it to better use.

She sent Arron and his friend off on foot with hard words and a slap of her blade. Let them walk back to Verlein, or the Highlands, or wherever they belonged. She told the taverner's boy to fetch her horse; he glanced at his father or master for permission, got only a bewildered shrug, and went into the barn. *I still have a horse*, she thought with mild surprise. She remembered gambling it away somewhere, but perhaps she'd won it back. Or perhaps it was a different horse—but it was Comfrey led sleepy and rankled from the barn, and her saddle on his back.

"Which way is Tilgard?" she asked, taking the reins.

The taverner pointed downland. In the bluing light, she saw that the road followed the stream. That suited her. She'd have her wash, and clean and oil her blades, and the morning sun would dry her. She started off, leading the horse although he nipped her shoulder hard.

"Who were they talking about?" the taverner called after.

"Who sent them, you mean? That bladed Souther."

" 'Her shielders,' that man said. Was she . . . ?"

Kazhe kept moving. "Verlein n'Tekla," she called without turning. "You had the first of Eiden's shield in your tavern."

She left them to whisper excitedly about their new brush with legend, and contemplated the joys of stuffing legend's beating heart down its throat.

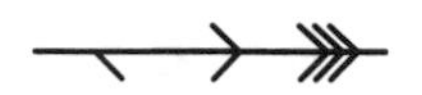

You must go back into the world.

This is the world.

It is not the world you came from.

I've always been here. This is the world.

It is not your world.

I don't understand. I've always been here. There is no place but this. I'm whole. I'm happy.

This is a passing place. Not a staying place.

I've always been here.

You dreamed yourself here. But you are flesh. You must go back to flesh.

I have flesh. Look. Hands, legs . . . I have flesh here. I can be flesh here! You have flesh . . . I can touch you . . . I can love you . . .

This is a passing place. Pass through.

Please. Don't make me go.

You must. Fare you well, child who is not.

Pass through.

The Fist

Kazhe burst into the Tilgard inn at midmorning and strode toward the big oak table where Verlein and two seconds were only just breakfasting. Eowi and Girayal. New recruits, when she had last seen them, and no one she had taught. Hah. Too easy.

"An ale!" she called to the innkeeper, whose wide eyes peered from the cookroom. "Make it two. And none of that black stuff. One for now, and one for after I break the first shield over my knee."

She dropped Eowi with an elbow to the stomach pit while he was reaching back for his longblade, and spun Girayal away with a kick to the hip so that her blade, coming into play, had only air to cleave. Her gloved hand closed on the blade of Verlein's battle knife, forcing it wide, while her forearm across Verlein's throat bore its wielder back against the wall. Fingers hooked around the knife's guard twisted it from Verlein's grasp, and she laid the blade on her own forearm, pressing the tip up into the soft flesh under Verlein's chin before the taller woman could land a blow or draw a different blade.

"Weapons turn on you if you misuse them," she growled.

"The ale was a mistake," Verlein managed through a constricted airway. "You have only till sundown to meet my terms."

"I chewed up your terms," Kazhe said. "They went in the midden."

"And you, from the smell of it."

"I took your message boys with me." Without looking, she said, "I'll drive this through her brain in the death spasm, Eowi," and he withdrew as noisily as he'd tried to sneak up.

"Stand down," Verlein rasped at them. "She won't hurt me."

"I wouldn't say that," Kazhe crooned.

"Don't you want to know what the mission is?"

"Not on your terms."

"State yours, then."

Kazhe shoved back and flipped Verlein her knife. "Outside."

The shielders obliged her on a nod from Verlein. Kazhe crooked a finger at the innkeeper, who stood frozen with two mugs in her hand, then swore and walked over to take one from her. She picked up an elderflower fritter on the way by, and washed it down with the tepid ale. "Ahhh," she said, wiping her mouth with the back of her hand. "Better already. My thanks."

Eowi and Girayal had positioned themselves to either side of the door, which opened inward. Kazhe ducked out and back and let them tangle with each other in trying to grab her, then cocked her head at Verlein and waited.

"Good training for them," Verlein said with a shrug, and gestured them back to her side.

Kazhe stepped into the grassy yard. Comfrey was tied to a hedge around the side of the building. Tilgard was a pleasant village, all whitewashed stone, thatched roofs, dark-leaved trees. Far enough into the heaths and downs that neither bogs nor sea was anywhere near. Salt air made her ill, and she never wanted to see the rocky coastline of the Fist again. "You and me," she said, flipping knives into a neat column in a mulberry's trunk. "Longblades. You best me, I do whatever it is."

"And if you best me?"

"Then I win."

Verlein removed her own shortblades from belt and thigh and boots, laying them down with care, and the cheit with them. "You needed a cause to fight for, once."

"I fight for the bloody thrill of it. But since you asked . . . I'll have that cheit back, too."

Verlein looked up sharply. "I don't think so."

Kazhe grinned. "Does my little dagger make fools take you for a blademaster?" She shrugged out of her crosswise harness and slid the oiled, ancient scabbard off the magecrafted kenai, the weapon that had been her father's, the weapon no blademaster bequeathed until death. "Or are you just sentimental?"

Verlein drew her long tapered blade and thrust forward in answer. Kazhe, flinging the scabbard aside and adding her left hand to the kenai's grip, countered with a bark of glee.

Verlein's opening thrust was arrow-straight and aimed at the belly, meant to prove the merit of her blade's design. She gripped it one-handed and turned her body, presenting a narrowed target—as though they stood on a practice strip, as though they fought along a single line. Had she abandoned the eight directions of movement? In her obsession with meeting straight-on invasion, had she conceived battle as only advance and retreat?

Kazhe passed forward and to the left and bore Verlein's blade down easily. The same motion served as a cut to the legs. Verlein sprang back to save her thigh and stop Kazhe bearing in on her from the side. Kazhe followed onto her right foot with a rising false-edge cut. Verlein half-bladed to block it, left hand on the weak of her blade. Kazhe did the same, and grinned at the shriek of iron on iron as they vied to slip past each other's point of resistance, to yield to the strong and draw the other off balance, to dart over or under and hook blade with guard or lever arm with hilt. Verlein made a bid to grapple. Kazhe sprang free and spat at the ground. This would not descend to wrestling. This was a contest of blades.

They resumed their guards at middle distance.

Verlein's flat stance was strange. Kazhe danced around it, testing her footwork, making her pivot, trying to force her back into a square-on stance. Verlein persisted in turning her body, shoulders angled to legs when she passed forward. Power derived from the alignment of hips and shoulders. It was a dramatic change in style, a weakening of all Kazhe had taught her. Kazhe moved fluidly through guards, seeking a way in. Verlein, voiding and winding and disengaging, never met her full in the bind, never jeopardized her weaker weapon. Instead she exploited her longer reach, her slimmer, swifter blade.

A tapered blade. A thrusting blade.

Verlein counted on her fluid wrist to be more deft than the two hands with which Kazhe levered and spun her grip. She turned her body to protect it as she maneuvered herself to dart in for the thrust or the harassing slice, again and again.

Verlein was a shielder. She was meant to be holding a shield in that off hand.

Or a dagger. A cheit.

Understanding at last, Kazhe attacked with full intent.

Burning, exhilarated, she turned Verlein in circles, backed her against trees, broke her stance again and again, made her leap and hop, sway and duck. Then she slashed under a high assault for a clean cut across Verlein's midriff, taking a slice to the shoulder for it, gasping with the ecstasy of pain—laughing to see Verlein's eyes fly wide.

To Verlein, this was a demonstration. A first-blood bout to prove supremacy of style. She'd let Kazhe attack the blade while she waited for her to tire. The first cut should have ended it; the two cuts should end it in a draw.

Verlein had not forgotten the eight directions—six forward and back on the straight and diagonal, one to each side. But she had forgotten the ninth direction.

The ninth direction was down. To death.

Kazhe drove in through a reddening haze, heedless of the damage the longer blade would inflict should she blink or falter. Under her own gruff, powerful exhalations she heard Verlein order her to stand down, as if she were one of her toy fighters. Under the next "Hup!" and clang of iron, it sounded like an offer to yield. But there was no yielding here. There would never, ever be any yielding.

Only a ruse of feigned yielding. The teacher's oldest trick: the invitation to underestimate. Would Verlein remember the hard lessons in the fields? Or had the sight of the drunken wreck wiped the memory clean? Still appearing to give her all, Kazhe hunched her shoulders and let her point drop below eye level in middle guard. Just a tad, a nearly imperceptible change of angle. She set Verlein's next thrust aside and failed to press through. She dropped her elbow in hanging guard, let her cut fall just shy, flopped her arms into low guard and let her blade point brush the ground. Just enough to signal that, ravaged from drink, out of practice, short on sleep, off her stride, she was beginning to flag. She drew Verlein in with each strike made too close to her own body. She invited her in, with elbows too bent, cuts too short. She passed back, but not quite out of range. When Verlein, still wary but irresistibly tempted, committed to one flung-out cut at the legs—meant as payback for the belly slice, delivered with only the pommel retained in her grip—Kazhe stepped in, whacked Verlein's forearm with the cross of her hilt, and lifted her blade above her shoulder to deliver the strike of wrath.

"Die, Verlein," she said, and brought her blade down with all the power of her body.

Verlein dove headlong past her. She groped for her fallen blade, failed to snag it as Kazhe pivoted, and rolled aside just a hair before Kazhe's reversed blade would have brained her with a hammer blow. Disarmed, she scrabbled to regain her feet and put a tree between herself and the vicious madness that was Kazhe, shouting for her seconds.

Kazhe let them grapple her, let them drag her away from Verlein, but would not release her blade even when one of them cracked a pommel on her knuckles. The blade was part of her. She was the blade. There was no word for blademaster. The word for blade and wielder was the same. She was kenai. She was the blade.

"There are no bouts, Verlein," she said through blood after Girayal whacked her in return for a peremptory kick. "There are no terms. There's only dying, and not dying. You've forgotten that."

"The drink has cracked you. You were never like this."

"I was always like this. That's why you loved me. Come on, Verlein. Pick up your hazel switch. We're not finished."

"We're finished, Kazhe. I am going to tell you what to do, and for once in your bloody benighted life you are going to do it."

"Or what? You'll hand me the pieces of your *broken heart?*"

"I'll hand you the pieces of this broken land. The Khinish are going to march, Kazhe. The Ennead's ghost is whispering in their ear, inciting them. I'm going to the Strong Leg to stop them. Destroy the ghost, and chances are they'll pull their thrust and go back where they belong. Terrorize that poor innkeeper into pouring drink down your throat, and my shield will fight the Khinish and the Strong Leg will soak in blood."

"You had to best me. Those were the terms. I owe you nothing."

"You refused the terms. The shield bested you." Verlein gestured at the seconds who held Kazhe's arms.

As though just noticing them, Kazhe buckled one with a heel behind the knee, freed that arm by cocking its elbow under the woman's jaw as she fell, dispensed the other with a groin strike, then asserted her space with a lazy sweep of blade. "Relying on shields is only one of the flaws in your new technique."

With a hiss, Verlein opened her arms and her empty hands and moved inside the blade, close enough for Kazhe to smell the scallions on her breath, the sweat on her body. "You listen to me. It's going to be them or us. If the Khinish carve out supremacy, they'll have us in irons. You will do whatever I tell you to do in order to keep them off us."

"The Khinish are olive growers. They have no reason to carve anything."

"The Khinish were formidable conquerors once. Warriors who invaded and took control of other lands."

Control.

Kazhe blinked. "You want to *rule.*"

"No. I command. I already have that. I want to save us."

Kazhe shoved away and turned to sheath the kenai. "You want to wield me like a blade."

"You are a blade," Verlein said. "You are kenai. The only one left." She strode halfway to where Kazhe was picking her knives one by one from the flesh of the tree. "Be good for something. *Do* something."

Kazhe sheathed the last knife in her belt as she sheathed Verlein's words in her mind. Newfangled shielders and ancient warriors: Two forces vying to conquer a land that had never been in dispute. Two forces vying to conquer *their own land*. Spurred by some surviving member of a corrupt mage cadre, or merely inventing justifications for war—it didn't matter which. All that mattered was that one of them would win.

Kazhe turned with a roundhouse punch that sent Verlein sprawling on the grass. She watched unseeing as blood gushed from the shieldmaster's nose.

No one had ever ruled this land. Not even the Ennead, manipulating their web of mages from their dark fastness. No one.

Her blade was sworn to protect. For as long as there had been people of light, there had been kenaila—their shadows, their blades, pledged to kill in their defense, to take the stain of death on their souls in order to keep the mages safe. Pledged to die for them.

Most of them had. Kazhe should have, too. She should have died with her father in the silken grasslands of home, when the Ennead's turncloak kenaila came to kill him. She should have died with Torrin in the magewar. But she had not. And, day after day, the balance of noon had come before the blade called her to its justice.

Now she knew why. There was one thing left to defend, protect, preserve. One thing still to die for.

"You will not rule," she said. "You will not rule the world that mages made. And you will not rule *me*."

She mounted her horse, ignoring his irritable nip at her foot when she reined him from the tasty hedge, and rode straight through the shielders, scattering them.

That was her answer. That was her vow. *I will ride through your forces with the forces I will raise, and I will scatter you, and your enemies, and there will be no ruling then*. Whether Verlein would understand it, she didn't know. She'd been a slow study, though relentless. She let words sway her when she should have looked only to actions.

Kazhe had no use for words. Only deeds would save Eiden Myr. Only a victor who refused to rule.

Or be ruled.

• • •

"She won't do it," Verlein told Worilke, deep in the afternoon, in the concealing shade of a mulberry tree.

Worilke shook with a rage that Verlein had never seen in her. "She must! Or you must send someone else! Who is your most stealthy second?"

"I will spend no more time on this. I don't care what's goading the Khinish. I'm a fighter. My job is to stop them. You take care of your old illuminator. She's not my concern. I leave for the Strong Leg tonight."

"Lerissa must be your concern, Verlein. She is your rival. Stop the Khinish, if you will. But use that victory as a stepping-stone. *You* must take control."

"You're as bad as Kazhe! I don't want your bloody control, when will you understand that? I'm pledged to watch. To defend. I'll defend against our own, if I have to, but then I'm done, Worilke. I'm going back to my coast to watch and wait, and to the spirits with all of you!"

"You would let the menders take control? The runners? The heirs of the Ennead's warders and reckoners? Their *proxies*, Verlein. Even now, I have word that runners are forming their own holding. That would make two—one white, one black. How long until they have three? How long until they dissolve your shield and leave our coasts defenseless?"

Verlein mopped at her nose, which had begun to run bloody again. The pain was bad. Nearly blinding. She wanted to strike out, but she didn't know at what. Worilke was an aged, withered woman, powerless now except for her. Or because of her. Verlein kept her for her counsel. It had always done well for her, until now, and Worilke couldn't be blamed for the wild, burning arrow Kazhe turned out to be. Let her fall, and burn. The rejection smarted, and she'd bear the bent nose of it as a lifelong reminder. But Kazhe was of no more interest now than some scheming remnant of the Nine. She had a battle to fight.

Yet what lay at the other side of it? Could Worilke be right—could there be more gain in winning than simply winning for its own sake? She wasn't Kazhe, to fight for the bloody sport of it. She wasn't Kazhe, to fight with no concept of the consequences. Why not use victory to establish permanent dominance? Why not?

"It's either you, the Khinish, or the proxies, Shieldmaster. Identify your opponents and eliminate them."

Slowly, in pain, Verlein nodded. "And Lerissa?"

Worilke sighed, fingering a pouch she kept always at her belt amid folds of robe. It held banewort, Verlein knew. A useless substance; it killed only mages, and the magelight was dead. But Worilke never touched it directly. "I will see to her," she said. "Summon Teyik for me. He'll arrange it." Then, looking down at the shape of the hard, dried roots imprinted on the fabric of the pouch, the linen shiny from the oils of many touches, she said, "And more besides, and more efficiently, perhaps." The grin she raised was ghastly, insane. "Time for Freyn's justice."

Verlein left her to her mutterings. She'd get nothing more of use from Worilke now. In the morning her madness would have lifted. Let her sit in her wagon and speak to herself of old, dead things through the night. Teyik, her old steward's son, would look after her.

She called for Girayal and Eowi and began preparations for the Strong Leg journey.

In the end, she could trust only herself. In that much, Kaẕhe and Worilke were both right. If someone was going to rule—if her blades were going to allow the rule of anyone—it had to be someone she trusted to do right by Eiden Myr.

It had to be her.

Kaẕhe regarded the tankard in her hand, her knuckles blanching on its handle, the dull nothing it reflected and the ale it no longer held. "*You* will not rule me," she said, very softly, and rose, and left the Low Arm public house, and got back on her horse. He bit her arm, but he bore her true.

The next morning, on a ferry bound across the water that lay between her and the myriad grasses of home—between her and the proud, loyal folk she would forge into a blade, a bladebreaking blade, the greatest blade, a breaker of armies—she sent the tankard spinning end over end into the sea.

Every part of him hurt. His hands hurt. His head hurt most of all. His eyes hurt, when he came near light. He stayed away from light.

There were bigthings moving in the tunnels. He heard their tread. He heard their talk. He heard the whisk of their cloaks. Sometimes they brushed his face like wings.

He was small. He shrank from light. They didn't see him.

He sniffed his way. Torches smelled of tar, lamps smelled of oil. Lightless tunnels smelled of damp stone and safety. Damp was good. He heard damp trickling down a wall. It had a bad smell, but he was very thirsty. He lapped at it. Then he was sick. Then he was hungry. He sniffed his way to where something frilly grew in long wooden cases filled with earth. He ate the frills. They tasted like mushroom. He pressed his hot face into the cool ruffled freshness, down into the loamy soil. Earth was nice. Stone was nice. The banks of ruffles made a soft bed. He slept.

He woke to shadow so deep it seemed to move. He reached up. He wasn't afraid of the dark. He was good at the dark. Dark hid you.

His hurt hand touched something thin and sharp, and he screamed.

Bigthings pounded down the tunnels toward where he was. He scrambled off his bed, whimpering, ducking low, batting at his head to keep the thinsharps off him. A door opened and light flooded his good dark place with its ruffled woodsoil beds. He crawled deep into the darkness by the floor and slid out the way he had come in.

The bigthings didn't get him. The thinsharps didn't follow.

Tears were salty. Not good to drink. He went back to the trickle and then past it. He came to a wall. Spaces opened on each side. He could feel spaces on his skin; he could hear them. Spaces sounded different from walls.

He went into one. It went for a long way. At the end of it was a hole that whispered. Air came up through it from far below, like someone breathing. It was nice. He sat with his feet dangling over the edge for a long time. The hole went down a long way. The hole was an old, old thing. It had a smell, not exactly like the ruffles, but close. He liked it. It made him feel as though he knew things. He stayed there so long that he got sleepy again, but he thought he might roll in by accident, so he left there and went past the trickle tunnel, hoping for a softness to lie down in.

Instead there was a wonderful, wonderful smell. Warm things. Treats. It came from an up tunnel, but there was light there. He winced and drew back. He screwed his eyes down tight, leaving just a crack to see through, and tried again. It hurt. It scared him. He heard bigthings up there.

He was hungry, and hurt, and tired, and he longed for something he couldn't name, something to go around him. But there was only stone. He tucked up where the floor met the wall, and slept.

When he woke, there were thinsharps. He ran away, and lost them in the twists and turns. The tunnels changed. It took a while to find his way back to where he was. Then he tried to find another way to the warm smell. But the tunnels hadn't changed enough for that. He learned the new tunnels—where there was light, where there wasn't, where there were bigthings, where there weren't. The warm smell and the trickle made one line now, and the ruffles and the whisperhole made another. He learned where other tunnels connected in shadow, high up in holes too small for the bigthings but just right for him. But in three awakes he couldn't find a way to the treat. And every time he woke up there were thinsharps, and it took more twists and turns to lose them.

He tried to be good. Lightless kept him safe. He even went back to the ruffles, because they were the only thing to eat where there wasn't light. The thinsharps weren't there anymore, but bigthings came again. His mouth filled with spit every time he went near the warm smell.

He got to nine awakes and then lost count, and then he couldn't stand it anymore.

He crept up, on hands and knees at first as he was used to, then slowly rising to his feet because it hurt his hands, learning how to push himself from one shortfloor to the next. The light grew worse. He put a hand over his eyes and cracked his fingers. There were no bigthing sounds. This might be an asleep, for them. His heart raced faster the closer he got to the warm smell. He felt as cold as stone. He wanted to eat the warm smell and then wrap up in it and sleep safe. A thing that had a smell like that would be very soft.

It came from behind a door. No sounds within. Doors were forbidden if they were outer doors. Only inner doors were allowed. But the smell . . . He pressed the handle down and crept through, silent, silent.

"You there!"

The shout stopped his heart in his chest.

He twisted to scoot back the way he had come, but the loose door moved, tangling him up. The floor here was smooth and his bare soles slipped instead of digging in. This was a chamber, not a tunnel. He was good at tunnels. He was all sliding and tangled here.

A big hand slapped onto his back and closed on rags and skin. It dragged him farther into the chamber so that another big hand could take his wrist. He had to follow his bent-up arm. It was a tiny scrawny arm in the huge hand of the fat bigthing.

"What do you think you're playing at, this time of morning?" She bent down to peer into his face. Her cheeks were like rolled dough. Her lips were fat. Her eyes were milky marbles with blue swirls and tiny black holes. He opened his mouth to scream.

"Look at the state of you. Whose child are you? What happened to your hands?"

An answer tried to come out of him. But it couldn't.

"Come on now, little fellow, who do you belong to?"

There was an answer. There was. He had a thing to say, he knew. But he'd lost it. He'd lost it! Rage rushed up like a great wind from the whisperhole. He snarled and bit and kicked, but when the woman snatched her hand back from his teeth he forgot to run away, and he was biting and punching himself instead.

"Easy, now, easy, for spirits' sake, love, stop that now."

He snarled, and sobbed, and tore with his teeth and punched with his fists. But the big woman didn't hit him, or shout, or make a bright light. She engulfed him. Her thick arms scooped him up and pulled him in so that he sank into the doughy softness of her.

Something warm. Something to go around him. This wasn't exactly it. But it was close.

It murmured like the whisperhole. It moved in a rocking motion, but didn't trip and tangle like the door. It surrounded him, but wasn't cold like a tunnel. It was warm. It felt safe.

After a while, it gave him a soft sweet thing to eat, and then another, and then no more because he'd be sick.

It put something cool on his hands and wrapped them up clean. It hid him from some other bigthings that came. It made them go away. It said hard things to them but nice things to him.

He liked it, even though it made him cry.

Maybe he could stay.

The Knee

Pelufer started awake a moment before she heard Nolfi's warning.

She was in a bed, not wrapped in blankets in some field. There was a wall at her head, not a hedgerow tree or bush. She was jammed against Elora's back, with Caille sprawled half across her and the covers kicked into a tangle at their feet. Though the window was shuttered and the air was close, she was in a good solid room under a sturdy roof in the house of Jiondor's cousin, and until some danger sense woke her she had thought they might finally be safe.

"Get up!" Nolfi whispered through the window slats. "Wake up, get up. Someone's turned in from the road."

Elora stirred and muttered in sleepy protest. Pelufer jumped up to open the shutters, then sorted quickly through the hand-me-downs left for morning wear, tossing the biggest clothes onto Elora. "Who?" she said as Nolfi leaned in the window.

"Two of them. On foot. I couldn't see any more before I ran back here."

Nobody else would be making for an offroad farmhouse in the dead of night. Pelufer dragged their travel sack from under the bed. She stuffed in clothes for Caille and threw it to Nolfi.

"Is it morning?" Elora said, tugging blearily at the tunic lying on her, trying to make sense of the dark.

"Get Caille's shoes on." Pelufer stripped off her nightshirt and pulled on droopy hose and too-long shirt. "Give her to Nolfi."

Elora understood, then, and moved quickly.

The farmstead was well back from the road, up a winding path through coppice oaks that made good hiding. They'd arrived at midday, and Pelufer had spent the afternoon exploring furlongs and headlands, fixing an escape route in her mind while Elora, claiming a need for time alone, had sat watch by the path. Pelufer had shown her bolthole to Nolfi just before supper, then took the evening watch while Nolfi napped. Jiondor's relatives had not questioned their behavior. They were children, and still new here.

Elora passed Caille to Nolfi through the window. Pelufer climbed out after, into the dim light of a half moon diffused through haze. Elora was just behind, with her shoes in her hand. "Put her on my back," she said to Nolfi, and Caille, who had been working up to sleepy tears, wrapped arms and legs around her and laid her head down to go back to sleep. Elora used to carry her that way all the time. She was too big for it now, but there was no choice. The plan was for Nolfi to stay behind and tell the killers they had gone, so they would not wake or harm Jiondor's folk.

There wasn't time. They heard the huffing of a dog straining at a lead, and then the dangerous man and flowery woman emerged from the oak-bordered path into the farmstead's front yard.

They had tracked them with the cowdog. Seeing how it stayed by Caille in the tavern, the woman must have made its master trade it.

"Get the dog!" Pelufer said, snatching up the travel sack.

"I'll try," Nolfi said, and pushed her. "Go!"

They ran, dodging around the side of the house and through the shadows between sheds.

They heard words, a scuffle, an oath, a yelp, an outcry.

"Nolfi . . ." Elora moaned.

"Don't turn," said Pelufer. Skewed bars of yellow light fell beside them and then away as they raced between vegetable and herb gardens. The relatives had woken, lit a lamp. "Don't stop."

Faster even when Elora wasn't carrying Caille, Pelufer took the lead. She relied on memory and shape-sense to navigate the baulks and gores. She stayed by the hedgerows where she could and avoided the dewpond on its rise. At the end of the farthest field, they crossed a headland, jumped a ditch, and scrambled up a woodbank. At the woods' edge, Elora took over. She made a way through dense briar and hawthorn that had nearly stopped Pelufer's exploration; it simply yielded to her, and Pelufer squeezed through in her wake, leaving no sign of their passage. Elora moved quickly through pollard hazel and ash, never tripping on roots, never crashing into trunks in the dark. She could feel the wood, through her skin, through the soles of her feet. Pelufer hung on to Caille's nightshirt and followed, blind except for Elora's shine.

"Rest," Elora said, halfway in. They were in timber trees now, mature ones past time for logging. On the other side the woodland opened again into pasture, and across the pasture was the road Pelufer was aiming for. "She's too heavy."

Caille was squirming to get down anyway, jostled from sleep and now frightened and upset. Pelufer tried to calm her and explain things while Elora caught her breath.

Back through the woods, they heard the dog rasping.

Caille's head came up. "He wants me."

"I know," Pelufer said. "If you touch him, can you make him go home?"

Caille shrugged. Her body felt stubborn and resistant. Pelufer sighed and tried again to explain. Caille refused to understand the danger. She was getting angry at her sisters for being tense and afraid all the time. She hadn't liked being on the road and she wanted to go back to the farmhouse.

The dog was getting closer. They could hear the killers' boots crunching through underbrush. Pelufer thrust the sack at Elora and hefted Caille up against the front of her with a grunt. "Ready?"

With Caille's weight transferred, Elora was as swift and light-footed as Pelufer was heavy and plodding. The woods invigorated her; in the midst of their thriving growth, she came to life, all fear and weariness lifting. Pelufer followed the ruddy shine of her. When she stopped and turned, letting Pelufer catch up, her eyes gleamed like rubies in the darkness.

Pelufer unlocked her hands, deposited Caille, and stood panting for a moment. Then she said, "Elora," and took a breath.

"What?" Elora couldn't stop moving. She spun in circles, dancing from tree to tree, her head flung back and her long hair flying coppery around her. She was drunk on living woodland. They had dwelled too long in town and poisoned forests.

She looked the way Pelufer dreamed her mother looked.

"We can't just keep running. As long as they have the dog and we have Caille, they'll find us."

Caille frowned. "No kill," she said, a sullen warning.

"No, no, I wouldn't hurt the dog," Pelufer said, too quickly. "I want you to send him home. But we have to stop the man and the woman for a little while to do it."

She looked to Elora then, but Elora was full of the night and the forest, and her shining eyes weren't fixed on the right things.

"You have power here," she prompted. "You have to use it."

Elora stopped still, facing the depth of trees. "I have love here," she said. "It can't be used the way you want."

"Fine," Pelufer said, thinking *Pest, pest, stupid pest*. "I'll do it, then. Just stay out the way." Her sisters and their poxy should-and-shouldn'ts. This was *real*, this was *important* . . .

She looked up into the branches overhead, and saw what she needed. She was a good climber, and her side teeth were strong. The creepers here were strong enough to hold, but not so strong she couldn't gnaw through them. She had it set up in a few long breaths. A trader's solution. Ingenuity. She stationed herself by the base of the tree, and kept telling herself how clever she was so her hands wouldn't shake so badly.

The dog's choked panting came first, the scrabble of its feet, followed by the hard tread of boots. They weren't trying to be stealthy. The dog writhed and tried to bark. The man loosed it. It ran to Caille's hiding place, then turned and snarled. The killers advanced on the spot, saying they wouldn't hurt anyone, they only needed some help. Just another step . . . one more . . .

Pelufer hauled down on the vines with all her weight. A pair of dying branches ripped free and came plummeting down in a whoosh of leaves and twigs. The man and the woman went down under them.

Pelufer hefted a branch she had chosen for a club and braced herself. Either they would get up, or names would come.

With a cry, Elora rushed out to pull the branches off them.

"Elora, you idiot! Get away!"

The woman thrashed free. Elora fell back with a cry. The woman looked around wildly, then lunged for her.

Pelufer swung the club. The blow took the woman in the ear. This time she didn't get up.

Elora flung herself down between the man and the woman. "Spirits, sweet spirits, don't let them be dead . . ."

"They're not dead," Pelufer said, relaxing. Caille would have gone spare if they were, and . . . "I'd have felt it."

"They're breathing," Elora said as if she hadn't heard. She freed their packs and shoved them aside. "Caille, come here. I need you to tell me if they're all right."

"Don't touch them, Caille," Pelufer said, kneeling by the long pack the woman had been carrying.

"We have to help them," Elora said. She cleared broken pieces of branch away, her hands lingering a little on the shattered wood, as if its hard flesh could tell her the extent of the damage it had done to the soft human flesh. "Caille . . ."

"Don't touch them, Caille!"

Pelufer's tone was so sharp and so hard that Caille shrank into herself. She looked from Pelufer to Elora, her shape uncertain in the gloom. The cowdog sat by her, a blur of white head and ruff, its black body blending into the dark.

"We'll go while we have the chance," Pelufer said, unbuckling the woman's pack. Quick, she had to be quick, take what was worth taking and be gone before they woke up.

"We can't leave them like this."

"They hurt Nolfi."

"We'll make sure they're all right and then go check on him."

"We have to go, that's what all this was for!"

"We can't just run all the time. We can't just *escape* things."

Pelufer cried out, slamming her hand down on the half-opened pack. "Why *not*?"

"Because you have to be responsible for what you leave behind you in the world."

Father's words again. Father, who'd left a trail of vomit and drink spill through his last years. They'd saved themselves this time. They didn't need him. They had to get out of here.

Her hand hurt. She looked down at the pack. It was hard enough to hurt her hand when she slammed it. She reached inside, questing through layers of cloth wrappings.

"Those farmers were kind to us. They took us in. We'll check them and Nolfi and then we'll take the dog and go." Elora was pressing leaves to a cut on the man's head. "If we tie them . . ."

"You were willing to run a few breaths ago!"

"I was scared. I was wrong."

The woods had changed her.

Pelufer set the pack down and picked up the club. A queer, delicious feeling went through her arms into her body.

"Tie them, then," she said softly.

Pouncing on the compromise, Elora started lashing the tough creepers around their ankles. She didn't look up. She didn't see Pelufer's left hand lock in above her right, testing the resistance of weight against grip.

When the killers were trussed at wrist and ankle, Pelufer said, "Take Caille. Go back to the house. Make her wait while you look. If it's bad, don't let her see."

A low whine started in Caille's throat, echoed by the dog. Elora, understanding in a rush of horror, took hold of her, trying to shield her. "No."

"They'll always find us," Pelufer said. "They'll always hurt the people we leave behind. Anyone who helps us."

"We don't know that they've hurt anyone!"

"Names came off them both. They killed. They both killed."

"Pel, we have to *fix* them! We'll tell someone, there must be keepers somewhere, we'll tell them—"

"We promised Mamma. We promised Padda. Fixing them would give it away. Telling someone would give it away."

"Then we'll give it away! Oh, sweet spirits, Pelufer, put that down, *please.* We have the dog, they can't track us anymore . . ."

"They'll find a way."

"*We don't know what they did!*"

"I know what they did." Ardis, Traig, Areil, Bendik, all dead by the woman's hand. Deilyn, Niseil, Astael, Sowryn, Vaen, Coenn, Daeriel, Perchis, Vebryn, all dead by the man's hand.

"No kill," Caille pleaded. She was crying. Elora was crying. But Elora must have seen some sense in it, because she was holding Caille back. She was crying because she didn't have any arguments anymore. These people had killed, and they would kill again, and they would never stop tracking them.

"Pelufer," Elora said, "if you do this, you'll be speaking their names for the rest of your life."

Pelufer thought about that as she raised the club. She had to let it fall almost right away. It was too heavy. But if she swung it, she only had to give it a good wrenching start and its own weight would pull it the rest of the way. She could do this. She could end the threat. She'd always wanted to be a fighter. Fighters killed people. Fighters killed each other. What difference would two more names make? She'd already clubbed the woman once. . . .

She was on her knees. She dragged a leg forward to plant a foot, to push herself standing. She might have only moments before they woke. She might not be able to do it if their eyes were open. She had to strike now.

"*NO KILL!*" Caille screeched, breaking free of Elora, and flung herself on Pelufer. On one knee, Pelufer couldn't balance against her sister's barreling impact. She fell beside the woman. Not close enough to touch. But she dropped the club. And the woman woke up. There was no slow awakening. She was dead out, and then she wasn't.

She rolled toward Pelufer. Pelufer scrambled out of the way, pulling Caille with her, then shoved her sister toward Elora. "Take her! Run!"

The woman's bound hands closed like a pair of tongs around Pelufer's ankle. From the edge of her eye Pelufer saw Elora heft their sister and retreat. Darkness swallowed them. She kicked out but couldn't connect—the woman swerved or ducked her head, she was quicker than any grownup had a right to be. Pelufer flipped over, wrenching her ankle around, but somehow the woman kept hold. Pelufer scrabbled backward. The gnarled roots of an ancient tree came around her like arms. Not fair, not fair—the forest was supposed to help her, she was Elora's sister! But the tree stopped her backward-crabbing flight, and the woman's hands would not release her. She couldn't kick now. Her legs went tingly-numb and limp as the bubbles expanded in her blood and behind her eyes.

"No," said the woman. "No more running."

Pelufer could barely hear her over the rush of sound from her own mouth. Efrein, Liya, Istriel . . . a dozen names came out of her, and she was retching, choking, and the woman would not let go. She couldn't kick, she couldn't struggle, she couldn't shove or scratch her way free. She couldn't do anything but let the names go through her, and wait till they stopped, till she could breathe again.

"Is that it?" the woman said as the fit eased. "You only say them once and they stop? What happened to Areil and Bendik this time?" She gave Pelufer's ankle a jerk. "Come on, girl, I asked you a question. I killed someone named Areil and someone named Bendik. Who were they? Are they gone? You only feel them once?"

"*No!*" Pelufer cried, seeing Elora loom shining over the woman. The man's carry knife glinted in her hand.

The woman rolled again, bowling Elora's legs out from under her, then push-hopped through the bracken to the club that lay where Pelufer had dropped it. Twisting her bound hands, she locked palms and fingers around the base of it, and got to her knees. Her ankles were still tied. She couldn't run. She knelt, brandishing the club.

"I won't hurt you," she said. "We'd never have hurt you, you fool girls. Stop trying to kill me."

Elora had ahold of Pelufer's shirt and was hauling herself upright. She was looking into the canopy overhead, gauging angles and weights. Tears streaked her face. What Pelufer had done with vines and weak branches, Elora could do with one touch to the trunk of a sound tree.

"No," Pelufer said. "No, Elora, stop. You don't have to." She saw the dim shine of Caille huddled in the shadows. Someone had to go to her.

"I won't let her kill you," Elora said, every word an agony.

"It's all right." Pelufer didn't know how to explain. She got up and walked unsteadily toward where the man lay, but she didn't touch him—not yet. Instead she knelt down by the pack she had half opened. Her hands knew what they would find now, groping past layers of clothes and oddments. She pulled out a long cloth-wrapped object, uncovering one end to reveal a wire-wound grip. Uncovering more, she found the scabbard, and freed enough of the long weapon that its blade gleamed silver in the dappling of hazy moonlight. She stared at the liquid run of half-light along the metal, the shadow of the fuller, the edge so sharp it cut her to look at.

"She was a fighter," she told Elora. "That's why she killed. All the people she killed were trying to kill *her*."

Elora, pushed past all bearing, let out a string of profanity that would have made their father proud. "*You didn't know that before?*"

"I ran away," Pelufer said, sheathing the blade with a shiver and then looking at the woman. At Risalyn. "I ran away too soon. I should have learned from the spirit wood. If I don't run right away, if I stay and . . . let it . . . finish . . . I know more."

"Then you bloody well better touch the other one," Elora said, "and don't let go till you know all about him, too." She got up to fetch Caille. Pelufer only realized that Caille had been shrieking when it stopped.

"How about untying me first?" said Risalyn, laying the club down and offering her wrists.

"Not till we know about him," Elora said, throwing her a hard trader's look.

"I can tell you that he hasn't come to yet," Risalyn said, "and that you might kill him yet if somebody doesn't fetch the cloak from his pack and get him warm, at the very least."

Pelufer leaned over to comply. She was shaking, as much from cold as from the fit of names and what she'd almost done right before that. Things were growing steadily more visible as gray morning crept down through the treetops. Dawn came colder in the Highlands than in Gir Doegre. She laid the man's cloak across him, then found a coat in his pack, too, and threw it to Elora to put around Caille, though she wanted to keep it for herself.

Then she tucked the cloak around the man.

Only a few names came. She had already said the others in the spirit wood. They didn't come again. But she held on, and let the memories go through her, the snatches of life embedded in the last intense sensations before death. That's what the names were: the last burning flares of self, the explosions of spirit as they left the body. When you killed, it left a shadow on you, a burn mark. Where people had died there were burn marks, too, and where the bonefolk had consumed them.

After long breaths, she drew away, and sat with her knees against her chest, hugging her legs. Caille and Elora tried to comfort her, but she shook them off. She didn't want anyone to touch her right now.

"Well?" said Elora.

"Some died on a blade. They were angry. They were trying to kill him, and they were angry that they got stabbed instead. Some of them—" A whimper came out of her, and she pressed her forehead into her knees, fighting hard not to raise the axe in her mind and cut those limbs off. They were bad ones. "Never mind," she said. "It's not important. The others . . . most didn't know that . . . it was him."

Risalyn nodded as if she understood this, and was about to speak when the man's eyes fluttered open and he arched in pain against his bonds and spoke her name. In response she said, "You're all right, Yuralon. Your hard head has saved you again."

He looked from one to the other of the girls, then tried to raise his head to look at Risalyn. His eyes rolled up and his head sank back. It seemed he'd passed out. Then he said, "Someone's made a gelatin mold of my skull."

Risalyn grinned and was about to return some banter when Pelufer said suddenly, "They were grateful."

"What?" Yuralon said sharply, then groaned, then gritted his teeth as if even groaning hurt. "Who?" he managed, with tight care.

"Diandre and Korras," Pelufer said. "I didn't feel them in the spirit wood. I didn't hang on. I should have."

"What do you mean, they were grateful?" Risalyn said, all humor gone.

"They were relieved. They were happy. Soliri was too, but she didn't know it was you. But it was, wasn't it? And Rajulon, and Thandra, and . . ."

"What is she on about, Yur?"

The man looked at Pelufer for a long time, and then winced and turned his head away as far as he dared move it. But he said, "Thank you, child. I had hoped . . . but there was no way to know. It seemed a kindness. It was meant to be a kindness. Yet one always doubts."

"They were sick," Pelufer explained. She looked at Elora. "He was a fighter, too. Those names that came off me in the spirit wood, those were the . . ." She had no word for it. "They were harder deaths. Scarier and more sudden. All deaths are sudden, I guess, but those were . . ."

"Violent," Risalyn supplied. "Shocking."

Pelufer nodded. "Those other ones weren't. They were quieter.

They didn't burn in as hard. But they're there. He killed them. Because they were sick. Or hurt. They were in so much pain. They felt so horrible. All they wanted was to go."

"Mercy killings," Elora breathed, as if it was the most terrible thing she'd ever considered.

"You don't know, Elora. You don't know how those people felt."

"Maybe they could have been cured!"

The man tried to shake his head, then thought better of it and said, "No. We had done everything we could."

"You're not menders," Elora said. It was an accusation.

"We never said we were," Risalyn replied. "Not the way you mean. We don't wear white—not that we would, not in the Strong Leg, anyway. You people have a twisted way of hanging on to tradition."

Pelufer said nothing, and tried not to look at Elora, but she could feel the shape of her, the anger and the guilt. There was suddenly so much she wanted to say—about workings and people like Mireille, about spirit woods and people like Anifa, about things that everyone took for granted that maybe weren't the way they thought—but she wouldn't have known where to begin.

Risalyn said, "But we're trying to be menders, in a different way. We've learned what healing arts we can. We make our way as healers, as we can—doing penance for all the folk we killed, I suppose, though Yuralon takes that harder than I do, as far as I'm concerned we were all trying to kill each other in the magewar and I was just better and faster. But it turned out the sides weren't as clear-cut as we thought. And it turned out that there are still some folk running about who are angry at mages for something. We don't know what. But we're trying to mend it. And if that means killing folk who kill, better the deed should be on our hands. They're already stained."

There had been no sound in the brush. The cowdog sat quietly. The fighters hadn't looked up. But at those last words from Risalyn, Pelufer felt some shift in the space between the trees behind her, and she twisted around hard. Standing there in silence, blended almost imperceptibly into the tree trunks, was a man perhaps two nines and three, straight-backed and handsome, with black hair and pale skin and eyes the dark blue of the deepest sapphire on a stonemonger's stall.

"Who are *you*?" she burst out, and then her sisters and the fighters saw him, too.

He surveyed the downed, trussed fighters and said, "I came to rescue you from them."

"We don't need rescuing," Pelufer said.

"So it seems," he replied.

"I don't see a blade on you," Risalyn said, with a grin that looked like a snarl, just as Elora asked darkly, "How much did you hear?"

"Enough to deduce what your friend Jiondor would not tell me. And I do without blades, for the most part." He smiled at both of them. Pelufer saw Risalyn cock her head, reevaluating, and she didn't need to turn to feel Elora melt. He was too beautiful. She would have to be the one to judge him. "Jiondor should be along shortly, with the farmholders who sheltered you," he went on. "They fell behind me in the dark. Your friend Nolfiander showed us the route as well as he could with a turned ankle, but when I saw the glow up ahead I didn't need him anymore."

"He turned that ankle trying to snatch the dog," Risalyn said with a wider grin. "Brave young fellow. But we were determined to catch you. He came to no harm."

Pelufer should have been relieved, but she and Elora were both staring at the stranger, all thoughts of scuffles and night chases fled.

"Glow?" Elora said softly.

Pelufer swore under her breath and got to her feet. "That would have been the moonlight," she said. "There was a break in the clouds." No one had ever seen Elora or Caille as she had seen them. No one *could*. If he had . . . The thought filled her with more terror than any of them knowing about her knack. Too many people knew, now. It was all right if they knew about her. She could take care of herself. But if he had seen Elora . . . if he had seen Caille . . .

The man looked at her for a breath, then made his face go gentle and replied, "No doubt." Turning to Risalyn, he said, "I'd like to know more about these killers you say you're trailing."

"Would you, now?" she said, cocking her jaw. "Why don't you tell us what you're doing here at all? These girls don't know you. You're no friend to them."

"Nor were you, until some extraordinary events took place. And I can't help but notice that they have not untied you."

Pelufer rectified that. She'd rather have Risalyn's blade arm free, whether this stranger was armed or not. But Risalyn went immediately to tend Yuralon. "Who are you?" Pelufer said again to the stranger.

"My name is Louarn. I'm a crafter, a traveler. Jiondor will vouch for me when he arrives." He looked around. "They must have lost their way. But the wood isn't large. Our voices will carry. They won't be long."

"You keep changing the subject," Pelufer said. "Who *are* you? What do you want with us, or them?"

"I thought they were killers. I thought you had proof of their deeds. I misconstrued the kind of proof you had, as I found out from Jiondor on our journey here—but he did not divulge your secret. Perhaps I can explain it all to you in more comfortable surroundings."

Pelufer said, "You don't want them to hear what you have to say. You don't trust them. They don't trust you. Jiondor's not here. Nolfi's not here. You could have said anything to them. Why did Jiondor come? Maybe he didn't. Maybe you're lying." By the time she finished, her own words had scared her. *Time to go, Elora,* she thought. *Time to go!* But Elora was tired and melty, and Caille was exhausted, and she couldn't make this decision by herself, and Elora didn't want to run anymore. Maybe Jiondor *would* come . . .

"Here," the stranger said. "Take my hands. Let me prove myself. What can I do to you, one man alone? Your bladed friend would skewer me in a heartbeat—see, she's strapped on her weapon, she's ready to spring to your defense. My name is Louarn. I'm a crafter. I've harmed no one. I'm trying to find folk who may be doing harm. It's a perilous search. I do not trust easily. Neither do you. I understand that. You sense haunts, do you not? You sense those whom a killer has killed. I have not killed. Take my hands. See for yourself."

Pelufer nearly growled in frustration, but with the secret out, it was all there was to do. She could not gauge him from his stance, let alone his voice; he seemed calm, blameless, earnest, but there was a craftedness to it, as if he was a created thing, a fashioned seeming. And if he could see . . .

There was more to him than there appeared to be. But at least she could satisfy herself that he had no deaths on him.

She walked up and placed her hands in his.

And felt the bubbles rise inside, felt her belly roil, her mouth open. Saw his eyes go wide. Felt his hands twitch, then grip hers hard. She couldn't have let go; she was stuck to him, lint to rubbed wool in winter, a tongue to a frozen iron bar.

Then the names came.

Pass through.

He came into the world on a wail of bereavement and slammed into a wall of cold. He fell, curled into a ball, and rocked himself, whimpering. After a time, the whimpers subsided. He sat up. The forest was wrong. The smells were wrong, the colors were wrong. Blue sky beyond green leaves. Air brushed against him like a living thing. There had been no moving air where he had come from.

He examined his body. His limbs were long and ungainly in relation to his trunk, but looked too short. His hands and feet were too large for them. There was hair at chest and crotch, downy along forearms and shins and thighs, a patchy stubble at chin and cheek, a tousled mass at the top of his head. He fingered the cartilage at his ears, the bone of his nose. He had not become what he had hoped to be.

Yet he was whatever he was. He got up, and set off through the wood.

He was empty. He knew that feeling. Hunger. He filled his belly with peaberries and sheepherd's lettuce and his mouth with the taste of tart sugar and gall. He drank deep of icy runoff. Light angled down through the trees like spears, then was swallowed by shadow. He dug a hole in bracken and humus and slept covered in fir boughs. When the light returned, he found a woodsman's shack. He ate moldy flatbread, and belted baggy, musty cloth on himself for a second skin to keep off the cold. He gathered cones and seeds and kindling from the forest and brought them back to the shack. Rain came, fragrant and soothing. The light went. He made a fire in the small round iron stove, boiled acorns into a paste, smeared it into his mouth with his fingers. He slept wrapped in coarse blankets and dust, then swept the shack out and scattered a layer of green needles on the floor. The next day, he foraged farther. He came to the edge of a field. He saw people there, shaped like himself. He wondered what they could tell him about this unfamiliar world that he seemed to know without knowing it. But he stayed clear, kept to the forest's edge, moved on silent bare feet through the underbrush. He returned to his shack empty-handed and with his heart beating hard, and lay down to sleep hungry.

Moments later he startled awake because he had begun to dream. He didn't remember dreaming before. In the crooked half-light between worlds, he'd glimpsed a blackness, a cobbled-together thing like an assemblage of old sticks. He thought it spoke to him, one word, which he tasted on his own lips as his body spasmed back into the waking world:

Tchatichoch.

Danger.

He heard it like an echo in the shack, though the dull flat wooden walls would reflect no sound of dreams; he heard it echo in the resonant chamber of his skull and knew that he had spoken aloud.

Danger. Dreams were a danger. There was danger in dreams.

He must not dream.

He tried and failed to sleep dreamless. The dream always darkened, took on shape, opened into a realm of its own, fraught with significance and power. Deep, ineffable forest lurked along the byways of sleep. He trained himself to wake each time the darkness threatened. Though maddened with weariness, he did not give up. After a threeday he began to dream while waking. Things moved among the trees, along the ground, at the edges of vision. Things that were not there. Dream-things, impinging on the realm of waking. In the middle of a task, his eyes would slide closed, and the black stick thing would clatter toward him.

After a nineday, he learned that those snatches of sleep were enough. He sat wrapped in his blanket on the doorsill in moonlight and watched the movement of leafshadow on the ground. When he heard the clattering stick figure approach, he jerked awake, and looked for repetition in the curds of cloud crossing the moon, in the shadowed valleys of the moon's silver disk. In place of dreams he gave his mind pattern. The striations in an old oak's bark. The twists and curls of a complicated knot. Spirals he carved on stone with the frisson of doing a forbidden thing. He would lose himself in waking vision, following the spiral, tracing the furrows . . .

He wove puzzles, braiding twig and stem and vine into intricate workings to trick the eye and capture the mind. He studied the construction of the shack, how the woodsman had made it, how the nails and joinery worked. With a whittling knife and an old axe and other spare tools, he built another shack on its model, hardly aware of what he did but emerging from the dream with a memory of making in his hands, a sturdy construct to admire.

He must find other models. He must have more to occupy his famished mind. That was the only way to keep the dreams away. Or to replace them.

This world was made on a different model from the one he'd known. He could barely remember that world anymore. Understanding this one would be the work of a lifetime. It would keep him safe from himself.

He set off into it.

The world was more different than he knew.

He came into the fields where folk worked, and they drove him off. He came into the towns where people traded, and they shunned him. He lurked in ditches, behind walls, along byways, listening to them speak. He practiced softly to himself until he believed he had copied the patterns correctly. But when he approached travelers on the road, in daylight, simply to ask where work might be found, the men cursed him and drove him off with stones. Holding wads of cattail to his bleeding head, he crouched under a hedge and made a careful comparison. He was not garbed as they were. He was filthy and matted. They had meat on their bones. His stood out starkly. Bones and tatters looked right to him, but not to them. He must find better food, and better garb, and a place to bathe himself. Objects and structures were not the only constructs to be puzzled out. He must master folkways, too.

Food came first. In the forest there was enough to eat, but towns and tilled fields afforded little more than roadside fodder, and that wouldn't fatten him up sufficiently to make him presentable.

He looked across the fields, the delicious greenness of new soy set out in neat rows against the rich black of turned soil. Too young to eat. He waited until his head stopped bleeding and the sun dipped below the edge of a rise. Then he made his way across the fields, careful of the tender plantings, and came silent on his unshod feet to the edge of the barnyard.

A dog eyed him warily. He held out a hand and beckoned softly before it could bark. Suddenly it came toward him, tail giving one hesitant sweep and then its whole body bursting into a wagging wiggle as he scratched its ruff and stroked between its eyes. "Go on now," he told it, voice low. "Go on to your bed now and lie down, there's a good fellow." With a last lick at his hand, it obeyed him.

He glanced around, sniffed, then went straight for the root cellar. Rich starches would be a good start for him, wrapped in leaves and baked in a fire's coals until they could be chewed.

He was standing with a turnip in one hand and a white potato in the other, weighing which to choose and how to bag them, when he felt the tines of a hay fork in his back.

He went to sleep in the doughy woman's arms, and when he woke up there were no thinsharps. There was a different softness under him, a different wonderful smell, sweet and rich and fresh. He sat up in a pile of long yellow bendable things. They were scratchy but they were good to lie on.

He turned his head. His eyes went wide and his mouth opened.

It was the biggest thing he'd ever seen. It stood on all fours, and instead of hands it had hard round feet, and its legs and arms bent different ways from his, and the arms seemed to be legs too. It had a long neck, and a long head, and its ears went straight up. It snuffled at his chest and his neck. Its nose was soft. Its whiskers tickled his face. He laughed, and it blew air through big nose holes and tossed its head and swung it down to the scratchy sweet things he was lying on. It started to eat them.

He tried one. It smelled good, but it didn't taste good.

Then he saw the other. It was half the size of the big one, hiding behind it, peering out at him.

He looked into its dark, liquid eyes, and was filled with an aching sweetness.

"That's Purslane," said a kind, low voice.

He did not look up. He could not tear his eyes away. Slowly, he held his hand out, with the long thing he'd been tasting, what the big one liked to eat. The little one came toward him on spindly legs. It sniffed the long thing but didn't take it. It sniffed the wrappings on his hand. He dropped the long thing so he could touch it and it clattered backward. But he kept his hand out. It extended its neck, took a step, took another step, and then its neck was under his fingertips and then his arms were around it. He pressed his face into it. It was warm. It smelled good.

"He likes you," said the kind, low voice. "And a good thing, that. His mother slipped her stall again, the canny wench. She's not supposed to be nosing around little boys we've laid down to sleep in the hay."

He looked up, afraid they would take Purslane away. He looked up into eyes as dark and liquid and gentle as Purslane's eyes.

"Have you slipped your stall, young fellow?"

He blinked, then turned his face back in to the warm sweet neck, but Purslane pulled away and shoved his head up under his mother. A hank of hair on his backside twitched back and forth.

"He doesn't understand," the doughy woman said. She was standing by the man with the low voice. He was nearly as big as she was, but darker. "I don't think he's understood a word I've said to him." She knelt down to bring her round face level with his face. "I'm glad you were all right waking up on your own. I shouldn't have left you, but we didn't want to wake you with all our talking. Are you all right?"

He nodded; then, overcome by a yawning empty hole opening inside him, he reached his arms out to be held—then yanked them back, terrified that he would fall, and scooted against the wall, his heels digging into the hay. He wanted to punch himself. He balled his fists.

"None of that now, love," the woman said. "Hug yourself. Like this. That's right. Hug yourself tight."

He did, and he felt better. She scooped him up the way she had before, and she and the man with the low voice sat next to each other on squares of old hay, and she held him in her lap, and the man gave him a soft thing to eat. It wasn't as sweet as the warm things the woman gave him before, and it had harder things inside it that crunched between his teeth, but right now it tasted even better.

"Will you keep him, then?"

"Of course."

"If I could . . ."

"I know you can't."

"Just till his parents are found."

"I don't think we're going to find his parents."

There was a long silence, with just the sound of his own crunchings, and Purslane's mother munching hay.

"He must have run wild for days. I can't imagine what he ate."

"He's had a hard time of it, that's clear enough. But there's something about him. Something . . ." The man sat up very straight.

He shrank back against the doughy woman, but the man took his chin in one hand and lifted his face. The hand was warm, and gentle, but firm, not to be pulled away from.

"Eiden strike me," he said. "I know this child."

The Knee

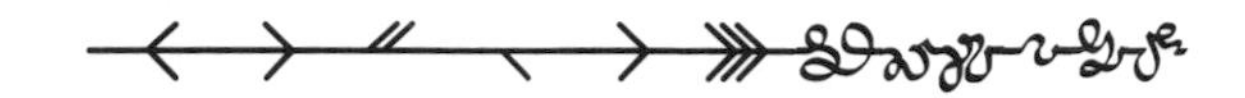

Who is he then?"

"I don't know what they called him. He's Pirra and Alliol and Ellerin's."

They looked down at him, then at each other.

"No reaction to the names," the woman said. "Are you sure?"

"They died on Ve Galandra. This boy's been untended at least that long."

"I never saw that child of theirs. Hardly believed they had one."

"They didn't let him roam."

"He's never seen a horse before, so that much rings true. And if he saw it happen . . . well, that would explain some things. But how would you know? What would a stablemaster be doing visiting the Ennead's head warders?"

There was longer silence then, and he looked up, trying to make sense of what was passing between the man and the woman. Something strained, strung tight. And then it relaxed.

"I fostered this child to them," the man said. "He takes after his father, though he has his mother's coloring. I know where he came from. But those are names he can't ever hear. Nor are Alliol's and Pirra's and Ellerin's, now they're gone."

"Should we send him away?"

"He's too little. Five and some, if I reckon the years right. It would be difficult to get him out of the Holding. They know the warders had a child. They'll want him, if he shows a light."

"Can you hide him?"

"I've done it before."

"He'll be happy here. He's in love with that foal."

"He'll need a name."

"You choose. You'll be his father now."

The big man regarded him with pursed lips, then said, "He reminds me of a man I knew, good man named Mellas, loved his horses better than he loved himself. That's a common name, a Heartlands name. He looks a Heartlander. It'll bring no attention on him."

The big man laid a hand on his head, and he leaned into its warmth, its strength and protection, and the doughy woman shifted him into the man's arms, and it felt a safer place, though not as soft.

"You'll be Mellas, my boy, and we'll make a runner of you, and keep you as safe as we can here until you can make your own way. Safe from the Ennead, at any rate, and spirits willing you won't show a light. You'll be all right, Mellas. You're with Bron now."

Louarn flung the girl away and held his hands before him as if seared.

"Mellas," he said, testing the name. So like, so like the thing he was supposed to say, and yet that wasn't it. But close. Close enough. "I'm Mellas." It shocked the man and the woman, because he hadn't talked before, and their faces made him laugh, and then they laughed, too, and he knew it would be good here. "I'm Mellas!"

"I'm Louarn," he said, reeling. He could feel the baker's doughy embrace, the foal's soft coat against his cheek, the stablemaster's hand warm on his head, feel horror and tragedy loom in the next breath, and he threw an arm out as though he could ward himself, as though he could unmake the unbearable griefs if he could just stave off their return. "Louarn," he said, "I'm Louarn. . . ."

"Now, I hope you're not thinking to eat those raw. Be in a world of sickness, you do that."

The tines withdrew enough for him to turn toward the man's voice.

"Made friends with old Skulk there, did you? He never minded me so well when I sent him to his bed."

"He's a good dog."

"That he is." The farmer gave him a wry once-over and set the hay fork on its points, propped against the cellar door. "What's your name, then, lad?"

He looked down at himself, the shreds and tatters clothing him, his bare dirty feet, his hands holding the tubers.

"I . . . don't know." He tried; he cast about inside for a name, but there was nothing. Only the shreds and tatters of another world. Pass through. "I think . . . I've come from a dream."

"Bollocks," the farmer said with a laugh. "From a hungry place, I'll

grant you that. May be a lot of those soon, with the light gone. If spuds were eggs, you'd be the old fox in the gooseyard, you would. Come along, young fox. Let's get you warm, get some clothes on you. Took a knock in the head, looks like. You'll be Louarn, then, till you remember, or until you become something else. 'Louarn' was a word for fox, in the Old Tongue. I remember that, from my prentice days. Never made a wordsmith, though I talk enough for three, wouldn't you say? There's a lad, now, sit on down there, we'll fill a good hot bath for you before you tramp those feet inside the house. Yes, I prenticed as a wordsmith, though whatever passed for a light in me turned out too dim in the end, couldn't cast for sprouts at my trial, and all the better for me when the light went, didn't hurt me hardly at all, you'd not believe what it did to the mages hereabouts. But I remember, some. That's all that trade'll be good for anymore. You'll be Louarn, and that's an end on it. Wrap up tight now, that's good thrice-shrunk wool, and give me these, you'll have them back cooked flaky and tender, and fresh butter from the churn. . . ."

"Louarn," Louarn breathed, staggering back another step, then swaying forward and going to his knees. "Louarn . . ."

never noticed the shy boy in the shadows

breaking the world in the saving of it

It'll be soon, son. Too soon.

Father's quill scritch-scritching on parchment, Mother's hand smoothing him into sleep, Father's weight on the bed until the weight of dreams took him. He loved bedtime. Now he huddled under the covers feeling that dreams were the only way he'd ever leave these chambers, and he woke alone and stumbled to the doorway and found

Father doubled over himself blackening and twisting like a lemon peel on a fire

a shadow of Mother in a bowl of dark water blackening melting

an opening in the wall, no floor beyond it, only little black stone not-floors, one after another, down and down, to ruffles whisperhole thinsharps

shivery air like a fizz of bubbles around a swimmer

Could he have dreamed awry, could the walls be softening? The only thing his dreams had ever wrought before was razored darkness. If he gave in to it, it would dissolve him where he stood. He would drown in memory as darkness pressed in and lose the only hope he'd ever have of making things right.

Don't you know me? Was the pain so bad that you forgot who brought you to this?

The tunnels turned, and the tunnels branched. How would he find the way? He had always known his way through the Holding, even in the dark where the torchman had neglected his duties. You dreamed these passages. They're a reflection of you. *It was a cruel mountain. It taunted him. This was a cruel dream. The stone looked smooth, but the chalk bounced over tiny bumps and his lines came out raggedy. He could return to the passageways he'd dreamed and drown in memory or he could go as far from the Holding as he*

knew no trade except for the fetching of mages but if some craftsfolk would take on a boy too old to prentice

the woodsman's shack the farmer's field the farrier's wagon the cooper's shop the saddler's bench the ironsmith's forge the tinker's cart the weaver's loom the chandler's wax the

My name is Croy. Want to know about bricks, do you?

never noticed the shy boy in the shadows

breaking the world in the saving of it

tried to burrow back into the dark, but it was beyond him now, and anyway there was no choice, his attention wouldn't tear away

"I'm Louarn!" he cried, curled around a pain so terrible he thought it would break him. "*I'm Louarn . . . !*"

The middle girl was sitting where he had cast her down. She had held on to him for a long time after the names came out of her. She had to hold on for a few breaths to get the full story, she'd had to do that with the Girdler, he remembered that, he remembered . . .

The oldest was trying to drag her back, babbling something about names and killers. But the middle one wouldn't be dragged. "Bad things . . . bad things happened to them, they saw . . . I can't . . ." She strained toward Louarn. He shrank away, but his body wouldn't come with him.

"Leave him to me," the sweetsmonger said. "He doesn't look good. Ill or mad, he needs shelter and looking after. We'll sort the rest when we're settled somewhere."

Louarn heard them as if down a long corridor. Their speech was conversation heard by a child with no interest or comprehension but remembered, interpreted, by an adult. His limbs seemed to be too large and very far away, but stunted, ill formed. The Girdlers stood guard, though one was digging for something in a pouch. He must not let them drug him. He saw a fist on the grass in front of his face. His own, at the end of a palsied arm. The other spasmed against his chest. His teeth were clamped. His drawn-up knees would not unclench. He could not control his body. He sensed through layers of other senses, overlays of sound-shadows and darkness.

"I've got to touch him again," the middle girl said. "To be sure."

Louarn heard a low keening come out of himself, but he was unable to move away from her.

"Be sure of what?" said the older girl, plainly terrified. "Names came off him, Pel, we know what that means—"

"Not anymore. Not after *them*." The girl crawled to him as if mesmerized. He could not stop her.

She laid hands on him, and went very still.

He felt nothing but the cold sweat on his skin, the tingle of blood in muscles and joints, an imminent convulsion.

"Boys," she said, blinking. "One had two years on you, Elora. One had a year on Caille. Another . . ."

"He killed *children*?"

"Come away, Pel."

"Sweet spirits—"

"No, it's not like that, get back, get off him! They were dead, those boys. Except they weren't. Their bodies went on and grew and got older. But it was the same body. The same person. I don't know how to . . ."

I'm not Flin?

Of course you're Flin, my sweet. You're you, you're Flin. . . .

You'll be Mellas, my boy, and we'll make a runner of you. . . .

You'll be Louarn, then, till you remember, or until you become something else. You'll be Louarn, and that's an end on it. . . .

The girl looked into him in awe, and said to her sisters, and the sweetsmonger, and the barrow boy, and the Girdlers:

"They're all him. The haunts inside him are all *him*."

His body convulsed. He felt hands on him—Jiondor's, Nolfiander's. They tried and failed to stretch him flat. One pried his mouth open to get at his tongue, lay a stick on it. He gagged, and writhed, and cried out horribly. He was all agony, one body with three vying to inhabit it, there wasn't room for three, he would crack, he would burst. Louarn was reduced to a single cool point of clarity within a burning maelstrom. He could no longer control the man's body, but he felt its torments as though they were his own. A crevasse of darkness opened, toothed with dark steps, *little stone not-floors one after another*, a void, an abyss, *drynumb coldweary hunger*, waking after waking with no escape, no progress, no certainty, no hope.

Vision filled with blood and dimmed to nothing. Bones snapped. A scream tore through the woods, in a voice that had been his.

Flin died in a fall down hard stone steps he did not understand. Mellas died of hunger and thirst lost in cold stone corridors he had dreamed within a dreaming mountain. Louarn had only suspended those deaths, delayed them, escaped them somehow for some temporary time. Now he would live them, and die at last.

He grieved. There were so many crafts still to learn. There was love—he had never felt love, he had wondered when it would come, why it hadn't, and now he'd never know. There was so much of the world still to travel. There was so much he wanted to know.

"No dying," said a child's voice.

New hands touched him.

His muscles unclenched their shattering hold on his bones, released his airway, eased his nails from his palms, uncramped his toes and groin and gut.

Hands touched him, touched his seized heart, returned its rhythm.

Hands touched him, knitted his long bones, reseated the displaced sockets of his spine.

Hands touched him, sealed burst vessels and cleared his eyes, smoothed away the bloody gouges in his palms.

Hands touched him, a child's hands, and his body was whole.

He sat up through a rusty mist, trembling. The pain lingered like an echo, then faded. After long breaths, blessed breaths, he leaned forward to cup the healer's face in his hands. "Spirits, child, what did that cost you?"

Her grin plumped pudgy cheeks into his palms. Her merry eyes, an unearthly shine of emerald and flame, eased back to ordinary hazel as he blinked. Her only answer was a giggle.

"Nothing," said the oldest girl. She was behind her sister and to the side, sitting on the ground, rocking with her arms clasped around her knees, tears on her face. "It costs nothing when it's the way the body wanted to be, when there's no death."

He didn't understand.

"Diseases are alive," she said, bitterly, spitting her explanation as though it was the only way to wipe the stupid awe off his face. "When you heal a sickness, you kill them, so it *costs* you. She doesn't like killing, as you may have noticed."

Standing tense beside her, the middle girl said, "This is what you wanted. Let Caille fix people. Tell people. Give it all away so nobody would die. You wanted this, Elora."

"I didn't."

"You did."

"Shut up!" Elora covered her ears, elbows tight against her knees, folded in on herself. "Shut up, shut up, shut up."

Louarn sat back gracelessly, stunned. His gaze rose to the naked blade the little girl did not see over her shoulder. The Girdlewoman must have drawn it when he leaned forward to touch the child. Ready to run him through if he looked to harm her. But the Girdlewoman hadn't known. None of them had known—not the Girdlers, not Jiondor, not the barrow boy Nolfiander. Their shock mirrored his own.

Not even mages had been capable of this. Not with a touch.

"I don't suppose she could do my head," the other Girdler said wryly. Yuralon. The woman had called him Yuralon.

The child looked at her sisters for permission. *She must have healed me of her own stubborn choice. They tried to stop her, to keep us from knowing.* Elora, the oldest girl, shrugged miserably. "Padda would kill us," she murmured, rocking. "But it's done now. Go ahead."

"Are you really all right?" the barrow boy asked, though he was moving to Elora, to stay helplessly by her as she cried.

Louarn nodded. The movement left him feeling he had three heads, as though two of them flew nearly free and then snapped back into place, elastic. "My body is, at any rate."

They watched with no less awe as the littlest girl pulled the tall Girdler down to her level and laid hands on his bloody head like a benison. He had spoken to ease the tension, not expecting her to do it, and now looked dazed. She glowed like an iron heated red in a forge's flame, and drew her tiny hands from a mended head.

Yuralon probed his skull. "Thank you, child," he whispered.

She shrugged, and sat by her sisters, pulling the cowdog into the circle of one arm. The other thumb crept toward her mouth; the middle sister, barely looking at her, batted it absently away.

"And you?" Louarn said, to the grieving eldest. "Now that we've seen all this, will you show us what you can do?"

"She can't do anything," Pelufer said, quick and harsh. She pulled herself tall, freeing her hands, prepared to defend her sisters however she must. "She was a love child, we had different fathers. She showed a light but now it's gone. She didn't even live with us until—"

The eldest rose slowly, cutting off the escalation of lies. She walked to a sack of blankets, lying half tumbled open a few threfts away, and withdrew two wrapped objects, which she put in Jiondor's hands. Then she stood by an old upright damson tree, one of a scattering beyond which mostly young ash was visible, suggesting some orchard or hedge demarcation overtaken by forest.

The sweetsmonger unwrapped two heads. Though each was only the size of paired fists, it took Louarn a moment to realize that they were made of wood, so lifelike were they. The planes of the features, the hairs on the heads, looked as though the wood had simply, impossibly, just grown that way.

"Nimorin," Jiondor said. "Prendra. These are their parents."

"Our mother made those!" Pelufer cried, squirming and jiggling. "She gave them to us before she died! Elora, *tell them*!"

Elora said, "It's done, Pel. They know. They might as well know it all. It's already over."

"Your alderfolk burned carvings like that," Louarn said, remembering what the spiteful girl Mireille had told him.

"They were afraid," Jiondor said. He looked sad, beaten. "They were afraid that work like this would keep the light from coming back. I'm glad you saved these, Elora. I've never seen such carving in all my life as a trader."

"It's not a carving," Elora said. "It's a working." She laid her hand on the damson trunk beside her. Her muted copper shine became a ruddy glow, like the light of a blood moon low in the sky, or the rich heartwood of the fruit tree she touched. Slowly, magnificently, the tree came into profuse bloom, clouds of white emerging on its branches.

Elora sank down gently as a fallen leaf and slumped against the trunk. White blossoms drifted around her.

Pelufer swore a streak and went to sit her up. She was pale and vague, half in a faint. "I can't believe you did that! That was so *stupid!*"

"That cost her," Louarn said.

Pelufer rounded on him. "It was the wrong time, that tree was done flowering a moon ago, she had to push it. She'll be tired for a day now. Just to answer your stupid poxy question! And after everything we did. I was *sorry* for you!" She was fierce and red-faced, her eyes wild. "A plague on you! A stinking rotting plague on you all! We kept those secrets all our lives! And now you'll try to use us, now everyone will want to use us, Padda *told* us, he *told* us, Elora, why didn't we *listen?* Never get beholden and never let anyone know what you can do, because your lives won't be your own anymore. He *told* us!"

"Padda's dead," Elora said, almost too low to hear.

"*Don't you think I know that?*"

"That's enough." Jiondor pressed the woodwork into Nolfiander's hands and got to his feet. "This is madness. We're going back to the house. We'll sort this out. There'll be no running and there'll be no blades. You two—give them over."

Louarn watched in amazement as the Girdlers handed their sheathed weapons to the sweetsmonger. One of the girls must have explained them to Jiondor when he and the boy arrived. Louarn didn't remember their arrival. They had come while he was swamped in the past. The people standing in this wood were connected now, bound together by extraordinary circumstance. But they were nothing to each other beyond the revelations they had shared.

"Will you let me carry her?" Yuralon asked Pelufer, gesturing to Elora.

"If she will," Pelufer grudged, still ready to fight or bolt.

"I'll take Caille," Nolfiander said.

Caille. The littlest girl was Caille.

"You can't," Pelufer told him. "Your ankle."

Caille looked up, sleepy but expectant, perhaps wondering if she might heal the sprain.

"No," the boy said. "I don't want it. It's too late."

"What are you talking about?" Elora murmured, raising her arms for Yuralon to lift her. The gesture sent a queer twinge through Louarn.

"Not now," Jiondor said, "when we're settled," but Nolfiander stood staunchly and replied, "She could have saved Sel. She could have saved everyone. She could have saved your father."

"I know," Elora said.

They walked in laden silence through woods and fields streaked with morning light. Yuralon bore Elora, whose shine was very dim now. Pelufer bore Caille, who walked the last bit when her sister could no longer manage, the cowdog trotting at their heels. Jiondor bore the girls' carrysack and the longblades, Risalyn her pack and Yuralon's. Louarn supported the limping barrow boy. The boy was nine-and-six years old; though he was brown-eyed and sandy-haired and a Souther, with the turned-up nose and impish look of the mid-Leg, still, Louarn thought, this was how it would feel to walk with Mellas beside him. Caille's five-year-old face plumping into a grin against his hands was how Flin's face might have felt. Pelufer had woken them. It had nearly killed him. Caille had saved his life.

A girl who communed with haunts. A girl who shaped living wood. A girl who could heal injury and illness. Two fighters become mercy killers and healers, yet still bladed, chasing magekillers. Two Gir Doegre traders who only wanted to help and protect.

And me. Whoever, whatever, I am.

A wood. An eerie, wondrous wood, where no winds disturbed the sweet air, where no leaves fell. The sky was lavender, the ground was black, the leaves were gold, the trunks were silver. The smell was chill, metallic, rich. They said he had dreamed himself here, but that was a lie, or a different side of the truth. They had brought him here. They were the only ones who could have found him. And they were making him go.

The trail had forked twice, and split again here.

This is it. You don't get in from the back. There is no back. You get in from the top. Or the sides.

He stood on a platform of shadow within a vast, roaring space, stillness within rushing void. This was the birthplace of shadows. Existence was a roaring void where shadows dwelled.

Half-formed links weakened and broke as the next loop in the chain failed to fit. He looked for repetition in the curds of cloud crossing the moon, in the shadowed valleys of the moon's silver disk. He wove puzzles, braiding twig and stem and vine into intricate workings to trick the eye and capture the mind. He whiled away the slow breaths till noon weaving box puzzles for the children, twistleaf puzzles

He was himself the puzzle he had been braiding all these years.

Had he pursued killers because he was haunted himself? Or because he had killed the parts of himself he could not bear?

Hang on, but don't look back. *Looking back was like looking down. He could not keep his balance if he looked back.*

"Tell us what brought you to the Knee, then." Risalyn's words returned him to the farmhouse common room, the table set with simple, hearty food, the whiff of the cookfire left to burn down.

He must stop lapsing into reverie. He feared it would take as long to sort through his memories as it had taken to make them. How many times would he have to relive it all before it became part of him? Would his memory ever be seamless, scenes recollected at need rather than intruding themselves as alien visions? Would he be forever torn in three?

He could not remember what memory had felt like before.

"By hit or miss, I followed the killings as far as Dindry Leng," he said. His voice seemed distant; his memories, Louarn's memories of what had happened most recently to him, were dimmed now in comparison with the intensity of Flin's life and Mellas's. His existence seemed a dry, two-dimensional thing, gray and flat. A half-life. A third-life. "When I realized that all the victims were mages, I headed for the place where the magelight had always been strongest. It seemed to me that there would be the most former mages there—the most folk in jeopardy, the most likelihood of flushing the killers. Gir Doegre was on my way. I had heard of two folk asking similar questions to my own in Dindry Leng. In Gir Doegre, I heard of those folk again, and concluded that they were the killers I sought. Those folk were you and your brother. I followed the girls because you would be following them, to retrieve what I believed were trophies—triskeles and a proxy's ring taken from the victims."

"They came from the spirit wood," the middle girl said. Pelufer n'Prendra, nine-and-two years old, wiry and thorn-sharp, with canny hazel eyes, fawn skin, blond-streaked chestnut bangs. And that shine to her. All three girls had it even at rest. No one else had mentioned it; he might be the only one who could see it. Not magelight . . . one of him remembered magelight . . . it was golden. . . .

He shook himself and moved closer to the dying fire. He could not seem to get warm. "You never told your alderfolk that. They deduced it—incorrectly, I believed. Risalyn collected what you had dropped. I believed she was retrieving her trophies, and her claim that she would return them to the wood was a lie."

"I did return them, on my way upland," Risalyn said.

"And I returned the rest of it," Jiondor added, raising a warning brow at Pelufer's annoyed wriggle. "She meant to trade it."

"They don't miss those things, you know," Pelufer said. "The dead don't care."

How much did she know about the dead? How much could she tell him? He saw now why Risalyn and Yuralon had been following her. She would be of inestimable value in the search for killers. But they must know more about her powers.

"It's disrepect nonetheless," Jiondor was saying, "and it's mended now, and that's an end on it."

You'll be Louarn, and that's an end on it.

"What brought *you* to Gir Doegre?" he asked Risalyn, to drown out the voices of the past.

"The same as you," Risalyn replied, "though we started at home, and our trail has muddied. The killings are legwide, now, and into the Heartlands. It's not one killer, or even one pair of killers, though perhaps they work in pairs or threes."

"Then the runners know," Louarn said, and Risalyn nodded. "They are better equipped for this hunt than any of us."

"Not anymore," said Yuralon. "We have Pelufer now." Risalyn's brother, a few years younger than her four nineyears. They were of a height, with tawny hair worn long and loose when possible, banded back tight when necessary. Their long heads swept forward into prominent sharp noses, the hatchet features typical of the Highlands Girdle. Both had eyes of dark quartz, though where Risalyn's were watchful, experienced, Yuralon's were smoked with old griefs. They spoke in a way that Mellas remembered—in the refined cadences of the Holding. Louarn was afraid to find out more, and longed to. Mellas's path might well have crossed theirs.

His path.

"You don't have Pelufer," Elora said. "You don't have any of us for anything." Already a slim beauty at nine-and-four, she shared her sisters' coloring but was more fey, more fine-boned. She'd be ripping hearts out of boys' chests in a couple of years—and that was the least remarkable thing about her.

Jiondor said, "You will not take that child into the kind of horrors I've heard described. I wouldn't let Risalyn take her when I thought she was a fighter. I wouldn't have let you have her if I'd believed you were a healer."

"Fighters," he said to Louarn in the tinker's wagon heading Kneeward. He spat the word. He'd held it in since their confrontation behind the tavern. "I didn't say so to the girls, but I thought they had been fighters in the magewar, gone off to join the shield, to keep the art of death alive in the name of protecting us against some imaginary threat from the lands-beyond. They're good girls. I would have fostered them. Always looked out for them, as I could. A lot of us did. My first pledge died. Beronwy, the woman I'm with now, she was a fighter in the horde. The magewar ended. The horde went off to form the shield. She came home. This is a place of peace. We don't hold with death arts here, though we tolerate bladecraft some, keepers are bladed, but it's mainly for show. I thought that woman would have forged those girls into weapons. That's not a thing to do to children. Said she was a healer, but I could see it in the way she held herself—just like Beronwy. Then it turned out the middle girl would have to leave town, she finally stole something so serious . . ."

"Triskeles. A proxy's ring."

"Yes. They wouldn't let her stay, after that. It only made them more determined to prentice her to that blade. I sent her off to some relatives, to keep her out of harm's way till I could make things right with the alderfolk. I thought the woman would give up, and that man with her. I know she saw something in Pel, there's a fire in that child and she'd trade her soul for a blade. All the more reason to keep her away from people like that."

There was more, and Louarn knew it. Something more about the girls than the man was willing to say. . . .

Now memories as recent as last night felt as alien to him, as vivid and yet distanced, as those of the boys he had been. Would it become impossible to tell which were theirs and which were his? *Louarn, I'm Louarn, I'm Louarn . . .*

"She can't go home," Risalyn said. "She committed a crime."

Jiondor replied, "I'm sure I can concoct a story close enough to what Louarn believed to convince my alderfolk. And if they can't go home they'll stay here, as planned."

"Will your relatives still abide that?" Yuralon said. "They were none too happy about this morning's events, and I fear that no matter how these children hide themselves, trouble will find them."

Jiondor's cousin and her pledge and her sons had left them to sort themselves out, having a farm to look after. These little girls would be more of a blessing than the farmers could know, if they earned their trust and the aid of their powers, but they could be a curse as well. Fate was no longer content to let them hide. It was a marvel that they'd concealed themselves as long as they had, in their crowded town. How many years of safety could they eke out on this peaceful farmstead? Enough to grow up?

I need them, for what I must do, Louarn thought, and then wondered what he meant.

"They're good folk and they'll do what's needed," Jiondor said, and Yuralon replied, "You may be asking too much. The Khinish are waking. The land is distressed. These folk will have troubles enough, without you putting this on them."

Louarn saw Pelufer's fingers move against her leg, as if she were fidgeting. Just a quick flutter, but he blinked as meaning came to him through it. She wanted to go with them, she said. He could read it the way scribes could read glyphs, with the unthinking ease of understanding vocalized words. She said she wanted to find those killers.

Under the continuing spoken conversation, Elora replied with slower, wearier fingers that Pelufer just wanted to be a fighter like that bladed man. But he wouldn't teach her. He was a healer now. He repented the terrible things he did.

Pelufer signed back that he still carried a longblade, that they both did.

Elora told her she wasn't going to touch it, and what about Caille? Pelufer might want to have an adventure, but Caille wanted to stay here.

Caille nodded vigorously, her mouth full of food, her hands passing treats to the dog. She had been watching the silent exchange and understanding it. Five years old. The age Flin was, when he lost himself and became Mellas. The age Flin was when he saw his parents die. What happened to these girls' parents? Where had they learned to speak in this silent, flap-fingered way? And how did he understand it?

Pelufer jerked her head toward Louarn without looking at him. She signed that Elora only wanted to go with him. She told Elora that the way she mooned over him made her want to throw up.

"Ew," said Caille, and the Girdlers and Jiondor glanced over, their own conversation faltering.

With a leer, Pelufer told Elora she was smitten. Elora signed that she was not. Pelufer signed that she was, her fingers pressing into Elora's leg, a physical gibe.

"What is that you're doing?" Risalyn said.

"It's a private conversation," Louarn said, hiding a smile, and added "apparently" too late to avoid the sharp glance of the middle girl. Not unlike the glance she'd given him when he mentioned seeing a glow in the woods.

Well, there had been enough secrets. His fingers found the movements almost naturally, using the edge of the table for . . . what? He didn't know. He didn't know what he was doing, yet he knew how to do it. Which one of him knew this thing?

Yet that was not the most important question.

Do I shine at all, myself? With angled combinations of one, two, and three fingers to each side of the table's edge, he asked them.

The two older girls' jaws dropped. It was left to the smallest one to answer. "A little," she said aloud, unperturbed. "But you could do something. It's more when you do things."

"What *is* that?" Risalyn said. "Some kind of signaling, I see that much, but . . ."

"I don't know," Louarn said. The signing interested him less than did the shine. "Where did you learn it?"

"Our mother," Elora said. Pelufer started to sign something hard against her sister's leg, then looked up at Louarn and froze. But Elora had taken the point. "She made it up, I suppose."

That was doubtful, but it could wait. He regarded the three powerful children with an intensity that kept the other adults quiet, waiting. "You thought you were the only ones," he said at last. "Perhaps you're not."

Looking uncertain, with Pelufer frozen beside her, Elora signed to him that they were the only strong ones. Children shined when they were small, but not enough to see in each other, and they lost it by Caille's age. Sometimes grownups shined, but only for a moment here and there. Crafters and farmers shined longer, but mostly when they were working, and they couldn't see her shine or her sisters'. He might be strong, too, if he could see it, she signed.

Everyone had it. Everyone had it to some degree. But he could *see* it.

He told her with his crafter's hands that he was a crafter but he couldn't do the things they did. After a hesitation, she signed back that maybe he could learn.

"If someone doesn't start saying things I understand, *out loud*," Risalyn said, "I am going to do something very nasty."

"Don't shut us out of this, Louarn," said Jiondor. "We have serious decisions to make in this room, and we'll make the wrong ones if we keep things from each other now."

"You don't talk like Girdlers," Elora said promptly to Risalyn and Yuralon. "You come from the Head."

Pelufer grinned at their startlement, broken free of her paralysis by briefly getting the upper hand over the grownups. "Elora has a knack with accents," she said, and then signed to Louarn that it wasn't one of *those* knacks, just a trader knack.

Good, thought Louarn, *any indication of them bonding with me bodes well*—and then some deeper part of him, the runner part of him who had lived in fear of manipulation all his life, recognized that as the manipulative thought of a man who tried to craft things to his own ends. Louarn, the lad-of-all-crafts, had crafted everything around him, right down to his own appearance and comportment, and had fled every time he felt himself beginning to feel. *You are a very superficial man, Louarn.*

Then a wave of nausea swept him, and he thought, *Spirits, I shall go mad.*

"We were trained as fighters for the Ennead," Risalyn said.

Jiondor made an inarticulate noise that Louarn recognized as a swallowed "I knew it!"

"Born of High Girdle stock into a steward family in the Holding," Risalyn went on. "They bladed us in secret, some as guards, some as assassins. Ours was one of three reserve groups, about to be sent in to put down the stewards' uprising. Then some comrades of ours came across a gaggle of . . . wounded mages. The Ennead had . . . used them ill. Terribly. It showed us the truth of the Nine. Some of us turned on them. Belatedly, I'm afraid. And we tried to help those mages. But some were beyond help."

Pelufer repeated several unfamiliar names. "Yuralon killed them. Those ones beyond help. They asked him to."

"That was the beginning, yes." Risalyn answered; Yuralon seemed unable to speak of it.

Given the expression Pelufer tried to hide from her sisters, she knew how those mages had been used. Louarn gripped the sides of his chair. One of him knew, too. Spirits help the child if she had been inside the minds of those folk.

Elora was frowning. "The Nine weren't bad. That's a lie spread by the Lightbreaker's folk."

Risalyn and Yuralon could find no way between them to answer.

"That's what they've taught you to believe, here in the Strong Leg," Louarn said. The nausea had grown much worse. He pressed a cloth to his mouth, and then managed, "Mellas saw it for himself. Flin's parents were killed by the Nine. Believe me, Elora. Those were not lies."

Jiondor said, "I'd like you to tell my Beronwy that, sometime. She fought in the horde that stormed the Holding. She thought she was doing right. She's near convinced she had a hand in breaking the light herself, now."

"A lot of people from the Strong Leg joined Verlein's horde," Risalyn said. "But when the light went, people were angry. They had to blame someone." She paused. "I fought beside that horde, in the end. I may know this Beronwy of yours."

He wanted to tell them. He so badly wanted to tell them that it was he who led those mages up out of the depths of the mountain. But it hadn't been he. It had been some boy hiding inside him. A shy boy in the shadows of his mind. He remembered doing it. But it had not been he.

And still he found himself wondering which of them had asked Yuralon's mercy. The acerbic wordsmith? The wry illuminator? He hadn't learned their names. Perhaps it didn't matter, and was best not known. Their courage had moved Mellas deeply. He would grieve to know that any of them had been lost.

He blinked at a dislocating spasm. The stablemaster, the baker, the other fosterlings—what had become of them? Did they still live? Who could tell him?

Menders. Menders had taken over the Holding. Some of them must have been stewards or warders. Some of them must know. Could he bring himself to go back there, to find out?

"At any rate, we have a job to do," Risalyn was saying. "We must determine which of us is in, and which of us is out."

"The girls stay here," Jiondor said. "Nolfi's road is down to him. I'm going back to Gir Doegre, to my pledge and my trade. I kept your secret, Pel. I'll keep Elora's and Caille's as well."

"I know," Pelufer said.

"Thank you for coming after us," Elora said, with a tired but still cutting glance at Pelufer to remind her of her manners. "Thank you for sending us here. You've gone to a lot of trouble."

"You're good girls," Jiondor said, gruff, embarrassed.

"Pelufer wants to go," Louarn said, to force the issue. "The others seem not to."

"I didn't say that," Elora put in quickly, and then blanched as she remembered that he'd understood Pelufer's teasing about her being smitten. He caught himself midway between giving her a smile and giving her a look of gentle reassurance. Neither would have been genuine. He dropped his gaze.

What am I? What am I if I am not the man I have crafted myself to be?

Jiondor said, "I'd rather hear it from them, if it's all the same to you."

"We'll go," Elora said. "We'll go find these killers. It's something we can help with. Something we can do." She glanced at Nolfiander, and then said, "We could have done a lot of things, and we never did, because we had to keep the secret. I think maybe it's time to start doing things that need doing."

"That's not fair!" Pelufer said. "What you said wasn't fair, Nolfi. You don't know everything."

Nolfiander had been completely quiet, soaking and wrapping his ankle, then sitting staring into the cookfire's embers. "You could tell me," he suggested, in a low voice, without looking up.

"She couldn't save Father. He poisoned himself. He left us, he ran away, he ran away by dying. He wouldn't let her fix him. He couldn't stand that Mamma was gone, and he went to be with her."

To Louarn, perhaps to Risalyn and Yuralon, Elora said, "Our mother died in an accident when Caille was a baby. Our father died of drink and a broken heart two years ago." She spoke dully—reciting a tale.

"She could have saved Sel," Nolfiander said.

Again Elora translated, as if making words out of the past could neutralize it: "Seliander was his brother. He died two years ago, too. That was the rasping cough."

And again Pelufer protested. "She was only three years old! Saving Sel could have killed her!"

"No," Caille said calmly, one cheek stuffed with grapes. She proceeded to stuff the other cheek and then sat poking them to see what would happen.

"It could have," Pelufer insisted. "She'd have to kill a sickness like that. She wouldn't kill the mites and borers that ate our shed. She might kill sickness, but it would . . . what did you say? It was something a trader would say."

"Cost her," Louarn supplied.

"And then she'd have had to do everyone else! *That* would have killed her!"

"He was my brother," Nolfiander said.

Elora was sliding down in her seat. She had borne the responsibility for them too long at too young an age, Louarn thought. Thieving, irrepressible Pelufer had tried to style herself a provider for the family, but Elora felt the burden to the spirit far more keenly. The secrets, the choices had weighed on her. And if she was smitten with him, it was a brief flare, a young girl's reaction to a pretty face in the midst of much fear and excitement, in the euphoria of the greenwood that fed her soul. Anyone could see that the barrow boy was the one she cared for. But she kept herself apart from him. She had let his brother die.

"She would have had to tell you," Jiondor said. "It was a hard choice, Nolfi. Don't you be hard on her for it."

"She never had to tell me a thing," the boy replied, still staring into the glowing coals. "I've told them that a dozen times. I always knew there was something. Have to be stupid not to know."

"Perhaps the girls didn't know what she was capable of, at three years of age," Louarn offered.

"We knew," Elora said. "She could do it when she was a baby. Padda cut himself once. He was minding her. He picked her up to bring her with him to where he could tend the cut. She touched it and it went away. Then he knew."

"She couldn't save your mother?" Risalyn asked, getting the whole question out though Jiondor hissed the moment he knew what she would say.

"No," Pelufer said, flat and hard. "It was too late. Mother was already gone."

Louarn understood. They could count the story on their fingers. Caille was five years old. The light was six years gone. She was conceived of the dying light, as the freedoms failed and women who thought they were warded came unexpectedly with child. She was an orphan of the vanished light: with no magecraft to ease her way, their mother had died in the birthing of her.

A sad tale, that. But one repeated in every village in every region. And yet it niggled at his puzzler's mind. A piece that did not fit. If she healed with a touch, would not her passage into the world leave her mother whole and healthy in its wake? Had they not laid the infant on her breast?

He could not ask that here. It didn't matter, perhaps; power was power, and that the girls were not its only possessors was the more staggering revelation. Elora had said that he might learn. But there had been no one to teach these girls. If something had happened after their mother's death, or during it, to increase their inherent abilities, to make them shine so bright . . .

"I would like to learn more about this shine of yours," he said. "And—"

"Shine?" said Yuralon.

Louarn found himself looking at Pelufer. She thought for a long time. Then she shrugged.

"They have a shine," he said. "A ruddy shine, like the golden shine that magelight had."

"Eiden's eyes," said Jiondor, amazed. "I don't see it."

"Nor do I," "Nor I," said the Girdlers.

Softly, Nolfi said, "I do. A little."

Elora's head whipped around. But he would not raise his eyes to her. She slumped back into her chair, her own eyes fixing on the table. Louarn felt a pang, and then something like a distant, pealing bell. It was time to go.

When he began to feel for them, it was time to go.

"It's the light, come back into the world," Jiondor breathed. "Just like they said it would."

"It's not magelight," said Risalyn. "I lived my life in the Ennead's back pocket. Trust me on this."

"What we've seen wasn't magecraft," Yuralon agreed, "nor anything like it. And the magelight was yellow. Louarn said this was red."

"It's a shine, not a light," said Louarn. *Tell them,* he thought. *Tell them who you were. Tell them who you are!* But he couldn't. It was too new. It was not him.

Pelufer said, "Mellas showed a light."

I didn't, there was no light in me, magestone glowed for mages but not for me, the illuminator thought there was a light but she was wrong, my life wasn't so hard that it would seal off my own—

Mellas hadn't remembered Flin.

When he was six, he would show a light. The moment he turned six, there it would be. He'd look down at his hand and see it glowing. He'd look up and see his mother glowing, and his fathers . . .

Magecraft had seared the skin from Flin's parents before his eyes. It was that as much as the fall that knocked his mind into darkness. He'd been almost six. The light had most often shown in one's sixth or seventh year. Some had believed it was there before that, but not strong enough to be visible. His mother had been sure he'd show a light. His father had prayed he wouldn't—the Ennead would have no interest in him if he didn't show a light. *Lightless keeps you safe.* He'd turned that; he'd turned it to mean that shadow kept him safe, and darkness. But Father had meant his own light, the light inside him. He could never show a light if he was to remain safe.

That didn't work out very well, now, did it, Louarn thought.

"That boy Mellas . . . the last thing before he went dark . . . the thing that burned in, the thing I feel when I touch you . . . I think it might have been the light dying. I think that might have been what hurt him so much."

"He was lost," Louarn said. "He was deep in a cave, no food or water."

"That didn't kill him, or you wouldn't be sitting here," Risalyn said.

Perhaps it was true. Perhaps there had been a light in him. Perhaps Flin had understood his father's warning perfectly well, deep inside, and hid his own light to keep himself safe. Mellas remembered . . . he remembered the shifting plane of lights, a realm of lights burning calm and true across the plane of the world . . .

"They were yellow," Pelufer said. "Or maybe gold. I'm not good at colors. They were like a candle flame. We're not like that."

"No," Mellas agreed softly, and Louarn let him.

"What, then?" Jiondor said. "What is it? What are they?"

"You make us sound like dogs! Like we're cowdogs or sheepdogs or—"

Jiondor was laughing. Despite all the heartbreak and tribulation here, he was laughing, and of course that was the right thing to do, the real thing to do—what else could you do when you had discovered a power that might replace the only power that had kept the world safe and well?

"Dogs are good," Caille said. "I'll be a cowdog. Like this one." She slipped another cheese wedge under the table.

"I'm sorry, Pel," Jiondor said. "I don't mean it like that. But it's wonderful, whatever it is! Merciful spirits, it's a miracle!"

"It's not," said Nolfi, and at last he turned.

Elora went stiff and but did not sit up.

"It's a threat," he said. "They'll never be safe, ever. Sel died. I don't know if I can forgive that. But maybe it would have hurt Caille to save him. She was so little. I don't know. I can't ever know, and anyway he's gone, there's never been any changing that and there never will." He swallowed, and went on, "She was so little, and she's still so little—"

"Ei!"

"It's true, that's why you're cuter and more special than anyone else, because you're the littlest. But they're all little. Now look, they're all angry at me. I'm a boy, Elora. I work a barrow because I have no one, because I have to do it to stay alive, to keep on in my parents' trade, and that's if I still have a place when I go back after all this is finished. But I'm a boy, I'm only nine-and-six, and I have two years on you and four on Pel. This isn't supposed to be happening to any of us. They're going to want you to save the world. They are. You know it. That's why you were crying. Everyone knows it. And they're going to be mad that you didn't save it already. Just like me."

"We can't save the world," Elora said. "I couldn't even save the forest. I did one tree, and I couldn't get up for days. That was all right, I told myself, if Pelufer would mind the pitch for once, just for a few days here and there, I could do all the trees, even if it took years. But it only got poisoned again. It still drank the water. It was so hard to make it better, and then it died anyway. I couldn't save it."

"What if someone could clean the water?"

"Maybe. If there was someone who could do that."

"Could Caille do that?"

"Maybe. I think she can do almost anything. But even if she could. Even if she were a grownup and big and strong. Even then, there's only one of her. She can't clean all the rivers and heal all the people and all the animals and . . . it's too much! Nolfi's right. We're just little girls. When we grow up, we'll be only three, and that's years away."

"I won't let you make them do it," Pelufer said. "People should look after themselves. They shouldn't be looking to other people to do it for them."

"It's important to help people, Pel," Jiondor said.

"Not if they'll take your life away because of it. Not if they'll make you do more than you can do."

"Your father frightened you very much, didn't he," said Risalyn.

"Their father loved them very much," said Jiondor.

Louarn turned to Elora. "You thought it might be taught," he said.

She pursed her lips. "I don't know why I said that. I never thought about it before. I've never seen anyone like you before." She blushed, but went on, "We could try."

"Good girl," he said, softly, though in truth he was reluctant to say anything to her for fear of trying reflexively to charm her.

Jiondor said, "If such skills as these could be taught . . ."

". . . we could heal the world," Yuralon finished for him, with Risalyn adding, "And no need to realize their father's fear, for if all shared in this there would be no using them—or abusing."

"There's something else, though," Nolfiander put in. His brown eyes were sad but steady under his forelock of sandy hair as he came around the table to face the girls. "It has to be asked, Elora. Caille can kill sickness. Can she kill people?"

"No kill," Caille said.

She remained absorbed in a precarious structure of bread crusts she had been assembling on her plate, and Louarn could read no expression from her. An adorable child, but inscrutable. Had she been taught those words? They were the words of a baby, and they issued from her instantly. Had her father felt compelled to put that stricture on her? If so, there were profound dangers here.

Elora answered then. "She never has, so I guess we don't know. But I don't think so. I think . . . I think that if you killed someone, it would kill you."

"But she could do harm?" Louarn cast it as a question, not a statement. "She could inflict such damage as she healed?"

"No!" Caille cried, and this time it was clear: not a parent's injunction, but an appalled denial. Such a thing would be anathema to her.

But it could be done.

"It would hurt her," Pelufer said.

"Do you know that for a fact?" Risalyn asked.

Pelufer started to answer, then stopped, looking sullen.

Nolfiander said, "It made Elora tired to make the tree bloom. It made her tired to weaken the planks to get out of the tavern. That's how you did it, isn't it?"

Elora nodded. "It's wrong to do unnatural things. Wood is still alive even after you make houses and tables and tools out of it. Metal is alive after you mine it. Stone is alive. Everything's alive. There are right ways for it to go, and wrong ways. When you push in a way things aren't meant to go, it's no good for you. If I hurt a tree, I don't think I'd just be tired. I'd be hurt too."

"Is that why crafters shine?" Louarn felt iron shaping under his hand, wool spinning into yarn, beeswax layering into candles, brick sliding into place in a broken hearth.

"When they're doing it right," Elora said. "Yes. I think so."

And when they're doing it wrong, it tires them, and frustrates them, and drains them, Louarn thought. He'd seen it many times.

Risalyn said, "I can give a man my hand, or kill him with it. Every power comes with ill uses as well as good. We lost all the protections of magelight because the Lightbreaker decided it was the only way to stop the Ennead doing harm. This is a safer power, I think. The harm you do comes back on you. I can't say the same for magecraft. Or blades. Or hands."

"The harm we do does come back on us," Yuralon said quietly.

Her mouth twisted in sad, knowing agreement. "Yes. But not so persuasively, perhaps. Not for everyone."

Jiondor cleared his throat. "I was going to say that if such skills could be taught, they might be honed, too, like any other skills, and maybe Pel could learn not to say the names aloud, so that she wouldn't betray herself to killers who might hurt her."

He's coming around to it, Louarn thought. *He's almost willing to let them go.*

Pelufer seized on the prospect of control. "How would I learn a thing like that?" she asked. "How long would it take?"

For some reason, everyone in the room looked at Louarn.

How would I know? I'm a journeyman crafter, and a haunted man with dreams you know naught of who may soon prove quite insane. Do not look to me. Yet it was an interesting question. A puzzle, a challenge. "A few days of practice, I'd say. Somewhere quiet but haunt-ridden. A spirit wood, to start. Then the streets of an unfamiliar town. With us to protect you, perhaps drown out any slips, you might master it, assuming it can be done." While he still had their attention, he brought the matter back to the larger question. "As I was going to say many breaths ago: I would like to learn more about this shining craft, but there is a task at hand, as Risalyn long ago gave up reminding us, and we must choose our paths before the farmholders return. If Pelufer is willing, I might devise a plan. We have Risalyn and Yuralon to shield and heal us. Caille and Elora need not show their powers. My only fear is for Caille's comfort and safety in the traveling, but perhaps there would not be much. It was the Knee where I was bound. We're in the Knee now. We have only to position ourselves in a more populous place." A place where there were former mages. A lot of them. Gir Nuorin might do. "But we must move quickly."

"This is the reckoning, then," Risalyn said, and took a survey of the group. The two older girls were determined to go, for their respective reasons. Louarn couldn't quell the satisfaction that gave him; though he'd taken as little hand in it as he could, still he had crafted this, if only by his presence. They would not have gone with the Girdlers alone. He was getting what he wanted. The youngest girl made no objection, though she bade a sad farewell to the dog, which might have been an oblique indication of reluctance. Jiondor was returning to Gir Doegre, as he'd stated. Louarn's path, and Risalyn and Yuralon's, was clear.

That left only Nolfiander, the barrow boy, undecided.

"I should go back," he said. "My barrow's untended. I was going to try to protect Elora's pitch, too. But . . . well, I'm in it now, aren't I? I guess I'd rather come along."

Louarn wasn't sure whether the oldest girl would object to him putting himself in danger, object to his presence on some pretext to cover conflicted yearnings, or embrace his company as loyal friend. When she went once again to dig a hand down into her blanket carrysack, and drew forth a third working to hand to the boy, it was the last thing he would have expected.

"Sel," the boy breathed, uncovering the young man's face shaped in living wood.

"Bring him home," Elora said. "Bring him home safe, and watch our pitch, and mind your family's trade—and keep that dog while you're at it, too, if it's all right with Risalyn, she traded for him fair and square and his master couldn't have been fond of him if he gave him up. Go home, Nolfi. We'll come back to you. Gir Doegre's where we belong."

Risalyn made a gesture of offering to Louarn. "There's your reckoning," she said. "Do we leave at morning light?"

Do not look to me, he thought again, more harshly. But he nodded, already devising strategies, calculating travel time, the needs of young children, what stories they would give to explain themselves. "If these good landholders will put up with us on their common-room floor for the night."

The sunset angled smoky red through louvered shutters in the Bootward wall, as if the embers in the hearth had flared to light the room. The farmers would return any moment. Jiondor told Pelufer to fetch water for the kettle and went to build the fire back up to cooking heat.

"May the spirits speed you down your road," he said, shaking his head. "And may you all come safe home, wherever home may be."

II

Storm

The Belt
The Girdle
The Druilor Piedmont

Kazhe's boots sank into the muddy shore of Lough Elin, leaving prints that sagged and smoothed almost as soon as her soles came free. Where reeds had choked the water's edge, the going was less sticky. The lough looked solid, congealing with red algae that mages had once kept in check, collecting windblown plant matter and soil that, left untended, would form a sucking bog. Far out in the middle, draggers poled their way on flat boats, fighting the encroachment as they could, working to keep channels clear.

"At least we can eat the stuff," said her companion, a tall redhead dressed in black. "But it tastes like snot."

"I've had worse," Kazhe said, watching a heron wing its slow way across the surface. Not much room left for birds, here. But the draggers aided the waterfowl as much as they aided Elingar's trade with its neighbors around the lough.

"You said you needed help," the woman said, crossing in one long stride a sinkhole it took Kazhe a tussock-hop to clear.

"Quiet help," Kazhe replied. "I might be mistaken to look to a runner. But your master wasn't available. It cost me enough to find that out. You folk aren't cheap."

"He's not my master, and he's on Khine."

"Ah." If the runner knew why, it would make this easier. But of course she did. She was a runner. "I need to know how your pigeons work."

The woman laughed aloud. "I would tell you they eat, they flutter their wings, they take to the air, it just happens—but you'd knife me for being flippant. They're not looms, Kaẓhe. They're not even pigeons, most of them."

"How they find their way," Kaẓhe growled.

"That's a trade secret." Laughter danced in the runner's blue eyes. She said, "You might not have the knack for imprinting a bird, and it takes time. They don't find their way home, as they used to. They find the people they love. If you need to fly messages, you'll need birdfolk to do it for you."

"Only one message," Kaẓhe said. "And given what you say, it would mean sending one runner to the Boot and giving one to me."

"Logistics are my job, not yours. But you're going to have to tell me what you need to know."

"And where I plan to go."

"I don't have to know that, though I'd very much like to."

"You'll find out anyway. If you sent someone with me, they'd get word to you."

"Most likely. But only to me, as their sender. We're not leaky sieves. I'd say you'll have to risk trusting three of us."

"Not four? You wouldn't tell the man who isn't your master?"

"I might." The woman stepped up onto a grassy sward, stopped, and regarded Kaẓhe with folded arms. Waiting.

"I'll need to know when the Khinish march. I'll need to know fast. And I don't know where I'll be."

The woman nodded, looking out over the lough and back toward Elingar. The incessant rain had abated, leaving the summer air close and sticky, but storm clouds still roiled across the sky, black and gray as rock doves' wings. "Perhaps they won't march," she said. "Perhaps they'll sail, or not come at all."

"Trying to talk them out of it, is he?" Kaẓhe suppressed a sneer. Pelkin was wise, but no match for the Khinish.

"He'll fail," the woman replied. "So will anyone who tries to stop them. Still, I'll go with you. We'd be safest sending two to the Boot, each with a couple of my birds. The weather's bad, and getting worse. One bird can't be assured of getting through."

"You're one of these birdfolk?"

"I am. I love the birds. They do what I can't do. They fly."

"You would ally yourself with me, one woman alone, though you say no one can stop the Khinish?"

"I don't know that you're trying to stop the Khinish. I don't know what you're trying to do. You're probably insane. But I know that above all you have always sought to protect. The Belt was my home, when I started. Perhaps I'm just feeling protective, posted here."

"Or tethered."

Karanthe n'Farine smiled. "That too. Come on, Kazhe. Let's go pick some other runners you can trust. Or use. However you want to look at it. You're not one woman alone anymore."

The Girdle was unrecognizable.

In the lands Kazhe had known, grasses rippled under the caress of wind, the wind sighed sweet and lonely, the rivers wound slender and sinuous. Now all was muddy, trodden, tilled, battered by downpours. The rivers bulged, their curves flooded straight, bordered in mudflats marred by reeds and rot. Rice paddies terraced what had been gentle grassy rises. Horses huddled under tarps, rain-beaten and miserable; folk huddled in tents staked down tight, with so many structures built up around them that moving on would be a task too involved to consider. The many-colored grasslands had gone drab and dour. The sighing wind shrieked, and pummeled them with rain, then died to a dripping whisper only to writhe and whip and pummel them again. Her herd-band folk had become rice farmers. The plains of her home had become a swamp.

"The land defies us," said a low voice, so achingly familiar that Kazhe froze, unable to turn. "It doesn't want to grow what will grow in this flooded place. It wants its horses back running free, it wants its folk to roam. But it thwarts them. It no longer knows what it wants."

"Benkana," she said, and still could not turn.

His arm came around her from behind, embracing shoulder and chest. He laughed when Comfrey nipped him, and scratched the spot under his mane where he liked it best. It was a rich, infectious laugh, one she'd never thought to hear again. He rested his chin on the top of her head, pillowed by his beard. After a moment, she crossed her forearms over his, pale skin on dark, pressing tight.

"I knew you would come home," he said. "So I waited. Sira's here, she left the Jhardal band, and a few of the others as well."

"This looks more like your home than mine." He came from the Lowlands in the Weak Leg, jungle verging into swamp by the Low Sea.

"Maybe that's why I stayed. Give you plainsfolk a hand with your new terrain."

She spun around in his arms and kissed him with a ferocity he returned threefold. Her hands slid under his horsehair vest, her short nails scraped down bare flesh. He had to bend to reach her lips. It arched his body away from hers. She slid her arms around his neck to hoist herself and mount him standing. He boosted her with locked wrists. After long breaths, she abandoned his mouth to say, "I don't know for how long, Benkana," and she could see in his dark green eyes, in the subtle deepening of squint lines in his brown skin, in the hardened jaw under his black beard, that he knew she meant it in more ways than she had words for.

"I take what's offered," he said, and kissed her again, hot and deep. She had forgotten how sweet, how hard that draught of flesh could be. Once she would have ridden him straight to their tent, or taken him right here in the rain. But she was practicing restraint now. Just for a while. Just for a short while, till the job was done. Far too soon he eased her down so he could greet the runner Karanthe, reunite Kazhe with her old friends, find out what had brought her here and what might lie in store for them.

There were eight of them now. Within days, quietly contacting relatives and old friends of her father's, she had made them two dozen. Gritting her teeth, sheathing old hatreds, she made brief visits to other villages, to the children and siblings and pledges of the turncloaks who'd killed her father. She was gratified to find cheitla and tainla among them, many earned; but there were no kenaila. Those blades lay where the kenaila who bore them had fallen, and would not be wielded again. It was better that way, for her. When she returned with the last she could find, her cadre numbered more than three dozen.

She drilled them hard, out in soaked grazeland in pelting rain, far from scanning eyes. She did not promise to make them kenaila; a kenai trained only three, one in each blade and one of those in all three, and she had neither the weapons to bestow nor any intent to teach them cheit or tain. "But I'll teach you the first way of the kenai," she told them. "I'll teach you to disarm." She left it to them to hope for more. She drilled them in shield and spear and longstaff, the wooden weapons, knowing that they would follow her whether she bladed them or not—some because they had loved her once, and some because they believed she meant to muster a horde of kenaila. They hoped for much more than she would offer.

"You're too far," Karanthe said, "unless you plan to engage them in the Druilors."

Kazhe made no nod or reply, only sipped her blistering spiced tea. She listened to the beaded partition clack slowly quiet again after

Karanthe's entry. She listened to the maddening, endless drip from the hut's leaky roof. But she listened to Karanthe, too.

"By the time a bird gets to me, they'll have marched past the Boot. In the time it takes you to quit the Girdle and skirt the Druilors, they'll have come up the Strong Leg. Is that your plan?"

Still Kazhe did not reply. But the next day she drilled her cadre for the last time on the plains. The day after, they set out for the Druilors, three dozen and more on tall, long-bodied Girdle mounts, spears and staffs wrapped, shields bagged beside their saddles. They camped alone, avoiding villages, easy in their dog tents, plains Girdlers relieved to be on the move after two years of staking down ever tighter where they'd been. The few who had blades kept them sheathed and packed. For the rest, Kazhe said, they were bound for the far side of the Blooded Mountains, where there was iron aplenty, and smiths who knew what to do with it.

They wanted blades. She would give them blades. Not kenaila, not cheitla, not tainla. Her kenai, the greater blade, one of a kind, was her own and would part from her only in death. Her cheit, the dagger, the tooth, was still at Verlein's belt, though she would have it back in the end. Her tain, the lesser blade, belonged to Benkana, who had learned all she could teach him long ago and was the one successor she had chosen well.

She would give them blades of her own invention. Bladebreaking blades. And she knew just the ironsmith who could make them.

Sowmid waned in a scowl of clouds, discomfited rumbles from the mountains, rumors of plague and magekillings, mad tales of bonefolk stealing children.

Kazhe lifted the new-forged iron and, with no warning, extended her body over an outstretched leg in a deep thrust that left the tip of the blade fingertip-deep in one of the smithy's support beams. The ironsmith and her prentice were too startled to move; after a moment, the prentice said, "Oh," and took a step back.

"No good," Kazhe said, withdrawing the weapon and her body to resting position, then laying the ill-balanced blade down. "The weight has to fall nearer the tip."

"But then it overbalances," said the smith, indicating another blade, an earlier attempt to follow Kazhe's instructions. "You lose control. It leads your hand wild."

Kazhe bit down on an oath. "It *must* lead your hand. The weight must be where the thrust goes."

"This is a bladebreaker. That's what you said you wanted. A blade with no edge—"

"I know what I said." She kept her voice calm, her words measured. A tone that might be taken for patient, that's what she was after. "I'm not asking for a lead ball on the end of the thing. Denser metal, that's all. It should fly before me on the thrust. I should launch it like an arrow and be pulled after."

"Why can't we just work on copying your blade?" asked the prentice softly.

Kazhe saw the yearning in his young eyes. His fondest, greediest wish was to forge a blade like hers. Second to that, he wished only to hold hers again. The touch of it was like a fine, sweet wine. One sip, and next thing you knew you were fighting for the jug—anything, *anything*, for just one sip more.

Briefly she considered handing it to him, letting him run his finger along the swirls and currents in the strange metal—letting him, and his master, feel again the exquisite imbalance, the way the foreblade pulled toward the target from the moment the thing was unsheathed. But she had given them enough opportunities to learn the shaping of it by feel. The trouble was that they were not fighters. They had never been trained in the use of these weapons. Until they were, all the explanations and descriptions and examples in the world were not going to drive the point home.

"I don't want another blade like this," she said. "I *have* a bloody blade like this. Keep working on the bladebreaker. And get it right, or by all the spirits I'll pull Auda Bladesmith out of the bonefolk's bellies."

She turned to go, thinking, *That was not what I meant to do*. She had seen the diminishing effect of bluster. She knew she must not lose her temper when she was armed. But if they would only do as she told them, and stop insisting on their own forsaken—

No. This was not the way.

At the threshold, she made herself turn back, and hoped that shoulders slumped would resemble shoulders softened.

"You can't copy it," she said—then gave them the gift of the secret, and if it knocked the hope out of them perhaps it would also clear the ideas from their heads so her instructions could get in. "It was magecrafted. A blade like this will never be fashioned again."

She traded the heat of the forge for the lesser heat of the day. The seasons had been unpredictable in recent years, if her blurred recollections could be trusted, but the heat could only get worse as summer approached. She was stuck with it, and the poisoned Druilor runoff, and the loss of Auda Bladesmith to an infection the weakest triad could have cured.

She moved to the next smithy, here in this town of ironmongers, and found the problems similar. Perhaps it was more magecrafting than metal that made her blade move as it did. Perhaps the weapon she wanted could not be made by ordinary craft. She pondered that, briefly, while the ironsmith haggled with her over the price.

"All right," she said at last, acceding to his wishes—to a trade she should have hoped for all along, even suggested. It seemed so obvious now. "I'll train your daughter *and* your son, in return for the weapons to arm them and six others. Whether they follow where I'm bound will be up to them."

Smithy by smithy, she acquired additions to her cadre. In the Strong Leg, all folk had heard rumors of the Khinish waking. All folk wanted to be armed. If it suited her, if she was suited to leading it, she might muster a full-blown uprising before the Khinish even set foot on the Boot. But slaughter was not her intention. Training the nonned she had now, the two nonned she would have before she was through, was dangerous enough.

When she brought them to their new training ground, in a poisoned dell between long Druilor feet that hid them from the roads beyond, she said, "You've done well. The least of you, armed with a longstaff, can work a ribbon of nine shielders. But the Khinish may be tougher. I've taught you to disarm. I've taught you to incapacitate. Now I'll teach you to kill." She paused, and looked at their faces. "Wipe those grins off. It's no gift. It's a taint, a stain. A curse. Respect the blade—and beware the shadow it will bring on you."

"I don't know how long I can hold on," she murmured to Benkana, lying sweat-soaked atop him in their shed behind a smithy. Her folk were scattered through nearby villages, to avoid arousing suspicion by camping as a group. There were nearly two nonned now. Enough to be mistaken for an armed force.

He grunted, like a small quake underneath her. He'd already been nearly asleep, exhausted from drilling his third of the cadre. Sira had the other third. "To what?" he said, when he'd disentangled her voice from the onset of dreams.

She didn't have the words to answer him. Sanity. Clarity. Patience. Evenhandedness. Telling people not to strain themselves when all she wanted was to brawl, and drink, and kill. "To not being me."

"You're kenai. You've always been kenai. You always will. It's what you are." He shifted her off him and lay on his side, head propped on one hand, the other tracing swirls through the sweat around her collarbone. "Is it your blade you fear to lose?"

It was so simple for him. He was a good man. He worked hard, and he fought for what he believed in, sometimes when he didn't even know what it was—when he was only following someone he loved, someone he trusted, someone he'd die for. He'd followed Torrin that way. It was how they'd met.

He didn't understand the lusts that fired her blood. He didn't understand rage. He didn't understand how it felt to *want* to kill. To want to die.

"You can't lose it," he said. "It will always come back to you. It finds ways to hide itself, keep itself safe, and then return to your keeping." She thought of the taverner handing it back to her. He was right; it was the blade that had contrived that. "The blade is you, Kaẓhe."

"Then yes, it's the blade I fear to lose," she said, or perhaps only thought, as sleep began to carry her off.

Something snapped her awake. Her hackles rose; a tingle swept through her limbs; she went stiff. Benkana felt it, and in silent unison they rolled from their bedding. Blades came easily to hand. They crept from the smiths' shed, Kaẓhe on point, Benkana watching her back. She hardly felt the stray bits of metal that dug into her bare feet. Her knees flexed. Her nostrils flared. There was danger nearby. Someone intended death. She could smell it like blood.

Her own blood sang.

A sound, from the right. The slightest tick. It might have been lips parting in sleep. Karanthe slept in the barn where the smiths' draft horses had been kept. Glanders had taken the horses. Comfrey and Benkana's Eyebright were in a makeshift paddock with the other mounts, away from where there had been sickness. A rustle—feet in straw? Benkana moved beside the door. Kaẓhe reached her off hand toward it.

The scrape of edged metal being lifted.

She hauled the door across its rollers. Two forms crouched in the gloom. Kaẓhe came in low, Benkana high. The form on the right shot up to full height and raised something that glinted. Benkana's blade swept over her head and clanged hard against denser metal. The weapons scraped one on the other. She rammed a shoulder into the form on the right, then sprang back to bring her blade into play. A knife gleamed dully, rising up and away from near the floor. She dodged at the same moment it was hurled. A heavy clunk came from the right—a weapon flying loose—as the knife whispered past her bare shoulder. She drove forward and down with her blade. It grated through bone and sank into softness.

Ignoring the outcry, she pulled out, swung her blade around. Benkana was reeling back with empty hands. It was his weapon that had flown loose. An axe cut the air horizontally where his belly had been. Its wielder was right-handed. The swing opened his right side to her. She thrust for the kidney. The blade slid in. The axeman was still pivoting through his swing. His spine caught the side of her weapon. He shrieked. The blade jarred free. He fell.

She drew back into position, balanced, scanning the shadows. The axeman was between Benkana and his blade. Rasping. Not dead yet. Still a threat. Benkana crept forward and took up the axe. They listened. A sob, a death rattle, then nothing.

Three dark forms lay on the barn floor. Benkana moved to the middle one. Kazhe covered him. Sleepy, frightened voices outside were responding to the noise. "It's Karanthe," Benkana said as candlelight bore in—the smith and her pledgemate.

The light revealed a barn spattered in blood, two dark-cloaked figures drenched and still, and Karanthe emerging, woozy, from unconsciousness as Benkana lifted her up to sit.

Kazhe searched the dead. The axe, the rope looped over a rafter beam, and Karanthe's triskele in the axeman's pocket told the story of what had been meant to happen here, but it took Karanthe to translate it for them.

"They've been killing runners," she said, when they'd gotten her inside the house and poured some tea into her. "Killing them, taking their triskeles, and . . ." She stripped off her black tunic and hose and gave them to the smith's pledge, who'd offered to rinse the blood out before it set, then sat with Kazhe and Benkana and the smith at the cookroom table while the older children ushered the younger back to bed and the smith's prentice talked to the townsfolk gathered outside, awaiting a cart to take the dead to the bonefolk. With the children gone, she finished, "And cutting their hands off. Almost as if to stop their haunts casting, or some such nonsense. It's madness."

"Where has this been happening?" the smith said. "We heard rumors, but there's every sort of rumor going around, half of them wild imaginings."

"Here, in the Boot, in the Heartlands, in the Girdle. In sowmid there were two in the Elbow. We follow trails and then lose them. We don't know how many they are or how they're organized or why they do it. It tailed off just after Wantons' Eve—do you call that Brightfire here? We hoped they were done, or caught, or dead."

"Now two of them are all three," said Kazhe.

"I wish we could have questioned them."

"I'll take them the way they are."

Benkana asked, "You think there's someone directing them?"

Karanthe shrugged. "There's no pattern. But there's more than one group. I'd like to know how they're connected, and what they have against people who used to be reckoners."

"Have they killed menders? Scribes? Scholars?"

"Not that I've heard, but I don't know. So many people die. People die with no one knowing; if they're not found before the bonefolk come, they disappear, and no one knows how they went."

"Why didn't you tell us this?"

"I hoped it was over."

Benkana looked at Kaẕhe, knowing her mind. "You can't protect all the former mages in the world."

"That's what kenaila do."

"And what about this other thing you're doing?"

The fervor abruptly ebbed from Kaẕhe's limbs, leaving her sitting naked at a cookroom table in the middle of the night. She'd wiped the dead's blood off on their own clothes, but her blade, propped against her chair, needed cleaning and oiling. Though it was sweltering even in the dark hours, she felt a need to wrap herself in something clean and dry.

Two nonned fighters, trained for one purpose, awaiting her direction—awaiting a message from the Boot. They were not trained kenaila. She could not train two nonned kenaila. Only two nonned kenaila could do that, and it would take years. They were trained for one task, one mission.

"I'll see it through," she said. But for the first time she felt doubt. Suppose Verlein or the Khinish won their decisive battle here in the Leg? It would fall to the victor to protect the runners. Let them bear the responsibility. A burden on that scale was the last thing in the world she wanted. *Let* someone bloody take over the world. Let them run it. Let them cope with this.

Yet if mages were dying . . .

There are no mages anymore. "People of light," they called them here, as if even to think the word "mage" was to overstep some superstitious bounds. *Call them what you will, they're gone, and they're never coming back.*

What idiocy, to kill them—

Unless . . .

"Your light *is* really gone, isn't it, Karanthe?" she asked carefully.

The runner nodded. "Yes. It's really gone."

So much for that. "Maybe they're still angry at the Ennead."

"For what?" said the smith. She was not one of the ones who had been with them six years before, in the Blooded Mountains. "For dying?"

Kazhe shared a look with Karanthe, then sighed. That story was too much to tell. "It doesn't matter. It's late. Men died here tonight. I don't suppose you recognized either of them, did you?"

To her surprise, Karanthe frowned. "I feel I saw them once, when they were younger. And less dead. But I can't think where."

"Then that doesn't matter either, unless it comes back to you. Could have been anywhere. I'm going back to bed. It's either that or one of your Longdark flings, the way I'm dressed."

They thanked the smith and her pledge, apologized for the disruption; she and Benkana left them insisting that Karanthe sleep in the house. Then there was a flutter and a cry. They turned back, blades ready, and found Karanthe, still in her silks, fumbling to wrap a dishcloth around her arm so that the hawk flapping unhappily around the room could perch there.

Fastened round its leg was not a message, but simply a token: a band of silk ribbon, dyed slate and rose to match the bird's plumage.

The runner looked at Kazhe.

"They're moving," she said.

The Khinish had woken.

Gir Doegre

Silks draped in luscious waves over the posts of stalls, linens and felts and flannels and tweeds and velvets in layered folds below, bundled textiles sandbagging the front of shops. Gauzes and crapes heaped and piled with negligent charm; gossamer scarves and wormsilk bed nets and lace table covers in soft profusion, a diaphanous billow and flutter. Woolens and braid rugs, carpets and throws, drifts of balled yarn. Brass doorplates and hinges and knobs, urns and candlestands, even oarlocks and cleats and stanchions—ship fittings, in this landlocked place equidistant from maur and sea. Pewter tableware, teaware, candleware. Playing stones and luck stones and counting stones and whetstones, mortars and pestles, earthenware, clayware. And everywhere tools. Trowels and spades and hoes, hay crooks and hay knives and hay hooks and hay forks and barley forks, flails and reaping hooks and sickles and scythes, here where the fields were dying and the crofts abandoned. Mortise axes, chisel axes, felling axes, hewing hatchets, shingling hatchets, lathing hatchets, jiggers and froes and drawknives, here where their softwood had rotted and what wasn't made of cedar or stone was made of tin. Thatchers' tools where they roofed with metal to keep vermin from spreading disease. Wares displayed with salacious decadence on streets somehow crowded, though illness had taken a hard toll.

This place must have been a wonder, in its day.

"There has to be *something* you want," Adaon said, coming up behind Dabrena where she stood at a coppersmith's stall, in a trance of velvet-sheened kettles and pots, platters and tureens.

Grieving spirits, she thought. *I cannot wipe this irritant off even for a morning.*

She hadn't ridden six leagues from the holding, on a gelding named Vervain with a packhorse in tow, when she'd caught sight of the bald head, dark gray over light gray scholar's garb on a short, thickset body strolling loose-limbed down the trail ahead. Now and then he'd stopped to listen, or examine some deadfall or rock formation of incomprehensible interest. When she'd come to within a ninefoot of him, he'd turned, and even from that distance his pale brows and pale eyes were startling against the dusky complexion. "Mender!" he'd said, as if welcoming her—with a forced show of delight—into his own spruce-vaulted home. "And where are you off to, packed for so long a journey? The Neck?"

It was a less than subtle gibe, with the Neck so near, and she responded coldly. Yet somehow in the next few breaths, as she walked her horse by him, he had talked her into offering him a ride. How the excess of the spare animal was understandable from one so cloistered. How a denizen of the isolated holding would naturally be ill at ease with company on the road. She didn't know why she'd let his challenges provoke her. It meant redistributing her gear so that he could mount the hard-gaited packhorse. It meant suffering his nonstop chatter. If she'd known he'd been a seeker before he went to the scholars' isle, she'd have ridden him down and not looked back. But she should have known. Seekers stopped at Senana when they bothered stopping anywhere, but a few had found their way into her holding, and she was familiar with their antics. She should have recognized him for what he was.

She'd seen seekers do remarkable work. She'd heard them together, honing plausibility from absurdity. They took crackpot notions and grated them down on facts. They produced, through dialogue and debate, hard results that chambers full of scribes working problems on sedgeweave could not. They had not been mages, did not think like mages; they did not even think like scholars, which was probably why Graefel was glad to see the back of this one. But there was more to their thoughts than folk credited, at least when applied to practical tasks. There might be more to Adaon than unendurable ribbing and unfathomable interests.

Not that she'd seen it if there was. What he thought was winsome had long since worn thin. She had grown accustomed to his presence on the road; he'd distracted her from guilt-ridden musings on the past and dark forebodings of the future. But she was in the Strong Leg now, though still in the watershadow of the Druilors. She had work to do, a mystery to solve. And what awaited her in Glydh, in the Knee, she must face alone.

She startled as his arm reached around her to pick up a barn lantern. The round holes were of simple cut, not stars or diamonds or floral shapes; there was no patterning to anything in this town beyond the workings themselves. In the Oriels, through Heartlands and Belt and Girdle, even around the high side of the Druilors, there were decorations and designs—painted on gourds, carved in chairs, enameled on tin, hammered in copper. Everything here was plain. Reports had told her that Strong Leggers resisted the liberation of magecraft's tools harder than most, but this was more than she expected. So much beauty wrought here, of so much talent, but none of it ornamented. It seemed strange to her, and stranger still that it should be strange at all. Mages had hoarded ornamentation for aeons. She had grown up in a dyeless, patternless world. Yet how quickly the forbidden had become the ordinary.

Except here.

"I've never seen such craft," Adaon said, examining the seamless soldering, "unless it was out of a tinker's wagon, and like as not that wagon came from here."

Neither had she. Perhaps they diverted the decorative urge into more painstaking basic work.

The purveyor swelled with pride. "Like as not it did. We're a metals town, copper and tin mostly and enough bronze to keep Bronze Long alive, but if it's iron you're after you'll need to go up Dru Myrle way, toward the Blooded Mountains. Poor selection here."

"Is it iron you're after?" Adaon asked, peering at her over her shoulder, his head level with hers and canted suggestively.

Trust him to find something lascivious in an inert element.

"It's peace and quiet I'm after," she said, elbowing him away as she turned.

She came face-to-chest with a man wearing a blade at his hip.

"Good day, mender," he said. "Good day, scholar."

It sounded as though he were bidding them farewell.

"Good day," Adaon said brightly. "How can we aid you?"

"Respect our ways," the man said, unaggressive but firm. He was broad-shouldered, slim-hipped, tall for a mid-Legger, with the region's impish features but no trace of humor on them. A local peacekeeper, if she remembered the nomenclature of Porfinn's last report. Porfinn, she remembered quite well, had disappeared in this leg over the winter. "Clothe yourselves plainly, or move on."

Dabrena gritted her teeth. Such a small thing to ask . . . and yet her whites defined her. In white, she knew who she was. *I lost my light,* she found herself thinking. *You won't have this from me too.* It was absurd. She must defer to the man. She was the visitor here. It was a new world now . . . and yet this vestige of the old seemed the most alien thing about it.

Apart from people roaming around bladed.

She inclined her head. "I'll change as soon as I've picked up something more suitable."

"Now would be wiser," the man said.

She blinked at him. "Here?"

"You're a nonned steps from any short where they trade in clothing."

Adaon said in her ear, "I think he's angling to see you in silks. Can't say I blame him."

The peacekeeper folded his arms, and Dabrena blushed to think he'd overheard. Where she came from—the Fingers, the holding—no one cared if you went buck naked. Why should this gall her so? Adaon and his blighted infantile humor!

"I was a warder once, and I wore white," she told the peacekeeper in a cold voice. "My wearing it now will deter the light's return no more than wearing it then effected its departure."

Adaon clucked at her and warned softly, "Better to show the man your silks than intimidate him with holding rhetoric."

"It's for your own safety, mender," the peacekeeper said, implacable. "And yours as well, scholar."

"It's not 'scholar' really," Adaon said. "I'm a seeker by nature, you see, I only—"

"Then divest yourself of dyes," the peacekeeper said, in deadpan mockery of Dabrena's speech, "and you'll be welcome to partake of the keepers' tithe. It's at the Tufted Duck today."

Adaon's eyes went wide. "I think he just told me to be a good seeker and go begging," he said to Dabrena. Voice high and aggrieved, he told the peacekeeper, "We don't really subsist on alms, you know, we pull our weight like any journeyfolk—"

Dabrena nudged him and lifted her chin to gesture beyond the bladed man, toward the three bladed folk who were moving to join him. A murmur rose up, heads turned in their direction. Before they knew it a crowd would form.

"Eiden's eyes," Adaon whispered, "next thing they'll mob us!" He turned his broad face to her and mouthed, *Run for it!*

They ran for it. Down the long street, dodging drifts and clumps of customers, keeping out of the path of carts and wagons. Dabrena caught hold of his wrist when they came to the clothing-heaped street and dragged him with her when he would have overshot. Abruptly a tangle of dogs and children and sticks came under her feet and sent her into a spectacular sprawl through the sticky mire of mist-damped dust. The children, unharmed, continued on in a burst of jeers and protest, leading the little dogs to jump over the sticks they held ever farther ahead.

"Get up, get up!" Adaon said, turning her over, taking her hands and hauling. She was dead weight. She could not brace herself or rise. She was laughing too hard. "They'll string us up, I tell you! Run for your life!"

Every single thing he had said since he came up behind her at the copper stall had been a windup. He was having her on, he was having the peacekeeper on, he was having her on again now.

"Get up!" he begged, but he was losing control of his panic. His lips were starting to twitch. "By all the blessed spirits, mender, get up!"

She got her feet under her and staggered behind him to the nearest stall, gasping, "It's all right, it's all right, *I'm not white anymore*!"

He turned from rummaging through breeches to examine her with a critical eye. He brushed at the great smear of brown that was the front of her, smacked at her soiled knees, and shook his head. "Not brown enough," he pronounced, and looked down at his dove-colored self. "Too gray!" He pulled off a boot and hopped on one foot as he haggled with the astonished trader behind the stall, then handed across his entire carrybelt for collateral. Balancing with the stockinged foot raised, he fingered quickly through dun and beige linens and knits, choosing and discarding until he had two tunics and two pairs of hose in roughly the right sizes. He thrust Dabrena's at her, stripped off his dove tunic, wrestled off the other boot, and peeled off his hose. "Go on," he urged, "go on!"

She followed suit, standing on her toppled boots to keep her socks out of the dirt, and when the peacekeepers rounded the corner, two scratching their heads, one shaking his, she and the seeker were smoothing new garments, fastening belts, sliding back into boots, to present sober, acceptable, and utterly drab attire to the guardians of propriety.

There'd never been so much as a glance from Adaon to her silk sark and drawers.

"You could have bribed the keeper," he said, between a slurp of greenbriar soup from a plain tin spoon and a slug of dark stonenut brew from a plain tin cup. "I know just what would have shifted him."

They had finally stopped laughing after the keepers sent them on their way, and packed their colors safe with their gear in the farrier's barn where the horses were stabled. Then they'd returned to the inn where she'd arranged lodgings for the night, an indulgence after well over a moon on the road in miserable weather.

"If I'd known you were hoarding tallies good over half of Eiden Myr, I'd have charged you for your passage," she said.

"I'd have worked my passage off anytime," he replied, holding the leer for only a moment before it lapsed into a chuckle.

She flipped the spoon in her fingers and moved bits of walnut around the dregs of her cucumber soup. "What are you looking for, Adaon?"

"I've been looking to make you laugh for a moon now, and let me tell you, it was no easy thing."

"What are you really looking for?"

"Do you really expect an answer? I'm a seeker. I seek."

"Oh, please."

"I'm looking for everything. I look at everything. The world is astonishing and wonderful. Look at this soup! The way the greenbriar thickens it, the way the vegetables soften on cooking. Why do you think they do that?"

"You filled my ears with that same babble over three mountain ranges, Adaon. I asked you a question."

"You've been head of that Head holding too long, I think."

"You think too much."

"I talk too much, too. Wouldn't you rather let me eat this astonishing soup?"

He held his spoon in the overhand way she'd tried to teach Kara not to. She was suddenly back in the spare lamplit dining hall where she'd eaten with her child for six years.

"And no mooning over your daughter," Adaon added with his mouth full. He swallowed, wiped a dribble from his chin, and said, "Tell me how this is different from your journeying. You did journey after you took the triskele?"

She let him have his diversion. It diverted her from the flare of phantom pain in her missing limb, the place where there had been a child attached. It never stopped aching, but now and then, just now and then . . . "Not for the full year," she said. "I did the Heartlands, the Belt, and the Low Arm. Kept ahead of reckoners for nearly five moons before they caught me and sent me to the Ennead's Holding. It was a game, to see how long I could elude them."

"I knew you'd had experience in fleeing from figures of authority!"

She smiled. "It took me that long to talk myself into becoming a warder. The call was inevitable. There's not much light in the Fingers, but when it flares it flares bright. Flared, I mean."

"Slip of the mind."

"Mmm. I'd been harvestmaster at nine-and-eight. The next season I took the triskele. Ran off journeying that very night. Thought I'd go on forever. Thought that was what I wanted." She'd lapsed back into the brief bursts of speech that characterized folk from home. When her own words echoed in her mind, it was the first time she'd heard that kind of speech in years.

"It's different now," Adaon said, and tilted his bowl over his mouth to scoop the last drops in.

"Yes," she said. "Now I'm plagued with a rejected scholar."

"I wasn't rejected!"

" 'Bloody spirits, go on then, if you want it so much, but leave me in peace'?"

"That's very close, Wordsmith. But Graefel affects more of a Holding accent than you do."

"Don't call me Wordsmith here. They'll string me up."

He laughed. "There's hope for you."

"You weren't a mage. You went to the scholars to learn the great truths the codices would reveal."

"Something like that. I learned to read and scribe. The codices aren't all they're cracked up to be."

"So what are you looking for?"

He threw her a sly smile. "Nicely turned."

She watched him for a long time when he spoke no further. He was waiting her out. There was no reason to play into his hands. There was no reason to trust him; there was no reason not to. There was every temptation to underestimate him. His eyes, pale as ice in the ash-skinned face, betrayed nothing he did not want them to.

He made me laugh. How long has it been, really, since I laughed?

The knowledge that he might have been working her made her abruptly, deeply, weary.

At the same moment, he gave a small nod in concession, as though she had outlasted him, and said, "I saw the child's map, Dabrena. You don't need to pull it from that carrybelt to show me. When I see a thing, I remember it. It's brought us to the same place."

She frowned, shook her head. "The map is a whimsy. Something Kara said did bring me here, and *I* brought *you* to this place. But it's just a stop on a journey. My destination lies farther on."

"Is it? Does it? Look at the map again. Not here—they'll string us up, remember? In the privacy of the room upstairs. That map is centered on this town. That map is *of* this town."

She blew air through her lips. "I think that map is whatever your fevered imaginings want it to be, seeker. You were keenly interested in real maps we'd made in the holding. You have some idea in your head, and you think my daughter's fantasies support it. I think this is at last where we part ways. Though I do thank you for the laughter."

With raised brows—mocking? suprised? he had become unreadable—he pushed back in his chair and stood to gesture her toward the stairs. A movement as gallant as he'd shown her in the holding, but peremptory, and challenging. Intensity came off him like heat. He could as easily have been daring her to bed him as to disprove a theory

She laughed aloud to think that this was seeker foreplay.

He did not laugh back this time.

"All right," she said, and rose, but she gestured gallantly for him to precede her up the stairs, and hoped that she wouldn't have to send him out hunched over his groin to sleep with the packhorse.

The slope-ceilinged room barely admitted them in addition to the two narrow beds and small chest that already occupied it. A triangular window over the chest between the beds let in a watery gray light. Adaon sat on the right-hand bed and dragged the tin chest into the light with a teeth-grating scrape. The metal bedframe whined at his weight. Though hardly more than her height, he was a broad man, thickly built. He was larger than himself. His presence made the small room smaller.

Dabrena sat lightly on the other bed and opened her carrybelt to draw forth Kara's map and lay it on the chest. The banded surface was uneven, so she did not smooth the sedgeweave out.

"You see?" she said. "Such a fuss over a child's invention."

"Look at it." He didn't point, didn't even touch the map to hold the curling edges down. He leaned slightly toward her, with his elbows out and his dark hands braced backward on his thighs.

She rolled her eyes, and then she looked.

"Yes," she said after a few long breaths. "It could be here. It could also be Gir Youris, Gir Myrle, Gir Anad—any mid-Leg town wedged among hills along a river."

"Are we in the Midlands?"

"More or less."

"More less than more. We're in the mid-Leg, yes. But the Highlands follow the bulge of the Knee. The Druilors have bottomed out.

Their foothills are away Headward of us, and the Cors are away Bootward. Below us is all bottomland. Above us is a flat stretch cut off by the Elfelirs. We are on what amounts to a plain. Yet around us are eight hills, positioned as on your daughter's map."

"The body of Eiden is a strangeness. Its topography isn't a natural thing. Someone crafted it this way, some ancient folk, whoever carved out the holding in the Aralinns, whoever shaped the land in human form. Eiden himself, perhaps. Or some folk who lived here long before Galandra led her mages into exile."

"I'm not trying to explain why these hills are here."

"You should be."

"And I will. But you must admit that the child's representation can only show this place. See how vague it is elsewhere, how misshapen."

"All except the Knee."

"The Knee is clear, and even to scale, yes. Yet it lacks the detail of this area."

"This was drawn by a six-year-old!"

"A talented one, enamored of maps, perfectly capable of drawing an accurate one, who knew precisely what she was doing."

"This was not where Tol—" She bit her lip. "This was not where I was meant to go."

"Then indeed our ways must part. I am where I was going."

He sat back, relaxed his shoulders, laced his fingers loosely between his legs. She got up, leaving the map, moving to lean beside the door.

"What will you do here?" she asked.

"Keep looking. I'll start at this hill, where Kara's drawn in a circle of trees. Woodhill, they call it. Appropriate."

"Why there?"

"How did Kara know there was forest on that hill? It's not on any of your menders' maps; they don't detail terrain that closely in this leg. Yet there's forest on Boothill and Pointhill, too, and she didn't illustrate those."

"You were already leaving the holding when she showed you the map. You already knew where you would go."

"I had two choices. The Strong Leg or the Haunch. Her map intrigued me enough to choose the Strong Leg first."

"Why the Haunch?"

"Because the reckoners are drawn there. But they're looking in the wrong place, too, if Pelkin even knows to look at all."

"*Looking for what?*"

He got up, rising fluidly from the knees, and moved to the door.

It brought him to within a pace of her. "If it's there, I'll let you know by sunset," he said. Then he glanced at the window, and grinned. "That gives you most of an afternoon with the room to yourself! Perhaps that keeper is due a break. The slim hips, the fair hair, the stoic demeanor . . . he'd be a nut worth cracking, wouldn't you say?"

She swore at him, and he left the room laughing. "I'll be sure to knock!" he sang from the stairs.

The room was stifling. She rolled the map back into her carrybelt, then went down into the common room, left the inn. Adaon was nowhere in sight. Old folks sitting on the porch were talking about illness coming to Lowhill again. She was a mender; there would be something she could do. She started off to fetch a pack of herbs and dressings from the farrier's and offer aid. But the symptoms sounded familiar. She turned back. She asked the old folk for details. It was Rikka paralytic fever, though in Rikka they called it Elia's seizure and here they called it the fire palsy. It had moved around Maur Lengra since winter. Highly contagious during first onset, then inert from the fever stage through death, which occurred in perhaps a third of the cases. Her menders had not yet found a reliable treatment when she left the holding. "Got old by staying away from trouble like that," one of the men said. "Best you do the same."

He was right. She had to live long enough to find Tolivar's treasure, to see Kara into womanhood. She would not get through the quarantine cordon; and there was nothing she could do, no information she could add to what they knew. Hating herself, relieved, guilty, she went back into the inn with a vague notion of getting just pleasantly tipsy. At least the drink here wasn't watered; tending drip pits expended more effort than just serving the stuff full strength, and poisoning customers was generally bad for trade. Listening to the innkeeper gossip with an idle taverner from down the road, she managed one cup of hard pear cider before the dark absurdities of rumor turned her stomach. Khinish killing people of light in their beds, runners stealing children . . . the only plausible news was of a terrible new sickness running down rivers from Fist to Belt, and it only made her frustrated that she was not in her holding, receiving reports, coordinating a response.

She walked up the stairs and back into the stifling room, took out Kara's sedgeweave, and sat heavily on the bed. She was still staring at the map when the light from the sunrise-facing window was no longer enough to see by.

Three hard raps came on the door, and she jerked nearly out of her skin.

"Ho inside!" came a lusty voice. "Unsheath that blade, now, and tuck it away. . . ."

"Oh, just come in, Adaon," Dabrena said, coarse and irritable.

He opened the door slowly, peered around it, then entered and shut it behind him. "Was he that quick? No cuddle after? No juice in him for a second round? There's no flush to your cheeks. . . ."

"You couldn't tell in this light. How did you fare?"

"There's a glade, but it's guarded. I couldn't get in. I'll have to petition their alderfolk. Naturally I'll argue them into granting admittance. They'll grant anything, to get rid of *me*."

"Guarded?"

He crooked a smile at her and leaned against the door. "Makes you think there might be something there after all, doesn't it? But it's their boneyard, their hauntwood. They've had trouble with thieving, someone taking the objects the bonefolk leave. So they've posted bladed keepers."

A place they carried their dead so that the bonefolk would come, just as in the holding they carried them to a special chamber. Not uncommon, in populous places. The bonefolk would not come if the living were near.

A forest of the dead. A forest of haunts.

But Tolivar was from the Knee. . . .

Still, who knew where the dead might roam? Some would say he should have been unable to leave the rock he died in.

And who knew what the dead might tell each other. . . .

"We can still get in."

He cocked a brow at the plural, but didn't comment. "I couldn't sneak in through the woods, I make far too much noise."

"There's another way."

"Show me."

"We'll have to wait till full dark."

Nodding thoughtfully, he said, "Supper first, then?"

"Not a good idea."

After a disgusted, despairing groan he produced an exaggerated retching sound.

Now it was her turn to nod. "There's been a run of paralytic fever in Lowhill. They'll be carting dead out tonight."

"And us with them. Charming." He crossed to his bed, lay down supine, and laced his fingers under his head. "Tell me, then: How long *have* you been keeping celibate?"

She closed her eyes. "You and I, Adaon, have very different notions of how to amuse ourselves."

He wiggled in delight and crossed his legs at the ankle. "We certainly do! You could have had *three* keepers in the time I was away!"

"I was referring to conversation that passes the time during an enforced wait. For example: What made you become a seeker?"

"Burning, restless curiosity and a tendency to grow quickly bored. We had this conversation at midday. Is it the loss of the first freedom? Afraid to come with child?"

"I have a child."

"She's a beautiful child! Make more of her! Go wild, bed anyone you fancy."

"You, for instance?"

He made a rude noise. "Anyone you like. What's to stop you? You're a mender, surely you know there are ways of preventing—"

"Eiden's spleen, Adaon, it's not that. Just leave it, will you?"

"Perhaps you couldn't be parted from the girl long enough to have any fun."

"Tread carefully there."

"Or perhaps there *was* no one you fancied."

It was almost completely dark in the small room now. The window was a portal on indigo, the poisoned river rushing two stories below it. Adaon, when he sat up, was like a shade rising from its resting place. She remembered her vision of him in the holding, the stunted reversal of a boneman. He leaned forward, legging the chest out of the way. In his dark skin, in the gloaming, the whites of his eyes were lurid under the pale shadows of brow.

"You have to want *something*, Dabrena," he said softly.

"Your overtures stop here."

"I'm not suggesting that it be me. I'm not suggesting that it be that kind of pleasure. But there has to be pleasure. Not just the cold iron of responsibility and abstinence."

"And what pleasure do you take, Adaon?"

The white of his grin opened below the whites of his eyes, then winked out as he rose and turned for the door. "Right now? Tormenting you. In a few breaths, hugging the dead. Are you sure they're not contagious?"

They awaited the cart in the dark by the side of the Knee Road, crouched by a wilted hedgerow.

"How will we get on it?"

"Run behind, grab on, jump in."

"They'll hear us."

"Not over the sound of the team. Not if we do it right."

"Suppose there are outriders with lanterns?"

"Then we give it up and find another way."

"We might have to stay till daybreak."

"That will delay the bonefolk."

"I might need to have a good look round."

"And two perfectly good beds back in that inn."

"We don't need a bed."

"Don't try to exploit this."

"It was your idea."

"I won't shift you in a boneyard."

"It would keep us warm."

"It's sweltering out."

"Don't talk like that, I'm getting aroused."

"Looking at vegetables gets you aroused."

"Come to think of it, it does. Say 'lentil' for me. Just once. Please."

Heartache silenced her. She had bantered with harvesters this way once; it had been she accosting them with ribald insults and encouragements. She had bantered with vocates this way once. She had bedded every pretty boy she fancied. Now handsome, muscular keepers held no allure, and it took the turn of a moon to leverage a laugh from her.

What have you done to yourself, Dabrena?

It was a jolting, nightmarish ride. The corpses were shrouded, but they hadn't been washed; the odors of their illness clung to them, and the one on Dabrena's side was still warm. The driver passed the keepers' post with only somber acknowledgment, and no one looked within. They hopped out just as the wagon slowed but before it stopped and silence could fall. The glade was shrouded in fog; they didn't have to move far to stay concealed.

There seemed nothing remarkable about the place. It smelled like a wood, it felt like a wood.

"Well?" Dabrena whispered, after the driver and her helper had laid the bodies out and turned the team and the wagon had rattled off. It didn't take two oxen or a wagon that size to cart five bodies. They'd had more before, and expected more tonight.

She felt Adaon shake his head, and she settled in for a long night in the rough.

Another wagonload arrived at what might have been midnight, though she had no way of telling except that it felt she'd slept for a long time. She jolted awake at the sound and lifted her head from

Adaon's shoulder, glad to miss any leer or smirk in the dark. The driver and her helper murmured in consternation to find the five bodies still there. "Why don't they come?" Dabrena heard one say. "Tell the keepers to stand farther off."

She woke again at dawn sprawled half across Adaon, another wistful reminder of her vocate days, and raised herself before he woke as well. Fog and ground damp had soaked into her. She scooped a squirming insect off her neck and shook out her hair. The dead were still there, eight of them wrapped in their shrouds, unmolested by the wildlife. It hadn't been so bad a night as the old folks on the inn's porch had feared. She prodded Adaon. He was tough as the proverbial log. It was light enough to see, though too misty to see much except for some astonishing broad trees, and she wanted to be out of here as soon as he'd had his look round.

He came to after a harder jab, groggy, as if returning from some far realm, and looked as though he had no idea what he was doing flat on the ground. When he saw who was leaning over him, he sat up suddenly, backpedaling through wet bracken, and held his hands up as if to placate her.

She made a face and held her finger to her lips, then gestured around the glade: *Go on, have your look.*

With the brisk nod of someone making a show of being awake when he was not, the seeker crept off on hands and knees into the roiling fog, as if he were feeling the ground for some sign the earth would give him of its nature.

There was a soft crackle to her left, and then the prick of a blade tip in her shoulder. "So you're why they didn't come."

She raised her head slowly, taking in muscled calves, hard thighs, a cocked hip. She continued upward past a broad chest to the impish features of a chestnut-haired keeper—features arranged into a sternness that did not suit them. "Are you *all* this handsome?" she said. Her voice sounded dreamy and dull in the fog, thick with sleep.

"Get up," he replied, and called across the obscured clearing, "I've got your explanation over here, Onlorin."

Dabrena obeyed him, steadying herself on the trunk of an ancient, hollowed yew. She felt unbalanced—drunk on mist and mysteries. It hadn't occurred to her that getting out of here would mean getting caught, but once it did, she was irrationally pleased. She would distract the keepers while Adaon crawled and groped for . . . whatever he was crawling and groping for.

"What are you doing here?" the keeper said.

"I was sleeping," she said.

"By yourself in a spirit wood."

A sadness swept through her. "I was hoping for Tolivar," she said. "But he didn't come."

"A tryst?" the keeper said, utterly disgusted.

A tryst. She started to laugh, and then sobered. "More of a quest." Best not mention treasure, they'd have her up for thievery then.

"She's some kind of seeker from the sound of it," he called again to Onlorin, who grunted from his invisible position. To Dabrena he said, "This is a serious matter. You've kept the bonefolk off, dishonored our dead. I don't know what restitution you can make for something like this, but that's for the alderfolk to decide." With a hand on her back, his blade held low in the other hand, he pressed her along the tree line toward where she supposed the road was. She went willingly, then stopped and turned. "I would have bedded you, you know."

"What?"

She shook her head at his exasperation. This was important. "I would have bedded you once. But then the baby came, and Tolivar went, and none of that mattered anymore. I had to grow up."

"You have a ways to go, from what I can see." He called to Onlorin again to cover his position, and acknowledgment came back through the mist. Dabrena let herself be herded and did not turn or speak again until there was a thud and an oath and a rustle and another oath from the glade behind them, and the second keeper came out of the mist with Adaon by the collar. "Look what I tripped over," he said.

"Is this your Tolivar?" Dabrena's keeper asked.

"No," she said, and sighed. "He's Adaon. He's alive."

"All right," the first keeper said, gratingly patient. He took Adaon in hand. "I'll take the two of them back to the . . ."

A queasy vibration undulated below their feet, and passed.

The keepers stared at each other. Adaon stared at the ground. Dabrena stared at the trees.

The birds had gone silent.

It came again, like a wave passing deep in the earth. This time it stuttered, as if snagged on something, and wrenched to the side, staggering all four of them.

Adaon swept Dabrena with him as he broke into a trot down the sloped, curving road. The keepers shouted after them and started to pursue, but the earth wrenched back the other way, and they all reeled.

Adaon kept his hold on Dabrena, caught a hazel trunk with the other arm, and hung on until it passed. They made the main road before the next small quake, but that one knocked them into a ditch.

By the time they scrabbled out of it, the keepers were running past them. Ignoring them—just trying to get back to town.

"What *is* it?" Dabrena said, her head swept clear by incipient panic.

"It's a quake."

"They don't have quakes here."

"They do now. Hang on."

She hung on to the ground, going to hands and knees in a bid for stability. But the ground shook her off, and she'd rolled two jarring threfts down cartwheel ruts before the shake subsided. The earth itself could not be trusted.

"If it gets any worse, some of these trees are going to fall." She sat up as Adaon came down next to her in a crouch. "Did we do this? Did we do this by chasing the bonefolk off?"

"Of course not," he said, unconvincingly.

"What did you find? Anything?"

"No." He gathered her against him as another ripple went through the ground, vertigo made tangible. It was less this time. "That was an aftershock, I think."

Dabrena shrugged free. "We've got to get the horses, get out of here."

"I can't leave Gir Doegre yet. This is where it is. I just don't know how to prove it."

The billows of mist took on a greenish tinge, then went white again, and thinned. "They've come," Dabrena said.

"And gone," said Adaon. "Let's go back. It's wider there, less chance of treefall striking us."

They climbed back up the slope, swayed only briefly by a mild aftershock. The glade was cleared of its dead. Small handleless iron tools were left where they had lain, and a circle of counting stones on a string, shining wet. The fog was not so heavy now, more a passage of tattered mists on currents of air they couldn't feel. The day was already laden with heat. Dabrena's wet clothes were heavy on her body, though the tunic was a summer linen and the hose a light, breathable knit of silk and flax.

"What did you think you'd find?" she asked Adaon.

He walked the periphery, testing the curve or levelness of the ground, examining the growth pattern of yews and hazel and bonewood, peering through them to the younger stonewood and ironwood that dominated the rest of the hill. "A shape," he said. "A sense. A flatness. A newer place, I suppose, though I may have had it backward. And there's no telling how many nonneds of years it's been. Plenty of time for a grassy mound to become an aging forest. They haven't tended this wood, just left it alone in the midst of a forest they cut. That's not healthy for it in the end, though they did keep the stonewoods from overshadowing it."

"Now you sound like one of us."

"They're dying. Even the trees renewed by harvesting for wood and lumber. They shouldn't be."

"Their rivers poison them here. They carry minerals from the Druilors that magecraft doesn't clear anymore."

"These aren't river trees. No river runs under this hill. They drink rainwater."

"The clouds and fog are deceptive. They're in the middle of a drought here. It hasn't rained in . . ." She was embarrassed to find her hand twitching to reach for a codex she didn't have, to find a fact she didn't carry in her head. ". . . a long time."

"Ah. Thank you, mender. That explains some of it."

"Perhaps I could be of help in other ways. If you would tell me what you seek."

He came over to crouch by where she sat in leaf litter, her hands pressed to the sides of her head. "You're in pain?" he said.

"My head's pounding. I think I'm hung over. I'd like to know what that fog was spiked with."

"The truth, from the sound of it."

"For me, but not for you."

"I don't need drunken mist. I'm a seeker, I always speak truth."

She laughed, then winced at the pain. "You do not."

"Yes, I do." Smiling, he added, "Not that a great deal can't be twisted by the inflection." He sat beside her, heavily, as though the weight of the heat and this ancient place was affecting him, too. "I'm looking for the Triennead holdings, Dabrena."

She stared at him, her mind wiped blank.

"You must have thought of it," he said, seeker hubris surfacing briefly. "One could not have been enough. There had to have been three. Three holdings would have balanced each other, checked each other's excesses, resisted the formation of one misguided hidebound hierarchy vulnerable to corruption. All the most powerful things come in threes. The first mages would have established three holdings. Seekers have argued this theory for years. Of course no one listened to them. Graefel was ready to banish me for pressing the issue."

"The Ennead's Holding defended Eiden Myr against the Sea of Storms," she said, trying to grasp it. "One holding, at the Head. That's all there ever was. That's all we needed."

"Three holdings, evenly spaced throughout Eiden's body. Centers for healing, learning. Accessible places where folk could seek knowledge, and share it." He looked sidelong at her.

She swallowed. It had become very hard to breathe. "Wishful thinking," she said. She stared at the ground as if she might sink in, trapped, drowning in earth.

Adaon blocked her view, rolling up onto his knees before her, leaning forward, his hands pressed tight between his thighs. His pale eyes burned. "There's something here, Dabrena." His voice was hoarse, breathless, his speech rushed and intense. "In that town and under these hills. Refugees flock here and stay for no good reason. Gir Doegre draws people. The Haunch draws people, reckoners in particular. It drew them even when there was light. Sauglin was a meeting ground for journeymages, a place the untriaded went in desperation, craving power, craving light. They sensed it there, under the ground. They sense it still. And it's here. Can't you feel it?"

She had felt inebriated, then drained. Now her heart raced, her blood pulsed. *There has to be* something *you want*. . . .

"I was sent here to find treasure," she breathed.

She'd thought the treasure might be people. Someone who had miraculously retained a light, perhaps. But if it was the contents of a second holding, buried under the aeons and the earth . . .

A trove of stored codices. Codices no one living had ever seen. Codices that would fill in everything they had been missing because the only texts they'd had to go by predated the mages' exile from the outer realms.

"History is treasure," Adaon said.

For him. He was a scholar after all, delving the past. For her it was practical knowledge they could use to mend and cure. Her folk pored over ancient herbals, but the plants matched few that grew on Eiden's body—they were mostly herbs and roots and flowers of the outer realms, rendering the text useful only as paradigm, not practical guide. They pored over descriptions of ancient crafts, but many of the woods and stones were unknown to them here. It was only partly the fault of uncertain translation. The words weren't wrong. There was simply nothing in their world that corresponded to them. Reiligh had worked wonders with grafts and crossbreeding, but his success owed more to his own natural talents than to anything they'd learned from the ancient world. What Adaon's theory and Tolivar's treasure and Kara's map combined to offer was the missing link in a referential chain: codices that had been kept during the reclamation of Eiden Myr from wasteland.

"We'd have to dig," she said, getting her knees under her, sinking her fingers into the mulch.

"Not by hand," Adaon said. His thighs pressed tightly against his fists. "And not here. This is a sacred place now."

"From the side, then."

"Perhaps. But only with the alderfolk's permission. It will not be given easily. And there are eight hills."

"You'll argue them into it. You'll charm them."

"Perhaps."

"But . . . Adaon, they can't know. They can't, you mustn't tell them—they'll destroy anything that's left. There won't *be* anything left, what am I saying . . . nonneds of years under the ground, any wardings on them broken with the light . . ."

"There will be something. But it may be too great an assumption to believe they kept records at all."

"They did. They had to. The prohibitions on permanent scribing must have come later. They never made any sense. All that time, through all those golden years of magecraft, there were codices in the Head. The last Ennead kept records for years, made copies, and it never harmed the craft. Superstition, like keepers keeping people from wearing dyes. The first mages must have known better. Superstition came later, from ignorance, from forgetting. . . ."

"You want those codices. Spirits, look at you—"

"You want them too. You must. You're a scholar . . ."

"I gave up my grays for one tail-eye glimpse of a pretty girl in silks. I want to know *why*, Dabrena. What happened, why the Triennead fell, who lived and who died in the dim mists of the past. I want to restore a lost age into our keeping. We do not know what we are unless we know what we were, why we were, why we changed. It's the *knowing*, Dabrena, don't you see? What I want is to *know*. . . ."

They were kneeling face-to-face, hot and soaked, breath coming hard, Adaon's hands clenched to keep from touching her, Dabrena's clawing into the earth.

He managed a wan grin. "And you thought vegetables excited me."

She swayed toward him.

He swayed back, blinking.

"Adaon . . ."

He murmured, "I only meant . . ."

She pressed her mouth against his, pressed him back into the yielding ground cover. His heart pounded wildly under her breasts. She smoothed one hand over the sweet curve of his head, explored the tense ridges and furrows of muscled neck and chest and arm with the other. She slid her leg across his thighs, levered her hips over with the other knee, sank down. Under his body she felt Eiden's body swell to welcome them.

Adaon took her by the shoulders and moved her off him, rolling them onto their sides, gasping as her lips came away. "No," he said. "You will not have me in order to make a point."

"There's no point but that I want you."

He caught her wandering hand. "This is use. Don't use me this way. Please."

"*You*, Adaon. Not some pretty keeper to prove I can still take risks."

He searched her eyes. Evaluating, not pleading. "I want more than this from you," he said. "More than I can have."

"Don't be so sure of that." She kissed the jumping pulse in his throat, digging one hand under his hip and curving the other around his rear to keep him still as she fitted herself to him, ground gently against his hard length. She nearly lost herself to waves of sweetness.

"Don't," he begged, gripping her hipbones, forcing her back. When she growled, he gave a ragged laugh. "I won't last that way, love. It's been a long time."

She had been close. She couldn't wait anymore. She fumbled his tunic up to get at his waistband, undo the string; an impatient thrust of her hips in his hands urged him to do the same. He complied, but more slowly, distracted by her caress as she freed him from the impediment of fabric or unwilling to let her rush. He kissed her, deeply and thoroughly, with a kind of amazement—as if this was one moment of bliss the spirits had for some unknowable reason blessed him with, and he was prolonging it, because it would end, because it would never come again.

She smiled against his mouth, an irresistible, joyful smile, and extricated her tongue, and took his hands from where they belayed her, and said, "The sooner we do this, the sooner we can do it again."

He surrendered then, and she let him cover her, let him control it, in smooth even thrusts that swept her up to the brink in moments. She drove her face into the thick flesh of his neck and let out a deep groan as ecstasy peaked and vision fractured. He followed without a sound, one great silent shudder. As he eased his weight to the side, she began, impossibly, terribly, to laugh. It jounced him out of her, and he rolled onto his back. An uncertain smile flirted with hurt.

"If I'd known my rusty technique would produce this hilarity," he said, "I'd have saved myself a moon's attempts at cleverness and kept my grays in the bargain."

She kissed his ear, his pale-stubbled jaw, trailed her hand down wrinkled linen in a frustrated wish to stroke his chest, and said, still laughing, "That is the only thing in your life, Adaon, that you do in complete silence."

He let his head fall back and relaxed with a sigh. She caressed the spent softness between his legs, exploring him, toying with the notion of a second time. Then, reluctantly, she sat up and grasped the bunched tangle his hose and silks had become. He protested, but raised his hips at her insistent tug, so she could slide the hose up and snug the drawstring.

"The quake's over," she said, fixing her own clothes. She stood to give him a hand up, grunting. He was dense as a tree. "Despite every effort, we failed to make the earth move again. The keepers should have been back by now."

"Good thing they weren't sooner. Sleeping here was crime enough. I can only imagine what they'd have made of *that*."

Dabrena surveyed the peaceful glade, drank in the deep, ancient quiet. "I think the dead might have been rather pleased."

He brushed twigs and leaves from her clothes, turning her to clear the back and comb his fingers through her hair. Her eyes slid closed under the caress. His arms came around her, and his lips touched her ear. "I don't suppose you meant what you said."

She swiveled to face him. "I did. This doesn't have to end, Adaon."

He smiled, hopeful and wry and sad all at once. "It will, Dabrena. It will end. But I will love every brief precious moment while it lasts."

She kissed his broad lips, left corner and right, top and then bottom, loath to give up the taste of him. He squeezed her tight, and she felt arousal swell against her groin. With a moan, she gave him her tongue, but he drew back after barely two breaths, placing thick fingertips on either side of her chin.

"All right," he said. "I believe you. But alderfolk now."

She was slow in releasing him.

"Codices, Dabrena," he sang, gently taunting.

"Lentil," she threw back at him, and struck off down the path to the main road.

She came into the crowded haze of midday Gir Doegre with the seeker's arm draped over her shoulders and glints and gleams of visions sparkling across her mind's eye: new holdings, new knowledge; exchanging their lodgings for space to spread out for a leisurely, thorough encounter; what it would feel like to hold ancient vellum no one had seen in generations, to open to the first recovered leaf;

striding into a place like Lowhill with lifesaving remedies, their rescuer, their savior; what Adaon's skin would feel like bare against hers, the broad dark whole of him; history and codices unearthed and restored; coming home to Kara a better mother, a better woman, with that charming scholar at her side, to whisk her off into a wide world full of wonder and invitation. The restrained panic in the long streets, the shuttered windows and absent wares along the short, the keepers massing along the Boot Road, all jarred so badly that she simply could not comprehend them. As reaction to an earthquake half a day gone, none of this made sense. The quake had passed. Why were folk running, why the looks of fear? They didn't have quakes in this region, but many had fled quakes elsewhere; memory and ignorance might combine to produce such anxiety. But why all the keepers? Why had the traders packed up their wares, breakable and unbreakable?

"The Khinish have *woken*!" a woman cried when Adaon waylaid her, as if she'd had to say it twice and he still hadn't heard. "They're coming. The shield is tightening to meet them. There'll be fighting here, or near enough. Spirits, let me go!" His attempts to calm her failed, and she tore free and disappeared into the mists and milling crowds.

Dabrena's heart went cold. "The Khinish."

"There've been rumors of them waking for some time now."

"It's Streln, their headman, he saw things on his way Headward . . . but we've seen nothing of the sort, it's madness, it makes no *sense*. . . ."

But of course it made sense. That was the point he'd been making, when he held her daughter to the blade. Not that pacifist Dabrena would gladly sanction violence if the outer realms threatened her home . . . but that he, Streln, Khine, could hold all Eiden Myr to the blade.

Verlein had killed the man he ordered to do it. Verlein was moving her shield in now to stop him. A blade to pierce Khine's throat before it could do any harm, whether it intended to or not.

"We've got to get out of the road," Adaon said.

They made their way, bumped and jostled, down Bronze Long, to the inn where they'd taken a room. Dabrena needed a moment to think, to sort out motivations and intentions and plan her response. She'd need runners . . . birdmasters . . .

The innkeeper was brusque and acerbic; he'd let the room when they never came back, but they could have it again now, all right. "And there's a girl been in looking for you, so."

The holding, messaging her to tell her what she now already knew. "Where is she?"

"Running up one long and down another trying to find you, I

imagine. No, I take that back—she's right behind you."

Dabrena turned as Beadrin came up. She was a holding girl, one of the stablemaster's fosterlings from before the magewar, stayed on to do what stewards had once done. She ran messages for them, but never this far—they'd have employed a runner for a trip like this. Dabrena frowned at her, trying to wait until she got her breath. Her eyes were shifty, as if she'd done something wrong. Or carried some news she feared, for all her desperation, to deliver.

"Tell me," Dabrena said.

"It's Kara," Beadrin said. "She's . . . They've taken her."

All the blood left her limbs. She remained standing only because she was already standing, because no breath of air brushed her. "The Khinish," she said.

"No, no . . ."

"Who?"

Whatever Beadrin saw in Dabrena terrified her. "R-R-Reiligh . . ." she stuttered, and could get no further.

Dabrena slammed her into a chair, one fist in her collar, one hand on the chairback, tilting it but not letting it fall. She shoved her face down to the girl's. "Not Reiligh."

"Rei—" she choked. Her arms windmilled.

Dabrena's fist tightened convulsively at her throat. "Reiligh didn't hurt her. Reiligh didn't lose her. He watched. I left him to watch. *Reiligh wasn't the betrayer!*"

"I—don't—what—" The girl was strangling. Her fingers clawed Dabrena's wrist. Dabrena clenched tighter.

"Let her speak." Adaon lifted the back of the chair with one arm, the other hand closing over her fist, pressing between thumb and foreknuckle until it opened. His elbow moved her back, and he crouched in front of the gasping girl. "Tell it," he said, his voice low and flat.

"Reiligh left her with Loris, they were in a scriptorium and he was called out to discuss something he didn't want her to hear, but it only took a few breaths and he went back in to fetch her, and . . ."

Beadrin faltered. Dabrena twitched, and Adaon barred her from the girl. "Get your breath," he said, "and go on."

"Reiligh found Loris . . . giving her to the bonefolk. The boneman took her . . . he . . ."

She couldn't say it. It wasn't fear of Dabrena's rage. She hadn't even been there to witness it, but it was so horrible that she couldn't get it out.

"He killed her," Adaon said.

To find out. Only to find out.

The breath between that probing statement—*he shouldn't have said it words make things true words have too much power*—and the girl's answer was the longest of Dabrena's life.

"No!" Beadrin cried. "I don't know. I don't know what it does to the living! No one knows! They don't take the living! But . . . oh, spirits help me . . . I'm sorry, Dabrena . . . Reiligh made me come. . . . They took her. The boneman took her. He . . . fed, or . . . I don't know! She's gone! I'm sorry!"

Dabrena fell back a step. One part of her was shaking her head in complete disbelief at this inane tall tale. Another part of her grieved for the girl's distress. Beadrin had been fond of Kara, kind to her at times, offering to amuse her, take her riding, but Dabrena would never allow it. She had kept so many fond people from getting close to Kara, and now none of them could get to her at all.

She had trusted Reiligh—

"Loris." The word came out a moan. "It was Loris." Then, suddenly crouching, reaching for the girl's hands past Adaon, she said, "Is Reiligh all right?"

Beadrin nodded. "He broke Loris's jaw. He said that was stupid, because then he couldn't talk, but that he still had a perfectly good scribing hand. He locked him up. I don't know if he told anyone. I don't know if Loris explained himself. I don't know anything. Reiligh sent me to you. He said to tell no one, that no one but him knows where you are. So I came."

"How long?" she asked. Her voice sounded very far away.

"A nineday. I did it in a nineday. I slept in the saddle. I took horses from runners. I told lies."

"You're a good girl, Beadrin. None of those lies will come back on you, I'll see to it." She tried to sit back on her haunches and found herself sitting on the floor. Adaon lifted her into a chair and called something to the innkeeper.

"I have to go back," she said to Adaon. It came out so strangely, as though she were begging him for something.

"She's not there," he said. "They'll be searching. If I'm wrong, they'll find her with or without your help."

"The betrayer was Loris. I have to go put things right."

"I don't see how. But you know best. Or you will. Here, drink this."

She shook her head, then snatched the tin jigger from him and dashed its contents at the back of her throat. "She's dead," she choked, tears springing out of her eyes, from the liquor's burn or something else.

"We don't know that."

"The bonefolk take the dead! They take everything, flesh, bones, the lot! How could you not be dead after that?"

"She was alive," Beadrin said. She was crying now, too. She hunkered down beside Dabrena's chair. "She was kicking and biting Loris when the boneman scooped her up. Reiligh said. She gave a good fight. She wasn't dead." This was clearly not sufficient consolation for the girl. Dabrena pulled her close and let her cry.

"What should I do? Where can I even start?"

Her words hung in the air. The only answers were silence, the girl's exhausted sobs, the muted hubbub from the street, and the thin razored silver keening threading deep through her mind.

GIR NUORIN

"You ate the last of the jellied balsam."

"Did not."

"Did too!"

"Did *not*!"

"Stop that, both of you."

"But Ris—"

"Caille ate it. Look, it's smeared all over her. And you stop grinning, you greedy imp."

"You'll turn into a lardball if you keep that up. A bulge in the Bulge!"

"She eats *everything*, Eiden's whole body won't be big enough for her to live on."

"You'll have to have your own limb, Caille! Then Eiden will have three legs, he'll walk like people in a sack race."

Pelufer inflated her cheeks and crossed her eyes to demonstrate Caille's fate. Risalyn and Yuralon laughed aloud, Caille and Elora giggled; even Louarn had to smile, though he hid it behind his mug of unsweetened roseroot tea.

They sat at breakfast in the Ruffed Grouse's greatroom. It was a large meal, befitting the third day of Longlight celebrations. The two-story stone inn was at the upland end of Gir Nuorin's Bulge, the curve in the Knee Road where it bent around Lough Nur in the middle of a picturesque plateau in the Elfelirs—the Sudden Mountains. On the mountain side of the Bulge were the inn, the ironsmith's and farrier's, the saddler's and cartwright's, a tavern and a public house, and behind them an array of paddocks backed by peaks; on the lough side were shops and crafteries, and around the other side of the lough and along the mountain river that fed into it were crofts and stone cottages. Out past those, where the mountainside rose in a forested incline from the plateau, was Gir Nuorin's spirit wood. At the downland end of the lough were its public dock and market grounds; past that were a few fields and an old quarry, after which the road descended steeply into forest.

Louarn, aged two nines and three—far younger than he'd thought he was, or felt—surveyed his tablemates with what he feared might be a grandparent's fondness. Were they becoming a family? The thought came unbidden and disturbing. The girls had torn through a spread of food that the six of them together couldn't have afforded a moon ago, Longlight or no. Cloudberry compote, honeyed fir, frost-grape jam, and three different breads to smear them on in addition to hands and faces; cherry-plum sauce over stewed apples rolled in parchment-thin wheat-flour pancakes; mashed turnips, soft-fried velvet mushrooms, and white-cheese spinach layered inside a butterflake crust and flavored with red pepper and dill. The advantage of unseasonable heat was early ripening, and drought did not trouble the spring-fed Knee. Risalyn and Yuralon discussed downleg illnesses that as yet had not affected Gir Nuorin, debating compresses and decoctions that out of context sounded almost appealing. If there had been sunlight through the gauzy curtains, if the slightest breeze had stirred them, if there were not a pressing weight of overheated air, this would be an idyllic end-of-sowmid morning, and he might be some affluent uncle enjoying the company of relatives before an ordinary workday.

The girls were often taken for Risalyn's get, no doubt owing to the hair; sometimes folk took the adults for a pledged threesome, a common arrangement in the Heartlands, or assumed that Risalyn and Louarn were the mother and father, since she and Yuralon were so obviously related by blood. But they slept by gender; though all three adults traded watches, they'd let two rooms for the moon they'd been here, one for Risalyn and the girls, one for himself and Yuralon.

It had seemed a foolish extravagance at first, though the Girdlers turned out to have no trouble paying their way with herblore. But at this point they might have made an offer on the whole inn. There were no peacekeepers in this town, no alderfolk, and superstition was far less virulent than in Gir Doegre; though Elora traded her workings on a shadow market of her own creation, most townsfolk knew and made no protest. How could anyone object to such beauty? She rendered faces with uncanny expressiveness, capturing the essence of personality in living wood. In rounded burls, right on the tree, she worked tiny replicas of trees detailed down to the last leaf; her birds seemed on the verge of flight, and Pelufer had broken one posed with outspread wings, trying to sail it through the air across their room. Elora had mended it with a touch—the wood flowed back into itself just the way it had been worked, the way it wanted to be. The mending had taken no toll on her.

Louarn had built them a stall and workbench on the market grounds. Elora did the haggling; he fronted as the craftsman. He loved woodcraft, close detailed work most of all, and his birdhouses and toys and puzzle boxes, made on the spot and to order if requested, moved as quickly as the more practical wares traded by those around them. They had made a good life for themselves here, strange as it was to think so, strange as the circumstances were, and brief the time that had passed, briefer still the time that might remain.

Contentment was a danger. Elora flirted nearest to it. She was a keen trader and an inspired crafter, and she ran their business with pleasure and a sure hand. But she was a child—and he sensed that she was, now, only waiting to grow up, only waiting to become old enough for him. He regretted the barrow boy's absence. A deep-seated awareness of their own transience had kept them from opening a shop and taking up residence above it. Elora urged that next step with increasing frequency and enthusiasm—and the only argument Louarn could raise, against expansion and entrenchment that made all the sense in the world, was that their success as crafter-traders was an ancillary benefit, unintentional . . . irrelevant.

They were stationed at the forefront of a busy market in a well-traveled town, on the one road from the mid-Leg through the mountains of the Knee. The Knee had been drenched in magelight. But in all this time their trap had not been sprung. Pelufer worked the stall day after day, hating it, desperate to be out boating the lough or hiking the wooded river or—her heart's desire, as yet unmet—drilling in bladecraft. She contrived to touch everyone who passed them in the market. She took the tallies and the trades, she handed across the goods; she hawked their wares, skipping out to pull the reticent playfully toward the stall. She was good at it—she was a traders' daughter—but bored and restless. And not one of the hands she touched had been a cold killer's.

He'd feared she might turn up ill-doers who had no connection to the magekillings. But the worst she'd come across had been a couple of former bindsmen, and farmers who'd put ailing, agonized livestock out of their misery. Now that she had control of her power, she could feel the deaths of calves and kids and lambs, cattle and geese, sheep and goats, as well as those of human animals. The stray shielders who passed through, bladed and trained to kill, had been mercifully unblooded.

He welcomed the dearth of killers. He welcomed the dearth of bad tidings; they had heard of no further magekillings. But he was deeply frustrated. It seemed all was for naught. He was plagued with memories he might have preferred to leave buried, given a choice; tendrils had grown between him and the children as tendrils had grown from the soles of his feet, seeking to root. For as long as he had been solely Louarn, he had avoided entanglement. He had denied fondness. Knowing why, knowing what he had lost, in the past, that had made him so wary, was no consolation whatsoever.

Still he surveyed them with fondness—unwelcome, uncomfortable, unavoidable affection. Their young faces glowed with a health all too rare in these hard times, their fawn skin scrubbed clean of street dirt in clean mountain water; their good clothes were tidy and fresh. Elora, successful and shining and almost content, with her long streaked silken hair and sweet fey looks, would grow out of her puppy love and bloom into an extraordinary woman, a precious gift for Nolfiander or whoever she gave her heart to when the time came. Pelufer, brimful of energy, sleek and wild as a young horse, seemed unharmed by her dark shining talent, which she had mastered with admirable dedication; she would succeed at whatever she applied herself to. Caille was still too young to assess, but if she could channel her tremendous power in safety, she might do anything. Assuming, he thought as he watched her gnaw cloverbread, she didn't gain a nonned pounds before she turned six.

Caille returned his gaze calmly. "You're shining," she said.

They all looked at him.

"Spirits, you are," said Elora, and "You're nearly as bright as when you work!" said Pelufer.

Was that what it was, then, that shining ruddy light they shared? Was it affection, compassion . . . love? He could certainly identify this additional new feeling: embarrassment. They had determined that his shine was brightest when he was crafting—wood, metal, it made no difference—and had increased now that he was aware of it. He'd thought it was love of crafting that caused it, some sweet mix of ability and pleasure. He knew it went somewhat beyond that; he shone when he befriended animals, too, something Caille had been quick to point out. "*Made friends with old Skulk there, did you?*" the farmer had said, the one who'd given him the name he bore now. "*He never minded me so well when I sent him to his bed.*" But there was more to it. There was the melting love-at-first-sight when he'd met the foal Purslane, the overwhelming sense, when pressing his face into that brown velvet coat, that he had come home.

And there was the unendurable pain of the horse Purslane dying, broken in a mudslide in the Black Mountains.

That was why love was not permissible. That was why the distant chimes sounded. These children and Girdlers were cursed with siblings to love, no choice in it, an accident of birth. He was different. Fortunate. He could choose to walk away.

He need not pursue the shining, or court the pain it promised.

"Now he's remembering," Pelufer said, in a bored drone. "He's always like that—happy and then sad."

"And the shine winked out," Elora said, puzzled. She had taken the firmest hand as tutor, with Louarn her prize pupil and the two Girdlers her challenge. She claimed that Risalyn and Yuralon were beginning to shine when they worked their herbcraft, though Louarn had not seen even the dimmest glow in them. Perhaps their bladedness interfered. Or perhaps the girls had keener eyes.

"I was thinking about a new thing I might try making today," he said. "Something to ease the aching back of a poor sleeper. A set of wooden balls on dowels . . ."

"You were not," said Pelufer.

"I was too," he lied, falling into their patter—the crafted man, the man who could blend himself into any situation, become unnoticeable. But they knew him too well. They knew he didn't talk that way. They laughed.

"Breakfast is over," he said, and rose from his seat. He was transparent to them, his insides becoming more visible by the day. He despised the development. If that made him seem testy, so be it. They had work to do, the blasted make-work that had succeeded beyond all expectation. He would do his work, and find his killers, and move on.

While Yuralon took the girls to wash up and collect their gear, Risalyn waylaid Louarn. "Speaking of poor sleepers," she said, "how long has it been since you had a good night's sleep?"

"I've been short-tempered," he said, attempting to relax a tensed jaw. It only set a tic going in his cheek. "I apologize."

"I don't mean just now. Yuralon says you're always up when he wakes up, even when you're not on watch. You doze fitfully for a few breaths and then jolt yourself awake."

He frowned. It was an effort to remember, and he was tired of remembering, battered by memory, sick of it. Not letting himself sleep deeply had been second nature for so long that he'd forgotten why he did it, just as he'd forgotten why he blended speech patterns and gestures and styles of dress. "Six years, I suppose."

She blinked. "*Years?*"

He found it hard to produce his wry, self-effacing smile for her. He found it ever harder to craft himself for any of them. "The side effect of a troubled childhood."

She pulled a face. "I don't care what happened to you, and I know a good bit of it now. Everyone has to sleep." She paused, thinking it through. "Everyone has to dream, Louarn."

Yes. That was it, of course. The dreams. The shadows. He'd told the Girdlers, at last, about leading the mutilated mages out of the Ennead's casting chambers through tunnels he had dreamed into existence. He'd told the story as though it happened to someone else. They weren't as surprised as he'd expected. Yuralon had tended those mages—put some of them out of their pain—and they had mentioned the boy they'd followed. A sad, haunted boy, they'd said, yet brave; a sound lad who rose to a challenge. He'd regretted divulging the secret then, not least because they in turn had filled in what he'd missed while wandering the labyrinth—the revitalized stewards' revolt, the arrival of the rebel horde, the Khinish taking Lerissa Illuminator into custody. He had burned to know what became of those he'd known. Now he knew that the gentle stablemaster Bron and the kindly baker Drinda had died on Ennead blades. Now he knew that one of the Nine who had terrorized him still lived. He was heartened that all but one of Bron's other fosterlings had survived, though held briefly hostage by the Ennead, then doubly pained that the one who'd died had been an infant. He'd grown up in a dark, diseased rock steeped in cruelty and secrets. Now that he knew who had lived and who had died, he wished he didn't. Louarn-alone had not been a happy man, but he'd been content in his craft-hungry, puzzle-hungry wanderings. So much better to be that ignorant, empty man than whatever trebly-haunted creature he was now.

"I have bad dreams," he said at last.

Risalyn snorted. "Don't we all. Dream them, Louarn. Face them. Dreams are offal, they excrete the things our minds can't bear."

"My dreams come true."

"So you said. But you're not the boy you were. It might be time to try again."

With that she left him, and he moved, sluggish, through the unendurable air to fetch his tools.

Pelufer, already bored, set the last crate of their wares on the market ground.

"He's shining more," Elora said, unfolding the clever hinged worktable that clever Louarn had built onto its clever hinged legs so they could open out the stall's clever side baffles and get the clever awning up. "He's learning."

Pelufer groaned. "Louarn Louarn Louarn! Go puke your lovesickness on someone else."

Smitten with that haunted man, when he was just itching to be away from them, when loyal Nolfi waited at home. Pelufer liked Louarn too much, too. She liked Yuralon too much. She liked Risalyn too much. But they were still on their own. Still orphans. Caille and Elora were forgetting that. She wouldn't forget. She would get everything she could from them, learn everything they'd teach, and she'd pay every bit of it back by finding the people they were after, and then they'd be square. Then, when Risalyn and Yuralon went back to being journeyhealers, when Louarn took up his wandering lad-of-all-crafts life again, it wouldn't matter.

Pelufer stooped to pull some puzzle boxes out of the crate and handed one to Caille, for something to do besides watch ants in the grass. Yuralon, helping unpack their gear, was asking Elora about the language of their hands now. Elora was turning the questions as only a trader could. But in truth they didn't know where the secret fingerspeech came from. Mother had made a game of it, when they were little. It was their baby talk, she thought. But then Louarn had understood it. Louarn had been able to answer. And his fingers had an accent that his voice didn't. It was a shape accent, not a sound accent. He had a perfect, accentless voice, Elora said. You couldn't pin down where he came from, not from the way he spoke. But it was too perfect, as if he'd had to learn to talk from scratch when he woke up that last time with no memory. Where had he gone, in between? Somewhere that other people used the secret fingerspeech. But with an accent.

She plunked the boxes on the table. Enough poxy blighted Louarn! They hadn't told him everything. Probably he hadn't told them everything either. Her haunt-memory from him ended with Mellas lost in the tunnels. After that, he was only whatever he told them he was. She liked those boys he had been. She felt bad for them, and wished she could meet them for real. Louarn was kind, and he wasn't so fake around them anymore. But she still couldn't gauge him, not well. He was too many shapes all at once.

And there were more important things. As Yuralon came up from his squat by their carrycase with a handful of tight-wound tops, she asked him, "Will you show me how to stand on guard today?"

His body skewed into the hipshot stance that meant he was aggravated. A balanced stance meant danger if he was being serious.

She'd worked on that stance, the rare times she had to herself. Knees flexed, weight on the balls of the feet, arms relaxed but not dangling. Ready for anything. She only needed a longblade in her hand.

"You know Jiondor made us promise."

"*Don't you be teaching any bladecraft to that young Pel, now!*" Jiondor had told the Girdlers. "*I don't care how much she pesters.*" Feh! "How come you can have blades and I can't? You learned when you were my age. I'm no different from you."

His shoulders lowered. "Yes you are, sprout."

Caille tapped her on the ankle and handed the box puzzle back. "Did it," she said.

Pelufer sighed. She did all his puzzles fast. She didn't even think about them, just felt how they should go. Elora could do it too, the ones made of wood anyway. Pelufer had yet to solve one.

But I know how people fit inside other people. As she had a nonned times before, she wondered what that was good for.

"I could make a trade of being a killer hunter," she said to Yuralon as he and Elora finished snapping the awning in place. "Then I'd need to know blades, wouldn't I, to protect myself."

"Why don't I show you some plants, before the place crowds up," he said. His arms swung down from the awning and he looked around the market. "I spy . . . three so-called weeds that could be harvested for healing. I dare you to find them."

"Oop, sorry, customer." Pelufer ran off toward a woman who hadn't even stepped onto the market grounds, walking in long strides down the road from the Knee. Maybe she wouldn't learn *everything* they had to teach her.

Only when she was close enough to start crying their wares did she see the scabbarded blade on the woman's back. She swallowed the cry and dropped to a stroll. A shielder, on some important errand. They never wanted anything Louarn had made. She looked down the road and saw Louarn and Risalyn coming around the bend. They were walking as if pulled up by strings on their heads. Craning their necks. She started to turn, and was stopped by a hand on her chest.

"Best keep the road clear," the bladed woman said, pressing her firmly onto the patchy trampled grass of the market commons.

Pelufer took a deep breath, held it, let it out slowly through her nose. Any names that came would bubble up from inside her, but they would go into her head, not her mouth, and she would keep them there, in a special place that Louarn and Yuralon had helped her clear for them, a place that could hold all the names in the world, all the memories and selves in the world, and never fill up, and never do her any harm. She waited to feel a name come up into that vast quiet space, a soft harmless burst, a soap bubble.

No name came. She opened her eyes without knowing she'd closed them. Louarn and Risalyn had stepped off the road, too, just past the last craftery on the lough side, where the market started.

She turned, and looked up the Knee Road.

There were two more shielders, and three more behind them, spaced at a dozen threfts. A wedge, to clear the way.

Behind them, just coming into view where the road dipped down again before switchbacking through the mountains to the Knee, were row upon row upon row of shielders. Ranks of them, three abreast. They were all brown, as if they'd rolled in soil, but it was their clothes, all the same dull color, as if they'd need to keep hidden in some brown place, or to know each other from some other shielders. Or some other fighters.

She stood rooted to the spot, staring, watching them come. They weren't in step, but they stayed together, stayed in their ranks. Blade after blade. The shield was moving. They must have marched all night, or been camping just past the far dip of the road. Her heart began to race.

"Pelufer." Louarn came up beside her.

"No."

He sighed. "Then I'll stay with you."

They watched together. The front ranks were about to pass them and still more were coming. Dust rose where they walked, hazing the view like the fog at home, even though it wasn't a very dusty road. There were just so many of them. She tried to count rows and lost count before two nines, and then it was too late to start over.

"This must be all the shielders from the Knee," Louarn said. "Three lookouts every ninemile, posted in shifts . . . an outpost every three ninemiles, six to a post . . . there must be four nonned shielders around the Leg coast, and this nearly a nonned of them."

"Where are they going?"

She felt him shrug. "I could guess. But I don't know. Risalyn's gone to find out what she can. She knows some Knee shielders."

The Khinish are waking. She remembered the sound-shadows of promise and menace around the longs at home. She'd heard them again, louder and more certain, from folk all over the market, through the open doors of the tavern and the public house and the smithy, from elders exchanging gossip over cold sweet-birch tea in the Ruffed Grouse.

They were going to fight the Khinish.

"Gir Doegre's down this road." Her voice had gone very small.

"That's no place to stage a battle, among those hills," Yuralon said. He'd come up on her other side and she hadn't even noticed. "They'll cut down to the Boot Road, most like. Engage them somewhere on the flats downleg."

She saw again the dangerous man, the fighter, the bladed killer. She had not seen him in that shape for a moon now. She had forgotten that shape, for all she tried to copy it. She had not come even close.

The awe and dread of the marching ranks thrilled her with a terrified yearning. "Teach me, Yuralon. Please. Before you go."

"I'm a healer now," he said, and she could hear from the angle of the sound that he was saying it to the heedless marching ranks, not to her. Or maybe to hear himself say it, so he'd believe it. Risalyn had told Jiondor the same thing after his no-bladecraft speech, and he'd said, "*I know what you are. Just mind my words.*"

I know what you are.

The forge had fallen silent, the saws at the lumber mill, the axes splitting firewood; the banter of traders had long ceased, the calls of excited children had fallen off, all the sounds of morning muted by the speechless passage of those brown bladed ranks.

"Come, Pelufer," Louarn said. "That's the last of them now. They're not stopping."

"They've a long march ahead of them," Yuralon said, as they turned her between them and marched her back to the stall. That felt like an even longer march. Away from everything she wanted to be. Bladed, brave, invincible, dangerous. The stall was diminished; she came up to find it smaller, more drab than it was already.

"So many," Caille said to her, to share the wonder. She didn't know what they were marching off to do.

So many, Pelufer thought, watching the dust die down, her hands idly ranking toys in even rows along the table. But there'd have been one more, if she were a grownup, and could do what she wanted to do, not what she had to do.

She listened without interest as Elora made their first trade of the day, and picked up the wooden item without looking, knowing it by shape and position. Her eyes on the dying dust trail of the marching shield, she reached out for tallystones at the same time she offered up the item she held. From habit, reflex, she brushed the customer's hand, unthinking, uninvolved, her head filled with the low rumble of passing feet.

Croy burst into her mind, a perfect shining soap bubble.

The girl forgot the signal, but Louarn, considering chisel versus gouge just behind her, felt her go stiff, then flail to the side and back with a hand. He turned. He gripped Yuralon's upper arm with the hand that held the chisel. He fixed in his mind the details of the two customers just walking away. The taller one: a dark woman with dark braided hair and a cloak unsuited to summer. She presented a blunt-nosed profile. Attending to something the shorter one was saying. The shorter one: a swarthy man in shirt and breeches with black bowl-cut hair. He was hesitant, perturbed. He held up the toy he had acquired.

"He felt something from her," Louarn said. "He knows."

Pelufer was still trying to speak. After all their training to mute her reflex, she could not get the names out now. But the names made no difference.

"They were avoiding the shielders," Yuralon said. "Laying low, trying to look natural."

Louarn dropped the chisel, held the gouge down straight by his thigh, and moved to the left as Yuralon moved to the right. Custom was thin yet, but the grounds were filling. If they could come on the pair in a quick decisive swoop from opposite sides, they'd have a chance of doing this quietly even without Risalyn.

As he stepped away from the stall, Pelufer choked, "Croy."

He kept moving. He denied the frozen numbness that entered his veins. Croy the bricklayer. Croy his master. Croy the good man who'd craved Neck brandy he could never afford.

He moved with speed but no rush, weaving among traders and sparse customers as if on an angled trajectory off the killers' path, striding off on some business. He kept Yuralon in his side vision—lost him behind a sourfruit sledge, found him again, paralleling the pair. They were hurrying now but had not broken into a run. The moment Louarn angled toward them he must be prepared for them to bolt.

They were heading for the dock. The boats were all pleasure craft and slow shellfood dredgers. There would be no escape that way. But if they could trick a pursuer into the water they would gain ample running time. And flush the pursuit, as well—the dock was empty of all save a boat tender, with no one else approaching.

Yuralon moved in. Too soon—Louarn wasn't in position. There must have been something he didn't like about the dock. The woman, nearer but turned toward the man, didn't see him.

The man did. He broke—shoving off the woman, dropping the toy, making for the fields in a dead run that took him directly across Louarn's path.

Yuralon grappled with the woman. Blows fell; someone cried out; they staggered toward the dock.

Louarn dodged behind the tall stand of a rope vendor. He waited a breath, listening, gauging the footfalls. Then he burst out in a headlong lunge between pottery and a turner's bowls and tackled the fleeing man.

They went down hard. Breath gasped out of them both. Louarn moved an arm he could barely feel and sank the gouge into yielding belly flesh, just shy of breaking through shirt and skin. He pushed up, braced a hand on the man's collarbone, positioned a knee under the gouge, moved the gouge up to chest level. "Be still and I won't hurt you," he managed at last.

"What in all the spirits are you *doing*?" Rough hands hauled him off the man, who scrambled up quick as a bug and raced off in a new direction—through the market, downland toward the fields, the quarry, the woods.

With an oath, Louarn shook off the ignorant rescuers and gave chase. He'd rather let the man run his breath out while he had him in sight, but once he made the woods he'd have the advantage. Louarn had to catch up before that. He'd lost the gouge, but he was still wearing his tool belt. Plenty to threaten the man with. Plenty to kill him with.

No.

He killed Croy—

No.

Belatedly he realized that, while he could follow the trail of crushed barley the man would leave through the summer-high cornfield, he could be easily ambushed from the side if the man doubled back. He had lost the element of surprise that was his only ally. He was not a fighter. He was in over his head.

Still he followed. He plunged into the swath the man beat in the tawny forest of stalks. Any moment a weight would hurtle into him from the side, drive him down, he'd feel the bite of a knife, add all his names to those the killer already bore. But he hadn't counted on how much easier it was to follow a swath than bushwhack it bodily. Suddenly the man was there before him—he'd pulled up—there was clear space beyond him—

Louarn had learned the hard lesson of the ground. He didn't tackle. He drove forward with his left shoulder, arms clasped, putting all his weight and momentum into it. The sharp impact of bone took the man midway down the spine and sent him reeling forward, his arms scooping at air. Louarn stumbled after him, then caught his balance.

The man hung as if in the air, prostrate but humped, like a cat with its back up. It took a moment for Louarn's eyes to resolve what they were seeing.

The man had stopped short at the sight of a pollard oak, ancient and thick and low, overtaken by rising ground as the fields were marled and manured year after year, losing its heartwood, studded with old branch stumps, staghorned from some period of neglect yet still fuzzed with new growth. One of a row of such oaks that divided the field they'd been in from the next, too tall to hurdle but too short to see through the screen of ripening barley. Louarn had caught him just before he could shift to skirt it—in that one moment of surprised hesitation at bursting into the clear to find an obstacle in the way.

Louarn had driven him onto the tree. He lay draped over its low crown, impaled on the spike of an old dead branch.

Pelufer stared at the cloaked, not-right woman walking toward their pitch.

She wasn't the one who'd been with the man the names came off. That woman had long braided hair, this one had short smooth hair. But she was coming from the direction the braided woman had run off in. Louarn ran after the man, Yuralon fought with the braided woman, some traders took the braided woman in hand; Yuralon followed Louarn and told her and Elora to stay put, that Risalyn was coming. But the braided woman had broken away from the traders. They hadn't chased her. They were confused and threw their hands up in disgust. Pelufer had seen the braided woman coming. She'd run out to trip her. She'd tried to hold her for Risalyn. She'd clung to the woman's ankle, a dragging weight, so she couldn't get up. But the woman had beaten her off.

It was a stupid thing to do. The braided woman could have killed her. New names roosted like bats in the safe cavern in Pelufer's mind. The braided woman had killed nine people of light. Between them, she and that man had killed more than two nines. Tellers, singers, scribes, farmers, crafters. All the things that people of light became when their kind of light was gone.

She'd made a fool of herself, clinging to the braided woman's leg. She'd been unable to speak when the first name came off the man, in the rush of all the other names. She'd forgotten the signal. She'd touched killers in her training, but mercy killers, former binders. This had been the first time her new control was put to the test, and she'd stood there with her mouth working and no sound coming out. But the flush was fading from her cheeks. The braided woman had another partner. The smooth woman. Who was walking toward them now as if she knew. As if the braided woman, running past her at the back of the market, had said, "It's those girls, they know, they know what we did."

"Is Risalyn coming?" she asked Elora, keeping her eyes on the approaching woman.

Elora had been dabbing at her forehead with a linen handcloth. The woman had bruised her when she beat her off. Kicked her. She barely felt it. Feeling stupid and angry, she wouldn't let Caille fix it. "Yes," Elora said, and waved with both arms, the handcloth fluttering from one hand. The kind of thing you did when you had something important to say, when the person you were waving to should hurry.

It needed to be the kind of thing you did when you were in a lot of trouble and help had to come *right now*. "Wave harder, Elora," she said, and picked up the chisel Louarn had dropped.

That only made Elora reach for Caille. "Pel . . ."

She flicked her gaze toward the Bulge. Risalyn was trotting now. Not fast enough. She needed to be running. "Don't look. There's a not-right woman. Smooth hair, cloak on her. Take Caille to that secondhander's pitch. Quick but don't run. Now."

Elora didn't argue. She hustled their sister off fast. Pelufer made one more calculation of angle and distance. Her sisters would make it to the shelter of the toolman's elaborate pitch. But the woman was going to get here before Risalyn did. If she ran, the woman would know there was something to run for. But maybe she would follow her and leave her sisters alone. If she ran to Risalyn, they'd both be too far to get to Elora and Caille in time if the woman went there. But Elora and Caille could run. Caille was quick and slithery.

The chisel still clutched in her fist, Pelufer ducked under the table and took off straight for Risalyn.

Then Risalyn knew. She reached behind her head. She was wearing her blade. She'd gotten her blade from the inn and strapped it on. It came free in a fluid iron arc.

The woman behind Pelufer was running, too. Gaining. Risalyn had seen her. That was why she drew her blade. But she wouldn't draw on someone unarmed. The smooth woman was cloaked on a day as hot as a furnace. To hide a longblade. It had to be.

She couldn't chance a look back. She would fall. She had to run, just run, straight ahead, toward Risalyn, as fast as she had ever run in her life.

She outdistanced the woman in a burst of speed. She was nine-and-two. No grownup could catch her.

"Pass me," Risalyn called.

She passed, and heard a sound she'd dreamed but never heard before: the ringing clash of blades.

She skidded to a halt, and turned. Everyone in the market turned. Someone laughed, thinking it was a shielder demonstration. People murmured. The murmurs darkened. This was no demonstration.

Pelufer stood transfixed by the play of iron, the angles, the footwork. They danced a circle in the trampled grass, probing for openings, swinging and blocking, high and low, crashing together and pausing as if stunned, then breaking apart for a renewed windy flurry of attacks and responses, too fast for the eye to follow. It was a dance of bearing and balance and edge, a dance of shapes.

She brought the chisel up in a blade grip. She took a step forward, as if she would dance, too.

The smooth woman lifted her weapon so fast that it was coming straight down to cleave Risalyn's head before Risalyn could take the opening to thrust into her body. Risalyn brought her blade up hard to block the blow.

Her blade broke. The tip fell like a shard of ice.

There was shouting. Pelufer's body jerked as two people ran by, one on either side of her. She had not been in her body. She was still not completely in her body. Some part of her was reaching out, through the shared medium of grassy ground. Not toward Risalyn, but toward the smooth woman. Seeking something, like an opening. Not finding it. Blocked. There was an opening. A way in. Somewhere. If she could find it.

Risalyn sprang away, but the woman had anticipated the move and swept a foot out to trip her. Risalyn fell so hard on her back that she bounced, stunned loose-limbed, on the grassy ground. Her bladeless hilt left her hand. The woman loomed over her.

Maybe it wasn't the ground. Maybe it was the air . . . she knew metals, she was born of a metals town, but that was tin and copper, and iron had to cleave through air before it met flesh. . . .

The woman's back had come around to Pelufer. Pelufer couldn't see the blade now. But she could read the curve of spine and shoulders, the jut of elbows. The contraction, the drawing-back. She could feel the cold iron, feel the grip draw warmth from the woman's hands, feel the blade draw strength into the tang and along itself to the killing point. The blade drove at Risalyn—

And was deflected by a sharp chop from a blade borne in from the side by one shielder, while another shielder ran the woman through.

Pelufer felt that blade enter flesh not as if it were her own flesh, but as if she were the blade.

Somewhere off to the left, Caille was screaming.

Then the ground tilted up and jarred her hip and head and shoulder hard, and she was nothing.

Louarn startled at a sound behind him—the rustling, wary tread of Yuralon, less heedless of the threat of ambush in the cornfield though he was better trained to meet it.

"Weeping spirits," he said, confronting the impaled man.

Louarn knelt by the bowl-haired head. Blood and drool dripped from the man's mouth, but he was breathing. "He's alive," he told Yuralon, who came to kneel by the other side, soaking wet. He'd gone into the lough. "What's your name?"

"Can't . . . feel," the man said. "Breathe." He seemed able to move only his head.

Louarn blanched. "I drove my shoulder into his back," he said. "Perhaps the spine . . ."

"You may have snapped it, or the branch may have severed something." Yuralon had opened a pouch at his belt and was fingering through it. "It's a mercy to him, either way."

Louarn sat heavily on his rear. "I wouldn't have killed you," he said, uncomprehending.

"Kill . . . myself before . . . tell . . ."

"Who ordered you to kill mages?" Yuralon asked.

No answer came.

Louarn got up with some idea of hoisting him off the branch, stanching the wound, fetching Caille, healing him. Could Yuralon heal him? Elora had been trying to help Caille teach them. . . .

"Stand off, Louarn," Yuralon said, shaking powder from a drawbag into his palm. "It's too late for that. He has only breaths."

Louarn crouched by the man's head, at a loss for what to do or say. He didn't know which one had carried Croy's name. Those hands might have taken Croy's hands . . . those hands might have broken Croy's skull . . . but he could summon no outrage in the face of what had befallen this living body.

Yuralon slid a hand around the man's head to cover his mouth, let him exhale protest, then pinched his nostrils shut. The head gave a weak jerk. Yuralon waited a breath, then brought his powder-sprinkled palm under the nose. When he opened his pinching fingers, the man inhaled.

"Did someone order you to kill mages?" he asked.

After a moment, there was the suggestion of a nod.

"Who?"

The man struggled against whatever drug Yuralon had forced on him, but it acted quickly, and he was too close to death to fight it very hard. "Ennead . . . last . . . one . . . one left . . ."

"Why?" Yuralon's questions were delivered with grinding, inexorable dispassion.

". . . magelight . . . Galandra's . . . warding . . . protect . . . kill the light . . ."

"Kill the light? The magelight is dead."

". . . not dead . . . chance of . . . return . . . for some . . . she doesn't know . . . who . . . kill . . . all . . . herself last, her . . . steward will . . . do it . . . time . . . comes . . ."

"This makes no sense," Yuralon said, frowning, and drew the use knife from his belt.

"No," Louarn said.

"He's dead anyway."

"Let him go."

"We can find out the rest from the girl, but only if it was my hand that killed him."

"I killed him."

"Not enough. An accident." He lifted the head by the hair. Louarn saw a bloodied smile on the man's lips, and grasped the fighter's knife arm, leaned in. "A mercy killing," Yuralon said, his composure unyielding. "He's asked me for it. He's bleeding his life out. Let me end this, that we might end a greater threat."

Running footfalls crunched over downed stalks back the way they had come. Louarn looked up wildly. Risalyn would halt this act, Risalyn—

The woman who came hurtling out of the cornstalks was dark and braid-haired. A longblade sang over her head.

Louarn fell back at the shove that freed Yuralon to use his knife. The fighter came up under the woman, driving into her belly as she swept her blade through where his head had been. The tip tore the air in front of Louarn. The blade went flying into the barley beyond him. He looked over to find her dying on Yuralon's knife, which had angled up to her heart.

The impaled man was dead.

"I told them to hold her," Yuralon said, easing the woman to the ground. She too was soaking wet. "I told them she was a thief. They were traders, theft threatens them all. They looked like they were obeying me."

"She might have fought free," Louarn said. "She was bladed."

"She was no fighter. She came in wild. A child could have taken her." He withdrew his knife with a teeth-aching scrape of blade on bone, then closed her glazed eyes before he wiped the blade clean.

"Folk fear longblades. The sight or feel of it under her cloak . . ."

"It wasn't under her cloak when I wrestled with her."

"Then there is a third. We must go back—the girls—"

"Easy. Risalyn is with them."

Staring at the dead woman, Louarn said, in an odd voice, "Now Pelufer can divine her name from you."

"Yes. And perhaps more."

Louarn got up. "Take care of the girls," he said.

"You can't do it alone. She's on Khine. A far journey even from here, even without Khinish forces to reckon with."

"I'll find a way. A wandering crafter. You reek of the blade. I'll have more chance alone."

"Let us see you through the fighting. There may be no way to skirt it. We'll be going there anyway. They'll need us, as healers or fighters, one or the other. We know folk in that shield."

"Take care of the girls."

"Come back with me. Let's see what the sprout can add to what that snort of foolswort got from this one."

"I have to go through before the battle starts. I can pass the shield. But I have to go now."

"You have no pack, no provisions, nothing."

"You'd be surprised how well I can survive off the land."

"We can't stay with the girls."

"Someone has to stay with them."

"They fended for themselves for years."

"At home, with folk aiding them without their knowledge."

"They'll be all right here," Yuralon said. "Elora is thriving. They're well off. They can sit tight until it's over."

The shield had passed. The fighting would not come up here. They'd engage on the flats somewhere to Bootward. "I'll be back," he said. "As soon as I can. Tell them that." Once the words were out, there was no retrieving them. They shocked him. But they were said now. "See them safe, Yuralon."

"See yourself safe, Louarn n'Mellas n'Flin. Lerissa Illuminator was a stone-cold viper. I dread to think what the Khinish have forged of her."

Pelufer woke up in her bed in the inn with a glorious familiar warmth flowing through her and Caille's pudgy little hands on her face. She smiled. "Hello, Caille."

Caille smiled back, shining. "Hello, Pelufer."

"Welcome back." It was Risalyn, sitting on the other side of her. Elora was standing by the door, talking with Yuralon, looking very much like a serious grownup. That was annoying.

"Did you close up the stall?" she asked Elora, and got a curt nod: *Of course. I wouldn't leave everything out untended.*

She turned to Risalyn. "What happened?"

"There were three people we think were killers," Risalyn said. "One of them fell and was hurt. He died after telling Yuralon some rather confusing things. Yuralon killed another one, who attacked him. A shielder I know killed the third. That part you saw."

"Where did the shielders come from?"

"They were at the back of the column. A clever tavern girl went after the shielders crying that two women were having a bladefight in the middle of town and someone should stop it. One of them knew me and came running, with a comrade of his running after. Knew me, and knew it must be me, if there were blades involved." She grinned, and the hairs went up on the back of Pelufer's neck.

"They hadn't gotten very far."

"A lot of things happened very fast. And big hordes of people go slowly on foot. It's not a forced march yet."

"If they're gone I can't get the woman's name off the shielder who killed her."

"I know. I'm sorry."

"Where's Louarn?"

There was a silence then, and in the end it was Elora who answered, in one harsh word: "Gone."

No. Not dead. He couldn't be dead. "Where?"

"To Khine," Yuralon said. "That's where we think the killers' master is. But you can—"

"How are you feeling now?" Risalyn broke in.

Pelufer frowned and sat up. "I'm fine, I'm always fine. Caille fixed me. She always fixes us, even when we don't ask for it, when we're sleeping. She's a pest. That's why we're never sick. What happened to me?"

"I don't know. You fell, or fainted."

Caille said, "You were shining."

Shining . . . She wished she could remember what she was trying to do. All she could come up with was a cold taste of iron, and some feeling of reaching out. "I don't know why," she said. "Did Caille fix the woman who got stabbed?"

Risalyn seemed taken aback. "I didn't think . . ."

Elora was still standing by the door, the shape of her body hard and bitter and distant. "She can't fix death."

"No kill," Caille said, abruptly resentful and sulky, and climbed into the bed next to Pelufer.

"It wasn't good for her to see that," Risalyn said.

"She's seen plenty of death. Death happens all the time. She just gets mad when people make it happen. People are supposed to know better." She snugged Caille close and said, "What did you stop Yuralon from saying?"

"I killed the woman with the long black braid," he said. "I'm not sorry, Caille. She was trying to kill me. But I carry her name now, I expect."

Pelufer nodded. She tried to make it a brisk, grownup nod, to show that she knew what she was about and they should get on with it. But she didn't want to feel that woman's name. She didn't want any more names in her head. So many had come off that woman. Now that woman was a burn mark on Yuralon. She didn't want to let that into her. "All right," she made herself say.

Caille scrambled from the bed and eeled around Yuralon to go to Elora. "I'm hungry," she said. "I want Louarn." It came out muffled. Her face was pressed into the skirt of Elora's tunic.

"So do I," Elora said, and Pelufer saw tears spill onto her cheeks, but her chin came up and her eyes flashed, forbidding Pelufer to draw attention to it.

They were tired. Everything happened so fast. They'd had a scare. All the running around, and people dying. And all the names. And the shield marching through. She wished she was back at breakfast arguing over who finished the last of the jam.

She waited while Yuralon's weight settled on the edge of the bed, balancing Risalyn's. Then she laid her hand on his arm.

I'm out of trim, Louarn thought, slowing to a walk, bending to ease his aching back. Half a day on the road and already he was flagging. He'd pushed it, true—he'd trotted as often as walked, and when he'd walked it was in long strides, eating up the ground between him and the shield, then putting as much ground between them as he could. He had a good lead on them now, turning at the fork in the woods onto the cutover to the Boot Road. He should meet up with it a league or two Bootward of Gir Doegre. He'd still like to return to that town someday, to plumb its secrets. Perhaps the girls would have returned there, by the time this was over, and he'd have the excuse of going there to find them.

If he survived.

The pressure of air was unbearable. Bad enough he was soft from too long living well in a safe, prosperous town. But the heated air had the incongruous consistency of congealing lard. The dense cloud cover pressed down like a weight of stone. He wished again that he had taken the shorter way, through the Elfelirs to Glydh, and shipped for Khine. But he might have waited days for a coaster bound downleg, and it would be a trading vessel with a schedule of ports. He could not wait on trade, or trust that the Khinish fleet was letting ships round the tip of the Boot. Overland was the only certainty.

His ears pricked up at the welcome rumble of wheels behind him. A few breaths later, he was sitting braced against the front panels of a stock wagon, his teeth rattling like the wooden slats with every jarring bounce, surrounded by braced, jouncing, complaining sheep, who persisted in trying to press toward him, though milling was not advisable under the circumstances. Sheep were not sensible creatures. He pressed the smelly rear of one firmly but gently away, and smiled as another butted its head into his shoulder.

Jounced and jarred, he rubbed the velvety black head, and could almost feel himself shine.

"Are you all right there, sprout?"

The voice came from far away. She was in a cavern, with a terrible dark coldness, a malevolence, a hatred. A name. Elya. The braided woman.

"She's gone pale. Take her hand off you."

Somewhere far away, a hand that belonged to her clenched tight on a warm arm. The pain of the dead could hurt sometimes, but it wasn't real hurt. The dead were no threat. The harm the dead had done was slight, and mostly to themselves, save for a few fighters Risalyn and Yuralon had killed, and they'd been angry and frightened, not . . . bad. This was a badness. Elya. Elya. Elya.

The badness held what they wanted her to find out.

She reared back, raised an axe. There was the tree, it was still there, but it had a new limb—rotted, galled, and stunted. One blow of the axe and the black limb would drop away.

"She's shining. Leave her. Let her do her working. It's what she does."

Elora's distant voice brought her back to the task. She dropped the axe, reached out, and grasped the cold, decaying limb.

Hatred. Blood and death. Hiding the hands so the bonefolk wouldn't have them. Killing the light. It hated light. It came from a dark dead place, a black rock—she'd been to that rock, she'd been in those places, only through someone else. She had a shine of her own. It would hate her, too, if it could see her. But it didn't know she was there. It was only a memory, an echo, a burn mark. It couldn't hurt her. Its hurting days were done.

It hated dying. It hated being killed. It hated the searing pain of the blade—she knew the blade, she'd been that blade, she remembered how it felt to go in, the terrible fierce wonder of cleaving flesh. Now she knew how it felt to be killed by it. She lost her balance, frightened. She gripped the limb harder. Her hands sank in. It was spongy now, rotting from the inside. Just a thing in her mind. A thing she made to make sense out of a surge of life that wasn't her own. Just the burned-in shape of a self. That was all. A sick rotting self that was falling apart in her hands.

She hurled the limb into the cavern, and came out.

"Elya," she said, releasing Yuralon's arm. Her voice sounded strange. It echoed in her head. "She hated light. She came from the same place as Flin and Mellas. She was loyal to a woman of power. She hated the woman's light, but she would do anything for her. Kill for her, die for her. I guess she did both."

Risalyn handed her a cup of pear juice. She drank greedily, then passed the cup back, and said, "She killed people of light because that old dark powerful woman told her to."

Both Yuralon and Risalyn went ramrod-straight.

"*What?*" Risalyn breathed.

"A gnarly old black-skinned woman. She . . . she looked like she was from the Heel. Like Elya."

"This was an order she gave long ago," Risalyn said. "Years ago. Before the magewar. Yes?"

"No," Pelufer said, cocking her head, waiting for that to come out of the haunt-memory. "Not so long ago." Her eyes went wide. "They think the light is going to come back! They're killing anyone it might . . . come back *to*."

"Everyone thinks the magelight will return," Elora said. She was on Risalyn's bed now with Caille asleep in her lap. Pelufer must have been away for a long time. It hadn't felt like it. "Everyone around Gir Doegre, anyway."

Yuralon and Risalyn were staring at each other, as if they could talk with their minds through their eyes. It was eerie when they did that, but she and Elora did it too, and probably that looked just as eerie. "It's not Lerissa," Risalyn said.

"No. Not Lerissa. An old black-skinned woman with the look of the Heel. It can only be Worilke."

Pelufer didn't know those names. She'd hardly known there was an Ennead till everyone was talking about how they were all gone.

"She couldn't have survived," Risalyn said. "We'd know."

"She hid herself," Yuralon said. "Even six years ago she was a canny old thing. She's out there somewhere, spinning her webs. Sending people to kill as many mages as they can before the light comes back. She is mad. It's not coming back. The brightest thing in Eiden Myr is in this room with us, and whatever it is, it isn't magelight. Who would follow such mad instructions?"

"She sent us to kill people, too," Risalyn said quietly. "Our own Holding stewards. For reasons just as mad. And we would have, Yur. Spirits help me, we would have done it."

Pelufer had almost forgotten that they were trained by the Ennead to guard them. "But you didn't," she said.

"I killed my own comrades instead," Risalyn said. "Yuralon and the others tried to turn them to the truth. When they couldn't, I fought them, side by side with the horde that became the shielders."

"Then you were lucky," Pelufer said. "You got to fight for the right side."

Risalyn looked over at her shattered blade. Someone had laid the pieces on the chest that held their clothes. Pelufer wished she had a talent for metals like Elora's talent for wood. She could have fixed the blade, then. Caille could do it, but she wouldn't.

Again something teased at her, again the taste of iron came into her mouth.

"I don't think there's ever a right side when you're dealing death," Risalyn said.

"The gnarly woman is on Khine?" Pelufer asked, to work the iron taste away. "That's who Louarn went after, to stop the killings?"

"No," Yuralon said, and rose. "He's chasing the wrong survivor. There were two, and we didn't know it."

"Killing the killers isn't enough. She'll send more." Risalyn swore. "How are we going to find Worilke in all of Eiden Myr?"

"We go after Louarn, then," Yuralon said. "Stop him risking his life on a mistake, at least. Start over, search for Worilke however we can, track down killers wherever we can, and hope she'll give up or die and we'll have wasted our time. Runners and menders will help us. We need aid now. This is too large for us."

Pelufer thought it might make sense if one of the fighters went after Louarn and one tried to find the gnarly woman, but she knew they wouldn't split up any more than she and her sisters would. And they were stronger together. They were stronger still with Louarn. Clever Louarn would have known what to do. Louarn had become their center. They needed him back.

"We retrieve Louarn," Risalyn agreed, and stood up. "He has

only half a day on us, and he started on foot. I'll see about horses."

Yuralon voiced the last remaining doubt. "Barumor and Sevriel are going into battle. Cheveil and Eshadri, too. Maybe all of them." All the folk who'd been or become their comrades in the Holding, whichever side they'd started on. "We should be there."

Risalyn, who loved the blade more than Yuralon did, who was less certain about right and wrong but never about whether the fight was worthwhile, said, "We left them. We didn't join the shield. We're healers now."

After a moment, Yuralon nodded. It was a funny kind of healer who wore a longblade, Pelufer thought, but if the blade cut out a festering piece of Eiden's body to keep its poisons from Eiden's blood, she supposed it made sense enough.

By late afternoon they had acquired horses and new travel gear. "You must stay here," Yuralon said for the ninth time, in the road outside the Ruffed Grouse. He looked dashing and confident on horseback, with his long tawny hair loose, his blade strapped openly on his back. "What happened in the market today will blow over. Make up a story. You're good at that. Ply your trade and keep yourselves safe until we come back for you."

That was something they could do. Pelufer wanted to see the battle, but not so much now as before the bladefight in the market. She had a queer feeling about blades now—part longing, part terror. But they didn't want Caille anywhere near a battle, or evil gnarly women. They were almost happy here. They could wait, while the grownups saved the world.

Risalyn lifted Caille down from the saddle of her own horse, and mounted while the huge head was lowered to snuffle Caille's hair and neck. He was a handful, the farrier had told them, but Risalyn said she liked his spirit and his compact Highland build. He didn't look compact to Pelufer, and he'd tossed his head and moved his feet a lot until Caille came over and petted him.

Elora drew her a few steps off. She was nervous around horses, and Pelufer had to admit that she was too, a bit. They were so much bigger than donkeys, and none of them knew how to ride a big horse with a saddle. Something else she should have found a way to make Risalyn teach her before now. Risalyn would have taught her bladecraft. It was Yuralon who kept their promise to Jiondor.

"They'll bring Louarn back," Pelufer said to Elora as they watched the bladed healers ride away.

Elora was lost in her own distant thoughts, her shoulders stiff as if she bore a weight on them now and wasn't used to it yet. "I'd like that," she said, in a soft voice.

They should have gone inside then, or reopened the stall for what was left of the daylight. But they just stood there, the three of them, her and Elora side by side with Caille in front, looking down the curving road.

Louarn could not get past the Khinish.

They had blocked the main Bootward road and every detour. They were closer than anyone had realized. The shield had waited until they were at mid-Leg before they'd moved to tighten the noose. Now the Khinish knew they were coming. They had locked the center of the Strong Leg down tight.

All night as he traveled Louarn heard irrefutable word of this from angry traders and journeyfolk sent back the way they had come. The Khinish were rocks. They were immovable. There was no getting past them. Inns and stables and barns were filling up; soon folk would have to camp in fields to wait out the trouble. Most gave up and turned for home. Others stayed—some on pressing business, some to be near the novelty of battle.

As he puzzled out the deployment of forces, he developed a grudging admiration for Khine's methods. They had halted their upleg march with stolid purpose. They had cleared a field of battle. There would be few casualties among the common folk. Sheep and cattle were found far upleg of where they belonged, driven off their grazing land. There would be confusion in the wake of this, but as little destruction as possible. They did not want to harm Eiden's body. Louarn didn't understand what they did want, but it wasn't to wreak havoc. Perhaps the fragmented rumors of a dispute with the Head holding were true.

It didn't change the fact that he had to get to Lerissa Illuminator.

He remembered her, through Mellas, albeit vaguely. An aggregate of things the boy had heard, from proxies, from his master. Lerissa was complicit in what the Ennead had done to him; what Seldril and Landril had done, all nine of them had done. Though he'd had no direct dealings with her, she was in him, a shadowy figure. He believed he would know her when he saw her.

He would bring all his dark history to bear in stopping her.

He had to get through.

Just before dawn, after a long arduous survey of the position of watchfires and torchlights beyond Gir Mened, he brazened it out. He came around a cowpath to where one man was stationed. Affecting his best Holding demeanor, he said, "I am a personal runner for Lerissa n'Lessa l'Rigael. I carry urgent news for her," and stood as one who had utter confidence in his errand and the access he would be granted.

"Are you," said the Khinishman. Sun-bronzed and solid, half again Louarn's nine stone and every ounce of it muscle. There would be no fighting past this one. "I suppose then you would know that she is called Lerissa ti Khine."

Louarn snorted in disgust, opened his mouth to answer, and sprang wide around the guard, making for the pasture beyond.

He was snatched back by a heavy hand and hurled stumbling several steps to sprawl on the ground.

"None of that, friend," said the guard. "If you've a message for the woman, go find something to scribe it on—good luck to you there, in these parts—and come back to me. I'll see it's sent."

He rose, cowed, nodding, and turned back the way he'd come.

Out of sight down the dark path, he cut through the hedgerow into a scythed field. Haycocks were just perceivable as darker dark under the heavy clouded sky. He would flit from shadow to shadow, as noiseless as could be. One man, one small solitary man with no mount and no pack, would be able to creep through their cordon.

Halfway across the field, he heard a creak, a twang, and a whistle, and an arrow tore through the sleeve of his shirt. It caught at the fletching and flopped point-down. As he pulled it free, he felt blood well from the furrow it had gouged in the skin of his upper arm.

"The next is for real," a voice called, from somewhere off to the side and up—atop one of the haycocks.

It was inconceivable. They could not shoot that well in the dark. They could not have enough archers to post in every field around their periphery.

Perhaps he had been unlucky, or had tried too obvious a route.

He could not trust their uncanny marksmanship so far as to risk another warning shot loosed in some other field.

He could not get past the Khinish.

The first thought Pelufer had when she woke into the watery half-light before dawn to Elora snoring and Caille talking was that Caille had sneaked her little friend into their room, the innkeepers' youngest, Lusonel. For a few breaths she just lay there. And though annoyance gouged through her at being woken—Caille *knew* how light she slept—she held herself still. She felt bad about how they didn't let Caille have any friends at home, and she and Elora had agreed that they would be nicer about it here. Caille was getting better at not saying or doing things that might betray them. They'd decided she was getting old enough to start trusting.

Caille said, "Eiden doesn't like the fighting. We have to go there, but they'll say no."

No one replied. Was she talking to herself?

Caille said, "Pelufer too! She can fix it better. She almost did before."

Pelufer opened her eyes, and saw long inhuman fingers move slowly, as if making an extra effort to be clear. The fingers were talking about her. They said that she wasn't ready, that a teacher was needed. They said she was too big.

Pelufer sat up through air as heavy as a blanket.

A great bent creature stood crammed into the one corner not piled with the tools and clothes and crafts they'd moved from Louarn and Yuralon's room when they gave it up.

At its feet stood Caille, tiny by comparison, looking up at it with her fists on her hips in a perfect imitation of Elora scolding someone.

"She woke up," Caille said. "You *have* to take her now. Take us to the fighting!"

The pale creature would not. It could only send her ahead, its fingers said. It could not take Pelufer. She was too big.

It was a boneman.

She'd seen a boneman once. It wasn't the same one. The face was the same, near as she could tell, but the shape was different. Harder. Like those twins at home that nobody could tell apart but her. Grown-ups always made the bonefolk sound like monsters. Better watch out, the bonefolk will get you. Don't be naughty, the bonefolk will get you. But the bonefolk never harmed anybody, least of all little children. All those stories that were going around were the worst sort of daft stupidity. The bonefolk were only interested in the dead.

She was full of the dead.

Why was this one fingerspeaking to Caille?

How did this one know how to fingerspeak?

Why was this one standing in their room?

There was no one dead here. Elora was fine, snoring away in Risalyn's bed. Nothing would rouse her but a shake and a poke. The door was locked. She could see the bolt in its slot.

"Did you let him in?" she asked Caille.

Caille shook her head.

The boneman loomed in the corner like a distorted shadow thrown by a very bright light low to the floor. But he was the opposite of a shadow. He was pale as the moon, all except his great sad dark eyes, which had no whites at all. There was no hair on him. He had no ears and no nose, just holes where those should be, two for the nose and one for each ear. He had cheekbones and a jaw, but there was something funny about his mouth. She thought it was a him, like the other one, but tattered fabric covered just enough that she couldn't be sure. He was as still as stone. He didn't even blink. His long forearms were crossed in front of his chest and his long fingers were curled up loosely as if he was holding something, but he wasn't.

She stared at him for what felt like a long time. She wasn't afraid. She was amazed and fascinated. But Caille was up to something. There shouldn't be a boneman in their room. Elora would go mad.

The last time she'd seen a boneman, the only time she'd seen a boneman, their lives had changed forever.

Wait out the battle, Louarn told himself, returning to the cowpath and thence to the back road. *Another day, another nineday, what difference does it make?*

It would make a very great difference to any people of light who lost their lives because of his delay.

He tried again. The Khinish would not be wheedled or cajoled or charmed. He tried the truth and, no surprise, they laughed at him. He created a diversion, sabotaging the axle of a chalk wagon so that it toppled as its driver turned the team and its contents spilled out all over the road. The Khinish were sympathetic but did not move to help. Running out of back roads to try, he bribed a wine trader to make a fuss at the roadblock, and then he set a fire in a hedgerow; in the humid midmorning air it smoked rather than blazed, but the confusion and the screen of smoke got him past the roadblock. Then an arrow took him in the calf. They dragged him back, retrieved their arrow at considerable agony to him, dressed his wound, and packed him off with the angry trader, who said he could have burned a whole field down, and whacked his shin with a blackthorn stick every time he shifted his weight as though to jump off the cart.

A league and half a day lost, the noon heat steaming him into wilted defeat, he was put out of the cart in Gir Mened and handed into the care of peacekeepers. They marched him off limping—the pain was considered no more than he deserved—and locked him in a storage shed with a gourd of water to reflect on the consequences of making a bad situation worse.

They knew him now at every stop point, and the locals had had enough of him.

He could not get past the Khinish.

Face them, Risalyn had said of his dreams.

She had not fully known what she was suggesting.

Mellas should have died in the treacherous tunnels of the Black

Mountains. He was starving, hallucinating . . . dreaming. He had dreamed himself free. He had dreamed himself to another place. When he came out of that place, back into the world, he was no longer in the Black Mountains. He was somewhere else.

You're no longer the boy you were. It might be time to try again.

He had controlled himself, denied himself, suppressed himself too long.

He had power. He had need. It was time to see what this power of his could do.

What it would feel like, after six years of surviving on fragmented, intermittent naps, to sink luxuriously into soft, drowsing, engulfing slumber?

Several times he spasmed awake, the reflex of years not so easily unlearned. Lying flat on the stony bare dirt floor of the shed, hearing the smallest sounds from outside as though they were amplified by a great cave—oxen cropping the dry grass, a washline creaking under a fresh load, even what sounded like the Girdlers' voices calling his name—he despaired. He would never overcome the distracting multiplicity of sounds. He would never sleep. He had lost the knack for it, forgotten how. He might never sleep again. He

"Why are you here?" Pelufer asked.

The boneman made no reply.

She asked again, with her fingers this time.

The boneman picked Caille up.

It wasn't an abrupt movement—Caille was just suddenly in his arms, cradled like a baby. She blinked, then settled herself. "Pelufer too," she said. "To fix things."

Pelufer was out of bed before Caille had the last word out. "Put her down."

"Pelufer too!" Caille warned, watching Pelufer with suspicion. "And Elora, or she'll be angry."

The boneman's liquid dark eyes closed like lips, and his round mouth opened. No sound came out.

Caille started to glow.

It wasn't her shine. It was a green glow.

Green as the glow of bonefolk feeding.

"Put her *down*!" Pelufer's shout was loud enough to wake the whole house. She heard voices, doors opening along the hallway. She reached up to take Caille under the arms and lift her down. Caille didn't look so sure she wanted to be there anymore. She held her arms out to be taken. But the boneman had her tight around the middle. Pelufer clawed at his arms. They were fleshy but cold. They felt like plant stems, as if there were no bones inside them.

The glow increased. Caille let out a wail. Fists pounded on the door. Elora cried out in groaning sleep-tangled horror. Pelufer kicked the boneman, punched his legs and his sides and anything she could reach past Caille. He didn't react. She fumbled through Louarn's things, came up with the chisel. She held it overhand and stabbed it into the boneman's leg and side. "You're hurting her! Let . . . her . . . *go!*"

Somewhere else in the inn someone shrieked. Elora shrieked, too, falling out of bed, scrambling up to dig her nails into the boneman's arms, tear him with her teeth. He didn't react. He didn't move. He didn't bleed. He didn't feel it.

The green glow was so bright that they could hardly see. Caille was yowling, reaching for them, kicking and squirming. They could see her bones as if all her flesh had become translucent, or as if the green glow was coming so bright from inside that they showed right through muscle and skin and clothes.

Pelufer swore and stabbed and tore, and every wound she made was not-made before her eyes had blinked, and then she really couldn't see, she was blinded by the phosphorescent glare, and then it was gone, first Caille was gone and then the glare was gone. The boneman's arms were cradling air. She flung herself on him and plunged the chisel into his heart and his neck and his face.

The wounds closed. He did not blink. His long fingers folded over her arms and lifted her dangling away from him, though she spit and writhed and kicked with enough maddened force to throw off six keepers. He set her easily, gently, on the floor. He caught her neck in one hand, the way you'd fork a rabid animal, and caught Elora's in the other. He held them off—and he backed up, as if no wall was there at all.

He sank into the stone. Back, head, legs, arms . . .

"Stand away!" someone shouted from the hall. The door burst inward in a crashing spray of splinters and a thunk as the bolt hit the floor.

Pelufer's face came up against the stone as it absorbed the last of the boneman, and she was pounding and gouging the wall, and Elora was pounding the wall and sobbing, and the boneman was gone, and Caille was gone.

The Menalad Plain

In the deep darkness before dawn, Verlein ordered the watchfires extinguished. The Khinish kept no watchfires, but her folk had scouted their periphery the day before, and none had passed the great circle of her shielders during the night. They had been sentries for six years, and were as keen-eyed in close quarters as over the distance of sea. The battleground was established. There remained, now, nothing but to set the shieldwall, then gauge the coming assault when daylight revealed the Khinish formation.

They waited for us. They stopped and waited for us, on ground they knew they could control. It was an oddness; like her folk, they were most at home on rugged ground—coastal sand, fens, rocky outcrops. Nothing was to be gained for either side in fighting on the flat, except a clear field of play. Only a few sparse hedgerows stitched the quilt of pastureland, suggesting boundaries, not dense enough to hem in grazing stock. She'd been sure to position her shield beyond those, and upslope where she could, on the seaward side. Trees and tufted undergrowth, such as there were, would hinder only her opponent. She would control this day. She would contain the Khinish. But they had not entrenched, and their goal was to move up the Leg, not hold one scrap of ground. Waiting made sense if you had a vast horde to organize into fighting units, but her scouts had estimated no more than three nonned Khinish.

Another two nonned were on their way up from the Boot, three days behind the main force. When they arrived, the Bootward arc of her shield would be in danger of attack from two sides, and she would be outnumbered by a nonned where now she outnumbered them by that much.

She would finish this today.

"Silk over silks under rings," she told the nearest folk, and the reminder whispered along the circle and out of hearing, like a receding wave. Silk would stop an arrow from long range, and if the flesh yielded beneath, the silk could be pulled to draw the arrowhead from the wound. Over that, their mail tunics were light and loose enough not to kill them all in the heat, and protected as far as wrists and knees. Their hardboots were impregnated with resin, some reinforced with metal or a wound-wire crosshatching. Gloves were mandatory for all, to assure a good grip in the sweat-pouring humidity. An assortment of helms gleamed in the last embers of watchfires before they were shoveled under. Most of layered, hardened cloth, some of iron, some of molded bootbush reinforced with metal plates or wire. She was most concerned about their necks; though some buckled on bootbush collars, there was no protecting the soft flesh under the chin and over the breastbone. Only their skill with shields and weapons would keep the Khinish spears from their throats.

Only their skill with shields and weapons would keep the Khinish from Eiden Myr's throat.

They could have hacked the trees down. They didn't. She knew that meant something, but not what. Had they already chosen their angles of attack? It was a game of bumperpuck, with her shield the rim around the board. Where she came from, they played the game as a wild free-for-all, with hand disks to knock nine pucks through a hole in the opposite rim. When the game was over, you counted the pucks on your side, and whoever had let the most through was the loser. On Khine, they played it as a slow game of angles, turn by turn, with an extra disk as a shooter and one objective being to snooker your opponent's disks behind the bumpers. If the hedges were bumpers . . .

She shook herself, settling her ringed tunic closer on her body, shrugging off the kind of thoughts Worilke would entertain. As commander, she had to think strategically. But not everything was a teller's allegory, and she could not read the Khinish mind.

There were no angles. There was her shieldwall, and there was the Khinish charge. Her folk would hold or they would not. If they did not, either they would cut down the Khinish who broke through, or they wouldn't.

Live or die. Win or lose. Two simple outcomes. It might all be over by noon.

So why did she feel like the shot puck and not the hand disk?

Her invisible shielders had become gray ghosts in the gloaming. "Form up," she said. "Pass the word." She wanted the impenetrable ring of her shield to be the first thing the Khinish saw at dawn.

They had their instructions. To break the line was to fail. To fall back was to fail. To allow the line to ripple or distort was to allow it to weaken, and so to fail. They must stand fast under the first charge, their long kite shields overlapping to create a single unbreakable barrier. After the first impact, they could loosen to engage in small melees and hand-to-hand, but they must hold the line. They must be ever aware of those beside them. They must never fall back, only stand firm or push forward. The archers behind them would shoulder their bows after three rounds of firing into the Khinish center; thereafter they would range at will behind the line, cutting down any groups or singles who broke through. *Let one or two fight past if the alternative is to retreat,* she'd told them, and her seconds had passed the instructions along. *Leave them to the rear guard. But don't let so many through that the rear guard becomes the line.*

Her jaw set and grim, she pulled her own shield from where she had lodged it point-down in the ground for something to lean against during the long night hours. Strapped onto her left forearm, it covered her body from chin to shin, curving slightly to deflect all but dead-center blows. It was ash, light but hard, and would not be hacked through; most others were of lime, some ironwood, and all were iron-banded from behind, sanded smooth and waxed in front, to present a slick surface with the fewest protrusions for a point to catch on. It was broad enough to overlap the shield to her left. If the shield to her right failed, she would have room to bring her weapons into play without failing the fighter on her left. One section of the arc to Toeward comprised left-handed shielders. She had placed two of the most agile at its ends, to fight left or right as circumstance demanded.

She had done what she could do. Evrael's fleet patrolled her coast along the Sea of Charms and the Leeward Sea, and her folk along Maur Lengra on the Weak Leg side had been swapped out one-in-three for archers, to defend the maur better should invasion break through the fleet and come up that waterway. All was protected. Teach these Khinish a lesson, send them back to their island with their tails between their thick legs, and she could send her shielders back to the coast where they belonged.

Or lead them to the Head, and take the holding.

That was what Worilke wanted her to do. She had not said it

outright, but Verlein knew full well what came next if she was to establish command of Eiden Myr. Her folk in the Haunch stood ready to occupy Pelkin n'Rolf's ramshackle excuse for a runners' holding. Her folk in the Hand stood ready to row to Senana. Show Pelkin n'Rolf, Graefel n'Traeyen, and Dabrena n'Arilda who was master, and she would be most of the way to taking Eiden Myr in hand.

But first things first. That decision would wait until she saw how her shield handled the Khinish. She must win the battle for this scrap of grazeland before she chose whether to serve or take charge. Worilke was tucked safe away in a nearby town. Verlein would win this battle and decide her next move alone.

"Girayal," she said. "Eowi. To me." As they flanked her, she moved to take position in the first rank of the line, dead center of the route to Headward. *To get to the rest of Eiden Myr, they'll have to go through me. But I am only one shield in the shieldwall. Down the first shield, and the seconds fill the gap. Down the seconds, and the thirds will have you.*

The earth shuddered beneath her. It had done that constantly since they massed yesterday. As if Eiden shivered under the march of fighters' feet across his body.

She hoped he didn't mind a little blood.

There would be no daybreak over the flooded maurside. In this cloud-smothered leg, there would be only darker gray and lighter gray. But she could tell the ground from the sky now. Just a few more breaths, and she'd be able to see the deployment of forces on that ground.

Her shielders locked into position, shield on shield. To either side, they stretched from visibility into darkness, but in each breath she could see another pair to each side. The light was coming faster now.

The eighth of nine days of Longlight. Tomorrow was the longest day of the year. She had not paid attention to the holiday until she'd heard some of her shielders talking about what their folk would be doing at home. Solstice-stone vigils in the Elbow, tiltboard wrestling in the Fist, ninespice puddings in the High Shoulder, exchanges of gifts and compliments in the Belt. In her Weak Leg home, they'd be making good on debts and trying again to settle old arguments.

The festival of Longlight was a time to take active, positive steps to restore balance in the community. The thought made her laugh aloud. *That's what we're doing here, all right.*

Again the ground rumbled. This time the sky echoed it. She could see the clouds now, thick and dark, tumbling over each other like stones in a flood. Rain would help her. It hadn't rained here in two years, or so the locals claimed, but farmers were always overstating things—she'd heard enough exaggeration as harvestmaster to last the rest of her life, and she knew storm clouds when she saw them. Her scouts claimed the warmth-tolerant Khinish were far overdressed for the unseasonable heat, no doubt padded in wool-stuffed linen meant to keep her folk's blades out of their bellies. Rain would waterlog them, while her silk-clad folk remained unweighted by anything save shields and mail. This was looking better and better.

Her folk, hearing her laugh, seemed to hearten. She felt confidence run through the shieldwall like a current. They were linked, they were strong, a great unbreakable circle. Let the rain come! Let the winds come! Let the Khinish come!

At last she could see them, a darker gray on the graying fields. Moment by moment their details resolved: iron helms; round metal-rimmed shields with spiked bosses; stuffed linen jerkins, shining as if lacquered, under dull iron links; and on their legs fish-scale iron plates sewn into leggings and boots. Each one of them seemed to carry not only a curved blade at his side but a shortbow and a lance-tipped spear. Heavily armored, heavily dressed, heavily armed. They would not be outmaneuvering her folk. Typical Khinish: they would fire their volleys, they would set themselves, and they would charge, counting on sheer bullheaded weight and momentum to propel them through her shieldwall.

Her folk would hold. Behind her were two more ranks of overlapped shields: spearfolk, doubly armed with javelins and longspears, then a second rank of blade wielders. Behind that were the archers, awaiting her call, and the drummers who would send the signal round the great circle and across. She could almost see it in full now; only the far side remained obscured, and that was more the fault of her low vantage point than the inadequate light.

Pride swelled through her, and in its intoxicating mist swam visions of highest command, of organizing all Eiden Myr to hold off the incursions of whoever or whatever might come at them from the outer realms. Girayal on one side, Eowi on the other; better trained, now, since their hard lessons from Kazhe, and after this better trained still. This engagement would forge her folk into the fighting force she had driven them to be, dreamed they would be. Those who lived—and it would be most of them, it had to be, she had trained them too hard to part with them now—would turn seasoned, battle-ready faces to those outer realms, all the stronger for this fierce weathering. Perhaps Strelniriol te Khine had done her a favor, in his thrust for control. Perhaps mad, bullheaded Streln was the best thing that ever happened to Eiden Myr.

Then the Khinish took formation.

"Drummer!" Verlein called, and heard a brittle tattoo in response—he was careful not to trip the eager archers, though they had not yet strung their bows. "I need Harinar, old Tarunel, Cheveil, Lannan, Eshadri, dark Barumor, Sevriel, little Gilris, and Jia."

Nine of her best folk. Nine seconds who were post commanders. Nine who had fought beside her in the Holding, though two of those had been the Ennead's before they were turned. She needed bloody Yuralon and that sister of his, too—they were in the Leg, Cheveil had saved their lives in some brawl on his way downland, and he at least was still armed with a blade her smiths had forged in the Blooded Mountains six years ago—but they had styled themselves as healers now. They might as well be wearing white.

The Khinish had formed into three wedges. She would not underestimate how maneuverable those wedges could be, not given Khinish discipline. It didn't change everything, but it came close. She'd trained her folk in the boar's snout, but she hadn't expected that sort of finesse from the Khinish. A head-on straightforward charge in two or three lines, that would have been their style.

She had expected them to expect a straight, massed shieldwall from her, stretching across their Headward route, too wide to flank. And perhaps they had—the way they formed up suggested to her a last-minute adaptation to the sight of her circle. She had forced them into wedges by surrounding them, by denying the grace of retreat. Her circle challenged them; her circle told them that they would not be allowed to run home once stopped, but must be thoroughly beaten.

She had not intended that. She had intended to contain, to strangle if necessary . . . and to surprise. She had hoped to intimidate by surrounding them. *What did you expect, they'd lay down their arms and apologize for all the trouble?*

No. She had aimed for uncertainty, not a change in tactics. Never underestimate the puking Khinish, there was the lesson. Those wedges would drive right through her shield, and in containing them her circle would become three circles, and the battle would disintegrate into a formless brawl.

She needed wedgebreakers. Now.

It was a game of bumperpuck after all. In Khinish style, the pucks were wedged in the center, and one player got to break. But in Weak Leg style, it would be fast and furious thereafter. She must exploit the break for all it would give her.

Light, rapid, complex drumticks ran around the circle. Names were difficult for them. She felt the infinitesimal shift as nine fighters slipped from the front rank and the rank closed the gaps.

While they were making their way to her, a man stepped out from the front of the Khinish wedge that was pointed directly at her.

Streln, their headman, waving a blue cloth over his head.

Wave that dyed cloth a little higher, she thought, *and I won't need my shieldwall—these bloody Leggers will mob you for me.*

"String the bows," she told her drummer, and heard the signal repeated, strong and clear this time.

Little Gilris slipped in behind her, unnoticeable. Streln was still advancing. As if she were commenting on his approach, she said to Gilris, "Wedgebreakers. Do you understand me?" Gilris did. "I called eight others," Verlein told her. "Form three groups back where you were, with the heaviest sprinters around you, and have replacements ready to fill the gap from behind. You'll break out as soon as their archers let fly or as soon as those wedges charge. Take them in the sides. Break them before they hit the shieldwall. Understood?" Gilris understood. "Tell the others. It looks like their leader wants to have a chat."

Streln stopped midway to her position.

"I'm not a six-year-old to be dangled by my tunic," she called out to him, feeling Gilris slip back through the ranks, hidden by their shields.

"Shoot me now, if you fear me so," he called back, and held his arms out. "Surely you have someone who can hit me at this range."

To Girayal, who knew the signals, she said, "They depend more on their headman than you do on me. Loose the arrows if those wedges advance, and make sure one of them gets him."

Then she stepped forward, ash shield covering her, right hand on her throwing knife. When the wall had closed behind her, she walked to Streln.

Three times nine paces and four. He made no move until she was standing five paces from him, and then only inclined his head. Even so, she felt a reaction in the shield. But no bows creaked.

"You are a gamepiece in a bid by Evrael to become headman," Streln said, as though giving a teller's rendition of the concern that had only just begun to nag at her. "Whatever your agreement, he has breached it. Make way and let me get those spies and menders off your shoulders for good. I'll reinforce your shield, and no ditches to dig."

"A little late for that offer," Verlein said. "Imagine my eagerness to yield to you here, in front of all my folk. You've had ample time to message ahead for a meeting."

Delay could avail him nothing, and it gave her wedgebreakers time to organize. What was he playing at? His second wave was three days away, a day even by horseback. Apparently his folk agreed; closer, she could see the frowns, the tight shoulders, here and there a shifted stance. Impatience, concern . . . disgust? Was this not the first thing he had done or ordered that went against the grain?

"Look at me, Verlein," he said.

Not "Shieldmaster"? He seemed very strange, very tight, as if he were fighting something within himself—forcing words past lips braced against them. But his dark eyes were foreign, unknowable.

"I'll look where I please, Headman."

The next words came without a struggle, drenched in his familiar arrogance. "Then look up that paltry slope you think you own, past your folk, to the blond head there. Patrolling your shores, is he?"

She looked. He wasn't trying to hide. He might have just ridden out, as if on command, to sit his horse and watch the battle. Or join it, with the seafolk mounted awkwardly around him. There was nothing awkward about the longstaffs balanced across their saddlebows.

Was this betrayal? It was too late to matter. Six seafolk who could barely sit a horse would make little difference in this engagement. Evrael had deployed his ships, according to her scouts. He didn't have to be on them. If he'd called them off, her coast was unguarded; running back wouldn't change that today, and she might as well rout the Khinish while she was here.

"Your delay makes no sense," she said. "Yield, Streln, and in return I'll let your folk go home alive. Or make me a sensible offer, let me reject it, and let's get on with this."

Streln glanced to the other side and raised a brow in mild surprise before his eyes narrowed. She did not follow his gaze. She'd had enough games. But perhaps so had he, now. His head snapped back to her and with an eerie intensity he said, "Remember Eldrisil. Rout my folk or be routed, it's the same in the end. Remember Eldrisil, understand him, and he will not have died in vain." His throat closed up as he was speaking; the last words came out a rasp. His bronze skin blanched, his pupils contracted. He looked like a man fighting shock.

Battling some inner agony, and spouting babble. "I've had enough of this, Streln," she said, half drowned out by a grumble of thunder. "This parley is over." She didn't care if he could hear her. The sight of her spine would convey the gist. Would she make it back to the shield without an arrow in the spine? She would not back away from him like a deferential subordinate.

If he managed some strangled plea or insolent riposte, she could not hear it under the anger in the sky.

Rain, she thought, as she walked, and waited for the iron point to enter her back.

Rain, she thought, as she reached the shieldwall.

Rain, she thought, taking her place, checking the six wedgebreakers in sight, catching one nod from each of the closest.

"Ready archers," she said, and the command was relayed, and yew and elm bent as bowstrings drew back.

A thrill went through her body and seemed communicated into the earth, which quivered beneath her. *Don't thwart me, Eiden,* she bade him in silence, as Sylfonwy and Morlyrien conspired against the Khinish over her head. *Let me end this, and see you safe.*

Streln took the point of the wedge opposite her. He raised his arm. There was no blue cloth now.

"Archers—" Verlein began.

His arm swept forward.

"—let fly!" Verlein finished as, with the hum of a nonned bowstrings, the Khinish archers loosed their shafts. The song of their flight threaded over the deep many-stringed twang from her own bowfolk, and then all was drowned out by the swell of three nonned Khinish voices bellowing the charge.

Their strange horns called thin and redundant behind the pounding of their feet, and arrows cut several blasts short.

"Brace!" Verlein called, and heard the deep drums carry the word, and knew that too was redundant, for the shieldwall had gone taut as a bowstring, hard as a mortared stone wall, tight as the interlocking rings in their tunics.

The charge came on.

Each wedge moved as one, unnatural, uncanny.

Her wedgebreakers were nearly there, loosed with the arrows. A second flight of shielder arrows rained into the moving wedges, but whatever they hit they did not halt. Weight, momentum, and grinding commitment drove Streln's wedge straight at her. The other two had turned just before the charge, seeking to surprise sections of the shieldwall that had not braced for the worst. The wedgebreakers, small quick groups, had shifted trajectory to compensate. The third flight of arrows picked off some Khinish in the rear ranks.

The wedgebreakers smashed into the wedges from the sides.

She could see only the effect on the one driving toward her. Cheveil's group and Gilris's severed the rear wings right off the wedge. They went down in a tangle of shields and spears with a diagonal cut through the straight ranks. The severed wings held formation in smaller wedges—and broke away, charging the shieldwall to either side of her. Insane, they were too few, but they moved as one, impossibly, and there was no calculating the effect of surprise on braced shielders who might have stiffened too much to adjust to being harried rather than charged.

She could not watch or call to them. The main body of the wedge had also held formation, and covered the last threfts in three eyeblinks, aimed straight at her.

They crashed against the shield.

Verlein was lifted off her feet.

A shield cracked, or a bone.

Streln's breath rasped her neck as it came out of him in a whooshing grunt.

She was borne back, flat against the shields behind her. She could not move her arm to reach a weapon. Feet scrabbled for purchase in the grass behind her dangling feet. The feet behind those were cleated, and held, as her body and the body behind her absorbed the crushing weight.

She could not remember what it was to breathe.

The rear Khinish ranks drove forward around the wedge point, smashing into the shields around her in a spreading ripple.

Hold, she tried to tell them, *hold, hold, hold*, but there was no air in her.

She could not see. Shorter Streln had driven her shield up into her face. She tasted iron and blood.

A spear quested over her shoulder, seeking Khinish heads before the smashup broke apart. Grunts and cries came from behind her, but not beside. They'd crushed the breath out of themselves. She would never come back to earth. She would hang suspended between breath and death forever.

To the left and right, at the edges of the impact point, blades rang, a spear haft snapped, a woman cried out dying, a man cried out wounded. From far away, outside the muffling crush, came the scrapes and thunks and clangs of bladeplay, oaths and grunts and screams. A curved blade whipped downward, blind, from over her head, and found Girayal's, and looked for more as blood gushed out to drench her neck and shoulder, then dropped into the crush after a stab from the shielder spearpoint.

The shieldwall around her bent like some massive ancient willow limb, and held. The second and third ranks surged up from behind her in a mighty groaning effort and pressed the Khinish back. Abruptly they gave way. Verlein fell free and forward. She kicked out, on some untrainable instinct, so that her own shield braced her at the base when she came down and she could push herself upright instead of toppling headfirst. Girayal lay crumpled and cleaved to her left; Eowi had fallen onto his shield. Her eyes on the Khinish, she hauled at his belt but couldn't lift him along with his shield. He was stunned and limp. The Khinish wedge was dented into a square, retreating fluidly. In the next blink, it broke apart. Some backed off and brought shortbows into play. She would not fall back. She couldn't haul at Eowi anymore, she had to rise to the next attack. "Roll!" she shouted. He did not seem to hear.

The shield line came up beside her spaced for close quarters. The second rank hurled their javelins on her order. Khinish screamed, and fell. Arrows flew. Shielders fell to the sides and behind. More Khinish danced in, wielding spears and blades. Eowi rolled just in time to take a spear on his shield rim instead of in his back.

Her shieldwall had held, and tightened, for as far as she could make out in her peripheral vision in the moment before Streln's curved blade slashed toward her neck.

She jerked her shield around, and the curved blade bit wood a hair shy of her shoulder. She twisted, trying to pry it from his hand, but the blade only carved a furrow in her shield rim and slid free. She shoved her shield out in a vicious bid to smash his face, but he had danced back—they were all dancing, moving in and out again, tempting the line to warp. Her archers were done, and waited behind her spearfolk with blades ready. Holding, not jumping in. Letting the first rank do its job. *Good*, she thought, *good*, and she wanted to tell them that, but Streln had moved on and some other Khinishman was hacking at her now, and she met him in the bind, seeking always to exploit some weakness in the curve of those blades—but a quick deft spear thrust from beside her took him in the chest, and in the moment's respite she could only glance around her shieldwall to take stock.

we have them surrounded we withstood the charge we outnumber them four to three we have only to tighten on them tighten until they're backed up milling together let's see them dance and harry us then

"Forward a pace!" she cried, and the drums called out the order, and the shieldwall tightened, so much that some first-rankers were squeezed out. Her first mistake knifed through her gut as she saw them elbow their way forward instead of falling back to join the second rank. *To fall back is to fail,* she had told them, drilled them, but she had not thought it through as far as this, bloody wretched spirits strike her—forced out of the shieldwall, they were flinging themselves into the fray, engaging the Khinish inside the circle, quickly overwhelmed.

"Fall back to make way!" she called to her drummer, but there was a hesitation, that was not a command he knew, he had to send it slowly like a name and she didn't know whether the other drummers would make sense of it to pass it on or her people would understand it.

Bloody balls, bloody balls, Eiden's bloody balls—

Then she caught a clear view across the battleground, to the other side of the circle.

There was no other side of the circle.

The far Khinish wedge had driven through. The far side of the field was an incoherent melee.

There was nothing for it, nothing at all, nothing else she could do. She would have to call the charge.

A curved blade found a join and cleaved her shield down to the iron band above her arm.

She twisted down on reflex to avoid the cut. The shield tilted. The blade whipped out of its wielder's hand and twanged crazily, stuck in the shield. She brought her longblade up as she shifted for a view of the attacker, and cleaved him in return. A spearman beside him stabbed her in the shoulder. She fell back before the barb could bury itself, then drove forward with her cloven, blade-twanging shield and knocked the spearman to the ground. It drew the shieldwall with her, and she felt an irrational surge of rage, the bloody obedient idiots she had trained, couldn't let her push an attack and return to position but had to stay blindly with her.

There is no bleeding circle anymore!

She flung the unwieldy shield from her at the feet of an onrushing Khinishwoman, tripping her into a tumble that ended under the blade of the shielder to the left. She didn't know who was around her anymore, seconds or thirds, Girayal was dead and Eowi was lost in the fray and names and faces were lost with them, there were only shielders and Khinish, and as shields were hewn or dropped there were only straight blades and curved blades, silks and padded jerkins.

There was no circle anymore.

Her blade arm was not working well. Something wrong with her shoulder. Blood and punctured mail, at a glance. She drew a longknife left-handed, but for another moment there was no one to fight, there was a pile of dead Khinish in front of her and the battle seemed to have spread along the line. She blinked sticky dampness out of one eye with some dim memory of being smashed in the face.

Call the charge. There's nothing left to do. Form up and call the charge and take their main force down. The ones in the back will have to fend as they can.

Movement caught her eye from the downland side. Another gap in the circle, blast it, it was all going to pieces. Folk on horseback. A line of horses. Not Khinish, not seafolk, not Evrael, he'd been on the other side. Horses had no place in a battle. No one would fight from horseback, they'd just hamstring the beasts or cut them out from under them, a Khinish blade could behead a horse in one swing, there'd be no point to that, killing good stock, dead horses to no purpose, dead horses piling the battleground.

In the deepening gloom that might be her vision failing from blood loss or might be related to the claps of thunder muted in ears deafened by screams and bladeclash, she saw a head of white-blond hair.

Someone behind her was lifting her arm, pressing a wadded cloth to her shoulder, tying a binding around it. Some irritating second-ranker trying to stop the blood. Two Khinishwomen came at her and fell on blade and spear from either side of her. The neck. They should all have protected their necks better. Some had taken it in the head or limbs, but it always seemed to be the neck that did it, they bled out right away—

Kazhe.

Call the charge.

Kazhe, who was lost, irredeemable, maddened by drink, ungovernable—

Call the charge.

Kazhe, her blademaster, who had taught her and led her and forged the beginnings of a rebel horde for her and then abandoned her to follow the Lightbreaker to his death, come in this darkest hour to fight by her side as she was meant to—

Call the charge.

Kazhe, dismounting, handing her horse off to someone, but just standing there while others gathered around her from nowhere, at least a nonned armed fighters but not formed up into any kind of—

Kazhe, watching her shieldwall crumble—

Kazhe! she tried to shout, through the darkness and the wasp stings of raindrops, past the ringing iron and the cries and the agony in her head and in her shoulder.

The blond head turned, and even from this distance Verlein could feel the ice-blue eyes burn through her gratitude and wonder like the inexorable deadly bite of frost.

"Verlein!" someone screamed from nearby, a small muffled cry in her fading ears. Almost offhandedly, she ducked the wobbling spear meant for her head. It was a longspear, no good for hurling. That was good. They were getting desperate, misusing their weapons.

She came up to see Streln staring at her from across a field of their dead and dying.

She sheathed her knife and moved her longblade to her off hand.

She drew breath, deep life's breath, rank with blood and effluents and the sweat of terror and exhaustion and the heat that grew worse with the coming of the hot unnatural rain.

She called the charge.

The Menalad Plain

A Khinishman saw them. In his dark, battered face, his eyes went wide. His lips moved in the shape of an obscenity. In the nick of time he remembered the woman he was fighting. He beat her back. Another Khinish fighter bore in beside him—man or woman, you couldn't tell one from the other now half the time. They had the shielder outnumbered two to one. But the Khinishman broke off and started toward them.

"Stay down," Pelufer told Elora, pressing her deeper into the tufts of grazebane where they were hiding, at the base of a tree. As if Elora would move anyway. Her ankle was swollen and purpling, and her foot dangled grotesquely. Not sprained. Broken.

The Khinishman was coming closer. He was maybe six threfts away. Lightning branched across the sky. What if it hit the tree? But they couldn't leave the tree, the tree was all that had kept them alive, shielding them from the first pounding assault. Nobody would charge right into a tree. If they moved two feet from it they would be trampled. Even if Elora could run and dodge. Arrows fell everywhere, wildly now. The tree was spined with them. But Pelufer had to sit up, remain visible, or the Khinishman would lose her in the confusing dark melee.

Would the other fighters let him pass, if he ran bearing the body of a young unarmored girl, with another little girl in tow? Would arrows be more likely to hit them if they moved, or if they stayed still at the burled base of the arrow-spined tree?

The Khinishman fought his way over, smiting longblades and whirling to kick the bladefolk away, ducking one spear, cracking another in half with his curved blade.

He loomed over them, terrifying in his stiff, blood-soaked, iron-sewn clothes, a gigantic muscled armored killer. His mouth worked, but Pelufer couldn't hear what he was saying over the crashing thunder and the crashing battle. When he touched her, she would be drenched in names, maybe too many to swallow, but maybe he wouldn't be able to hear those either, maybe that wouldn't stop him rescuing them.

She made way for him to pick up Elora, saw that he saw the bent ankle and drained face and understood, saw that he was swearing at them but that he was glancing around for the best route to make a run for it once he'd picked up Elora.

An arrowhead sprang out of the front of his neck.

He crumpled, his mouth still working. His eyes were shocked and then sad, so sad, as though he'd been a good man who tried hard to do right, a good man who'd done his best but left so much undone.

Pelufer wailed in blind frustration, and tugged at his body until it lay on its side, a buffer to trip anyone who would run them over without seeing them.

Caille had wanted her to fix this. Caille had thought she could fix this. She tried, she tried so hard, she tried to find that reaching-out feeling she'd had when Risalyn fought the smooth-haired killer, but it was gone, there were too many. There were only killers around her now, nonneds upon nonneds of killers.

They had left Gir Nuorin a day behind the shield. They had to trick the innkeepers to sneak away. The innkeepers wouldn't leave them unattended once they knew that all their grownup minders were gone, not with Caille missing. It wasn't as if the innkeepers had done any better at protecting their own daughter—little Lusonel had been taken the same as Caille. But little Lusonel had reappeared by mid-morning. Just walked out of her room as if she'd been there all along. She couldn't tell them where the boneman had taken her. A strange wood, she said, and described a place that couldn't possibly exist. Silver trees, golden leaves, purple sky. A beautiful woman with a glowing ring. It was a fairy story, a tellers' tale. Lusonel had to be making it up.

None of the grownups believed her.

A lot of other children had been taken, too. All around the same age. Only one other came back. She was found wandering near the quarry, stunned, unable to tell them anything.

It wasn't Caille.

Lusonel loved fairy stories. Pelufer believed that what she said was true in a way the grownups couldn't understand. The bonefolk were taking the children wherever they most wanted to go. Or sending them. Whether they changed their minds or not.

Caille had asked the boneman to take her to the fighting.

It was the only place they could go to look.

They'd meant to creep around the edge of it, searching, during the day and night before the battle. They'd thought they might see the coppery shine of her, if they got close enough, and if she was trying to do something with her power from a hiding place. Catching a ride from Gir Nuorin with a tinker bound for Gir Doegre and then slipping away down the cutoff toward the Boot Road, they'd caught up with the shield, and rode the rest of the way hidden in one of their supply wagons. When the shielders called a halt, when the news came up the column that this was it, this was the fighting ground, they jumped out. They moved through dense thickets and hedgerows as only Elora could. They searched and searched, getting their bearings, even asking about a little lost girl. Folk told them there were scores of little lost girls these days, and they should get off home before they joined them.

They tried walking straight down a road. Khinish guards turned them back and warned them about bowmen and said all kinds of things about the trouble curious girls could get into. "It's going to storm," they said. Typical awayfolk, thinking it would ever rain in the Leg. "Go on off home now." They'd searched as far as they could Bootward, then came back Headward. But before they could go on around to the Toeward side, the shield moved in, surrounding the Khinish center, and they were caught in between.

Then night fell. Elora said they should ask the nearest fighter for help, shielder or Khinish. Pelufer said no, they'd hold them somewhere then and they'd never find Caille. In a last-ditch attempt to get out of the bind they were in without grownups taking them in hand, they'd moved too fast in the dark, and Elora had stepped in a hole and gone down with a bad sound of bone giving way. Pelufer had dragged her under this tree just as dawn was beginning to lighten the roiling black sky to roiling gray.

Now they were where the fighting was, and Caille was not. Whatever Caille thought she could do, she couldn't. Whatever Caille thought Pelufer could do, she couldn't.

From off to Headward, a drum boomed.

There was a pause, a silence at the center of tumult, as if seven nonned folk had all drawn breath at once. Pelufer stared at the trunk too smooth to climb, at the branches too far up to reach, at the tree Elora couldn't have climbed anyway with a broken ankle. Away above them, the sky was raging, spitting rain, coiling itself to unleash a deluge. She couldn't remember the last time she felt rain on her. She couldn't believe that Khinishman had been right. Lightning flashed, and the thunder that exploded on its heels seemed to rumble in the ground, a deafening response to the boom of the drum.

The shielders were shaping themselves into a line, and then another line behind it, and another line. Down Bootward small groups were still bashing at each other, and some Khinish broke away to nock arrows and aim for the gathering shielders. The rest made wedges of themselves, like in the beginning. The two hosts were going to charge straight ahead in a final bid to destroy each other.

A whine came out of her, felt rather than heard. Their boundary hedge, their three wych elms tufted by wild grazebane grass, stood right where the two hosts would meet.

"Stand and lean," Pelufer said, crouching to push Elora up by the armpits. Elora braced against the elm, pushing with her good leg, and between the two of them they got her upright in three jerking humps along the bark. Pelufer's back was one-third to the shielder side, but it was the only place where the burls at the nicked and gnawed base left some room for feet. She pressed Elora flat and reached her arms as far as they would go around the trunk. They would become the tree, perfectly still, blended, an obstacle easily avoided. The surging waves of fighters would crash and swirl around them.

Lightning flashed again, in a world going dark. Eerie blasts sounded on the Khinish side, like inhuman cries. Elora groaned from the pain of her ankle, a sound lost in the din. Thunder drowned out the pounding bootsteps of the charging hosts. Pelufer couldn't tell how close they were. She pressed her face into Elora's shoulder and squeezed her eyes shut tight.

The ground bucked. It sent her stumbling away from Elora. Elora clung to the tree somehow, or it to her, some trick of her power. Another heave of the ground knocked Pelufer down. Her face was slammed over Headward by the first gush of hard rain.

The shielders were scattered and downed but trying to get up and re-form. A twist of the head as she sat up showed her the Khinish doing the same. They would not let the storm stop them. They had come here to fight. Why? Why were they fighting? What could possibly be worth all this?

A blade in the hand and a job to be done with it, something deep within Pelufer said.

Elora was shouting at her, but she couldn't make it out. She got her knees under her, but the rain drove her down. They'd never see her now, in the stormdark, in the battle. The only ones who would notice her would be the ones who trampled her.

Elora might not be able to hold on to the tree without her. There might be time to crawl back to her before the fighters got their feet and lined themselves up to charge again.

But she could feel something . . . something in the ground under her hands, something connecting her to all that metal, all that blood . . . it was that feeling, that reaching-out feeling . . . if she could—

Arms caught her, and lifted.

She floated up into the air, unable to see who had her. She floated higher than any human arms could have held her. She felt a prickling tingle all over, as if she were coming apart, but it didn't hurt. Blood and strength and energy rushed through her. The earth rumbled again, losing its balance beneath them. The ranks of Khinish swayed back, like grass under a breeze, and went down. She saw them as ripples in a myriad array of tiny perfect points. It was like the glittering you saw when you passed out, but she wasn't passing out, she was more alive and more aware than she had ever been in her life.

And stricken through the heart.

"Elora! *Elora!*"

She heard back, in her ears or in her mind, a voice like a dry breeze, a voice like the shake of rattleseed, words distorted and slurred but understandable: "She has the way."

That meant nothing what did that mean there was nothing Elora could do or she would have done it already she was just standing there while nonneds of killers swept down on her if she couldn't hold on to the tree they would trample her she had a broken ankle what if she couldn't hold on—

The world disappeared in an ecstatic, heartbreaking whirl of pinpoints.

Elora stared at the boneman after Pelufer was gone. She didn't look at the Khinish or the shielders. She wouldn't be able to hear their pounding charge. But in moments, when the groundshakes eased, they would close like parted waters, and her death would come with them. At least Pelufer and Caille had gone on ahead. She swallowed the cry that came up like bile. She didn't believe that Caille was dead, not in her heart of hearts, but she didn't believe Pelufer's construction either, that the boneman had sent Caille where she wanted to go. She'd had to do something. She'd had to believe something. So she'd come here, because there was nothing else to try. But Caille was gone. Pelufer was gone. She might never see them again. She was alone.

The boneman stepped in close—one step, on his stork-long legs—and held out a spindly-fingered hand, awkwardly, trying on a human gesture, trying to reassure her. Would he take her now, too? Dissolve her like the dead, dissolve her alive? She realized she was screaming at him, screaming that there were nothing but dead bodies around him, couldn't he find something better to do than take her sisters from her? She was sobbing, and swearing at him, words she would have smacked Pelufer for saying, words that would have killed her father if he heard them come out of her mouth.

The boneman worked fingers against his chest, oblivious of her rant: *I go. Do what I do. Follow.*

He took another long step, right up beside her, and then a third—stepping right into the wych elm.

That was where he had come from. He had come from behind the tree. She hadn't seen him come out. He went into trees and came out of trees the way the one who took Caille went into stone.

The fighters had lined up again. The shield boomed. Khine howled reply.

She was leaning on the tree. It was an old tree. Solid and enduring. It held its arms up high over the animals that pestered it. Its bark was wrinkled into sinuous furrows like the flesh of an old woman's neck. It didn't mind the arrows much. Wych elms were unpredictable, dangerous, canny; she didn't think it would drop a limb on her, but she couldn't be sure. She hopped and twisted herself around. The pain was terrible. She tried to ignore it. She laid her hands on the trunk the way she would if she were doing a working. But this time she didn't think about bloomings, or healings, or beautiful things, or things she loved. She didn't think about pain, or mangled bodies, or wicked blades, or driving rain, or quaking ground, or lost sisters, or misery, or terror. She just thought about the tree. Flesh, like her. Spirit, like her. Alive, like her.

The old wood welcomed her. Made way for her.

She was Elora, and she was the tree. She was the soft-hard woodflesh, the furrowed skin, the languid flow of life's fluids from roots to crown and crown to roots. She was the seeking roots, the basking leaves, the slow accumulation of rings of years. She was unthinkably old, and absurdly young.

She was the tree, and she was Elora, and she wanted to live.

She leaned in.

As the voices of drum and horn and death tailed off behind her, she sank through.

The Menalad Plain

Razhe rode the quaking ground as easily as she'd ride Comfrey standing on his back. Her light-clad plains Girdlers did the same beside her, heedless of the downpour that battered the reeling ranks of shielders and Khinish. It had rained on them like this for nearly three years. They had adapted. They were in their new element now.

Half her forces stood with her and half stood across the battleground, come out of their hiding places while the shielders and Khinish engaged. She had two nonned. The Khinish had started with three, Verlein with four. Now she and they looked evenly matched.

They had killed more than enough of each other.

She could watch and see if the spirits defeated them, tilting the ground while smiting them with rain and wind; she could wait for one side to claw a semblance of victory past its own losses, then rout the victor, as planned; or she could stop this now.

If not for the drenching, Khine would win handily. Verlein had misjudged them. She'd thought they would bear down in one great domineering force—aggressive, armored, bent on marching over her. She'd thought she could withstand their first charge, then tighten her circle and crush them. But the Khinish were cats, not bulls. They gave way when least expected to, wheeled their tight maneuverable wedges, shifted bearing on a word. They thought and moved as one, yet each could act alone. At home, in peace, their hierarchies were complex, unfathomable, entrenched. In battle, their fighters were independent and equal, linked like rings in mail, sensitive to each other's movements, shifting to cover each other and change the attack with an intuitive sense of where both their comrades and the opponent's weak spots were. Like kenaila, each bore three weapons, and they switched among them at will; there were no archers to command separate from the spearfolk, no spearfolk to be directed separate from the blades. And they saw no disgrace in retreat. They withdrew in order to lure and encircle; they harassed with feints and spears and arrows, then darted in for the mortal blow. They looked like an ironclad wall, but they fought by weaving and crossing, delicate fingers playing upon a loom.

Verlein's ranks could not stand against that. But the Khinish had underestimated Verlein. They had scoffed at her homespun fighters, her hand-me-down bladelore, her glorified sentries. They had not expected to meet a rugged, disciplined force with a backbone. They had not expected the shieldwall to hold. And they had not expected the spirits of earth and water and air to besiege them.

Let them kill each other off, Kazhe thought. *Let them destroy each other, and good riddance. I need a drink.*

But they had killed too many good folk. And she had a point to make.

She strode across the bucking, rain-drenched pasture while the two hordes struggled to recover their feet and gather themselves for a third try at their scrambled charge.

Her folk arrayed in two ranks, one facing the Khinish, one facing the shielders. Their instructions were simple and echoed their training. Disarm. If that doesn't work, kill.

Their intent was clear.

She stated it anyway.

"You will not rule!" she called across to the Khinish. The headman would be somewhere in the center of the front rank, and if he was dead the rest would still hear her. Her voice was raised only to carry to them, not to challenge. Her presence was challenge enough. "This world has never had rulers. As long as I live it never will. And I am kenai." She drew her blade. The swirling metal was a creamy silver in the gloom, slicing raindrops in its arc over her head. "You cannot kill me."

Riding the bucking ground, she turned to Verlein, who stood linked arm in arm with her seconds to keep from falling. "You will not rule, Verlein! Have you told your shield what you mean to do? Have you planned their route to the Head, or the Haunch? Is your shield attacking them even now? Look at me. I am an end on it. You've become the invasion you feared. *You* are the outer realms, Verlein. You will not rule!"

Fatuous speeches. She'd have spat at the ground, but the rain made it pointless. Torrin's haunt would be busting a gut if it wasn't sitting on the stones that crushed him in the Fist, gazing out to sea forever. But she had to make the effort. Folk deserved to know their options, and understand the deaths they chose.

She couldn't hear the commands from the shield or Khine, but she heard the drum, she heard the horn, and she understood the arrows that flew wild from both sides.

She shrugged, and plunged her blade straight up into the air.

Her ranks divided. One took the shielders, one took the Khinish.

She went at the Khinish side, the stronger opponent.

She danced.

A parry here, a twist there, and two curved blades flew free. A nick here, a tap there, and two blade hands lost their grip. Her blade scythed ash hafts like wheat, lopping off lance heads, riving spears in two. She'd cleared a path through three ranks of them within moments and withdrew before she could be encircled. She let them fill the gap that she might nick and tap and parry some more. She began adding kicks and punches, small flourishes, flamboyant ornaments. Nothing like a broken nose or a sprained knee or dented groin to make a fighter think twice, no matter how he bristled and clanked. Blade spinning, she mowed through a rain of arrows from a clutch of bowmen, then sliced through the line of bows with one horizontal sweep, leaving the archers bruised and welted as their own weapons whipped back on them. It was a pleasant, playful dance. Her blood whined for the kill, but she gloried in the steps, the fluid movements, the ease with which she saved them from themselves. *No need to die. Not today. Not if you choose to live.*

But beside her, her folk were struggling. Trained up fast, they were good, but inexperienced. It was harder to incapacitate than kill, much easier to lose yourself to bloodlust than work at disarming an opponent bent on killing you. They began to fight. They couldn't help it. As the Khinish pushed forward, they began to fight harder. Snap a spear and they'd draw a blade. Break a blade and they'd retreat to draw a bow. Crack a bow and they'd draw a knife.

She redoubled her efforts. Bloody spirits, she'd take them all herself if she had to. But each one bore three weapons. Each one had to be disarmed thrice. And each one who took her measure moved down the line for easier pickings.

Her folk began to flag.

Behind her she heard cries. She heard the tenor of the battle change. She felt Benkana's side, the shield side, lapse into protracted bladeplay, no metal shattering against the bladebreakers. She heard him call to rally them to their purpose. They tried to obey. Overwhelmed, they failed.

Disarm. If that doesn't work, kill.

She'd created an arc around herself, the Khinish yielding to her and pressing up harder on the folk beside her. She glanced to left and right and saw that the arc was closing into the line behind her. At the edges where shield and Khinish met, they were battling to the death. In the center, her folk disarmed them, and they fell back, snatched up fallen weapons, took blades and spears from the dead, and flung themselves at the corners of the eye shape they had made. The corners elongated. The oval around her flattened. Her folk were coming back-to-back. The battle lines were forming again. They were ragged, they were stumbling under the elements' onslaught, but they were engaging. Fighting. Dying.

Bloody spirits!

She too had misjudged. She, who had lived her life full of rage, full of bloodlust, had misjudged the power of rage and lust to kill. She had tried to stop an arrow in flight. She'd lopped off its head and stripped its fletching. And still it flew, seeking flesh to cleave, hearts to stop.

She had been a fool.

The realization filled her with fury, and then a terrible joy.

Blood rushed hot through her veins, bursting its dams, a flood of ecstasy the strongest drink could never match.

If that doesn't work, kill.

Kill.

Kill.

"Die, then!" she cried, in crashing failure and exultation. "Die, you bleeding pustules!"

She unfettered her blade.

In a whirlwind assault, she made a mockery of the wind that raked the pasture. In a rain of blows, she made an irritant of the needling rain of water. She killed them before they could kill each other. She killed them in pairs, one edge cleaving a Khinishman, the other taking a shielder on the backswing. Her folk, all those who dreamed of becoming kenai, surged in her wake. They made a mockery of Verlein's secondhand training. They made an irritant of Khinish weary from a morning's battle.

At her back, Benkana fought with the easy, untiring grace she had taught him. He bore his blade of Druilor iron double-handed, moving fluidly through high and low guards, sweeping lesser blades aside and slashing legs and arms to halt their wielders. He was still incapacitating them. Most of his foes would bleed to death before the fighting ended. But still he did not kill them. Of all of them, he held to their purpose. Behind her, he held on. As if waiting.

Waiting for what? she wondered idly, flippantly, catching a crossguard, stepping in, levering it free and some fingers with it, delivering an off elbow to the sternum and then hacking through the neck conveniently presented when the opponent doubled over. *For me to kill them all? That shouldn't be a long wait.*

He stayed with her, sensing her movements, mirroring her, guarding her back. She'd wasted her time with those two nonned. Give her this man at her back, and she would cleave armies. Give her this man at her back, and all the would-be rulers and all the outer realms combined would rule never so much as a blade of Eiden's grass.

Then she felt him stiffen, through the brush of his back against hers as they danced.

"No," she heard him say, and she sent a shielder flying with a boot to the ribs instead of bothering with the time a thrust would take to withdraw from those ribs. She spun, but he spun with her, and then she saw Verlein, right arm dangling, bladed in her off hand, dancing sidelong to come around to his front again.

"Betrayer!" Verlein spat, and Kazhe heard her longblade ring against Benkana's. "Of all of them, Benkana! Not you!"

"Don't make me kill you," he begged, barely audible in the melee. "Stand down, it's over, Verlein. . . ." Pleading with her as he fought her, as Kazhe worked to clear room around them. He was distracted by this, he would not protect himself, Verlein was his old comrade, they had grown up in neighboring villages and she had brought him into Torrin's fold. Only Verlein and Benkana had come back alive from that first foray into the Black Mountains to assassinate the Ennead, the foray that Kazhe had scorned, the failed foray that had driven Verlein to muster a magewarded horde to storm the Holding in earnest.

"Leave her, Benkana!" Kazhe snapped over her right shoulder. "Let me turn! Leave her to me!"

"No," came a stone-hard voice from behind her to the left. "She is mine."

"On your right, Benkana!" Kazhe cried, spinning left, spinning him away from that stone-cold voice.

She felt the curved blade pass through his neck as though it cut her body in two. She saw the blade. It passed over her head. It tried to take her on the backswing, as Benkana's body sank to its knees behind her. She smashed it with her blade. It cracked jaggedly apart as Benkana's body toppled to the side. She carried through on her spin and saw the Khinishman already driving at Verlein, a longknife coming into his right hand as his left let the grip of his shattered blade fall away.

The point of Verlein's longblade came out of his back as Kaȥhe's blade went into it. They withdrew as one, and stood staring at each other, stunned, as the man crumpled from between them. His longknife fell with him, still locked in his hand. Where it had entered Verlein's side, a dilute red stain spread into the sopping silk. She took a step back, and sat down in a hard splash, still staring at what they had wrought.

The battle raged away from them, folk fighting indiscriminately now, slashing and hacking at whoever came within reach, half the time no longer recogniȥing even their own folk.

The leaders of the three battling hordes lay strewn around the body of Benkana.

Kaȥhe crawled to him. She put him back together, tenderly. She laid out his limbs in the position he most often slept. Sprawled, as though his dreams took up a lot of room. The rain might have been hot tears, or hot lava, the way it burned. She slid his eyes closed and held his head to kiss his lips. When she released it, it rolled to the side.

She sat back on her haunches, and screamed into the boiling sky.

The sound was nothing, swallowed by the screams of a nonned deaths.

She felt them. She felt every death as though it were her own. She felt every nick of blade on flesh, every slash, every cut, every thrust. She was each body, and she was every blade. Their iron sang through her veins. The blood they soaked in was her own. She was the blades, and she was the death the blades dealt.

She groped for her kenai. It came into her hand as though it slid there of its own. A coppery glow swirled through the watery silver rivulets in its metal. The color of blood suffused it. Her blood suffused it, and the blood of every soul it had severed, and the blood of all the flesh it had tasted.

Every body on this field was Benkana's. A good man. A quiet dreamer. A simple worker, a loyal friend, a fierce and gentle lover. A living soul who believed, and strove, and died before his time.

Every living soul on this field was Benkana.

She knelt by his body and raised her blade. It flared with the pulsing crimson of blood, and rage, and power. She was kenai. She was the blade. She was every blade in every hand. The earth connected them, through their bodies. The air connected them, through their blades. They were all one. The same purpose. The same terror. The same rage. The same lust.

"*No more!*" Kaẕhe screamed, into the screaming tumult.

The sky cracked open. The wind shrieked. A tree exploded, lightning-riven. The rain boiled, steaming on the ground, searing necks and ears and cheeks.

In every hand, in every scabbard, in every boot, on backs and at sides and lying on the field, iron melted.

Blades and arrowheads and lance tips liquefied and washed away on the flood. Spears splintered into sawdust and whipped away on the wind. Bows disintegrated and were gone. Arrows fell to fragments, then to dust.

The first way of the kenai was to disarm.

There was no second way.

Kaẕhe knew, now, what her father had done. He had been the last true kenai in Eiden Myr.

She had seen his blade, this blade, her blade, glow red as ruby, red as blood, and seen the iron of his enemies melt away. But the kenai, the blade of a kenai, would not be melted. His killers had borne kenaila.

Kaẕhe had taken up his blade, and killed them.

But she had not been kenai until this day.

"He didn't live to teach me the last of it," she bent to tell Benkana, smoothing his long hair over the grievous breach in his body, so that he appeared almost whole, almost sleeping. "He showed me, but I didn't see. Now I've learned it, but I can't teach you." She laid her blade down with the hilt on his chest, saw the ruby gleam flare and then fade. It was meant to be his. He was never meant to go before her. He was meant to guard her back, and mourn her when she gave her life for something she loved more than life, more than him.

Softly, only to him, only to the dying rain, the dying wind, she sang the words her father had taught her, the words that had been only sounds to her until the night he died:

Vabresi lioskdor.
Venaiveitsi liriknaishu.
Vinaislasi licherldei.
Shenaiprasi liyulshi.

Torrin Wordsmith had translated those words for her, on hearing her sing them. His face had filled with light as he realiẕed that the sounds she made were the glyphs he had read on some ancient leaf without knowing how to say them. He had bequeathed to her the gift of their meaning, their soft sweet elegy:

May earth mold the meat of your heart.
May roots bind the will of your days.
May grasses sing the gift of your flesh.
May winds receive the breath of your life.

From a time and place where folk buried their dead, he'd told her. Consigning them to the earth that bore them, returning them to Eiden's arms.

Then he'd given her the rest of the words, the prayer of the kenai, long lost to her folk over all the leagues and ages:

Where there is a greater, there is a lesser.
The true arm needs no blade.
The true arm cleaves all blades.
The true king crowned is king no more.

"I didn't understand," she told Benkana. It was what he had been waiting for her to do. She wondered if he knew it, or only sensed it, in some deep wordless corner of his heart. "But now I do. I'll come to you, Benkana. When it's time. I promise you."

She rose, and took up her blade—the blade that would never again taste flesh or blood. The parched field had soaked in blood, and soaked in rain, until it was full, and still the rain fell, and still blood ran in the flood. But the battle was done. There would be no more death this day. The hordes stood shocked, heads bowed or turning slowly in bewilderment. They were beginning to understand how many of their comrades had died.

Verlein sat where she had fallen, water pooling around her. The wound to her side would not kill her, if cleaned and dressed. Kaẕhe could kill her with one kick to the face, snapping her neck back.

"I only wanted to watch the horiẕon for sails," Verlein said.

"You wanted to rule," Kaẕhe said, as though someone else worked her mouth, "or you would never have let it come to this. What changed you?"

Verlein's eyes rose from fallen Benkana, her childhood friend, to Kaẕhe, who was her blademaster. "Rather ask who changed me," she said. She pushed herself up, stiff, feeling every bruise and cut, holding her bleeding side through breached mail. Step by slow step, she slogged across the pasture. Some of her shielders caught her up, made a litter of clasped arms, carried her.

Kazhe looked one last time on the body of Benkana, and sheathed her blade. Then her eyes fell on the man who had killed him. She blinked to see an arm twitch. She flipped him over and he gasped. He'd been drowning in the floodwater.

She could break his neck, or turn him again and let the water have him.

She spat on him, and strode away through the blood and the rain and the dead, and left the plain of Menalad to the bonefolk.

The Menalad Plain

The weapons were simply gone. All of them.

Dabrena felt her way through every step she took on the battleground with Adaon, groped around the downed fighters whose wounds she tended, certain that blades and bows and spears must have been flung somewhere, that what the towheaded fighter with no apparent allegiance and a blade of blazing crimson had done was no more than a trick. They hadn't been able to hear what she'd shouted, but perhaps it was something so persuasive that all the fighters in the field dropped their weapons onto the flooded ground. Or perhaps, Dabrena thought, binding a gashed leg that would need stitching, she had some arcane ability to move objects with the force of her will.

Verlein was carried from the field in the arms of her shielders, as if victorious. Her olive complexion had gone ashen under a plastering of black hair. Dabrena did not call out to her. Once again she had killed a foe who could have been incapacitated. But why hadn't the towhead done it sooner? How much bleeding and maiming and death did it take to convince someone a battle needed stopping?

It had been no trick. It had been some form of power, however belatedly unleashed. Dabrena moved to the next downed fighter, then the next; she applied cleansing herbs, set and wrapped and bound, and nowhere on ground or body was there a weapon. The only possible answer was that they had disintegrated—dissipated, like illuminated leaves after a casting. A power such as that would rival magecraft.

A power such as that could replace magecraft.

Or maybe it had been an enchanted blade, like the magic plows and sorcerous brooms in the tellers' tales. That would be just as easy to believe, at this point.

"Go, follow her, find out what else she can do," she said to Adaon, as the short towhead walked away across the field, shaking off the folk who tried to follow her . . . even comfort her, from the look of it. She must have lost comrades. But so had every other fighter here. Dabrena wanted to tell them, *It's no more than you bloody deserve, the lot of you, look what you've done!* But she was not herself. And that woman had ended the battle, taking their sharp deadly toys away. *You'd think if they wanted to fight so badly, they'd keep it going with a rip-roaring brawl.* But whatever killing furor had fueled their pointless battle was spent now. They were wounded and weary and shaken and bereft. They were appalled at themselves, most of them. Appalled at what real warfare and real death had turned out to be.

"She'll be easy enough to track down later," Adaon said. "I'll stay with you"—as if agreeing with her when he was saying just the opposite. He'd done that in the holding, too. She remembered. But it had been cheerful, just shy of insolent. Now he was quiet and intense. He knew she was trying to get rid of him.

He knew what she planned to do.

She tied off a sling and checked the supply of linen strips in her pack. Not enough. She had more back with her gear, but the horses were in a paddock in Gir Mened and the gear was stored in a tavern's attic. "They've got to get them to shelter," she said. "We can't tend to them properly out here."

And the bonefolk won't come until the living go.

"They're starting to," Adaon said, and pointed.

Her pulse slowed when she saw that he hadn't read her mind and hadn't meant the bonefolk. Two tall Highland Girdlers with long ponytails draggling over empty scabbards on their backs were taking charge of those who'd rushed onto the field to help the fallen. They seemed to be healers, though they were no menders of hers, and the scabbards were a puzzle she wouldn't soon solve; apparently related, the pair looked fresh, as though they hadn't fought, and she thought she remembered them standing not far from her vantage point during the battle. There had been a crowd of bystanders by noon, when it ended. Under the Girdlers' direction, aided by other fighters where they were able, those bystanders were helping the wounded limp back toward Gir Mened, or carrying them in their arms, or cutting poles from hedgerow trees and rigging litters.

Under the sheeting rain, the killing field was a shambles. Shields broken and whole littered the torn ground, amid helms and leggings, mail mounded or strewn, sodden piles of padded linen, blade belts and harnesses and sheaths. Had the fighters divested themselves of the useless accoutrements of battle because of the power they had witnessed, because they were disgusted with the whole thing, or merely because they were tired? If they expected to fight again, they'd want their gear. None of it came cheap. Could what they'd lived through here today have prompted them to swear off battle forever?

Dabrena had tended the wounded in the Ennead's Holding after the stewards' uprising and after the rebel horde rampaged through. She held out no hope of their discouragement being permanent. That towheaded bladebreaker could not be everywhere in Eiden Myr at once, if what she'd done could even be repeated. They'd have their chance again, any of them who'd acquired a taste for it.

She found it hard to care. She forced herself to care. She forced herself to do her work, her menders' work, and pay attention to it, and be suitably appalled by what she'd seen here.

You'll be with her by dark. If she can be followed, it's only a matter of hours now.

A gruff outcry raised her head again. Ah. Evrael te Khine had found his headman. Dabrena had wondered when she'd stumble over his body. Out of place in his fleet garb, flanked by seafolk, Evrael was kneeling near where the towheaded woman had kneeled when she raised her crimson blade. How ironic it would be if some act of Streln's had prompted her astonishing feat.

I don't want him dead.

I just want my daughter back.

"The weather's letting up," she said to Adaon. If she didn't occupy her mouth, her mind, her hands, the razored keening in her mind would overwhelm her, and she would be unable to do what must be done.

He obliged her by looking around, then said, "I wouldn't count on it lasting. The earth has barely settled. From the color of the sky it's going to storm again thrice as hard. And those clouds are nothing natural. Not in the way we think of it, anyhow."

"Next you'll be telling me the spirits are angry."

"Perhaps they are."

She glanced at him as if to say, *I'm too tired for your nonsense*, but there was no twinkle in his eye. There had been no twinkle in his eye since the stablegirl Beadrin had found them in Gir Doegre. What was happening to them, and to the world, he regarded as deadly serious. She found it frightening. She looked away. The world wasn't her problem now. "I shouldn't have brought it up."

His pale eyes were looking through her—past her, as if into some other world.

She turned, her belly going cold.

They ringed the upland half of the field, silent in their shreds and tatters, sheeted in rain that hardly appeared to touch them. In the gray light of storm, their pale flesh was a glaucous white. They were cadaverous, ineffable.

Waiting.

"We've got to go," she said, tying off the bandage around a head wound. "This one's the last. Help me lift him."

Other stragglers and litter-bearers and walking wounded had moved past them, leaving the field nearly empty. The two tall Highland Girdlers were moving their way. Dabrena waved them off. *We've got this*, her gesture said. *We're coming.*

They continued toward her, as if to speak.

From the direction of Gir Mened, where the bystanders had stood along the road, a woman came running. Mid-height, slim, chestnut-haired, a local, she struggled over the muddy field in a worker's wooden clogs. Partway in she pulled them off, hopping, hardly slowing. Two men trotted after her, as if to catch her but not trying very hard, their faces grim.

The Girdlers moved to intercept them. "Clear the field!" the woman called, and the man called, "They're only here for the dead!"

The local woman veered away from them, straight at the nearest bonefolk, and flung herself at one of them, and shrieked, "*Where is my son?*"

The words sliced through Dabrena's heart.

A very calm voice in the back of her mind said, *No. That is not the way.*

The men had stopped by another one of the bonefolk and seemed to be questioning the creature. They siezed hold of it, and it flung them off. There was no feeling to the act. It might have brushed off flies, or overeager pups. Their faces looked perpetually sad, but like masks, unreactive.

The woman was beating at the two nearest of the bonefolk with her alderwood clogs. They took no harm from it. As the Girdlers came up behind her, one creature enfolded her upper arms in its long hands and set her away almost gently.

"They cannot speak," Dabrena heard a Girdler say. "They cannot answer you. Let them do what they've come here to do. There are friends of ours in that field. Don't let the crows have them."

"They know where he is," the woman said. The stridency was gone from her voice. It was torn and bitter, weary of weeping, weary of shouting. She only wanted her son back.

"If they do, they cannot tell you," the Girdlewoman said, as the man moved to reason with the two local men. "Come away now. Let them take our dead."

"Your dead are dead. If my son's alive, I'll have him back!"

"You cannot hurt them. You cannot cut them. Leave it. Come back to town now. . . ."

Dabrena and Adaon had lifted the wounded fighter. He was sodden and heavy and slippery, still wearing his mail, but Adaon's thick body bore the weight of his shoulders with ease, cradling the wounded head against his chest. Dabrena had him under the knees, standing between them, but she lowered them so she could turn her back on the altercation and walk forward, toward the road, toward the town of Gir Mened, which she did not plan to see again.

"Don't do this, Dabrena," Adaon said.

"He needs to get out of the rain."

"You know what I mean. It's madness. It can't work. At least wait and see if she comes back. Some of them came back."

Some of the local children had come back. Not all. "It's the only way," she said, giving up pretense.

"There hasn't been time for further word to come from the Head. They might have returned her by now, and your man there with no way to tell you. Wait and see."

"For how long, until it's still the only way? What better chance will I have than now, in the midst of all these dead?"

"They may stop if you interrupt them."

"I guess I'll find that out."

"You'll die, Dabrena." His voice caught. He cleared his throat. "Most likely, you'll die."

She stared ahead, at the road, at the line of bladeless keepers now trying to stop other angry townspeople from rushing the bonefolk. "Then I'll die," she said. There would be a riot if the keepers did not hold firm, and she'd lose her best chance. "She's my daughter."

"Let me do it." His words came rushed now. Once they got to that line of keepers and gave their burden into other hands, there would be no more discussion. She would slip away from him, and he knew it. "Say you try this and you die, because you're tricking them, because you aren't doing it the way they intend, and then she comes back, delivered safe to her bed in the holding, and you're gone, never to return to her. What sort of heroism is that? Vain foolish sacrifice that leaves your daughter orphaned. I'll go. I'll fetch her back for you."

Adaon and his bloody ironclad seeker logic. He'd talk the spines off a hedgehog. "You're too big. I'm small enough to slip in. I'm faster. You'll bungle it."

"I won't. Not this. Not for you."

They'd reached the line. Arms reached for the wounded fighter, fresh strong arms to take him off to whatever dry place they had prepared to tend the wounded. She tried to turn to Adaon then, but keepers had hold of her, were pushing her toward the crowd. A hand pressed on her head to duck her under the cordon rope they had stretched, more symbol than barrier, between trees where the road gave access to the field from the Gir Mened side. She was hemmed in and couldn't see Adaon. She couldn't let them force her in with the others. By the time she came around and regained the field from some other side, the bonefolk would be finished, and it would be too late. She could lurk around the wounded, but it would never be like this, spirits willing there would never be so many dead in one place at one time again. There were at least two nonned dead in that field, and perhaps three dozen bonefolk. Such a massacre had not happened before in memory, if it had ever happened in Eiden Myr at all. There was a chance the bonefolk would have to adapt their methods. There would be no other opportunity like this.

She resisted the hands. She opened her mouth to summon some imperious objection, just enough to make them hesitate, just enough for her to slip away.

"Dabrena n'Arilda?"

She managed to turn, still on the field side of the cordon. Keepers' hands fell away as the two Girdlers came up, handing the distraught woman off to one of them, the men off to another. Just in time, from the looks of it; the men were regretting their own pliancy and seemed ready to bolt back for another go.

Somehow Adaon had stayed by her. He was tough as a stump, immovably resistant when he chose to be. It would have been easier if the keepers had parted him from her, and his heartbreaking, inarguable offer with him.

"Dabrena Mender?" the Girdlewoman said again.

"Yes," Dabrena said, unable to place her, trying to take in the field, the distance, the bonefolk while seeming to pay attention.

"I thought it was you I saw. You're a long way from the Head."

"Yes," Dabrena said again.

"You might want to have a chat with Verlein n'Tekla."

"I have nothing to say to the shielders."

"Not even if they're moving to take your holding again?"

Bloody spirits. The keepers were herding the townsfolk away, bearing them back with firm words and arms spread wide, clearing the road so the bonefolk would not sense any observers. "Those shielders won't be taking anything for a long time."

"There are other shielders."

"Yes," Dabrena said. "I know." *Let me go, let me go—*

"Dabrena," Adaon said. "Go back with these folk. Talk sense into Verlein before she gets her breath. Leave the rest to me."

From somewhere in the midst of the retreating crowd of townsfolk came a woman's hoarse, bitter weeping.

The Girdlewoman said, "I don't know what you're doing here, but you're here, and word among the shielders is that the Head and the Haunch are next. They await only the command. They don't like it. Besieging holdings isn't what they joined the shield to do. You'd have their thanks, if you kicked their leader while she's down. So long as no one speaks of it afterward." She held up the cordon rope, an invitation to go back, to leave the bonefolk alone, to find Verlein. In a moment it would no longer be an invitation. Whatever these Girdlers were, fighters or healers, they had comrades on that field.

"Adaon n'Arai will see to her," Dabrena said. It hardened into an order as it came out, and continued to him: "You're my pledge and you speak for me. Work your charm, run your rings around her, threaten her, do whatever you must to save my holding. Send Beadrin to the runners, have them warn Pelkin, then find that blond bladebreaker and—"

"Mender," said the Girdleman, gesturing under the rope.

The bonefolk had moved onto the battlefield and formed a loose, wide circle around the dead. They took no notice of the four humans who stood a dozen threfts away by the road. A greenish mist seemed to gather around their feet. It might have been a phosphorescent glow suffusing the rainspray at ground level.

Dabrena inclined her head and gestured to the Girdleman: *After you.*

Adaon, dark as the day, pale eyes unblinking, gave her one sharp nod. He would follow her orders. *I love you*, he mouthed, and moved to duck under the rope the Girdlewoman still held up—a distraction, a show of good faith, putting his body between theirs and hers.

Dabrena turned, and sprang into a run, boot heels cleaving purchase from the rain-soaked ground. The luminescence before her grew, with intensity and proximity. Was it balking surprise that straightened the bonefolk's bodies, or the beginnings of confusion, or only the motion of throwing their heads back? It looked like ecstasy, or anguish.

She vaulted between them, and dove into the dead.

The Menalad Plain

"Let them take me, Evrael."

He did not look up from the hollow his seafolk had lifted Streln into before he'd sent them off. The bonefolk were feeding. He could see the virid glow reflected in the rain and perspiration on Streln's dark face. "They will not dine on you this night," he said, and bound long strips of cloth around the poultices he'd packed into the dual blade wounds, front and back. As shipmaster he had practiced healing arts since well before there were menders, and as binder he'd been well acquainted with what became the healer's tools.

"But death frees me, Evrael. I see . . . clearly, for the first time in . . . years."

Evrael ground his teeth. He remembered that clarity. It was the clarity mages felt when they cast passage for the dying. That glimpse into the next plane. Evrael had always mistrusted those visions—those shared hallucinations of a dying mind. He did not trust the existence of any plane but the one he inhabited. Such false clarity Streln could do without. He would live, muddled and obscured, and do his best with his limited mortal sight, as did every creature born to earth. He would live.

"It is . . . such joy to look on your face again." Streln tried to grip him by the shoulders, but his arms had no strength. Evrael told him to be easy, to rest, lest he work more blood out of the wounds.

"The wounds leach her poisons from me," Streln said. "Sweet

raindrops wash the . . . crystal from my mind. I'll have rest aplenty when this has passed. To sleep free . . . of the fetters . . ."

The binding complete, Evrael scanned the area for some shelter from those drops. They had been hot, and now were going cold, and might turn to hail as the weather turned. He must get Streln under cover before the true brunt of the storm hit. He should not have sent his seafolk off. He'd thought he was clearing space for a private farewell, keeping the pale carrionmongers at bay. But there would be no farewell. Streln had not hung on this long, with such grievous wounds, to succumb to them now. He would not permit it.

They had badgered him to take command of the Khinish forces—what was left of them. The Khinish did not know how to be leaderless. They did not know what to do without a strong figure to follow. With Streln down, they were beheaded. With their weapons destroyed, they were limbless. Evrael had never before felt scorn for the Khinish, much less this cold rage that verged on hatred. He'd barked out a few harsh orders, sent them off to wait in Gir Mened until the wounded were travel-ready and then march seaward to be shipped home. Let them sort out the details, they were capable of that. Streln's life was the only thing that mattered to him now.

The man should die, for what he had done. The man should die, for marching on the mainland. The man should die, for not standing down when the fight was lost. The man should die, for all the Khinish he had led to their deaths.

But he was Streln. He must not die.

"Lerissa," Streln said.

"Fear not," Evrael replied. "I'll ship you back to her."

Streln laughed, a spray of blood. Not good, not good. There were herbs . . . but they did not grow here . . . he had none with him . . .

"Please refrain," Streln said, an echo of his old, tight-humored self, and then he gasped and said, "A crystal, that traps the eye and thence the mind. Herbal draughts that weaken and enslave. Fear those, Evrael. Kill her, though they banish you for it. Kill her and go home."

"Khine is my home." *You are my home. . . .*

Streln's hard features opened into a wondrous joy, then spasmed into focus. "She is stone, Evrael, stone. A mesmeric stone that throws light in hypnotic patterns. Fear it. Save the children. Eldrisil . . . It was all I could do. I could not tell you. Her fetters would not permit it. The pain . . . I could have borne the pain. But they locked my mind. Then I saw the child. I thought . . . I hoped . . . you would understand . . ."

Evrael did not want to hear this. Their predicament was grave and growing worse. This was a time for action, not explanation. That could wait until they basked on the slopes of Khine, watching olives ripen, shaping clouds in the image of their dreams, as they had when they were young. . . .

He shook off the sun-drenched vision. Streln was slipping, and pulling him after. "I don't need to understand," he said. "I only need you to live."

"You *must* understand. The children . . . You must stop it, Evrael. She seeks . . . control. She will take them all . . . she will twist their souls . . . destroy them . . . as she did me . . ."

There had been a glamour on his mind. But Evrael had known as much. Whether she cast it with a stone or a drug or her own languid wiles made no difference. But Eldrisil . . . he had mentioned Eldrisil . . . his man, sacrificed in the holding, the man he'd ordered to hold a child to the blade . . .

In a flash of comprehension very much like the experience of casting passage, it came to him what Streln meant, and what he had done.

Lerissa n'Rigael had some dark plan for Eiden's children. Streln had guessed it, or been told, but her powers had kept him from divulging it. So, in front of Evrael, the one man he trusted to see him truly, he had done a thing so heinous that it could only lead to questions. Evrael had been meant to ask those questions. Evrael had been meant to recognize the demonstration for the warning it was. *There is a threat to our children. Look into it. Find out what it is. I cannot tell you.*

Evrael had failed him.

"You understand." Streln patted him weakly on the hand. "Kill her, Evrael, and the . . . children will be returned. They will be our salvation . . . not warriors . . . not rulers—"

A gout of blood issued from his mouth, then nearly choked him. The fit of coughing that followed strained the bindings on his wounds, and a bloom of red soaked through the poultice into the cloth.

This was beyond his skill. He eased Streln back into the turf and made to rise. "The bonefolk have gone. I will retrieve those healers—"

"No. Stay, Evrael, my brother, my old friend. Stay by me now. It . . . is over. I reap . . . what I have sown."

With a groan, Evrael moved close, seeking to shield him from the elements, warm him—press his own life force into the failing body. He caressed the beloved brow in a gesture the Khinishman would have mocked him for, in a stronger time.

"Don't be . . . a soft-bellied Headman," Streln rasped. "Strive with honor, Evrael te Khine."

He could not tell whether Streln meant to insult his Head blood or exhort him to courage in meeting his destiny. He would not be headman. He would be no more than he was, shipmaster, landholder, serving beneath and beside a worthy headman—*this* headman. Streln would recover. Streln would lead. This was an error, now set right. Lerissa's glamour had cleared from his eyes. He would be again what he had been, the man Evrael had known, the man Evrael had loved, the man Evrael loved still and would have loved if he had cast all Eiden Myr into the abyss. He *must* recover. He had duties. He must lead the Khinish home. Khine required his service. It would be a grave dishonor to decline. *Do not disgrace yourself, Headman. Do not leave your post.*

He was prone on one elbow now, his left hand cradling the dark head. "Streln," he gritted through clenched teeth, his right fist twisting the iron rings bunched over the Khinish heart, "*do not leave me.*"

Streln smiled, looking straight into his eyes. "I loved you always, Evrael," he said, and died.

GIR MENED

There was a tavern. There was always a tavern, or an alehouse, or a public house. The world could be coming to an end and still there would be some aleman or taverner or publican to serve drink.

And thank all the absent spirits for that, Kazhe thought, striding through the doorway, bloody and bruised and soaked to the skin. The unlit interior was thick with vapor. She drew it deep into her lungs, felt it penetrate through her sinuses, seep into her head. Outside, the storm catching its breath, inhaling for another blast. Inside, the pungent mists of forgetfulness, peace. The world was coming to an end, and there was the taverner, pouring out his wares.

This was a spirit house. No reek of Souther garlic here, or yogurt soup, or vinegar. No ales, no stouts, no wines. No cane or fruit, milk or grain; nothing pulped and encouraged to rot. Only spirits. Distillations. Fermentations boiled or frozen until only their essence remained. A place of purity, and drowning.

She strode to the long servingboard and took a three-legged stool between gray elders hunched over their cups. The tavernkeep cast a wary eye on her, then blinked and looked closer. The tight corners were packed with fighters, waiting out the storm, waiting out the recuperation of the wounded. Drinking in grim celebration of being alive. Drinking to lost comrades. Drinking to calm shattered nerves.

They had told her tale to the taverner. They knew who she was, and what she had done this day.

She couldn't claim as much.

After an assortment of brandies and ciders, the taverner reeled off the specialties of the house: barley mash distilled with fennel, molasses distilled with anise, mare's milk distilled with coriander. Might as well drink her own horse. Come to think of it, where had Comfrey gone? Eiden's puke, she'd lost him again. All the beast had ever done was bite her, but that was more than she could say for the sodding blade.

It pressed against her back like a second spine. It weighed nothing now; it had gone light as a leaf. But its harness dragged on her like a stone nineweight. She'd tried to sheath the thing in her belly, to be rid of it, but she could remember only the urge, only the drawing of it, never what happened after. Next thing it was there on her back again, in its scabbard. Denying her its justice

"That," she said, pointing to the clear drink before the man on her left. He circled it protectively with an arm; she grinned at him, and he dragged himself and his stool another foot away down the board. "There's no scent off that one."

The taverner hefted a jug, poured a swallow into one of the measuring tins they drank from in these parts, and waved it under her nose. She nodded, satisfied. No horsy herbs to raise her gorge. "But you can keep that thimble. Give me a growler."

He raised a brow, dumped the jigger into a tin cup, then measured in another jigger. She laughed in his face, reached over his head to snag a good tall mug from the rafter hook where it hung by its handle, spat into it and wiped the dust out with her shirttail, and slammed it onto the servingboard. He went pale, but he transferred the cup's contents, then topped it off from the jug and drew back, as though she'd have the jug from him and all.

She warmed the pewter with her flesh, covering the rim until its circle scored her palm, then inhaled the captured vapors. No need to pollute this with spice or herbs. The white burn of pure potency was sweet perfume.

Thank all the good spirits for spirits, she thought, bringing the curve of rim toward her lips.

She set the mug down.

Evenly spaced around the darkling tavern were three iron candlestands wrought for nine. A girl moved from one to the next, lighting eight of the fresh tapers in each. A queer time of day to remember Longlight; maybe the stormdark confused them. Might be another of the Strong Leg's strange customs. Or maybe they were just low on wax.

Kazhe raised the mug to her lips, tasted metal, and set it down.

There would be only one sip. There would be the first, and all the rest, and between them time and pain and self would expand and contract with their own sense, their own reality. One sip was a nonned sips, nine nonned. One sip, one blink, and six years would be gone. She had only stepped out of the river. She had only to step back in, and be borne away.

She poured the drink into her throat.

The first swallow was shock. The second was panic. On the third her throat closed, gagging, denying what she had done; the third was surrender—it was swallow or choke. On the fourth it was too late. On the fifth she'd nearly drained the mug, might as well see it through. The sixth was rage, and hatred, and the vicious rapturous punishing jubilant plunge into annihilation.

Firestorm exploded in her head. The liquor's white burn spread through her chest, incinerated her heart, scalded her belly in an acid wash. Hot blood bloomed in her face, seared down her limbs to pulse in toes and fingers, cauterized all wounds in its path. She hissed out molten vapors and felt the slow burn of a grin. Give her strikers and she'd belch fire.

She pushed the mug at the tavernkeep.

"Again," she said.

The second draught was icy. A thread of frozen silver trailed down her backbone. Cold liquid sloshed gently through the swollen folds and crevices of her brain. She let her head fall back, spread her arms, let ice numb strains and bruises. Her eyes slid closed, and all was frosted darkness, the glittering frozen peace of a winter's night.

Fire and ice. This was more like it.

"More like what?" said a quiet voice from beside her, almost lost in the first clatter of hailstones on the roof. Sira, leaning on the board, addressing her while watching the room, in the fighter way. Her old friend from the Jhardal band, the folk who had roamed closest to her folk, who had met with them three times a year for trading and dancing and drinking. So she had lived.

Kazhe came back to the servingboard, but she didn't look at Sira. "Like death," she said, tapping the rim of her mug, lunging halfway across with bugged eyes to startle the taverner when he was slow complying. "But better." So much better, because you could feel every razored inch of it.

"You've bought us all our deaths, disarming us," Sira said.

"I saved your stinking lives."

"Not soon enough."

Not soon enough for Benkana. She tilted the filled mug, observing the lack of enlightenment therein. Torrin would still be down there somewhere, swimming in the depths, falling, falling. Would Benkana join him?

This had nothing to do with Torrin or Benkana. This was between her and the razor. It always had been.

"Why didn't you tell us what you planned, Kazhe? Incapacitate, you said, and we tried. Then you started cutting a swath through them. And when we followed you, you gelded us."

"You shouldn't have followed me."

"You shouldn't have brought them here. They trusted you."

"They *wanted* me!" Kazhe snarled. Sira was getting in her way. Benkana and Torrin were getting in her way. "They thought I would make them kenaila. They'd have done anything."

"You'd have promised them anything."

"I promised nothing."

"And delivered on it. Empty hands. Not so much as boot knife left to cut their throats with if they get enough drink in them to try us."

Shielders and Khinish and her own folk were arrayed in their corners like boxers on hazeled ground. But that was a Longdark custom, and in the Fist, not here. Or was she in the Fist? That had been stout. They served stout beer in the Fist, rich and dark, not this clear decoction of fire and ice. There were no brigands here. Or they were all brigands here, all except the doddering locals who'd kept disease and age at bay by steeping their flesh in preserving fluid. All yearning for her blade, and loathing it, and fearing it.

All she wanted to do was swallow it.

"Make friends with them," she said. "Find the camaraderie of the storm." In the grasslands of their birth, all tents were home in a storm. You never left an enemy out to die, not on the plains. "Stand them a drink and toast to fallen comrades!" She made the most of the brief fluid loquaciousness the razored acid bequeathed as lure and incentive. She needed no lure, no incentive. And there would be no basking in song or story, or false maudlin companionship, or dancing, brawling abandon. "Celebrate the climax of the bleeding light. Restore balance in your lives in this skewed time."

"We followed you here. Don't turn your back on us."

"The war is over. Go home."

"You sacrificed our people for nothing! And now you send them home? To say what to their families? How do we explain the ones who don't come home?"

I didn't know. I didn't know the power I had. Don't you think I'd have used it, if I'd known? Don't you think I'd have saved your children? Don't you think I'd have saved Benkana?

No. She'd done what she'd done. There was only the razor now.

"They'll still accept you, Kazhe, if you tell them why. If there's a reason. If there was a plan, a point. A greater purpose. Tell them, and they'll still love you. . . ."

It was her father's fault, for not teaching her the trick. It was his killers' fault, for taking him before he'd had the chance. It was Khine's fault, for thinking they could impose their ways on the mainland. It was Verlein's fault, for thinking she could stop their implacable advance with her tall shields and tapered blades. It was their own fault, for not doing their job, for being forced into deadly bladeplay when they were meant to *stop* the battle.

It was Torrin's fault, for breaking the light and bringing them to this.

Snatching up her mug, she spun on her stool and raised it. "To Longlight!" she said, and inhaled some razored acid. No one drank with her. No surprise there. She hopped down and strode to the nearest Khinishman. "And what are you when you're at home?" He returned her stare in stony silence. She drew her blade and pressed him to the wall with the flat of it. He cocked his head and said, with no expression, "I am a landholder, and a cooper by trade."

"A cooper!" Kazhe drew away to point her blade at one of her folk. "So is Chaela! Imagine that! And Effad there next to her, he's a potter, surely there's a potter among you Khinish, or a stoneworker—someone must have crafted all your faces."

"There was," said a Khinishwoman from somewhere in the candle shadows. "He died today."

"As did two quarriers of ours," a shielder said.

"You see? You're not so different after all. Just ordinary folk misled by flawed leaders. To the spirits with us!" Kazhe drank to that, upending the mug, running her tongue around the inside of the rim for the last razored drops. Then, flinging it aside, she grabbed the nearest shielder, a slight, pretty girl no older than she herself had been when she met Verlein. The girl was tougher than she looked, but a good hard yank sent her spinning into a handsome Khinishman's lap. "Chat her up," she said to him. "A good bedding's the only sensible answer life gives to death. We're all the same between the sheets."

She pushed past Sira, who was moving to put a stop to her. Sira caught her by the arm and spun her around. "Or you could have a brawl!" Kazhe crowed, giving a careless shove that sent Sira stumbling back into two of her fellows who'd risen behind her. "Settle the whole bloody thing with fists."

"We'll forge more blades," a Khinishman said.

"Good on you! Keep those smiths in business, don't let the likes of me be taking the bread from their tables." She leaned across the servingboard to the taverner, who had shrunk against the wall. "I'll have the jug now, thanks." She thought she'd have to spring over the board and wrest it from him, but he gave it up willingly, hoping he'd be shut of her.

She did not disappoint him. Slinging the jug over one shoulder, she strode to the door and flipped the latch with the point of her indestructible, feather-light blade. The wind slammed in, and a shielder dove across his comrades as the door crashed against his seat.

"You can't go out there!" Sira said, moving close, but not touching the door, unwilling to put flesh in the way of the blade. Hail littered the floor like tiny playing stones escaped from a drawbag and was swept inward on a burst of freezing rain. "Close the forsaken door, Kaẓhe!"

"You might as well make friends," Kaẓhe called to them all. "You're stuck here for a while. Try dancing instead of brawling!" With a thrash of her arm to be rid of Sira's concern, Sira's righteousness, she was free, surging into the rain, the dark of late afternoon, the empty road.

Alone, the way she should be. Alone, as Torrin had left her.

Bladed, and gelded.

But armed with a jug of raẓored acid.

Could have saved them all if she'd figured it out sooner. Could have stopped the battle in the first place. Love and grief, were those the ingredients? Did there have to be grief, and rage? Why couldn't she have loved Benkana and still have him be alive?

Bladed, and gelded. Warrior and peacebringer. She had cut off her own blade arm. Never again to feel nonneds fall under her onslaught. Never again to rage, to kill. She was rage, she was death. Never again to fight, to *win*. What else was there? To protect? She could not protect Torrin. Kenaila existed to protect power, compassion, light. They were light's shadow. They took the stain of death upon themselves so that mages would never have to. But a true kenai subverted death. A true kenai melted weapons before they could strike. A true kenai castrated herself, invalidated her own blade. She had destroyed herself. She had bequeathed herself the only possible reprieve. She did not want a reprieve. She was the shadow. There was no more light now to cast that shadow. There was no more excuse to kill, not when she could disarm. But all she knew how to do was kill. . . .

She was too small for this. She was too plain for this, too simple. She was her rage, her lust, her loyalty. She knew what she was for, when she followed Torrin. She knew what she was for, when she gathered a horde to deny control of Eiden Myr to any force that would take it. She didn't know what she was for, now. She was a tool, she was always meant to be a tool, a blade was a tool, she was the blade. Now there was nothing to serve. Invasion would never come. That was a teller's tale, a night terror. The outer realms were dead, abandoned. She would not stand waiting at the coast for sails that would never come in order to justify knowing how to kill. She was a killer. There was nothing for her now. Benkana beheaded. Torrin martyred. Herself gelded. No purpose to her. But she could still lift the jug. She could still work her throat. She could still swallow the razored, acid blade, again and again, pounding, tearing, avenging, punishing.

Sira screaming at her through the raging storm, a rain-smeared outline, come from nowhere though she'd been there for some time, screaming at her to stop, was it to stop hewing stone with the blade? She apologized—she hadn't meant to hew the stone, she'd meant to smash the blade, sweet spirits, who knew the thing could cleave stone now? No wonder it wouldn't shatter. The grieving puking blade wouldn't shatter! And what was she doing holding it? She'd flung it away in the tavern, she'd flung it at those righteous, squabbling children and told them what they could do with it and raged off into the night, but here it was, refusing to break on granite solstice stones, bloody pestilent thing, she'd break it, all right, she'd shatter the thing, there was nothing she couldn't destroy, nothing—

Sira falling back from her, stumbling away into the storm in a smear of reluctance, no choice, she remembered now, she'd hissed something to her, there'd been a moment of deadly silence in her raging mind and she'd said, "Go, Sira, go before I kill you," a plea and not a threat, that was unworthy of her, but it was past now, and she'd been talking about someone else, and she was in a smithy and she'd thought it was in the Druilor foothills, a smithy where they quenched their iron in poison, that had appealed to her, but it wasn't Dru Youris after all, it was still Gir Mened, or Gir Mened all over again, and she'd tried to make the blade glow, she'd tried to melt all the blades in the benighted smithy, melt them before they could tempt or taunt, but they wouldn't be melted, the power wouldn't come, and for a moment after the anger passed she felt a surge of hope—not gelded after all!—but then the smith who'd been cowering in a corner came at her with an axe where she was whirling in the center of the room, and crimson light surged down the blade and the axe was gone and the smith was stumbling after the vanished weight and sobbing to know his death was on him and she stopped whirling and cocked her head, sad in a distant way, sorry for him, and she'd have clapped him on the shoulder and said some comforting word except that when she moved she saw an arcing ruby glitter trail the blade, and the sight filled her with such awe of its beauty that for a time she stood just waving the blade back and forth, passing it in a gentle sweep before the newly bladed keepers who burst into the smithy, emptying their hands, watching the glittering, ruby trail the swirling crimson blade left in its wake—

There was no warmth to it. She huddled freezing and soaked between cracked, blazing sky and shrieking wind and rumbling earth, Eiden tearing himself apart and her at the center where it was coldest, she was cold, so cold, and there was no light in the blade now, and no warmth, just the chill of iron and the chill of the jug, but she'd forgotten the jug, her veins filled to bursting, yet somehow it stayed with her just like the blade, and there was warmth, and there was burning, there was the razored acid wash down gullet and heart and lungs and gut, surging in her limbs, and here was strength, here was fuel for her to fight the storm, that was the acid's justice, that it fueled you to go on when you flagged in your own destruction. It was sweet burning justice. Sweet, burning punishment.

She was a torch in the storm. It could not quench her. She could only be quenched in fire and ice, and oh, what a light she would cast while she burned.

III

Shine

P*ass through*

Louarn came into the realm of shadow as though gliding into dark waters.

He knew fear, then sensed the thing he feared to sense: the clacking, dragging steps of the shambling stick figure.

It had stalked the edges of his sleep for six years. A blackness, a cobbled-together thing like an assemblage of old sticks. Now he had entered its realm of his own volition. It approached with the inexorable arrhythmic cadence of doom.

This was the dark place where you fell between waking and dream. It opened between the realms of consciousness and sleep, a crevasse—a crevasse of whispers, like the whisperhole in the mountain where he spent his childhood; a crevasse of thorns. A roiling stew of memories and imaginings and fears. This was where the shreds and ash of terror sifted down to, forgotten in the daylight. A crack in the path between outside and inside. When you entered the realm of sleep, you let go of the external and turned inward; you were engulfed by the internal, turned inside out; you relaxed the clenched will required to maintain your waking self in the harsh bright world. You opened yourself to the mutable, the profound; you consigned yourself to deeper impulsions. But sometimes you were caught, you tripped, you took the path too steeply, and next thing you were plummeting into bristling edged spine-pillowed night, and you recoiled, you spasmed back into your body with the sense of just having fallen off a cliff.

This was where you fell, when you fell the wrong way into sleep.

It was smothering yet vast. It was temperatureless but cold. It was yielding but spiked, a needled corpulence, swollen, hollow. It was a place not of sight but of shape. Sound came as shape: the clattering of bones, the clacking of sticks, the rickety approach of long loose skewed things that held together when they should not.

A bad thing, Mellas's small voice said, breaking upward, not yet firmly set into manhood.

Yes, Louarn replied, gentle, grieving. *It is that.*

Can we get away? Mellas asked.

You can't get out from the top, Louarn said. *You can only get out from the back, or the sides.*

Together they crafted a tunnel. It was a long tunnel. It led quickly upward into light, a white light that fractured on sharp extrusions in the crystalline walls and became six lights, melding one into the other, one from another. Flame-golden magelight was there, heartbreakingly beautiful to see again after all these years, verging out of the yellow. The little girls' ruddy-copper shine was there, too, verging out of the red. And from the blue came a color so brilliant it looked silver, glowing with a touch of the magestone's glow.

Louarn moved enchanted through the shimmering light, the angled refractions, the tickling spangles. Mellas fell behind. The shambling clacking stick-thing was still there, still following, though it moved in a limping agony and Louarn moved with the swift exhilarating speed of mind and heart and spirit through the passage of light. Mellas cried out, as if the light pained him. From within him came a muffled echo: Flin's cry, his terror of the light, the heartrending cry of a frightened, uncomprehending child.

Louarn turned and in that turning embraced them, drew them into the shelter of his strong-crafted self. He continued on into the pure white light, the serene coruscating blend of all lights, all colors. He drank in the light; he sailed on it, borne as by a sweet bubbling current, effortless and joyous, flying on thought, swimming through light.

His selves cast three shadows, each a different tint and hue, each a different size and shape, all the same. In the pure white light, he refracted all colors, and all his shadows were known.

The passage would take him wherever he most desired to go.

pass through

The sky was dark lavender with no hint of stars. The trees were a softly shining silver; their leaves were gilded. The homefolk were luminous, standing among the silver trunks, a fleshlike forest within the metallic one, a grove of bonefolk. All else was black stone, deeper than nightstone, a coal black that drank in light and reflected nothing. He might sink into such porous stone. He might sink forever, unable even to dream himself free.

He knew this place. *This is a passing place. Not a staying place.* A wood. An eerie, wondrous wood, where no winds disturbed the sweet air, where no leaves fell. The sky was lavender, the ground was black, the leaves were gold, the trunks were silver. There was a fresh chill scent of stone, with a tang of metals and the time-steeped richness of rock in an ancient cave.

The woman who crouched near him was holding out a hand, curled loosely downward, as if someone had lifted it politely to drop a perfunctory kiss upon it. But she was holding it up to a child—a stunned, transfixed child, blinking at her, blinking at the ring on her third finger, not yet certain whether to wail in terror or sigh in wonder.

The ring bore a pale stone set in blackened silver. It exhibited no change upon proximity to the child. But as the woman, sensing Louarn beside her, dropped her hand and turned toward him, startled, it produced an unearthly moon-white glow.

The woman gasped, her eye drawn by the flare of light.

Louarn came fully awake, sitting up on soft-coal stone.

In the ring, the stone's flare faded.

The woman looked into his face.

It was his earliest memory. The cream-pale skin, the dark blue eyes, the rich fall of sable hair—a girl little older than Mellas, a sparkling jewel in a waterfall of night, gazing down at him through a woman's face carved into an awesome beauty by time and trials. He was looking through her into the past, all the haunts in him stunned by the sight of that first sight, two nines of years ago and three—the first memory, the only memory, of the third child inside Louarn, the nameless child who had only this one perfect vision through unformed, imperfect, infant eyes, who had lain silent and forgotten inside all of them for all this time, its single memory too fragile, too imperfect, too profound, too small to share.

"Mother," said Louarn.

The bonefolk watched unblinking. Far away, Louarn could hear the laughter of children at play. An incongruous sound. The nearer ones sidled closer together, seeking comfort amid strangeness past all understanding. Perhaps they believed they were dreaming.

The woman rose to her feet with a swish of silk, gazing down on him—imperious, but with the barest hint of doubt pinching the smooth flesh between her dark brows.

Louarn rose, as well. No leaves, no grains of earth clung to his clothes to be brushed off. No pain shot through his wounded leg or stung his gouged arm. He was whole—healthy, perfect, and whole.

He stood gazing into her long-lashed dark blue eyes with his.

Don't you know me? Was the pain so bad that you forgot who brought you to this?

"Take them back," the woman said, flashing him a chiseled profile as she spoke over her shoulder to the bonemen, waving a white hand in the direction of the huddled children. Like small animals caught in lampglare, the children froze, then tried to bolt, but the bonefolk moved in long fluid strides to scoop them up. Mellas remembered the green glow, the shining bones beautiful and supple in connection. Louarn blanched to see living children handled so. He opened his mouth—

"It doesn't harm them," the woman snapped, and then the children were gone, and the bonefolk who had passaged them melted into the surrounding stone. "The folk will see them safely to their beds, or into waiting hands. They've been gone barely an afternoon as they reckon time, but that's long enough for hysterical parents to spread tales that could hinder further collection."

Louarn's eyes cleared, as if mist had blurred them. Mellas blinked, and saw the Ennead illuminator he'd expected—a construct of overheard descriptions, but an accurate one, a recognizable one. Deep inside, Flin yowled in bereft fury, raising his arms for his mother to rescue him, his silent raging voice demanding his mother, his real mother, his real fathers, his real life, his own safe bed.

"I am not your mother," the woman said, an afterthought.

No, Louarn responded from the depths of his heart. *No, you are not.*

"Yet you may be flesh of mine. The resemblance is undeniable. You look older than he would be, yet there's something boyish about you still. That was a quality of Evonder's. And you bear his face as well."

"*He takes after his father, though he has his mother's coloring. I know where he came from. But those are names he can't ever bear.*"

"Evonder," Louarn breathed, and Mellas remembered kindnesses when he was small, a gentle hand ruffling his hair—a man he yearned for without knowing why, a man whom Bron his master told him he could trust when push came to shove but must stay away from in the meantime because he was one of the Nine.

I am a child of the Ennead, Louarn realized, locking his knees, which had gone weak. *The Ennead who terrorized me. The Ennead who burned my parents alive before my eyes.*

"The stone glowed for you," the woman said, assessing him with a cool gaze tinted now with greed, and hatred. "Only for a moment, but I saw it. The children were lightless. As am I. It could only have been you."

Mellas had shown a light. But the magestone had not glowed for him. He had stood in a solid corridor of it and the glow had faded. But the pale stone on the woman's hand—a bit of magestone, cut from the mountain, set in blackened silver—had glowed.

When he was dreaming.

He had not yet come fully awake. The fractured crystalline light of the passageway through sleep had still infused him. One brilliant bluesilver thread of it infused him still, as his puzzler's mind set the last piece into place.

Mellas had shown a light, to the one mage who loved him well enough to believe in it. Mellas's magelight could actuate a casting only when he was dreaming. As the dream fell from him, his light subsided—went back into hiding, into the shadows, into his deepest self, where Flin had secreted it. But Mellas's magelight was not all that fueled the power of his dreaming. There was the earthy copper shine, as well, the crafter's light, the heart's light. And there was a third light—the most powerful things came in threes. A bluesilver light . . .

Mellas had nearly died of hunger and thirst and madness, trapped in the dark corridors of his own mind. Outside, Galandra's shield was broken, and a world of mages was cored of its light by the searing burst of power released in its breaking. But Mellas, in that blinding agony, with other powers to call upon in addition to his besieged magelight, dreamed himself free.

Dreamed himself here.

Dreamed his own magelight safe, protecting it from the ravages of the coring.

Dear spirits, Louarn thought. *What am I?*

"It was me," he acknowledged, at long last, to the woman who was the mother of his flesh. "The stone glowed for me."

"Why did it fade?"

Something tearing deep within him, some long-held yearning pecking free of his heart's shell and leaving it cracked, he produced his most blinding, disarming smile. She was only a means to what he wanted. She was only someone to be charmed. He said, "It has been erratic, since the magewar. I'm afraid it comes and goes."

Lerissa n'Rigael—Lerissa Illuminator, Lerissa ti Khine—arched a hawk's-wing brow at him and said, "When it comes, then, you are the only adult left in Eiden Myr to show a light. How did you shield it?"

With a shrug, he turned a circle to survey their alien surroundings, using the leisurely movement to drop a hand to the use knife at his belt. "I have no idea. What is this place?"

Her gaze flickered to his blade as he came around, and she smiled. A smile as chilling as it was stunning. That would be a useful smile, if he could learn it. "A place of the dead, where there is no dying. Your little blade will do you no good here. Neither of your little blades, come to that. I'm old enough to be your mother, after all."

He found himself laughing. Such an Ennead display of verbal twists. So she had noted his charming, crafted smile. He would not seduce what he wanted from her.

That was all right. What he wanted was to kill her.

He drew the blade and ran its edge experimentally across the pad of his thumb. The wound closed in the wake of the blade's passing, before a drop of blood welled up. "Interesting," he said, and sheathed the weapon. He should have deduced it. All was healed, here, all the wounds of his travels, small and large. He looked down at his palm; the flesh had always been smooth, Flin's burn scars gone, the triangular bite from the shard of broken clay lamp Mellas had held in his last moments—healed when he emerged from this passing place into the world to become Louarn.

What would become of a body that came here dismembered? What would become of it if the bonefolk had been denied the hands?

"You'll have to go back to Khine sometime," he said, trying on Lerissa's smile. "You'll be mortal in the mortal world. And believe me: I can follow you anywhere."

In fact, he was not certain of that. He was new to the powers of dreaming. In the past, they had worked their will through him. He was far from mastering them. He might pass back into the world of flesh, but emerge anywhere—Gir Nuorin, the Head holding, Gir Doegre, Croy the bricklayer's house, anywhere his heart might lead him without him controlling it. Why had he landed in the Heartlands and not the Holding when he passed from here before? The Holding had frightened Mellas and frightened Flin . . . but why the Heartlands?

"Mellas—that's a Heartlands name, isn't it?"

"Yes, Illuminator."

"I don't know what they called him. He's Pirra and Alliol and Ellerin's. He reminds me of a man I knew, good man named Mellas, loved his horses better than he loved himself. That's a common name, a Heartlands name. He looks a Heartlander. It'll bring no attention on him."

Pirra, Alliol, Ellerin. His foster-parents were Heartlanders. Those were Heartlands names. They must have portrayed their homeland to

Flin with love in story and memory, and instilled that love in him.

He went where he felt safe, where he most deeply yearned to go.

He had no desire to go to Khine. But Lerissa need not know that. And eventually he would master this power. She could not kill him for fear of his magelight, as she had killed Croy and the rest. Not while they were here, in this place of the dead.

"Oh, you don't want to follow me to Khine, love. Far too many blades there, wielded by folk who know how."

"From what I saw, most of those blades were guarding a few acres of pastureland in the Strong Leg."

"It keeps them busy," Lerissa said, with charming diffidence, and a cold light in her blue eyes. "We'll keep you busy as well, I think. I don't suppose you were trained a mage?"

She doesn't care a whit what happened to me. Her own child, fostered out. I could have been dead for all she knew. Shocked at the naïve idiocy of his heart, he said, "Why shouldn't I have been?"

"Oh, you most certainly should have been. A grandchild of Rigael n'Saeron l'Portriel, a son of Evonder Bindsman, you should have been cherished, cosseted, groomed for the Ennead. But my redoubtable father only wanted you out of the way, that you not impede my own training. A mother's cooing and doting were not at all what he had in mind for me in the two years prior to my taking the triskele. He was a hard man, Rigael. With any luck, it's his blood in your veins, not his lightless bedmate's." Again she assessed him. "Astonishing, truly, and laden with irony. For years I sought to learn what had become of you. I planned to found a dynasty, a grand aristocracy of magecraft for a new age, and your light, your lineage would have been a cornerstone. And now, out of all the children, it is my own child, come back to me a young man, who may be the only one capable of . . ." She smiled, as if she had forgotten herself. Teasing him with suggestion, innuendo, half answers. She was working him. He would let himself be worked, so long as it seemed they were heading in the right direction. "Well, you're no longer integral, if you ever were."

He tipped his head in gracious acceptance of this reduced usefulness, which he knew was precisely counter to what she was considering now.

"You have not given up your dream of an aristocracy of mages," he said. "Not if you are collecting children of light."

"Not an aristocracy. Not this time." She smiled. "An army."

He took a stab at what he suspected. "Khine's wasn't enough for you?"

She answered him without answering. "When the light went, I became interested perforce in more conventional means of achieving my goals. The Khinish provided the material I needed. Ambitious, strong-willed folk, so instinctively steered toward domination. A riot here, a murder there, and up the Leg they went, determined to take charge. Strelniriol was most accommodating. A persuasive herbal I learned from my old bindswoman, Freyn—she was a poisoner, did you know that? She killed Rigael your grandfather. Poisoned his wine, because he didn't love her. Naturally, I killed her for it. They're both here somewhere. Shall we take a stroll and find them?"

Deeply chilled by the implications, he took her hand, stalling for time, massaging it, caressing the knuckles, turning the ring so that the stone was squarely on top. She permitted it. Delight flashed in her eyes as she watched the manipulation of her flesh, as though she was pleased to find his technique so assured. "Quite a feat, persuading these bonefolk to do your bidding," he said. "Or are they using you?"

"Both, of course. And yes, the ring was my entrée to them, as well as allowing me to test the children for signs of light I can no longer see. Did they foster you in the Leg? You won't have learned to scribe, in that case, and we'll need to rectify that first thing."

"I do not know how to scribe. Entrée?"

"It is proof that I can redeem them. I thought it a trinket, a memento of my former life, a little piece of the Holding, where veins of it run deep. A stone that glowed in the light of mages; little use, with no more light and no more mages. Yet it whispered. The magestone whispers. Would you like to hear it?"

He did not respond, but perhaps his eyes betrayed something of the memories tumbling over themselves in his mind—the whisper-hole, the well of secrets, the crevasse that spoke promise and mystery from the depths of ages, that made Flin feel as though he knew things; the whispering magestone tunnels he'd dreamed in the base of the Ennead's mountain, the tunnels that tried to drown him in the past. She didn't know he'd fostered in the Holding. She didn't know he had his own memories of magestone. She held the ring up to his ear, like a conch, just brushing his lobe with the cool, waxy stone, and he heard it again: the soft murmur of words and voices beyond understanding.

She smiled at the effect this produced. "It's memory. These stones are memory itself. Evonder your father reasoned it out, or intuited it, more like; and he was fascinated by it. He believed that magestone contained echoes of the minds of the race long lost, those who crafted the body of Eiden in their own image."

Louarn struggled not to react visibly. If this was so, then he himself was magestone, the vessel for the memories of the long-lost boys who dwelled inside him. He knew how powerful those echoes were. He leaped ahead to her point, and only came upon more questions, and swallowed them, waiting, letting her tell it.

"One night I sat alone by a dying refugee child on Khine; I had eased her pain with my herbals, and I had meant to comfort her, but I failed to pay attention, and she died without my realizing. I had rather a lot on my mind, and there was nothing I could have done." *And you were concerned only with the appearance of ministering to her,* Louarn thought. "The bonefolk came before I could absent myself, and they felt the presence of the stone, and reacted to it, and then I knew."

The bonefolk were the race long lost.

"They crafted the Holding from the black stone of the Aralinns. They crafted our impossible mountains, our unnatural terrain. They made the stone forest in the Belt and the Memory Stones in the Heel. They crafted the Eiden Myr landmass in their own image." She paused for effect. "And then they fell. And now they are what they are. I can make them what they were. But I will need magelight to do it. And so they bring me children."

"How will you redeem them?"

She glanced over her shoulder and held a finger to her lips, eyes dancing.

A pretense, that she would not tell him because the bonefolk might hear—clearly they understood the spoken tongue, they had ears though they did not speak, they responded to her spoken bidding—and effect their redemption themselves. A pretense, that she would not tell him because he might depose her and fulfill the bargain in her stead. He gave her a conspiratorial smirk, with just a hint of hesitation, to say that he understood, that he must defer to her but now dared to hope they would share a special understanding.

It was quite clear that she had no means whatever of redeeming these sad, fallen folk.

"Now wouldn't you like to meet your father?" she said.

A calculated jab, and it worked all too well. He wanted nothing more, and feared nothing more. He let bored diffidence blank his face, then brought his eyes back to the ring, as though he coveted it and could not resist another look. "The bonefolk leave all metal and stone. How could that ring have gotten here?"

"Clever lad," she said. Mocking. Then she shrugged. "Magestone isn't stone, apparently. It came with me in its drawbag. And the setting isn't silver from our world. It was crafted here, for me, by the bonefolk, from one of their silver trees. It blackened when it went around my finger. A change in its own essence when it touched living flesh, or some subtle gibe of its crafters at me, there's no telling. It serves its purpose."

"To test the children."

"Yes." She made him wait; made him ask.

He acquiesced. "How did you know the light was returning in the children? Did the stone glow for one of your refugees?"

"The first children of the broken wardings turned five this past winter—conceived on Ve Galandra six years ago. They will just be showing their lights now."

"You may miss some who haven't begun to show."

"We shall repeat the sweeps periodically, as anxious parents forget their terror and relax their guard. It's not that I must have them all immediately. It's that I must have them before they see the lights in each other."

"And alert their parents that the light is in fact returning."

"That the light is reborn. It will never return to those of us who lost it. We are permanently cored. Seared. But it will shine twice as bright in the next generation. Particularly to children of those who were mages. What cannot bloom in the parent will bloom in the child. Pruned back, the magelight will flower all the more profusely. That verse came to me in a codex retrieved from an errant scholar over the winter. The exiled mages lost their light when Galandra cast the shield, too, you see. But only those who were alive when the casting was done. In the next generation it came back stronger. 'Cut back hard, light's vine blooms thrice as lush: The children shine. The children shine. The children shine.' Well, it was quite moving in the original, but that's not a language you would understand."

For spirits' sake, then, why was she killing these mage parents?

"You keep the children here?"

"It's a lovely place, don't you think? A peaceful, pretty landscape from some tellers' tale. They need not eat, they need not drink. I don't yet know whether they will grow, but they never sicken, and cannot die. They run and play, within boundaries I have set—this place appears to be infinite, we wouldn't want to lose any—and once they turn six I will set about teaching them their craft."

"It is a place of the dead. That is no place to raise children."

"I'm not raising children. I'm training mages. And the dead don't bother them." She drew back with his hand in both of hers, bending prettily when he did not move, her arms extended, a display of lithe flirtation—girlish, breathless. "Come. Come and see."

He could no longer resist. He let her pull him through the silver trees, to the top of a soft-coal slope, and he looked out.

Rank upon rank of the dead, for as far as the eye could see, and farther. Flesh and clothing of every color, bodies of every size, laid out as if sleeping. Healed, and perfect. Like pebbles on an infinite shore, soft human stars on an inverted fabric of sky. This hill they stood on was some construct of the bonefolk's, a gold-and-silver forest rising above the endless plain of the dead. Similar hills shouldered up to either side.

This was where the bonefolk sent the bodies they consumed.

"To what purpose?" he murmured.

She heard him, in the unmoving air. "I have no idea. A memorial? A collection? Fuel for some future use? Their spirits were passaged to bet-jahr, or haunt the mortal realm."

Magecraft had passaged spirits . . . what else might it do, what more might it be capable of in its new blossoming? If a power arose that could unite haunts with their restored flesh . . .

Lerissa should know. She did not. She could bid the bonefolk, but she could not understand them, or they would not tell her everything. There was a breach here. He could exploit it. He had understood them, somehow, when he was here before, when he was Mellas . . . but he could not remember . . .

Somehow, he could exploit it, when his mind caught up with him, and he could take everything Lerissa had, everything she had constructed, and craft it to his own use.

"Do you know how limestone forms?" she asked, taking a step nearer to him. "Shells collect at the seabottom. The waves grind stone to sand. Time and pressures and shifting earth compact those particles into mountains. That's what these bonefolk did, in their glory. They crafted mountains. They are stoneweavers, these folk. They hear the thoughts of stone, they enter it bodily, they plumb its essence."

He'd seen them move through stone. There was stone under all the ground in the mortal world. They could go anywhere. Yet there was no sign of their passage through turf, no divots, no tearing. Bonefolk were known for lurking in forests. And he had not seen enough bonefolk here to collect all the corpses in his ailing world. All these dead, and they might be only the ones who died near stone, or enclosed in it. If there was more than one kind . . . if there were forest bonefolk, and water bonefolk . . . if she had subverted only this one group . . .

Another breach to exploit, more potential to leverage one thing against another, but he must have a few breaths to think, and the sight of the dead legions had nearly blanked his mind.

"It will be the third age," Lerissa said, moving close upon his right, pressing in so that he felt her soft breast against his upper arm.

"All those lives, all those shells, like grains of sand, the dead of twice nine nonned years. The next nine nonned have just begun. Imagine what lofty peaks we might craft of them, you and I."

He breathed deep, and what came to him was the shock of her scent.

It was his mother's scent. It touched the oldest, deepest part of him—the part that Pelufer had been unable to name because it had no name. The newborn infant he had been, just come into the world of sight and smell, laid on his mother's breast to breathe her scent and look into her face for one instant before Evonder took him off to Bron to be fostered, as Rigael had ordered. His body knew her. His body yearned for her embrace.

She is not my mother.

Moving around behind him, she smoothed a hand over his hair, down his neck, along his shoulder and arm. She was beautiful, and deliciously cold, and under the frisson her touch evoked his flesh burned for hers, and yearned for hers, all at cross-purposes.

She is not my mother. My mother's name was Pirra. My mother loved me. This woman is not my mother. I can bed her, if it will get me what I want. Evonder did; why shouldn't I? I could turn this seduction back on her in ways she's never dreamed, disarm her with passion when she thinks to cloud my mind with it. She does not know how I have gotten what I wanted all these years.

Or he might join her, make that only the first, symbolic joining in a partnership that could craft all the world to their own ends.

To his own ends.

If he could control her, he could put it all to rights. Harnessing the magelight of the children she had collected, seeing to it that they were treated with compassion and trained to treat the world with it, he might heal all the world's ills, calm the quakes, redirect the weather, conquer the blight and plague and drought and flood. One benevolent leader could change it all.

Why shouldn't it be him? He was still half intoxicated with the pure white light. He possessed magelight, and the same earthy copper light as the Gir Doegre girls, and he had the girls, as well—the eldest enamored of him and easily charmed, the youngest and most powerful an ally by virtue of their shared light. Only the middle girl would be troublesome, and she, an orphaned child who had fended valiantly on her own, was struck with pity for the orphaned children who dwelled inside him. He could turn her however he wished. And the bluesilver light, connected somehow with the puzzles he made, with the medium of thought . . . he could fan that silver flame, quicken it, find others who possessed it, delve its powers. He would be the first man of a new age, an age in which all lights were kindled, all powers available. Who better to restore the world that was, than he? Who better to make it more than it had been? Who better than a crafter, to craft the third age of Eiden Myr?

If he slept, if he dreamed, he could change the world.

He was dreaming now, a waking dream of peaceful fields and pliant skies, and with one word, one turned seduction, one choice, he could make it all come true.

He swallowed his gorge, and turned to Lerissa.

From behind them, in the trees, came the phosphorescent tingle of the passaged, the ragged ends of tantrums tailing off into wonder, the sniffles of frightened children frozen in lampglare.

Lerissa dropped her shoulders in an affectation of regret. "Only a brief interruption," she said. He felt her breath on his lips. "Then by all means we shall resume."

A child's voice called his name, questioning.

Caille.

Lerissa did not know his name. Lerissa did not know any of his names. Lerissa had not given him a name.

They turned as one and approached the children grouped loosely among the silver tree trunks and pendulous golden branches. As the others had, they moved closer to one another, away from the strange surroundings and the bonefolk and the unfamiliar adults.

"Louarn!" Caille called again, from the midst of them, and for a terrible moment he thought she would run to him. But she kept still, looking from him to the trees, to the bonefolk, to the other children, to Lerissa. She seemed very small and alone without her sisters, and her face was smeared and swollen from tears, but she dragged one thumb-stretched sleeve across her eyes and the other under her nose and, receiving no response from him, turned on the bonefolk with a stamp of foot. "I said to take me to the *battle*!"

Lerissa had turned her head three-quarters to Louarn, her lips forming a question for which words had not yet come, but the child's behavior was so odd in comparison with that of the other children that she forgot Louarn, or glanced off the flat stone of his expression glimpsed from the corner of her eye. She began to coo to the frightened children, approaching them with tender, silken softness, no threat in her bearing. Just that hand held out, as if in expectation of a kiss. Or obeisance.

No one could tear their eyes from her. She was beautiful and terrifying. She began on the left, holding the ring before each child. The second, a boy, she drew gently out of the group and pressed into the care of the bonefolk with whispered reassurances that he would see his mother soon. The third showed no light.

Louarn stepped in close behind her. He saw the ring glow for another boy. These were Knee children. The light had been strong in the Knee.

Caille was in the middle. A little girl from the back had come up to clutch her arm. The innkeepers' child, from the Ruffed Grouse in Gir Nuorin. He could not remember her name. Caille told the girl not to be afraid, and the fierce, wary face she turned toward Lerissa looked exactly like Pelufer's face.

If Caille showed a light, and stayed here, her powers would be revealed. There was no injury here to heal, but Louarn did not know what else she might do. *Almost anything,* Elora had said. And she could not be trusted not to speak of it, without her sisters keeping watch. He could feel Lerissa's excitement build as she made her way, casually methodical, toward the center of the group. She sensed Caille. She wanted Caille.

Caille was next. She did not look at Louarn. Her eyes were fixed on Lerissa. Wary, and hardening, as her chin jutted out and her fists clenched at her sides.

He encircled Lerissa with his arms and drew her up and back. He closed his hand on her hand, brought it to his lips. "Let me," he said, kissing her palm, her wrist. Moving to slip the ring from her finger.

She disengaged. "Not yet, love."

He caught her wrist, playfully. "The dawn of a new age," he said. "Let me share it."

She twisted her wrist, and he tightened his hold and bared his teeth, and her eyes went flat, and he endured the slap and would have stepped in to kiss her, stepping between her legs so that the knee could not come up into his crotch, but there was a patter of feet and a murmur from the children and Lerissa wrenched free of him and called out to her bonefolk, but they were only turning their long torsos from one side to the other, arms raised, as if in confusion, confounded by an invasion of mice, and there were children everywhere, running, swooping in through the trees—

Bearing the new ones off.

"Hold them!" Lerissa barked to the bonefolk who had the boys who'd shown a light, as she grabbed the nearest children by the hair. "Help me," she growled to Louarn, and "Bofric!" she shouted.

One of the children she held was the innkeepers' daughter. Caille tried to haul her away, but Lerissa would not release her grip on the girl's hair. The girl shrieked in pain, and a wink later Caille let go as though she'd touched a hot iron. Then an older child with blunt-cut honey hair swept Caille away with a whoop of glee, and they were gone, vanished among the trees.

Two-thirds of the new arrivals remained.

Quickly, Lerissa tested them; she culled half their number and sent the others home. The child from the inn was among the latter. Louarn bit his tongue to restrain himself from some attempt to send a message with her.

"What *was* that?" he said, when she'd parceled out her charges and turned to him at last, before whatever banishment or scolding or seduction she had chosen for him in the meantime.

"A minor difficulty." She smoothed her saffron robes. "Of no concern."

"It's of concern if they're liberating your—"

"Where will they go? The ones who show a light will still be in this realm; the others are simply unnecessarily denied their passage home. She's doing them no favors."

The honey-haired one. It had to be. She was older, and she swept through with the assurance of command, the others following in her wake as she'd run off. It was a familiar pattern, observed among countless children during his travels. There was always a ringleader. "Who is she?"

"A little girl who shouldn't have come here. My man in the Head holding sent her to me in a thoughtless panic. I wanted him with me, and sent one of the bonefolk for him, but it apparently caught him at an inconvenient time. He sent the girl on, planning to follow. It was stupid of him, and he's paid for it since. He miscalculated her age. She was already born when we were cored, there'll never be a light in her. I would have sent her back, but she got loose, and now she harries us. She steals new children from me, ganging them together who knows where. She's seen too much now, I can't permit her to return, and she's terribly quick. Even my bonefolk can't catch her."

It hadn't seemed to Louarn that they'd tried very hard. If these raids happened from time to time, they should not have been taken by surprise. That surprise had been feigned to cover a failure to act. *They aren't doing everything you bid them,* he thought. Perhaps they were working against her in whatever small ways they could, unhappy with what she had them do but still trying to keep her sweet in case she could actually deliver on the vague redemption she promised.

"She seems to think she's their rescuer," Lerissa said. "Perhaps she believes I'll kill them. I've called out to her, I've told her that I'll send the lightless home and take the best care of the others, but she doesn't respond. She thinks it's a game."

Oh, I doubt that, Louarn thought. *I doubt that very much. I think she's fighting for her life, and fighting for the lives of all these children. Brave girl. Good on her.*

And then, in a flash of connection so quick that it took him a moment afterward to isolate the disparate pieces, he realized: *She will be able to converse with them now. Now she has Caille.*

He had understood the bonefolk in this place when he had passed through from being Mellas to being Louarn. He had understood the fingerspeech with which the Gir Doegre girls spoke to each other in secret.

They were the same thing.

And Caille could translate.

Something lifted from him, some heavy veil, a blanket of iron.

Lerissa said, touching him suggestively, "That was untoward of you, trying to wrest my ring from me. Arousing, but inappropriate. Yet perhaps I may forgive you. Come with me now. We've kept your father waiting long enough, and after that I have something to show you, something that will change everything. Something far more astonishing than any chip of magestone."

Bofric arrived, the aide she'd called for, a knob-nosed older man, breathless and far too late. He must have run from another hill; the captured children must be kept on that other hill. He showed no expression upon seeing Louarn, no spark of recognition, though Mellas had known him when he was a Holding steward; but he exuded an animal antagonism. Whatever Lerissa was to him, he did not like the idea of sharing her. They said nothing to each other, and Lerissa made no introduction, merely gave Bofric a set of instructions and entrusted the magestone ring to him. Though he had not witnessed their struggle, he turned his gaze on Louarn as he took the ring, and triumph flared there.

"So," Lerissa said, "no more interruptions," and led Louarn down onto the plain of the dead.

They were equally spaced, a perfection of arrangement as unnatural as their physical perfection. The lavender sky, lightening to violet though no sun appeared, should have tinged their flesh with the color of a bruise, but their skin looked healthy, infused with blood and vigor. He touched one body and found it neutral in temperature, with nothing like the clammy chill of a corpse. But none of them breathed. None of them lived. They were just flesh, smooth and whole, preserved as if in alcohol or amber, though their clothes were dry and clean. Laid out as if sleeping, though there was no sense of sleep about them. Even the slackest sleeping face showed life, and these showed none. Their spirits were gone on, or left behind. Yet if these were shells, they were the most beautiful shells he could imagine.

"Rigael," Lerissa said, pointing out a man devastatingly handsome, but stone-faced, pale under a shock of black hair. "Your grandfather." If there was a grandmother near him—Lerissa's maternal name had been n'Lessa, hadn't it?—Lerissa declined to point her out. Perhaps she still lived, somewhere on the mainland. Louarn quashed a surging impulse to go find her when he returned. Lerissa was not his mother. Neither Rigael nor his mate had any connection to Louarn beyond the flesh. He must remember that. He must keep it very clearly in his mind. Their history was not his. *His path had well and truly branched away from theirs now.*

"Portriel," Lerissa said. "Rigael's mother." In death the woman's face appeared somehow joyful, perhaps the expression it had died with. "A stubborn woman, and formidable in her day. But my Ennead cowed her in the end."

She had not led him far, it seemed; perhaps this was where all the dead of the Holding were gathered, perhaps their position here in this infinity of flesh had some relation to their proximity in the mortal realm, or how close in time they had died.

"Evonder," she said, with what sounded like a wistful sigh, gesturing at a fair man dressed in robin's-egg blue. "Your father."

Louarn tried to feel nothing, but he remembered that boyish, haunted face, and knew it for his own. The hair was sandy, and the eyes were closed, but they were the same. A kind hand ruffling his hair . . . all he would ever have of a father who had never known him.

"Vonche and Naeve and Daivor," Lerissa said. "They were cousins, as you can see from the resemblance. Daivor got Evonder on Naeve, though she claimed he was Vonche's. One day, perhaps soon, his brother Evrael will appear here. I will cherish that moment more than I can ever tell you."

Evrael was the fleetmaster of Khine. Had he joined in the battle on the Menalad Plain, or perhaps somehow stopped it? *He is my uncle,* Louarn thought, and then thought, *No. These are no folk of mine.*

There were proxies he knew, warders and reckoners he'd called as vocates. There were stewards he knew. He did not react to them. He let her show him her folk, her Holding folk. The bodies of the remainder of the Ennead he looked upon without interest, keeping a tight rein on what would burst out of him if he did not maintain control.

"There are only seven," he said.

"Yes," Lerissa said. "I left Worilke to a rebel onslaught, attended by an ancient steward. She would not have talked or fought herself free. She was paralyzed with shock from some vision she'd had of Galandra during the hein-na-fhin. Perhaps they dragged her away, drowned her or killed her out in the woods somewhere, and the other bonefolk took her. It's of no matter to me."

The other bonefolk. "She was your wordsmith."

"Freyn there was my binder and my second mother, pledged to Rigael my father, and I cut her throat. Never assume alliances where you can assume even deeper grievances, love." She cocked her head. "It healed nicely, don't you think? But it was such a lovely smile."

He had seen enough.

Lerissa said, "Now you lead."

"I don't know the way back."

"We're not going back. We're going on. There's a stream I want to show you. But we're not finished here. You go first, now."

He resisted, baffled and frowning. This boded ill, but he could not find the harm that must be in it. If he got them lost, he would dream his way free and leave her wandering.

He moved down the rows, between them, in what felt like random steps.

The body of Brondarion te Khine came up on his left.

He swallowed hard. He continued on. There was one of the mutilated mages he had led out of the Ennead's torture chambers. Restored to beauty and power, though her unpassaged spirit, liberated through Yuralon's mercy, would haunt the mountain still. He saw another, and another, and among them the bladed stewards who had died in that brief bloody confrontation in the passageway—he remembered Saraen, their leader, and the man with the craggy face who had opposed him. He had seen the bonefolk passage these folk. He had seen these bodies consumed, dissipating in a light so bright it made him wince. This was where they had gone. This was the other side of the green glow of bonefolk feeding.

In front of him appeared an infant of three moons. A baby girl, tucked up as in her cradle. One of the newest fosterlings of Bron's. He remembered her. He'd been fond of her, a sweet burbly child. Her swaddling seemed insufficient in this open space. He almost reached to pull off a garment to cover her with.

She's not there, she's not there, he told himself, and ground onward.

On his right he passed three Lowland Southers, and he blanched. He did not remember their names. They had frightened him badly, on that last journey back to the Holding. His own razor shadows had killed one . . . but that must have been some doing of the Ennead's, some manipulation of their mountain, like the mudslide that killed the two others and his horse Purslane, because whatever that man's name had been, Pelufer had not spoken it when she touched him. He felt relief at that, unlooked-for, and fled from it, increasing his pace. He must not let this affect him. These folk were dead. Images of what they had been. Constructs. Vessels.

Shells.

The farther he roamed, the more faces he recognized. Was this how it was? You found your own folk, somehow, through the intrinsic nature of this place? This was no good, no good at all—

He fell to his knees in front of the bodies of his parents.

His mother, and his fathers. Dressed in immaculate snowy velvet and crisp linen. Beautiful and whole, their burned flayed flesh restored to pink-cheeked health. They looked like Heartlanders—the fair, even features, the rich thick hair dark as the coal on which they lay. Their eyes would be blue and green under the lids. Bron had fostered him to folk whom no one would question as his parents. Why had they hidden him? Why had they trapped him? Why hadn't they given him a bolthole, taught him to survive, *why had they left him alone in the dark tunnels?*

Inside him, Flin wailed. Oh, to see them animated again, to see them full of spirit, to see his mother's face light up with that beaming silly smile, to see Alliol stern and loving, to see Ellerin wink at him. . . .

"Oh, my," Lerissa said. "They fostered you to the head warders. The bloody fools."

He rose, deeply shaken, his heart broken inside his chest. Denial was useless. She had seen what she had seen. He nodded.

Her arm came around him, maternal, comforting. "All right, love," she said. "It's all right. We'll go now. You've had enough. It's hard, the first time, I know. But I have just the thing for you. Just a little farther. Back the way we came. We're leaving now, I know you want to go, it's over now, no more hurt. There, now. Sit down here, by this sweet stream. Let me show you a wonder."

He hadn't watched where she'd directed him, just went where she pushed, sat where she told him to. He had never felt so weary. He was weary in his deepest spirit. So long since he had slept . . . real, healing sleep, deep and long . . . years, years of fighting it . . .

"No," he said, raising his head. *I will not succumb to this now. I am what I make of myself. I am a crafter. The man I have crafted is stronger than this.*

"No? But look, listen—isn't it marvelous?"

She waved a slender arm over the crystalline stream that flowed through a delving in the coal before him. It sang sweetly, a gentle, healing song. There was humor in it, and delight. He moved closer, and looked into its sparkling currents, braiding and unbraiding in rivulets of diamond brilliance. A draught of this pure stream would be a draught of healing, a draught of immortality. . . .

Lerissa knelt to scoop up water in both hands, and raised the hands before him. The water she held looked perfectly still.

She tossed it at him. He swayed back.

It thumped, solid, on the black ground before him.

"Go ahead," she said. "Pick it up."

He did.

It felt like magestone—cool, waxy, alive.

"You can mold it," she said. "For a little while, before it fully hardens. Look." She took the chunk of frozen stream and pressed it in her hands, making a square of it, then molding that into a pyramid. It shaped like wet clay in her hands, but it was crystal clear, and in the sourceless light it sparkled like the running stream. "Now it's hardening," she said. "It happens rather quickly, once it starts." She'd flattened and extruded her pyramid into a shape that his eye could not define.

"Look," Lerissa said, holding it before him now in all its adamantine brilliance. "You can make of it whatever you wish. It's intoxicating, isn't it? And it can be brought back to the other world. Like the magestone, it can pass from one side to the other; it's like the bonefolk, it exists in both places. It proved useful to me in the mortal realm. I needed to start a little war in the Strong Leg, you see, as a distraction, while my bonefolk stepped up their collection. It's getting too close now; soon the children *will* be able to see each other's lights. I must harvest as many as I can before that happens. Pelkin will lay hands on them otherwise, and I can't allow that. He'd removed himself to Khine when I was last there, trying to talk that idiot hall out of their war, so *he's* distracted by his own doing. But it won't last. Nothing lasts, love. We must take what we need and forge what we require of it. . . ."

In the clear depths of the crystal he saw tiny explosions, white starbursts, coruscating lights. He could not draw his eyes away. He had never seen anything so beautiful, so pure. Like the crystalline light in the passageway of dreams . . .

He blinked and struggled out of the depths of purity. Bells were sounding, far away, warning bells. He'd always heeded those far warnings of his mind. He turned, sought some avenue of escape in the infinite coal-dark plain, and behind him, so close it startled, saw the nearest row of bodies. Flesh . . . but no more human than the molded crystal Lerissa held . . .

Croy was lying not two threfts from him.

Croy the bricklayer, who'd lived in a house built by his own hands. He'd died in that house, a house of bricks, of stone, and the bonefolk had come for him there. To passage him here.

Hands. The body of Croy, whole and healed, had both hands.

"Wh . . ." He turned to Lerissa, forcing his mouth to work. "What happens when the bonefolk don't take their hands?"

"You're tired, love. Let the crystal heal you. Let the crystal take the pain away."

"Why do you . . . castrate them? Why do you take away their . . . means of casting if as adults they will never . . . again have their light?"

"You're the only adult in whom I have any interest, love. You're a powerful boy. A good boy. A clever man. We'll do so well together, you and I. Just let the crystal take the pain, the weariness—"

He gripped her by the shoulders, saw a flicker in her eyes, doubt and surprise, as if she'd expected something else of him, as if she didn't understand what he was saying. She *must* understand. She must explain to him! "*Why do you cut off the hands if they only regain them on the other side?*"

He saw baffled innocence in her clear blue eyes for the first and only time, and knew how great a mistake he had made.

She had no idea what he was talking about. She was not the one who sent the magekillers. He'd learned her plans, he'd found his mother, his dead, his earliest memories, he'd learned so much . . . but he was on the wrong mission. This was not his mission. He came here because a magekiller claimed fealty to an Ennead mistress. But only seven of the Nine lay here. Worilke was missing. Worilke was alive. It was Worilke he should have sought, Worilke he should have dreamed his way to, they'd never find her in all of Eiden Myr, only he . . . only he . . .

"I am in the wrong place," he said.

"Here," Lerissa said, and smoothed the crystal down the line of his jaw, brought it into the line of his sight. "Here, love. Here's the right place."

Pelufer found her father right away.

He'd looked ravaged when he died. He had puffy circles under his eyes, his skin was sallow, his hair was greasy, his nose was swollen with burst veins, he'd gone all jowly, and his body was bloated and starved at the same time. She'd forgotten how he'd looked when she was little. A man in the prime of life, the traders would say. A solid body, fine chestnut hair, smooth toned brown skin, a muscular body filling out the clothes that had hung loose on him when he died, and a face . . . well, a face that looked from the outside the way hers felt from the inside. They'd always told her she took after her father.

Caille wasn't with him. That was a relief. There were a lot of other people she knew when they were alive, and they were together in families here, even though they died at different times and in different places. If Caille was dead, Caille's body would be with her father.

But living Caille wasn't here either. They'd sent her somewhere else.

And she couldn't find her mother.

The groves were beautiful. This was the true bonefolk's wood, not the spirit wood at home where the newly dead were left for them to collect. But it wasn't a wood. There were no bushes or saplings or plants. There was no undergrowth, only grass soft as goosedown. It was a realm of tended groves. Light filtered through the canopy in drowsy, mote-speckled shafts, shifting as time passed, as though a sun moved overhead. But there was no sun. The sky was a suffusion of golden light seen in glimpses through the leaves overhead, no sky there really at all. There were no open places, no clearings where you could just stand and look up. One grove melded into another. And none of the trees were the trees she knew.

There were some with bark like blackstone and golden fruit weighing their soft boughs among leaves of jade. There were some shaped like oak, but their trunks were creamy and it wasn't acorns that littered the ground, it was the flutternoses that came from sowmid flamewoods—except flamewood keys were red, and these were white. When she saw trees with the spiky leaves of flamewood, the leaves were blue and the bark was like marble and there were silver acorns everywhere. There were groves of flowering trees, where blossoms drifted like rose-colored snow and filled the air with a perfume so sweet it made her heart hurt. There were groves of harvestmid trees, copper-leaved with bark like rust, and groves of evergreens, their needles shining black and their heavy cones a dark blue whose color she couldn't even name until she finally came up with indigo.

And among them all, everywhere except the emerald grove where she'd first found herself, were the bodies of the dead. Nonneds upon nonneds of them, more than she could ever count. Still very dead, but whole and perfect. She was glad for that. She was glad to see Sel's body look like the Sel she remembered, not the thing that disease had made him. But it didn't mean anything. There wasn't any sense of haunting here. There were no names, unless she said them on purpose when she passed by people she knew. There was no one here.

No one human.

There were others. She felt their shapes, shifting through the trees like motes through the light. They felt like a frown. Confused and not very happy that she was here. But they stayed away. They let her roam. They made no sound. The only sound was the rustle of her feet through grass and blossoms, and the slow bending of boughs and leaves under their own weight. No breeze stirred. No breath, except her own.

She wasn't afraid to get lost. As long as she could see, she couldn't get lost. Her path was a shape, too, and she could follow it back the way she'd come. But when she decided to return to where she'd started, she was just there—it was the next grove she entered, even though the next grove had been purple hazel with silver pears. She was back where the grass was green as an emerald on Mireille's stall, and the trees had brown-gray dappled trunks like real trees, and leaves like sowmid limes, and no funny-wrong nuts or fruit.

Elora was standing there with the boneman, like two people who'd been talking for a while.

"Caille?" Pelufer asked—relieved, but not relieved enough.

Elora said, "Lornhollow thinks he knows who took her and where, but he can't send us there."

"That's Lornhollow?" Pelufer said, pointing at the boneman.

The boneman said, "I am Lornhollow, in your naming."

So she *had* heard him speak. She didn't know bonefolk could speak. She thought she might have imagined it before. He wasn't very good at it—his mouth was a queer shape, too round, and it didn't have lips—but he managed it somehow.

"If you can't send us to our sister, send us back," Pelufer said. "We'll find our own way."

"You cannot," the boneman said. "You do not have the way of stone."

"Then you do it!"

"We are woodfolk. Those are stonefolk. They are different."

Pelufer swore, slamming her arms against her sides, and whirled around looking for something to throw or break, but there was nothing. She was so sick of being looked after when she didn't expect it and didn't know and hadn't asked for it! She didn't ask the boneman to rescue her and Elora. She might have figured out what the reaching-out feeling was, she might have stopped the battle if he'd given her a chance, but no, he had to just send her here, and wherever it was and however safe it was, it wasn't where the other one sent Caille. It wasn't good enough. No matter how good anyone's intentions, they never saved her all the way. They never rescued her enough. Like every other time, she'd have to do it herself.

"Is it a safe place, where they took her?" Elora asked, moving away to touch a tree. "Like here?"

"No place is safe," Lornhollow said. His slurred speech sounded as sad as his big dark teary eyes looked.

Elora was still moving, going between trees now. She was in one of her trances. Woods made her drunker than Father after a jug, and these groves were golden, enchanted, perfumed. It would only be worse here. "Don't, Elora, don't get lost in this," she said, trotting after her to stop her. Movement was strange here. Elora might walk off into some other grove and Pelufer might not be able to find her. But she was right there, right in front, so close that Pelufer blundered into her. She was staring down at their father.

"Where's Mamma?" Elora said.

"I couldn't find her." Saying it made it hurt. It hadn't hurt before;

finding Mamma was just a thing she needed to do, and it wasn't as important as finding Caille and so she didn't let it touch her when she failed. Now it did.

Lornhollow came up beside them, moving in a slow, intentional way, rustling the grass with his long bare feet, so that they would sense him. He could have moved like the others, in a shifting silence. He was trying to be human for them, a little bit. As much as he could.

She didn't care. She didn't care. He could be as nice as he wanted and try as hard as he wanted. If he couldn't take them to Caille he was no use and they had to go.

"Prendra's flesh is not here," he said, in his dry, slurred, mournful voice.

Pelufer's heart took a turn. "They took her to the spirit wood. We were there. We saw it."

Lornhollow looked down on them from his height of more than seven feet. Tall as a tree, pale as mist. Luminous, as if there was something inside him that made him shine the way they shined when they did workings. "Prendra is here," he said.

"How do you know her name?" Elora asked, still vague, still entranced.

"I knew her," Lornhollow replied.

"Is that why you rescued us?" Pelufer said. "You were watching us, because we're her daughters?"

"I watch," Lornhollow said.

There was no telling what he meant. The way he spoke wasn't the way they spoke. The sounds came out in the shape of their words, but they didn't fit exactly. They were like someone giving you a plate because it was the closest thing he had to the kind of bowl you were used to, and you wouldn't recognize the kind of bowls he used. But it didn't hold what he needed it to. It was just a platter to present something on. It wasn't the right thing.

Pelufer stepped away, and looked up at him, and in the secret silent language their mother had taught them she asked him why.

With his long, facile fingers, Lornhollow told them.

"Watch" would not have described the way he'd been connected to them. "Children" meant so much more than new people their mother's body had made. "Because" would not have conveyed the obligation or the longing or the affection. "Love" would not have been enough if he'd said it, not for joy and pain that went as deep as roots. "Her" meant their mother, but so much more. His fingers were fluid and eloquent, and the shapes they made said things he never could have said with his mouth.

Elora sank into the downy grass and touched Padda's body. "You're not . . . our father, are you?"

With her head bowed, Lornhollow could not fingerspeak to her. "This is your father," he said, curling his hands loosely in front of his chest. "You are flesh. We are woodfolk. We are different."

"Where is our mother?" Pelufer asked—softly, in awe, as though she already knew.

Lornhollow uncurled one spindly finger, and pointed it at her.

"In me?" she whispered.

"All of you. You have the ways. She gave you the ways."

"Everyone has the ways," Pelufer said. "All little children have the ways. Crafters have the ways when they're doing it right. I saw a man with no shine to him at all pick up a dog that a cartwheel rolled over, and he shined, he eased the dog's pain and he wrapped up the shattered leg and the dog bit him in the beginning but later on it licked him and the whole time he was shining. He had the ways."

Lornhollow lowered his head and his arms. From the shape of it she knew she was babbling and he expected better of her. "You have more," he said, and his shape said *You know that perfectly well.* "She gave you more. She gave you hers. I gave you hers."

Slowly, like a giant heron folding itself down into a nest, the boneman folded his legs under him and sat in the grass by their father's body. Sitting, he was eye-to-eye with her.

"Look up, Elora," Pelufer said. She sat beside her sister and turned her toward Lornhollow. "He's going to tell us but he has to do it with his hands. You have to look at him."

"I don't want to know," Elora said. "I know too much. I know enough. I don't want any more. It's going to hurt."

"It won't."

"It will."

"All right it will. But I want to know."

"We have to get Caille." A calculated plea—she hadn't been so worried about Caille a moment ago, but she knew Pelufer was. At least the trance of the forest was wearing off.

"He's going to tell us what Caille *is*."

"I don't care, I don't care what we are, I just want Caille, I just want Mamma, I just want to not hurt."

"Don't look then," Pelufer said, but of course Elora looked, and with his fluid hands Lornhollow gave the story to them.

When the folk dissolved the bodies of the dead, they sent them on to these waiting places, leaving the spirits to go where they would. In the age of people of light, the spirits had already been sent on, most of the time, and all the bonefolk did was transport and repair the bodies. But when that light was gone, the spirits stayed behind in Eiden's realm. The bonefolk made the bodies anew. They learned the bodies, every particle of them, and made them right, and sent them on; Pelufer could not tell the order of those things, they were all one the way Lornhollow conveyed it, and there was terrible pain involved and glorious pleasure. Even his fingers could not shape the full extent of what it was like. Pelufer understood that. She couldn't explain her knacks to people even when she tried hard. But she understood what he said next: that there was power in those bodies. The force of life. The force of their hearts, she thought he said. And Prendra made him promise that when her spirit left her body, he would give that power to her girls. The world was turning dark and hard, with no mages to protect them anymore. She gave her heartforce to her children, to make them strong for what was to come.

Pelufer remembered. She remembered bundling up the new baby, sneaking out of the house with Elora in the lead, the way her foot hit that bad board even though she knew it was there and it let out a creak but Padda didn't hear under the sound of his grief. She was five, and Elora was seven. She had to be very careful with the baby, and once they came to the woods Elora took her because she was bigger. They went to the woods because while the baby was growing inside her, Mamma made Elora promise that if anything happened to her and they took her to the spirit wood, Elora had to take Pelufer and the baby and follow. Pelufer was scared, and angry at Elora. Elora was always so good and always did what Mamma and Padda told her. But when they got into the woods, she forgot about being scared and angry. She had never seen a boneman. She stared in wonder from the place where they were hiding, at the edge. She saw the boneman pick up their mother the way their mother picked *her* up, the way you picked up something you loved very much. The bonefolk were nicer than people said. The boneman looked so kind. But then her mother went away, just turned into green light in the boneman's arms and went away, and something passed through her like a wind, the sweetest strongest wind in the world, the most wonderful feeling she had ever had. But Mamma was gone. The boneman had made her go away. And Elora and the baby were glowing green now. What if the boneman took them too?

Elora couldn't hold her back because she had the baby in her arms, and Pelufer scrambled into the clearing to get her mother back, to stop whatever the boneman was doing to Elora and the baby, to punch him and bite him—only midway there she started spewing names, and the boneman must have gotten frightened and left, but she didn't see what happened because she was choking on the names, and Elora had to come and get her out of the wood and get them home. It was hard to carry the baby and get Pelufer out of the wood too. Elora told her that later. She told her that Pelufer could never ever go back to that wood. She was angry and scared about it. But she was proud of herself. She was proud that she did what Mamma wanted.

She was already starting to try to be Mamma.

Pelufer saw all that, remembered all that, through the shapes described by Lornhollow's hands. That night was when they changed, when they got their knacks. Caille got the most because she was the smallest and newest. That night had changed their lives forever.

He'd met their mother in that wood. He'd come for the dead, when she was a young girl, and had not sensed her creep up on him. It was—embarrassing, humiliating, to be seen in the act of working the dead. Like people shifting each other. You weren't supposed to watch when people did that. Mamma and Padda always kept their door closed. The bonefolk wouldn't come if someone might watch. It was their great pleasure and their great pain. Some were more shy than others. Lornhollow had been very shy. The girl had startled him badly. But something made him stay. She was so young and so shining, and she wasn't afraid of him. Time passed. He met her again, and again. His folk disapproved. They did not linger by the living. It wasn't right. It wasn't done. But Lornhollow did it. Her folk would not approve either. They had to be secretive and careful. But one of them saw. Another girl. Prendra tried to show the other girl that Lornhollow was good, tried to teach her the language of fingers she had learned from Lornhollow. Lornhollow tried to talk to her in the language of sound he had learned from Prendra. But the girl ran away. She threatened Prendra. Lornhollow was afraid of what would happen, what would befall Prendra. He lingered closer. He would send her away if she came into danger. But Prendra told him she had seen to it. She did not tell him how. Only that he was safe, as if his safety and not hers had been the worry, and that the other girl would not trouble them again.

"Mireille's mother," Elora murmured. *That* was the old grievance between them. Jenaille had been a stickler for convention. Every little rule, every little proper thing. She guarded decorum like personal property. Prendra consorting with bonefolk . . . she'd have gone spare.

"I'd like to know what Mother said to her to make her keep her mouth shut," Pelufer said with a grin.

Sadly, Elora said, "No wonder Mireille's the way she is."

Typical Elora, to pity that spiteful girl. It was Lornhollow Pelufer pitied now. "You gave her up for us," she said. "You didn't send her here."

He did not reply. Maybe he couldn't.

"Did Padda mind?" Elora asked.

She meant was Padda jealous. Pelufer wouldn't have thought of that.

Lornhollow told them again that bonefolk and humans were different. Bonefolk could not mate with humans. Bonefolk did not mate. That was a thing of life, a creation of life, a pleasure of flesh that was alien to them. What he and Prendra shared was not like that. But Nimorin knew of them. He was pained by them. He tried to love Lornhollow too, and could not. He feared that Prendra loved Lornhollow more than she did him, as if she didn't have enough love in her for the both of them and the girls too. She gave all her love to all of them. Her love was limitless, like this place. She was love. That was her shining.

"But the bodies . . ." Elora said. "You send them here to wait. To wait for what? To get their spirits back someday? To put the haunts back in them?"

If that was why, then Padda could live again, and Mamma could not, and Mamma had given up everything to make them strong.

Lornhollow didn't know. The bonefolk didn't remember why they did what they did. It was their sacrifice and their reward. It was pain and pleasure. All beauty was both pain and pleasure, as was all love. They did not know what would happen. They no longer knew what they were, what they had been, why they were. They simply were. They did what they did. They'd failed in some grievous way long ago, and so they did what they did. That was all.

"It is what is," he said aloud.

"Why are you stealing children?" Pelufer asked.

Lornhollow gestured that he stole nothing, and Pelufer sensed irritation in the shape of it—insult. He would get up in a moment, she could tell. He didn't like this. He didn't want to talk about it.

"The others then. You're woodfolk. The stonefolk took Caille and Lusonel and those others. Why? Where?"

To their place, Lornhollow told them. To their waiting place. Because they were bid to. It was wrong to move the living through the ways.

"You moved us," Pelufer said.

"Only you," Elora said. "I came myself. I can do it, Pel. I can move through the trees like they do. It's wonderful and frightening. I want to do it again, and I don't. But he only brought you. He broke his own rule to save your life."

Pelufer scowled, but she couldn't explain about the battle. She couldn't explain the feeling she'd had there at the very end that maybe there *was* something she could do to stop it, maybe Caille had been right after all. Lornhollow did a kind thing, and it . . . cost him.

"Thank you, Lornhollow," she said. Elora didn't even have to glare at her or pinch her first.

Lornhollow blinked—his eyes closed and then opened, even though they had no lids and he never blinked, not the way people blinked now and then to wet their eyes. His eyes were always wet. She wondered if that blink was a kind of smile.

She smiled back—

And then he was up, she hadn't even seen him get up but he was up and backing away, fading between the trees, or into them, moving with the bonefolk's swift silence.

Stricken, she said, "What did I do? I didn't do anything, I swear, I only smiled—"

Elora was scrambling to her feet and looking back the way they had come, and then Pelufer realized that she'd heard something, too, it just took a moment to come through to her. Lornhollow hadn't been insulted, he'd been startled, like a woodland animal, and he'd fled into invisible safety.

"We'd better go see what it is," Pelufer said.

"We'd better not," Elora replied. "Stay here, Pel. We don't know . . ."

"It could be Caille!"

"He wouldn't have run from Caille."

They could hear someone now, moving around the emerald grove. It was both right beside them and incalculably far away. They could walk right toward it and end up in some other grove if they wanted to. In fact, if Elora did that, she probably would end up in some far grove. They were already in some far grove. You moved the way you needed to move, here, and if Elora was afraid of whoever was rustling around over there, she wouldn't be able to go there.

"I'm going to go see."

"No! We can't split up."

"We can always find each other, Elora. We can always find Padda. That's how it works here."

"I know. But no. I'll go with you. You might need me, somehow. It's a forest. It's where I belong."

She had a point there. But she still might not get to the emerald grove, not if she really didn't want to go there. "All right," Pelufer said. "Just go back to Padda if things go wrong."

"We have to find Caille," Elora said, miserable.

"I know. I'll find a way, Elora. Maybe that's the way, over there, whatever that is. I have to go see."

With Elora following—watching her back, and hiding behind her at the same time—she crept back to the edge of the emerald grove.

A woman was examining the periphery. She never moved far from the center of the familiar trees. She wasn't yet ready to strike off and go exploring. She was stunned, confused, her limbs loose and not completely obeying her. She put a hand in front of her mouth to feel her own breath, then laid the palm on the dappled tree trunk before her.

She wasn't wearing any weapons. She was hardly taller than Elora, and nearly as slim, with honey-brown hair cut blunt at the shoulders and a hairband dangling at the bottom of it. She had a pretty face, from the side anyway. She didn't look like any kind of a threat.

Pelufer stepped into view. "Who are you?" she said.

The woman turned, putting the tree behind her, and Pelufer was taken aback by the hard authority in that harmless-looking body. She had a desperate shape to her, hands clawed, neck and jaw bunched with tense muscles, squared shoulders. But she checked whatever impulse ran through her. "I'm Dabrena n'Arilda," she said. "I'm a mender. I'm looking for my daughter."

Elora said, "She's from the Hand, but she's spent a long time in the Head."

"Good with accents, are you?" the woman said.

"You're alive," said Pelufer. Did the bonefolk ever make mistakes? Take the living by accident?

The woman patted herself down. "Apparently so, to my own surprise. And so are you. What's your name?"

"Pelufer. This is Elora. How did you get here?"

"I jumped into a pile of dead bodies while the bonefolk were feeding."

"They weren't feeding. They were sending them here."

"Then why aren't they here?" She looked around, still having trouble reconciling wherever she'd been with where she was now. It took grownups longer to adapt. "There were nonneds of them. . . ."

"They go where they belong. With their families, mostly. You can find the ones you know, if you want to." She was thinking of the woman's daughter. She might have been stolen, but she might have been dead, too. Sometimes grieving people did try to fling themselves on the bonefolk.

The woman blinked. "Can I, now. That's very interesting. Did the bonefolk bring you here?"

"Yes. But they don't bring. They send, and then they come after."

The woman sagged with relief. "Then my daughter's alive."

Stolen, then. "Probably. But she's not here. These are woodfolk. They aren't the ones stealing children."

The woman rubbed both hands over her face and let out a bitter laugh. "After all that, I jumped into the wrong circle of bonefolk?"

"I guess you did. But we're going to try to go there. The other ones took our sister, too."

The woman stood up straight. Ready to take charge. "How do we do that?"

Pelufer sighed. "I don't know yet."

She thought the woman would get upset. She was tight as a wire. She must have wanted her daughter back awfully badly, to jump into a pile of the dead while the bonefolk were working. That would have been a scary thing to do. But Pelufer would have done it to rescue Caille, if she'd thought of it. It was a clever idea. She wished she had thought of it.

The woman just said, "Ah," and went back to examining the forest. Back where she started.

Pelufer opened her mouth to tell her about Lornhollow, then shut it. She turned to Elora, raising her hands to finger some questions at her. They had to decide what to do now, and what to do with this woman, and how much more to tell her.

The bonefolk surrounded them before she could form the first question with her fingers.

They were just there, like another grove appearing inside the grove of trees. Pelufer was lifted off the ground before she could blink, and Elora was lifted away from her. The bonefolk crowded in around the woman, Dabrena n'Arilda, trapping her. She didn't try to run. She stood there as if she could stare them down. She was tiny among them, they were so tall, but she was fearless and determined and Pelufer could see that she was thinking hard.

"They're going to send us back, they don't like us being here, we're not supposed to be here," Pelufer told her.

Elora's hands fluttered at the bonefolk—she and Pelufer weren't harming anyone, let them go—but the bonefolk didn't respond.

"Can they understand me if I talk to them?" Dabrena frowned at Elora's fingers, now pressing into the arm of the boneman who held her—a firmer way of speaking, so he couldn't ignore her.

"I don't think so," Pelufer said. "Not these ones."

"Let them send us then," Dabrena said. "We're in the wrong place anyway, from what you say."

"She might be right," Elora said, giving up on the fingerspeech.

"It might be better if we went back and tried to find some stonefolk—"

Lornhollow pushed his way through the circle, flanked by two other bonefolk. The circle loosened a little, opened up. They were trying not to let Lornhollow come too close to them, and Lornhollow was trying not to go too close to Dabrena. His fingers were working, and the surrounding bonefolk became a semicircle so that they could all see what he was saying. One of them took Dabrena in hand at the same time that they let Elora and Pelufer down to stand in the grass, but they didn't let any of them go.

"That's Lornhollow, our mother's friend," Elora said.

"Our friend," said Pelufer. "But I don't know those other two."

One of the bonefolk who flanked Lornhollow said, "I am Thorngrief, in your naming, and that is Bindlegore. We stay by Lornhollow and learn your noisy speech, to speak and to hear."

"Can the others understand us?" asked Elora.

"Not to speak or hear. But they will understand your hands if you use them."

"I did, they didn't listen," Elora said.

Lornhollow's gestures had continued, and some of the others were gesturing back to him. They looked very animated, for bonefolk.

"What are they saying?" Dabrena asked. "I feel I could almost make it out, but . . ."

"It's too fast, I can't follow it," Pelufer said. "Can you, Elora?"

Elora shook her head, but said, "They're arguing."

"Yes, I gathered that," Dabrena said. Then suddenly she stiffened, and the boneman behind her tightened his grip so much that she swore at him. "I know those signs," she said. "Sweet spirits. Those are Stonetree runes. They're forming Stonetree runes with their *hands*."

"This isn't good," Elora said. She was starting to get the gist of what they were debating. "They want to send us back where we came from, but Lornhollow's upset. He says things are very bad there. He says we'll die if they send us back there."

"There was a battle," Dabrena said. "It *was* very bad. But it's over now."

"Not a battle. Something else . . ." Elora swore, and Pelufer's eyes flew wide. She'd never heard that word from her sister. "I can't make it out. A kind of tearing thing, or a breaking thing."

No, that didn't sound good at all. And the argument wasn't going Lornhollow's way. He was jittering and distressed. The other bonefolk were moving farther away from him, closer to each other, all except for Thorngrief and Bindlegore, who stood by him. Thorngrief had a longer face, and Bindlegore wasn't quite as tall or thin. Given time, she'd learn to tell them apart. But there wasn't going to be time. The boneman lifted her again, cradling her, until she tried to fight free, then holding her hard by the middle. She knew she couldn't hurt him. She'd tried that before, with Caille. She couldn't fight something that didn't feel pain, that couldn't be wounded. Why shouldn't they go home? Why would it be so bad if they went home?

Lornhollow let out a sound, and the other bonefolk recoiled.

The one beside Pelufer started to lift Elora.

Elora didn't fight him. She got a look on her face as if she was staring into another world, the look she got when she did a working, and she walked right through his arms.

A shudder went through all the bonefolk, even Thorngrief and Bindlegore, and then they all went very still.

Elora stood in the middle of the semicircle of bonefolk and said to Lornhollow, "They want us gone. Tell them to send us to the stonefolk's place. Then they'll be shut of us."

"That is not done."

"Why not?"

"It is not done."

Pelufer called, "He didn't say it can't, Elora, he—"

"I know what he said," Elora snapped over her shoulder. "Shut up, Pelufer. This is what I do. Let me do it."

"She's a trader," Pelufer told Dabrena, to get some of her dignity back. "She's a good bargainer. You can't outplay Elora on an even board."

"She's nine-and-five," Dabrena said, unconvinced.

"Nine-and-four," Pelufer said, with a grin despite herself.

"It is not done to move the living through the ways," Elora said to Lornhollow. He was jittering again, not a human movement, more like something a cricket would do. At the same time, he was fingering *Wait, wait* to the other bonefolk. "But you moved Pelufer. It is not done to move the living through the ways. But you would have moved Prendra if she'd been in danger. It is not done to love the living. But you loved our mother. Send us to the stonefolk, Lornhollow. Your folk don't have to know. Tell them you'll get rid of us, but it has to be you, you won't let them touch us, you don't trust them. Obviously they don't trust you, so that shouldn't surprise them too much. You'll be giving them what they want. They want us gone from here. You'll be getting what you want—keeping us safe from whatever's going on at home. Do what is not done. You've done it before. It's the right thing. It's the only thing you can do."

Pelufer's jaw dropped. Elora had grown up a lot more than she'd thought, while she wasn't looking. That was annoying.

Anybody should have caved in to what she'd said. But Lornhollow was still resisting. He was fingering things to Thorngrief, too quick for her to understand. Thorngrief had been in the real world, their world, more recently than Lornhollow. He seemed to have a better idea of what was going on.

Thorngrief said aloud, to keep the other bonefolk from understanding, "We do not know what the others do with the small living ones. Their place may not be safe."

Pelufer glanced at Dabrena, expecting her to react—watching for her reaction to see whether she herself should be upset. If they hurt Caille . . . if they'd done *anything* to her, even scared her . . . But Dabrena wasn't yelling or struggling. Her body had gone to stone. Her face had no expression, but her cheeks were bright red. Pelufer understood: Everything hinged on the decision that Lornhollow made now. They *had* to get to Caille. They'd thought she was as safe there as they were here, but she might not be. They couldn't afford to go back home and fight through whatever was wrong there to find stonefolk they could trick into taking them to her. They had to go there *now*.

Lornhollow had to send them.

Thorngrief said, in his stilted, rattleseed voice, "We would have to go too. One of us ahead and one behind. To guard."

"Two behind," said Bindlegore, just barely understandable.

Agitated, like a leaf on a trembling aspen, like a mantis on a branch, Lornhollow said, "It will seem an attack if woodfolk go there. An intrusion. A terrible breach. It is not done!"

Dabrena said to Elora, with almost as little inflection as the bonefolk's voices had, "It appears the bonefolk split into factions at some point. They remain separate from fear of propriety, not fear of harm. Blind adherence to propriety makes rifts in our own world, too. It would not be an intrusion. It would be a courageous act of offering. He could build a bridge to his brethren. He could be the first one brave enough to reach out. Sometimes that's all it takes, one brave soul. Tell him."

Softly, Elora said, "He heard."

Lornhollow was shy. Lornhollow was not the type to be the one brave soul. They saw the way he ran away from Dabrena at first. Like a striped squirrel, or a ground sparrow, or a dormouse.

Lornhollow's jitters got much, much worse—and then they ceased. He fingered rapidly to the surrounding bonefolk. With a sense of grudging irritation, the others withdrew. Pelufer and Dabrena were released to stumble over to Elora. Pelufer turned and watched the rest of the bonefolk slide into the trees. The impossible sight of it made her eyes hurt. But Elora could do it, too.

She felt she hardly knew her sister anymore, after today.

"I will go first, to shield you," Lornhollow said, and then fingered it, slowly so that they could understand. Thorngrief and Bindlegore would send Pelufer and Elora, then follow.

"What about Dabrena?" Pelufer asked. "Her daughter is there."

"I do not know you," Lornhollow said to the woman, and Pelufer didn't need his fingerspeech to understand everything that "know" conveyed.

There was a long silence. Dabrena said nothing, holding herself tight, as if aware that she could not influence this decision, that any appeal she made would only weaken her position. Pelufer would have ranted and raved. That was interesting, she thought. Sometimes . . . sometimes, if you just waited for people to think it through . . .

"But you spoke wisdom," Lornhollow said at last. "You fear for a child. I fear for a child. We are one."

"Send me first," Dabrena said. "So that the girls can arrive together."

Lornhollow turned his hand palm-up in a gesture that Pelufer read as "All right," and then held his arms out, and took her by the shoulders when she came to stand before him.

It was the most unlikely possible sight, the vibrant living woman giving herself voluntarily into the hands of death. But Pelufer was beginning to think that the bonefolk had a lot more to do with life than with death. She couldn't imagine what terrible thing they could ever have done to deserve sadness and punishment. She'd like to help them, if she could, someday. But it might not be something she could do.

Maybe it would be something Caille could do.

They were going to go get Caille.

Dabrena n'Arilda, her jaw set, as though she wasn't particularly happy about being dissolved into green light again, disappeared in a surge of phosphorescence so strong that Pelufer had to cover her eyes, and even then saw the veins in her own eyelids. When she peeked through her fingers, Lornhollow's head was coming down, his eyes were opening, and if a boneman's face could look awed, then that was how his looked.

"I know her now," he said.

Then he was gone into the trees, maybe down into their roots and from there into the earth and stone. Did he really know how to get to that other place? Should they have tested it first, had someone go and come back?

Too late, too late. Pelufer and her sister walked to the two remaining bonefolk, and passed out of the forest of the dead.

And came onto the plain of the dead, a vast black plain of coal or sand, with hills far in the distance, and so much sky that Pelufer staggered under it, and so much space that there was nothing to hang on to.

Lornhollow wasn't there. Thorngrief and Bindlegore didn't come along behind. They must have come through somewhere else. They weren't familiar with this place, the difference between sending here and coming here. Had they come through at all?

Pelufer clutched at Elora, trying to make sense of the purple light and endlessness. It smelled different here. Like wet stone, and dry stone, and dust, and sand. Age and erosion and endurance, ancient and timewashed. The outline of trees capped the distant hills with a spiky fuzz, but it didn't look like real tree fuzz, it looked more like some metalworker's suggestion of trees. But in that there was something she could hang on to. She was born of a metals town, a child of metalcrafters. Something deep inside her resonated to copper and tin, pewter and bronze, and most of all to the tempered iron of blades. Metals came from stone. Metals were a kind of stone. Her flesh and her spirit responded to this stone and metal place. She'd have her bearings in a breath or two.

She could sense that Elora was entirely out of her element. Elora's spirit resonated to wood. She had been all right in the forest where they'd been, even though it wasn't like any forest in the world they came from. The colors were strange and the trees were strange, but they were trees, they were something she could know if she had time to learn them. Here there was nothing familiar to her. She looked lost and scared . . . and then she didn't, then she went very straight, as if on a surge of relief, as if she'd spotted something that made sense to her and centered her in the midst of the alien infinite. Something she could hang on to.

"Louarn!" Elora cried, and dragged Pelufer forward.

A stream delved the matte-black ground, clear and sparkling and disappearing into nothing where it left the range of sight. Beside it sat Louarn, his knees cradled in his arms, his hands grasping for something held just out of their reach by a stranger.

Pelufer dug her heels in.

She had never, ever seen anyone as not-right as that stranger.

Grunting and slipping on the unnatural ground, Elora hauled her toward them. She called Louarn's name again. The stranger looked up. Her eyes were blue, and beautiful, and utterly malevolent.

Louarn looked up, too. His eyes were exactly the same blue, in a face exactly the same shade of pale, under a tousled shock of exactly the same dark hair.

There was no recognition in his eyes.

The sweet voice had stopped murmuring to him, gentle words of kindness and encouragement, sensible words, wonderful words, describing how all his talents would at last be put to use, how she would help him weave his powers into something indomitable and grand. *Don't stop,* he wanted to say. *Tell me what I am. Tell me what I can be.* He knew what he was. A superficial man. No more than what he had crafted of himself. Inside that he was a lonely wanderer, lost and divided. She would give him purpose. She would mold his ghosts and powers into a unified strength. He had told her everything: the shadows, the dreaming, the haunts, the shining, the crystalline passageway through realms, the three lights. She would know what to do with them. She would take the hard decisions from him. There would be no love, no pain. Love only led to pain. She would free him of all that. She would lead him through the treacherous labyrinth, back into the pure light.

He turned his head, seeking the sound of her voice, but his eyes were filled with starbursts and he could not see. He was lost, he was lost without her, she had abandoned him like all the others, why was he never a good enough boy to keep, to stay with, *what was wrong with him?*

"Mother," he whispered, pleading. "Tell me what to do."

• • •

Dabrena saw the little girls. She saw the woman and the young man. She saw the girls start toward them, the older one dragging the younger one, the younger one resisting.

She looked down at the body lying at her feet in warder's snowy whites. She had arrived here, seen the dead, taken three steps toward them, and there he was. Just as he had been when they met, the wicked boyish face, the soft brown hair. His sailor's hands, his bindsman's hands, still bore their calluses, though the rest of his body was healed of what she knew the Ennead must have done to it. He was wholly and completely himself. The young mage she had been called a vocate with. The warder she had triaded.

"Tolivar," she said. It came out a choked groan, so much guilt and heartbreak that it couldn't all fit through her throat. The whole of this infinite place would not be room enough to contain what she had done to him, her best friend, the father of her child.

A shout drew her attention. The girls were struggling with each other. One of them had cried a name. It was not a name she knew. Let them struggle. She couldn't leave Tolivar. She might not be able to find him again. She had to fetch Kara, show her her father, but she could not leave him. She had left him once, to fetch the baby, as he'd bid her to, and this was what came of it, this body lying here without breath, without spirit. She could not leave him again.

She must. She knew she must. But if she looked at him again, she would be unable to tear herself away. She would stay here by his side through all time, and that eternity of penance would still not atone for her betrayal.

Just one more look. Just one last look, to remember him as he had been, young and beautiful, not the pinched downtrodden gray-skinned man the Holding had made him. One last, sweet look . . .

She started to lower her eyes. Then, in the distance, by the stream, the young man's head turned, and she got an unimpeded view of the woman's face.

Lerissa n'Lessa l'Rigael, illuminator of the weather triad that had cast the first freedom off her. Lerissa Illuminator of the Ennead—the Nine that had destroyed the world she'd known, the light inside her, the future she had strived for . . . and Tolivar.

"Elora, please stop, this isn't right, she isn't right, we didn't come here for Louarn, we didn't come here for this. . . ."

Elora kept hauling on her. Pelufer made herself dead weight, just sank right down into the ground, and she was too heavy for Elora to drag.

Elora flung her arm down and kept going toward Louarn, either to save him from the not-right woman or because he was the only familiar thing on this terrifying plain.

The not-right woman sat back from him. She raised a clear stone she was holding, as though it would defend Louarn against Elora. She didn't know who Elora was, or what Elora was, or what Elora would do, but she didn't want Elora near Louarn. There was something about the clear stone that would stop Elora if she got close enough.

Pelufer scrambled up. She would have to tackle her sister before she got to the clear stone. But the distance was already too much. She would never make it in time.

"Elora, stop, please stop, she's not right, she'll hurt you!"

Elora ignored her. She wanted Louarn. She wanted a grownup, to help them find Caille, to help them navigate the world. Pelufer was always holding her back from going to the grownups, and now she was finally so tired and scared that she wouldn't listen anymore.

The not-right woman smiled, and offered the stone. A pretty trinket to bribe a child.

Dabrena came striding in from the side and caught Elora in her arms. Holding Elora's face against her neck, she looked the not-right woman dead in the eye and said, "I've cleaned up enough of your messes, Illuminator. Let the boy go."

Louarn could see through the starbursts now, in fits and glimpses, and what he saw was through Mellas's eyes: the warder who had called him "that lightless boy" in a voice hard and cold as stone.

Dabrena. Her name was Dabrena, and her cousin was Ilorna, one of the mages he'd led out of the Ennead's chambers, and Dabrena had tried to follow them, calling to her cousin, but she'd gotten lost in the tunnels. Just like him.

He tried to greet her. But the soft voice was telling him to sleep. To dream. He was the only one who had any power in this place. There was no death here, not with metal or stone or hands. But he could dream his razor shadows. They would have power here. They came from a deeper place than this, an older place. A place of primordial darkness.

The place you went when you fell the wrong way into sleep.

Tchatichoch. The word bubbled up unbidden, bursting against the murmuring flow of the sweet, low voice. Danger. There was danger in that voice.

It was a far older, far more powerful word than what the soft voice murmured. It burst into dark song, a melody of caution, a gust of chill air through the mind, to waken, to blast the cobwebs away.

Dabrena saw identity return to the young man's eyes, and knew him. The boy who could dream passageways in mountains. The boy who'd had no light, until he'd slept, and dreamed. The boy who, dreaming, had more power than her whole triad combined.

"Don't you know her?" Dabrena said. "Don't you remember what the Ennead did to you?"

Pelufer came up beside Elora and Dabrena and flung an arm out in front of them, a helpless, involuntary attempt to shield them from whatever Louarn was gearing up to do. He had come abruptly back into his own shape, and it was a shape of so much authority and power that he might do anything, anything at all.

Louarn stared right at the stone the not-right woman was holding.

The stone exploded.

Shards of crystal rained down. They turned into droplets as they fell, but they had been crystal when they burst apart, and most of them had flown at the not-right woman.

They'd torn into her face and eyes and hands. She screamed. The wounds closed up right away, but she'd felt the pain of them. She fell backward, writhing, as if she could still feel the pain. It took a breath to ebb away even though the wounds were gone.

Louarn took two steps, towering over her, then went to his knees and dug his thumbs into her throat.

"No," Pelufer said, "no, don't—" No matter how bad the not-right woman was, killing her would leave a burn mark on Louarn. It would scar him, he shouldn't do that, he shouldn't scar himself like that—

But he couldn't kill her. He choked off her air and must have crushed her windpipe, but she just kept looking up at him, and then she smiled, a smile that said *Go on, have your tantrum, little boy. You cannot harm me.*

This was a realm of the dead. You couldn't kill people here.

Louarn fell back, gasping and trembling, as if the effort of destroying the stone, or the dark killing fury that had gripped him, had been too much. Elora went to him and put her hands on his shoulders, intending to comfort. He shook her off roughly, and she crept back to Pelufer and Dabrena, injured and diminished. Louarn said, "I'm sorry, Elora. I'm sorry. I meant no harm. I am not myself. You must go fetch Caille now. She's here, safe and well, on one of the hills. But you'll have to search for her."

Pelufer looked back toward the distant hills, and all she could see were bonefolk. Rank upon rank of bonefolk coming toward them.

Louarn struggled to regain his composure in the face of this new threat. What looked like nonneds of the pale, tattered folk had descended the hills and were crossing the plain. How long before they were surrounded? Distances were mutable here. The only escape lay through the dead, but the dead seemed farther now, at least a dozen threfts before the first row of bodies, and they could not outrun pursuit in any event.

Lerissa rose and plumped out her silk robes, brushing at nonexistent dust. "There will be no searching, no running, and no rescuing," she said. "My bonefolk will not allow it."

Louarn assessed their progress. The bonefolk could move preternaturally fast. But they were stalking toward them, like herons browsing through dark water, making no effort at haste. Why were they moving so slowly?

As if to prove his point, three bonefolk were abruptly upon them. But they did not rally to Lerissa, though she gave curt beckoning. They came up close beside Elora and Pelufer, and Dabrena, who was between them. Ignoring Lerissa entirely, they turned to confront the inexorable advance of the others.

Pelufer grinned at Lerissa and said, "We have bonefolk too."

Louarn's heart surged with affection for her, irrepressible Pelufer, rebellious and brave and insolent as he had never been. The kind of affection Lerissa's crystal had leached from him, blanking him to everything but the imperatives her insidious murmurs instilled. The distant bells did not sound, warning him against fondness, against attachment. It was not time to go. It was time to stay, and fight.

But the three bonefolk the children had befriended would not be enough to stand against the nonneds who bore down on them.

Dabrena stepped out from between the two girls, leaving them in their bonefolk's care, and confronted Lerissa, who awaited her inhuman minions like a queen from one of the ancient codices awaiting her footmen.

"I commend you, Warder," Lerissa said. "Diverting that last Great Storm was an admirable feat. I embrace this unusual opportunity to thank you for it. My triad was occupied in an attempt to subvert the leading triad's attack on the outer realms, and we failed to fulfill our mandate to protect Eiden Myr. You saved us. We owe you our lives."

Flattery had always been one of the Ennead's great strengths. Finding the thing you were secretly proudest of and stroking you for it. To an observer it would seem absurd to fall for such an obvious tactic. But when it was exerted on you, it tugged at every yearning for approval you had ever had, every close-held pride. You expected confrontation and confronted praise. You expected anger and confronted sympathy. You expected chastisement and confronted admiration, and it disarmed you. Made you grateful. The Ennead had never been powered by their blinding light. The Ennead's great talent had been to warp the human soul.

"Then indeed you owe us your life," Dabrena said, with every ounce of Holding bombast, combined with the feral grin she had learned from Verlein. "One of us shall endeavor to collect at the first opportunity."

Lerissa made a dismissive gesture with a beringed hand. These were empty words, empty parries on a battlefield where no physical wound was fatal.

But the attempt had to be made. "Tell me where my daughter is, and perhaps there will be some clemency."

"Clemency?" Lerissa purred. "They gave me clemency on Khine, and you see what became of that. You don't want to grant me clemency, love."

"Then a quick death rather than the slow flaying you've earned."

"Ah. The threat of pain. They gave me pain on Khine as well, and the results were the same. Have you forgotten that you would have no daughter had my triad not cast the freedom off you? I remember every casting, and every subject. I cast you warder, Wordsmith. Your body loved the freedom. It did not give it up gladly. If we'd left it to you, there would have been no child at all."

The young man said, "All the children are in the hills," as though he'd sensed that she would react to this and was cutting in to subvert Lerissa's influence. Louarn. Elora had cried out for Louarn, though that had not been his name when Dabrena met him. He was some friend to those girls, and he had rendered her fine service in the Holding, though as she recalled she had scorned him. He looked to be some relative of Lerissa's, but his vain attempt to strangle her attenuated suspicions of a blood alliance. "If your daughter is here," he went on, "then she is safe with the others. Lerissa's intent is to control the returning light, not destroy it. Whatever happens here, no harm will come to them."

"The light's not coming back," Dabrena said. "I had a light. Believe me. I know."

"Not yours," he said. Sadly, she thought. "But it shows in the next generation. Any child born after the magewar will show a light if it is in her. Many already do. I've seen it. Each of the stolen children held in those hills made a fragment of magestone glow."

Dabrena glanced at the approaching bonefolk. They were moving slowly over a vast distance, like men walking on foot when they could have flown down a swift river, but there were only heartbeats now before Lerissa took charge by sheer strength of numbers. The revelation about the light's return was staggering, but she must not stagger. She must save the other children. There was no question of that. She must keep them from the Ennead's last pair of hands. But in this moment only Kara mattered. "My daughter was born three moons before the magewar," she said to Louarn.

Before he could answer, Lerissa said, "And you may have her back at any time. I would not incur the enmity of the menders. Indeed, we have the same goals, and I would welcome an alliance. I will require tutors for my girls and boys, and who better than the dedicated, fine minds of the Head holding? Certainly not those stodgy scholars, who can't see past the points of their own quills. Your daughter is in the hills, Warder. Just say the word and I shall reunite you with her, and send you home with my blessing. Only my bonefolk can send you back to your mountain holding. Any other route of return carries untold risks."

So that was it. Lerissa was abducting children in order to hoard the next generation of mages. Imprint them on herself, determine their loyalty from age five, age six, and in a dozen years command them, and take control of Eiden Myr—perhaps the whole world, outer realms and all. Dabrena's menders would be no part of that. They would fight it in any way they could. But she had to get back to them. Whatever had gone wrong in the realm of the living, she could not mend it if it killed her before she could travel up to the Head. Lerissa could send her directly home. Kara could be safe in her own bed within breaths.

It would mean stranding Adaon in the Strong Leg.

She had derailed him from his purpose of finding the Triennead holdings and made a proxy of him. It would mean leaving him to talk Verlein out of attacking her holding, with no idea what had become of her or Kara until a runner could reach him, if runners could even be safely dispatched.

It would mean abandoning him to his fate, alone and without her aid in a world gone awry in ways she could not guess. It would mean abandoning Beadrin the same way, after promising her protection, after all the runner girl had endured in order to reach her in time.

It would mean leaving the captured children here, with no guarantee of being able to liberate them.

But it would see Kara safely home. Once Kara was safe, she could take on the world.

Lerissa had the upper hand. Until Kara was safe, Dabrena was forced to negotiate with her. She had not fared well the last time she had negotiated with the Ennead for Kara's life. But she'd had no choice.

With nonneds of bonefolk descending upon them, under Lerissa's command, it appeared she had no choice now, either.

She opened her mouth.

Before she could speak—and she was never certain what she would have said—she saw that Louarn was was looking past her with surprise in his gaze and a smile beginning to twitch the corners of his mouth. "I think now you'll see why Lerissa would be so gladly rid of your daughter," he said, and pointed.

Dabrena turned.

"That's why they move so slowly," Louarn said, coming up close behind her, speaking only to her, excluding Lerissa entirely.

Because they were keeping pace with two little girls.

One of them looked like a smaller version of Elora and Pelufer.

The other one was Kara.

They were not being herded, like hostages.

They were leading.

Her daughter had come to rescue *her*.

Pelufer took a grim satisfaction in seeing the not-right woman realize that the stonefolk weren't hers anymore.

She was crafty at first, but that wore off fast—talking to bonefolk who didn't want to know was like talking to a stick. So she ordered them and yelled at them and threatened them. She told them that they'd never have their redemption, that they'd be cursed forever to do penance for their terrible crime by cleaning up the dead leavings of human life. For a moment Pelufer hoped that the woman would say what that terrible crime was, because she just couldn't figure out what bonefolk like Lornhollow and Thorngrief and Bindlegore had possibly done to make them feel so guilty. But the woman didn't say what the crime was. She didn't know. She only knew that they thought they had done *something*. Claiming that she could make it right was a ruse.

It just went to show how nasty she was, that she compared the dead to turds someone had to clean up. What the bonefolk did wasn't like that at all. She didn't know why they salvaged the bodies and made them whole, and they didn't know why, either. But it was a lovely thing to do, and a silly thing to insult them for. There wasn't even anything wrong with cleaning up turds. The whole argument was stupid.

Still, she could feel Lornhollow perk up at the making-it-right part. He hadn't known about that. He was tempted. They must have all been very tempted, to go so far as to interfere with the living when they were mostly just very shy of them. And it might be possible to make it right, to make the bonefolk whatever they had been before. If the light was coming back in all the children the stonefolk had stolen, then a lot of things might be possible. The way the traders talked at home, people of light had been able to do just about anything. If people of light came back into the world, people with magelight, then she and Caille and Elora could go on hiding. Nobody needed to know about their shining. Nobody would need their shining. Nobody would try to use them to fix all the troubles in the world.

Pelufer didn't understand why that didn't make her happy.

Watching Lerissa's downfall, Louarn thought: *The children shine. The children shine. The children shine.*

Her bonefolk had ceased to do her bidding. They stood as stony as their own medium as she threatened and beseeched them. She did not stoop so far as to sputter, but the clear light of defeat came into her eyes, followed by cunning calculation.

When she bolted, it was too fast for him to stop her, though he'd sensed it coming. None of the bonefolk moved to retrieve her. She fled out into the limitless coal plain and disappeared from view, perhaps wishing herself away with her dead father, or some dead ancestor even farther off. If he could puzzle out who she would flee to, he could be there in three steps. But he didn't know if he wanted to bother.

"How far can she run?" he asked Caille.

"Forever," she said. "It goes on forever."

"Can they fetch her and send her back to Khine?"

"If they decide they want to," Caille said. "I don't know if they will."

Louarn didn't think he wanted them to. She'd be better off spending eternity here, where she could do no harm. But as long as she was alive she would contrive to do harm, no matter where she went.

This temporary vanquishment would not be sufficient.

He would not try to persuade the bonefolk to return her to the mortal world in such a way that he could kill her. He would not become their manipulator, as she had been his, and theirs.

"You can tell them I don't believe she meant to make good on her promise to them," he said.

"I already told them that," said Kara. Dabrena's daughter, all of six years old, no bigger than Caille although she had over a year on her, with her mother's dark honey hair but brown eyes that must have come from her father. "She lied a lot." The sight of her mother had deflated her, and though she'd embraced her with relief, it was also with a discomfort that bespoke more than the embarrassment of greeting a parent in front of one's peers. She seemed eager to boast of her achievements, to tell her mother all about her escape, her raids, her adventure—and yet she ducked her head as if in expectation of a blow, as if her mother might blame her for her own abduction.

"Not everything she said was a lie," Louarn told them. This was between Lerissa and the folk she had tried to swindle, now, and they had the right to know everything he could tell them. "And if she'd decided to keep her bargain, she might even have found a way, with enough mages."

He glanced at Caille before he could stop himself, and he saw her understand that he was wondering what magecraft combined with her own power might be capable of, though he said nothing.

"I told Kara about me," Caille said. "She's my friend."

"She'll have to show me, back home," Kara said. "I don't know if I believe her, either, but she's my friend too and it's all right if she fibbed about that. She said she could talk to the bonefolk and tell me what they were saying back, and that was true."

That was how these youngest girls had convinced the bonefolk that what they were doing was wrong. They had already known it was wrong. They had already been unhappy about it. They had already been aiding Kara's rebellion where they could. But when Caille came and opened communication in both directions, they could no longer see the children as objects, or as livestock to herd as the sheepherd bid them. The children became real to them, as the bonefolk were becoming real now to Louarn and Dabrena and the older girls. That reality was stronger for them than Lerissa's suspect promises, no matter how badly they longed for those promises to be the truth.

They had sent the stolen children home. Lerissa had two human henchmen; they'd sent them back where they came from, but Louarn could not extract an adequate description of where that was. Caille and Kara had stayed, Caille determined to rescue Louarn. The only remaining task, it seemed to him, was for the bonefolk to send these humans back to Eiden's realm. He could return through his dreams, and he must do so as soon as possible. Worilke was there, somewhere. Ordering the death of mages from some insane, deluded, flawed assumption about the light's return. This sojourn had delayed him. He must finish what had begun when he left Croy Brickman's house in Dindry Leng.

But the bonefolk still surrounded them. They stood unmoving, as though waiting, or as though great thoughts were passing through them or among them, invisible to human view. For a moment Louarn wondered whether it had something to do with him. He had passed through this place before. Did they remember him? Did they remember his pleas for love, his pleas to stay?

But it had nothing to do with him at all. Part of him, the practical man, was relieved. Another part of him, the lost boy who was no longer Mellas but had not yet crafted himself into Louarn, felt a rush of loneliness and hurt, as though they'd turned him away all over again.

Pelufer tugged on the tatters that clothed the boneman next to her, and inclined her head toward the others. He shuddered up and down the length of his long body, and then he took a step forward, flanked by the other two who had stood with Pelufer and Elora.

The bonefolk began to fingerspeak to each other.

"Do you understand them?" Dabrena asked Louarn. The way he watched them suggested that he did, though their signing went too fast for even the girls to follow, and they were all signing at once, as if they could all read the gestures of every one of them concurrently, with a field awareness no human would have had.

Louarn nodded. "More or less. They are trying to . . . make peace? Mend a rift? I cannot define it. The ones nearest us do not belong here. Their arrival was . . . a great shock. They're trying to sort out the ramifications."

Dabrena nodded. "That sounds about right." She told him the names of the forest bonefolk, and what she'd gathered of their history with the girls, and as they spoke they moved half-consciously away from the children and the bonefolk, to keep their conversation off to the side of the momentous event unfolding. "Do you realize that what they are signing with their fingers are the runes of Stonetree?"

"Stonetree?" Louarn said.

Dabrena smiled, bemused to realize that for all his apparent talents and his Holding history, he did not know scribing. How in the world were they ever going to get people to learn to scribe, or even to read? Was she mistaken to assume that they needed to? "The runes the Ennead used as their own, though they learned them from a codex. The runes they carved along their casting tables, though in upright rows, which was not their intended rendering. The runes carved along the edges of the Memory Stones in the Heel. We know that they were designed to be carved in stone or wood, we know that each rune represents both a tree and the first sound of that tree's name in an ancient tongue, we know what those names were in that tongue . . . but we never knew whose tongue it was."

"Perhaps it was the bonefolk's, once."

"Yes. That is what I was wondering. And if that is the case, it gives an interesting interpretation to a seekers' conjecture that Stonetree was the scribing system of the indigenous race of Eiden Myr, predating the mages' exile. It was not a system the mages brought with them from the outer realms. It was translated by someone long ago into scribing we understand, glyph for glyph, but without explanation, probably as a learning tool."

"Then someone made contact with the bonefolk in some prior age," Louarn said, "perhaps the way the girls' mother did. And perhaps the bonefolk are that indigenous race."

He said it as though he already knew that they were.

"I would like to speak more of this with you, in more relaxed circumstances," she said. "And introduce you to . . . my intended pledge, who would find this more than interesting." She paused, and then said, "Do you remember me?"

"You were a warder," he said. "I remember. I heard you calling, through the tunnels. But they branched. Your cousin wanted to go back for you, but the other mages knew they must forge onward."

She nodded. She had thought as much. His tunnels had led her back into the Holding. Back to her infant daughter, though she could not thank him for that, for they had also led to her betrayal of Tolivar. If she had not gone back, those children would have been rescued anyway, her daughter would have come back to her anyway, but the other infant—the one she believed was her friend Dontra's baby, fostered out—would have lived.

"You're remembering," he said. His voice was gentle, and filled with an unspeakable sadness. "I'm sorry. I know what that is like."

She wanted to laugh at the same time her heart was breaking. He was charming and breathlessly handsome, this young man, the kind of pretty boy she'd once have gleefully bedded and then thought no more of, the kind of pretty boy who'd think he was wrapping her around his little finger and never know that she was only permitting herself to be charmed. The boy she remembered from the Holding had been nine-and-six, still struggling toward manhood, a haunted child who could barely speak. The difference between that boy and this young man made the gulf of years real to her as it had not been before. Before today, the past had been frozen in her memory, the way the bodies of the dead were frozen here—perfect, unchanging, unchangeable. She had relived those first steps to follow that haunted boy again and again, her journey through the labyrinth his mind had dreamed, her desperate journey to retrieve her infant daughter and its disastrous completion. Each time, she had returned to that same haunted boy, that same labyrinth of magestone tunnels, and started the journey again, and they never changed. But here he stood, six years older, changed past all imagining.

The words came out like a hard hot flow of tears into a dark basin. "Tolivar and I came down to the Ennead's torture chambers to aid the illuminator who came to rescue you, who'd been a vocate with us. We did so at the request of your master, Bron, the stableman, because she'd told him we were two warders who could be trusted. We left our baby daughter with his fosterlings in some stewards' care. But in our absence the Ennead captured those fosterlings, and our baby with them. Unknowing, I went back to retrieve her, while Tolivar stayed with the illuminator and Bron to fight. We agreed upon a meeting place. I found the fosterlings, all right, and I found Kara. And the Ennead had me. They wanted the illuminator. I would not tell them where to find her. So they took Kara from me, and held a blade to her. Still I would not tell them. I didn't believe that even they would kill a child. So they took an infant of the same age from among the fosterlings, and . . ." She could not say it.

"And they killed her," Louarn supplied. "Her body is here. I have seen her. She was a sweet-tempered child. I was fond of her. It grieved me deeply when I learned her fate."

"And they killed her," Dabrena said, because it was not enough for him to say it. "They killed her in order to get the information they wanted from me. I should have just given it to them. I was a warder, I was an Ennead proxy, it was my job. Tolivar could fend for himself. Tolivar was a grown man, responsible for himself. That infant was at their mercy . . . but I could have saved her . . . I betrayed him anyway. . . ."

His hands on her upper arms were a shock. He had not seemed the kind of man who would touch you, grasp you tight that way and say to you, "*The Ennead killed that child, Dabrena.*"

"I could have stopped them. I could have given them what they wanted before they killed her."

"It happened too quickly. I knew them, Dabrena, I knew their methods, I was one of their victims too. They had killed that child before you could blink, to shock you into submission. You could not have saved her from them. There were nonneds we could not save from them, none of us. They were a great evil, and great evil does harm, and we cannot blame ourselves for the harm it does."

Her eyes were locked with his, and she saw him blink, saw him listen to his own words, and knew that he blamed himself for as much as she blamed herself for—perhaps more. But it was not enough. His sins were not her sins. His sins could be reconciled, whatever they were. Hers could not. She would not permit it. They were too grave.

She shook free and finished her tale, spitting the words out now: "I told them where the illuminator would be. Tolivar was with her. They captured them, and tortured them, and Tolivar died, horribly, in the depths of a rock he came to seeking light and love and power. He was a sailor, and he drowned in stone. And not two days later came a rescue party, to liberate those fosterlings, and Kara, and me. If I had not gone there, they would all have been saved."

"If the rescuers had come sooner, they would all have been saved, and you as well, and your friends," Louarn said. "If you had not entrusted your child to stewards in order to save a friend, she would never have been there at all, and your friend would have died—and myself as well, as it happens, and possibly everyone in the outer realms. If you had not heeded the vocate call and gone to the Holding, your Tolivar might have lived. If I had not distracted my parents before a critical casting, they might have lived. If Lerissa had not given me up, if Bron had not fostered me to them, they might have lived. I was a child, it was not my choice to make, yet I will never forgive myself their deaths, even though it was the Ennead that killed them. If I had run away, just ridden away into the Heartlands and prenticed myself to some kindly farmer when I was Pelufer's age, I would not have delivered countless vocates into the Ennead's hands. Still they would have heard the call, and heeded it, and gone. Yet I will never forgive my own complicity in delivering them, even though it was the Ennead that killed them. You be stronger than that, mender. You go find your Tolivar, and kneel by him and praise his sacrifice and accept his forgiveness. You do that for your daughter's sake."

"You don't understand," she said, an old habit—what felt, now, like the oldest habit of all.

"Ah," he said softly. "But I do. If you've listened, you know I do."

"Mother!" The sweetest sound in the world, the sound of that voice, calling her, wanting her.

Kara, running over to tell her about the amazing reconciliation between the woodfolk and the stonefolk. Dabrena listened, awash in amazement—amazement that her daughter would return to her, safe and whole and eager to share what she had experienced while they were apart. She had only to let go. All the harm she had ever done was in trying to hold this astonishing, brave child still.

Then Kara grew hesitant. "Father's here," she said.

"Yes," Dabrena said, and smiled at her.

Heartened, as she always was when her mother didn't burst a seam, Kara said, "I look like him!"

Dabrena's smile grew wider despite herself. It might take some time for Kara to unlearn that expectation of burst seams, but there was hope. "I know," she said.

"Do you want to see him?"

"I already did. But we can go together, if you like. To see him one more time before we decide about leaving here."

Kara nodded, and led her off by the hand. She did not look back at Louarn. She would make no promises.

"But you *have* to!" Pelufer cried, and looked to Louarn for help. Lornhollow was being impossible.

All but three of the stonefolk had gone. There were dead waiting in what they called Eiden's realm, there was a job to do, and it *was* frightening that so many left to do it, because that meant there were a lot of dead, and she wished she knew how they knew, and she wished she knew exactly what was going on at home, but whatever it was, it wasn't fair to keep them here because of it. Louarn would be able to convince him. Louarn could talk with his hands. Lornhollow would have to respect that, if nothing else.

Lornhollow was fingering that he didn't have to do anything, and that he had promised their mother to watch over them.

"You can't keep us here against our will," Elora said. "That's the same as what the stonefolk did, and they just agreed how wrong that was."

Pelufer nodded vigorously. Trust Elora to solder a seamless argument. But Lornhollow said it was not the same thing at all, that protecting them was quite different from holding them for use by another, and that everything in Eiden's realm had changed, and they must wait to see what happened before they could go safely back.

Louarn caught the last bit of it as he came near, and he fingered something to Lornhollow, and Lornhollow fingered back in surprise, and then the stonefolk and the woodfolk and Louarn were all fingering too fast for her to follow, and she was ready to scream.

"Be quiet and let them talk," Elora said.

"Let the grownups make all the decisions," Pelufer said. "That's always what you want to do."

"Not always. But sometimes. And this is too big for us."

"It is not!"

"It is too and you know it."

The fingers stopped, and Louarn turned to them, but then he said, "Hold a moment," and they had to wait for Dabrena and Kara to come back from whoever's body they went to visit. Caille said Kara had grown up in a stone place and had never been anywhere but there and here. Pelufer had trouble imagining that, even though, until they went to Gir Nuorin and then down to the battlefield, she had only been outside of Gir Doegre a few times in summer to go swim in the maur, and that was when they had Padda *and* Mamma, so it was a long time ago. Until they went to Gir Nuorin, Caille had never left Gir Doegre, so Kara's story sounded reasonable, even though Gir Doegre was a town and Kara's home was inside a mountain. They had become good friends, much better friends than Caille and Lusonel the innkeepers' daughter. Pelufer wondered if that was because Lusonel wasn't as smart as Caille, and Kara was, or if it was because Caille had to be careful to keep their secret from Lusonel, and with Kara she could just be herself. It was complicated, having to wonder things about Caille. It used to be that all she wondered about was whether she was warm enough and had enough to eat and didn't have too many holes in her clothes.

Dabrena and Kara joined them, and Dabrena and Louarn shared some kind of a look, and Pelufer thought that if Risalyn and Yuralon were here, or maybe if they were all back in Gir Doegre with Nolfi and Jiondor's family, this would be like a happy ending in a teller's tale. The light would come back, and their shining would be safe, and they could all just go back to being traders and crafters and healers, and as long as there was an honest day's work to be done, it might almost be a little bit like how things were before, when you could go to the maur and play in the sand and the surf and there'd be someone there, someone you knew and trusted, someone besides just yourselves.

Again she felt that strange discontented yearning, and now it was herself she was wondering about, why she couldn't just be happy about happy endings, and that was a lot more complicated than wondering about Caille.

"Lornhollow feels that it is too dangerous to send the girls home," Louarn said. "He loved their mother and feels protective toward them, perhaps to a fault, given the powers he bequeathed them. Elora had . . . the ways, they call it . . . the means to passage herself home, but only in the woodfolk's realm. Here she requires the bonefolk. Thorngrief and Bindlegore stand by whatever decision Lornhollow makes. These three stonefolk, whose names are . . ." He struggled. He didn't have the words to translate their finger names into word names. Lornhollow had to supply them. "Irongrim and Slatespike and Writhenrue are willing to send Dabrena and Kara back to their home in the Head holding, but they will not defy Lornhollow's wishes this soon after the beginnings of a renewed relationship between their folk." He smiled. "None of them have promised *never* to defy each other's wishes or oppose each other's goals, a straightforwardness I admit I find appealing."

"Louarn!" Pelufer cried. "We have to go home! Nolfi's back there, and Risalyn and Yuralon and Jiondor and Beronwy and—"

He held up a hand. "You need not list them all. I know what is at stake. Dabrena has folk back there too, and even if we knew no one in all of Eiden Myr, their lives would be just as important. Hear me out. The Head holding may be the only safe haven in Eiden's realm right now. Lornhollow will not oppose the stonefolk sending you and your sisters there. But—I said hear me out, Pelufer—he and I are both aware that you will reject that option out of hand, and so this is why you must *be quiet and listen* while I tell you: The people you care for may already be dead. There may be nothing any of us can do, not even Caille, and—not even me. If we go back there, we may all die, and die in vain. In fact, it seems rather likely from what the bonefolk have told me that dying is exactly what we'll do. Wouldn't you rather live, and wait out the cataclysm, and go back whole and able to heal the damage?"

Pelufer stared at Elora for a long time, and Elora stared back.

Dabrena said, "Send my daughter to the holding."

Kara said, "No! I'm staying with you!"

Dabrena looked as though she wanted to cry.

Lornhollow said, "Your mother gave you her ways that you might live strong in a hard world."

Thorngrief said, "Let what must be, pass through. Or we will return you only to follow and fetch your bodies."

Pelufer looked at Caille. Caille's head came up, defiant. If they tried to send her to the safe mountain, nobody would be able to hear for a nineday. Pelufer knelt down so that she was eye-to-eye with

Caille, and said, "But wouldn't it be better to be sure you'd be alive to fix it?"

"I *can* fix it," Caille said, and folded her arms over her chest, and would say no more.

Elora said to Louarn, "They will send us back, won't they. If that's what we decide."

"Yes," Louarn said. "They feel they've meddled too much in the affairs of the living, and not enough. Your lives are your own, to do with as you choose. You belong where you choose to be. They will do whatever you ask of them."

"Where is it worst?" Dabrena said, as if she already knew. Pelufer already knew—it was worst in the Strong Leg, where the battle was. Caille was right. Eiden hadn't liked that battle. He'd already been sick, and angry, and he hadn't liked that battle at all.

"Where we came from," Louarn said. "All of us but Kara."

"I think we stay together now," Dabrena said. She meant all of them, and everyone knew that, and no one said otherwise.

Pelufer nodded at Elora, and Elora said, "Then we go back."

They were going home.

Gir Doegre

The wind smashed them flat. Rain came down like rocks pouring from an upended bucket. The roar was deafening.

Pelufer's face ground against roots and rocks. A stick gouged a furrow from the corner of her eye back to her ear. An instant reminder that this was the real world. Wounds did not heal here as they were made. She went to push herself up against the deluge, and pain shot up her arm. She'd put a hand out at the last moment to break her fall, and probably sprained the wrist.

If the wind was this bad here, in the shelter of the spirit wood, what was it like down the hill? Or outside of Gir Doegre, where there wasn't any shelter of hills?

She turned on her side and groped for Elora through the dark. The hill underneath her hip and shoulder trembled as Elora's hands fumbled to grasp hers. She was shouting something. Pelufer couldn't make it out. Pelufer held her palm up flat and pressed Elora's fingers against it. Elora signed that they had to keep the others from hurting themselves when they passed through.

Pelufer didn't see how, but then Louarn was there, stumbling and going to his knees on her other side, and Caille, who had tucked up into a ball, was between her and Elora. They put their arms around Caille and dragged her through the pointy, muddy bracken, out of the way of where Dabrena and Kara would fall. Pelufer was starting to be able to see a little. She made out the blur of Louarn crawling on all fours the other way, to try to catch them.

He caught Kara, but Dabrena fell hard. Pelufer thought she heard a cry of pain, but it could have been the wind. It was a horrible wind, shrieking, keening, a moan of anguish and loss and rage. It was Eiden, wailing his agonies. It was Sylfonwy, singing his death, and Morlyrien crying it.

Lornhollow had gone first. Why hadn't he reached for them when they fell? She twisted around, raised her injured arm to shield her eyes from the blinding downpour. Lornhollow was there—easing to the ground a brittle bonewood tree that had ripped free at the roots and would have crushed them where they'd fallen. Elora poked her, and she saw the pale runny blurs of Thorngrief and Bindlegore emerging from yew and bonewood. They were so tall, so spindly-thin, the wind should have lifted them and flung them away, but it seemed to pass over them as over a blade, or their bodies were shaped in a way that cut through it, or they just weren't entirely *here*—enough of them was always in their own realm to keep this one from harming them.

Inside the pounding rain and the thunder and the rumbling in the earth, Pelufer felt the brush of names. She'd already said them all once, they shouldn't have come again, but they did, breaking like soft bubbles in the safe cavern of her mind. It hadn't been like that before. She could tell differences in them now—some fresh and strong and redolent, some older and burnished with a patina of age, and many more, so many more of them, ancient and fragile, like flaked gilt, as whispery as dry leaves.

That wasn't the only difference, in these first gasping breaths of their return from the bonefolk's realm.

Dabrena and Kara were shining.

It was only a little bit, just the dimmest shine, like sunset reflected in dull tin, but it was there. Brighter in Kara, because it was always bright in children, although she was just getting to the age where it would start to disappear. It must have always been there. Everyone had *some* shine. But either it got stronger because of the bonefolk, or Pelufer was stronger and so she could see it now.

She thought no more about it, just accepted the gift. In the dark of storm, she'd be able to see their shine even if she couldn't make out their forms.

Lornhollow and Bindlegore helped them move back toward the relative shelter of the trees. Thorngrief stumbled over something, went to lift it, then changed his mind and left it where it was. The bonefolk weren't luminous here the way they were in their own realm, but their pale flesh was visible in the sheeting dark. Their tatters hung down, soaking wet. The rain did touch them. They were much stronger than their bony frames looked.

Three bonefolk, and the six of them.

But only one Caille. She had said she could fix this. But she had not known how bad it was. She had said Pelufer could fix the battle, too, but she couldn't, not before she would have been killed. Caille was only five years old. She was only a little girl.

They should go home. They should go down the hill before all these trees fell on their heads, and get to Nolfi, and Jiondor, and make sure they were all right.

Lornhollow crouched down in front of them like a wading bird in a watery world. He signed that this was a place of power. He signed that this was where they got the ways.

What was she supposed to do with *that*?

The ground shook again, harder, trying to buck them off. They clung together, and Louarn's hands moved over them, making sure each of them was linked to the others. They heard a tree go down back in the plain woods, a long tearing wet crash through sodden dying leaves and branches. It sounded like a tall tree, one of the stonewoods probably, they were shallow-rooted, and it took some smaller ones with it.

Again Lornhollow pressed them back, and back, and Pelufer felt wood enclose her. There was shelter from the rain, here inside a hollowed trunk. It was one of the massive, ancient yews. She hadn't noticed that any of them were hollow. She should have looked for hiding places like this. The tree must be twice nine threfts around, and all its heartwood gone, leaving a gnarled cavern where six could just huddle if they jammed close. She felt Elora relax, drugged and slowed by the surrounding wood. To find out if she could be heard, to wake her sister up, she said, "How old is this tree, Elora?," and her words echoed dully back, audible within the storm.

Elora leaned her temple against the twisting wood, and said, "As old as this hill. I don't know how old that is. Ages."

Lightning flashed, illuminating the bonefolk outside in glaring white, their eyes black hollows like the inside of this tree. She could feel everyone jump as a tree exploded, cracking, shrieking as its blasted trunk split and the parts of it tore away from each other. That had been close. Had it been a tree like this? The stonewoods and ironwoods were taller, they'd draw the lightning, wouldn't they? And the bonewoods in among the old yews and the hazel understory?

The ground wrenched again, and they felt the deep complaint of the yew's roots. The wind gusted so severely that Lornhollow and Bindlegore swayed. Another glaring flicker of lightning was accompanied by a crack of thunder so loud it seemed the sky must have shattered, and the ground rumbled reply, and the rain whipped across the bonefolk with renewed fury, sheeting sidewise along the gusts, spitting hailstones.

It was getting worse.

"We didn't come here to hide," Louarn said. "We had a place to hide."

"*Can* you fix this?" Pelufer asked Caille. Though Pelufer and Elora were pressed close against her, she was shaking with cold, soaked to the skin. Pelufer felt Kara's arms go around Caille from behind. Dabrena and Louarn were in back of her and to either side, jammed in at an angle. Pelufer felt Dabrena's hand on her shoulder, squeezing tight, and in the next blaze of lightning she saw Louarn's hand on Elora's neck. They were all connected now, to each other, to the tree, to the earth. They all had a shine, bright or dim. The bonefolk were arraying themselves around the tree, laying hands on it, maybe even merging with it. Whatever they were going to do, they had to do it now.

"Eiden hurts," Caille said, doubtful and plaintive. She had been so determined before. But they'd never let her use her powers before, not really, not to their utmost. And they had forgotten that Caille felt pain through touch. They had all completely forgotten that Caille felt pain as if it was her own.

Pelufer turned her head toward the ruddy woody shine that was Elora. "Maybe we should just try to go home," she said.

"No!" Caille cried. Kara said something encouraging to her, right in her ear, that Pelufer couldn't hear, and Pelufer felt the queerest rush of jealousy, that someone else could talk to Caille the way they did, and exclude them. Caille nodded. "It hurts," she said. "Eiden hurts. I want to fix him. But I'm scared."

"We'll help you," said Louarn. "We're here. Draw on us, if you can."

Caille nodded. Pelufer couldn't tell if she was responding to the rich assurance in Louarn's voice, or if she really could draw on their shining somehow if her own wasn't enough.

Whatever she'd heard in what Kara and Louarn said to her, Caille's shine began to swell.

First Pelufer felt a healing go through them. The cut by her eye sealed up and the throbbing in her wrist eased. She was going to tell Caille to stop, not to waste herself on that, but Dabrena had been in a lot of pain, and Caille wouldn't be able to work through pain like that. Dabrena gasped as her bones knit back as they were meant to be—she hadn't really known what Caille could do, but now she did.

Caille's shine got brighter. A shine didn't really cast light, their hollow was just as dark, but the shine expanded until it was as if all six of them were shining bright, all blended, like the rivulets of heat in a banked hearth, or the glowing tip of an iron bar drawn from the forge fire and laid on an anvil—like a mist of molten copper, like the color of a burning heart.

And then Pelufer wasn't looking out at the drenched, pummeled, lightning-slashed spirit wood anymore. She was beyond it, and above it, and inside it flowing outward. Into the world. She knew it, every tortured fingerspan of it. The entirety of Eiden Myr. The sea crashing at its edges, the tides sucking out, the massive waves forming offshore, rearing up to swoop in and smash down on the coasts. Gales tearing up trees, tearing up houses, whirlwinds spinning wagons and sheds, flinging cattle and people to their deaths. Fissures opening in the earth, swallowing cottages. Earthquakes everywhere, Eiden's limbs writhing in agony, thrashing in rage. Like ripples through his muscles. As if he was trying to tear himself right up out of the sea. This was like the way Louarn was when she gave Flin and Mellas back to him, when his body tried to rip itself apart. Seizures and paroxysms. Swollen rivers flooding their banks, sweeping everything away. Sheeting, slicing, stinging rain. Hailstones bigger than fists. Blizzards in the summer Highlands, two threfts of water in the Girdle. All the Belt flooded, all the loughs trying to connect up into one river from the Highlands to the Dreaming Sea. Gold and iron boiling in the veins of the Blooded Mountains. Magestone sloshing like silver freezing slush in the veins of the Black Mountains. Great pieces of the chalk Oriels crumbling into avalanches on the towns below, bowling down those fleeing up the mountainsides from the river bursting its banks. Ships stove to flinders on rocky coasts, coracles sucked out to sea like leaves. The swamps burning with Galandra's fire, burning themselves up, exploding. Furnaces bursting in the Weak Leg. The Fingers cramping, the Head throbbing, the Shoulders hunching, the Fist clenching, the Neck spasming, the Heartlands seizing, the Legs shaking, and the worst of it here, because of all that bladed death.

And in the Fist. Why in the Fist? It was terrible there, trees and fences toppled, chasms splitting the gentle downs, houses collapsed in on themselves, livestock drowned or crushed or tangled in a terror in thorny brush or broken fencing, and all the wildlife scattering, birds grounded by the winds, moles and rabbits drowned in their holes, hives smashed, rats swimming for their lives . . . The Fist was where it twisted, the Fist was where the land and sea and air had been twisted, and then the twisting was broken, and it untwisted like a taut string snapping back, and everything was wrong after that, unbalanced, with no one to right it, and the flexion kept twisting and twisting until it came to this.

From Fist to Head and Highlands and Lowlands and Legs, Eiden's body was racked with agony. Air and water raked across it in swirls and whirlwinds and blizzards, snowstorms and rainstorms and windstorms, and those bashed against each other, towering battles in the sky, while the sea reared up around the whole twisted shape of Eiden, poised to strike it.

Caille's tiny body had gone taut as that string before it snapped. *Stop!* Pelufer tried to cry. *Oh, stop, stop, it will break you!* But she could not control her own body. She was more than her own body. She was part of all the flesh around her, and the wood, and the ground beneath them, and the air around them, all the elements linked, all the elements combined.

And then *she* felt what her sister could do.

It was only a blink since she'd healed them. Pelufer, and then Dabrena, and any cuts and bruises and welts on the rest, any broken bones or skin. That blink had encompassed all of Eiden Myr. Now it was the next blink, and in that blink Caille's power was unleashed.

It flowed out the way Pelufer's senses had flowed out, and took her with it.

The pain was eased. The deep structures of stone were realigned and set right, the quakes smoothed quiet, the fissures sealed. Eiden's muscles unclenched, his limbs relaxed, his head sank bank. As the agony subsided, the winds lost their breath and their power and died away. The air settled, warmth flowing where it was supposed to, cold flowing where it was supposed to, breezes and currents carrying heat and chill where they were meant to go. The sea's great waves collapsed in on themselves in the absence of the fury that had fueled them; the sea rocked, lapping over the shores in long tongues, then found its level again, caught the rhythm of its ordinary waves, its ordinary tide. The earth set about absorbing and distributing the water that had drenched it; the rivers carried their swift swollen burdens to the sea, and emptied them there, and eased back in their courses.

Eiden sighed, and settled into his ocean cradle, calm.

Wreckage was everywhere. Devastation was everywhere. Drowned and broken animals and people. Shattered structures, flooded fields and pastures, tumbled stones, swaths of felled splintered trees. But the injuries began to mend. Where there was life, healing followed. Fractures knitted. Punctures and gashes closed. Contusions, abrasions, lacerations . . .

It was too much. The mortal wounds were healed, but the smaller ones, the strains and wrenches, the bumps and bruises, those would heal themselves, she had to stop now, it was enough, it was too much, next she'd be healing the illnesses they already had, the fevers, the disease, it was too much, it would hurt her—

"Stop," Pelufer croaked, finding her throat again, her lungs. "Caille, stop." It was not a plea. It was an order. Caille did what she was told when it was important. Pelufer found her legs and her arms and her eyes and turned them to Caille, to gather her up, embrace her in the sunshine that was streaming down between fluffy white clouds in a blue sky, hold her close and tell her she was a good girl, the best girl in the world, Mamma's girl, Mamma's best, tell her how much they loved her and how proud they were and how they'd never let it come to this again, they'd never let this happen again, she never ever had to use her powers again if she didn't want to, she could just be an ordinary happy baby girl and they would grow up together like a proper family and swim in the maur and pet dogs and donkeys and eat berrybread until they couldn't move—

Caille came into her arms limp and lifeless. Her little pudgy face was slack, pale as a corpse. Her eyes were rolled back in her head. Her tongue hung out. Her head lolled.

Her shine was gone.

"No," Pelufer said. She heard Elora's outcry as across a vast distance. She felt one of the grownups trying to pry Caille from her arms. She wouldn't let go. "No, Caille," she said, kissing the little face, kissing it all over the way she did when Caille was toddling because it always made her squirm and giggle. "I promised Mamma. Mamma will kill me. Don't die, Caille. Don't be dead! I promised Mamma! I love you! *Don't go!*"

Deep in the cavern of her mind, she heard the whisper of Caille's name.

GIR DOEGRE

Dabrena wrenched the grieving child off her sister. The bonefolk took hold of her. She was maddened, raving, uncontrollable.

In the way.

The older sister tried to block Dabrena. Dabrena caught her wrists in a vise grip and gave her one sharp jerk—snapping her neck straight, snapping her to attention. "I am a mender," she said, staring the girl down hard. "Move away."

The girl obeyed, lurching off on her knees, in shock.

Dabrena was in shock, too. What this little child had done, what she had sensed this little child do, was staggering.

She was a mender. She would not stagger.

Let her go, some part of her mind said as she cleared the child's throat, pressed her tongue back into place, positioned her head. *That was the triumph of a lifetime. She gave her all. Let her go.*

She drew in the breath she would have used to say no, and bent to pass it through the child's lips into her lungs.

Do not treat her body so. Her spirit fled. Let it go peacefully. Its job is done.

"No," she said, and worked the still heart, and passed breath again into the lungs. She would breathe for her, until she remembered breath. She would work her chest until her heart remembered to beat. This was menders' work. No light, no shining. A practical remedy.

The child remained still. No breath, no pulse. Pale as death. Kara watched frozen from the back of the tree hollow, amazement draining into despair. She was giving up.

Dabrena would not give up.

"Wake up, Caille," she said, with the flat, no-nonsense insistence of a parent's demand. She slapped one cheek, then the other. "Caille, wake up!"

"She's not going to wake up," Kara said. The way you said a thing you feared, not a thing you were certain of. "Neither of them is going to wake up."

Louarn lay slumped beside Kara at the back of the hollow. His chest rose and fell. He was alive.

Dabrena passed breath to the child, then worked the chest and said, "She will wake up. She must. There was too much life in her."

"She gave it all away." Tears spilled over onto Kara's cheeks.

Dabrena passed breath, worked the chest, and said, "She didn't. She couldn't. It's like love. You can never give it all away." She passed breath, and said, "Wake him up, if you like. He can help me."

"No!" Elora cried. Lornhollow caught her in his arms to stop her interfering, but he said, "Do not wake him. He is helping you now."

Dabrena shook her head. She had no idea what that meant. She passed breath to the child. She worked the chest. Life would come. Life would return. Life had not gone. The body had only been shocked quiet, breath and heartbeat suspended. "Wake up, Caille," she said, in the tone of the last warning. "Wake up!"

Caille and Louarn woke gasping, flailing out with their arms, as though they had been falling, as though they had been in the same precarious place and were dropped abruptly back here, or back into their bodies, and still felt the fall, still felt they had to grab themselves back from the abyss.

Dabrena sat hard on her rear, stunned.

"Mama?" Kara said, moving into her arms as Caille's sisters ran to her, as Caille's face flooded red and she let out a piercing wail—as the bonefolk, who had steeled themselves to passage her body, sagged with the release of tension.

Dabrena held her daughter and said, "Yes, sweet?"

"If I'm ever hanging by my fingernails from a very high place, it's you I'd like to rescue me."

Dabrena let out a bark of laughter as tears sprang from her own eyes. "Well, I left you, and I lost you. It was my worst nightmare. But we do seem to have lived through it, don't we?"

Pelufer suddenly stumbled off three paces, went to her knees, and retched.

Motioning for Elora to stay by Caille, Louarn went to steady her, and wiped her mouth when she was through. "You had a scare," he said. "But she's all right, Pelufer."

"It's not that," Pelufer rasped. "Not just that. It's . . . I can't . . ." She closed her eyes, swallowed, and took a deep breath. "It's the haunts. So many haunts. They're all different. Some are new and some are old. They're not . . . just *names*, anymore." She winced, and pressed the heels of her hands against her temples. "I was so worried about Caille I guess I ignored them. That's good, right?" She appealed to Louarn as to a master who had helped her learn to control a talent she didn't understand. "That means that I'll be able to ignore them on purpose."

"Yes," he said. "You learned to make the cavern in your mind to put the names in. We'll find a way for you to learn to live with this."

He seemed to be holding himself back—from voicing curiosity about this newly blossoming, or newly expanded, talent? Dabrena was certainly keen to know more. But it was Elora who said, "What *is* it?"

Pelufer swallowed again, and blinked several times, hard. "They're talking to me. They're speaking, Elora. I can hear them."

"Can you talk back?"

"I don't know."

Louarn helped her sit back, off her knees. "Don't try right now. We'll work on this later. Are they very loud?"

"No. Just whispers."

"Then tell them you can't talk right now, and keep thinking your own thoughts, very hard, to keep them at bay. All right? Now, can everyone get up, so that we can get Pelufer out of this haunted place?"

Kara bounced to her feet. But it was not at Louarn's urging. She went straight, as though every hair on her body had stood on end, and said, "He's here."

Dabrena went cold inside.

"He's here, Mama," Kara said, turning to her. Eager to share it. Desperate for Dabrena to believe.

Louarn was staring hard at them. He looked at Pelufer, who had put her head between her knees and crossed her arms over it, then back at Kara, then at Dabrena, quirking a brow at her. She gestured helplessly: *I don't know*. Could her daughter hear haunts, like the older girl? Was it just her father she heard? Or was it no more than a powerful imagination, excited by what she'd seen the older girl go through?

"Mama," Kara said. Begging her. To do *what*? To call out to Tolivar, to run across the clearing and embrace his chill shade, what?

She wanted to ask if Pelufer could hear him. But Pelufer was overwhelmed by nonneds upon nonneds of voices. She'd never isolate the thread of one, not a man she hadn't known in life.

Dabrena had opened her mouth to say something terse, something curt, to stop this nonsense now, when Pelufer raised her head and said, "He's very loud. He's what all the clamoring was about. He's Kara's father."

"No," Dabrena said before she could stop herself. Kara's face fell. That was too bad. She wanted her parents to be together. She couldn't have that. You couldn't have everything you wanted in this world. She might as well learn that.

"Can't you hear him?" Pelufer said, her eyes not quite focused, her brown face gone pale. "It's only the one."

"We said goodbye to him in the bonefolk's realm," Dabrena said, to put an end on this.

In a small voice, Kara said, "He wasn't in the bonefolk's realm. He's here."

"*I can't see him,*" Dabrena ground out. "I can't hear him!"

"There's nothing to forgive you for," Pelufer said.

Dabrena went very still.

"You protected the baby," Pelufer said. "Now you have to let go."

"What does that mean?" Dabrena said, searching the clearing and the air and Kara's face for some sign of him, finding none.

Pelufer turned toward her, unseeing. "You're hurting him. Stop doing that. It hurts him and it keeps him from moving. He wants to fly before the wind."

"What hurts him?" Dabrena whispered.

"The way you hang on. To things. Guilt. What happened. Let go. Let him go." Pelufer groaned, and her eyes focused. "I don't know! *You're* the one, *you* have to figure it out."

As long as she denied forgiveness to herself, she remained in control. As long as betraying him remained an unforgivable act of weakness, it was her own. If his death was on the Ennead's hands, then he'd died for nothing. Nothing. Not even because she had betrayed him. And Dontra's child had died for nothing. Not because she'd held out too long, not because she hadn't been quick or canny or strong or brave enough to beat the Ennead, but simply on a whim of the cruel, the careless, the vicious.

Dying had not destroyed his spirit.

She was the one doing that.

"I understand," Dabrena said. Talking to the air, she couldn't believe she was talking to the air, but she said, "I understand, Tolivar. I'll try. I can only try."

There's a girl, said the old, familiar voice in her mind.

"There's a girl," said Pelufer, and shook herself all over, like a dog shaking off water, and got to her feet as though nothing had happened. "Can we go now?" she said to Louarn. "It's gone all quiet."

With a cautious glance at Dabrena and Kara, he said, "Yes. Let's go while it's quiet."

Dabrena forced herself standing. Kara patted her on the arm and gave her a smile. Perhaps, for once, she had managed to say the right thing. Perhaps she ought to be silent for a while rather than ruin it.

Pelufer helped Caille and Elora up, and said to Caille, "I felt *your* haunt. I felt your spirit knocked loose."

Caille gave a wary shrug, wiping her nose on her sleeve before Elora could catch her arm and press a cloth into her hand.

Pelufer was grinning. "*You* took my jacks! That lost set I blamed Elora for all that time! It was *you*, you little sprite!"

Caille put on a perfectly innocent face, and said, "I'm hungry."

Pelufer snorted. "Trust *her* to think about food when the whole world almost came to an end. And her with it. But I'm hungry too."

"She's hungry *because* the world almost ended," Louarn said. He'd moved toward the bonefolk, to say his farewells, but now he cocked his head at Caille. "She should weigh nine stone, the way she eats. But she doesn't. It goes to fuel her powers. You're hungry because you just used yours. You girls never get sick, do you? She's using her powers all the time. She just doesn't tell you."

"Well, she won't be using them for a good long while now," Elora said. "We're going home, to see how everyone fared, and we're snugging you into a bed for a nice sleep."

"Food first," Caille said, at the same time that Thorngrief gestured at something on the ground, half sucked into the mud, covered in bark and leaf mold and twigs, and said, "One more use for her powers, perhaps. I cannot send this one through the ways."

Dabrena, curious even though she wished to be away from this hauntwood, took Kara to see what it was. Louarn and Pelufer followed. Caille did not seem interested, and tucked herself against Elora, her thumb on her cheek and her fist against her mouth. Elora sat, to make a lap for her.

It was a body, not yet dead. Sunken like a drowned rat into the ground. Dabrena and Louarn hefted it out and turned it, laying it on the longblade harnessed to its back. Though steeped in mud and tannins, the hair, once white-blond, was recognizable, as was the face.

This was the towheaded woman who had melted all the blades to end the battle.

They checked her carefully. She was breathing, but unconscious, not sleeping. Mucus slimed her mouth and eyes. Dabrena leaned down for a sniff, and came up quick. "Don't light any fires around this one."

"She needs care," Louarn said. "We must warm her, dry her. We must get her into the nearest town."

Dabrena would have said don't bother. But she had seen what this woman had done in the battle, however belatedly. They shouldn't leave a power like that to die on a hilltop. "The nearest town is Gir Doegre," she said, "and she's not going to make it."

"We'll carry her."

"That's not what I mean. She's dangerously cold, and her blood is poisoned. And there's this." She widened a tear in the woman's shirt to reveal a blade wound, newly bleeding. "The mud and the cold must have sealed it, but she'll bleed out now. It's a marvel she's alive."

As she reached to rip cloth from the woman's clothes to improvise a binding, Caille struggled off Elora's lap and came up wearily beside her. "I can fix this," she said, though with no enthusiasm.

Dabrena believed her. She had felt her heal all the body of Eiden. And even if that had been a dream, some spectacular shared hallucination, her own broken rib had not. She'd fallen on that stone, right there, when she passed through from the bonefolk's realm, and felt the rib crack. It was not cracked now. Jammed into the hollow yew, she'd had one leg stretched out between Caille and Pelufer, and she'd felt the healing flow into her. So like and yet so unlike the healings mages cast. This was power of a completely different kind—a different taste, a different texture. The difference between fire and earth.

But this power drained its wielder as magecraft had not. Mages wearied in an ordinary way, their eyes and hands tiring from the physical practice of their craft, and sometimes their creative powers ebbed. But this power drew directly on the force of its wielder's life. Caille had nearly died. Caille had been dead for many breaths. And she was hungry. She had not restored her depleted strength.

"That wound was self-inflicted," Dabrena said to Caille, and gave the hilt of the longblade a shake to illustrate. "This woman wanted to die."

"No she didn't," Caille said. "Or she'd be dead."

Dabrena couldn't argue with that. But Caille's sisters never missed an opportunity to argue. Elora declared that Caille was *not* healing any drunken suicidal woman, and Pelufer said it wouldn't cost Caille to do it, she'd only be putting the body back the way it was meant to be and the woman was passed out so there wouldn't be any pain to feel, and Elora said she'd only put Eiden back the way he was meant to be and look what that cost her, and Pelufer said that that was different, Eiden was upset and hurt in ways they couldn't understand, and Elora said so was that woman if she tried to kill herself, and Pelufer said that that didn't count, she was unconscious, all Caille had to do was purge the drink from her and seal the wound, and it was up to her anyway, they had to stop making decisions for her all the time.

While they were arguing, Caille laid her small hands on the woman's body.

Dabrena had seen wounds healed before. Dabrena had healed wounds herself, and done far more, as mage, as warder. With eight other warders, she had diverted a Great Storm that was the equal of what had just swept across Eiden Myr—and part of her wondered if the storm just past was some echo of the Storm she had denied. Diverting or beating back a great force, as she had done with that Storm, as Verlein had tried to do with the Khinish, was not enough. It had to be disarmed, as this woman had done, as Caille had done.

Watching Caille work, she felt a profound respect for powers she had never known existed, and was humbled. She had thought that magecraft was the only power in the world worth having—the only glory to be attained—and that in its absence they would be forever diminished.

She had been wrong.

The woman opened startling ice-blue eyes, took in the two adults and four children clustered round her and the three bonefolk beyond, and scuttled backward, spiderlike, on palms and heels. Then she reached behind her and drew the longblade from its sheath. Blinking, trembling with cold, holding the blade in one hand as though it weighed nothing, she groped her midriff with the other hand.

"No, you didn't dream it," Dabrena said.

The woman turned the gleaming blade in her hand, looking for blood on the tip. There was none.

"It went into the metal," Caille said, then laid her head against Elora and went promptly to sleep where she sat.

"That child healed me. How do I know that?" the woman demanded.

Dabrena said, "I have no idea. I hope you'll thank her sometime."

The woman scowled.

"Who are you?" Pelufer asked. Her eyes followed the blade, entranced. Elora regarded her warily.

The woman let the blade sag. "No one," she said. "I'm no one at all."

"You are," Pelufer said. "You're someone. What kind of blade is that?"

The woman rolled her eyes and tried to get up, but failed, still disoriented.

"A magecrafted blade," Dabrena said. "I saw its like, once. It was only a dagger, but the metal swirled in that same hypnotic way. Verlein n'Tekla bore it."

The woman spat off to the side. "I'll have that back from her someday."

"You were her blademaster," Dabrena said, remembering Verlein's claims in the holding on Spindle Day.

"I tried to be. We both failed."

"A blademaster," Pelufer breathed. She moved closer to the woman. The woman watched her with a frown, but did not move away.

Abruptly she offered the longblade hilt-first to Pelufer. "Here," she said. "Have it."

Pelufer's arms floated up as she took the grip in both hands, expecting weight. "It's like a feather!"

"Since the battle. Yes. But it cleaves stone. Bloody irritating thing. It's indestructible." She looked at Caille. "Is that your sister?"

Pelufer nodded, turning the blade from side to side, enraptured by the creamy metallic currents.

"The blade's yours," the woman said. "I have no other payment to tender for my life."

The words were grudging. She had not wanted her life. A shattered jug lay not two threfts away, unremarked upon. The woman had drunk herself into a rage in the storm and run herself through. At least she had the grace to recognize what had been done for her, asked or unasked.

"Really?" Pelufer said. "Mine? I can keep it?"

"If it lets you." The woman managed to get to her feet.

Elora started to protest, but Louarn quieted her.

Pelufer held the blade for a long time. At last she rose, and said, "It won't," and offered it back.

The woman gave a harsh laugh. "Of course."

Pelufer said, in a vague, puzzled way, as though the words were not her own, "It isn't time yet."

The laugh died on the woman's lips. She gave Pelufer a good hard look, squinting, head cocked. Pelufer obviously longed for that blade.

The woman had obviously dealt with many folk who longed for that blade. But something about Pelufer gave her pause.

It gave Dabrena pause, too. Why would a child who could hear the dead covet a weapon of death? Or was that no stranger than healers who wore blades?

The woman shrugged. "Please yourself," she said, and sheathed the blade. But the evaluating look never quite left her.

"We must return," Louarn said to the bonefolk.

"As must we," Lornhollow replied.

The blond woman rubbed her eyes, questioning her sobriety in the face of talking bonefolk. Dabrena smiled and would have patted her on the shoulder, offered a joke to ease the moment, but the woman stepped back from her, wary as a wild dog, unwilling to be touched. *All right*, Dabrena thought. *But I'll know more of that bladebreaking power of yours before this day is out.*

"If there is blessing or farewell among your folk, I never learned it, but I give it to you now," Louarn said.

Lornhollow signed *Pass through*, and he and his fellows merged backward into the trees. Back to their own realm, or on to some other hauntwood. There would be many, many bodies to be passaged.

"They didn't say goodbye," Elora said.

"I suppose they don't," Louarn replied. "Or that was it. Pass through. Perhaps it's a wish, and a bidding. Perhaps next time we meet, we can ask them."

Elora gave Louarn a shy smile.

"This way," Dabrena said, striking off toward the logging road she remembered from her sojourn here with Adaon. He'd be pleased to know that the world had been saved right here, where they'd had their joining. She was desperate to see him, thrilled and a little nervous. She wanted to tell Kara about him and she wanted it to be a surprise. She'd left him in Gir Mened, several leagues Bootward of here, by the battlefield; she hoped she wasn't delayed long in Gir Doegre, and that Kara's parting from Caille wouldn't be too hard. They would see each other again, and often, as she and Adaon dug in Gir Doegre for his Triennead holding. She would not separate her daughter from this friend her own age, this remarkable friend with whom she'd rescued the stolen children and saved the world. Theirs might be the bonding of a lifetime.

"Hold it!" she barked, flinging her arms to the sides, pressing Kara back on one side, Elora on the other. Behind them, Louarn with Caille in his arms just managed not to bump her, and Pelufer and the fighter stopped before they ran into Kara or Elora.

It would have bumped them over a cliff.

Where the logging road should have let out onto the thoroughfare from the Knee to Maur Lengra, passing downland into Gir Doegre, it simply stopped.

The Knee Road was gone.

The storm had ripped off the entire side of their hill.

Below were rocks and trees lying skewed and tumbled on a shelf, and beyond that was a slide of earth and rubble.

Where the roads from Knee and Boot crossed and became Tin Long and Copper Long, forming the angled corner of Gir Doegre's wedge, was only a wasteland of wreckage. Small figures moved around the rubble; some were bent over shovels, digging, and others were crouched, digging with their hands. Dogs' barking carried up on the clear air. They were looking for buried survivors.

"Grieving spirits," she said.

It was too late to keep the girls from looking.

"That's our home," Elora said.

"I'm sorry," Dabrena said. "I didn't know."

"The town looks all right," Pelufer said. "But that whole corner is jaxed. And the road. And it took some of the Kneeside."

"A shantytown," Louarn explained.

"Nobody would have stayed there in the storm," Pelufer said. "Nobody. They'd have been smarter than that. The inns and taverns would have taken them, and the waysiders and the folk from the ground pitches."

She said it the way you said a thing that you prayed for, not a thing you were certain of.

"How far is this town from Gir Mened?" the blademaster asked, and when they told her, she said, "How in the bloody blazes did I manage that?"

No one replied. Then Pelufer said, "Look! That's Risalyn! There's Yuralon!"

She shouldered past them, intending to wave, and when Elora snatched her back from the brink she turned and ran toward the clearing. "There's another way! Come on, I'll show you!"

Dabrena turned with Kara, eager to put the precipice behind them, and just caught the strange look in Louarn's eyes as Pelufer's words drifted out among the trees. It was very like what he had called, as he led the mages into the tunnels he had crafted. Dabrena gave him a reassuring smile, and together they followed the girl, with the grumbling bladebreaker in tow. Elora ran on ahead so that they wouldn't lose track of Pelufer.

It was a long way down and around. If there had been paths, they were washed out. Fallen stonewood trees blocked them, and the bladebreaker cut their way through when there was no choice among storm-delved gullies, piles of downed trees, and some impenetrable thicket. Dabrena had never been good at forests—crofts and fields had been her bailiwick at home, and for six years she had known only the inside of a mountain—and she was relieved when they came out onto the Boot Road and had only its mud to contend with. Logging crews were already clearing trees that had fallen across the road. Louarn asked one of them what day it was, and received an array of queer looks and the answer "Longlight," which any sane man would have known. But their faces softened when they looked at the children. They assumed they had been rescued by the three sodden adults. They could hardly know that it was the other way round.

They had been in the bonefolk's unchanging realm only one night. It was midmorning of the day after the battle. Longlight. The summer solstice. The longest day of the year.

The day of light.

They came at last to where the rescue crews were digging for survivors. They had found a few, and ministering to them Dabrena saw the two bladed Girdlers who'd acted as healers on the battlefield.

The Girdlers were more surprised to see Dabrena than she was to see them. But they greeted Louarn and the girls like family.

Elora introduced them, and the Girdlers gave Dabrena the fighters' feral grin.

"Mender," said the woman, whose name was Risalyn, as she hefted Caille for a sleepy hug. "I have never in my life seen anyone do a thing as daft as that."

"It worked out all right," Dabrena said. "Did my pledge get to see Verlein?"

The man, Yuralon, nodded. "And talked her out of storming your holding, from what we heard," he said. "But—"

"Your holding?" said Pelufer, staring at Dabrena.

"Dabrena n'Arilda is the head of the menders, from the Head holding," Louarn said. "That sounds funny, doesn't it? She was a warder in the old times. She's a very important person."

"You didn't tell us that!" Pelufer said.

"No," said the blond bladebreaker, stepping away. "You didn't."

"I told Caille," Kara said, and Caille nodded her head against Risalyn's shoulder.

"Verlein looked in no shape to be storming anyone's holding," the bladebreaker said, frowning.

"And who are you?" asked Risalyn, handing Caille off to Yuralon. To free her hands—there was a new blade in the scabbard on her back.

Bloody fighters. Like cats, they were.

"No one," the woman said, as she had before. "I'm no one at all. But I knew Verlein once. I saw her . . . yesterday."

"She's the bladebreaker," said Dabrena, with a strange satisfaction. "She's the one who stopped the battle by disarming all you folk."

"*She* melted the blades?" said Risalyn.

"And not before time," said Yuralon, his face darkening. "We lost comrades in that battle."

"As did we all," the bladebreaker growled. Stock words, from a fighter. She did not explain herself.

Pelufer was standing with her mouth agape and some new understanding struggling to life in her eyes. Whatever it was, she couldn't voice it. Dabrena caught her eye and cocked a brow, inviting her to speak, but she stood as stubbornly mute as the bladebreaker did. They looked like two of a kind. Dabrena wondered if that was what the child was realizing.

Then Yuralon dismissed the bladebreaker with his gaze and turned it back on Dabrena. "Mender," he said. "Verlein is here, in Gir Doegre. Her folk brought her here last night, before the worst of the storm hit, but I could not determine why. Your pledge sent a runner girl off somewhere and then followed Verlein, and we came with him. He explained everything to us. He spoke with Verlein. He persuaded her to call off her siege, as you bade him. Her shielders were glad of it. But this morning we heard a rumor that she had changed her mind. We were unable to find her. All the public houses were crowded with folk sheltering from the storm."

"All right," Dabrena said. "I'm grateful for your report, and for your befriending Adaon. Those public houses will be emptying out. I'll find Verlein and speak with her myself. Where is Adaon?"

"That's what I was trying to tell you." Yuralon glanced at Risalyn. "He was a busy lad last night. He feared for you, I think, and could not sit still after he'd done what you'd asked. He found the head alderfolk of this town and asked them for permission to dig. They were distracted, what with the storm, and he pestered them until they said yes just to be rid of him."

"That sounds like Adaon," Dabrena said. "He knows how to pick his moments." Her smile died when Yuralon did not return it. "No," she said. "There was a storm. There was a storm to end all storms. He wouldn't have . . ."

Her eyes were drawn up the rubbled slope to the shelf on which trees and rocks lay piled.

"Eiden's eyes," she said. "*That's the holding.*"

"The holding?" Louarn asked.

"The Strong Leg's Triennead holding," Risalyn said, echoing what Adaon had explained to her. "The seekers believed there had to have been three enneads and three holdings once. Adaon—her pledge—he thought one would be here, and one in the Haunch. He'd seen a map, he said."

"My map," said Kara. "I showed him my map. Where Father said the treasure was." Her small hand slipped into Dabrena's, and she pressed close. She knew. She understood what the adults around her were saying. She'd put it together. She knew.

"Where is Adaon?" Dabrena said again.

A wince shadowing her eyes, Risalyn pointed at the destruction of the hill. "He got his permission and he left us. As daft as you hurling yourself on the bonefolk."

Yuralon said, "He thought you were dead, mender."

Risalyn said, "The storm was very bad. The quakes. The wind. We thought we were going to die. We all braced for death, in our own ways."

The first cart piled with bodies was struggling off up the Boot Road. How they thought they were going to get those bodies through the forest to the bonefolk's wood, there was no telling. "Is he in that cart?" Dabrena said. "Tell me. Let me say my farewells."

"No," Yuralon said. "We've watched. They haven't pulled him out."

Yet, he did not say, but it was in his voice.

"Louarn, take Kara, please," Dabrena said. "Kara, please stay with Louarn for a little." Kara protested. Louarn spoke quiet warning. She barely heard it. She couldn't, she couldn't—this was between her and her loss, between her and Adaon, she couldn't consider the rest of them right now.

As in a trance, she walked toward the rubble and up the slope, picking her way over rocks, through the skewed piles of tree trunks. She'd walked in such a trance through the crowded streets of Gir Doegre the day they'd arrived, she and Adaon. Awed by the myriad of goods, by the surfeit of wares in a town weakened by disease, a world bowed under misfortune. Awed by the bursting color and texture of life and trade, despite all the troubles that had befallen them. And Adaon had said, "There must be *something* you want. . . ." And there had been. In the end, she had wanted him.

She slipped on the slick surface, earth drying in the late-morning sun over an underlayer still soggy. In her mind, she was lying in bed with him, the night before the battle, the night before the last time she would ever look on his living face.

"Who was Tolivar?" he asked. He'd heard her say the name, in her mist-drunken babbling, to the keepers who had rousted them from the spirit wood. Is this your Tolivar? they had asked, and she had said, No. That's Adaon. He's alive.

"My best friend. And occasional bedmate. Kara's father."

"You grieve him like a lost pledge. Or you try to."

"He was my bindsman. We were triaded warders. With Selen n'Mirin, you met her briefly in the holding."

"Plump, motherly woman."

"Motherly. Yes." She blinked. "I try to?"

"He wasn't your lifemate. You weren't pledged."

"I thought we would be. Someday. When I was older. When I was ready. I was two nines and one. I was a child. Promiscuous and thoughtless."

He laughed. "And you're an old woman now."

"I am," she said. "A widow woman with a child and a holding depending on me. I should not have left it."

"You should have left it long ago."

"You're a journeyer, Adaon. You don't understand about roots."

"I understand about chains. And you're a journeyer too."

"That was a long time ago. Another youthful dream. You're a seeker. You keep your dreams forever. You're still young. You always will be."

"I have four years on you at least."

"I'm older than I look."

"You're two nines and six if you're a day."

"Two nines and seven," she said. It sounded like nothing. But it was the difference of a world between who she had been and who she was now. "I'm two nines and seven."

He made a face. "I stand corrected," he said, with absurd formality. "But I do have four years on you. I'm three nines and three. Where I come from, that makes me a grownup." Then, more gently, "Dabrena. A harvest-master at nine-and-eight, a vocate at two nines, a mother and head warder at two nines and one. You did a lot of living for a child. But if you believe you're an old widow woman, burdened with a child, battered by a hard world, oppressed by a weight of black stone, then that is what you'll be. Go ahead and believe it, if you like. I can't stop you. It's not my place, even as your sworn irritant. But for what it's worth, that is not how I see you."

"It was once."

"Never. I swear it." He grinned. "The woman who made love to me in a sacred glade was neither promiscuous child nor old used-up woman." The grin widened. "Neither was the one I had just now."

"But when you were first galling me . . . you didn't want me then. I would have sensed it."

"When I met you, I thought you were a tight-strung snob with delusions *of authority. It was my responsibility to tease you. You needed loosening up. Then I began to feel for you."*

"*Desire?*"

"*Pity.*"

"*Oh.*"

"*And respect. You'd done yourself more harm than any nine enneads could have done, I thought. But there was more inside you than that. I hoped you'd let me see it. I hoped you'd open to me, in the odd moments, if I kept you off balance. It was somewhere in there that I realized my own mocking advances had backfired. I wanted nothing more than to . . . well, let's say crack the tight nut of you, which is both too blunt and not blunt enough. But I knew you'd have nothing to do with me. I dismissed the notion, stopped considering it. It was interfering with my teasing. And I was nothing to you. It would never happen.*"

"*You saw me softening. You must have.*"

"*I saw you beginning to realize that there might still be pleasure in the world. I told myself that if you found it against a wall behind a tavern with some pretty local, I'd be glad for you. I like to think I would have been.*"

It had all been to distract her from the loss of her daughter, and from what they both knew she planned to do, the daft attempt to follow her. But it had been no less true for that.

Now it was coming true.

She saw it, in a flash across her consciousness as she pushed and slid and clawed her way up a steepening incline, ignoring the shouts of panicked rescuers. She saw herself become the old callused woman she'd thought she was. She felt it happening already. She would become it in earnest, widowed, broken, bereaved past recovery. She'd found him, he'd opened her to the world again, she'd found happiness after all the dark years only to have it ripped from her. It would harden her past all cracking.

She could not permit that future. For Kara's sake, and for love of his memory. She would not become that closed-in woman, she would not allow the heart he'd restored to shrivel and blacken. He opened her to the world. Above all he would want her to embrace it. She'd never hear the end of it from him if she let his death sever her from joy.

She would go on. She would stop and look at deadfall, rock formations, vegetables in her soup. She would engage the world, question it, make demands of it—gall it. She would laugh.

Because she'd loved him, she would be strong enough to go on after losing him.

I promise you that, Adaon. She only thought it at first, and then she was saying it, again and again, "I promise you, I promise you,

Adaon," as she came to the top of the slope, to touch the Triennead holding that had meant so much to him that he'd rather die than wait just one more day to find it—so much that he'd rather die in the attempt than be killed in the riving of Eiden without ever having touched it at all.

Stone came under her hand. Carved, crafted stone. Stone shaped by human will. Triennead stone, still humming with ancient power even after the breaking of the light, the failure of the wardings.

"If you'd only waited another day, Adaon," she whispered. "If you'd only believed you had another day." It was the sublime moment of a lifetime, to feel this stone come under her hand. She stood with her boots dug into a slippery slope, touching the ages, poised on the brink of the future.

"Spirits willing, you lived to touch this, too."

"All those lives," Pelufer said. "All those ancient lives I felt. That's who they were. The people of light in that other mage place."

"The mists," Louarn said, agreeing with her. He was holding Kara's shoulders tight. She wanted to follow her mother, but that kind of grief had to be faced alone, and she could only stand and watch. "There was something about Gir Doegre. Some mystery. A puzzle to be solved. All the magelight that must have been gathered here. All the lights who must have died here, one by one over time or in whatever cataclysm buried that structure so that a hill might grow over it. There should not be hills here. Perhaps the others house structures, too. Buried by time, or built that way, to keep them cool and safe. Your entire town may have been the holding. And its power still drew people, still called people, over all the ages. That's why the itinerants stayed. Your waysiders. That's why when the weather turned bad there was always a mist here, more than the river could have accounted for, or the humid air."

"All those *lives*," Pelufer said again. She wasn't interested in structures or mists. Gir Doegre was what it was. Her home. Her parents' home. A tradertown. But the haunts . . . all those ancient, whispering haunts . . .

"Yes," Louarn said. "And if you can gain control over their voices, you might learn why they died, and when. You might tell us more than any codex any scholar ever read."

"I don't want to solve your *puzzles*!" Pelufer burst out. "I *can*'t solve your puzzles! I could never solve a single one of the poxy things. I just want . . . I just want . . ." Feelings swelled inside her and could not be sorted or understood. She did not know what she wanted.

Only that she wanted, terribly, desperately. To be something. To be someone. There was someone she was supposed to *be*. She'd never had Elora's power, she'd never had Caille's power, but when Lornhollow gave them their mother's ways, he'd given just as much to her. All she could ever do was spew names. But there was more. She knew there was more. She'd never minded, before, not being as much as her sisters were. She'd been the quick one, the thief, the provider, the one who didn't mind getting her hands dirty and getting in trouble so that the other two could go on shining and being powerful and safe. But now she knew that there was more, and it was all tied together with what she'd always been, but that wasn't enough, now there was *something*, and if she didn't become whatever it was she would always have this swelling yearning feeling inside her. She would never be . . . happy.

"I want a prentice," the blademaster said, quietly, from right beside her. Not as though she wanted one the way Pelufer wanted, but simply as though she lacked one.

The woman had been watching her the entire time. Watching the expressions go over her face. As if she understood what was going on inside her, the way Pelufer could understand the haunts once they had named themselves.

"The blade doesn't want me," Pelufer said. "I could feel it."

"Yes," the woman said. "So could I, when my father let me hold it. But it came to me in the end. Too soon. He died before he could teach me its true use." She laughed, a hard, coarse laugh. She was a hard, coarse woman, much harder than Yuralon, much coarser than Risalyn. They were both looking at her, listening, wary, ready to snatch Pelufer from her hard, coarse clutches. She grinned at them, the most careless, soulless, dangerous grin Pelufer had ever seen. Risalyn's and Yuralon's feral grins were only faint echoes of that grin. Speaking louder, for their benefit, the woman said, "I only learned its true use yesterday. A little late. Maybe it's not so late for you. You say you can hear haunts. Good. Then you know that taking a life stains you. This blade was crafted to take that stain. I think you've already tasted the stain, whether you've taken a life or not. I think you know that stain the way I know the shadow of my own hand. I thought I *was* that stain, that shadow. But lo and behold, this blade was crafted for something more. I think it would be willing to show you, if you're willing to learn. We could learn together." As if her own words were too much for her to stand, she snorted and said, "Eiden's bloody balls, it's got to go to *someone* when I die!"

"You're kenai," Risalyn said suddenly.

The woman nodded. "Yes. I am kenai. I am the blade."

"There's only one kenai left in the whole world," Risalyn said.

The woman said, "Yes. Since my father died. The other kenaila killed him, and I killed them, and now there's only me."

"You trained Verlein," Risalyn said. "You trained Cheveil, and Lannan, and Eshadri."

"Friends of yours, are they?"

"Eshadri and Cheveil, yes. They were."

"I grieve their loss."

"And I grieve yours," Risalyn said. "You're Kazhe n'Zhevra. You were Torrin n'Maeryn's bodyguard."

The woman spat into the dirt. "I'm Kazhe," she said, and looked at Pelufer. "Do I have a prentice?"

Awed, Pelufer nodded.

The woman clapped her on the shoulder, gave one hard squeeze, and stalked off into the crowds down Copper Long.

"Jiondor will kill you!" Elora hissed.

"Jiondor never made that woman promise not to teach me blades."

"She's a drinker, Pelufer, just like Father. You can see it in her cheeks and her sliding eyes. She's probably heading to a tavern right now. She was up on that hill drunk in the storm. That's just the kind of thing Father would have done. She's just like Father!"

"Just like Father," Pelufer said, and grinned. "And I've had a lot of practice with that, haven't I? I'll do all right with her."

"Blades kill people, Pel! You can't kill people! *You can hear haunts!*"

To Elora's shock, Risalyn said, "Who better then to have the use of blades? Who better than someone who knows the harm they do? We saw what Kazhe's blade did. It destroyed every weapon on that battlefield. I wish she'd known how to use it sooner, but from the looks of it she wishes the same. That would be the right kind of blade for Pelufer, I think."

"Pel could have stopped the battle," Caille piped up drowsily. "I told the boneman to send her there, but he wouldn't."

"We went there, Caille," Elora said. "We went there looking for you."

"I wasn't there," Caille murmured, already drowsing off again.

"I know," Elora said softly. "But Pelufer didn't stop the battle."

"I didn't have time. I couldn't figure it out. But I felt something, Elora. I *felt* something. I felt it when Risalyn was fighting that woman in Gir Nuorin, too."

Elora threw her hands up, and Yuralon said, "That's her power, Elora. You have wood and trees. Caille has flesh, and life. Pelufer has metals—blades. And death."

"She's only nine-and-two," Elora said, looking ready to cry.

Risalyn patted Elora on the shoulder. "I wish I'd seen my way as clear when I was nine-and-two."

Elora looked at Pelufer, and said, "I don't even know you anymore."

Pelufer blinked. She'd thought the same about Elora, more times than she could count in the last few days. She didn't know what to say.

Elora's hard shoulders went soft. "But that's all right. You'll always be my sister. We'll work it all out somehow."

"Yes," Caille said, from deep in dreams.

"Oi!" Dabrena called to the rescuers who were trying to struggle up to her, expecting any moment for her to come sliding and crashing down the slope. "Bring me a shovel, one of you!"

"There's no one up that far!" a woman cried from below.

"It's not bodies I'm after!" Dabrena called back, and turned to start groping along the stone, looking for something that might have been a window once. She would finish the task for him. She would open the first way into the past.

She lost her foothold and nearly did slide down the slope when a spade burst through the earth not two feet to her right and two pale eyes peered out from the gloom inside.

"Not even this body?" said a muffled voice. "It's awfully glad to see yours."

Dabrena clawed and flailed and dragged herself up over the ledge that was the holding's roof. For long moments, as Adaon dug his way out through the window below her in a racket of breaking shutter slats, she just lay there, waiting for her heart to slow and feeling to come back into her limbs. When his arms and shoulders lifted his bald pate up through the hole he'd made and his grinning mud-smeared face popped up beneath her, she said, "*I am going to kill you.*"

"Not before you imperiously order some local to fetch you a lantern so you can come in here and see what I've found," he said.

Then she kissed him, leaning out over the ledge, faint with the beloved taste and scent of him, alive, alive—and slipped over the edge and grabbed him round the neck and shoulder just in time, and nearly lost her grip anyway, but hung on, laughing, dangling and kicking, kissing his ear, his head, his thick neck, anything she could reach.

The rescue woman made it up to them at last, in boots with cleated iron strapped on, and helped Dabrena flip over and set her rear securely on a lodged rock. "Sweet Eiden's breath," the woman said, "a survivor!"

"Not quite," Adaon replied, winking at Dabrena. "I beat you all out here, that's all, the moment the weather changed. I pulled who I could find out of the mud, and then I went round and found a way in where it's not so treacherous. There's a nice staircase made of tree trunks, if you just go round that way a bit."

"You weren't out in the storm?" Dabrena said. "Risalyn and Yuralon were afraid that you'd—"

"That I'd gone completely daft? Well, I thought about it, I admit. I did come out here, armed with lantern and shovel. I thought we were done for. I wanted to spend my last moments trying to reach my goal. But the storm got much worse around midnight. It beat me back. I took refuge in the nearest cottage to wait it out." He looked around. "Convenient of the weather to start the excavation for us, don't you think?"

"You're both daft," the woman said. "Get down from here. There's real work to do."

Adaon looked at Dabrena. "Well?" he said. "Come on, now. Imperious. Your best holding bluster. I know you can do it."

Dabrena cursed him cheerfully, then said, "Come down and say hello to Kara. Look, she sees you, she's going mad down there."

"Well, we can't have all three of us in that condition," Adaon said. "And I suppose we really should be helping with the rescue."

"It's over," Dabrena said as they started down, hanging on to each other, heels dug in, sliding down by the rear. "They're only digging for the bodies now. Most folk got out of their shanties and into proper shelter."

"The first cottage I sheltered in lost its roof," Adaon said. "Torn right off, and everything inside tossed like a salad. I carried a boy with a broken arm to the next cottage. His sister had a bad gash on her head. I think her skull was cracked." He looked sidelong at her. "I don't suppose you know anything about why that boy and girl are good as new today?"

"It's going to take some explaining," she said, as they came down far enough to stand, and walk-slide the rest of the way back to Kara and the others.

Some searchers had broken off to help clear the Knee Road, but most stayed, with their dogs. Risalyn and Yuralon joined them, after hearing Adaon's account of himself and offering to kill him for Dabrena if she wasn't up to doing it herself. Kara had to be restrained from telling him her entire adventure right then and there. Unwilling to give his attention up, she pointed at a gray-black pall in the Haunchward sky, and said, "What's that?"

He regarded it thoughtfully, then for some reason looked at Louarn. Louarn, as though responding to words Adaon had spoken aloud, said, "There *are* sulfur springs at the head of Maur Lengra."

"And a caldera, though old and weathered," Adaon said. "And the soil is rich, and the growth a verdant green."

Louarn nodded. "There must have been a volcano under there."

"A volcano?" Kara asked.

"A vent for molten earth deep under Eiden's body," Dabrena said.

"They were known to erupt at times, spewing boiling rock," Adaon said, his throat tight, as though he was trying not to laugh.

"It sounds like me," said Pelufer.

"Among other things," Louarn said, and Adaon grinned.

"I hope it didn't hurt too many people," said Elora.

"It doesn't look like it was a very large one," Adaon said. He was losing his battle with laughter. "Or the whole sky would be black with ash."

"It should make for lovely sunrises over the next couple of ninedays," Louarn said, succeeding far better than Adaon at keeping his face respectful of Elora's concern.

"A volcano in the Crotch," Adaon said—and finally he couldn't resist: "At least we know for certain that Eiden's male!"

News traveled as fast as sound in the tradertown, and friends of Elora and Pelufer and Caille came rushing up to them. With promises to meet everyone again in the Mute Swan, the traders' tavern, after supper, the girls went off happily with the sweetsmonger Jiondor and the barrow boy Nolfiander. "It *would* be Mireille who spotted us," Pelufer said as they moved off into the crowds that were lugging repair supplies one way, covered dishes of food another, a controlled mayhem that would have looked all at cross-purposes to anyone but Dabrena, who knew how such things worked. "Let's just get you home and fed before the alderfolk demand a word," Jiondor said, as their voices faded into the cries and calls and sounds of shovels, hammers, saws.

This town had lost no time in throwing itself into its own repair. But she would have expected no less, from what she'd seen before. Their wrecked stalls would be put right by the next day, all their wares displayed once again.

Dabrena, with Adaon and Kara, was left standing beside Louarn.

"Will you stay for a while?" Dabrena said, starting off down Copper Long in the vague direction of inns and public houses and food and rest.

"How would you know I'd go?"

"I can see it in your eyes. You're already gone. You're a journeyer."

"A lad-of-all-crafts, so," Louarn said in a Strong Leg accent as they passed Hunger Long. Then his face hardened. "I set out some time ago to do a thing. It remains undone."

"We all have a great deal to do. Excavate that holding. Tell Pelkin about the light's return." She gave Adaon a look that said, *I know, I know. I'll explain everything.* "Rebuild."

"A thing more urgent than any of that, I'm afraid." As they turned onto Bronze Long, Louarn cast his gaze about as though he was looking for a quiet place in which to do it. The boy who could dream passageways. The man who could dream little girls' spirits back into their bodies. Dabrena had breathed for that body, worked its chest, to hold it ready. But they'd saved the child together. It would never make up for the baby's life she had forfeit. But it was something to be grateful for.

"Well," she said, "my first stop is with Verlein, since she's right over there, leaving that inn. Won't you come with us? We could use your . . . varied talents, in putting a stop to her delusions of conquest once and for all."

Louarn turned, only half paying attention, perhaps making a connection in his mind between a vacated room in an inn and a quiet place where he could go to sleep and dream his powerful dreams.

Then he went rigid, and said, "Kara. Fetch Risalyn and Yuralon. Now."

He saw Verlein. A woman Mellas knew. The woman who had stabbed a man by accident seven years ago in the Neck because she was trained to a fine edge with blades she was far too inexperienced to wield safely. The woman who crossed the Black Mountains intending to assassinate the Ennead. The woman who would have used him if she could, a boy in the nine-colored cloak of an Ennead runner. The woman who'd fought shadows beside him, who'd nearly died in a mudslide with him, who'd spoken the truth when Purslane stood crippled by a shattered hock, said that it was best done quickly, putting him out of his pain. He remembered that now, though in his tortured memory it had been the mud that killed Purslane, and he had looked on this Gir Doegre landslide with an old blade going through his heart. But it had been the illuminator's hand, with a knife. He had been unable to do it himself. And that woman, Verlein, had turned back from her death mission, beaten by shadows and the mountain. That was the last he'd seen of her. That was seven years ago. She looked profoundly changed. So was he. He still had nothing to say to her.

But the hunched, cloaked woman she was bundling into a wagon . . .

Louarn caught only a glimpse of wrinkled black skin, ornate white braids, and glittering black eyes. It was all he needed.

He bade Kara fetch the Girdlers, and crossed the intervening threfts at a dead run.

With a cry, Dabrena gave chase, but his legs were longer than hers, longer than Adaon's, and he dodged through the crowd like a pike through water. He shoved Verlein away, spun the old woman around, and slammed her against the wagon. Instantly several new-forged blades were at his throat and back. Ignoring them, he said, "You ordered the magekillings."

Worilke n'Karad, Ennead wordsmith, bequeathed upon him a slow, lazy smile, and whispered, "Yes," too low for anyone else to hear.

"Louarn, what are you *doing*?" Dabrena said, coming to a halt, out of breath, just beyond the shielders.

"Hello, Warder," Worilke said.

Louarn did not turn to see Dabrena react, though he heard the hiss of air through her teeth. Adaon must have stopped halfway to guide Kara to them with the Girdlers. He need only delay until they arrived, with their own blades.

"Hands off her," Verlein said. "Now."

Louarn obeyed, and turned inside the ring of blades. "Hello, Verlein."

She frowned. "I know you," she said. "But I don't know from where, and I don't care. Step aside, very slowly."

"So that you can join your forces in the Head to take Dabrena's holding? Or is it the Haunch you're aiming for first?"

Verlein's frown deepened. "I told you to step aside."

"That's Worilke n'Karad," Dabrena said. "She was the wordsmith of the weather triad of the Ennead."

Verlein's fighters seemed to falter, though their blades held steady enough on Louarn.

"She's an old, sick relative of mine who needs to be away from this place," Verlein said. "You've mistaken her for some ghost of your past. The Ennead died six years ago."

"No," Dabrena said. "Lerissa Illuminator still lives. We've always known that. And now here it seems you've kept her wordsmith for a pet. How interesting, that my proxy should dissuade you from your holding conquests one day, and the next you just happen to be in company with an Ennead mage when you change your mind."

Risalyn and Yuralon came up on either side of the shielders surrounding Louarn. Verlein swore. "Where were you lot yesterday when I needed your blades?" she said.

"We don't fight for you," Risalyn said. "We never did. We fought the Ennead. Do we still have to?"

"*You* were in the old Holding," one of the shielders said to Risalyn. "Is that one of *them*?"

"Why don't we take this inside," Yuralon said. "Blades down, all of you. That man is unarmed."

Risalyn cast Verlein a significant look, and Verlein said, "Yes, all right. Inside. Eowi, Gilris, Jia, keep guard out here, don't let anyone conscript this wagon, I'll be needing it."

She turned on her heel and walked into the inn, and Louarn understood: The Girdlers were guarding her command. They did not want her shielders to lose faith in her. "We'll sort this out," Risalyn said to the one who knew them, as she and Yuralon took hold of Worilke.

"But *is* she?" the shielder demanded.

"I'm not sure," Risalyn said. "We'll let you know."

If they had to kill her, then she was Worilke. If not, she was some old relative of Verlein's who would disappear into obscurity while the first shield returned to her post.

Louarn did not think that the rumors that would spring from this could be quashed, or that Verlein would ever be entirely secure in her command again. But no ships had come, no invasion had manifested in six years. Perhaps disbanding the shield—or the ascent of some new commander—was not the worst that could happen.

Not if a remnant of the old Ennead had been whispering in her ear for six years.

A crowd had formed. Louarn moved past the shielders, away from it, toward the inn's entrance, but sensed that Dabrena was not coming, and turned to find her staring past the shielders, at a woman in black who stood by the head of the wagon's team of mules.

"They can wait for me," Dabrena said.

"We'll go with Louarn," Adaon said, taking Kara's hand.

Dabrena nodded. "I'll be six breaths, no more."

With a shrug, Louarn went into the dim interior of the inn.

"What are you doing here?" Dabrena said, as the runner Karanthe n'Farine moved to her side. One of Pelkin's closest, and one of the runners Dabrena had been a vocate with in the Ennead's Holding. The vocate who had vied with her for Tolivar's affections. He had bound all three of them together in a core of friendship and competition, as only a binder could. But then Karanthe went for a reckoner, breaking the triad they should have been, leaving them for warders, leaving the Holding, joining the Lightbreaker. It was still a strangeness to see her in black.

"I came to this leg with Kaẕhe n'Ẕhevra, who came to stop the war," Karanthe said. "Which she did, though not till after losing her lover and half of all three armies, and then stormed off on a tear. I've been out here looking for her. She's not in Gir Mened, and one of her comrades said she'd gone Headward. This is as far as she could possibly have gotten in that storm. I don't know why I bother, really. She was mad when I knew her and she's mad now. But I'm glad to see you."

Ignoring that last, Dabrena said, "*That* was the Lightbreaker's bodyguard?"

"His name was Torrin," Karanthe said. "And he broke the light to save the world."

"He broke the light. He was the Lightbreaker. You helped him." She shrugged. "Your bladebreaker is here, I've seen her. Try the taverns. She had one blast of a hangover, but someone healed it. She's all fresh to start again."

"You never did believe in healing hangovers. Who's doing healings these days?"

"It's a long story. I have business inside."

"I saw. That *is* Worilke."

"Yes."

Karanthe said, all in a rush, "I'm sorry, Dabrena. When I sent you that message, I didn't know you didn't know about Tolivar, I hardly knew how to scribe yet—"

"I have business inside. Go find your bladebreaker. We may need her in the Head."

She left Karanthe standing in the road.

Dabrena's eyes were slow adapting from the sunshine outside. The windows laid bluish squares of light on the planks, but between them was only darkness at first, speckled by the arcs of nine-tapered Longlight candlestands. She found a seat saved for her between Louarn and Kara at a large round table in the center. Despite the innkeeper tending some shaken customers, out of earshot, and a serving girl waxing tables and looking often out the front door, and the smell of Strong Leg food and drink, she felt a temporal vertigo, as though she were back in the old Ennead's presence chamber, hosting shielders and runners and Khinish. How long had it been since she slept? Since the night before last, when she slept in Adaon's arms. She needed food and rest. She was in an ill temper for this.

Risalyn and Yuralon sat to either side of Worilke, a diminutive, wizened form barely visible in the dimness. She had managed to stay invisible for six years. Shielded by the shielders, while she worked her insidious will on their leader. Verlein was separated from her by Risalyn and an empty chair, with Louarn on her other side. Adaon sat between Kara and Yuralon. Eight of them at a table that would seat nine. Perhaps she should have invited Karanthe in. The ironies were numerous.

"So she's alive," Verlein said. "Why does that trouble you so? The past is over and done. Let the poor ill woman alone."

"She doesn't look ill to me," Dabrena said. "She looks old. Arthritic, a curving spine, underweight. Even magecraft couldn't do much more than ease the pains of age. She's stuck with those. But the only ill thing about her is the deeds she did over that long life."

"And is still doing," Louarn said.

"We caught some of your folk in the Knee," Yuralon told Worilke. "A woman named Elya and her cohort. They told us you had sent them out to kill mages."

"There are no mages now," Verlein said.

"Those who were mages, then."

Verlein made a rude noise. "No one is killing folk who were mages. You ran across a madwoman with some old grudge."

"We have now," Risalyn said.

"Someone has been killing runners," Dabrena said. Pelkin had told her that in the holding. With a cold feeling in her belly—did it go farther than that? had she missed this crisis, in her absence? had Streln been trying to tell her this, back at the beginning? would Karanthe have told her more if she had not cut her dead in the road?—she echoed Pelkin's words: "Whether they meant to target former reckoners or not, they were killing folk in black."

"Not only folk in black," Louarn said. "Tellers. Singers. Farmers. Crafters. Alderfolk. Downmongers. A man named Croy, who was a bricklayer, a kind man who harmed none. All mages, once. Not proxies. Just mages. Journeymages. Ordinary village triads. And not one of them with a light that worked."

"Most were killed or disabled with a blow to the head," Risalyn said. "And then the hands were cut off and flung away or hidden, usually in some rubbish heap. As though to prevent them ever casting again. Even after they were dead."

Dabrena's stomach turned. She had not known. She should not have left her holding. Yet she might do more here than she ever could have from there, hearing some delayed report of this, if there had even been someone to render one.

"Why, Worilke?" Louarn said. "Even madwomen have their reasons. *Why?*"

"When I was a girl in the Holding," Worilke said, toying with a pouch at her belt, "some still received visits from their relatives outside. There was a boy I used to play with, in a little-used gallery where the sun shone in during winter afternoons. Too cold to work in, but a lovely playroom. I had planted some winter-blooming bulbs in an urn where they could take the sun. When the first buds came up, I was beside myself with pleasure. So was he, I thought. But when they were just about to bloom, he said, 'My cousins are coming tomorrow. You'd better hide this.' I didn't understand, though a frisson of nameless fear swept over me. What were these cousins, that I should fear them? The urn was stone, far too heavy to move, and how would the cousins even find it, occupied in taking meals with their visiting families? They were only flowers. What would anyone have against them? I was more distressed that I would not see my playmate during their visit. The next night my pretty flowers were torn up, the bulbs flung out the window into the sea. The cousins, I thought. The cousins destroyed them after all. I had not met them, not seen them during their visit. But they rampaged through my Holding, destroying whatever they could find that was fragile and vulnerable. It didn't occur to me until later to wonder how they had found that little-used gallery, unless my playmate had told them of it. To curry favor? For fear of their wrath? From the same irresistible perversity that makes a man on a cliff sway forward, as if he'll let himself fall, just to see how it will feel? There was no telling. But the cousins came, shadows in the night, and destroyed the fragile lives I had tended." She lifted her glittering eyes to look around the table. "The cousins will come," she said, and gave a terrible, chilling smile.

Risalyn threw her head back and swore. Louarn and Yuralon squinted at Worilke in a failed attempt to make sense of this allegory. Verlein said, "See? She's mad, leave her in peace." But Adaon said, "And so you uproot the blooms yourself, so that the cousins cannot have them? Better it should be your hand that destroys, for then at least they are still yours?" Worilke fixed on him with her sharp eyes, suspicious of him, because he had it right. Quietly, he said, "That assumes that there will be a blooming. Bulbs hidden under the soil present no temptation to . . . the cousins."

"The light will return!" Worilke said. "It was scribed in Luriel's codex, the one that was stolen. When Galandra cast her shield to isolate Eiden Myr from the outer realms her mages had fled, it shocked the light from all of them. But within a nineyear it was back. I read it in Luriel's codex!" She tapped her brow. "I forget nothing. Steal all the codices—*burn them*—it will make no difference to me. I read. I remember. The light returned to Eiden Myr. It will return again. Ignorance, vain foolishness, to break Galandra's shield! It had a lifespan. It was a living thing. That fool boy shattered it and shocked the light from every mage in Eiden Myr. It would have dissipated in due time, like any casting. Twice nine nonned years it held, until he broke it—only twice, not thrice! It was meant to hold another nine nonned. We would have had time to make ourselves strong, to thicken the mageblood, stiffen our lax training. We had become weak. If that fool boy had left well enough alone, my Ennead would have scourged those outer realms, and by the time they crawled their way back from oblivion we would have been strong. Unassailable! Mages all, with no lightless among us. Powerful past all dreaming. But he broke it. He broke it, and I saw the face of Galandra, and I felt her great imperative: Protect." The swelling of pride and outrage left her, and she sank into herself, went crafty and cunning, twisting the pouch in her hands. "He left us with nothing, that boy. But the light would return. The invasion would come. Our human shield would not withstand it. They would come, and conquer us, and root out any light they found. But if they found no light, there would be nothing to fear. We might return to the world as ordinary, lightless folk. Diminished, all our glory lost, our great future vanquished. But alive, and safe." Seeing no comprehension on the faces around her, she said, in a plea for understanding, "They would root out our light! That is why we fled from them!"

"You were rooting it out first," Adaon said.

"But why the hands?" Louarn said, still frowning, still struggling. "What purpose in removing the hands?"

As though sheer viciousness needs explaining, Dabrena thought in irritation. *As though the methods make a difference!* "Never mind that," she said. "Why the *adults*? What purpose in *that*?"

Worilke regarded them with scorn. They were children asking stupid questions when the obvious was right in front of them. "The light will *return*," she said. "Suppose my stewards bungled a killing? How often would they get a second chance? They must not have their hands when the light returns. Dead or alive, they must not be able to cast." Offhand, she added, "I've chosen death, myself. There was a light in me as well. Better to die, than live unable to cast. Death was a mercy on them."

"How generous of you to refrain from sparing yourself," Dabrena said. Her bad temper at last succeeded in irritating Louarn, who threw her a sharp look to say she was not being helpful. "You'll notice she answered your question, not mine," she threw back at him.

"I don't understand why the age of the victims is at issue," Adaon said. Nipping their wick before it could flare up. "Perhaps Worilke doesn't, either."

Louarn stared at Adaon for a moment with no expression on his face, which Dabrena was learning to recognize as the indication of something clicking into place in his mind. Abruptly he turned to Worilke and said, "Your assumptions are flawed."

She snorted. "Luriel's emended codex," she said, as though shooting an arrow at him.

This was a weapon Adaon the scholar understood. "There are references to such a codex," he said, "but it is not in the scholars' possession."

"Of course not. The bloody thing was stolen, I told you that. And I know who took it. It probably went into the sea with him, buried under a chunk of the Fist."

"The Lightbreaker stole the codex?" Adaon said, his pale brows rising. "That's interesting. We might retrieve it, then, if we tracked down those who—"

"The codex was flawed," Louarn said to Worilke, cutting him off. "Or your memory of it."

"Within a nineyear the light had returned," Worilke said. "Must I recite to you the specifics?"

"It would be helpful," Adaon began, eager for some tidbits of this lost codex, but Louarn said, "No. Simply tell me this. In whom did the light return?"

Worilke smacked the table. "In the mages, you idiot child!"

"Did it say so, specifically?"

"It didn't have to." She sighed, and slowed her speech, prompting a remarkably dense prentice: "Who else would show a light but one who had a light to show?"

Dabrena pressed her lips together to quell the impulse to interject. She saw where Louarn was going. Let him choose the road.

"Did the codex say whether the light returned to some before it did others?"

Now Worilke's eyes narrowed. "It did not return to all," she said warily. "But return it did."

"I do not dispute that," Louarn said, with a smile that would have melted the glaze off a fired pot. "But your illuminator, Lerissa, had a codex, too. Also stolen, I suspect, and from the scholars this time," he added as an aside to Adaon, who accepted the information with a nod. Only then was it clear that Louarn had deduced that Adaon was a scholar, and had probed to see whether he had taken the codex. Dabrena turned to him; he shook his head, shrugged, and mouthed, *If only*.

"I sent a gift of banewort to Lerissa," Worilke said. "If she lives, it won't be for long."

"She wasn't there to receive it," Louarn said.

"You've seen her?" A complicated array of expressions flitted over the dark lined face.

"I have," Louarn said. "And I have seen magestone glow. She has proven what her codex contends."

"For whom?" Worilke said, leaning forward. "For herself? She must not regain her light before—"

"For children," Louarn said. "For children born after Galandra's shield was broken. It did not glow for Lerissa. Lerissa was rendered lightless in the breaking, as were you, and Dabrena—even Dabrena's daughter, who was an infant at the time. The fragment of magestone glowed for the children of the vanished light. The children born because the freedoms failed. The children who were not in this world to be affected by the searing release of power when Galandra's warding was breached."

"Coring and sealing can be reversed," Worilke said dismissively. "They are never permanent."

"Then you, as wordsmith, should understand that that is not the correct term, merely an analogy. The light was not sealed off inside our mages six years ago. *The magelight was extinguished.*"

"Not obliterated. Stunned dark. It will recover."

"Then why didn't Lerissa's magestone glow for her?"

"Perhaps it returns more slowly in those of us stunned by the breaking."

"I cannot dispute that possibility," Louarn said. "Only time will tell. But according to the codex Lerissa had in hand, the light will return only in the next generation. How did you plan to geld that light? Kill all the children? Dismember them?"

Dabrena let out a hiss, reflexively reaching over to Kara, but her daughter was watching the debate with intense fascination, no sign of distress in her at all. Dabrena let it pass.

"No need," Worilke said. "When my stewards' work is done,

there will be no one left to teach them. All the light in the world is worth nothing without the skills to actuate it."

"It didn't occur to you that they might redevelop magecraft, all on their own? Scribing is available to anyone who would learn it. Vellum and sedgeweave are traded widely. In most of Eiden Myr, there is no superstition against painting or color or pattern. Your craft's strictures have been lifted. What would stop them?"

"You think magecraft was the scribbles of a child on parchment incorrectly prepared, materials randomly chosen, words unstructured into effective verse forms? You know nothing. Be gone from me."

"You'd have had to kill all the reckoners," Dabrena said. "The runners. They've built a holding of their own, in the Haunch, with the express purpose of keeping the arts of magecraft in use, light or no. I thought Pelkin was wasting his time. It seems he was not."

"I would have killed them," Worilke said, deflating. Defeated. Was it a ruse? "Every last black one of them, and you warders as well. The proxy system was a dangerous dispersal of power. One ennead was sufficient." Before Adaon could speak on the breath he drew, she said, "At any rate, you've thwarted me now. You've caught me out. The invasion will come, and Verlein's blades will fail to halt it, and the first triad that casts with the return of the light will bring the rain of terror down upon us all over again, and Galandra's vision of peace and safety will go dark at last." For a moment Dabrena had thought she saw again the ebon-skinned, muscular woman Worilke had been, redolent of authority, redolent of light, impatient with nonsense. But it lapsed into the sullenness of a cracked old woman denied an expected treat.

"You used me," Verlein said. "You hid in my shadow while you killed mages who might have protected us."

Worilke shrugged. "We all use each other. I gave you good counsel, where I could. Perhaps we were meant to redeem each other, you and I. Two cold killers, with Eiden Myr's best interests at heart."

"You counseled me to take the menders and runners in hand. Not to set things right, as you claimed, as you knew would sway me. But so you'd have easy access to them all, to kill them."

"They're still warders and reckoners, whatever they call themselves now. Yes. That would have saved a great deal of time and trouble. A pity." Worilke drew a morsel from the pouch she had been fiddling with and popped it into her mouth.

"We have not defeated her so long as any of her killers remain at large," said Yuralon.

As he said the last words, Verlein, who had not finished her exchange with Worilke, said, "I should have killed you six years ago."

At the same moment, Karanthe's voice called from the inn's doorway, "See who we've got here, Dabrena!"

And at that same moment, Dabrena knew that what had looked like a bit of ginger root in Worilke's hand had not been ginger root at all.

Verlein lunged for Worilke with a knife.

Risalyn met the lunge, and they wrestled for the blade.

Yuralon drew Worilke from her chair and away from the struggle. "Stand down, Verlein!" he said. "She has to call her killers off!"

Adaon drew Kara away in similar fashion, as Louarn said, "What's that at her belt, Yuralon?"

"Don't touch it!" Dabrena cried, pushing her way past chairs to get around to Worilke. While Yuralon held the old woman, though she gave no struggle, Dabrena pulled her sleeves over her fingers and pressed the worn, oily linen of the pouch around the human shape of a root within. "It's banewort," she said. "An emetic, Yuralon, do you have one?"

"Freyn's justice works far too fast for that," Worilke said through a grin tightening into a rictus.

Yuralon shook his head, his attention distracted as Verlein and Risalyn crashed against the wall and spun into a table. There was a clunk as the knife flew free, then a disgusted oath from Verlein. Dabrena turned in a desperate bid to sieze on something that would make Worilke vomit up the poison root she'd swallowed, and saw the bladebreaker, with Karanthe behind her, hustle a man into the light from the window. She knew him . . . she knew him. . . . "Bloody raving spirits," she said, and turned back, snatching a pair of gloves from Yuralon's belt and tugging one on. She'd have to stick her fingers down the cursed woman's throat.

"No," Worilke said. Her eyes were fixed past Dabrena, at the man Kazhe and Karanthe had brought in. Her face contorted with pain, she doubled over, saying, "No, no, no," then choked on an agonized gasp.

Dabrena took another look at the man. "That's Teyik," she said.

"Our laundry steward from when we were vocates in the Holding," Karanthe said vaguely, trying to make sense of the melee. "Valik's son. Valik was Worilke's steward."

The man seemed torn between an attempt at bewildered innocence and an undisguisable desperation to go to Worilke. He chose to bolt; Kazhe held him firm.

"Valik's dead," Dabrena said. "He was old. . . ."

"The son's her steward now," Louarn said, from behind Dabrena.

Yuralon said, "The impaled man claimed her steward would kill her when it was time."

"I told you . . ." Worilke choked. The banewort's poisons worked in moments when applied to the skin. Dabrena could not imagine what they were doing inside her gut. ". . . to go . . ."

"It wasn't time!" Teyik cried, pulling toward Worilke. Yuralon gestured for Kazhe to free him, and let him take the dying woman in his arms. He sagged to the floor, keening. "I tried to go, I tried, but the runner said you wanted a word with me, what could I do, how could I know? Once I saw, it was too late, they caught me and held me."

Worilke's death rattle had already come and gone. She never heard his explanation.

"He was only her . . . servant, her minder," Verlein said. Her struggle with Risalyn had ended when the knife flew loose, or perhaps when Yuralon's words sank in, about not killing Worilke before she had called her killers off.

Worilke had known that her stewards would be the next question. A veteran of a cruel Ennead, she had not trusted herself to hold out under torture. Her steward Teyik was meant to carry on for her. Of course. An aging woman in a troubled time . . . a woman kept under close watch by the shieldmaster . . . a woman unable to manage the logistics of directing widespread killings . . . she would have had to have one reliable, mobile agent to work the rest.

"He'll know who all her killers are," Dabrena said. "She died to keep him a secret." She looked up. "Thank you, Blademaster."

Kazhe snorted, and went off to put an arm around the distraught innkeeper and move him back to his servingboard.

More slowly, Dabrena said, "Thank you, Karanthe."

"Take care with him until they're found and stopped," Louarn told Yuralon, as Risalyn came up beside him.

"We'll handle it," Risalyn said. "But we could use some help getting this out to the cart."

Her gaze turned to Verlein. Verlein shook her head.

Teyik carried the body.

Dabrena held Kara in a long hug, far past the point where she was squirming and groaning to get free. At last she let her go, and said, "That's Karanthe n'Farine l'Jebb. That's who you were named for, Kara."

Kara blinked.

"Did you think I must be a dead person?" Karanthe said. "Head custom isn't to name firstborn children for the living, is it?"

Kara shook her head.

"Your mother and father thought I was dead when they named you," Karanthe said. "Lucky for me they were wrong." She gave Kara a wink, but the gaze she turned on Dabrena said, *Though perhaps, to your mother, I was dead, after a fashion.*

Dabrena introduced Karanthe and Adaon, then drew him and her daughter into seats at the disarrayed table, implicitly inviting Karanthe to sit as well. "Do you think all our stewards were Ennead agents?" she said. "Lenn was Naeve's, I figured that much out."

Karanthe sat, and began to relax. "Probably. Wynn n'Miser l'Niggard, now, it's hard to say whose pocket he was in."

"He was our materials steward," Dabrena told Kara and Adaon. "Tighter than a fist."

"What about old Knobface?" said Karanthe. "Remember him, the lessons steward?"

"That was Bofric," said Dabrena.

"I knew *him!*" said Kara. "He and Loris worked for the scary woman with the glowing ring."

Karanthe's slim brows went up, and Adaon wiggled down into his seat, plunked his elbow on the table, and put his chin on his fist with an expectant look.

Dabrena laughed. "It is rather a long story," she said. "Does anyone have any tallies? I think we'd better get the drinks in. And a meal wouldn't go amiss."

Karanthe produced a drawbag full of tallystones, dangling it provocatively.

"Merciful spirits," Adaon said, his eyes bulging. "Let's order quickly, before the keepers make her spend it on plain clothes!"

Dabrena had not forgotten how beautiful Karanthe had been at two nineyears of age. But seven years later, she had matured into a stunning woman. Black did suit her awfully well.

Pretending to ogle the drawbag, she said to Karanthe, "Have I told you yet how good it is to see you?"

Louarn left mender and runner to their reunion meal with the scholar—whom he suspected must also be a seeker, though where his allegiance lay could not be easily determined in this region where dyed garb was ill received—and sat down alone at a small table between the servingboard and the door. He had no bag of tallystones, only his smile and his blue eyes, which with any luck would persuade the serving girl to slip him a bowl of soup and forget to take payment. If not, he would see whether that keepers' tithe was still on offer. But he wanted to hear what passed between the shieldmaster and the blademaster. It was unlikely that Verlein would persist in any bids for domination, but he'd get a more genuine sense of that from eavesdropping than from confronting her. And he did not want her to remember where she knew him from. Mellas did not ever want to talk to her again.

"Worilke was what changed me," Verlein said.

Kazhe, rolling a cup of Strong Leg wine in her palms, did not even look up.

"I had tucked her away safe here," Verlein said. "I came back here to break with her. Maybe kill her, if my own wound didn't kill me first. And still she talked me back round to taking charge of the holdings. In the morning my wound was healed."

"That wasn't her doing."

"Whose, then?"

Kazhe shrugged.

"Well, she's dead now, and her schemes with her."

"No one left to tell you what to do. Maybe you can still find that one on Khine."

"She's nothing to me."

"Suit yourself."

"I only wanted to watch the horizon for sails."

"So you said. You'd best get back to it."

"I will." Verlein waved the wine-bearing innkeeper away. "Come with me, Kazhe. I need you."

"I told you what I think of your fool shield."

"Not to shield. To teach."

Kazhe laughed aloud, then peered into her wine, as though some message had tried to manifest there.

"Not shielders," Verlein persisted. "Me. I'd like to finish our training." She pulled a small dagger from her belt; even in the dimness, Louarn saw it undulate, as though the metal were alive. "I'd like to earn that longblade of yours. Try to make up for . . . Benkana. Learn how to destroy an opponent's blades."

Kazhe's hands tightened on the cup until the tin gave under her whitened fingers. Then she set the cup down. "You can't," she said. "You have to want to win more than you want to fight. You have to want to stop the fight more than you want to win."

"I could want that," Verlein said. "For peace, for safety, I could learn to want that."

"You could never want any of those things," Kazhe said, sliding from her stool. "And I have a prentice."

She walked away, leaving her drink untasted.

After a long moment, Verlein laid the dagger beside it, and went out to her waiting wagon.

Rising quickly, Louarn retrieved the dagger before the innkeeper saw it. The serving girl had just started toward him with a look of interest. He shook his head, gave her a regretful smile. A glance showed Dabrena pleasantly engaged with her family and her friend.

He left the inn and stood at the side of the busy longstreet. *Perhaps the Weak Leg,* he thought. He'd never been as far as the Toes. He would find some way to slip the dagger to Pelufer without becoming entangled in pleas or farewells. She would return it to its rightful owner. Perhaps someday, if they met again, he would plumb the secrets of this ancient blademaster tradition.

He'd left tools and belongings in Gir Nuorin. So had the girls. He could go fetch his own, leave the dagger with their gear in assumption of its eventual retrieval, and take ship for the Toes from Glydh, at the top of the Knee. There might be vessels back in service by then.

"Where to?" asked Dabrena, coming up beside him.

"Glydh," he answered, knowing that telling her invalidated it. Ulonwy, then. Or he could cadge rides to the Heel and take a simple ferry across Maur Lengra.

"What a nice coincidence," she said. "Kara has grandparents there. We were considering a visit ourselves. It's important to stay close to family. We forget that, in the holding."

He handed the dagger to her. "This should go back to Kazhe," he said. "Will you see that she gets it?"

Dabrena took it, and said, "Don't go far, Louarn."

Not *Don't go.* Not *You can't leave.* Not *Please stay.*

Just *Don't go far.*

"I'll try," he said.

Dabrena nodded. "That's all any of us can ever do."

GIR DOEGRE

Their new stall was a thing of beauty.

It fit perfectly in its Hunger Long slot between Jiondor's sweets and Dalle's pies. Dalle's stall had been nearly demolished. Starting yesterday—Longlight—they'd rebuilt it right up against Riflin's, eliminating one of the tight alleys Pelufer had used as an escape route in the old days. Jiondor's stall had needed work, too, and between the lot of them they got it shifted over a threft, right up against Galtrelor's. That left the perfect space for a stall that required only room for three girls to sit and cry their trades. There would be no wares to put out. Not at first, anyway—Pelufer had found, as they worked on the tin assemblages of the foodmongers' stalls, that she had more than an affinity with metals, she had a knack, maybe even as strong as Elora's knack for wood. Battered by haunts' names and working hard just to survive, she'd never known there was more to her than names and scrounging and thieving. But she wouldn't have time for any workings, not for a while, and she might not have Elora's talent for them, in wood or metal or anything else. And Hunger Long wasn't the place for metalworking.

Hunger Long was a place to satisfy hungers. And Harvest Long, its old name, had been a place to share bounty. If their plans worked out, it would be Harvest Long again soon.

"I wish I could smooth the wood," Elora said, regarding the pocked awning supports with a critical eye.

"Don't," Pelufer said. "It has to match the other."

"I know. But not forever, I hope. Still, I wish we'd had Louarn to help us build it."

"You had me!" Nolfi said. "And Jiondor and Riflin and Dalle and—"

"All right!" Elora laughed and gave him a playful shove, then blinked, blushed, and went quiet. Nolfi's eyes were shining. He'd practically turned inside out with happiness when Elora came back. Elora wouldn't miss Louarn's pretty face for long.

Pelufer missed Louarn so much she couldn't talk about it. He'd said he'd help her learn to cope with all the voices. Well, maybe she could learn on her own. Maybe what he'd already taught her, to find ways to live with uncomfortable things, could be applied to anything. But she was still furious with him for not saying goodbye.

All afternoon, and through supper, and all night she'd waited to hear the familiar tread, waited for him to come back from his wanderings and ask for a place on Jiondor's common-room floor. They'd even put out bedding for him. Jiondor's little sons had helped them. But he'd never come. They'd slipped out during the night—all the dogs were sleeping with Caille—and fetched the lumber for their new stall and put it by Jiondor's. When they crept back in, there was no dark head on the pillow, no body curled up in the blankets. Just Jiondor, arms crossed, tapping his foot. Demanding the whole story from them.

Pelufer fell asleep while they were explaining what they'd decided, but Elora must have kept talking, and Jiondor must have listened. First thing in the morning they were up and banging planks together, helping the other traders and being helped in return. Kara came and played with Caille while they worked, so Dabrena and Adaon could go off on some digging expedition, and when they came back they were so excited and terrified that they had to go straight to the alderfolk with some proposal, so Kara got to stay with Caille. Pelufer thought they should probably take Elora, but Adaon wasn't half bad at talking people round to things, so she supposed they'd do all right. But if the codices they were worried about were anything like workings, they were going to have a job of it. Good thing that black runner had gone off to fetch some friends of hers. They would need them, with Mireille around.

On the other hand, they had Kazhe. She would defend whatever they'd found under Woodhill. She was the most dangerous, intimidating person Pelufer had ever met. A thrill went through her just looking at Kazhe, like the thrill she'd felt when she first held Risalyn's longblade. And her shine was a dark blood red. When the whole hill business was sorted, their training could start. She'd do that for half a day and work the stall the other half. She wouldn't even be tied down to the stall, not if things went according to plan. She'd be moving around Gir Doegre all the time, and Elora couldn't complain, because it would be on business. If things went according to plan.

"All you need are seats, and you'll be all set, so." Jiondor was admiring their handiwork. "How about stepping behind there and giving it a go? Custom's starting to pick up."

Pelufer looked at Elora, who nodded and called for Caille. "There's something we have to do first," Pelufer said, looking across the low traders' wedge toward the river and Lowhill.

"I understand," said Jiondor. "Will you want company?"

"No, thank you," Elora replied. "It has to be just us."

With Caille between them, they cut hand in hand down Vanity Short, past the scents and creams and hairbrushes, and crossed Bronze Long with care. Between the Swallow and the Chimney Swift there had been a footbridge over the river, but the storm had washed it out, so they went back down Bronze Long to the maurbridge, and made their way from there into the shambles that was Lowhill.

Their cottage, toward the center, was wrecked.

The cottage to one side of it had slanted over in the storm, and the tin roof had gone clear through the common room at an angle. Wind and water had done the rest. The people who had lived there must have picked through their salvageable belongings yesterday; they were nowhere to be seen. The whole hill was quiet, with most folk tending first to their shops and stalls, no one preparing meals at this hour, no one emptying drip-pit tarps or turning middens. And there had been illness here, while they were gone. Lowhill had never been as rife with haunts as Highhill or the Kneeside, but Pelufer felt them now, like the shreds and tatters of a boneman, gossamer lives and names and thoughts passing through her. The fog had lifted, but for Pelufer there would always be a mist clinging to this town, fogs curling in the cracks and corners. It was all right. There were only two voices she was listening for now—and so intently that the others couldn't overwhelm her.

She touched the wreck of their childhood home. Gone, now, like Mamma's workshop. All the structures of the past demolished, collapsed. They had only themselves to live in now.

"Do you hear them?" Elora said, watching her carefully. When they'd gone to Jiondor's house last night, where his pledge had died of the bilechoke—his sons' mother, though Beronwy was their mother now—she'd gotten a nosebleed. That's how powerful it was between Jiondor and the woman's haunt. But afterward Jiondor looked two stone lighter, and Beronwy had gentle tears in her eyes, and the little boys couldn't stop talking about how they'd spoken to their other mother. And the mother's haunt was gone. She'd been able to say goodbye, and it freed her. That was worth a nonned poxy nosebleeds.

"One of them," Pelufer said.

She heard her father.

He was calling their mother's name.

"Mamma?" Pelufer said, putting her other hand on the wreckage. "Mamma? It's Pelufer, and Elora. And this is Caille. The baby. Look how grown up she is, Mamma!"

Caille found some other child's broken toy in the rubble inside what had been the front doorway. She handed it to Elora. A spinner, made of oak. Elora fit the pieces back together. The seams flared copper, and sealed. "We'll find them and give it back," she said, returning the mended toy to Caille's care.

A man, headed for the river with a basket of muddy clothes, had caught sight of Elora's working. "What was that?" he said, veering closer. "What did you just do?"

This was it. A scary moment. Half a lifetime of keeping the secret . . .

Elora squared her shoulders and said, "A mending. There's more where that came from. Go to the stall between sweets and pies on Hunger Long when you've done your wash, if you're interested." She swallowed, clutched Pelufer's wrist, and said, "Tell your friends!" Then she turned back quick, covering her mouth, her eyes bulging.

Pelufer swayed, feeling a swell of trader pride that did not come from her. "Good girl," she said. The wreckage blurred. She felt she was looking into some other place—some invisible place beyond what was in front of her, or inside it. "Good trader girl," she said, and then reached out to grab Caille and pull her into a rough hug.

"It's him," Elora said, going pale, as Caille squirmed free.

Pelufer nodded. "He's not saying much. He's proud of you. Never miss a chance to show your wares. That's his girl. But . . ." It was fading. For a moment he had noticed them, like a fish nosing to the surface of the river, but then he submerged again, and all Pelufer could hear was him calling Prendra's name. "He wants Mamma." The world came back into focus. "Where's Mamma, Elora?"

"Tell her we met Lornhollow. Tell her he misses her. He did what she asked him. He made us strong. Caille saved the world."

"Not by myself," Caille said, examining the crazing in a chunk of plastered wall.

"And we helped. And she eats enough for six, and she's beautiful and strong and healthy. Tell her that, Pel. Tell her good things so she'll come."

Pelufer shook her head so hard her hair fluffed. "I can't . . . She's not . . . She's not *here*, Elora!"

Elora blew out a hard breath. "The bonefolk don't passage the spirits. She's *somewhere*. Why would she leave Padda by himself?"

"He's still calling her. He's been calling her for a long time, I think." The father she had felt in the spirit wood had been protective and strong and even stern with her. But she had been in trouble then, or so she thought. That got his attention. It took that much to wake him from the long dry dreamy loneliness of waiting for Mamma.

"He doesn't want to be here," she said. "We're not here anymore, no one he loves is here. But he doesn't know where he'd find her otherwise. She's not at her workshop. Her workshop's gone. Oh, Elora, *where is Mamma?*"

"In the stall? Would you feel it if she were?"

The wood for their stall had come, originally, from what was their mother's workshop on Heelhill, the shed they'd lived in after they traded this cottage away because Pelufer couldn't stand the feel of her father's haunt—the absence of her mother's haunt. Her mother had never haunted this place. Her mother had never haunted the workshop.

"He left us to be with her, and he couldn't find her." She had never felt such a profound sadness. It hurt, deep in her heart, like a real physical pain. Ripping away from Elora, she whirled around on the devastated Lowhill slope and cried, "Mamma! *Where are you?*"

Elora hissed—she'd have every keeper in town running to save the poor lost child—but Pelufer didn't care. Let them come. Maybe that would get Mamma's attention. Why didn't she come? Why wasn't she here? How could she have left their father all alone? She wasn't with Lornhollow, she wasn't in the bonefolk's realm, she wasn't in the spirit wood or the planks of their stall and she wasn't *home*, she wasn't *here*—

I'm here, love.

"What?" Pelufer whispered.

I'm here. I've always been here.

Elora said, "What is it?"

Pelufer held a hand up and closed her eyes. Haunts' voices came from places. Haunts *haunted* things. They had location. But she couldn't tell where this one was.

Here, love. Look in. Look quick! I have to go now.

Pelufer sank to her knees.

The voice was coming from inside *her*.

Elora rushed over and said a lot of things about how they shouldn't have come here and of course it was too much and they'd go back to Jiondor and Nolfi now and start their new lives.

Pelufer said, "I found her. She's here." And put her fist on her chest.

"She's haunting *you?*"

"She . . . It . . ." Pelufer listened, and said, "You and Caille have so much of her. You look like her, Elora, you have all her goodness, Caille has all her love. . . . It was a way to . . . know me . . . and be with us, because she loves us, because she left us so early and . . . But . . ." She rubbed her hands over her face, and then felt a grin come on, a grin that wasn't her own but was exactly like her grin, and it was Mamma's grin, Mamma's mischief, all this time she'd thought that her thieving and rule-breaking came from her father's side, but it was Elora's shoulds-and-shouldn'ts that came from Padda, and it was Mamma who had lurked in the spirit wood and fallen in love with a boneman, it was Mamma who broke all the rules by making him promise to give her strength to her children, it was Mamma who did everything you weren't supposed to do and drove poor straitlaced Jenaille to distraction. It was Mamma who broke all the rules, and she couldn't resist that in Pelufer, and so she'd hidden inside there all this time, to be with them, all three of them. Because you haunted the place you most wanted to be. Because you haunted the things you most loved.

"She has to go," Pelufer said. "She misses Padda. Nimorin, Padda. I . . . She didn't know he was waiting, calling. Now she knows. She's . . . sad, and happy, so happy she can't . . . I can't . . ." She made herself focus on her sisters. "We're getting to be big girls now. We're big brave girls and we can take care of ourselves, and she misses Padda so much. She's going now. She's . . ."

Don't go! her heart cried, at the same time that she felt a wondrous flood of joy wash through her, and then wash back, from the cottage, from Padda.

He'd called for so long, and now Prendra had come.

What happened then was beyond Pelufer's ability to comprehend. It was so instantaneous and complex and deep that it made her realize that no matter how she might think of herself, she was still only nine-and-two, and not even nearly a grownup yet.

But she understood the last bit. She understood the feeling of air being sucked out of a room, like when you yanked the front door open and you heard the loose shutters on the windows bang inward.

"She's gone," she said. "They're gone."

Elora looked stricken. "They can't go! We didn't get to tell them we love them!"

"They knew. They knew, Elora. They knew everything."

"But . . ." Elora couldn't put into words all the things she had expected, and wanted, from this.

"They're not like us now," Pelufer said, getting up on shaky legs. She felt blood running down into her mouth. Elora groaned and pulled out a cloth, tipping her head back, sopping at her nose. "They love us, but they know we're all right," she said, muffled through the cloth, the way the names used to be when she hid behind her kerchief to keep people from hearing them. She let her head down when her neck started to hurt, and pressed the cloth up tight to hold the blood in. "She was with us through all of it, Elora. She saw Caille grow up. She saw your workings. She saw what Caille did. She was proud. Padda wasn't worried about us, but he was there when it counted, and now they're together, that's what they wanted, and they've gone. They'll find us if they need to." She looked down at Caille, who had been picking around the edges of the cottage the whole time. Caille knew she was loved. She knew it so deep inside that she didn't need to talk to haunts or hear last words or worry whether people knew all the good things she had done.

We did that, Pelufer thought. *We made her like that. And Mamma and Padda know it. And they're proud.*

Someday, she would find a way to explain that to Elora.

And find out what it was Elora's heart had wanted from their parents' haunts, and tell her that she already had it, and always had, and always would.

Mireille was standing behind their stall when they got back.

Her face was red and her eyes were shiny, and Pelufer had the perverse thought that Mireille had a shine, too, and hers was for getting other people into trouble.

"Don't you have a stall of your own to tend?" Pelufer said, knowing full well what Mireille would say.

"I used to! I expanded it and all, but the storm blew it down and before I could rebuild *someone* walked off with my lumber."

"From what I heard, you didn't lift a finger yesterday to start rebuilding," Pelufer said.

That scored with the traders around them, who didn't think much of laziness. Mireille said, "I could hardly do it by myself. And now I can hardly do it at all, can I, with *all my lumber* hammered here into your new stall!"

Caille had run around behind Jiondor's to see what Kara was doing and show her the mended toy. Elora was wilting under the stares of the other traders. Mireille's accusation was serious. Pelufer only grinned. "Why don't you go fetch Alderman Denuorin and make your claims to him?" she said.

With a toss of her head, Mireille went off to do exactly that. "Plaguing the alderfolk beats a day's honest work," Pelufer said to the other traders, and went to stand behind her new trading board, as though she didn't notice how they *humph*ed down into themselves.

"You're playing with tin sheets and no gloves on," Jiondor said quietly.

"Healings and mendings!" Pelufer cried out into the long, her voice weaving into the cries of stewmongers and soupmongers, rootmongers and juicemongers. "Feed the spirit and talk to haunts!"

Now she was getting stares, all right. She raised her voice, cutting through the murmurs, startling the gawpers back a pace, and cried their trades again. No one came forward. At first no one had any idea what she was talking about. That was all right. It would take time.

Mireille took hardly any time. She blazed her rude way back through the gathering crowd practically hauling the alderman behind her. Anifa would have none of her, and the other alderfolk were too busy to entertain yet another of Mireille's tantrums. But Denuorin was a kind man who could never say no.

"That's my lumber," Mireille said. "See there, the cuts where the tin used to sit? That was the extension on my stall, and no sooner was it blown down than Prendra's lot swooped in to have it off me. I want it back, and I want my stall repaired for my trouble."

"That could have been anyone's tin seated in those cuts," Denuorin said. "How do we know for certain this was your stall?"

"Where else did the planks go? They're not on my pitch. Ask *them* where they got the lumber for this new stall."

Denuorin asked.

"From Mireille's pitch," Pelufer said promptly, and enjoyed the gasps and consternation. They had a nice batch of gawpers now.

Mireille threw her arms out—*You see? I told you!*—then crossed them over her chest and waited on Denuorin.

"And where did you get the lumber, Mireille?" Denuorin asked. "Might it have been someone else's before it was yours?"

"From a scrapmonger," she said, frowning. "I have no idea where he got it!"

"Which scrapmonger was that? Ollo? Elidorlin?"

Her eyes narrowed. "It wasn't one of ours. A passing trader."

"That's very interesting." Denuorin pulled half a shattered plank from a carrybag slung over his shoulder, and held it up beside their stall. The gray weathering was almost identical; the pocks and holes from mites and borers were the same. "Now, this piece comes from Heelhill, where Prendra n'Anondry, these girls' mother, had her copperworks. Jenaille and Prendra were never on very good terms, were they?"

"My mother had nothing to say to them."

What a liar! Pelufer thought, but she kept her mouth shut. For now.

"After their father died and they traded their cottage away," Denuorin said, "these girls lived in that shop. That shop was knocked down by someone with a hammer, shortly before they went away up Gir Nuorin. Elora took me for a walk up Heelhill yesterday afternoon, so. We had a look round. Someone had taken most of the lumber, but a few scraps were left, tossed into the bushes by the storm. We retrieved this one."

He waited. Mireille waited him out, giving him nothing.

Denuorin sighed. "While they were away up Gir Nuorin, you expanded your stall, Mireille. Which scrapmonger did you say you got the lumber from?"

Mireille only hesitated for a moment, but to Pelufer that moment was priceless. "A thieving one who knocks workshops down, apparently," she spat.

"I'd say you were sadly taken," Denuorin said. "You might be more careful who you trade with in future. Stick to Gir Doegrans, where you can. Trade local and you'll never go wrong."

He laid the piece of plank down on their trading board and, without further word to anyone, went back to his own business on Pewter Short.

Mireille wasn't through. "I'm very sorry for what happened to your mother's shop," she said to Elora. "But you abandoned it when you went off. You left the lumber there for the taking. If some scrapmonger took it, worse luck for you. But I traded for it fair and square. I'll have it back now."

Pelufer stepped out from behind the stall.

Elora calmly responded, "You made no effort to repair your stall, which amounts to the same thing. Anyone would think you weren't going to bother. That doesn't mean that someone could come along and take the parts that rightfully belonged to you. We just took the parts that rightfully belonged to us."

"I demand restitution," Mireille said, ignoring Pelufer moving toward her. "How was I to know where the scrapmonger got the wood?"

"If there was a scrapmonger, then you were cheated," Elora said. "Go demand restitution from him."

"And how will I find him? You stole from me! I demand restitution from you!"

Pelufer reached out for Mireille's arm as though she was going to try to reason with her in a more friendly way, but once she had it, she didn't let go, even though Mireille tried to jerk back.

"Your mother told you never to lie, Mireille," she said. She looked past Mireille, letting her eyes go out of focus. "She haunts you, did you know that? She's asking you a question. She wants to know if you've forgotten that mendacity is the only affront worse than impropriety."

"Get your hands off me! You can't hear my mother's haunt!"

"She can hear haunts," Elora said. "She always could. That's why she was in the spirit wood that day."

Mireille's conniving outrage was like a sheet of metal she held out before her to push her way through all the obstacles in the world. Pelufer saw it dent and crumple in the middle. Jenaille had been scared of the bonefolk, and of Prendra. Her kind of hate came from fear, and she passed that on to Mireille. Mireille was scared now, and Pelufer let her go. But Mireille held her ground. So Pelufer added, "Now get away from Prendra's lot, she says. I don't want you associating with that bonefolk's get!" Then she pretended to come back into herself, appalled at how the haunt had insulted her and her sisters, and braced against the stall. Had her ruse worked?

Mireille went dead pale. That was answer enough. Pelufer was sure she'd won. Elora leaned forward to whisper, "Her mother wasn't in there." Pelufer, pretending to whisper back something affronted, said, "She might as well be!"

Elora covered her face with her hands. Through her fingers, Pelufer heard a snort of laughter.

The gawpers were swayed. You could see the ripples of curiosity move across them. Could the little girl really hear haunts? Could she hear their own haunts, speak to their own dead? Mireille had provided Pelufer with the perfect chance to show her wares.

But Mireille would not give up. "You leave my mother out of this," she said.

"Your mother is the reason you hate us, and knocked our shed down, and used our lumber," Elora said, as young and sweet and injured as could be.

To wrest the crowd's sympathy back to her, Mireille cried, "None of this changes what I'm supposed to do for a stall now! You stole from me. I need that lumber to put my stall back up. It won't work the way it was, not since the expansion. My family has tended that stall for three generations!"

That was a persuasive plea. It wasn't fair and it made no sense, but it worked on every trader's sympathies. Pelufer had wanted to humiliate Mireille, make her leave them alone, and cry her new trade all at the same time. But she would never get rid of Mireille by humiliating her. They had gone about this all wrong. They had worked from spite of a spiteful girl. *Don't try to use someone who would use you. It twists on you.* If she'd just done a working on Mireille's old tin stall, to make it fit again, Mireille might have been satisfied. She'd have thought she got something out of them, and got away with hurting them too. She'd have thought she won, and she'd have left them alone.

Offer to put her poxy stall back together, Pelufer told herself. *Do it. Say the words.*

She couldn't. Mireille made the alderfolk burn Elora's workings. Mireille destroyed the only shelter they had left, and did her best to run them out of town, and stole the lumber while they were gone.

She knew what she should do, and she just couldn't do it.

"I think you'll find your stall repaired and waiting for you to set out your wares," said a familiar voice from the crowd beyond Mireille. "Perhaps you should have stopped by there first this morning."

Mireille whirled. "You!"

Louarn gave her the stunning smile that Pelufer had never trusted. She'd never been so glad to see a thing so beautifully crafted. "It's made of tin, but that is what you started out with, yes? The stall your mother tended, and her mother before her, was made of softwood, and fell to the rot last summer, as I recall."

When had Louarn ever met Mireille? And why was the old stonemonger Loralir on his arm like a favorite aunt?

Mireille shot an accusing finger at him. "That man trades the badges of people of light on a shadow market! The keepers were after him!"

Louarn's smile turned gently pitying. "The keepers were after me because you set them on me, love, and where you got the idea that there's a shadow market in mages' gear, I can't imagine."

Mireille actually sputtered.

Loralir said, "Why don't you go back to your stall, dear?" Loralir had the stall beside Mireille's. They'd been competitors forever, but Loralir was unimpeachably prim and proper, and she'd coexisted about as well as anyone could with Mireille. "He did mine, too, you know. Was just finishing up yours at dawn when I came out to have another go, and he had mine up in a jiffy. He's a lovely boy. And he's going to take something in trade for the work he did for *me*. Whether he wants to or not." Ostentatiously, she pressed something into his hand, and Pelufer could see that Loaurn was genuinely taken aback. "I won't hear no for an answer this time. Nobody helps me twice and gets away for nothing." She gave him a quick peck on the cheek and was off, back to set out her wares and return to business.

As Mireille slid away, quick to avoid the issue of payment and probably wanting to check his work, Louarn looked at what Loralir had put in his hand, and started to laugh. "I have really got to learn not to turn down gifts."

"What did she mean, 'this time'?" Elora asked.

"I did her some small service on my first visit here. She tried to repay me with this. I declined. I thought it a useless trinket. Neither of us knew what it was. But I know now." He called to Kara and Caille to bring over the children they'd been playing tag with. "Were any of these children in the bonefolk's realm with you?"

"Tofro was," Kara said. "But nobody believed him, so he won't talk about it."

Louarn knelt before a chubby boy whose lower lip was already coming out in a stubborn pout. He said, "I look a little like the scary woman, don't I? But I'm not like her, not much anyway. I'm Kara and Caille's friend. They'll vouch for me. See? Do you believe me?" The boy looked at Kara and Caille, who were nodding, and then he shrugged. "Good lad," Louarn said, and opened his hand.

In his palm lay a waxy, pale stone, irregular in shape, as though it had been hacked out of a bigger stone. When Louarn held his hand up near the little boy, the stone glowed like moonlight in the middle of the day.

"That's magestone," said a waysider in the small group of lingering gawpers.

Louarn nodded. "Yes it is."

"That stuff is only supposed to glow for people of light."

Louarn nodded again. "And so it does."

For a few breaths more, the gawpers gawped. Then they were gone—to tell the alderfolk, to tell their friends, to flee, Pelufer had no idea. Only one or two were left now, their jaws hanging open.

Louarn thanked the boy and stood up. Despite the assurances, the boy thought something would happen to him, the way it did the last time he saw a stone like that. He looked surprised to be finished. Then he and the other children tore back into their game, Kara in the lead, calling over her shoulder to Caille to come join them.

Caille stood watching Louarn.

"Would you like to know what the woman's ring would have told about you?" he asked.

Her eyes on the stone, Caille shook her head, but she kept standing there.

"Are you sure?" Louarn said.

Eyes still on the stone, Caille shook her head again.

Pelufer went over and crouched down next to her, throwing a loose arm around her, saying nothing.

Caille looked slowly up at Louarn, and nodded.

He closed the stone in both hands, knelt in front of Caille, and said, "Pick a hand!"

It was a game he'd played with her in Gir Nuorin, a silly baby's game that she only liked when Louarn played it. It was completely silly now, since the stone was in both hands. She giggled despite herself, and clapped her hands on both of his.

He opened them. The stone lay pale and lightless in his palms.

Pelufer let out a breath she hadn't known she was holding.

"I guessed right!" Caille said, and darted off to rejoin her friends' game.

"I think she's glad because otherwise she'd have something that Kara was supposed to have, and that wouldn't be fair," Pelufer said, watching her go. It was so strange to see Caille surrounded by friends. Frightening, and wonderful, and sad. She supposed she'd get used to it eventually.

"That's very astute of you," Louarn said, and she found him looking at her with his head cocked.

She was about to rake him raw for letting them think he'd left them forever when one of the last gawpers touched her lightly on the shoulder, then snatched his hand back. Both she and Louarn stood up. "Can you really talk to haunts?" the man said.

Pelufer swallowed. Elora giving secrets away was one thing. Doing it herself was another. She'd cried their trade across the whole long, but that was to shock everyone. This was different. With an effort of will, she made her head go up and down.

"What would you take to talk to my family in Highhill?"

Pelufer could not begin to think.

Elora swept in to haggle with the man. It depended on how many haunts there were, and whether they were there or not, and of course whether he was satisfied, but they worked out a range, and next thing she knew Pelufer was headed back to Highhill, the scariest place of all next to the spirit wood.

Jiondor had said she might make a trade of this.

Well, they'd find that out now.

• • •

She was back at noon with real tallystones in her pocket—stones she'd earned, not stolen. She was ready to present them to Elora, their very first takings, but she found the stall so swamped with custom that she had to squeeze between two stalls down the row and come up along the alley behind them to reach it, and then everybody was too busy to listen to her.

Louarn was arranging work for her, and Kara was sitting under the trading board, hiding while she scribed on a board with a piece of charcoal. Caille was watching in fascination. "Their names," Kara said when Pelufer squatted for a closer look. "In order. You'll never keep them straight otherwise. But you need someone who can scribe better than me." It did seem to be hard for her, and her tongue stuck out while she worked the charcoal with her hand. But Pelufer had never seen anything like it. Marks that told you the order of customers! Now, *that* was a useful knack. It would leave all kinds of room in your head for remembering other things.

Elora was explaining the rules for healings for what sounded like the dozenth time. "One healing per customer for now," she said to a man with a scrape on his head. "You might want to save it for something important. And you have to bring someone with you to help. The point is that other people can do it too. We're going to teach you. So healings are free, but every one has to be a lesson, and you can't come to us for small things."

The scraped man went away, but another man came forward, with a sickly-looking child and dark circles under his eyes that attested to the difficulty in caring for him. "My boy's got Saron's palsy," he said. "He'll take his healing now, assuming this isn't a barrel of backwash. You can give whatever lessons you like to me."

Elora peeked under the board. "Are you ready, Caille?"

She must have turned dozens of small injuries away, if this was the first time Caille was doing a real healing.

Caille nodded, and came out.

The crowd that formed to watch her work made an immediate problem obvious: nobody could get through Hunger Long while this was going on. But the sooner the word got out, the better. She and Elora had decided, and Caille had agreed. The only way to protect their powers was to give them away. If they weren't the only ones who could do what they could do, they wouldn't be overwhelmed by people wanting them. If they weren't the only ones, they wouldn't be in danger because they were the only ones. They had to hide in plain sight, by making their powers commonplace. Everyone had *some* shine. There was no reason they shouldn't learn to use it, or use it better if they already could, or find it again if they'd lost it when they grew up. And there might be a lot of strong ones. Maybe not as strong as they were, but as strong as Kaʒhe, or Louarn, or even stronger.

It meant they were going to have to learn to explain how they did things. That was going to be hard. Jiondor was the one who pointed that out. But he also said that he learned more about being a trader from starting in to teach his sons about it than he ever had just doing it. It made you think about what you were doing, and do it better. They were learning more about the shine all the time. This would help them. So they'd get something out of it too.

A good traders' solution, that was. Pelufer liked it.

Caille stood next to the boy and looked at Elora. Elora nodded. Caille took the man's hands and put them on his son. She put her hands over them. Pelufer didn't think the man had much of a shine, although the little boy had a lot, even though he must be seven or eight and he was sick and wasted. But the man saw Caille shine. He must have. His eyes flew wide as copper plates. And then he started to shine, too. He started to believe that maybe this wasn't a barrel of backwash. He started to hope that his son might get better. He started to let himself want it. And then all his love and his longing and his strength began to . . . shine.

Caille couldn't explain what she could do. But she could share the feeling of it. That might be a better lesson than all the words that Pelufer and Elora would ever be able to come up with.

Their first customer went away more than satisfied. That gruff, exhausted, suspicious man went away awed and laughing and mopping his eyes, with his son healthy for the first time in his life. He'd thanked Caille so much that he'd scared her and she'd crawled back under the stall, and Elora said that he could thank them by trying to do what Caille had done, and she hoped he'd come back and let them know if he did, or if he had any questions. She was such a good trader. She was in her element here, behind her wooden stall. She wasn't just shining with her shine. She was shining with happiness.

"How did you fare with your haunts?" she asked Pelufer at last, holding a hand up so the customers would wait a moment. It was a good technique. Get them excited, then make them wait.

Pelufer grinned. "He bawled like a baby," she said. "He never got to say goodbye to his grandparents, and then there was his pledge, and his father, and his sister." For a moment her grin left her, as she thought how terribly many dead there were in this town, how many had been lost to the fevers and coughs and poxes. But they weren't lost, she told herself. Their selves went on. And maybe there'd be something they could do about it, someday. There were all those bodies in the bonefolk's realm, with no one knowing what they were for. They were going to have to work on that, once they got themselves established. "Anyway, he feels better now. But I never saw so much blubbering in my life."

"You're going to see a good deal more, I expect," Louarn said. He'd sent the rest of the hauntseekers away, and carefully wrapped the board Kara had scribed the names on. "You've got two days of work lined up for you. That was all the room Kara had on her board."

"It's because I scribe too big," Kara said from under the stall. She had some string and was showing Caille how to make a cat's cradle. "And you need sedgeweave and quills and things. What kind of place doesn't let people scribe on sedgeweave?"

"That may change as the light returns," Louarn said. "But for now we follow the rules."

He didn't look at Pelufer, but she knew the way his brow would have arched and the face she would have made back. He was almost all one shape now. It was different from the shape he'd had in the beginning. That one was flat. This one had volume. Like a sheet of metal turned and cut and soldered so that it could hold things. Some things would still bounce off him. But some things would fall in, and be held.

She suddenly felt too full of joy to be still. She had to *do* something—run, or jump up and down, or dance in and out of the stalls and alleys and shorts the way she used to, only this time calling hellos to the traders instead of snatching their wares. She would dance, the way she used to. She had left, and seen the world, and seen other worlds no one else got to see, and now she was home, and she felt as though she could dance forever.

"Hold on there, Pelufer," Louarn said. "I have something to tell you. All three of you."

Elora turned back to her customers, and Caille hunkered down into herself under the stall.

"I'm off up to Gir Nuorin to fetch our gear," he said, "and whatever Risalyn and Yuralon left."

Elora and Caille looked up. "That's it?" Elora asked.

"Yes. Just fair warning."

Or his way of saying goodbye. That wasn't good enough. Regarding him warily, Pelufer said, "Will you come back?"

Louarn smiled. "Yes. I can't promise it will be to stay. I'll go out again. Perhaps quite often. Perhaps for long periods. But yes. I will always come back here."

Pelufer danced.

KHINE

Evrael paced Streln's cool, uncarpeted bedchamber. Streln's house was constructed from the marbled blue stone of Khine. Perhaps that was one reason Evrael had always loved it here. It had the cool, clean chill of a stone holding, the temperature almost constant across the seasons within the thick stone walls, an environment that reminded him enough of home to replace it; but the stone was blue, not black, and it had always been warmed by the fires of Streln's presence.

It was cold now. The light in the chamber was aquatic, oblique; on the other side of the house, the sun blazed in a clear blue harvestmid sky. The day itself was sultry. Khine didn't feel the crisp bluster of harvestmid until winter had come to the Northlands. He'd never entirely accustomed himself to the offset seasons. On Khine, Longlight was midsummer; in all but the mainland's most southerly precincts, summer began with Longlight. The battle in the Strong Leg was known here as Midsummer's Folly. On the mainland, it was merely the battle of the Menalad Plain, and they didn't make much of the fact that it occurred during their Longlight festival. It was an event so contrary to reason that it had no place in the context of ordinary lives, and certainly not in the context of a celebration of life and light. Now, on Khine, it was harvestmid, which had started on Moonfire, what they called Sheaf Day in the Head. Ve Eiden, the equinox, harvestmid's peak, was a nineday away, and then harvestmid would be only beginning on the mainland. He felt unmoored from time, adrift. Position was relative, and he no longer had a lodestar to navigate by.

He walked to the window. The buffed bluestone floor was smooth and chill against the soles of his feet. A good place for sailors, Khine, where the stone was the color of sea and sky, where the custom was to go barefooted unless footgear was needed. He wore the loose nine-pleated pants of a ship's master, and nothing else but a ceremonial blade on a strap around his left shoulder—grief's knife, the blade Streln had worn to mourn his father. He'd let his hair grow out, according to the custom. On Ve Eiden, three moons after Streln's death, he would cut it, and go back to sea.

He had left the grounds of this estate only twice since his return. Once for the headman's memorial, and once more nine days later, to attend the hall that chose his successor. The new headwoman would render fine service. She came from an impeccable family and had many good works to her name. A woman of strength, compassion, and reason. There could have been no better choice.

He had denied the factions who would put him forward. He wished to return to sea as soon as propriety allowed. He planned to stay there.

At one end of the world, the mountain holding that had given him birth. At the other, this stone house, this cool blue bedchamber, where he had spent the brightest of his days and the most heated of his nights. He was weary of stone. Stone became permeated with the scents and tastes of ecstasy and pain, and exuded them thereafter. The sea washed all hurts away on the oblivion of tides. At sea, there was always a fresh wind, a new course.

Beyond the window, figs and olives hung ripe on their trees, grapes on their vines. The green terraces were acrawl with laborers—Streln's family, pitching in to maintain his land. He had bequeathed it to Evrael, according to his eldest brother, who mentioned some passing madness about the woman Lerissa, the details of which he seemed to have forgotten. It was moot anyhow; Lerissa had not returned from her last philanthropic journey, and was here to inherit nothing. Evrael had arranged for Streln's estate to pass to his youngest nephew, and for his own estate to pass to Streln's youngest niece simultaneously. Streln's family was large, and those youngest would otherwise get short shrift. Evrael had leased his land season by season when he was away at sea and could not tend it; the shipyard he had built was worked and owned by those in residence. He had held land only to assure his own standing in this community of landholders. But his ship was his own, and that was enough. If he lost his fleet command for lack of holdings, it was of no matter, so long as he was master of his vessel. He'd prefer a younger commander to run the fleet in any event, and would be looking for one suitable to put forward.

He was in the prime of his life, at six nines and two. He felt inordinately old.

With a sigh, he moved at last to the locked trunk he had found in the well under the stone platform of the bed. A trunk that had borne Lerissa's scent. A good blow from a ship's axe had opened it for him. Inside he had found an unusual codex, and inside that he had found the motivation for Lerissa's scheme.

It was wrapped now, and ready for a runner to deliver to Pelkin n'Rolf before it was sent back to the Isle of Senana, or wherever they were keeping the Head codices now. He had delayed long enough setting eyes again on a black-clad proxy. He called the waiting runner in.

The instructions he gave for the package's care and delivery were not complex, but the runner insisted on scribing them, and Evrael's brief message, on a sedgeweave scroll, so that he would get it right. *In my day*, Evrael thought, *our runners kept even the longest messages in their heads, and went where they were told without scribing the destination.*

The world had changed. He sent the boy off, and was again alone in the chamber where he and Streln had slept, the chamber Lerissa had appropriated. Streln's younger brother had her things removed before Evrael's return, though he had not known the trunk was hers. Evrael was grateful for that. But it made no difference. Streln was no longer here to fight for.

I should have fought for you, he thought. *I should have called her to an honor wedge and made her lift a blade in defense of her claim on you. I should have dishonored myself to save you.*

It was too late. It was far too late. Jealousy was ashes, and regrets were for the weak. He could not undo the past. A courageous man, a strong man, a Khinish man, went on, unbowed. With honor.

When he lifted his head, unaware that he had let it fall, Lerissa n'Rigael was standing before him.

He thought he was mad. Had she lurked here all this time? Were there hidden passageways unknown to him in this house of stone, as there had been in the Holding? Had she come back from some land-beyond? Or was she a phantom of his tight-held grief and rage, a manifestation of his unhealthy, cloistered mourning?

She stumbled slightly, like a sailor coming onto solid ground from a heaving ship's deck, and her hair and clothes were disarrayed, as though in a struggle. That was unlike her.

Why would he hallucinate a daughter of the Ennead in that disheveled state?

He wouldn't. He would not hallucinate at all.

"Evrael," she said, with some surprise, striving for composure. Then she seemed to realize where she was, and laughed. "So again it seems I come into your capable hands."

"So it seems," Evrael said, and stepped between her and the door.

"Will you deliver me again into your headman's care?"

"You seem to have returned yourself to his bedchamber with no aid required from me."

"I must have been gone some time, for you to make your way back into *that* bed."

"There was an absence in it."

"It's a large bed. There will be room for three."

He moved in close to her without touching, forcing her back with his height and breadth until her calves were pressed against the cold stone platform of that bed. "There are only two of us," he said. His breath lifted a strand of her hair.

Slowly, she raised her sapphire eyes, searching his face for signs of what he wanted—what would move him.

"Have you no crystal stone to capture my thoughts?" he said.

Her lashes fluttered—surprise that he knew how she had controlled Streln—and then she drew her lips back in a smile and her hand down his bare chest. It wasted no time seeking lower, more intimately. "You don't strike me as the sort of man who needs a crystal stone," she said.

"I have had quite enough of stone," he agreed.

Probing for response, she faltered when she could elicit none.

"And alas," he said, "I have never been aroused by women."

Her eyes flew wide as he took her by the neck and wrested her over his leg and to the floor. He wedged one hand under her chin, and whatever reply or protest she made came out a gurgle as he stroked the ceremonial Khinish blade across her throat.

"This was Streln's blade," he said quietly to her, as her lifeblood soaked the stone foundation of the estate she had usurped. "I consign to his spirit the blood it draws, and he is avenged."

He left her for the bonefolk.

He would grieve Streln his life long, but his days of mourning were at an end.

Gir Doegre
The Fist

It had been night in this holding for countless nonneds of years, as it rested in its long sleep inside the hill. When they shed light on it at last, it was as on a dream. A life imagined, yet fully lived; an ancient realm of alien objects and carvings and ornamentation, yet inhabited by people as human and ordinary as the folk of the town in its afternoon shadow. Ornate platters and goblets left set out for a meal. An overturned stool of strange design. Once-vibrant tapestries grayed with time, depicting scenery resembling the landscape they knew, yet different in dozens of details—windows on the past. The familiar rendered strange at every step. The folk of this lost age had been mages, folk of their own; but they were as wondrous and arcane as any folk from the outer realms could possibly have been. They illuminated their world, and inscribed it—in the stone of their chambers, in the metal of their diningware. Sculpted scenes ran along the ceilings, around each door, faces and animals and flowers and trees. Glyphs and pattern were everywhere. This had been the pinnacle of a culture. It had been plunged into darkness. They had opened it again to air and light.

It was also the highest sacrilege, by Strong Leg standards. Yet the alderfolk who stood beside Dabrena, here on their Ve Eiden tour, were not mortified.

Jeolle n'Jedona's face was slack with awe. Denuorin n'Amtreor beamed. Anifa n'Bendri appeared serene—satisfied in a sublime, peaceful way, as though something she had always suspected had come to pass. The junior alderfolk were smiling.

They were *proud*. Far from demanding a bonfire to destroy this nest of sacrilege, they had embraced it. Their reverence for people of light was rooted just as deep as their prohibition against the use of their tools. It would be a long time before the white and gray and black of menders and scholars and runners were tolerated in Gir Doegre, if they ever were, and longer still before color and patterning and scribing were permitted to the lightless. They might never understand that the carvings and inscriptions in this holding were clear evidence that nontriadic patterning did not weaken the power of castings. But as far as these alderfolk were concerned, it was the work of people of light, and they would cherish it, as they would cherish every child who showed a magelight.

This holding had been a center of magecraft and a well of light. They could not have been more happy that it had existed here under their feet for all these generations. Perhaps they saw its unearthing as a reward for their staunch defense of magecraft's instruments. As traders they had been quickly persuaded of its value as a local attraction. But their pride went deeper than self-righteousness or avarice. They were good folk, and they recognized the extraordinary when they saw it.

"It's beautiful," Anifa breathed, in the strangely scented air. There was as yet no cross-ventilation, but the interior would retain the odor of its long slumber even when thoroughly aired. A combination of Druilor and Elfelir stone, the peaty acidic damp that had seeped in long stains through the shuttered windows, and something else—the piquant scent of another world. The scent of time and the ages; the scent of history.

"Who'd have known people of light were capable of such work?" Jeolle said. "I thought it was all parchment and inked signs I knew nothing of."

"They made rings and pendants," said Denuorin, who was a pewterer. "I always admired those triskeles. I touched one once. It felt alive in a way my own metals never did."

"You've done a fine job here," Anifa said.

"Thank you for granting us access," Dabrena replied. "And for the time to clean it up before we presented it to you."

In truth, there hadn't been much to clean up. Some rodent bones, some ancient droppings, the remnants of an aborted nest; worms and insects hadn't found much to their liking in the bare stone halls. The seeping stains had been the worst of it. There was hardly any dust to speak of; dust was a byproduct of life, and no human living had been done here in nonneds of years. Earth had not filled the rooms. They had been preserved just as they were, stale air and all. Her first breath of that stale air had been a marvel. A draught of the past. Adaon had been drunk on it for three moons now.

What they had wanted was time to look, and catalogue, without the disturbance and contamination of visitors. Their own intrusion was disturbance enough. While they employed waysiders to excavate the front of the structure and provide safe ingress, they assembled a small crew to help with the interior. Stairways had to be cleared, the whole structure checked for soundness, and all had to be done with painstaking care, every detail recorded.

And then there were the triskeles. They had been nearly everywhere, though clustered, either because folk gathered together to die, or because the bonefolk had passaged their bodies in groups. Woodhill had been a grave mound, a cairn, a memorial to the dead. They had marked the location of every triskele on a map, then collected them all, with utmost respect, into a plain chest, now stored on the level below awaiting an appropriate place of honor. More than a nonned of them. More than a nonned mages had died here, and their triskeles were all that was left of their passing.

Now they could no longer hold off the hordes of seekers and menders and scholars who swelled Gir Doegre to the bursting point—and they would need trusted, expert help to mount an inventory of all the volumes stored here in their magecrafted, airtight vaults. The denizens and caretakers of this place had known that they might fall. They had not counted on wardings to safeguard the treasure of their lore. They had sealed their codices away from air and damp in stone chambers below ground level and in stone chests on the first and second stories. All had been carved with Stonetree glyphs to indicate their contents. She and Adaon had required the help of a stonecutter to open one, and what they had found still made her giddy. A set of herbals, three nines of them, perfectly preserved. Not in perfect condition; they had been used, in their day, marked and emended, wooden covers dented at the corners, bindings worn, leaf edges smudged with the oils of many ancient seeking fingers. In and of themselves those signs of human use took her breath away. And the contents—the renderings of familiar plants, the recipes and instructions . . . It was a mender's dream, a healer's dream, come true. Lore from what might have been Eiden Myr's most glorious age, restored to them.

Adaon had suggested Ve Eiden for the unveiling day. A tour for the alderfolk, by way of courtesy and thanks, in the morning when the sun shone through the maur-facing windows. The rest of the day, and the next, for the curious townsfolk—and then they would unleash their stonecutters, their seekers and scholars, their menders and runners, and open the treasure trove. The holding would live again.

She lingered in a sunlit corner on the second story as Adaon escorted the alderfolk back down the closest stairs and out. She traced a finger over the animal carvings in the stone as the alderfolk's steps receded, and smiled not to hear the thunk of Anifa's cane. Caille could not halt natural death any more than magecraft could, but she could ease the pains of aging, and Anifa's arthritic knees now moved fluidly and supported her weight. Ronim and Dontra waited below to begin showing Gir Doegrans through. This would be her last quiet moment here—perhaps ever, or at least until the novelty wore off and they could begin to work in earnest, and in peace.

From what she'd heard from the menders who'd come down to join her, and from what Adaon's scholar friends had told him, her own holding was much changed in these three moons. If Caille had not calmed the Longlight storm when she had, the Isle of Senana would have drowned, and its store of codices with it. As it was, it nearly had drowned. Folk in gray had watched in despairing horror as a great wave loomed incomprehensibly large on the horizon, so large it would have towered over their heads and swept Senana under before it broke on the High Arm's coast. Then the wave had melted into the sea. The residual water that slopped over them came up far enough to flood the floors of their dormitories on the hilltop. If they hadn't raised the codices nearly to ceiling height—or covered them in waxed tarps against the roof leaks and the driven rain that ripped through two layers of storm shutters—all would have been lost. When it was over, the decision to return them to the safety of the mountain holding in the Head was perhaps the first thing that Graefel n'Traeyen and Nerenyi n'Jheel had ever agreed on. They had been removed from the Head to keep them from the ire of any backlash against the Ennead—to keep them from people like Verlein. Dabrena had acquiesced in their removal. But they belonged where they had come from, not out on some windswept island, and the Head was safe haven for them once more.

Graefel might have always had designs on that Head holding. He'd followed the codices to Senana, but he'd always grudged their being stored there, and the authority their location conferred on Nerenyi. Nerenyi was pledged to one of the island's leaders. In concert with them, and Pelkin n'Rolf, and the Lightbreaker's advisor Jhoss n'Kall, she had arranged for both codices and scholars to be housed on Senana. Graefel must have been gratified by the opportunity to leave Senana and return to the holding that had once been the pinnacle of his ambitions. *Before you know it, he'll be running the place,* Dabrena thought.

That was all right. She missed her colleagues, but many of them had come down here, and this was a far better place for Kara to grow up. In the Strong Leg, where her father came from. She loved visiting Tolivar's family. They'd have to go up to the Fingers one of these moons, too, so she could meet her other grandparents. If there was time, it might provide an excuse to continue Headward. Or perhaps she would content herself with reports. She did not know if the black mountain was a world she ever wanted to return to.

Graefel had been a reckoner before he lapsed to pursue his personal goals. He would have no easy time of it with Selen n'Mirin or the other former warders. But if he ended up running that holding, fair play to him. In the three moons during which Dabrena had been in Gir Doegre, her menders had begun reporting to her here, of their own volition. She was their head, their nexus, whether she wanted to be or not. She moved, and they found her. It was heartening to know that she had neither clutched the reins nor held them merely by staying put. They were handed to her anew, each day, by the folk in white.

She'd be needing copies of the menders' codices. She would not send for the originals; those belonged in the Head. She had need only of their information. The master map of Eiden Myr could be copied and transported in sections. Each holding should have copies of it, and everything else up there, and everything that had been on Senana, for that matter—and everything that they found here. Each holding should be able to function in the absence of the others; no holding should function in isolation. She did not yet know why the Triennead had fallen, but like as not it was related to insularity. No more islands. No more closed mountains. Here was a chance to start fresh. To study the mistakes of the past and try not to repeat them.

And embrace the future. Reiligh had entrusted his garden to a prentice and had come down with a cartload of boxes—soil, seeds, bulbs, cuttings, entire plants. When she presented the chest of herbals to him, she thought he'd keel over like the tree he resembled. Each day brought a slew of discoveries, of "I knew it!"s, of beside-himself excitements. But there were times, when he sat quietly with Kara dozing on his lap, when she wondered if in truth he had come down here to be with her. Dabrena had known he loved the child, but she had not guessed how deeply, or that his despair at her abduction had been the equal of her own. She was, however, quite tickled to see one of those handsome sandy-haired muscle-legged keepers making excuses to help with Reiligh's new garden. Reiligh was beginning to look for him every day, the way a tree looks for the sun. There was a great deal for them here that they would never have found in the Black Mountains.

They were fairly certain that there were holding structures under Gir Doegre's other hills. This one seemed to be the library, with residence accommodations for only two families, the rest given over to reading halls and storage. Whether they would be permitted to excavate was less certain; there were people living on the town side of two of the eight hills, and three of the others were grazing land or tended woods. But if they could find a way to dig without disturbing what lay above, their chances with the alderfolk would increase. Though it was under duress, and though the storm's damage had rendered it unnecessary, the alderfolk *had* given permission for Adaon to dig into Woodhill. Woodhill was the hauntwood hill, the one that should have been untouchable. He would find a way to persuade them of the rest.

The miners helping Pelkin's folk in the Haunch would be helpful. There was a hill by the town of Sauglin—the town Adaon believed drew folk the same way Gir Doegre did, and a town that had always drawn mages—that might well be another buried holding structure. The runners were digging there, carefully and safely, to see if it was. The folk of Sauglin were enthusiastic, seizing on the possibility that they might have their very own holding. The Haunch had been unfriendly to mages in the last years of the light, but what they'd objected to was the Ennead's Holding taking the brightest of their bright mages and sending them only unresponsive proxies in return. To have a holding of their own would vindicate old grievances and give them their own center of power. In the meantime, the runners continued what they'd started in their quarters by Maur Gowra—a place to train folk in the use of magecraft's tools. It could all be easily transferred down to Sauglin if the opportunity arose.

Separation, isolation, overspecialization—those were the dangers. With Graefel and the oldest codices in the Head, the Head holding would attract scholars. She attracted menders, here in the Strong Leg. The runners congregated in the Haunch. That was all right. It was a good strong triangle, and they should build on it. Scholars came here, too, to see the newly unearthed codices. They would go to Sauglin if a holding ruin was found there containing records. Seekers visited all three places, and runners went everywhere. It would settle itself out. But if some prompting became necessary—particularly if Graefel required pressure to keep his holding accessible—they must be prepared.

She was aware that all her organizing thoughts were based on the paradigm of magecraft. She had been trained a mage and a warder. She thought like a mage and a warder. She knew that. And she knew that she must never forget that magecraft was no longer the only power in Eiden Myr. It never had been, as far as that went, but it was the only power they had tended, watering and pruning and training it the way Reiligh tended his vines and shrubs. They had only a new sprout of it now, and it would take a dozen years of careful work to see it bloom again. Meanwhile, this ruddy-copper light, this shine, had sprung up like an overlooked weed and spread with a weed's indomitable, glorious persistence. In three moons, Prendra's daughters had worked wonders, from their little stall in the center of town. What menders could not do with all their draughts and poultices, farmers and farriers, sailors and wranglers, sheepherds and cowherds and goatherds now did with a laying on of hands. Illness had abated since Eiden's storm, but whatever lingered was as often healed by heartcraft as by healers. Menders themselves were now working to increase their shine.

According to Adaon, the seekers had conjectured such a power, and some had witnessed it; they called it earthcraft. Louarn had begun calling it a heartlight and its powers fleshcraft. The girls simply called it a shine. Whatever nomenclature stuck in the end, it was a raw, new talent, a spreading wildfire. Those girls had struck Eiden Myr like lightning, and now their flame was fanned and fed. In comparison with that, magecraft had been stilted, restricted, stagnating. And dangerously elitist. She was eager, now, to prove that the Triennead had existed in part to prevent such stagnation, and that magecraft's senseless strictures had come upon them only in the ages since the Triennead fell. And that made her laugh—because it was a seeker's eagerness. Adaon had made a seeker of her after all.

She did not know how this new heartlight would fit in with the return of magelight. How complementary were they, how competitive? She believed Adaon when he said there must be a third power—Louarn had said the same, and knew more than he was telling—but she could only speculate upon what it was and what role it would play.

She feared it; she feared powers. However marvelous and benign, they carried the potential of conflict. She hoped it would be as simple as some earthcrafter and magecrafter arguing over who was to heal a broken arm.

Earthcraft would win, if it came to that; an earthcrafter could heal a dozen arms in the time it took to prepare and work a casting. And perhaps that was a blessing. To heal flesh, magecraft required the use of flesh—animal vellum and parchment, animal products for brushes and pigment and inks. Could earthcraft spare magecraft its killing aspect?

It could not replace magecraft, though it would compensate for it in the dozen years it took to train up prentices. Earthcraft could not ward against fire, or waterproof a cloak, or dozens of other things that magecraft had been able to do. They would always have need of both. The trick would be seeing to it that they coexisted in peace.

And what of that third power?

She wondered if the Lightbreaker had known the light would return. It was the difference between a spectacular error, unparalleled sacrifice, and the canniest strategy. She had spoken long with Karanthe about it, over several too many wines; as one of Pelkin's reckoners, Karanthe had been with Torrin Wordsmith and had believed wholeheartedly in him. She'd been quite taken with the notion of sacrifice—the sacrifice all mages had to make to keep the Ennead's darkcraft from destroying the outer realms. But if the only way to stop the light doing harm was to extinguish the light, then great peril lay in store for them. The potential for darkcraft would always exist. They would have to teach these children with care.

It had been a sacrifice in either event. Her light would never return. Pelkin's light would never return. Torrin's own blazing light would never have returned. She and Karanthe, who had based all their expectations and ambitions on their light, would be forever lightless. It was still hard to swallow, even with new hopes and ambitions in their place. Karanthe wanted Torrin Lightbreaker to be Torrin Martyr, a hero, a legend worthy of worship. Karanthe wasn't sure she liked the idea that he might have known the light would return—that what he had done might have been manipulation on such a vast scale. It wouldn't surprise Dabrena in the least. Torrin n'Maeryn had been a product of that Ennead and that Holding as much as any of the Nine had been. He had defied them, and fought to destroy them—but he had been one of them. She wasn't sorry he was gone.

She was startled to hear the next visitors coming up the stone stairs, and even more startled to see who they were.

Pelkin, with Karanthe on his arm, in a capacity Dabrena could not quite define but would certainly rib her about mercilessly the first chance she got. Louarn, at the back, like a reluctant shadow on Adaon's heels. And between them a slight, pink-eyed albino man she hadn't seen in years: Jhoss n'Kall l'Sirelyi, formerly of the Isle of Senana, formerly advisor to Torrin Wordsmith, come up from the Heel to have a look at this proposed new holding.

"Sunlight," Jhoss said to her after they had all exchanged greetings. "It suits you better than lamplight did."

"He talks about light quite a bit," Louarn said in an acerbic tone, examining the carvings around the door as though he'd rather go back through it.

Jhoss seated himself at the table in the center of the room, which was the common room of one of the two residences in this library structure. Pelkin complimented Adaon and Dabrena on their work here—still probing at Adaon, she noticed, still not entirely certain of him, like a grandfather unwilling to accept a granddaughter's sweetheart. Jhoss merely sat, and waited, and after a time conversation faltered in his silence, and they were all just standing there staring at him.

Dontra and Ronim brought a gaggle of Gir Doegrans through, and warned Dabrena that Kara already had the next batch in hand, determined to make herself a guide. Dabrena laughed. Kara would be an excellent guide; Kara knew this holding better than she or Adaon did. It didn't stop Dabrena's heart seizing each time she thought the girl had fallen down some hole they didn't know about, but she told herself they had to find the holes somehow, and she let the girl roam free. So it shortened her life by a nineday each time. She'd get used to it.

When they'd passed, Jhoss was still sitting there. Waiting.

"All right, you inscrutable man," Dabrena said at last. "Is it a meeting we're having? Important matters to discuss?"

"If you wish it," Jhoss said, and gestured to the other chairs around the table, as though they might take them or not and it was of no matter to him.

Dabrena winked at Pelkin and seated herself. "What fun! It will be just like that ill-fated meet we hosted in the Head on Spindle Day. We can call it the Council of Ve Eiden, in grave tones, and scribe interminable accounts in our historical records."

Adaon was laughing as he sat, and Pelkin was giving him a stern look, clearly of the impression that his bad influence was the source of Dabrena's cheerful flippancy. In fact it was only her good mood. She was in love, she was sitting in the sunshine in a Triennead holding rediscovered after aeons, the magelight was returning, there were new powers of healing in the world, the storm was over, Kara was happy and as safe as any inquisitive child could be. Adaon was drunk on the past; she was drunk on the present.

"Well, I do have some news to impart," Pelkin said, also seating himself—across from Adaon, which put Karanthe across from Dabrena. That would be useful for making faces, Dabrena thought. "Here and now serves as well as any other place and time. Shall I go first?"

"So long as someone does," Louarn said. He still stood by the doorway, though the table would seat six. The remaining chair was at the head of the table, or the foot, depending on how you looked at it and what you thought of Jhoss. Dabrena had a feeling that was important, but found the whole thing impossible to take seriously.

Pelkin put a threaded bamboo codex on the table, opened at the halfway point to reveal a strip inked in curling Celyrian script. "I received this from Evrael te Khine. He messaged that it had been in Lerissa n'Rigael's possession, and that it might explain the disappearances of children. He offered his help in finding them, should we need it. I messaged back that we would not."

Pelkin had heard the full tale from Karanthe, who had heard it from Dabrena, but Dabrena threw a questioning look to Jhoss. He nodded. He knew.

"That was the codex stolen from Senana," Adaon said. His arms twitched as he refrained from reaching for it.

"Take it," Pelkin said. "Read it. That's what it's here for."

Holding it so that Dabrena could read with him, Adaon did.

"This would have saved a lot of trouble if we'd gotten hold of it sooner," Dabrena said.

"I believe it was stolen with precisely that in mind," Jhoss said. "A scholar named Falowen n'Tedra disappeared at the same time this codex did, shortly after my own departure. I believe she intended to bring the codex to me. On the heels of her defection, Bofric n'Roric left the isle. I believe he intercepted it."

"He was Lerissa's man," Karanthe said. "One of her stewards from the Ennead's Holding." *Old Knobface*, she mouthed to Dabrena, and Dabrena made a rude gesture as a reminder of how they'd used to joke about the quickest way to earn the ring.

"Lerissa's agents Bofric and Loris remain at large," Louarn said. "With their master gone, we can hope that they will fade into obscurity." *And if Loris knows what's good for him*, Dabrena thought. Louarn added, "I had wondered about the codex. I'm glad it has resurfaced."

"It's moot now," Pelkin said. "We already know what it would have told us. But I thought you might find it interesting. I'll return it to the collection in the Head, unless you've any objection, Jhoss."

Jhoss said, "I have none. But you have news. Or so you said. This is not news."

Pelkin nodded, as though he had long ago ceased to be affected by Jhoss's peremptory quirks. "Evrael te Khine killed Lerissa n'Rigael for her subversion of Khine's headman and her conspiracy to provoke the battle of the Menalad Plain. I have since heard that he has been relieved of his fleet command for the act, but otherwise vindicated by the consensus judgment of the landholders."

Dabrena couldn't help but twist around to look at Louarn. He showed no reaction, lounging with careless impatience against the door, but she had only rarely seen his face betray anything he didn't want it to. "When?" he asked, and when Pelkin told him a nineday ago, he said, "How?"

"He did not specify, but I gather from his rather poetic mention of grief destroying grief that he used what they call grief's knife. A ceremonial Khinish blade, worn to symbolize the cutting pain of grief and the severing of mortal bonds. Strelniriol te Khine had been his lover and bonded brother."

Dabrena was still looking at Louarn. She cocked her head. He looked up at her from under his lashes and his forelock of dark hair, then raised his head. "Indeed," he said. "And all in the family. Evrael is my uncle. Lerissa was . . ." He paused, and smiled. "Lerissa birthed a child. I was that child."

Pelkin's head came up. "You were the babe Evonder gave into Bron's care?"

Louarn nodded.

Pelkin started to ask something, checked himself, and said, "We thought we'd never know who you fostered to, once Bron was gone."

"Your counterparts," Louarn said. "Pirra, Alliol, and Ellerin. The head warders. The Ennead struck at them on Ve Galandra . . . nine-and-six years ago. They were casting a warding, I believe, though I was too young to fully understand. Not to kill the Nine, but to save themselves, and me. They failed. I came back into Bron's care, after that. Do you remember a runner boy named Mellas, Pelkin?"

Pelkin squinted at him; then his face opened and he shook his head in wonder. "The weaves of the past are intricate beyond even my old illuminator's sense of path. Why did you change your name?"

"Now, that is a tale best left for some long winter's evening by a tavern fire," Louarn said. "And I know what Jhoss wants. I'd rather he have out with it, so I can say no and be on my way."

Jhoss said, "Yes. Good. Let us speak of light."

What he told them then, in his abrupt, stilted way, was a tale to rival Louarn's discovery of Prendra's daughters. Dabrena watched Adaon closely as Jhoss spoke, examining the play of expressions on his dusky face, the light of fascination that grew in his pale eyes. Jhoss's tale was a seekers' tale, a tale *of* seekers. The tale of a quest for the third light, though Jhoss had not known that when he started. He had sought a substitute for magecraft. He had not expected to find any light at all—not the way Dabrena conceived of light. He had sought to replace magecraft with the liberated tools of symbology. Finding insufficient support among the scholars on Senana, he had broken with Graefel and returned to the Heel. He had surrounded himself with seekers and scribes. He had developed a representational system of numbers. He had striven for a power of mind that Dabrena, even trained a wordsmith, could not comprehend. Something of his goals came to her as a shimmer on the horizon of awareness, but she could not have articulated what she sensed.

He concluded that his symbology would not fully develop in time to halt the droughts and floods and afflictions besetting Eiden Myr. It would require many more fine minds, working for many more years, to even begin to do whatever it was he envisioned. His seekers concocted many fascinating theories about the land's troubles. But they made less headway toward a solution than her menders had, working along similar lines and with the same tools—reason and the instruments of scribing.

"In the end," he said, "the shine of heartlight was required to ease the ills of Eiden's flesh, as it will continue to be required in the years to come. The lightless power of mind I sought cannot be developed in a moon, or a year, or six years, or a dozen, as I had dreamed. In a nonned, perhaps. Or nine nonned. Or twice that. And it is your menders who will do it, Dabrena."

"But there was a light," Louarn said, to bring the tale to its point. "Wasn't there."

Jhoss nodded, and waited.

Louarn made a sound that might have been a growl. Jhoss was forcing him to tell it. "And there is a light," he said, coming around at last to the chair at the end of the table, standing behind it. "A blue light, silver-blue, like the golden yellow of magelight and the coppery red of heartlight. Right, Adaon? Right, Pelkin, Karanthe? Any seeker will tell you that the most powerful things come in threes. Any illuminator will tell you that there are three primary colors. We have seen two of them. Of course there is a third. There had to be."

"Add red pigment in equal portion to yellow and blue," Pelkin said quietly, "and you get black."

"Add red light to yellow and blue," Louarn said with a strange smile, "and you get white. I know. I've seen it."

"You *are* it," Jhoss said.

There was a long pause.

"I have a power of dreaming," Louarn said. Acquiescing, again. Telling the tale because Jhoss forced him to, in order to have done with it. "Jhoss remembers. Torrin told him. Before she was his, Torrin's illuminator befriended a boy whose dreams were powerful enough to kill." He closed his eyes briefly. "I had a dream, a very terrible frightening dream, that Galandra's warding had been breached and the light was being seared from every mage in Eiden Myr. No, I didn't break the warding, Karanthe, don't look at me like that. Your martyr is safe. But I escaped the searing."

Jhoss said, "Louarn is the only adult in Eiden Myr who retains a magelight."

On a spike of envy, Dabrena said, "How?"

"I dreamed myself free. To do so, my dreaming must have been fueled by other powers as well. My magelight was under attack. I felt the coring, as though I were being disemboweled. I fled into another realm, and saved my light. Through a dream. A thing of the mind. Through what I conceived of as a passageway made of brilliant white light."

"You glow," Jhoss said.

"And so do you," Louarn said. "Silver blue. The light of mind." He looked at Adaon. "Can you see it? It's strong in you. Can you see Jhoss's? Or mine?"

Slowly, blinking, Adaon nodded. "Somewhat," he said.

"It will get stronger as you learn to look for it, just as the copper shine becomes more visible to those who learn from those girls down on Hunger Long."

"Wonderful," Dabrena said across the table to Karanthe and Pelkin. "Everyone gets to glow but us. Thank your Lightbreaker for me, if you ever run across his haunt, will you?"

"One light goes dim, perhaps another has the chance to shine," Louarn said to her gently. "In each person, as in the world we know. Magelight was quenched, after we had relied on it for twice nine nonned years. And in an eyeblink, relative to those aeons, up springs heartlight. The strongest copper shine in Eiden Myr is a child of the vanished magelight—a child conceived of the failed freedoms, a child whose birth was her mother's death in the absence of magecraft to smooth the way."

Dabrena noticed that he did not mention Lornhollow's role in the flaring of that light. None of them who knew had said much about the bonefolk. And they would not, without their permission. They had only just learned of their realms, their language, their ways. Much was required before they could share that with—

Abruptly Dabrena remembered something Pelufer had told her. Everyone had some shine . . . but her shine, dull though it was, and Kara's, which had started to dim as she left early childhood, had brightened after their passage through the bonefolk's realm. If that passage somehow excited the shine within them . . . if a heartlight could be liberated, or increased, by such a passage . . .

She saw Adaon recognize that she was holding in some important thought. She shook her head. There would be time for this. She would not interject her new seekerlike theory into whatever Jhoss and Louarn were having out.

"With magelight to rely upon," Jhoss said, "we neglected many powers of invention and intellect that we otherwise might have fostered. Twice nine nonned years of progress were lost. For lack of necessity. As the instruments of ink and sedgeweave were restricted to magecraft's use. I grieve those years . . . yet there is relief, as well. Of a burden. I made a great effort toward that vision of invention. Time thwarted me. But perhaps . . . that other path . . ." He faltered.

"That other path might have led to powers that would have harmed more than helped us," Louarn said. "But we'll be here all day with visitors gawping at us if we don't get on with this, Jhoss. The answer is no. Ask your question."

They must be glowing bright blue, Dabrena thought. *Working their mindlights like mad, weaving rings around things they haven't even said aloud yet. I'll take that red shine, if I get a choice.*

Karanthe, perhaps thinking along the same lines, or just responding to the sour expression on her face, stuck out her tongue. Dabrena grinned, and felt seven years younger.

Jhoss stared at Louarn with no expression. At last he said, "There is a mindlight. Seekers have it. Others have it. Some very bright. As bright, perhaps, as the brightest magelights were described to me. Those folk have powers. Not powers of symbology and invention, as I had hoped; those went to the menders, and they must pursue them. Not powers of dreaming, like Louarn's. But powers to reckon with. I have found only a handful. I continue to seek."

"What kind of powers?" Dabrena said, no longer amused.

Jhoss turned his corpse-pale face to her, with its strange pink eyes filled with incomprehensible visions, and said, "Powers to fear."

"Ah," Pelkin said. "Yes. I see." He rubbed his chin and jaw and let out a rough sigh. "Three discrete, fearsome powers. Three lights, growing day by day. Within a dozen years we will run the risk of great conflicts among them."

"Three primary pigments combine to black," Karanthe repeated softly.

"Three primary lights combine to white," Adaon insisted in return.

"Those will be our choices," Pelkin said. "To combine and complement, becoming something more brilliant in whole than in part. Or to go dark."

"A leader is required," said Jhoss. "A leader with all three powers."

"Louarn the White," Louarn said, in soft mockery of an old tale told by tellers at hearthside. "Or Louarn the Black. You put much trust in me, Jhoss, to assume I would be the former and not the latter."

"You spent most of your life in shadow," Jhoss said. "I need not hear your long tale in the tavern to know it. You have been Louarn the Black. If he were here, we would know him."

Pelkin plucked ruefully at his ordinary tunic. "Black is really a very rich color," he said. "I'm rather fond of it, myself." In response to Jhoss's hard stare, he said, "Yes, Jhoss, I apprehend the metaphor. But it seems Louarn is not interested in being this leader of yours."

"You always wanted a leader," Karanthe said suddenly, as another gaggle of visitors came through, rushed along by Kara, who was well aware that important things were being discussed in that particular common room. "Torrin made you want it, simply by being who he was. When you lost him, you went looking for someone else, and everyone you asked said no. Torrin would have said no, too, and somewhere inside you know that. Not even he was the leader you longed for him to be. You tried to become it yourself. And now you've grappled on to Louarn."

"Who has said no, twice," Louarn said, while Dabrena was smiling at the sailor terminology Karanthe had picked up from Tolivar. He did haunt them, in so many ways. "And now that the proposal is in the open, I say it for the third, most powerful time. I am a journeyer, no more than that. A lad-of-all-crafts."

"A lad-of-all-lights."

"Perhaps. But my search for their meaning and their powers is a personal one, and any good I may do with them will be as an ordinary man. My childhood was a living nightmare because of a corrupt Ennead that sought control. Our mages were seared of their light by that Ennead battling one of its sons for control. The Menalad Plain was drenched in blood by folk battling for control. Lerissa sought control by hoarding light. Worilke sought control by exterminating it. You seek control, Jhoss, and like everyone else you will come to know that you cannot have it, acquire it in proxy, or bestow it. Not in this land." He paused, as though he would go on and was grabbing hold of himself.

Spirits help him if he shows a little uncontrolled emotion, Dabrena thought. Then, with some sadness, *And now he'll go off, and break those three girls' hearts again.*

And then her eyes went wide as she saw it.

He had a magelight.

He was a binder.

She'd watched him, in the rebuilding of Gir Doegre. Watched

him work tin, stone, wood—watched him turn his hand to anything, with skills acquired in six years of prenticing to smith after wright, bricklayer after carpenter, chandler after weaver after cobbler. He'd told her of his wanderings, his insatiable hunger for new crafts. But in all his crafts, he'd never learned the binder's. He'd circled round it, never landing—never knowing, in a lightless world, that there was anywhere to land. His hands worked looms when they should have been laying sedgeweave, cut dowels when they should have been trimming quills. He was lad of all crafts but the one he was meant for. None of his prenticeships had been the one he truly craved.

He was a bindsman, in every sense. The preparation of materials would come easily to him, and solving the puzzle of each casting—which inks, which pigments, which implements to provide his wordsmith and illuminator to make their work effective. A binder bound his triad the way Louarn had bound those children, the Girdlers, the bonefolk, the way he bound everyone in this chamber. The way he bound, within himself, the three lights.

He might not have the voice for it. Binders sang, to complete magecastings. She didn't know if he could give himself into song the way that binding required. It was an opening of the soul. A revealing. He was as yet too closed a man for that.

But he could learn. He had a dozen years to learn, with the children of the reborn light.

You're a binder, Louarn. The words pressed against her wordsmith's lips, straining to come forth. *I don't need a light to tell me that. I loved a binder once. I know one when I see one. Take up the craft you were born to. You will never cease your wanderings until you do.*

She could not say it. The words would be no better than Jhoss's—an attempt to shape him into what she thought he should become. Louarn would have to find his own path to the manhood he was destined for.

"The answer is no," he said at last. To Jhoss, though Dabrena knew he would have said the same to her. "The rest is words. I leave it to you." With a perfectly executed Holding bow to Pelkin and Karanthe, he sought the doorway he had courted and made use of it. No glance toward Dabrena or Adaon, no reassuring wink. That boded ill for the girls' hearts. But every journey began with a departure.

One visitor had lingered in the shadows just beyond the doorway. Dabrena's eye caught on the movement as Louarn left. Had Kara lost track of one? She was so organized for her age, and quite bossy on what she felt to be her own territory. . . .

She heard the visitor's voice, and understood.

"The true king crowned is king no more," Kazhe said, and stepped into the room. "Hello, Jhoss."

Kazhe n'Zhevra and Jhoss n'Kall, in the same room for probably the first time since the day the Lightbreaker died. She and he had been with him from the earliest days, and had stayed by him, his strange pale shadows, when everyone else was off pursuing their own concerns. Jhoss's and Kazhe's concerns had been wholly Torrin. Jhoss desperately wished to see Torrin's ideas come to fruition, Torrin's goals met. Kazhe desperately wished to keep Torrin alive against impossible odds. They were the kind of people often overlooked by history, and the kind of people most deeply wounded by it. Leaders lost their lives, and left folk like Jhoss and Kazhe to live on and bear the heartbreak.

"That was part of the elegy," Jhoss said. "That you said for your father."

"Old verses of my folk. The kenaila—the blademasters—or whoever it was who settled the plains Girdle. Or both. Maybe it was a song, once. Songs are odd things, make me feel I've gone queer—they do to your gut what dinging your elbow does to your arm. We forgot the tune, if it ever had one. I had most of the words, but we'd lost the end. Torrin gave it back to me, once he figured out that what I was saying was the same thing he had read in some old volume. Funny. It turned out to be about me."

"Songs have a tendency to do that," said Adaon.

"Yes. Even the ones you like because you think they're not about you at all."

"We're just swimming in old verses today, aren't we?" said Dabrena.

Pelkin replied, "There was a reason the wordsmith's craft carried so much power. And the binder's song."

"And will again," Karanthe said.

"So what shall we do with these three powers of ours? The gold, the copper, and the silver?" Pelkin asked. "This is a metals town. Surely even leaderless we can think of something."

"Let them shine," Dabrena said. "Buff them as we can, give aid and counsel where we're asked, and let them shape themselves."

"There are risks," Jhoss said darkly. "Risks none of us can see."

"Tightening your fist on Eiden Myr won't reduce your risks," Kazhe said to him, and ghosts of old debates filled the air around them. The past clung to them all, like a haunt. Like a caul. "And there will be no rulers in Eiden Myr. Not so long as I live."

"Our folk have always done best when left to sort themselves out," Dabrena said. Deciding to apply her own advice to Jhoss and Kaẓhe, she rose. Adaon rose with her.

"Let them shine," Pelkin said, testing the words in his mouth as he stood up. Dabrena watched how Karanthe stood beside him, but still could not discern the nature of the bond. That was all right. She'd have it from her later, no matter how many jugs of wine it took. "Those may be the wisest words I've heard in a long time."

They slipped between groups of visitors and made their way down the stairs and out through the excavation scaffolds and back into the clear open sunshine of noon in Gir Doegre. The balance of the balance day of Ve Eiden, the harvestmid equinox. To Dabrena, for at least this one moment, all things felt in balance indeed.

"Let them shine," Pelkin said, and smiled.

Verlein slipped the band from her hair and let the wind comb it loose. It felt good to be free of restraints. It felt good to be free of Worilke n'Karad, and the Ennead's clinging webs, and the rigors of command. Her shield would not rally to her in battle again. She had let too many of them die, and stood by helpless while they were gelded, and rumors of her secret association with the Nine were now too rampant. She wondered if this was how Torrin Wordsmith might have felt, standing on this spot, or near enough, if he had lived to feel anything.

She let go of her regrets and her rages, let the wind take them. She was still first shield, though only in name. It was just another word, another squiggle on a piece of parchment. The seconds were the shield's leaders now, and she did not aspire to so much as command of a guardpost. She wanted only to stand here, in the Fist, and watch the seam between sea and sky for any ravel in its stitching. And feel the wind sweep her clean.

Beside her was a young shielder, just shy of a year past two nineyears of age, just shy of a year in service to the shield. A chunky, freckle-faced girl with long red hair, she was lighter on her feet than you'd expect, and had trained well with the blade. She was still smarting from not being called down to the battle in the Strong Leg, though Verlein had pulled only her own seconds from Fist postings; it had been far too great a distance, and the coastal watch could not be weakened in this of all places. Now the only battle this girl would see was one that sprang upon them from without—and like as not Kaẓhe would come and knock it down to a battle of fists.

Well, she'd do all right there, this youngster. Verlein had never seen anyone so handy in a brawl. And more than blades and battles, the girl had joined the shield, the moment she came of age, because she was keen to watch. There was no more farsighted or patient observer. She volunteered for double duty at any opportunity, and always worked the holidays. She was content, if that was the word for someone with eyes as restless as those, only when she was keeping watch.

Quiet and dedicated, she was Verlein's favored partner, and Verlein could not even remember her name.

The smell of the sea came up sharp in a gust of spray. Long mare's tails swirled the sky. Murres squabbled and purred in their rocky perches; gulls and terns wheeled and croaked. The sea rose and fell in easy swells. As the slow, steady breaths went by, the sun moved directly overhead, and their shadows were sucked into their feet. Noon of the harvestmid equinox. The balance of the balance day. The moment when time and light poised motionless, suspended . . . and then tipped over into the headlong fall toward Longdark. They were too far from the nearest village to hear the Ve Eiden chanting, and no one had come to hold vigil here beside them by the sea; this was Eiden's day, the celebration of earth and flesh, and they stood on Galandra's ground. Where Galandra's triad had cast the warding, and Torrin's had broken it. On Galandra's day, then they would come, to look out over the Forgotten Sea at the dark strip of the old world along the horizon. On Galandra's day, the celebration of spirit, then they would come.

Today, it was just her and the girl. Two ordinary shielders, devoting their lives to a watch that they could not help but hope was in vain.

Yet Verlein did not feel that the girl beside her aspired to futility. They spoke little during their long watches, and had spoken less on this sacred day, but now she hazarded to say, "What is it you watch for, girl?"

The broad redhead turned in mild surprise. "Ships, Shieldmaster."

"Ships?" Verlein said.

Her aim proved true; the girl's gaze dropped for a moment before returning to its task. "A ship, Shieldmaster."

"Perhaps it is not the same ship I watch for."

"We don't know what kind of ships will come."

Will, not *might*. Was that to please the shieldmaster? Her words were straightforward, but Verlein caught some emphasis in her tone. Determination. Conviction.

"I'm watching for one bristling with spears," Verlein said. She meant it half-humorously, and to prompt a more detailed response, but to her surprise she found herself describing a vision she'd never put into words: "A long ship, beamier than ours. Moving fast, with folk at banks of oars as well as tending sail. Square-rigged, I think, though I don't know why. With the sun behind it, so that it sails into its own shadow, so that it's a shadow itself against the glare. The darkness we fled, catching us in the end." She snorted. "What a load of manure that sounds when I say it, eh?"

She'd picked up the "eh" from the girl; she hadn't noticed when. A Norther tic. She found it funny.

"I see a small ship," the girl said. "One sail, one woman at the tiller. The sun's behind me when I see it, and the sail's let out in a triangle to one side, so that at first it looks like a shard of white shell stuck upright in the sea."

Her eyes still on the swells, Verlein clapped the girl on the shoulder. Not too hard. Companionable. "One of your folk went off in the ships that sailed to see the outer realms."

"The first," the girl confirmed. "The very first one. But she'll come back. She has to." Softly, not meaning for the shieldmaster to hear her, she said, "She never came to say goodbye."

Verlein squeezed the girl's shoulder. It was meant to be sympathetic, but it became a hard, convulsive grip as the two of them went rigid, staring at the seam between sea and sky.

At the first prick of sail on the horizon.

The Strong Leg

Do not look to me, Louarn thought in anger as he left the burrow hole of the past. A narrow track gouged through banks of earth led him back out onto the road, where crowds of Ve Eiden celebrants, fresh from their noon ablutions, waited their turn for a glimpse of history.

Jhoss wished to make a symbol of him. He was far too enamored of symbol. It was a tool—a useful tool, and a transcendent tool when wielded by mages, but still akin to a chisel, or a blade, or a loom. He would never again be anyone's instrument.

The stale scent of the stone interior clung to him. He shook his clothes to air them.

He had worked hard to craft himself. He was tired of being crafted. It was time to just be, and see what came of it.

When the runners and Jhoss had waylaid him, he had been on his way to breeze Dabrena's horse Vervain. Daily rides gave him an opportunity to learn the countryside and observe its changes; the vision of Eiden Myr that he'd been privy to during the storm had given him a taste for sprawling vistas, and he took pleasure in finding new hilltops, new views to enjoy. He had spent a good deal of his youth on horseback and most of the last six years afoot. There was nothing in the world like movement, and becoming one with the mount beneath you.

He fetched the gelding, swung aboard, and reined down the Maur

Road and into a lope as soon as traffic permitted. Gir Doegre's historic hills smoothed into the distance behind him, sinking with the outline of the Elfelirs, and before long there was only the green of pastures, the gold of grain, the russet of flamewood, the deep delicious blue of the harvestmid sky. Eiden had healed; in the hands of a small child, his agonies had eased, and the twisting of Galandra's shattered warding had been corrected. Mages had made this land a paradise. Perhaps it might be paradise once more.

He stopped in a small roadside village for a rest and to water the horse. Sitting by the trough outside an inn, he found himself abruptly beset by children. They always seemed to find their way to him, with their tongue-lolling dogs or capering pet goats. With stray bits of straw that had collected around the watering trough between evening sweeps, he twisted some quick braid puzzles for them, and their laughter so pleased the innkeeper that she brought him out a snack of pickerelweed seeds and a growler of ale, then went back in to fetch a carrot for the horse. They went on their way, refreshed and happy, and when they rounded the next bend in the road and cleared a buckthorn hedge, Louarn saw Maur Lengra laid out in the glittering distance.

He had come nearly eight leagues without realizing it. This was as far as he could ride today and still be back by dark.

He paused, looking down to where the road forked maurward and Heelward.

He had never been to the Toes. A ferry from the Heel would have him across the maur in less than a morning. He'd like to learn the smelter's craft. He'd never seen the Souther Lowlands, tasted their fermented palm sap, hung from the tough vines in their dark forests, smelled their exotic flowers.

He had no pack, no provisions. That was no deterrent. The weather in these Souther climes had not yet turned too chill for sleeping out, and he had always earned his way with little trouble, charmed it where he had to.

But Vervain did not belong to him. Dabrena rarely rode him, but she'd have need of him soon enough, to visit her family or her old holding, or to take Kara up to Glydh again.

Hands tight on the reins, he was about to turn back when a trebled thud of hooves from that direction warned him off to the side of the road just in time to avoid a young lad racing around the bend on a dapple pony.

"Ho, there, not so fast," he warned, but the lad was reining up at the sight of him. Apparently the rush was to catch him.

"You shine," the boy said, breathless and with no preamble. He might be nine-and-four or nine-and-eight, there was no telling, but the eagerness in his eyes was unmistakable.

"So do you," Louarn said, and waited.

"I heard about the shine," the boy said. "Like a flamewood leaf, when it's strong, and you can ease pain and cure colic and—well, I've done that, you see, and I thought I might—I might—"

"You do," Louarn said.

The boy licked his lips. "I'd like to do more. I'd like to learn more. I heard there was a place where they teach you. Where they shine bright. I'd like to shine bright. Sometimes our stock—things happen—if I could help—and my sisters are little and they're into everything and sometimes I worry that—and if the fevers came back, or—well, if there is a place, I'd like to go there, but no one seems to know exactly where it is, it's just a rumor like every other rumor—but I hoped—and when I saw you, and I saw your shine, I hoped—I thought—"

The lad must have kept a pack ready by the door, waiting for the moment when someone passed through with that shine. Waiting, and watching, and peering out from his dairy or smithy or stable, examining every stranger who passed through his little roadside village.

This lad could take Vervain in tow and return him to Dabrena while Louarn continued to the Heel on foot. Louarn could see the Toes. Sip fermented palm sap. Wander the dark forests.

"It's Gir Doegre you want," he said to the boy, whose shine was like Elora's eyes when she worked a delicate form in wood, like Pelufer's face when she stood up in fierce defense of what she loved, like Caille's hands when she stroked a cat's soft fur. "It's up the Knee Road, straight on, surrounded by hills. There's no missing it. But . . ."

The boy paused with thanks on his lips and worry in his eyes.

"But I can do better than that," Louarn said, and reined Vervain up beside the dapple pony. With a smile that required no crafting at all, he said, "I can take you there."

He set off at a canter for home, and called to the shining boy, "Follow me!"

NAMES

The Living

Adaon n'Arai l'Ivrel, a seeker and scholar
Anifa n'Bendri, a senior alderwoman of Gir Doegre
Annina, a runner who was a vocate with Dabrena
Barumor, a shield post commander
Befendry, a scarvesmonger in Gir Doegre
Belwyn, a woman who minds children in the Head holding
Benkana, a man from the Weak Leg
Berilise, daughter of the Chimney Swift publicans in Gir Doegre
Beronwy, Jiondor's pledge
Bofric n'Roric, a scholar on the Isle of Senana
Burken, a reckoner retired from the field
Caille n'Prendra l'Nimorin, a street child, five years old
Chaela, a fighter from the plains Girdle
Chaldrinda n'Poskana, an aide to Pelkin
Cheveil, a shielder
Cinn, a mender who was a vocate with Dabrena
Corle, a senior mender in the Head holding
Dabrena n'Arilda l'Desarde, head mender in the Head holding
Dalle, a piemonger in Gir Doegre
Denuorin n'Amtreor, a senior alderman of Gir Doegre
Diluor, a coppersmith in Gir Doegre
Dontra, a senior mender in the Head holding
Effad, a fighter from the plains Girdle

Elander, a Copper Long trader in Gir Doegre
Eldrisil te Khine, one of Streln's men
Elidorlin, a scrapmonger in Gir Doegre
Elora n'Prendra l'Nimorin, a trader girl, nine-and-four years old
Eltarion te Khine, a mender who was a vocate with Dabrena
Elya, a woman of Heel descent
Eowi, a shielder, one of Verlein's seconds
Eshadri, a shield post commander
Evrael n'Daivor l'Naeve te Khine, the Khinish fleetmaster
Falowen n'Tedra, a scholar on the Isle of Senana
Flin, nearly six years old, a child of Holding warders
Galtrelor, a foodmonger in Gir Doegre
Gilris, a shield post commander
Girayal, a shielder, one of Verlein's seconds
Graefel n'Traeyen l'Brenlyn, head scholar on the Isle of Senana
Harinar, a shielder
Herne, a runner who was a vocate with Dabrena
Ilorna, a Holding warder
Jeolle n'Jedona, a senior alderwoman of Gir Doegre
Jerize, a mender who was a vocate with Dabrena
Jhoss n'Kall l'Sirelyi t'Eiden, a beekeeper
Jia, a shield post commander
Jifadry, a soupmonger in Gir Doegre
Jimor n'Loflin l'Baile, an aide to Pelkin
Jiondor, a sweetsmonger in Gir Doegre
Kara n'Dabrena l'Tolivar, Dabrena's six-year-old daughter
Karanthe n'Farine l'Jebb, a runner who was a vocate with Dabrena
Kazhe n'Zhevra, last of a line of blademasters
Lannan, a shield post commander
Lerissa n'Rigael ti Khine, formerly an Ennead illuminator
Loralir, an elderly stonemonger in Gir Doegre
Loris, birdmaster at the Head holding, a senior mender
Louarn, a lad-of-all-crafts
Mellas, a Holding runner boy
Meloni, a seamer in Gir Doegre
Mireille n'Jenaille, a stonemonger in Gir Doegre
Narilyn, a senior mender at the Head holding
Nemrina, a weaver in Gir Doegre
Nerenyi n'Jheel l'Corlin, keeper of codices on the Isle of Senana
Nolfiander (Nolfi), a barrow boy on Copper Long in Gir Doegre
Ofalador, a Copper Long trader in Gir Doegre
Ollo, a scrapmonger in Gir Doegre
Pelkin n'Rolf l'Liath, head runner

Pelufer n'Prendra l'Nimorin, a street child, nine-and-two years old
Porfinn, a mender
Prenaille, a Tin Long trader in Gir Doegre
Reiligh, herbmaster at the Head holding, a senior mender
Riflin, a foodmonger in Gir Doegre
Risalyn, a woman from the Highlands Girdle
Ronim, a senior mender at the Head holding
Seldra, a Tin Long trader in Gir Doegre
Selen, a senior mender at the Head holding
Sevriel, a shield post commander
Sira, a woman from the plains Girdle
Strelniriol te Khine (Streln), headman of the Khinish
Tarunel, a shield post commander
Teyik, the son of Worilke's old steward, Valik
Tiloura, a coppersmith in Gir Doegre
Tofro, a trader child in Gir Doegre
Toudin, a stewmonger in Gir Doegre
Verlein n'Tekla l'Sayal, first of Eiden's shield
Worilke n'Karad, formerly an Ennead wordsmith
Yuralon, a man from the Highlands Girdle

The Dead

Torrin n'Maeryn l'Eilody, the Lightbreaker, a wordsmith

Gir Doegre

Aifrin, Altreille, Amtreor, Andorlin, Anondry, Bardor, Belu, Beoni, Diludel, Donfa, Eldomon, Erileka, Feraille, Fesalyn, Grotelyn, Herik, Jedfa, Jerulon, Jimni, Jimurin, Luander, Melledor, Morlor, Nemolle, Nilu, Noluorin, Nomulor, Ofrander, Ronderas, Valenya, haunts
Jenaille, Mireille's mother
Nimorin n'Belu, father of Elora, Pelufer, and Caille
Prendra n'Anondry, mother of Elora, Pelufer, and Caille
Seliander (Sel), Nolfiander's older brother

The Holding

Alliol, a head warder, one of Flin's foster-fathers
Brondarion te Khine (Bron), a stablemaster

Daivor, an Ennead binder (balance triad)
Drinda, a baker
Ellerin, a head warder, one of Flin's foster-fathers
Evonder n'Daivor l'Naeve, an Ennead binder (balance triad, Daivor's successor)
Freyn n'Eniya, an Ennead binder (weather triad)
Garran, a vocate
Gondril n'Rontifer, an Ennead wordsmith (leading triad)
Jonnula, a vocate
Landril n'Rontifer, an Ennead illuminator (leading triad)
Naeve n'*Bevriel*, Evonder's mother, an Ennead wordsmith (balance triad)
Pirra, a head warder, Flin's foster-mother
Rigael n'Saeron l'Portriel, Lerissa's father, an Ennead illuminator
Seldril n'Yelwyn, an Ennead binder (leading triad)
Terrell, a vocate
Tolivar, a warder triaded with Dabrena; Kara's father
Valik, Worilke's old steward
Vonche n'Reiff, an Ennead illuminator (balance triad)

RISALYN

Ardis, Areil, Bendik, Efrein, Istriel, Liya, Traig, haunts

YURALON

Astael, Coenn, Daeriel, Deilyn, Diandre, Korras, Niseil, Perchis, Rajulon, Soliri, Sowryn, Thandra, Vaen, Vebryn, haunts

GLOSSARY

bet-jahr, also *pethyar*: The spirit world.

binder, bindsman, bindswoman: A mage who prepared casting materials and sang a wordless melody over an inscribed, illuminated manuscript to complete a casting. Binders also bound their triads, psychologically and sometimes by blood relationship. Former binders have taken up a variety of trades, as healers, herbalists, producers of scribing materials, and so on; some have become singers, traveling to learn and entertain; some have become scholars, attempting to re-create from scribed sources ancient songs with words; only a few, unable to bear their inability to cast, have returned to their family trades.

bonedays: Three days a year (one in each season) when the dead are remembered and offerings are left for the bonefolk. Observances differ regionally. Binders often chose bonedays to harvest skins for vellum and parchment.

bonefolk: Mysterious fringe folk who dispose of the carcasses of people and animals, leaving nothing behind but any metal or stone.

Brightfire: A minor holiday also known as Spindle Day; the night before is known as Wantons' Eve. Considered the start of summer in some Souther areas and on Khine. We would call it May Day.

Celyrian: One of the old tongues that was lost over time but retained by wordsmiths as the language and scribing system used for magecraft. An ornate, flowing, alphabetic script, it is now the scribing system used most by the scholars.

cheit: A small, hooked, magecrafted dagger carried by a kenai. Plural *cheitla*.

Eiden: The animating and personified spirit of earth. Masculine in aspect. Anyone engaged in farming, animal husbandry, or material crafts is considered a child of Eiden. Formerly, anyone not a mage—not a child of Galandra—was considered a child of Eiden.

Eiden Myr: The world; now also, more specifically, the island continent on which a magecrafted society existed in isolation for twice nine nonned years.

Ennead: Nine mages, in three triads, bound to protect Eiden Myr from the Great Storms and other catastrophes. Also called the Nine, the Three of Threes. Lived and worked in the Ennead's Holding, in the Aralinn Mountains of the Head facing into the Sea of Storms, until their downfall six years ago.

Galandra: Galandra na Caille le Serith, the mage who founded Eiden Myr twice nine nonned years ago and six. Also, still, a mythological figure: the mother of all human beings, Eiden's pledge, and the mother and protective spirit of mages.

Ghardic: One of the old tongues that was lost over time but retained in the codices that are now kept by the scholars. A straightforward syllabary that's easy to learn, Ghardic scribing is gaining popularity for messages, recordkeeping, and trade in the common tongue.

Great Trines: Seekers have long maintained that history is full of trines, critical connected events that come in threes, and that there are three Great Trines, which have not yet seen their completion.

harvestmid: Autumn (one side of midder). The three seasons are winter, summer, and midder.

hein-na-fhin: "One of three." A dangerous, powerful casting in which three mages combine into one being. Such a casting was how Galandra's triad died, in order to create the warding that kept Eiden Myr isolated for twice nine nonned years, and how the leading triad of the last Ennead died, trying to subvert that warding.

illuminator: A mage who received an inscribed leaf from a wordsmith and materials (ink, pigment, brushes, pens) from a binder, and illuminated the leaf with patterns, illustrations, and kadri. Many illuminators have taken up decorative or patterning crafts, becoming carvers, ropemakers, weavers, and the like; others continue to illuminate, working with permanent manuscripts, or have become scholars, studying and emulating the old arts of illumination; some are now painters and portraitists, for a living or on the side; others, unable to bear their inability to cast, have returned exclusively to their family trades.

kadra: An ideographic symbol enclosed in a triangle. Plural *kadri*.

kenai: A blademaster; also, the magecrafted longblade carried by a kenai. Plural *kenaila*.

Longdark: The winter solstice. Also, the nine-day festival culminating in the shortest day of the year.

Longlight: The summer solstice. Also, the nine-day festival culminating in the longest day of the year.

mage: A worker of magecraft, in the time before the magelight was lost. Mages cast in triads using illuminated manuscripts, and wore triskeles to identify themselves as mages. Their magelights, which showed in the sixth or seventh year (age five or six), were visible only to one another, as a yellow or golden glow. Mages prenticed for a dozen years, underwent a trial, then journeyed for a year before choosing a triad. Their craft cured sickness, healed injury, eased childbirth, passaged the dying to the spirit world, controlled the weather, calmed earthquakes, preserved food, and warded against fire, weather, blight, and unwanted pregnancy. The loss of mages' power, symbolized by their light, is largely attributed to the actions of Torrin Lightbreaker.

the man who could not die: A tellers' tale immensely old. Stories recount his adventures through various imaginary realms, such as the land beyond the mist, the land beyond the rain, the land beyond the shadows, and so on.

mender: Any of a group of healers, herbalists, agriculturalists, scribes, cartographers, and crafters based in the Head holding and roaming throughout Eiden Myr. Menders attempt to compensate for the loss of magecraft through the consolidation and dissemination of practical knowledge. The warders in the Ennead's Holding re-formed themselves into menders, and continue to wear white.

midder: Considered one season, though it occurs in part between winter and summer and in part between summer and winter, midder is the time between the other two seasons.

moon: A month, which is twenty-seven days, or three ninedays.

Morlyrien: The animating and personified spirit of water, and more specifically the sea. Either masculine or feminine in aspect. Sailors and those who make their living from the sea are children of Morlyrien.

nonned: Nine nines (81). Twice nine nonned is 1458.

parchment: The skin of a sheep, lamb, goat, or kid used as a writing material.

pledge: To pledge someone is to vow a lifetime romantic and sexual partnership. Someone you have pledged is known as your pledge or pledgemate. Pledgings are no longer cast by magecraft, but are entered into nonetheless.

proxy: A mage who worked on behalf of the Ennead, either as a reckoner in the field or a warder in the Holding. Proxies wore black if they were reckoners and white if they were warders, nine-colored Ennead cloaks, and silver rings engraved with three circles inside a triangle.

reckoner: A proxy, trained in the Holding, sent into the field to manage other mages and report to the Holding (through the proxy circle or reckoners' chain) on weather conditions. Reckoners cast in threes but did not form permanent triads. They wore black.

runner: A professional message bearer. A network of runners, consisting largely of former reckoners, has formed out of the remains of the proxy circle. They continue to wear black.

scholar: A resident on the Isle of Senana, where the collections of ancient codices salvaged from the Ennead's Holding are now kept. Scholars are usually seekers or former mages (especially wordsmiths), dedicated to research, maintenance, and decipherment of the codices, their history, and their languages. They wear gray.

sedgeweave: Papyruslike writing material made of laid strips of reeds.

seekers: Itinerant folk, suspicious of superstition and convention, who try to discern large truths by applying rigorous logical inquiry to stories, legends, and empirical observations. Considered crackpots. Associate loosely with each other, usually arguing a lot. Put a silence on themselves when they need time to think.

sheddown: Down collected where it has fallen.

sowmid: Spring (the other side of midder).

spirit days: The dark of the moon; correspond to no phase of the moon (the moon's three phases are waxing, full, and waning).

stewards: Non-mage support staff in the Holding under the Ennead. After the Ennead's downfall, loosely applied to some of those who remained in the Holding.

stones: Any of various table games, often played in taverns, with pretty colored stones that would be called jewels elsewhere.

Stonetree: A runic system. When inscribed upright as discrete glyphs on a flat leaf, the runes look like trees, and each rune is named for a tree. Can also be inscribed as hash marks from a continuous horizontal or vertical line, more in keeping with the oldest examples, which were carved along the corners of squared or triangular stones. Also known as Lir-Wor, for its first and last glyphs, or Lir-Geis-Saor, for its first three glyphs. It contains no vowels.

Sylfonwy: The animating and personified spirit of air, and more specifically the winds. Of neutral gender, though masculine and feminine pronouns are used in reference.

tain: A magecrafted longknife, like a messer or saxe, carried by a kenai. Plural *tainla*.

threft: A yard; contraction of "threefoot."

triad: Three mages (wordsmith, illuminator, and binder) who formed a threesome to do a casting; also, three mages who were cast triad by reckoners, to make their threesome permanent.

Triennead: A postulated structure of three enneads, each maintaining a holding in a different region of Eiden Myr.

triskele: The pewter pendant worn by a mage, shaped as three arms curving from a solid center into a shared circle.

Ve Eiden: The autumnal equinox. Also the three-day celebration with the equinox as its middle day.

Ve Galandra: The vernal equinox. Also the three-day celebration with the equinox as its middle day.

vellum: The skin of a cow or calf used as a writing material.

vocate: An exceptional mage called to serve in the Ennead's Holding. Vocates generally trained for three moons or so—working together, bonding, and learning to think collectively—and then were sorted into reckoners and warders, known as "earning the ring." They wore gray.

warder: A proxy, trained in the Holding, who remained in the Holding to assist the Ennead in managing the weather and maintaining the physical premises of the Holding itself. Warders formed permanent triads and wore white.

wordsmith: A mage who inscribed the manuscript leaf in a casting. Many wordsmiths have become scholars, many others tellers and scribes; some, disturbed by new knowledge, have joined with the seekers to obtain more; many offer their recordkeeping and messaging abilities on the side, while plying a family trade; a few, unable to bear their inability to cast or in outright rejection of the widespread understanding and use of scribing, have returned exclusively to their family trades.

Special thanks to: Russell Galen, Teresa Nielsen Hayden, Patrick Nielsen Hayden, Fiorella deLima, Fred Herman, Wah-Ming Chang, Becky Maines, Rob Stauffer, Gary Ruddell, Carol Russo, Ellen Cipriano, and Ellisa Mitchell. Larry Cuocci for the jacket photo. Illuminator Karen Gorst and Kremer Pigments (www.kremer-pigmente.com), Michael Norris for pointing the way to them, and Bennett Liberty for the nifty show-and-tell; coach Enid Friedman of Hofstra University's fencing program, and John Clements and the folks from the Association for Renaissance Martial Arts (www.thearma.org) for the welcome and the basics, with hopes that they'll forgive me both liberties and missteps. Adrian Legg, Cliff Eberhardt, Patty Larkin, Solas, Dervish, Stephen Sondheim, Handspring®, Landware®, Yankee Candle®, the Dr Pepper Company, and Lyons Tea for essential ancillary materials to work by. The folks at SFF Net (www.sff.net, irc.sff.net) and DelphiForums' SF Literature forum (www.sflit.com). The folks at the Dempsey's *seisiún*, who welcomed me back after I disappeared for several months to finish writing; Joey and Frank and Art for keeping me in the music anyway. Sam, Jim and Tom, Chana, and Alex and Nicky, who are all the coolest. My mom, for more than everything.

And, always, Jenna Felice.